The Victor Canning Omnibus

The Victor Canning Omnibus

Ravette London

This edition published by Ravette Ltd
© Ravette Ltd 1986

Typeset by Input Typesetting Ltd
Printed and bound in Great Britain for Ravette Ltd
3 Glenside Estate, Star Road, Partridge Green,
Horsham, Sussex RH13 8RA
by T. J. Press (Padstow) Ltd., Cornwall.

ISBN 0 948456 09 4

Contents

The Python Project

Contents

CHAPTER 1

Sunshine in a Shady Place

His name was Hawkins and I knew him very well. I'd worked for him—or his company, rather—on and off for the last five years. He was always embarrassed when he had a dubious client—as though it reflected somehow on the good name of his company, though I couldn't think why because since they had been first established in 1870 they must have been gypped, swindled and cheated hundreds of times. After all, that's what most people think insurance companies are there for.

'I'm not saying there's anything wrong about her,' he said, 'but I just get a feeling. If she'd been an old customer I wouldn't be so sensitive, but she only switched her insurances to us about six months ago. Yes, I've a very definite feeling about her.'

Usually when he had that sort of feeling he was right, and he always came to me. It was handy to have someone do your dirty work for you.

He slid a glossy photograph across the desk to me and it skidded fast and fell to the floor. I reached down and retrieved it and felt my arm muscles stiff from my last session with Miggs. The bastard had enjoyed himself for half an hour teaching me new arm-holds and throwing me all over the gym. You couldn't see more than a yard ahead for the dust from the mats when he had finished.

I looked at the photograph without interest.

'I don't want a job. I've made some big money lately and it's put me off work.' It always did. Besides, outside in Northumberland Avenue it was spring, the cock pigeons chasing the hens around, the cab drivers watching the mini-skirts go by, and an icy wind coming up the street canyon from the river. I thought of golden sands, golden girls, golden nights in casinos, and wondered if they would do anything for the tired feeling I had in the mornings or whether just a bottle of the old tonic from the doctor up the road from my flat wouldn't be cheaper and more effective. Cheaper, certainly.

'What I want,' I said, watching Hawkins's moist, pebble-grey eyes on me, 'is a real lift. Salt in the blood. A different beat in the pulse. A sense of discovering a new man inside this weary old frame. Something you can't get from Ovaltine or Metatone but maybe from the Mediterranean. Certainly not from work. Not from chasing around trying to find out if some woman is trying to cheat your company over a jewellery claim. The odds are high that she is.'

I tapped the photograph.

'This is the most ghastly bit of Oriental bazaar work I've seen for some time.'

'It's Indian, seventeenth century, and it's worth about five thousand pounds. The eyes are diamonds, somewhere around fifty carats each, and each coil is studded along the whole length with emeralds. And the body-work is pure gold.'

'I still think it's vulgar. I don't want work. I want rejuvenation.' I slid the photograph back to him.

He fielded it with one hand, neatly, and flipped another photograph across with the other. For a moment there was the suggestion of a twinkle in his watery eyes.

'That's the owner,' he said. 'I brought it along because Wilkins said it was going to be difficult to get you off the ground. She's worried about you.'

'She always is. There's no pleasing her. Hard up or well off, she worries.'

I let the second photograph rest where it had skidded off the desk to the ground.

'You're lucky to have Wilkins,' he said. 'I'd give her a job any day at twice the salary you pay. I've written all the details of the owner on the back of the photograph. Incidentally, she's a widow and worth about a quarter of a million—and she's only twenty-seven.'

Just for a moment I felt a flicker of interest. But it died quickly. I just didn't have the blood count to boost my imagination into orbit. Wilkins was right. Something was wrong with me and it was going to be difficult to get me off the ground. Wilkins was my secretary—and also a partner in Carver & Wilkins. She was thirty-five, spinster, and lived in Greenwich with her father, a retired ship's steward. She had red hair, blue eyes, no dress sense, and mostly thought nothing of me. She was zero to look at and I don't

know what I would have done without her. She had a fiancé, a
Swede who was a Suez Canal pilot, and saw him about once a year.
I didn't think he represented any threat.

Hawkins said, 'Have a look at it. Or haven't you got the strength
to pick it up?'

'Just,' I said. I reached down for the photograph. It was face
down, the back covered with Hawkins's notes. The chair tipped a
bit and I nearly went over. I came back to a level keel with the
photograph, the right way round, a foot from my nose.

I didn't say anything. But somewhere inside me the motor turned
over, fired, missed a few cycles, and then steadied to a quiet tick-
over. I stared at the photograph, not hypnotized, but quietly, almost
happily, absorbed. Somewhere inside me a thin trickle of adrenalin
began to seep into the blood stream.

'This,' I said, 'is not a woman of twenty-seven.'

'Taken when she was nineteen. The year before she married. She
used to do that kind of thing, professionally.'

'Judging by this, she did it very well. Where did you get it?'

'Sources. Interested?'

He stood up, which I thought was taking a lot for granted. He
buttoned his overcoat and adjusted his neck-scarf which was red
with little white horses all over it.

'Could be,' I said.

'Good. Usual terms. I've left the company file outside with
Wilkins.'

'Any particular line?'

He put the photograph of the Indian piece of jewellery on the
desk. 'I think it was stolen, but not the way she describes it. Have
a word with her. I'm sure you'll feel better when you have.' He
nodded at the photograph in my hand. 'It's things like that which
cheer up a dull world.'

'Personally, on a freezing day like this, it just makes me feel
colder.' It wasn't true of course, but I didn't see why I should
admit that his tactics had paid off. Since there isn't much dignity
in my profession I had to cling to the little I could muster.

He looked at me, decided not to wink, and went out. Wilkins
was in ten seconds later, carrying the company file. I was still
holding the photograph in my hand.

She put the file on my desk, sniffed hard to keep abreast of the
cold she had picked up three months before, and said, nodding at
the photograph, 'Disgusting.'

'Absolutely. But maybe what I need.'

'For a reasonably nice person,' she said, 'you respond to the coarsest stimuli. Sex, alcohol and gambling.'

'Thanks.'

She turned away, but when she got to the door she paused and cocked her head back at me. I knew all about that pause and half-turn of the head and waited for one hand to go up and touch her hair. Something was coming.

'Mrs Burtenshaw, my sister, will take over next Monday.'

'Christ!' It was out before I could stop it. At least some reflexes were working properly.

She gave me a chilly look.

'Sorry. Why is she coming?'

'Because I am going to Cairo, to be with Olaf. It's my annual visit.'

Olaf was the Suez Canal pilot. His other name was Bornjstrom, or something like that. I'd met him once and kept a very clear impression of a blond giant, about eight feet tall and three feet wide, who made the ground shake beneath him as he walked. Any ship he went aboard was in danger of capsizing unless he kept dead centre on the bridge. Whenever Wilkins made her annual visit her sister came and did for me. And there is no more accurate description. She was three times tougher and more efficient than Wilkins and I couldn't get into the office if there was the faintest whiff of beer on my breath. In my present low state of health she was all that was needed for my sister in Honiton to be able to collect my death insurance money.

'Think he'll pop the question this time?' I asked.

Wilkins changed the chilly to her basilisk look, and said, 'I suggest you read the file before you visit Mrs Stankowski.'

'That can't be her name.'

'Her late husband was a Pole who made a fortune from scrap-metal dealing. He had a thrombosis almost two years ago.'

'Couldn't stand the pace.' I looked at the photograph. The subject was clearly death to anyone with a weak heart.

'Before her marriage she was a Miss Freeman. Gloria Freeman.'

Eyes still on the photograph, I said, 'Gloria. It's just the name I would have chosen.'

'I find it, myself, rather common. Are you going to see her today?'

'If I can find the strength.'

Wilkins looked at her watch. 'That shouldn't be difficult. They've just opened.'

I went across Northumberland Avenue and into the public bar of the Sherlock Holmes.

Although it had only been open ten minutes, Dimble was there. Half an hour later and I would have had to go to the Chandos Arms. Dimble had a strict routine for the lunchtime session. Everyone who knew him, professionally, that is, knew it. At any time of the day during licensing hours it was possible to say exactly where Dimble would be, or be between being. He was doing the quick cross-word in the *Daily Mail,* using a stump of pencil half an inch long. Dimble got the maximum use out of everything he possessed. When he struck a match he transferred the spent number into another box, saved the boxes and burnt them on his fire at night. He was a dedicated miser, about fifty, and never got crowded on a bus or the tube because he applied his miserly principles even to the matter of personal hygiene.

I bought a couple of Guinnesses and sat down two feet from him. I reached over and put one of the Guinnesses in front of him.

"Lo, Mr Carver,' he said.

"Morning, Dimble.' I raised my glass and drank to him. He looked at his and decided to save it for a while.

I put my glass down and passed him a photograph. Dimble's profession included knowing every fence worth knowing in London and having an unrivalled knowledge of the movement of stolen tomfoolery. Quite a big slice of my work was recovery and Dimble had worked for me often.

I nodded at the photograph. 'If you've seen that anywhere around lately I'm willing to pay for its return.'

He looked at the photograph without touching it and his face stiffened in Presbyterian disapproval. Then he edged it away from him with the tip of one finger and said, 'Contrary to most, Mr Carver—I have a higher opinion of you than that.'

I saw that I had given him the wrong photograph. Hastily I corrected the mistake. You'd be surprised how many people in Dimble's world have very old-fashioned ideas about women.

'Sorry,' I said. 'I meant this.'

Dimble picked up the other photograph and examined it. It showed the piece of Indian antique jewellery, an arm bracelet in the form of a coiled python. Stretched out straight, I suppose, it would have been about two feet long. Personally I don't go for snakes or for the snake motif in jewellery. I think both can bring you bad luck. Thinking that then, of course, I didn't know that I was casting my own horoscope for the weeks ahead.

'Haven't seen it around,' said Dimble. 'Leastways, not up until the day before yesterday. I'll ask and give you a ring.'

'Thanks.' I took back the photograph.

'Where would it have come from?'

I gave him Mrs Stankowski's address and he fished out a cheap notebook and wrote it down. He picked up his glass and drank carefully, timing himself for his departure for the Chandos Arms.

'How's Miss Wilkins?'

'Blooming.'

'Heart of gold that girl's got. Always sends me a Christmas card.'

'Once you're on the list, only death gets you off.' I stood up to go.

He cocked his head up at me and said, 'You didn't ought to carry that other photo round with you. Say you got knocked down and they went through your pockets? Look bad. I mean, at the hospital, and so on.'

I walked through the passageway under Charing Cross Station and got a taxi in Villiers Street. The cabby told me there was a sharp nip in the air and I gave him Mrs Stankowski's address.

I didn't believe in making appointments. That always gave people an hour or so to think about what they would say or not say. If she were not at home I could always call again. And again, and again, I decided, as I sat in the back of the taxi and studied her photograph. It was neither disgusting, as Wilkins had said, nor calculated to shock any doctor or nurse, as Dimble had suggested. It was just a reasonably modest study of a naked girl richly endowed by Mother Nature.

The cabby slid back the glass partition and from the corner of his mouth said, 'What you think of this business in China then? Old Mao and the Red Guards and seven hundred million of the little yellow bastards all trying to make up their kinky little minds which way to go. Some situation, eh? That's if you're interested in international affairs. Worry you stiff really, international affairs, I mean, if you thought about it.'

I always got the chatty ones. Always. Years ago I had decided that it was some sort of punishment settled on me by the gods and only they knew for what.

I said, 'The only thing worrying me at the moment is that you're going a long way round to get to my destination. That makes you a deviationist too.'

He closed the glass partition and frowned at me in the driving mirror. I put Mrs Stankowski away and smiled back at him. Suddenly I realized that I was feeling better, only a little, but better.

Upper Grosvenor Street it was; a fourth-floor flat in a place called Eaton House. The door was opened by a maid, about thirty-odd, with a strong Scots accent and an unfriendly glint in her eye. I gave her my card and asked if Mrs Stankowski would be kind enough to see me about her recent jewel robbery. She said she would find out, not letting any hope slip into her voice, and shut the door on me. I stood in the narrow hallway that served the three or four flats on that floor and waited. A plump woman, cuddling a miniature poodle inside her mink coat, came out of one of the other flats and I reached out and punched the lift button for her. The poodle yapped bad-temperedly at me. The woman nodded bleakly at me, then kissed the beast on its muzzle and stepped into the lift. I felt unwanted. What was I doing here anyway, I asked myself? At the moment I had plenty of money, which was unusual for me; although I admit that you can't really have too much of the stuff or fuss overmuch about the way you get it. But the last thing I wanted at this moment was a job.

The flat door opened and the James Barrie character said something like, 'Will ye cum in the noo.'

I did, wiping my feet without being told.

I didn't pay much attention to the hall, which was about the size of a large pantry, except for a semi-circular, marble-topped table with ormolu-crusted legs. I stumbled against this as a rug slipped under my feet and had to make a quick grab to stop a heavy eight-branched silver candelabra from going over. The Highland number frowned, not sure whether I was drunk or about to make a quick snatch-and-run.

The main lounge was very big, overheated, the air faintly laced with scent. The maid announced me and I looked around and made a quick inventory of the main features. Either side of the fireplace, on small tables, were a couple of porcelain lemon trees, the soft light gilding the yellow fruit. In a corner was a television set with the biggest screen I had ever seen. Next to it was a bar alcove, hard stuff on the lower shelf, a bottle of Chivas Regal rubbing shoulders with a Glenlivet, and the shelf above holding the biggest private

collection of liqueurs and aperitifs I'd seen in a long time. The
Slivovitz was half empty and the Strega Alberti unopened. The
whole alcove was backed with mirrors and flooded with concealed
pink lighting. I felt thirsty. The carpet was ivory and I could feel
myself slowly sinking in it. Just off centre of the room was a low
walnut table with some coffee-table books on it, and a centrepiece
in silver of a benign Buddha holding one hand on his navel and
looking as though he wanted, or had just taken, a dose of bicar-
bonate. At an angle to the window wall was a black-and-ivory-
striped settee big enough to hold about six people and ensure that
each had complete privacy. Sitting on this, her legs curled under
her, and wedged up on either side with black-and-white silk
cushions, was Mrs Stankowski. I had saved her until last, which
was just as well, otherwise I would never have noticed any of the
other things.

She was wearing a little jacket, collar high at the neck, which
tipped her chin up slightly, and lounge trousers, the whole suit
made of some silvery material. It was a perfect fit and looked as
though it had been sprayed on to her. Her figure had matured a
little over the last eight years but not to an extent that would
prompt anyone to shout 'objection' to the stewards. She had red
hair which made Wilkins's look like rust chippings from some old
tanker, and it was short and curly and full of bright lights and must
have cost her a packet every few days at somewhere like Vidal
Sassoon's. She had blue eyes, cornflower blue; and it's not my fault
if that's corny, because that's exactly what they were. In addition
they weren't very friendly, but I wasn't worrying about that. It was
a just challenge, and I realized there and then that that was what
had been missing from my life for quite a while . . . challenge.
Somewhere the adrenalin tap was turned on a bit more. She was
the most gorgeous—no, glorious—thing I'd seen for at least two
months. I gave her a warm smile and I could see that she thought
nothing of it.

'Sit down, Mr Carver, and state your business quickly.' She
pointed with a long ebony stick that had rested across her knees,
to a small gilt chair by the fireplace.

I sat down, knowing the chair would stick to me when I got up.

I said 'I've been employed by the London Fraternal Insurance
Society to try and recover the gold python arm bracelet which was
stolen from you.'

'I thought the police did that kind of thing?' She had a nice voice, a faint little gaspiness in it as though she suffered from a weak chest, though you would not have thought so looking at it. Somewhere, too, there was the echo of an accent, though I couldn't place it.

'The police rate of recovery is so low it hardly comes on to the graph. As you know, because you've been through it, they're very sympathetic, take down all the particulars and then—and you probably don't know—they go back to the police canteen for a quick one and forget all about it. So, insurance companies prefer people like me.'

'Why?'

'Because I get paid for the job and a commission on all recoveries. A sergeant-detective could recover the Cullinan diamond and still get only his pay packet and go on worrying about his hire-purchase payments.'

'The Cullinan diamond doesn't exist. It was cut up into one hundred and five separate stones.'

'It was a figure of speech.' But I was impressed, and followed it up. 'You know about diamonds?'

'A little.' The pale, creamy pink lips moved to something like a smile.

'Tell me,' I said, 'something about the Tennant Diamond.'

'It is a perfect yellow African stone measuring an inch by one and one-eighth inches. Sixty-six carats. But I'm not in the mood for quiz games. What do you want from me that I haven't already told the police?'

'With the greatest respect, the London Fraternal Insurance Society finds it hard to believe—though they would never say so, they leave that kind of thing to me—that while you and your maid were out someone entered this flat, using a key, walked off with a python bracelet from your dressing table and took nothing else.'

'It might have been someone who specialized in Indian antiques. Just like these art robberies. They select what they want.'

'True. But why did they leave old Buddha there?' I nodded at the coffee table. 'He's antique enough. And Indian.'

'He's from the Tanjore district. Seventeenth century. But don't ask me why he was left, or other things. I'm not interested in the psychology of the thief. My bracelet was insured. I've made a claim for the loss. Just tell the company to pay me. The thing is perfectly straightforward. You don't think I'm lying to you, do you? Yes, or no?'

I'd had that kind of question before—mostly from women, too. Believe me, it's harder to answer than 'have you stopped beating your wife yet?'

Of course, there was no doubt in my mind that she was lying. The police weren't happy with her story, and neither was Hawkins of the L.F.I.S. And having seen this place, I wasn't happy with it. There was a gold cigarette box on the side-table close to me, and plenty of other stuff around the room that any villain with an eye for tomfoolery would never have passed up.

'Well?' she said.

I stood up. Of course, the damned chair came with me. I prised it off and gave her a look full of confidence.

'I'm absolutely certain you're not,' I said.

'That's a very nice thing to say.' She was smiling.

'It took no effort.'

'But you only did it out of politeness.'

'*Noblesse oblige.*'

'Crap.' The underlying accent was stronger. I'm no Professor Henry Higgins, but I thought I could hear something North Country or Midlands in it. She raised her ebony stick and gave one of the cushions a whack. 'I only like people who tell the truth.'

I said, taking a chance, 'With looks like yours and a quarter of a million pounds, it can't happen often. You'll only hear what people think you want to hear.'

She gave me a long look, and said, 'Let's try again. Am I lying?'

'If I can recover the bracelet it won't matter either way.'

'Don't spare my feelings, Mr Carver.' She picked up my card which lay on a cushion at her side. 'Mr Rex Carver. Where the hell did you pick up a name like Rex?'

'I was told there was a two-week argument between my father and mother. He won. I've never forgiven him. I go round thinking I should have been a golden labrador. How come Gloria?'

'It's Gloriana, really. My father. He had a thing for Spenser. *Faerie Queene.*'

'Educated man.'

'Self-educated. He was an iron-puddler in a steel works at Scunthorpe. I think it was a puddler, anyway. He was a strict disciplinarian. Every Saturday night when he got back from the pub he used to beat my mother, me and my brother.'

'Made for a quiet Sunday, no doubt. And coming back to the

main point—yes, I do think you're being less than honest about the bracelet. Maybe it was stolen, but not the way you tell it.'

I began to move towards the door. If she could whack cushions with a wrist movement that Arnold Palmer would have admired, she could also throw things.

'Thank you.'

'Nothing to it.'

I put a hand on the door knob. It was a glass job with fancy brass filigree over it.

'Do you do anything else except recovery work for insurance companies?'

'Pay me the rate for the job and I do anything—except baby-sitting, unless they're above the age of consent.'

'Funny man.'

'Humour is the oil that—'

'Stuff it.' The accent was strong this time.

'As you say.'

'I do.'

'Goodbye, Mrs Stankowski—and thank you for sparing me the time.'

'It's the only thing I give away . . . usually.'

I inclined my head a few degrees, butler fashion, opened the door and went out. I couldn't make out whether she liked me or not. Anyway, it wasn't a problem I was going to go to a psychiatrist about.

Outside the door, granite-faced 'Will-ye-cum-in-the-noo' was hovering. She steered me carefully past the semi-circular marble hall table and opened the flat door.

I said, 'What's her problem? Thinking that nobody will love her, except for her money?'

She said, 'Ken this well, keep your gab steeket in guid company and gie your ain fish-guts to your ain seamaws.' At least, it sounded like that.

'You're dead right,' I said.

Dimble phoned just before five and said that nobody in the regular trade was handling a gold python arm bracelet at the moment. He would keep his eyes open and call at the end of the week for his money. I rang Hawkins and said that as far as I could tell—tell him, that was—Mrs Stankowski's story of the arm bracelet was on the level. He said what level? Knowing where that would lead, I pretended that the connection was bad and rang off. Then

I sat and thought a bit about Gloriana. Stankowski came too hard off the tongue. Her old iron-puddler of a father might have been a self-educated man, but so was I, having been to a Devon grammar school. '*Her angel's face as the great eye of Heaven shyned bright, and made a sunshine in the shadie place. . . .*' Spenser. Well, I had an idea—which meant I was feeling better—that there were quite a few shady places about. If you were going to pick up a little cash or excitement there were no better spots than shady places. Cash, at the moment, didn't too much interest me—though that would come naturally if everything else was right—but excitement did. It was better than strychnine glycerophosphate (0.0025 gr.) in the blood.

When I said good night to Wilkins she said, 'Try to be nice to my sister when she's here. She makes a great sacrifice to come.'

I said, 'Is she bringing that basset hound with her?'

'She has to, since there's no one to leave it with at home.'

I went on thinking about the long, mournful streak of dog. I'd be tripping over it six times a day and, since it favoured my desk chair, sitting on it even more often. I will say this for it, though—no matter what the indignity, it never bit. Just looked at me with sad, reproachful, blood-rimmed eyes.

I had a couple of whiskies in Miggs's office with him, on the way home. Behind his garage he had a small gymnasium. He had been a sergeant in the Commandos and for a couple of guineas a half-hour session gave work-outs to a mixed clientele, and taught some of them how to kill a man with bare hands—twenty different ways—in twelve sessions.

'Manston,' he said, 'was in for a refresher today.'

'I hope he dusted the floor with you.'

'He did. He asked after you, health, finances and sex life.'

'Tell him to keep away from me.'

Manston was an old friend of mine, though the friendship was usually in a bad state of strain. He worked in the same line of business, but in a much higher bracket. His monthly cheque came fat and regularly through the Treasury. He also knew thirty different ways of killing a man with his bare hands.

I took the Central Line home; home being a flat in a small street near the Tate Gallery.

Parked outside the house was a 1930 Phantom Two Rolls-Royce. It was ivory coloured and immaculate. There was a chauffeur, looking as though he were carved out of wood, behind the wheel.

He wore a black uniform with tiny lines of white piping on collar and cuffs.

Mrs Meld, next door to me, and a great friend of mine, was leaning on her gate waiting for Mr Meld to come back with the supper Guinness in time to catch 'Coronation Street'. 'Gives a bit of tone to the place, eh?' she said.

'One of your rich relations?'

'The only one with money in our family is my brother Albert. He keeps a whelk stall at Southend and drives a Ford Consul. No, it's a visitor for you, Mr Carver. I let her in your place.' She winked at me. 'Don't do anything I wouldn't do. Not with a red-headed type. Otherwise you might be biffed over the nut with a bottle. She was carryin' one.'

CHAPTER 2

Something Large and Bulky Fell Out

The flat consisted of a bedroom, a sitting room, bathroom and kitchen. From time to time, when I had had it, I had spent a lot of money on it. Mrs Meld came in and did for me in the mornings but somehow the place always looked untidy. From the sitting-room window, by risking a cricked neck, I could get a fair glimpse of the river.

When I went in there was no sign of Gloriana, except a new bottle of Vat 69 on the sitting-room table. I got two glasses and a soda siphon, and opened the bottle.

She came through from the bedroom, obviously the end of her tour of inspection, and said, 'Why on earth do you need such an enormous bed?'

'I sleep diagonally.'

I poured whisky into the two glasses.

'Water, not soda,' she said.

I went through into the kitchen for water and called back, 'Thanks for the present.'

'You seem to take it very much for granted.'

I came back with the water.

'It's happened before. People who change their minds sometimes bring a peace-offering.'

I fixed her drink and sat her in my best armchair with it. She looked good against the brown leather; red hair, a green tailor-made with mink collar and cuffs, and crocodile shoes. She smiled at me and then lowered the whisky in her glass in a way which would have made her old father proud of his daughter.

She said, 'How do you know I've changed my mind?'

I said, 'Where did you get that Phantom Two?'

'It was my late husband's. Jan was very fond of it and I've never liked to get rid of it.'

I said, 'Is it really a quarter of a million? It's important, you know, when it comes to fixing my fee.'

'Nearer a million.'

'Good. Now tell me about the bracelet.'

'You're a presuming bastard, aren't you?'

'I've been in this business a long time. I can read the signs like a Master Magi.'

'Magus. Singular. By the way, is the girl at your office always so cagey about giving your home address?'

'She can't get it out of her head that I'm not grown up and don't have to be protected. She's seen this, too.' I handed her the art photograph.

'Lord, those old things.' She reached down for the crocodile bag at the side of the chair and slipped the photograph in.

'Now, what about the bracelet?'

'It was taken, stolen by my brother. So, naturally, I didn't want to tell the police that.'

'How did he manage it?'

'My maid—the silly old haggis—let him in when I wasn't there. She dotes on him. He took the bracelet and five thousand pounds in cash from my safe.'

I shook my glass to get the soda bubbles working again. 'He makes a habit of this kind of thing?'

'When he gets the chance. But usually only small things like the bracelet. Normally he writes within a week, sending the pawn ticket and apologizing.'

'And you get them out of hock and forgive?'

'Normally.'

'My husband said one should always have a substantial cash float, just in case. Jan was—'

'I get it. You fond of your brother?'

'Very.'

'Why should he steal from you, then? Why not just give him a handout occasionally? You can afford it.'

'I did. Sometimes a hundred, maybe five hundred, once or twice a thousand. But in the end I got fed up.'

'Tell me about him.'

'He's a dreamer. Not poetic. Big-business dreams, big schemes for making money. It always seemed unfair to him that I had so much from just marrying.'

I stood up, took our two glasses and began to refill them. 'Well, you're not going to miss five thousand or the bracelet. Equally, clearly, this isn't one of the times when you are prepared to forgive—otherwise you wouldn't be here.'

'That's so.'

'Why?'

'All this happened two weeks ago. I haven't heard from him. I don't know where he is, and I'm worried about him.'

'Maybe for a bracelet and five thousand he reckons he should wait three weeks, perhaps a month?'

I handed her a drink and sat on the stool. She uncrossed and recrossed her legs for comfort two feet from my nose. I had a controllable desire to reach out and run a finger over the right patella and tibia.

'But he's always been very punctilious.'

'It's a good word. But you wouldn't be here, bearing gifts, and with a touch of *Femme* by Marcel Rochas behind each ear, over a matter of punctilio.'

'I said I was worried. He's left his job, and they don't know where he is.'

'Who are they?'

'He was a foreign correspondent for Intercontinental News Services.'

'Didn't he give them any reason?'

'They had a letter of resignation from him. It was written on Excelsior Hotel notepaper—that's Florence.'

'Was he based there?'

'No.'

'Well, five thousand's a good reason for chucking a job. When it runs out he can get another. I don't think there's anything to worry about.'

'But there is. I'm absolutely sure that something has happened to him.'

'Sure is a very strong word.'

'That's why I used it. He's missed my birthday. That was four days ago. Ever since we both left home, no matter where he's been in the world he's always sent me a cable.'

'A man of fixed habits.'

'In some things.'

'You want me to find him for you?'

'Yes.'

'I'm expensive—particularly when it comes to foreign travel.'

She stood up. 'He's my brother. I don't care how much it costs.'

I stood up, slopping whisky over one trouser knee.

'I'll think it over and give you a ring in the morning. The cost, I mean. What's his name? Freeman?'

'Martin, yes.'

'Where did he hang out in this country?'

'He had a room in a Dorset Square hotel. The Mountjoy. I phoned them. He gave it up the day after he took the bracelet and the money.'

I cuddled my left palm under her right elbow and led her to the door. For a moment I thought of asking her to stay for dinner, poached eggs on toast, with a thin smear of Marmite on the toast, delicious, and a bottle of Spanish chablis. Then I remembered her flat and the ivory Rolls and decided against it. She'd think I was after her money with some homespun approach.

Her blue eyes frankly on me, her lips slightly parted, the length of her body slightly hipped out in a *Vogue* pose, she said, 'You will do your very best?'

I said, 'Yes—if you'll tell me what it really was that made you decide to come to me between the time I left your flat today and now. And no malarky.'

For a moment she said nothing. Then with a smile she said, 'I knew I was right about you. I have an instinct about people.'

'Come to the point.'

'Half an hour after you left I had an anonymous phone call from some man telling me not to worry about my brother.'

'Then why worry?'

'Because the last time it happened—an anonymous phone call, I mean—he got mixed up in some awful currency affair in France and only Jan's influence put it right for him. Jan was very fond of him. They got on well together.'

'Thank you for being frank with me. How many times has he been in jail?'

It took her ten seconds flat to decide not to give me a backhander, and then she said, 'Once—when he was twenty-five. He did two years for some . . . well, it was something to do with the City and the share promotion. I told you. He's a dreamer, always after big money, big schemes. The trouble is he's hopelessly incompetent, really.' The smile flashed on. 'You will help me, won't you?'

'Absolutely. No matter how much it costs you.' I gave her my little butler bow and ushered her out.

I thought about her, all through the poached eggs and cheap chablis. And then I thought about brother Martin. Well, it all seemed straightforward enough. I just had to find him. That should be simple enough. How simple can you get? Here was a case, I thought, which I could take just for health reasons; no escalation to the dangerous heights of the Secret Service world of Manston and Sutcliffe, no excessive excitements—just find Martin Freeman. Somewhere—God damn it—somebody must have laughed at my innocence, knowing I was going to end up looking for another man, far more important than Freeman, a man who had been kidnapped—and for reasons which were to bring Manston and Sutcliffe down on me like a pair of hawks on a corn-fat dove.

Intercontinental News Services were around the corner from Fleet Street in Whitefriars Street. The weather had relented a bit and there were occasional strip-teasing gleams of spring sunshine. Walking the few yards from the taxi to the office, I thought I detected a suggestion of a new lift in my steps, something that in time might almost develop into briskness.

After a lot of delay and little co-operation I saw a Mr Addle who was the Office Manager. He lived in an office about the size of a big packing case. As I sat opposite him my knees almost touched his under the desk. His long grey face looked as though it had been moulded out of wet paper pulp and allowed to set hard. He had an absent look in his eyes and a rambling way of talking which suited me. All I had to do was nudge him now and again. I explained how Mrs Stankowski was worried about her brother and wanted me to trace him. Had he any views about the resignation?

His eyes wobbled, trying to focus on a point somewhere above my head, and he said, 'Not the first time he's resigned. Always comes back. Restless man, certain charm, though. Knew how to make friends and use people. Good at his job . . . well, good as most. Always trouble over his expenses, of course, but there always is trouble over expenses with all of them.'

'Did he specialize in anything, any particular field of news?'

'No. Anything he could pick up. Oh, well, maybe European political affairs more than most.'

'He'd been in trouble before, hadn't he?'

'Before he came to us. Impulsive, easily led. Always had some wildcat scheme for making a fortune. But then a lot of people have. You know, being Office Manager and responsible for staff . . . makes me a bit like a Father Confessor. Everyone comes to you with their stupid little confidences and problems. Particularly the secretaries and typists.' His eyes managed to focus briefly on me. 'Miss Lonelyhearts, that's me. Thank God I've only got another year to do. Got a bungalow down at Seaford. You can sit at the window and look out to twenty or thirty miles of nothing but sea.' His eyes wavered up to the wall a foot behind my head. 'Distance . . . lovely thing.'

'How was he on women?'

'Terrible, I'm told. But not here. I saw to that. Anyway, he wasn't here often. You should tell Mrs Stankowski he'll turn up. He's that kind. The turning-up kind.'

'Where was he based in Europe?'

'Paris, usually. Sometimes Rome. Beirut, too, for a while. Look, I can't tell you anything that'll help you trace him. He's just gone off.'

From Fleet Street I went round to the Mountjoy Hotel in Dorset Square. It was a quiet, modest place which could have done with a repaint job inside and out. Behind a little counter-fronted alcove which was the hotel desk sat a brunette of about thirty-odd, good-looking and pleasant, and with time on her hands. She was drinking coffee and reading a week-old *Observer* colour supplement. She looked up and gave me a bright, flashing smile full of false promises. Returning it in kind, so that we immediately became old and intimate friends, I said, 'My name's Addle. I'm the Office Manager of Intercontinental News Services. And I want to make some enquiries about one of our correspondents—Martin Freeman—who used to live here.'

She nodded sympathetically and said, 'I'm Mary McCarthy, American novelist—but, of course, you know that—and I've taken this job to get material for a new book I'm writing. You don't have to go out of the door and come back and start all over again. You can do it from where you're standing.'

'You know Mr Addle?'

'He's been in Room Twelve for the last ten years. Martin Freeman came here on his recommendation. My real name is Jane Judd—yes, I know it sounds like a strip-cartoon character, but I'm stuck with it. Actually I *am* writing a book and it's called *Why I Sometimes Don't Like Men*. Subtitle—*Homo Hoteliens*. They think every chambermaid is a whore, or should be, and every woman receptionist is longing for escape to an illicit weekend. You're lucky I'm in one of my chatty moods. Yesterday you'd have found me glum and dumb.'

'Today's model suits me.' I dropped my card in front of her.

She glanced at it and said, 'I read about you once. In an old copy of *London Life*—a symposium on private-detective agencies in London. All the magazines I read are old, left behind in their rooms by transients and regulars. What's that bastard Martin been up to and why has he left us?'

'Is your heart broken?'

'Chipped on one corner. I suppose he's been pinching from that sister of his again.' She held up a hand. 'This ring belonged to her once. Still does, I suppose.' It was a dress ring, a thin gold band with an oval-shaped piece of jade.

'She's cross with him this time. And he's given up his job. She wants me to find him. Any ideas? For instance—' I nodded at the small switchboard behind her—'what about a list of phone numbers that he used to call?'

'We don't keep a record.'

Probably they didn't.

'Well, anything that could help me.'

'Maybe—if you could help me. Summer's just round the corner. I was looking at some super beach-wear in Harrods the other day . . . I don't mean all the way, of course. But perhaps a contribution.'

I put two five-pound notes under the blotter on the counter. She stirred her coffee, looked up at me and I saw that she had gone glum. No smile. I slipped another fiver under the blotter. The smile came back.

'Martin Freeman,' she said, 'is a charming man, but potentially as crooked as Hampton Court maze. He never gave it any publicity, and certainly Mr Addle doesn't know about it, but he has a small place in the country.' She picked up a pencil and began to scribble on a tear-off pad. 'Don't run away with the idea of anything worth writing home about when I say "place". It's a crummy little cottage. Oil lamps and a chemical closet. Those were the things that put me off after two visits.'

She tore off the sheet and handed it to me.

'Thanks.' I gave her a genuine smile. 'One of these days I might get a small place of my own in the country.'

'Let me know sometime.'

'How long ago were you last at the cottage?'

She retrieved the fivers from under the blotter and began to put them in her handbag. 'Relations between Martin and myself have been very correct for the last year. I'm engaged to a P.R. man from Shell-Mex, but it doesn't inhibit either of us.'

'Thank you for your co-operation.'

'You *should* thank me. I refused it a couple of days ago to another man. He said he was from a hire-purchase company . . . something about a car Martin had bought. I didn't care for his manner. And anyway, Martin hasn't owned a car for all the years I've known him.'

'What did this man look like?'

'I kept on thinking of a well-beaten spaniel. Fifty-odd, shabby grey suit, mackintosh and well-rubbed suède shoes. Brown eyes, thin wispy brownish hair, London-Scottish regimental tie, white silk shirt with the collar frayed, and his heart not really in his job, whatever it was.'

'You should have been in this business.'

'Let me know if you ever have a vacancy.'

I went out, thinking about the London-Scottish, beaten-spaniel type. Given a change of tie there were a lot of them about, and one of their characteristics was that they would never get anywhere unless they really believed that it was important to girls like Jane Judd that summer was just around the corner and Harrods was full of super beach-wear.

The address on the sheet of paper read:

Ash Cottage, Crundale, near Wye, Kent.
Key under foot-scraper at back door.
Fire smokes when wind in north-east.
Drinks in cupboard under stairs.

Jane Judd was a girl after my own heart. There should be more of them around.

I phoned Mrs Stankowski and told her that I was doing some preliminary work on her brother and would call and see her the next day. She wanted to know what I had been doing, and what I still had in mind, so I pretended the line was bad and finally rang off. No matter how you get a quarter of a million, or a million, one of the things it does for you is to make you think that all your questions should be answered instanter. And let's face it, they usually are.

I called in at the office and had a ten-minute but not unreasonably acrimonious chat with Wilkins to put her in the picture. As I was going out to get some lunch she said, 'Well, at least this looks like a reasonably straightforward job.'

I said, 'In this business there is no such thing. Otherwise there wouldn't be any business. What about the chap with the London-Scottish tie? Debt-collector, or a divorce creep? Freeman been playing around? Or something really sinister?'

'I know which you would prefer.'

'Sinister? Why not? In my present condition any doctor would recommend it. Salt in the blood—'

'Don't start that.'

I had lunch in a pub, then went round to Miggs's place and borrowed a Mini-Cooper. An hour later I was in the green leaf and bare hop-poles of springtime Kent, going like a bat out of hell round the Maidstone by-pass, and convinced that it was better to hire a car and charge it up to expenses than to own one and spend daily misery in worrying over London parking places. I found Wye all right, but Crundale was more elusive because I was three times given explicitly wrong directions. It was half past four and a strong slanting rain, with a lick of sleet in it, was coming down when I got to Ash Cottage. At least, as near as I could get with the car. It was in a little valley, served by a dirt road that ended at a field gate. At the side of the gate was a wooden arrow stuck on top of a pole with the name—Ash Cottage—on the arrow and pointing up a low hill towards a beech wood. The cottage sat just in the lee of the wood. Coat collar turned up against the rain, I went up a muddy footpath for two hundred yards to the cottage. It was red tiled, wooden framed, with black timbers against white plaster, and had small diamond-lozenge window glass. A crack of thunder heralded my arrival. Behind me the footpath was becoming a coffee-coloured torrent. I took the key from under the foot-scraper, didn't dally to scrape my muddy shoes, and went in.

I found myself in the kitchen. Well, everyone says it's the most important room of the house, so why not enter through it? It was dark inside and I flicked on my torch and had a pleasant surprise. By the far door that led into the main part of the cottage was an electric light switch. I pressed it down and a light came on. Martin Freeman had had electricity installed since Jane Judd's last visit. I remembered then that there were poles all the way up alongside the dirt road.

Apart from being as crooked as Hampton Court maze, Martin Freeman was also untidy. The sitting room was large and comfortable, but there were old newspapers crumpled on the settee, and dirty glasses and an empty *vin rosé* bottle on a side-table. The open fireplace was a foot high with old wood ash and was decorated on one side with a pair of gum boots and on the other by an old cavalry sword which had been used as a poker. Against the window that looked up the hill to the beech wood was a dining table with a cloth half over it and, on the cloth, the remains of a breakfast set-up, yellow egg-spill congealed hard on a plate and a paperbacked thriller propped against a Worcestershire sauce bottle. An open stairway ran up to the bedrooms. Round the newel post hung a pair of nylon stockings. Halfway up the stairs was an empty beer bottle with a faded red carnation stuck in it. I began to get a confused idea of Martin Freeman.

The main bedroom had a large double bed, unmade, covers flung back, the pillows crumpled. Over an armchair had been tossed a dressing gown, black with a white lightning-stripe motif all over it, and a red pyjama jacket. I found the trousers in the bathroom next door later. Just at this moment I was interested in a pile of letters, opened, that lay on the floor at the side of the bed. It was easy to tell that Freeman went down for his mail in the morning and came back to bed to read it. His procedure was clear. He opened an envelope, read the letter or contents, stuck it back in the envelope and dropped it on the floor.

I sat on the floor and began to go methodically through the pile. The bottom one dated the accumulation as being four months old. Most of the stuff was bills—and all of the envelopes had been addressed to Freeman, care of Lloyds Bank Ltd, 50 High Street, Canterbury, and then redirected to the cottage from there. A January bank statement showed that he was £45.11.6. overdrawn. Sorting out what I hoped might be the wheat from the chaff, I was left with:

1. A New Year's card—postmark Firenze—inscribed '*Buon Natale e Felice Anno Nuovo*'. Signed: *Leon Pelegrina*. The message and name on the card had been printed and the name Pelegrina was struck

through in ink just to leave Leon. Obviously Leon was a friend.
The printed address in one corner read:23 Piazza Santo Spirito,
Firenze. Freeman's letter of resignation had been written from
Florence.
2. A letter, only a few lines, from someone called Bill Dawson. It
was on hotel stationery and in an hotel envelope—the Libya Palace
Hotel, Tripoli, Libya. It was a month old, and read: *'Long time no
see or hear. Tour out here extended another three months. What about it? Find
some excuse. We could make Sabratha this time. And you could have your
revenge on the Wheelus course. Additional incentive (?) the charmer is due in
Uaddan next month sometime.'*

Well, if Freeman had taken off, it might be to Tripoli. Sabratha
and Wheelus meant nothing to me. Charmer could be guessed at.

3. A statement of account rendered for £105.7.2. from a shipping
and travel agency—Phs. Van Ommeren, 118 Park Lane, London,
W.1. I might be able to check with them whether Freeman had
gone to Libya.

These were the only things that seemed to me might be of significance. There was plenty of other stuff—mostly from women—that
no man of discretion would have left kicking about on the floor.
However, it was clear—from the bank redirecting—that Freeman
hadn't let any except very close friends—apart from Jane
Judd—know about the cottage.

I did a quick tour of the bathroom and the other bedroom and
then went down to the sitting room. It was still raining outside and
getting dark. I found the cupboard under the stairs. There was half
a bottle of whisky there and a couple of bottles of soda water. I got
a clean glass from the kitchen and fixed myself a drink. I sat down
in an armchair and put the drink on a side-table. The ashtray on
it was full of golf tee pegs, and lying face down by it was a small
framed photograph. Tidy-minded, I stood it up. It was worth
bringing out into the light. It was a photograph of a girl of about
. . . well, not far off thirty . . . not that I was concerned with her
age. She wore baggy Arabian Night harem trousers, too diaphanous
ever to keep out a cold desert wind, and two heavily sequined
plaques over her breasts. On her head was a tiny turban with a
large jewel at the front from which sprang a whisk of stiff horse-
hair. She was slim, good-looking and would have made the Sultan
Schahriah's eyes pop. Scribbled in violet ink across the foot of the

photograph was the inscription: For Martin—Paris 1966. Apart from being good-looking, she had a good face, interesting, intelligent, and something about the set of her lips, even in the posed smile, that said she was clearly on the ball. I couldn't make a guess at her nationality, but she was certainly not Arab.

I took a drink of my whisky, felt in my pockets—amongst the letters and stuff I'd taken from the bedroom—for my cigarettes, and had them out when a voice said from the direction of the kitchen door behind me, 'All right then, let us be very civilised about our behaviour.'

Before I turned I knew that he was not English. The French accent was as thick and meaty as *pâté de campagne*. When I did turn I found myself looking at the business end of what, later, I learned was a 9 mm Browning pistol, manufactured under licence in Belgium, at Herstal, by the Fabrique Nationale d'Armes de Guerre.

I said, 'Considering that thing you're holding, I think that remark applies to you more than to me.'

'I don't trust anyone.'

'It's a good rule-of-thumb procedure, but it still doesn't make you civilized. I hope you've got that damned thing on "safe"?'

'Naturally, Monsieur Freeman.'

For a moment my instinct was to disillusion him. Then I decided to play it for a while. He might say things to Monsieur Freeman that he would never say to Monsieur Carver. And when he did get the name I knew that he was going to pronounce it *Carvay*.

I said, 'I'm not going to give you any trouble. There's some whisky and a bottle of soda left. Get yourself a glass.'

He hesitated quite a while and then decided to accept the invitation. He put the pistol handy on a chair near the stair cupboard and began to help himself, managing most of the time to keep an eye on me.

He was a biggish man, about fifty, and with most of his weight around the middle. He had a nose in the de Gaulle class and rather close-set, worried little green-brown eyes. Fiddling with his drink, he made flappy, almost womanly, flutterings with his hands and kept on humming to himself as though to keep up his confidence. He was all wrapped up, untidily, in cellophane, or that's what it looked like, until I realised that he was wearing one of those transparent light-weight raincoats and a sou'wester kind of hat over his own cloth cap. Rolled up, the whole weather-protection outfit could be tucked away in a tobacco pouch. His drink prepared he stood behind the chair on which his pistol rested and took a sip from his glass and, because of the way his eyes were, eyed me narrowly from above it.

I said, 'Why don't you take your wrappings off and sit down. You look as though you are collecting for the National Lifeboat Institution or something.'

He considered this, then put his glass down on the chair and began to slip his things off.

'Don't make any mistake, Monsieur Freeman. I am here on very serious business.'

He transferred his glass and pistol to the edge of the table and sat down on the chair.

'You'd better say what it is.'

'I'm from Monsieur Robert Duchêne.'

He waited for me to show surprise, but I didn't.

'Of Paris,' he said.

'You're French too, aren't you?'

'François Paulet. I'm surprised you are so phlegmatic, monsieur.'

'It must be the weather. And why are you from Monsieur Robert Duchêne, armed with a gun and dressed against all weathers?'

'Flippant, uh? It is an English characteristic, no? Oh, I know all about the English when I learn the language here many years ago. I was wine waiter, you know, at many restaurants. However, let us not bother with my history, considerable though it has been. From you I want what you have taken from Monsieur Duchêne. I have this—' he touched the pistol with a fingertip—'because of the delicacy of the matter. My client cannot call in the police because, as you know, the things you have taken were not all legitimately acquired by him in the first place. Notwithstanding, it is my duty to recover them.'

'By force?'

'If necessary. And do not be misled by my docile appearance.'

'Perhaps you'd better tell me what I have to hand over.'

'Certainly.' He smiled, and it was quite a warm, genuine smile, touching and appealing. 'It is good that so far we talk amicably. All business should be like that. Everyone would finish more quickly and get more money.' He fished in his jacket pocket and pulled out a sheet of paper and slid it across to me.

I reached for the paper and unfolded it. It was a quarto sheet, typewritten, and read:

Ancient Greek coins, the property of Monsieur Robert Duchêne, 2 bis Rue de Bac, Paris.

Item—one Electrum stater of Lydia.
Item—one Electrum stater of Ephesus.
Item—one gold stater of Croesus.
Item—one Daric of Persia.
Item—alliance of Siris and Pyxus, two.
Item—Knossos with Minotaur and Labyrinth, two.
Item—stater of Thasos, two.

There were quite a few more items, twenty-two in all, finishing with:

Item—one, gold 100 litrae of Syracuse.

I said, 'These have been stolen?'

He said, 'You know they have, Monsieur Freeman. By you. And it was, if I may say so, a great abuse of hospitality. No doubt you thought that since Monsieur Duchêne had acquired them for his collection in . . . a devious way . . . that you would not be pressed to return them. Legally, I mean. But Monsieur Duchêne has employed me to recover them for him without the help of the law. I may say I am an expert at such matters. A large part of my business is the recovery of stolen goods.'

I said, 'Monsieur Paulet, take a good look at me. I'm in the same business. The name is Carver, Rex Carver, and I'm after Monsieur Freeman too, to get back stolen goods.'

He looked at me blankly for a moment or two.

Then he said, 'You are not Monsieur Martin Freeman?'

'No.' I took out one of my cards and flipped it to him.

He looked at it and his face fell.

'Carvay,' he said.

'That's right.'

'Not Freeman?'

'No.'

'*Merde!*' he said. 'Why do I always get things cocked up?' I really felt sorry for him. In disappointment he had a warm, collapsed human appeal.'

'It was a natural mistake,' I said. 'I am in Freeman's cottage, drinking his whisky. I could have made the same mistake. Tell me—when did Freeman pinch these coins?'

'About two weeks ago. No, a little less.' He smiled suddenly and
leaned forward and held out a big hand across the table to me.
'Monsieur,' he said as I took it, 'it is a pleasure to meet someone
of my own profession on this side of the Channel. *Enchanté*. And
what was it he has stolen from your client?'

He had a grip like a vice. I rescued my hand and shook it to
ease the numbness. 'He lifted five thousand pounds and a piece of
jewellery from his sister. You understand, I tell you this in
confidence.' I could feel the old Gallic protocol taking over in me
too.

'But naturally, monsieur.'

'How,' I asked, 'did you trace this cottage? Freeman never adver-
tised it.'

'Haaaaaa!' It was a great gust of a knowing sigh and then he did
something I hadn't seen done for years. He laid the index finger of
his right hand against the side of his big nose and winked. I knew
better than to probe a professional man further. Then he stood up
and said, 'You have found many clues in this place?'

I waved my hand around and said, 'You're welcome to what
there is. I'll have another drink while you look round.'

'*Merci*, monsieur.'

Ignoring me, he took a leisurely look around the room and then
disappeared upstairs. I lit a cigarette and waited, and wondered
what there was in Freeman that made him go for antique stuff,
jewellery and coins. Nothing that sprang from a genuine love of the
past and its craftsmanship I was sure. He was just after cash. And
then I thought about François Paulet. He was a likeable number.
But in my profession to keep an overdraft down you had to have
more than likeableness. There was a touch of music-hall about
Paulet and a self-confessed habit of getting things cocked up that
marked him out for the lower rungs of the hierarchy.

He came downstairs after a while, looking shocked, and shaking
his head.

'*Mon Dieu!*' he said. 'It is incredible. To have affairs of the heart
is natural. But to leave the evidence lying on the floor at the side
of the bed for the world to see. No Frenchman would do such a
thing.'

'Nor many Englishmen.'

'But some of them were clearly married women. Why—' his
face cleared suddenly—'there is enough material there to keep a

blackmailer happy for life.' Then he frowned. 'It is a good thing that you and I are honourable men.'

'Personally,' I said, 'I've never ceased congratulating myself about it.'

I stood up.

'You are going?' he asked.

'Back to London.'

'You could give me a lift?'

'How did you get here?'

'I am by train to Ashford. Then a bus. Then I walk.' He smiled and my heart went out to him as he went on, 'Monsieur Duchêne is not generous in the matter of expenses.'

'I'll give you a lift back to London.'

'Thank you.'

He followed me into the kitchen and then paused and nodded to a door at the far end. 'What is in there?'

'I haven't examined it because I know. It is the chemical closet.'

'The toilet?'

'Yes.'

'Ah—then I will use it before our journey.'

He went over and opened the door. I must say that for a big man he was quick on his feet. As he pulled the door towards him something large and bulky fell out, and François did a backward jump of three feet.

I went to his side and looked down.

'*Merde!*' he said. 'Is it Freeman?'

'No.'

'Who is it then?'

'I don't know. Freeman is in his thirties. This man is much older.'

'He was propped on the seat, his head against the door. So when I open it—out he comes, *bim!*' Paulet sounded a bit scared.

I didn't think I had to make any comment. I knelt down by the man. I'm no expert but it was clear from the markings on the neck that he had been strangled manually. *Rigor mortis* had set in completely, so he had been dead for anything between twelve and twenty-four hours—after this *rigor* begins to pass away. I went through his pockets, but either he carried nothing on him or someone had cleared them after his death.

Behind me, Paulet said, 'What is to do? I am in a strange country and do not wish to be involved in this kind of thing.'

'Nor me,' I said, standing up. 'We'll just go quietly away, and I'll phone the police anonymously on the way back to London.'

I looked at Paulet. He was very much shaken.

'I think,' he said, 'with an effort I shall not be sick.'

I went to the back door and opened it, letting him pass me.

'For a man who carries a gun around, I should have thought this kind of thing meant nothing to you.'

He glanced back at me indignantly. 'But that is for show. It is never loaded.'

We slithered down the muddy path in darkness and a thin drizzle to my car. All the way I was thinking of the man lying back in the kitchen. He wore a London-Scottish tie, a shabby grey suit and well-rubbed suède shoes. Even in death he maintained his beaten-spaniel look.

CHAPTER 3

Neanderthal Man with Azalea

I phoned the Ashford police at a call box just outside Maidstone. Later, I dropped Paulet at the Strand Palace Hotel where he was staying.

He hadn't said a great deal on the drive to London. The sight of the dead man had shaken him. I went in and had a drink with him and he brightened up a bit. I think it was the sight of the waiters and being in an hotel. He was reminded of his old life.

I said, 'You should have stuck to the hotel business.'

'Yes, often I think that. Between ouselves, too, I made more money. You think Martin Freeman killed this man?'

'He might have done. But somehow it doesn't seem to be his style. Anyway, one thing I'm pretty certain about is that Freeman's not in England. He wrote a letter of resignation to his firm from Florence.'

'I think tomorrow I go back to Paris.'

'I should do that. If you like you can tell Monsieur Duchêne that if I ever catch up with Freeman I'll try and do something about his antique coins.'

'Thank you. And if you come there, look me up.' He handed me a business card.

The next morning from the office I phoned Gloriana and made an appointment to see her at twelve. I handed Wilkins the Bill Dawson letter and asked her to check on Sabratha, Wheelus and Uaddan. You never knew when you might not pick up some small lead. I also gave her the Phs. Van Ommeren bill and asked her to check with them what travel arrangements they had made for Martin Freeman. When she raised an eye at this I said, 'Tell them you're speaking from the Intercontinental News Services, and it's a question of checking for his expense account. Freeman worked there.'

When she had gone I sat and stared at the wall calendar. It didn't help me beyond announcing that the day was Thursday.

Why, I asked myself, had old London-Scottish tie been strangled in Freeman's cottage? Clearly—according to Jane Judd—he had been looking for Freeman and was using a thin cover story. I thought—from his condition—that he had gone to the cottage the day before I had, and met someone who resented his presence. Really resented it, too. I resented his presence too. If the police ever discovered that Paulet and I had been there, we should both be in trouble. I was used to being in trouble with the police, but Paulet didn't strike me as the type who would handle it very well.

Thinking of Paulet, I began to go over the Duchêne antique coin angle. That sounded like Freeman, all right. Any stuff his friends left lying around he felt free to pocket. Paulet hadn't put a price on the antique coins. But at the moment Freeman had five thousand in cash from his sister, a python arm bracelet worth another five thousand, which made him ten thousand pounds in funds, plus the value of the coins which would be . . . well, I didn't know. Not knowing always irked me. I got up and went over to the low wall bookcase by the door.

Wilkins, when we had been flush once, had spent over a hundred quid on reference books, most of which we had never used. Some had never been opened. I pulled out Volume 16, MUSHR to OZON, of the *Encyclopaedia Britannica,* and looked up the article on Numismatics. Perhaps I would get some idea of the value of the coins from that.

I didn't. But I got something else. A shock. Leafing through the article I stopped at the first photographic plate. It was a full-page illustration of Ancient Greek coins, photographed by courtesy of the Trustees of the British Museum. Each set of coins, reverse and obverse, carried a number. There were twenty-two sets illustrated. Below the illustrations a legend was set out referring to the numbers. I began to read through this and before I had finished the first line a bell began to ring. The line went: 1. Electrum stater of Lydia. 2. Electrum stater of Ephesus. 3. Gold stater of Croesus. 4. Daric of Persia.

I read right through and by the time I reached number twenty-two I was certain. It read: '22. Gold 100 litrae of Syracuse.'

The list of stolen coins which Monsieur Duchêne had given old Paulet had been copied straight out of the *Encyclopaedia.* For my money—none of your antique Greek stuff—it had to be a phoney.

I've had a few startling coincidences happen in my life, but this certainly wasn't one. Either Duchêne had given Paulet a phoney list and a phoney story to go with it, or both of them knew it was phoney. I considered the possibility of Duchêne stringing Paulet along, and then I considered the possibility of Paulet knowing the list was phoney. He seemed simple, straightforward, and a little more than inefficient. Well, that kind of act would make a good cover for whatever it was he or they wanted to cover.

I picked up the phone and called the Strand Palace Hotel. Lunch with Paulet might help to sort things out. After some hanging about, the hotel people told me that Paulet had booked out that morning.

Wilkins came back in while I was still getting nowhere.

'Sabratha,' she said, 'is the site of an ancient Roman town thirty-odd miles to the west of Tripoli.'

'It could be,' I said, 'that what is wanted on this job is an archaeologist.'

'Wheelus is the American Air Force base to the east of Tripoli. Wheelus course refers to the golf course which the Americans have built there. It's called Seabreeze.'

'Original name.'

'Uaddan,' said Wilkins, 'is the name of a hotel, which also has a casino, in Tripoli.'

'And what about the Van Ommeren people?'

'They were very helpful. Some of the account is a carry-over from old travel charges, but the bulk is for air-booking from London Airport to the King Idris Airport, Tripoli. Via Rome.'

'Date?'

'He bought the ticket over a month ago and had the date left open, saying he would make his arrangements direct.'

'He must have broken his journey and gone to Florence.'

'Van Ommeren say they would be glad to have Mr Freeman's present address.'

'I'll put them on the list. When do you go to Cairo?'

'Monday.'

She moved to the door.

'Until you go—and leave a note for your sister to watch it afterwards—I'd like any press cuttings you can pick up of the discovery of the body of a man strangled to death, at Ash Cottage, Crundale, near Wye. That's in Kent.'

Wilkins looked at me. That's all. Just looked.

Gloriana mixed me a large dry martini which I sipped at gently over the next twenty minutes in order to avoid having the top of my head blown off. She drank lime juice with soda.

She had her place of honour on the large settee, one leg curled up underneath her. She wore a short blue woollen dress and a gold band around her hair. On my way in the taxi I had debated with myself what I was going to tell her. Usually I like to keep a little up my sleeve for a rainy day. However, by the time I had the martini glass in my hand, freezing my fingers off, I'd decided to give her the truth. By now I was quite sure that there was something wrong with all this Freeman business. And let's face it, because of my low iron and vitamin content I welcomed it. I was beginning to feel that maybe life still had something to offer. It's instructive, too, to lay the truth out for people. Not all of them can control the reactions they would like to control.

She listened carefully as I went through the story, every detail, and I watched her carefully. The only thing I saw of interest was the gentle swinging movement of one long nylon leg over the edge of the settee.

I finished, 'Any comments?'

She considered this for a moment, then said, 'Only that he seemed to be getting himself into the dirt again. And I'll have to get him out.'

'Got a photograph of him?'

'I'll give you one before you go.'

'Would he murder a man?'

'No.'

'Bill Dawson—know him?'

'No.'

'Did you know about the country cottage?'

'No.'

'Did he ever mention any girl in Paris, probably a cabaret type? Favours Oriental gear.'

'No.'

'We're doing well. What about Leon Pelegrina who sends him a New Year's card from Florence?'

'No.'

'Tripoli—has he been there before to your knowledge?'

'Yes.'

'That's better.'

'He showed me something he did about a year ago. Some feature

article which his firm placed with one of the Sunday papers. It was
about the oil industry in Libya. I didn't read it.'

'Do you have any ideas about Monsieur Duchêne with his phoney
list of antique coins?'

'No.'

'And you've never heard of François Paulet?'

'No.'

'And this strangled type in the cottage. From my description,
does he seem to fit anyone you know?'

'No.'

'We're back on the old negative routine.'

She said, 'I know very little about my brother or his circle. That's
why you're here. I want you to find him.'

'Well, one thing I'm pretty sure of—he's not in this country. How
do you feel about footing first-class travel expenses all over the
place? And my fee?'

'What is your fee?'

'It might be a long job, so I'll give you the monthly rate which
comes a little cheaper. One thousand pounds a month.' I pitched
it very high.

'That's all right.'

It's nice to be rich.

'My secretary,' I said, 'is flying on Monday to Cairo to spend a
holiday with her fiancé. She could go via Tripoli, spend a few days
there and check whether your brother is around. I'd only charge
you half expenses for that since she's going out to Cairo anyway.'
Wilkins always paid her own fare so there was no reason why I
shouldn't do her some good. Whether she would take it on, of
course, was another matter.

Gloriana nodded, and said, 'And what are you going to do?'

'The police,' I said, 'are going to find that body in the cottage.
I thought I'd hang about for a day or so to see if they issue an
identification. Could help. Then I'd like to see Monsieur Duchêne
in Paris, and then Signore Leon Pelegrina in Florence. After that
I'll play it by ear, according to whatever my secretary turns up.'

'That seems reasonable. But I'd like you to keep in touch with
me. You can always phone. I'm usually here between seven and
eight at night.'

'I was hoping you wouldn't be tonight.'

'Why?'

'Because I was hoping you'd have dinner with me. I've got a

much better suit than this at home. And I won't let you down with my table manners.'

She smiled, which I hadn't expected, and said, 'Just for the pleasure of my company?'

'Absolutely. I won't give a thought to the million stacked up behind it.'

'I'd be delighted. Would you like another martini?'

'Not unless you and your maid are prepared to carry me to the lift. I'm a whisky man, really.'

She nodded understandingly. I got up, patted the antique Buddha on the head, gave her my little bow and went, saying, 'I'll pick you up just before seven.'

In this business it is important to establish cordial relations with clients. It gives them the feeling that you have their interests exclusively at heart. It has other side-effects too—not always pleasant.

I had trouble with Wilkins. I knew I would. She was very much a creature of habit. This was her holiday. Why should she spend it working?

'All right. You can add an extra week to your leave. And don't forget you'll be getting your expenses.'

'But Olaf wouldn't like me to be alone in a town like Tripoli. He fusses, you know.'

The idea of anyone fussing over capable Wilkins was novel —but who was I to argue? I know what love can do to people.

'You'll probably be safer in Tripoli than you are in Greenwich. But if you want the anxious Swede to stop from worrying ask him to join you there. It must be less than an hour's flight from Cairo. All you have to do is send him a cable, fix rooms at a Tripoli hotel—and I suggest the Libya Palace—and change your air ticket. I tell you this Stankowski thing could be a big job. With luck I can string it out to a month. That means a thousand quid in the bank and you could have that electric typewriter you want.'

'Well . . .' It was very grudging, but I knew that I had won.

'Thanks. Anyway, you ought to do more field work. You're miles better at it than me.'

She liked that. Not that it was news to her. She had a firm conviction that she was miles better than me at everything, except a few activities which anyway she wouldn't have touched with a barge-pole.

After that I went round to Miggs's place and fixed up for a

chauffeur-driven Rolls for the evening. He gave me tea out of a quart-sized enamel mug, a five-minute dissertation on the state of the second-hand car market owing to the Labour Government squeeze, flipped to a quick run-down of the present state of the Roman Catholic Church and its attitude to the Unity of Christian Churches, which—if he'd had it printed—would have gone on the Index right away and which, since he was a Catholic, didn't surprise me because they're always the best value when it comes to running down their religion or making jokes about it, and finished by asking what the hell I wanted a Rolls for.

'I'm taking a million out to dinner. Name of Stankowski, Mrs, widow, formerly Gloriana Freeman. I'm looking for her brother.'

'If that was the Stankowski who was in the scrap-metal business, watch out that she isn't like him. He was as bent as a bedspring.'

Going down the stairs, I ran into Manston at the bottom, arriving for another work-out with Miggs. He was wearing a bowler hat, dark suit, and carried a rolled umbrella, and he looked as usual like a coiled steel spring, and God help you if you were in its way when it went *zing!*

He said, 'Busy?'

'Moderately.'

'We could always give you a job. Permanently, if you like.' 'We' meant his Service, and occasionally they had roped me in to work for them and not once had I spent a happy moment on their payroll.

'I like a quiet life.'

He grinned. 'You're getting old. Sluggish too, I'll bet.'

As he spoke he raised his umbrella and swiped at the side of my neck with it. I ducked and let it go over my head. Then I went forward and got my right shoulder under his raised right arm, grabbed his wrist and let myself fall back so that I could use his moment out of balance from the umbrella blow to send him over my shoulder. It should have worked, would have done with most people, but in some odd way I found myself spun round, my face pressed against a wall and my right arm twisted up behind my back.

Still holding me, he said, 'You used to be better than that.'

'You've got it wrong. You used not to be so good.'

He released me, straightened his Old Etonian tie, and then offered me a cigarette. I lit it with a shaking hand. He saw the shake and said, 'You've been leading too sedentary a life. You really should join us and see the world. Also you get a pension at sixty.'

'Send me a telegram,' I said, 'the first time any of your blokes live long enough to qualify for one.'

As it was a nice spring evening I walked part of the way home, from Lambeth Bridge along Millbank and past the Tate Gallery. The sky was an even duck-egg colour, and the tide was coming in fast, making up towards Vauxhall Bridge, an even brown-soup colour. A handful of gulls hung over it, scavenging. I had a growing feeling that any moment now I might feel good to be alive.

Mrs Meld was hanging over her front-garden gate, taking the air, and watching her dog take its hundred-yard-evening stroll down the pavement.

''Evening, Mr Carver.'

''Evening, Mrs Meld.'

She jerked her head upwards to my place. 'You're going it a bit, aren't you?'

'You've got to be clearer than that, Mrs Meld.'

'There's another one up there.'

'A woman?'

'What else?'

'Why do you let them in?'

'What you told me, weren't it? Women can go in—not nobody else. Want to alter it, Mr Carver?'

I thought for a moment and then shook my head.

It was Jane Judd. She was wearing a light raincoat and yellow beret and was standing at the window, watching Mrs Meld who still stood at her gate.

'When that woman speaks about you,' she said, indicating Mrs Meld as I went and stood at her shoulder, 'there's reverence in her voice. Also I got the feeling that she would have liked to search me to see if I had any hidden weapons.'

'Have you?'

'Only this.'

She handed me a copy of the *Evening Standard*.

I said, 'Let's have a drink before we settle down to the crossword. And anyway I haven't got much time. I've an appointment at seven. So chat away. I presume this isn't a social call?'

'No. It isn't. I just decided that I'd been less than honest with you.'

'Don't worry about that. It puts you in the main category of my visitors and clients. Gin or whisky, or a glass of white wine?'

'Whisky, Straight.'

I poured it, straight and generous. She was putting on a good act but there was the suggestion of a shake somewhere in her voice.

'How did you get my address?'

'I phoned Mrs Stankowski.'

'And she gave it to you, just like that?'

'She did when she heard what I had to say.'

'Then let me hear it.'

She sat down on the arm of a chair and toasted me briefly with the whisky.

'I should have told you that Martin Freeman is my husband.'

I said nothing, letting it sink in. This Martin Freeman was quite a number. The more I learned about him, the more intrigued I became.

She said, 'You don't seem surprised.'

'Oh, I am. But I've learned not to show it, otherwise I'd be going round all day with my eyes popping. Why don't you wear a ring?'

'It was a secret wedding, nearly two months ago, at a registrar's office. In Acton.'

'Nice spot. What about the fiancé? P.R.O. at Shell-Mex?'

'He doesn't exist.'

'Why did you get married?'

'On an impulse.'

'No question of love?'

'Oh, that. Yes, I suppose so. But chiefly, well . . . I like him. He's charming. Good company. Makes a woman feel good and pleased with herself. And I was tired of hotel work and just the odd dates that don't develop beyond a tatty weekend in the country. I'm thirty-five, you know. You begin to think about security, home, kids. God, it sounds conventional, but that's what all women are at heart.'

'Freeman doesn't sound the security-giving type. Pinching from his sister, and a few others; a spell in stir for some City company swindle. I wouldn't have thought you'd have been taken in.'

'I'm impulsive. That's why I'm here. I trust you.'

'Carry on then.'

'He said he was on the point of a really big deal. Something that would make his fortune. The idea was to keep the marriage secret. He didn't want publicity and he might have got some. He's a bit of a name in Fleet Street. He told me he was going off for two or three months, but he would send for me. We'd live abroad for the rest of our lives.'

'Where?'

'He didn't say. I was just to trust him and wait for his call.'

'Well, why not carry on and do that?'

She got up and helped herself to another whisky.

'Because, frankly, I'm frightened. For two reasons.'

'Number one?'

She nodded at the *Evening Standard* on the table at my side.

'I've put a mark around a news item in the paper.'

She had. It was on the back page. Just a few lines, announcing the discovery of the body of an unknown man, strangled, at Ash Cottage, Crundale, near Wye in Kent.

I said, 'He was in the chemical closet when I got down there. The type with the London-Scottish tie.'

'God.' She breathed the word quietly but there was all the feeling in the world in it.

'You don't like being mixed up in murder? Particularly if you fancy Freeman might be involved?'

'You're bloody right.' There was a flash of the forceful, competent manner I'd known at the hotel.

'Point number two?'

She hesitated, took a sip of her whisky, and then said, 'This afternoon I had a phone call at the hotel. Some man, foreign, I think, who wouldn't give his name, but said he was a close friend of Martin's. He said that if I heard in any way that Martin was dead, I wasn't to believe it. He was speaking for Martin, and said that Martin would, as he promised, eventually send for me.' She looked hard at me. 'I really am frightened, you know. I don't want to get mixed up in anything . . . well, as I said, one of the chief reasons for marrying him was this security business. But I don't want that at any price.'

'So you came to me?'

'Who else? I mean, you struck me as being a decent sort. You're already looking for Martin . . . I just had to have someone to tell this to.'

'You told all this to Mrs Stankowski?'

'No. Only that I was married to Martin. What am I going to do?'

'Go home, take three sleeping pills and get a good night's sleep.'

'But what about the police?'

'If they get round to you—about the cottage, I mean—then tell them everything you've told me if you want to be out in the clear.

Mind you, if you're stuck on waiting for Martin Freeman to send for you, then you'll have to make your own decision how much you tell.'

'And do I tell about you?'

'Why not? I didn't murder old London-Scottish, and I'm just trying to trace Martin Freeman. However, if they happen to catch on fast to you, you might stall mentioning me until after midday tomorrow. Not that I think they will be so fast.'

'Why midday tomorrow?'

'Because I'm going to Paris on professional business and don't want to be delayed.'

I stood up and took her arm and led her to the door.

'Don't fuss. You've done nothing wrong. Just speak the truth and shame the devil. And, anyway, you'll have a new wad of material for the book *Why I Sometimes Don't Like Men*.'

She paused at the open door, smiled and just touched my arm.

'You're a good guy. Thank you.'

'If you get time, put that in writing and sign it. I'm often in need of a reference.'

She grinned, adjusted her beret with that nice little movement woman have with hats, and I knew she was recovering fast. Then she held something out to me.

'Would you let Mrs Stankowski have this sometime? You needn't say where you got it.'

I had the gold ring with the jade stone in my hand.

'I'll give it to her tonight,' I said.

I didn't. I drove, or rather was driven, in the Rolls around to Upper Grosvenor Street just after seven. I wore a midnight-blue dinner jacket, onyx cuff-links my sister had given me, and one loop of my back braces was held on to my trousers with a safety pin because the button had gone.

I went up in the lift feeling like young Lochinvar coming out of the West—S.W.1, actually. This Freeman thing was developing nicely along the therapeutic lines I needed. Could be, too, that there might come a moment when in addition to my Stankowski fee, there might be a chance to pick up some side money. Oh, yes, I was recovering fast.

The Scots number on opening the door to young Lochinvar soon put paid to any nonsense about so faithful in love and so dauntless in war, and she didn't care a damn that through all the wild Border his steed was the best. She'd have known the Rolls was hired anyway.

She put a photograph in my hand.

'I'm to give you this and her apologies for being called away for the evening.' That's a translation. I worked it out while looking at the photograph—of Freeman—which I'd forgotten to take with me that morning.

'Where's she gone?'

'The devil knows. I'm not told anything in this house.' Practice made the translation of that faster.

I went back down the lift, wondering if it were some other man, some laggard in love and a dastard in war. Frankly, I didn't care over much. Gloriana was high-flying game, too high for me in my present off-peak condition.

I got in the Rolls and had the chauffeur drive me around for an hour. Then I went home, opened a tin of ox tongue, made myself some sandwiches and coffee and sat and contemplated a bunch of mimosa that Mrs Meld had arranged in a vase on the sideboard. I considered Freeman.

For my money he was too impulsive, too careless, too given to friends making anonymous phone calls about his welfare ever to last long in the big league. He might, with luck, get away with some small racket. But I didn't read his character as closed, discreet and contained enough to engineer anything that would give the forces of law and order more than a temporary headache.

I was in the office the next morning at half past nine—early for me. In the outer office Wilkins said, 'I've got a hair appointment at half past ten. Is that all right?'

I nodded, hoping it would be, though what anyone could do with Wilkin's hair I couldn't imagine.

She went on, 'When I got in this morning I put a call through to the Libya Palace Hotel in Tripoli.'

'Why?'

'Because I don't see why Olaf and I should go there if a simple query could be settled by a telephone call.'

'Freeman?'

'Yes. They said there was no one staying there of that name.'

'He could be at some other hotel. What about the Uaddan?'

'I've got a call booked through to them. If it comes while I'm out you can take it.'

'He might not be using his own name.'

I tossed the Freeman photograph on to her desk. She examined it and handed it back. She had a trained memory. If she ever saw Freeman now she would recognize him.

I said, 'See if you can get me a booking on an afternoon plane to Paris.'

She nodded and then handed me a newspaper cutting. It was the paragraph about the dead man at Freeman's cottage.

'Why,' she asked, 'does everything you touch start getting involved and unpleasant?'

'Which part don't you like? The involvement or the unpleasantness?'

She didn't answer, because at that moment the telephone began to ring. I went into my office. She came in ten minutes later and said, 'That was the Uaddan Hotel. I got the same answer. No one called Freeman known to them. And Mrs Stankowski is outside, wanting to see you.'

'Show her in. Don't forget that Paris flight.'

Gloriana was wearing a beautifully cut black silk suit, a mink wrap round her shoulders, a tiny little black hat with a black veil that came just below her eyes, and a different scent. She sat down on the other side of my desk and I reached over and lit a cigarette for her. The pearls round her neck were as large as fat garden peas, all perfectly matched, and evidence of the handsome profit margins in the scrap-metal business. One day, I promised myself, when I got tired of the high excitement of the struggle for existence, I would find a young rich widow—beautiful, of course—and marry her.

I said, 'You broke two things last night. My heart and a dinner engagement.'

'Crap.' All of old Scunthorpe was in the word. But she said it with a smile.

'What happened?'

'At half past six a car called for me. It was from the office of the Lord High Treasurer.'

'Sounds like something out of Gilbert and Sullivan.'

'In the car was a man I know.'

'Young?'

'Forty-odd. His name is Apsley and he's a senior legal assistant in the Treasury Solicitor's office.'

'What did he want? To marry you or raise a loan to help pay back the war debt?' As she spoke I went over to the bookcase and fished out Whitaker's Almanac for 1965. Apsley was listed all right, commencing salary £2,391 rising to £3,135.

'I've known him for a long time and I think he would like to marry me—but he's not my type. He took me back to his office where there were two other Treasury officials. They wanted to know all about Martin. Did I know where he was and so on. Apparently they've an idea that he may be mixed up in some currency deal which isn't exactly honest.'

'Did they give you details?'

'No. They've no positive evidence yet. They just wanted to know where he was. Since Dick Apsley knows me they thought an informal approach to me was the best thing. I told them I'd employed you to find him.'

'You told them everything?'

'Practically.'

'What does that mean?'

'I didn't mention about his marriage to that woman . . . what was her name?'

'Jane Judd. Why not?'

'Well, I didn't see that involving her was going to help them.'

'But you told them about the dead man at the cottage?'

'Yes. I thought they took that very calmly.'

'And what did they say about me?'

'That I could tell you of their interest—though they have their own investigators—and if I wished I could go on employing you, but they'd be glad if I passed on to them anything you found out. What the hell is that brother of mine up to?'

'I'd like to know. How long were you there?'

'Two hours.'

'And afterwards?'

'Dick took me out to dinner. But we didn't discuss Martin any more. Except that I made it clear that I wanted to go on employing you. Do you mind if I pass them any information you find?'

'No.'

'You look cross.'

'I don't like official departments on my tail. But I'll learn to live with this one. Also, since they know about the dead man, I'm going to have the police around my neck at any minute.'

'I'm sorry.'

'Don't be. I hope I'm going to be in Paris before they get to me. But I'll be back.'

'And you'll keep me informed?'

'Sure.' But not, I thought, necessarily about everything. I didn't like this Treasury approach, largely I suppose because it wasn't typical form. And I'm a great one for form.

I was in Paris by five o'clock. I looked up Monsieur Robert Duchêne in the directory at the airport, but he was not listed with a telephone number. François Paulet was listed at the business address he had given me. I don't know why, but in the taxi going to 2 bis Rue du Bac to see Monsieur Robert Duchêne I suddenly had a comfortable feeling because in talking to Gloriana, although I had mentioned Duchêne and Leon Pelegrina of Florence, I hadn't given their addresses to her. Frankly, there seemed something a little fishy to me in the Gloriana-Treasury tie-up. More frankly, I recognized stage two of my usual client relationship—a nagging feeling that I wasn't being told the truth and nothing but the truth, that somewhere somebody was preparing to take advantage of me.

Two bis Rue du Bac was an open doorway next to a stationer's shop. Beyond the doorway was a narrow hall with a wooden board on the wall announcing who lived in each of the six flats that made up the building. Duchêne was listed in Number 4. I went up the bare board stairs through an atmosphere thick with the smell of ancient meals and tobacco smoke.

Duchêne had handwritten his name on a piece of paper and slipped it into the card holder on the door. I rang the bell and waited. Nothing happened. I rang again, and while my finger was still on the bell push I noticed that the door was off its catch. I stopped ringing and gave it a gentle push with my toe. It swung back and I went in. There was a little hallway, two doors either side and a door at the far end. A man's bicycle stood against one wall, a raincoat hung on a peg on the other and there was a small side-table piled with old copies of *Elle* and *Paris-Match*. The coloured cover page of the top one was given up to a head and shoulders photograph of Brigitte Bardot, marred somewhat by the fact that someone had added in biro a pair of spectacles, a drooping meerschaum pipe and a fancy-looking medal above her left breast. I didn't stop to work out whether it was the Croix de Guerre or the Victoria Cross. I was just thinking that this place didn't seem the kind of pad that went with a wealthy, if unscrupulous, collector of antique coins.

The big door at the end of the hall was also slightly ajar. I pushed it open with my toe and stood waiting. Nothing happened. Inside the room I could see part of a settee and beyond it a bureau. There was a knife-slit along the cover of the settee, the material was pulled loose, and three cushions lay on the floor, with covers ripped off and some loose stuffing material which had come from inside them on the carpet. The bureau drawers were on the floor in front of the piece, and papers and odds and ends were scattered about as though a small whirlwind had hit the place.

I left a nice big interval, listening hard as a safety precaution, heard nothing, and then went in.

Someone politely shut the door behind me and something cold was pressed against the back of my neck. I didn't try to move or turn round. Facing me from the window was a number who reminded me of a full-size model I'd once seen of a Neanderthal man, only this one wore a leather jacket and blue jeans, openwork sandals, a dirty white shirt, and had in his hand a flower pot which held a red azalea.

In the politest of voices he said, '*Bon soir, Monsieur Duchêne. Nous sommes très content de vous voir.*'

He got hold of the base stem of the azalea and pulled it out of the pot, bringing the roots and soil with it. He then examined the inside of the flower pot, shrugged his shoulders with disappointment, and let the whole shebang drop to the floor. The pot shattered and the azalea scattered its petals.

In English I said, 'You've got it wrong. My name is Apsley—Richard Apsley—and I'm from Her Majesty's Treasury Solicitor's office in London.' The esses whistled a bit but I managed to sound casual. I added, 'Also, this thing at the back of my neck is making me feel very cold.'

Neanderthal smiled and from such a grotesque face it came with surprising sympathy. In good English he said, 'Then in that case, or any case, we won't concern ourselves with you any longer.' He reached out an arm about four feet long, plucked a picture from the wall and began to tear off the backing paper.

I said, 'That's no way to treat a Picasso, even if it is only a reproduction.'

I never got his reaction to this. The cold steel was suddenly gone from the back of my neck. I was hit hard and expertly above and just to the back of my right ear, and went down and out to join the azalea on the floor.

CHAPTER 4

Girl with a Python on her Arm

Naturally, when I came to they were gone. But they'd left their mark, not only on me, but the whole flat. I knew something about turning a place over, but they knew more. It had been gutted. In the bathroom, where I staggered to get my head under the cold tap, the soap had been cut into small segments in case anything had been hidden in it. In the hall the magazines were all over the place and the tyres of the bicycle had been ripped open.

They only conceded one touch of neatness. Going back into the sitting room, I found that they had taken all the contents of my pockets—nothing was missing—and laid them out neatly on a low table. From my passport they knew that I was not Richard Apsley.

Shaky still, I went over to the telephone. Clearly this was a furnished flat which Duchêne had rented. That's why no name or phone number was listed for him. I rang Paulet's office and was lucky enough to find him in.

I said, 'I'm at 2 bis Rue du Bac. In a few moments I'm going to be strong enough to totter down the street as far as the Seine. You'll find me propped against the parapet of the Pont Royal.'

He asked no questions. Just said that he would be there. I tried out my legs by moving round the flat. I could find nothing that interested me, except a bottle of Armagnac in a kitchen cupboard. I pumped a couple of quick glasses into myself, and then went out into the world.

François Paulet, driving a small Fiat van—he apologized for it, saying that in his work it was less conspicuous than a private car (though it rattled enough to draw anyone's attention to it)—picked me up and took me down along the river to a small restaurant just off the Avenue Rapp. We ate overcooked veal and a limp salad, but the *vin blanc* was good. I told him what had happened, explaining that I had flown over thinking that a chat with Monsieur Duchêne might help me in my search for Freeman.

'You take it from there,' I said. 'What the hell were those men doing, who were they, and where the hell is Monsieur Duchêne?'

He called for the cheese board and then said, 'Monsieur Duchêne, I know, has gone to Rome. He travels much. The apartment is rented furnished and he is not often there. May I say that some of his activities—as I explained about the coins—are a little—well, irregular. But as far as I am concerned he has given me a straightforward job, to find Freeman.'

'It's not turning out like that.'

'I told him about you. Before he went yesterday. He said he would pay for any information you could give about Freeman and also that I should help you as much as possible —even to travelling, if necessary, though he warned me to keep the expenses down. What do you think? I mean about helping you?'

'I'm not doing much thinking at the moment.'

It was a lie, of course. I was. I was wondering whether I should drop into Paulet's lap the knowledge that the list of antique coins was a phoney. He might know it and he might not. I decided not to tell him. It would have been giving away an advantage which eventually I might use to my own good.

Paulet sat there, pulling at his big nose, his narrow eyes anxious to please. 'I would not get in your way. And it would be a privilege for me to observe your methods. Yes?'

'I'll think about it when my head returns to normal. What do you think these men wanted?'

He did the old Gallic handspread, palms up, and rolled his eyes. 'Who knows?'

'Have you any way of getting in touch with Duchêne?'

'No. He phones my office, or writes when he is out of Paris.'

'You've done other jobs for him?'

'A few.'

'Like what?'

'Monsieur Carvay—would it be ethical—?'

'All right.'

'If you wish, I could give you a bed for tonight. My wife and I—'

'You're married?'

He smiled. 'Well, not strictly. It is an arrangement . . . well, what I mean is that I am married, to another woman, but I live with this one. She is more my type and understands me. It is expensive, though, to keep two establishments going. Soon—if things do not improve—I may have to go back to the hotel business. You wish to spend the night with us?'

'No. I'm going to get a night plane back.'

'But you will keep in touch with me? About helping you?'

'Probably.' That was the best I could do for him.

He cut himself a large slice of Camembert and shook his head sadly. 'I do hope you will. In an emergency, you know, I can be very useful.' He grinned suddenly and tapped his head. 'Not much up here, maybe—but I have a strong body.'

'We'll see.'

I got back to my flat at four in the morning and slept through until nine. Mrs Meld woke me, standing in the bedroom door holding the kitchen alarm clock which was ringing its head off.

'Shut that thing off.'

She did, but the ringing still went on. It was the telephone beside my bed. As I reached out for it she said, 'It's rung about twice in the last half hour. There was a police car round here last night, about nine. How many eggs do you want?'

'Two boiled. Three minutes.'

She went and a voice over the phone said, 'Don't take too long over breakfast. You're wanted round here.'

I knew the voice. It was coming all the way from some grim little room in New Scotland Yard.

I said, 'I didn't kill him.'

'We know that. But the Ashford police would like a statement from you. I'm interested too. It's been a long time since I listened to one of your fairy stories.'

I was round there by ten. With my friend was an Inspector from Ashford. I gave them a straightforward account of my visit to the cottage and my reason for going. I didn't say anything about the stuff I had taken from it. It took some time because the Inspector wrote it all down and then I had to read it and sign it. This done, he pocketed the statement and left. I sat and looked at my friend. He smiled at me and said, 'Like to add anything off the record?'

It's good to have friends in high places who trust you. He was a Chief Superintendent, 'C' Department, and wouldn't be bothering himself with a tatty little murder in Kent unless there was a great deal behind it.

I said, 'You whistled your country buddy off pretty smartly.'

'I wanted to make him happy. He's got your statement for his

file. He can ask the Paris boys to get one from this Paulet man.
Just keep the file growing fatter day by day and it feels like progress.'

'Who was the murdered man?'

'Don't know.'

'Honest?'

'Honest.'

'When was he done in?'

'Late evening. Day before you got there. What did you or Paulet
take from the cottage?'

'Nothing.'

'Honest?'

I just winked, and went on quickly, 'You know the Treasury
have an interest in Martin Freeman?'

'Yes.'

'Can I go now?'

'Where did you get that bump above the right ear?'

'Paris, last night. On the *métro*. An angry commuter hit me with
an umbrella because I wouldn't give up my seat to a pregnant
woman.'

'That figures. You're only on your best behaviour with women
before they're pregnant. Thinking of doing more travelling?'

'I had it in mind—unless you're going to confiscate my passport.
Then I should make a stink. Taking away the tools of my trade.
Probably sue for loss of earnings.'

He shook his head indulgently. 'You can go anywhere you want.
Mrs Stankowski wants Freeman, the Treasury wants Freeman, the
Ashford police want him and I'd quite like to know where he is. So
carry on. Every little helps. You might turn up something, and, if
you're in the right mood, you might be honest enough to let me
know about it.'

He was being as bland and easy-going as butter that spreads
straight from the fridge. That meant that there was a hell of a lot
that he was not going to tell me.

I stood up. 'It seems to me that a lot of people want Freeman.'

'You'd be surprised. And because that's so, and because this
morning I quite like you, let me give you a little advice. Just watch
yourself on the *métro* in future.'

At the door I said, 'What did you get when you ran a check on
Monsieur Robert Duchêne—remember, he's another who wants
Freeman.'

He said, 'The Paris people have nothing on him. No record.

Neither have Interpol.' He grinned. 'I checked François Paulet, too.
He's about to be sued by his wife for arrears of maintenance under
a legal separation order. Otherwise, nothing. Help?'

'Was it intended to?'

'No.'

I went. Back at the office Wilkins told me that Dimble had called
to say there was nothing on the python bracelet and she had paid
him five pounds. She then said she was flying to Tripoli the next
day and that Olaf was going to meet her there.

I said, 'Look pleased about it. It'll make a change from
Cairo—and your expenses are being paid. All I want to know is
whether Freeman is there, or has been there recently. And anything
you can get on this Bill Dawson. Why does that name seem
familiar?'

'I wouldn't know.'

If we had done at that moment it might have saved us both a
lot of trouble.

From my room I phoned Hawkins of the London Fraternal
Insurance Society and fed him an edited account of the Freeman
affair. He said not to worry because Mrs Stankowski had withdrawn
her claim against them and he would send me a cheque for my
services.

I then phoned Gloriana and told her to tell her Treasury friend
that I had visited Monsieur Duchêne's flat and had been banged
over the head for my trouble, and that I was going to Florence on
Monday. I asked her if she would have dinner with me that evening
and she said she was sorry but she was going away for the weekend
and, no matter where I went, would I please keep in touch with
her. I promised that I would.

Then I sat and chain-smoked for a while, wondering why I was
getting the feeling that somehow I was being manipulated. It was
a strong feeling and—although it was a challenge and fast bringing
back that old zest for living which I needed—I didn't altogether
like it. It would have been a compensation if somewhere I could
have glimpsed a chance to make some side money for myself. For
a time I considered sending Paulet a telegram to say that I would
be in Florence, Hotel Excelsior, on Monday evening, but although
it was flattering to see myself in the role of a top professional making
a tyro's eyes pop with my expertise, I decided against it. He'd be
better off in Paris dealing with his wife's lawsuit. And, anyway,

there are different kinds of expertise and some that pay off in a sounder currency than flattery.

Mrs Burtenshaw, Wilkins's sister, was in the office on Monday morning. So was her basset hound, curled up on my desk chair and defying me with hung-over eyes to do anything about it. I didn't take up the challenge as I was only passing through on my way to the airport.

I said to Mrs Burtenshaw, 'Fisk will be coming in every other day in case anything crops up.' Fisk was an ex-policeman who gave me a hand now and then.

'Hilda,' said Mrs Burtenshaw, 'was very annoyed that you wanted her to go to Tripoli. After all, Mr Carver, a holiday is a holiday and people should be free to choose where they go.'

I said, 'You think she'll ever get round to marrying Olaf?'

'I should hope so. He's a good, sound, solid, respectable man with money in the bank.'

Practically everything I wasn't—and that's what she meant.

I said, 'If your hound in there gets bored sitting at my desk —and God knows I do at times—just give him a few of the confidential files to chew up. And thank you for coming in to help. I appreciate it very much.'

She fixed me with her steely blue eyes and said, 'I notice that whenever I do you usually contrive to be away. I think that's a very suitable arrangement for both of us.'

The air trip produced a fine selection of irritations; fog that delayed take-off two hours, then something wrong with the plane so that we had to be switched to another and then—because of bad weather—a switch to the Caselle airport at Turin instead of Linate at Milan, so I missed my train connection. It was ten o'clock at night when I finally checked in at the Excelsior in Florence. I had a late meal and went to bed. It was a bad idea, because sleeping too soon after eating always gives me wild dreams and a restless night. The next morning I was bad-tempered and my eyes felt as though their sockets were too small. Leon Pelegrina was listed in the telephone directory at 23 Piazza Santo Spirito. I called him from the lobby and when a man's voice at the other end said '*Pronto*' a few times I just put the receiver down. I didn't want to talk to him over the phone. I just wanted to know he was there.

Piazza Santo Spirito was only a few minutes' walk from the hotel, over the Arno by way of the Ponte Alla Carraia, down the Via dei

Serragli and then left-handed into the Piazza. At the far end of the square was the Church of Santo Spirito. It was a narrow piazza, with the space in the middle tree-lined and holding a few seats for those who just wanted to sit and stare and rest their feet. Number 23 was on the left not far from the church. A twisting stone stairway served the three or four flats into which the house had been converted. Halfway up at a turn there was a Madonna and Child set back in a wall niche decked out with some artificial flowers and lit by a weak electric light bulb. At the next turn up there was a heavy wooden door with a small brass plate carrying the name—Pelegrina. Below it was a brass knocker shaped in the form of Michelangelo's David. I took him by the legs and rapped his backside smartly against the door three or four times. I waited. Nothing happened. I repeated the treatment. This time I was rewarded with a shuffling sound on the far side of the door.

It opened slowly on hinges that needed oiling. Standing on the threshold of a small, very dark hallway was a large shape, oval, about five feet tall at its vertical axis and three feet at the horizontal. There was a round excrescence at the top of the oval from which came the glint of glass.

I said, 'Signore Pelegrina?'

'Si.'

I handed the shape one of my cards. He came forward a little into the light of the stairway to read it. The dim light threw up more details. He wore a monocle stuck in the right eye of a fat, reddish-brown face whose colour could have come from weather exposure, blood pressure, drink or all three. He didn't have any neck, his shoulders went straight up to his ears. When he readjusted his monocle to examine the card, his mouth gaped open like a goldfish starved of oxygen. He could have been anything between forty and fifty and he had wiry, almost curly dark hair which had scattered a fine dandruff dust on the shoulders of his jacket.

'*Inglese?*' His voice was a little hoarse as though he had lived in a damp atmosphere too long.

I said, 'Yes. I'd be glad if you could spare me a few minutes.'

He let the monocle drop from his eye, and frowned. There was a strong odour of Turkish tobacco about him and stains down the front of his velvet waistcoat. One of its fancy pearl buttons was missing.

In English he said, 'It is very early in the morning.'

'Well, you know the old saying. The early bird.'

He frowned again and momentarily there was a nervous tic in his right cheek. I had the feeling that I had worried him.

'I am not dressed for visitors.'

He looked clothed enough for me. Maybe he was referring to a pair of sloppy carpet slippers he was wearing.

'I won't keep you long,' I said. 'You speak very good English.'

'I should do. My mother was English, and insisted. She was a very insistent woman. That's why my father left her. Come in.'

He stood aside for me to enter, closed the door on us, and then passed me down the gloom of the little hall. He opened the door at the far end and ushered me into the main room of the flat. From behind me he said, 'I will be back in a minute.'

I was left alone in the room. There was no gloom here. Three sets of windows looked out over the piazza. It was L-shaped, with a small fireplace set in the smaller part of the L. By the window was a large divan. In one corner stood a grand piano with a purple cloth runner on the top and a silver-framed photograph dead centre on the cloth. There were a couple of well-worn armchairs, a long narrow table and, in another corner, a small roll-top desk, open, with a typewriter on it. I walked past the fireplace and examined the bookshelves beyond it. Two of the shelves were given up to paperbacks. English, Italian and French. The bottom shelf held a collection of English books, mostly, I noticed, about sailing or the sea. Flat on their sides at the end of the shelf were an old *Lloyds Register of Shipping, Volume I,* 1962–63, and on top of that a *Mediterranean Pilot of the Hydrographic Department of the Admiralty.* Over the fireplace was a big photograph of a coastwise tramp steamer, and above the desk another photograph of a steam yacht. I was moving over to look at it when Leon Pelegrina came back.

He had put on patent leather shoes and a different jacket. He waved me to a chair, picked up a cigarette box and said, 'You will probably prefer to smoke your own—unless you like Turkish?'

He sat down and we both lit our own cigarettes.

Without going into a lot of side details, I told him that I had been employed by Mrs Stankowski to find her brother, Martin Freeman.

At the first mention of Freeman's name he began to pick a few bits of imaginary fluff from the sleeve of his jacket, saw me watching him and stopped. I explained why Mrs Stankowski was worried about her brother, not having heard from him on her birthday, that he had left his job, and also that he had walked off with a valuable bracelet and some money. I didn't specify the amount. I said nothing of the anonymous phone calls assuring her of his safety, and nothing about Jane Judd and the Robert Duchêne angle.

I finished, 'Mrs Stankowski is not concerned about the thefts from her. Apparently Freeman had done this before. She is genuinely worried about him. I discovered that he had a cottage in the country and I found there a New Year's card from you. Since his letter of resignation from the News Service was written from this city it seemed reasonable to come and ask if you knew anything about him. How well did you know him?'

He put his fingertips together and made a steeple, eyed it, and then let it slip into a cat's cradle. Everything he said to me, I guessed, was going to be carefully considered.

'I've known him for some years, on and off. First in Rome, I think. He has many friends there. If he wrote this letter from Florence, I certainly didn't know he was here or see him. I've been away for a long time and only got back last week.'

'Can I ask how you came to meet him?'

'Through my daughter.' He got up and went to the piano and picked up the silver-framed photograph. 'She is in the theatrical profession and Freeman did some publicity work for her. Ever since then we have kept in touch loosely.'

He handed me the photograph. She was wearing jodhpurs and a shirt and carried a saddle over one arm. It was the same girl whose photograph in Oriental get-up I had seen in Freeman's cottage.

'I see. Where is she now?'

'I haven't the least idea. We had a quarrel about six months ago. Not our first. But always when it happens—' he shrugged his fat shoulders—'we lose touch.'

'Could Freeman be with her? Was there any romantic attachment?' It's a good phrase when you want to be polite, and I wanted to be polite with this man. I had a feeling that it would be easy to scare him and make him clam up.

'A little once, I think. But not now that I know about.' He nodded at the photograph in my hands. 'When I say that she is my daughter, let me make it clear that I have never been married. Even in that photograph you can see that she has a certain amount of, well, coloured blood.'

I nodded. It seemed an odd thing to tell me, a stranger—unless it was a way of sliding the conversation away from the main point.

Dads don't usually go out of the way to explain to my kind about their bastard, partly coloured daughters. He went even further.

'Just before the war I had a business in Italian Somaliland. I met her mother there. Beautiful, beautiful. When she died I naturally looked after the child.'

Big of him.

'How,' I asked, 'could I find out where your daughter is? Has she got an agent?'

'Yes. In Rome. Marrini Fratelli. They're listed in the book. Her stage name is La Piroletta. But I could probably do more for you. I could ring up a few friends in Rome who might know something of Freeman's movements recently.'

'I would be glad if you would. I'm at the Excelsior Hotel, certainly for tonight, and maybe tomorrow night. Could you ring me there?'

'Yes, certainly.'

He stood up, adjusted his monocle and gave me a little nod of dismissal.

At the door to the stairs, he said, 'Freeman's sister—she is paying you well for your work? I understand she is a very rich lady.'

'She's giving me the rate for the job.'

He smiled, and it was the first time he'd given me that benefit. Just for a moment, I sensed, he was completely relaxed.

'It must be a wonderful thing to have much money, too much money. One could do so much with it.'

'I gather that's Freeman's angle too. And, let's face it, mine. Always the big dreamers and schemers are the chaps who lack capital.'

The smile went. He pursed his fat lips and said, '*Certo. "Senza speme vivemo in desio."* That's Dante. My father made me read him. Without hope we live in desire. And that, Mr Carver, is a bad state for any ambitious man.'

He closed the door on me and I had the feeling that, despite himself, he had revealed something of the alter ego struggling for freedom inside him.

He hadn't called me by ten o'clock that night. I telephoned him at ten minutes past ten and there was no answer from the flat. I went up to my room to go to bed.

A man got in the lift just as I was about to press the button for the third floor. He was a big man with shoulders like the back of a truck. He had a large, bland face, and he wore a well-cut grey silk suit with a tiny white line in it, an immaculate white silk shirt and a yellow tussore tie. In one hand he carried a fat briefcase. There was something about him that made me think he was an actor. I'm a great one for instant diagnosis. In Rome I would have bet that he was straight from Ciné Citta with his contract renewed for another three years at double the salary plus a slice of the gross.

I raised an eyebrow at the board of floor buttons.

He said, '*Terza, grazie.*'

It was a nice voice, vibrant, manly, guaranteed to send chills of pleasure down the spine of any woman who needed her head examined.

We went up in silence. The lift stopped, the doors went back and I stood aside for him to move out. He shook his head and waved me forward. We had a silent courtesy duel for five seconds and he won. I went out and he stepped after me. I went away down the corridor towards my room. Behind me I heard the lift doors close.

At the same moment something hard was stuck into my back and the vibrant, manly voice sent a chill down my spine as it said, 'Just open the door of your room and go in without causing trouble. We do not want blood on this highly expensive corridor carpet, do we?'

I said, 'Nor on the one in my room, I hope.'

He chuckled. It's a verb which is used loosely. Not many people can really chuckle after the age of four. He could—a fat, babyish sound of pure, uninhibited pleasure.

I fished out my key to open the door and decided against a quick swing round to catch him off guard.

We went through the tiny hall into my bedroom. He shut the door behind us and said, 'Go and sit in the chair by the window.'

His English was good, but the Italian accent was strong in it.

I went and sat in the chair. He put his briefcase on the bed and, holding the gun in his right hand, he opened up the case left-handed. He took out two bottles of whisky. Vat 69. For a moment hope flowered in me. He took the glass from the water carafe by my bed, poured a liberal helping of whisky and then came and handed it to me from a safe distance.

'Drink.'

I did. Not all, but a fair portion. I felt I needed it.

'Hold this.' He handed me the bottle.

'Why?'

'Because it will keep both your hands in sight.' Then as I took the bottle, thinking it might be used as a counter weapon, he added, 'Also it is a good thing to have your prints on it.'

He went and fetched the other bottle and, for the first time, I noticed that he was wearing gloves. Holding gun and bottle in one hand, he opened it and then splashed some of the contents on the bedside table and the floor around it. A nice aroma filled the room.

I flung my bottle at him. He ducked and it hit the wall on the far side of the room, smashed, and whisky trickled down the striped wallpaper.

He said, holding the gun on me, 'I was hoping you would do that. It will make it more authentic.' He tossed the other half-empty bottle at me and instinctively I caught it to save my suit being drenched.

'*Grazie,*' he said. I knew why. My prints were now on this bottle.

I said, 'Care to tell me how this scene ends?'

'Accidental death of a drunk,' he said. 'The window behind you opens on to one of the inner hotel wells. A very long drop. Nasty. However, I'm in no hurry. Some men, knowing they were going out of the window for good, might, given the time, ask for a woman, or a good meal; some, I suppose, a priest. All I can offer you is ten minutes and the whisky from the bottle in your hand.'

He sat down on a chair by the door and kept the gun on me. From above it I had the benefit of his high-glazed smile.

I finished the glass of whisky and half filled it from the bottle. He nodded approvingly.

I said, 'I had you figured for an actor.'

He said, 'I am. People pay me and I act for them.'

'Steady work?' How did I get out of this? I was wondering. Or if I couldn't, should I finish the bottle? Why not? Where I was going, anyway, a reek of whisky on the breath wouldn't be held against me.

'Too much,' he said. 'As a matter of fact, I have to be selective nowadays.'

'Lucky you. Most of us scratch around for jobs.'

'I make plenty and pay no taxes. Also I meet interesting people. Like you, for instance. I shall be disappointed if the moment I move to hit you with this—' he indicated the gun —'you start to sob or plead. Some do.'

'I'll try not to disappoint you.'

'Good.' He shifted in his seat to make himself more comfortable, made a flappy motion with his free hand for me to go on drinking, and said, 'It is interesting that, about last requests. I consider it often. For instance—if you had wanted a woman and I could have provided any one you wanted, which would you have chosen?'

'You're a curious bastard, aren't you?'

'Well, fundamentally my work is without much variety. I try to give it some status, intellectual or philosophical. I find it helps both me and my client. Which woman would you choose? Some glamorous film star? Or society woman? Or maybe some nothing-to-look-at number of a secretary or typist who was more a bomb in bed than any of the big names ever could hope to be. Big names, you know, are like that. They have the habit of thinking all the time only of themselves, and that is no good in bed. The ego must be swamped, the body, the senses must dominate all thought, all personality.'

'You should write a book about it. That kind of thing sells well these days.'

'Maybe I will. I have had many experiences. Once, you know, I did a job for the Mafia. It was a man, a neurotic type, but good, sincere, a sort of religious man, in a way like Billy Graham—but much smaller. It was in the south of this country, Calabria, where he was giving the *contadini* ideas. He was a peasant himself. You know what he would have liked?'

'Go ahead. Astonish me.'

'A hot bath.' He chuckled. 'Unbelievable, no? A hot bath he wants, with expensive soap, bath essence and thick towels —because never in his life has he had such a bath. So now, which woman would you choose?'

I said, 'If you're serious about last requests, you ought to be naming yours.'

'Why?'

I didn't bother to answer. In the last ten seconds the bedroom door had been gently opening behind him and I had seen part of a face which I recognized. The door now went back with a bang and François Paulet was in the room. I sat comfortably where I was and watched. Not long ago Paulet had said to me that, although he was without much up top he had a strong body and could be useful in an emergency. His demonstration of it was a joy to watch. He wasn't handicapped in any way by the fact that my philosophical friend was as big as he was.

He smacked the man on the back of the neck and the gun jumped out of his hand and skittered across to my feet. I took my time picking it up. It was a .380 *pistolet automatique,* MAB *breveté,* model F, I discovered later. But at that moment I only had eyes for Paulet as he grabbed the man, jerked him to his feet and slammed a big right fist in his face and followed it with the left in his stomach. After that he went through a simple routine of throwing the man against one wall and then another, bouncing him once or twice on the floor and finally slinging him like a roll of limp carpet into a chair.

He stood over him and began to interrogate him in Italian, too fast for my limited knowledge of the language to give me any help. At first the man was reluctant in his replies. Paulet encouraged him with short jabs of his right fist and eventually they had a conversation which seemed to be satisfying Paulet. Paulet rounded it off by suddenly slipping his own gun out of his pocket and cracking the man above the left ear with the butt. My friend went out like a light.

Paulet turned and grinned to me.

'I did well, no?'

'It was a pleasure to watch. Have a drink.'

I held out the bottle. He drank without benefit of glass but with the thirst of a man conscious that he has done a good job and merits refreshment.

He nodded at the man. 'This *canaille*—your word for that escapes me at the moment—'

'Scum might do.'

'Yes, scum. Well, he is a professional killer who comes up from Rome today. Employed by a man here in Florence whose name he does not give. This I did not press because he had ethics like us and—'

'I know who the man is. And I think we ought to go right now and have a chat with him.'

'It will be a pleasure,' said Paulet. Then, rubbing the tip of his big nose with one finger, he looked down at the man. 'But first we must dispose of this. You think there is any more useful information to be had from him?'

'I doubt it. He was just trying to do a job.'

'You would like to hand him over to the police?'

'Don't be crazy. I wouldn't get out of this town for days with all their enquiries and processes.'

'In that case, we just get rid of him.'

He bent down, lifted the man and threw him over his shoulder. It sounds easy, but you try it. The man must have weighed over two hundred pounds. Paulet almost did it one-handed.

I followed him out of the room into the corridor. At the lift he rang. It came up and the doors opened. Paulet slung the man inside, reached round the corner of the lift and pressed one of the buttons, and jerked his arm back as the doors began to close.

'We,' he said, 'will walk down, while he goes up to the top floor. When he is able to, he can make his own explanations.'

We went down the stairs and there was a spring in Paulet's step. He was pleased with himself, pleased that he had given a demonstration of his potential usefulness to me.

I said, 'Thank you for getting me out of that.'

'A pleasure, Monsieur Carvay.'

I said, 'My room door was locked automatically when I went in with our friend. How did you get in?'

'I have, over the years, acquired a very large collection of hotel pass keys. Maybe it was a touch of vanity, but I wanted to come in and surprise you, to impress you. Perhaps because I sensed that there was a little reluctance in you to accept my minor services.'

'How did you know I was in Florence at this hotel?'

'I telephone your London office and tell the lady there that I have important news about Freeman for you and must get in contact. She gave me your address.'

I didn't tell him that I would check that. I did the next day, and Mrs Burtenshaw confirmed it. In my book Paulet was beginning to win his spurs but I still had a lingering doubt, probably unworthy, about which horse he was intending to ride.

We took a gentle stroll through the night, over the Arno to the Piazza Santo Spirito.

Repeated banging of David's bottom on Pelegrina's door brought no response.

I looked at Paulet. 'It's a very thick door.'

'We try the keys first.'

From his jacket pocket he brought out a bunch that was so big it would have made any ordinary man walk lopsided. He bent down, examined the keyhole, and tried one or two keys experimentally.

He half turned and smiled up at me. 'Locks, too, I have studied. This is a Continental variation of the English lever lock which your great Jeremiah Chubb invented in 1818. The important thing is not to lift the detector lever too high by using the wrong key.' He examined his bunch, selected a key and began fiddling with the lock. A few moments and two keys later, the door was open. He waved me in, beaming, his narrow-set eyes sparkling with frank vanity.

Leon Pelegrina was not there. He had packed and gone, and obviously taken his time about it. In the bedroom, which was off to the left of the hall, all his clothes had gone except an old dressing gown and a pair of pyjamas. The only things of interest—but not as far as Freeman was concerned—were the contents of the bottom drawer of the dressing table. It held a woman's silk nightdress, some female underclothes and a couple of whippy school canes.

Paulet put on a stiff, disapproving face, and said, 'One of those.'

There was nothing to be learned from the bathroom or the kitchen. In the big main room Pelegrina had done a thorough tidying-up job. There wasn't a personal paper or letter in the desk, though there was a pile of thoroughly burnt and stirred-up paper ash in the fireplace. The silver-framed photograph of La Piroletta had gone, and the box of Turkish cigarettes was empty. Missing, too, were the framed photographs of the tramp steamer from over the fireplace and the steam yacht from the wall behind the desk. Both pictures had been hanging some time because the wallpaper was less faded from light where they had hung.

I sat down in a chair by the fire and lit a cigarette.

'Who lived here?' Paulet dropped to the divan and the springs creaked.

I told him, gave him a brief outline of my conversation with Pelegrina, and explained about the New Year's card I had found in the cottage.

I said, 'I'm sorry I kept that from you. But at the time I didn't know what a sterling chap you were going to turn out to be.'

It mollified him a bit, but not entirely.

'Let us,' he said, 'have no secrets from one another in future. I wish to help and I wish to be frank with you. No?'

I nodded agreement. Well, that was all right. A nod is not binding. He could have been, for all I knew, putting some unspoken clause to the end of his declaration. If he were a good professional man he had to be, because frankness in our line never paid a dividend that raised the pulse rate through joy.

I said, 'He takes his daughter's photograph. Why?'

'Maybe it was a publicity photograph originally and would have her agent's name and address on the back.'

'You think that Marrini Fratelli are an invention?'

'I would bet on it.'

'You needn't. I checked the Rome directory at my hotel this afternoon. They don't exist. Now—why did he take the photographs? One coastwise steamer, pretty ancient craft by the look of it. Can't remember the name. And the steam yacht. I never got to have a close look at that.'

'There must have been a reason. Some day, we know. Clearly he was worried by your presence here and your questions about Freeman. Otherwise, why try to kill you? This Freeman begins to interest me.'

'That began with me a long time ago. I think you'd better get in touch with your Monsieur Duchêne and see what you can dig out of him. You can tell him about all this. In fact, it might be a good idea if I could talk to him.'

'I will try to arrange that.'

'You speak Italian well?'

'Fluently. In my youth I was a kitchen boy in the Hotel Principi di Piemonte at Turin and later a waiter at many other Italian hotels.'

It all came out pat. I knew he was a good guy, anxious to help me—but since suspicion had often meant the breath of life to me I couldn't forget the phoney list of coins.

'Have a poke around here tomorrow morning and see what you can learn about Pelegrina from the other people in the building.'

'A pleasure.'

As he spoke, an idea struck me. They did from rare time to time, out of the blue, like the first swallow of summer. I got up and went over to the bookshelves and nearly broke my wrist picking up the fat red leather-bound *Lloyds Register of Shipping, Volume I*.

I was hoping that there would be an index of ship owners. There wasn't. The whole thing was arranged alphabetically by the names of ships. I didn't feel like ploughing through the names of nearly four thousand ships and checking the owners to see if I could find a Pelegrina amongst them. I didn't have to. Sticking out from the top pages of the register was a small piece of marking paper. I opened the register at the marked place.

I ran my finger down the first of the two pages that lay open and found what I wanted at the bottom almost. The ship's name was *Suna,* but in 1959 she had been called the *Pelox,* and before that in 1948 the *Nordwell*. Under her earlier names she had flown the

Liberian flag, port of registry Monrovia. Her present owners—this was a 1962–63 register —were listed as 'Leon Pelegrina and Others'. Her gross tonnage was 1,366 tons, summer deadweight 662 tons. She'd been built by the Burrard D.D. Co. Ltd of Vancouver, engines by John Inglis Co. Ltd of Toronto, and her classification at Lloyds was marked 'LC class withdrawn'. A key to symbols at the front of the register said that this indicated that the class had been withdrawn by the Committee for non-compliance with the Society's regulations. From what I had seen of Leon Pelegrina, and knew of Freeman, if they were connected, that seemed about the right form. Non-compliance with regulations would have made a fine family motto for both of them. At the moment the *Suna* carried Greek registration.

I explained the details to Paulet.

He said, 'Pelegrina could still be in shipping. This I find out tomorrow, perhaps.'

I was about to tell him not to bother. I could do it by a phone call the next day to a friend of mine at Lloyds and, what is more, have him check in the Lloyd's register of yachts whether Pelegrina owned a steam yacht. Normally I wouldn't have been at all interested in Pelegrina's shipping connections. It was only the fact that he had troubled to take the framed photographs that made it seem possibly significant so far as Freeman was concerned. As I say, I was about to tell Paulet this when I heard footsteps coming down the small hallway.

Paulet and I stood up and turned at the same moment.

A woman appeared in the doorway of the room. She wore a loose, very short-sleeved white coat over a green silk dress that showed her knees and a nice run of legs. She held a small white pigskin case in one hand and a big white handbag in the other. Full under the light she was a treat to look at and would have passed A1 at Lloyds or any other place. Her skin had a dusky, velvety suggestion about it, and her eyes were wide and dark. Her hair fell just short of her shoulders and had a gloss on it like fine old mahogany.

Putting in all the charm I could, I said, 'Good evening, Miss Pelegrina.'

She said, 'How the bloody hell did you get in here?' It was a beautiful voice, low, vibrant, full of dark tones that really sent a chill down my spine without making me stop to think whether I needed my head examined. She hadn't said 'bloody' either. It was something Anglo-Saxon and straight from the barrack room. I was charmed, bewitched by her.

'The door was open and—forgive us—we walked in. We had an appointment with your father.'

'Is that so? Well, the bloody door is still bloody open—so just walk straight out. I don't want any friends or business acquaintances of my father's in my flat.'

She stood back to give us room to pass. I didn't move, though Paulet shuffled a few paces.

'I understood this was his flat. It's listed in the telephone directory as—'

'If it suited him he'd list it under the name of President bloody Johnson. But it's my flat, and I want a good night's sleep, so get the hell out of here.'

She dropped her case and made a gesture with her right arm towards the hall. I was going to argue, but her right arm made me change my mind. Around her wrist and encroaching on the end of her dress sleeve was a python gold bracelet which I would have known anywhere.

I glanced at Paulet. I knew at once that he had seen it.

'Come on, Paulet,' I said. 'We'll come back tomorrow when Miss Pelegrina has had a good night's sleep and is in a better mood.'

'Just get out and stay out. And when you next see my father tell him also not to come back. Tell him I'm having the lock changed.'

Her right arm waved again, imperiously, and we shuffled by. I'm good at scents, but I couldn't get hers. It was delicious, heady with all the magic and fascination of the East. I winked at her and she gave me a basilisk stare that would have put any of Wilkins's efforts in the kindergarten class.

Standing in the square outside was a white Ford Thunderbird that hadn't been there when we came in. It had a Rome number plate and thrown across the back seat was a mink coat. Before moving on I checked that the doors were locked against theft. They were.

CHAPTER 5

The Hour of Cowdust

From my room the next morning I telephoned Mrs Burtenshaw at the office. She was to contact my friend at Lloyds and get a list of Leon Pelegrina's shipping interests if he still had any. I said I wanted a reply by the afternoon.

After that I called Gloriana and told her that I had met Leon Pelegrina but he had been unable to help me about Freeman. This was true enough and I did not bother her with the incidental details. In fact, enjoying myself as I was beginning to, feeling the old *élan vital* coming back and not wanting to lose it, I had decided that I was not handing over any incidental details to anyone. I would stick to *bald* and, as far as possible, true facts. At the moment I didn't think that Gloriana was letting me in on the whole truth or, more charitably, didn't know it all herself. The Treasury angle seemed unnatural. So did the attitude of my friend the Chief Superintendent in 'C' Department of New Scotland Yard. Usually if I came up on the inside of any horse they were running I could expect to be bumped into the rails. Here they'd hauled off and let me through. Monsieur Robert Duchêne for my money was a phoney. Just at the moment I wasn't prepared to lump Paulet in the same category, but if I got a chance I was going to carry out an analysis for purity.

I phoned him too. He was staying in a cheap hotel near the Stazione Centrale. I told him to get round to Piazza Santo Spirito and keep an eye on things. Also, later, he was to try and contact Monsieur Duchêne. He said yes, yes, yes, full of eagerness. Too much eagerness, perhaps.

I gave him twenty minutes, and then I walked around to his hotel. On the way I thought about La Piroletta, and the python bracelet. Freeman was married to Jane Judd, and Jane Judd had been instructed that no matter what she heard she was to wait for the call from him to take off for pastures new. Pelegrina, I felt, could have been the man who had spoken to her and Gloriana on the phone, reassuring them about Freeman. As for Freeman . . . well, maybe he was the kind that kept one woman on a string while he played around with others, a game that usually ends up with a man getting the string snarled up around his feet and tripping over. In my book I was prepared to lay odds that the python bracelet was no love gift, but had been sold for hard cash.

At Paulet's hotel the reception desk was empty. The number of his room was 17. I took a look at the key rack. Number 17 wasn't there. Paulet had taken it out with him. That didn't worry me. I reached over and took Number 15.

On the second floor I fiddled around at the door of Number 17 with the Number 15 key, cursed aloud because I couldn't open it and then went to the chambermaid's room at the end of the corridor and asked her to open my room for me. I'd been given the wrong key at the desk. She obliged and took key Number 15 off me. The world is full of unsuspecting women always ready to help a man out of trouble.

I did a quick and neat turnover of Paulet's room. Quick, because there wasn't much to see, and neat because I didn't want him to know anyone had been in the place rummaging. I learned that he was in a poor way so far as pants and shirts were concerned, and was halfway through a *livre de poche* called *Vipère au Poing* by Hervé Bazin; that his second pair of shoes wanted resoling, and that men have a way of stuffing things in their dressing-gown pockets and forgetting them. For him I suppose there was some excuse because he had actually found the letter in his pocket. It had been put there by the woman he lived with in Paris—his estranged wife would never have written in the same terms. I sat down and applied my rather fractured French to it. The first sentence explained that she was packing it, unknown to him, in his dressing-gown pocket—so that he would have a nice surprise when he found it. After that it was mildly erotic in a pleasant way. The woman was obviously stuck on him. She signed herself Thérèse and had added a footnote which came out in my translation as:

You rightly have a high regard for Monsieur Carver's reputation, so please be careful. Men who are both pleasant and clever can be dangerous. I know this because that is the way you are. So watch yourself. To lose you, my darling, would make life empty for me. A thousand embraces. T.

Pleasant, clever, dangerous. I didn't know whether to be flattered.
It was interesting to know, however, that she put Paulet in the
same category. Very interesting. I made a mental note of the address
on the headed notepaper. You never knew when a detail like that
might be useful. If I had been Paulet, knowing me as he was
supposed to do, I would —if I'd been up to anything—have
destroyed the letter. That he hadn't was a point in his favour. Or
did it mean that he just wasn't quite clever enough to appreciate
how clever I was? I decided to defer a decision but to keep my eyes
open.

I went round to the Piazza Santo Spirito. Paulet was sitting on
a bench under a tree opposite Number 23. He looked gloomy.

'*Buon giorno*, François,' I said cheerfully.

'She has gone, Monsieur Carvay.' He nodded across the street.
The white Thunderbird was no longer there.

'You saw her go?'

'No. She went at eight o'clock this morning. This I learn from
the woman in the opposite flat. I pretend to be from one of the city
stores. Come to measure the big room for new curtains. With women
it is always better to be something to do with furnishings. That is
their world.'

'What did you get out of her?'

'Coffee. She is a compulsive talker and has bad breath. The
woman in the opposite flat, I mean. She wants my opinion on the
purchase of a new carpet, and she is watching us from the window
up there now, but that is all right because I said I have to wait
here for my assistant who comes from another job.'

'What did you get about the Pelegrinas?'

'The flat belongs to La Piroletta. She does some cabaret act, has
money, and is not often here. Just a flying visit like this one. The
woman does not like her but that is because she is beautiful and
this woman is not. Leon Pelegrina was there more often, though
not lately. His last visit was only for four or five days. She did not
like him either. She would not want to be quoted but she thinks he
is a crook and lucky not to be in prison. There was, some years
ago, a scandal about him over some holiday villa development on
the coast near Viareggio, but nothing was ever done about it for
lack of proof. Also, she did not care for his taking women into the
flat.'

'Where else would he take them?'

Paulet raised a sad eye to me. 'These women were *puttane*.'

'Well, he'd still need a flat—unless he didn't mind frightening the horses in the street. Come on, let's go.'

'You do not want to go in and have another look around?'

'It wouldn't help. Besides, I want to get down to Rome and take a plane to Tripoli.'

'Tripoli? But that will be expensive.'

'My client pays—for me. What about yours?'

'I must contact him.' He made a face. 'He hates spending money.'

'If you want results you've got to. Where is he?'

'I think in Naples.'

'What do you mean, you think? You know, don't you?'

'I am reasonably sure, yes.'

'Then ask him to meet us in Rome. I'd like to talk to him.'

'But why Tripoli?'

'Because I am reasonably sure that that is where Freeman is.'

'How you know this?'

I'd noticed that in moments of depression or excitement Paulet's syntax was inclined to slip.

'Later, perhaps, I'll tell you.'

Actually, in my pocket was a cable from Wilkins which had arrived for me early that morning at the hotel. It read:

M.F. DEFINITELY HERE SIX DAYS AGO STOP ADVISE ARRIVAL STOP ENQUIRY BLANKET LOCAL BOGEYS STOP REGARDS H.W.

It was the first time in her life that Wilkins had sent me her regards. Best wishes, of course, I got every year on a Christmas card, but that didn't count. And when it came to it she could use underworld slang with the best of them. The local police in Tripoli clearly weren't encouraging enquiries about Freeman. Wilkins didn't care for the police any more than I did, but she could be much more vocal about it, and I knew she would be—with me—the moment I arrived.

We took a train down to Rome that afternoon and we booked into the Hotel Eden together. Paulet was a bit fussed about staying in a four-star job, but I told him to relax and try and get in touch with Monsieur Duchêne. He went off to do this, while I had a large Negroni in the bar and sat considering the information which Mrs Burtenshaw had phoned me at the Excelsior just after lunch. My Lloyds friend had said that the only maritime interest Pelegrina had at that moment seemed to be a steam yacht of some vintage

called *La Sunata*—though the name had been changed a few times
over the years—which was Greek registered at Piraeus, and which
he let out on charter.

Monsieur Robert Duchêne arrived at the hotel at eleven the next
morning. Paulet had said that he would not want to carry on a
discussion in the bar or any of the hotel lounges so we held a
conference in my room.

He was a tall lean man, wearing big horn-rimmed glasses, and
he was in a bad temper. I put him at about fifty; his skin was like
stained vellum and he smoked long Swiss cigars, each one having
its own mouthpiece attached to it. He seldom took the cigar out of
his mouth, talking expertly around each side of it, which gave a
curious sideways waggle to his lips. It put them out of phase with
his words as though his speech was being badly dubbed. However,
he made himself clear in about ten minutes flat.

Talking exclusively to me, while Paulet sat humbly in the back-
ground, he said, 'I will be perfectly frank with you, Monsieur
Carver. I understand from Paulet that following your interview with
Leon Pelegrina an attempt was made on your life. Also my flat in
Paris was ransacked. All this is in some way connected with
Freeman, yes?'

'Yes.' His English was good, but I was trying to place the accent
behind it. It didn't sound like French to me.

'Then let me make this clear—but at the same time stress its
confidential nature. I am in the art and antique world. And by that
I do not mean I put in any appearances at Christie's or Sotheby's.
I buy and sell in a twilight world.'

'Nice way to put it.'

He frowned. 'There is always a nice way to put even the most
unpleasant things. Freeman stole certain coins from me and I
thought their recovery would be a simple matter. With simple
matters like theft and recovery without aid of the police I am at
home. Let the matter become complicated and I want no more to
do with it. Frankly, the coins were illegally acquired by me in the
first place. Equally frankly I do not wish to pursue their recovery
if it is to lead into deep and unfamiliar waters. In other words I do
not like my flat being searched and I do not like being involved in
an affair which has room for attempts on people's lives. I am
dropping the whole matter. Monsieur Paulet will be paid off, and

whether you find Mr Freeman is now a matter of indifference to me. Am I understood?'

I looked at Paulet. This had obviously come as a surprise to him. He looked like a small boy who has had a Christmas present taken from him because he had got it by a mistake in the first place. He didn't at that moment look like the man Thérèse loved and described as pleasant, clever and capable of being dangerous. He was just crestfallen.

I said, 'Since you've never been a client of mine, Monsieur Duchêne, it is a matter of indifference to me what you decide about Freeman. I still have my own client to satisfy. Would I be right in thinking you're not in the mood to answer any questions about Freeman?'

'On the contrary, Mr Carver, I will tell you what little I do know. I met him almost a year ago in the Georges Cinq bar in Paris, and he subsequently sold me a Rajput painting of the late eighteenth century. It was of the Kangra school and was called "The Hour of Cowdust". It showed Krsna returning with the herds to Brndaban at sundown.'

He paused for me to register how impressed I was and I did register—but something quite different. I was prepared to lay fifty to one in fivers that this long streak of snap and bite had me figured for an ignoramus when it came to art and antiques. And maybe I was. But what he hadn't figured—though Thérèse could have given him a pointer of two—was that what I didn't know about I checked against the best references. And I was damn well going to check this Rajput load of cowdust which he was throwing in my eyes. I could do it at the British Council library in Rome. He'd slipped up over ancient coins once, he could be doing the same over old Indian paintings.

He went on, 'I met him once in Rome after that, and then not long ago he came to my flat in Paris and tried to sell me an antique Indian python bracelet. We could not agree on a price and he left. After he had gone I discovered that he had taken a collection of ancient coins I was holding for sale to a client.'

'And you sent Paulet off to try and find him at his cottage in Kent, a cottage which, apparently, very few people knew about. How did you know about it?'

Duchêne rolled the cigar to one corner of his mouth and the movement produced a fair imitation of a smile. 'He got drunk the evening I bought the Rajput painting and he told me about it.

When drunk, Monsieur Carver, he was most tedious with his confidences. I say tedious because they were mostly about women. You will agree that women are only interesting at first hand. Is there more you would like to ask?'

'No.'

'Very well.' He looked at Paulet. 'I am staying at the Bernini-Bristol. Come there at three this afternoon with your account and I will give you a cheque on my Paris bank.'

He picked up his hat, dished out two brief nods, and left.

I looked at Paulet. 'You expected this?'

'No.'

'Well, it's happened. I'm sorry. I've enjoyed your company.'

'You would not care to hire me as an assistant?'

'No thanks. My client wouldn't wear it and I can't afford it. Anyway, it's now the hour of cowdust in the eyes. Let's go down to the bar and have a couple of double Rajputs.'

He gave me a quizzical look, but said nothing.

I stopped at the desk and asked them to try and get me a late afternoon booking on a plane to Tripoli. Paulet and I then had our drinks and he was a very subdued man.

'Always,' he said, 'when I begin to enjoy myself, or meet someone interesting, *bam!*—the guillotine comes down.'

'Stick a 10 percent surcharge on your bill for loss of expectations.'

I skipped lunch and went along to the British Council library. It was no surprise to me to find in the article on Indian and Sinhalese Art and Archaeology in Volume 12—HYDROZ to JEREM—of the *Encyclopaedia Britannica* a full-page reproduction of 'The Hour of Cowdust'. Well, well, even in the most careful of us there's always a point of laxness. But what, I asked myself, was it all in aid of? It wasn't the first time in my life the question had arisen and I knew that if I didn't come up with an answer then time eventually would reveal it—probably with unpleasant consequences.

The hotel desk had got me a reservation on the half-past-four plane to Tripoli. I said goodbye to Paulet and made the Leonardo da Vinci Airport by taxi with ten minutes to spare.

There were not many people on the plane so there were plenty of spare seats. I sat down on the port side close to one of the wings and we took off out over the Mediterranean heading for Sicily, Malta and then Tripoli. I settled back with a Pan book and promised myself that in an hour's time I would have a large whisky and soda. Just before the hour was up I began to get that feeling that someone was watching and taking an interest in me. It's a sense that becomes highly developed in my trade, like the sense of hearing in a good mechanic who notices at once from the note of an engine when it goes slightly off tune. I glanced across the gangway. A fat number in a mohair suit and a red fez, brown as a coffee bean, was sleeping happily. I turned to take in the seat behind me.

La Piroletta had the outside berth. The inner one held her handbag and a bunch of newspapers and magazines. She was dressed exactly as she had been in the Florence flat—except that she was not wearing thc python bracelet. And she was looking at me thoughtfully. Whatever expression she had on her face suited me. It was the kind of face that could make more than the most of any expression and still be beautiful. I gave her a smile and a nod. She just remained thoughtful then she gave me the faintest of nods and there was a tiny movement of her mouth which wouldn't have needed much more to make it a smile. Anyway, it was enough for me.

I got up and went back to her.

I said, 'I was just thinking of having a drink. Would you care to join me?' At the same time I handed her one of my cards.

She looked at it and then with a nice, flowing, graceful movement got up and moved to the inner berth. If you think that's easy to do, gracefully and flowingly in an aircraft seat, you can never have tried it.

I sat down and asked her what she would like to drink.

'Gin and tonic.'

I caught the stewardess's eyes and gave her order and while I did I was sorting out two problems. One, the line I was going to take; and, two, this business of coincidence in life. I don't have any great faith in coincidences—though I'll admit they happen more often than most people think. But with me, so far as business was concerned, coincidences generally turned out not to be. I decided not to lay any bets either way on this one. As for the line I was to take, I thought it might make a nice change to be reasonably honest and straightforward. After all, one mustn't get stuck in one routine all the time.

I said, 'You're going to Tripoli or further?'

'Tripoli.'

'So am I.'

'Where do you stay?'

'I don't know until I get there. A friend is booking a hotel for me. And you?'.

'The Uaddan.'

'I've begun to wonder what that name means.' I hadn't because I didn't care, but I wanted to keep the preliminaries on a drink-chat level so that she would not feel rushed.

'It is,' she said, 'the Arab name for some kind of mountain goat or deer. Something like an ibex, I think.'

The drinks came. I lit a cigarette for her. She sipped her gin and tonic and there was an unembarrassed pause in the talk while we both decided the next move in the game. Daintily she picked the slice of lemon out of her drink and sucked it. That, too, she did gracefully, and with a nice little wrinkle of her nose at the citric sharpness.

I said, 'I gather you haven't a very high opinion of your father?'

She considered this, then nodded.

'Why not?'

Without hesitation, and there seemed to be no question of her sincerity, she said, 'Because he's the world's champion scrounger and he has king-sized dreams in a pea-sized brain. But that doesn't mean I haven't a protective feeling towards him—so long as he doesn't ask me for money. At least, not too much.'

'You've got plenty?'

She looked at me, smiled and said, 'I suppose we shall come presently to the point of all this, but for the moment, since I don't actively dislike you and I like company when I'm flying to take my mind off the twenty thousand-odd feet below me, I don't mind talking. Yes, I'm very well off. And I did it all myself. How's your bank balance?'

'Reasonable at the moment—which is a rare state of affairs.'

'And you are going to Tripoli on business?'

'Yes.'

'Not, I hope, connected with my father?'

'Why do you ask that?'

'Because if you are you will either be cheated or lose your money.'

'I'm not in any deal with your father. I'm looking for a man.'

She smiled. 'I've been doing that for some time, but the quality isn't what it used to be. I suppose it's because they're mass produced or something.'

'If I can find time off work I might take you up on that. I'm one of the last custom-built models, real leather upholstery and at a hundred miles an hour all you can hear is the ticking of the clock. How much did you pay Martin Freeman for that gold python bracelet you were wearing yesterday?'

She took it without a flicker, shook the ice around in her glass, glanced out at the strato cirrus over which the setting sun was slapping gold and scarlet in action-painting frenzy, and then said, 'In lire the equivalent of two thousand pounds.'

'It's been valued at five thousand.'

'I got a bargain then.'

'It was also stolen.'

No flicker again. 'That's his problem. Not mine.' There was a touch of the father's daughter there.

'My client wants it back.'

'Your client can have it for two thousand five hundred pounds.'

'I'll consult her.'

'Her?'

'Yes. His sister. He makes a habit of financing himself out of her collection.'

'She's wealthy?'

'Very.'

'The price has gone up to three thousand. Now ask the next question.'

'Which is?'

'Where did I get to know Martin Freeman and why did I buy it?'

'Well—where did you and why did you?'

'He once helped me with some publicity work in Rome. He's a likeable layabout and the same kind of dreamer as my father. Maybe his brain is a bit bigger. I wanted to help him—in return for what he'd done for me years ago.'

'You go for him?'

'No. Even amongst the mass-produced goods he's strictly a reject—with me, anyway.'

'Somali mother, Italian father, you speak English almost too well.'

'My mother was an octoroon. I'm a fast studier, an international cabaret star, and English, French and German are obligatory. I weigh a hundred and thirty, have a Greek passport, and a star-shaped mole on the inside of my left thigh. If you are custom-built I might show it to you sometime. As for the Greek passport, I thought I would like to be a member of one of the most illustrious

civilizations of the past. By the way, I get most of my clothes at
Courrèges, don't care for oysters much, but am inclined to make a
pig of myself over *pasta*. I'd like another drink and suggest that
from now on we just keep to this kind of small talk. Unless, of
course, you want to tell me the story of your life?'

It was a sudden dismissal, and I wondered what had prompted
it. However, I didn't quarrel with it. Small talk suited me. The big
fat facts of life often show for a brief, shy moment in small talk.

'Suits me,' I said. 'As for the story of my life, I really think it
began when you walked into the Piazza Santo Spirito flat. Stout
Cortez and a peak in Darien and all that.'

'You will have to do better than that. Why not order the drinks?'

I did and we talked. I had a feeling that I was doing better, but
it was hard to tell. I didn't doubt that she felt that she had my
measure. And I didn't doubt that I hadn't anything like got
hers—except that she knew how to handle herself and wasn't going
to let anyone else do it unless he passed muster. And nothing came
out of the small talk, except the pleasure of making the time to
Tripoli pass quickly and enjoyably.

As we parted in the beginning of the stampede into the customs
sheds, under a dusky blue velvet sky lit with little yellow star sequins
and a crescent moon to symbolize the Arab world, I said, 'Some
evening soon, perhaps, we might make pigs of ourselves over *pasta*
and a bottle of Orvieto?'

'Could be, but it would have to be Chianti Ruffino.'

With a smile she flowed ahead of me and I couldn't help noticing
that the customs boys fell over themselves to deal with her and get
her through as fast as possible.

I came out into a warm night that smelt of dry dust, burnt-up
palm fronds, goats and exhaust fumes from the waiting taxis.

One of the taxis was under the charge of the faithful Wilkins.
She was wearing a woolly cardigan, a tweed skirt, sensible shoes
and a wide-brimmed straw hat so that she wouldn't get burnt by
the tropical moon. Just seeing her there gave me a warm feeling of
belonging and nostalgia. She certainly wasn't any Gloriana or La
Piroletta, but she was my girl Friday, one in a million, and that's
what a man has got to have if he's going to make a success of
business and have his filing system kept in order.

It was half an hour's drive in to Tripoli from the King Idris Airport.
The Arab taxi-driver took it at top speed and with the radio wailing

out snake-charm music at top volume. Now and again Wilkins and myself were thrown about as he deliberately just missed the odd pedestrian, goat or camel. Conversation was difficult but we managed.

I said, 'Why didn't Olaf come with you?'

'He has a stomach upset.'

I didn't make any comment. The taxi ride was bad enough; I didn't want Wilkins turning a broadside on me.

'Where am I staying?'

'At a hotel on the sea front called Del Mehari. I got you a room with bath.'

'Why not a room at your hotel, or the Uaddan?' La Piroletta was still very, very fresh in my mind.

'Because all of them are fully booked. This is a booming oil town and hotel rooms are at a premium. And, anyway, I thought you might like to stay where Martin Freeman and William Dawson had stayed.'

'How did you find that out?'

'Olaf was responsible. I told him about the case. We checked all the hotels to see if either man had stayed recently—with no result. Then Olaf said that if Bill Dawson had said in his letter to Freeman that he could have his revenge at the Wheelus course, then—if the hotels were covering up about them for any reason, which now I am sure they are—the police or whoever it was who had instructed them might not have thought to put a cover on the Seabreeze golf course, particularly as it is American owned. So Olaf said—'

'Let's go out and see if they did play there and enter their names in the book?'

'Yes.'

'And they had?'

'Yes.'

'Clever Olaf. He's in the wrong business.'

'They played there about twelve days ago and they both gave the Del Mehari as their hotel. But at the Del Mehari when Olaf and I made enquiries—'

'They just looked blank and said no?'

'Very blank. And since they don't use a hotel registration book but do each guest on a card which goes into a filing system we couldn't ask to see the register. How long do you think it will be before Olaf and I can go to Cairo?'

'Don't tell me you're losing interest? You've done so well.'

'I'm entitled to my holiday. Also—' an even primmer note came into her voice—'I don't like being followed by the police everywhere I go. The car behind us now is one which followed me out to the airport.'

I screwed my head round. Through the back window I could see headlights following us.

'Sure?'

'Positively.' Then disapprovingly, 'I thought this might be a straightforward case, but I'm sure now that it isn't. You know how much I dislike complications.'

'You, and Monsieur Robert Duchêne. What's Olaf's reaction? Doesn't he find it exciting?'

'I told you he has a stomach upset. I'm sure it's a nervous one. I'm worried for him.'

She had reason to be. In a man Olaf's size a stomach upset was no minor matter.

I said, 'Did you get anything on Bill Dawson?'

'Nothing, except—'

I lost what she said as the radio began to whack out an Arab nuptial dance or something and we swerved to miss a donkey loaded four storeys high with sacks.

'Except what?'

'Except that I keep thinking that I ought to know something about him. Something at the back of my mind. It is most irritating.'

'I get the feeling too. Maybe it will come. Did you check the hire-car services? This golf course is some way out of the town, isn't it? They could have hired a car to go out.'

Wilkins nodded. 'Olaf suggested that. We went round them all. And they were all very co-operative, looking through their books and apologizing when they had no record recently of a Freeman or a Dawson. All except one—it's a place near the centre of the town called the Magarba Garage. They just said at once without reference to their books that they had not hired out any cars to any such persons.'

'The police or whoever had been at them?'

'Yes. Did you bring any firearms in?'

That was typical Wilkins. She could call a spade a spade with the best of them, but a gun was always a firearm.

I said, 'Yes. It's strapped to the inside of my left leg now and damned uncomfortable.'

'Then if you don't want to become *persona non grata* I should get rid of it. Firearms can only be imported if declared on arrival and a licence obtained.'

'I'll be careful. And you've done a good job—or, at least, Olaf has. He's a bright boy. Why don't we offer him a job with us and then you wouldn't have to make the Cairo trip every year? Carver, Wilkins and Bornjstrom. Sounds good.'

'The car behind is coming up to overtake us.'

I squinted back. It was. And it did. And then about a hundred yards ahead it pulled up and a man jumped out into our headlights.

Wilkins said, 'The firearm.'

I jerked up my trouser leg and did some quick unstrapping. Wilkins took it from me and calmly put it into her handbag like a schoolmistress coolly confiscating a catapult.

Our driver hesitated for a moment or two, considered whether he would notch up another pedestrian on his steering column, and then changed his mind as the white holster webbing, navy blue uniform and peaked cap said 'Police' very plainly.

He pulled into the side of the road behind the police car which I saw now was a Land-Rover. The police corporal or sergeant or whatever he was came round to the side of the car and spoke through the driver's open window. Our taxi-man switched off 'Return to the Oasis' or whatever was playing and shrugged his shoulders.

The policeman came back to the rear window and signalled for me to wind it down. I did. A warm gust of night air came in and I gave him a big smile.

'Trouble, Officer?'

He was a Libyan, small, stocky, hard material all the way through and very correct. Even his English was correct.

'You are Mr Carver?'

'Yes.'

'And you stay where?'

'At the Del Mehari Hotel, when I get there.'

'This lady?'

'She is my secretary.'

'It is requested that you come with us, Mr Carver. Be good enough to ask your secretary to take your luggage on to your hotel.'

'I hope I'm going to be allowed to join up with it later?'

'Certainly.'

I wondered why they hadn't picked me up at the airport. The only answer I could come up with was that they wanted the minimum of

public display. Interesting, since I was only looking for a man
who'd stolen money and a bracelet from his own sister.

'Shall I be back there tonight?'

'Certainly, Mr Carver.'

I turned to Wilkins. 'Drop my stuff and come round and have
breakfast with me in the morning. Bring Olaf if he's in a breakfast
mood.'

I got out and the policeman waved the taxi on. It roared away,
leaving a dust cloud behind it and I could hear the radio going full
blast.

They put me in the back of the Land-Rover and we headed for
town. One of the things about strange towns is never to reach them
at night. You have no sense of topography or direction and if you
have to take quick action you are at a loss to know which way to
head. Not that I thought this might be necessary tonight. But you
never knew. Some of the politest police opening gambits lead up to
nasty end games sometimes.

There was a nasty end game this time. But not the kind I could
have anticipated. We drove into the town and I didn't try to make
any sense out of it until for a few moments we swung along a wide
esplanade with the sea on our right and the lights of shipping
somewhere way ahead from a harbour. Then we turned into a side-
street and pulled up in front of a blank-faced building with double
wooden doors. From a socket over the door projected a Libyan
national flag.

I got out with my police escort and he took me by the arm and
through the door. He said nothing and I went with him, his palm
on my elbow, feeling like some old man being helped across the
street by a good Samaritan. We went down a tiled corridor that
smelled of old cooking and stale tobacco, up a stone flight of steps
and then through a half-glass door into a large, low-ceilinged room.
One wall held what looked like a collection of large metal filing
cabinets. There was a bare, chromium-topped table in the centre
and sitting on one edge of it was another Libyan in a white overall.
My guide said something to him in Arabic and the man got up and
jerked a half-smoked cigarette into a drainway under the table. For
the first time I got the smell in the room and a flicker of familiarity
trembled inside me.

The man in overalls went over to one of the filing cabinets and
pulled it open. It didn't surprise me now to see it come out about

six feet on its rollers. He made a motion with his hand for me to come over. I did.

It wasn't a pretty sight. I stook there and took out a cigarette. The policeman who had come up alongside me held out a lighter. The man in overalls watched me guardedly. Neither of them said anything.

Lying in the container was a naked man. I inhaled smoke to get the chemical smell out of my throat and to fight down an edge of nausea. I'd seen plenty of dead men, and even a few who had been in the water a long time, but to stand there and look down at this one took more out of me than any of the others had. I let my eyes go from what had been the head down the length of the body to his feet. I did it deliberately, slowly, and with half of my thoughts a long way away. Then I stepped back, turned and heard the cabinet roll back behind me.

To the policeman I said, 'What now?'

He said, 'Please to come with me.'

I did, avoiding his helping hand, moving alongside him and wondering how Jane Judd and Gloriana Stankowski were going to take the news, because tabbed neatly round the right wrist of the body had been a label, marked—*Martin Freeman, British.*

CHAPTER 6

The Apprentice Tail

The room, though I didn't know it then, was in the Police Headquarters on the Sciara Sidi Aissa which was a street one block south of the waterfront. Almost next door, though I didn't know that until the next morning when I got a town map and began to take my bearings, was the Hotel Casino Uaddan, and a little further up the street to the east was the Libya Palace Hotel.

It was a small, high room with a framed photograph of King Idris of Libya over a fireplace which was piled high with old pinecones. On the opposite wall was a framed photograph of H.R.H. El-Hassan El-Rida El-Senussi, the Crown Prince of Libya, and just below it, flickering in the slight sea draught from the half-open window, a calendar of the Oasis Oil Company which told me that it was now April 21 and cuckoo time back home. I had to admit to a slight touch of nostalgia for the pigeons in Trafalgar Square, the tube rush in the evenings and Mrs Meld leaning over the garden gate. I always got nostalgia when I sensed that I was getting into something deep and far from home.

The man behind the desk wore a plain navy blue suit, a white cotton shirt and a black tie with a white stripe right down its middle. He was in his thirties, had a brown face as smooth as a pecan nut, pleasant dark eyes, a small, thin-lipped mouth, and short, wiry black hair. He looked as though no one had ever rushed him in his life, or was ever going to, because he had long ago decided that, paradise as the bosom of Allah might be, he was in no hurry to reach it—so the form for longevity was a calm, even-paced life and always keep your voice down. On the edge of his desk was a little wooden board which read 'Captain Iba Asab', in English, and below some Arabic writing which probably announced the same thing.

He watched my police corporal escort out of the room, and then gave me a slow nod which was a greeting and an invitation to sit on the chair lying just off his desk.

'Mr Carver?'

'Yes.'

'Captain Asab, Libyan State Police.' He put out an arm slowly and tapped the announcement board across his desk.

'And not without a sense of the dramatic. Why this build-up?'

'You have been inconvenienced?'

'Only to the extent that by now I'd thought I'd be having a leisurely drink at my hotel and changing my socks.'

He smiled. 'Moslems are especially enjoined to be kind and charitable to the *masakeen*—unfortunate. I regret, however, I have no drink to offer you. However, I will try not to keep you too long.'

'Don't rush anything.'

He gave me a look and said, 'At the moment you are a little uncertain. Perhaps of my attitude? Perhaps of your status? Do not worry. My only wish is to give you all the information I can to help you to bring your business here to a conclusion.'

'How's your colloquial English?'

'Fair to middling. I did three years at the London School of Economics—and ended up a policeman, which just shows that you can never tell which way the ball's going to bounce. I don't myself—but light up if you want to.'

I lit a cigarette and he slowly opened a drawer as I did so.

'Where was Martin Freeman fished out of the drink?' I asked him.

He pushed an open shallow cardboard box across the desk to me. 'A little way up the coast, west of the town, two days ago. He was fully dressed, a sports jacket and trousers and so on. That's all he had on him.' He nodded at the box.

I took the box and went through the stuff. All of it had suffered from water exposure. There was a British passport in Freeman's name, a leather wallet with about ten pounds in Libyan sterling, a couple of membership cards of clubs in Rome, a bunch of keys, a Ronson leather-bound lighter, a silver cigarette case with the initials M.F. on the outside and two water-pulped cork-tipped cigarettes inside.

'Where would the rest of his stuff be? He was a visitor here. He must have had a case or something at his hotel.'

'That we have been unable to trace.'

It could have been a lie, but whether it was or not didn't seem important to me.

'How did you know I was looking for him?'

'We were informed by the British Embassy here when we reported the recovery of the body to them. I gather, too, from them that your Treasury officials in London were interested in him.'

'Why?'

'The details are confidential, but, I imagine, irrelevant now. You can go and see them, if you wish, but they asked me to tell you that Mrs Stankowski is being informed of her brother's death and she will give whatever instructions are necessary for dealing with the body. In other words the affair is out of your hands.'

'Unless—when she knows the facts—she tells me she would like to know why, before being tipped into the sea, he was shot through the head.'

'Whether it was murder or suicide, Mr Carver—that is our concern. We need no help.'

'Got any ideas on the subject?'

'At the moment, few.'

'The body floated ashore?'

'Yes.' He reached slowly for the cardboard box and began to put it back in the drawer.

'So he could have been in the water anything from six days onwards?'

'About that.'

'What did the autopsy show? About the time in the water, I mean.'

'There is some doubt. The head wound complicates it.'

'Well I can tell you he hadn't been drifting around more than twelve days.'

He looked at me calmly, but it was the kind of calm that covered surprise. Tell this man that some forgotten old uncle out in the Fezzan had left him Solomon's treasure and there still wouldn't be a flicker; in fact, you could tell him anything and he would still be the same. But one thing was for sure—he was never going to tell me or anyone else anything that he had decided was best kept to himself.

'How can you know?'

'Because he played a round of golf at the Seabreeze course twelve days ago with a friend called Bill Dawson. You got a line on any Bill Dawson?'

'No. But thank you for the information.'

'Just that? Thanks. No questions as to how I know?'

He smiled. 'Tomorrow, maybe. At the moment I don't want to delay your whisky and soda.'

'I can wait. In the visitors' book at Seabreeze they both entered their hotel as the Del Mehari—that's where I am staying—and the hotel people told my secretary that neither of them had stayed there.'

He shook his head. 'Maybe they did. Some of my countrymen, Mr Carver, are lazy and inefficient. It is a young country. I'll look into it.'

'Check the Magarba Garage too. I think you'll find that Freeman or Dawson hired a car there some time in the last twelve days.' I stood up. 'And let's be as frank as we can with one another. Okay, there are lots of things you don't want to tell me. Fine, if that's how you feel it must be. But it hardly is the way to encourage co-operation from me—that's if there's anything I could do to help.'

'If I fancy you can help me I'll get in touch with you. But please understand that I do not wish you to encroach on what is now purely a police matter.'

Encroach. It was a good word. The trouble was that I had encroached already. And it was a good feeling. My late-night and early-morning lassitude was gone. La Piroletta had been the final dose of tonic to brighten the whites of my eyes. But more than health now I could hear distantly the rattle of a cash register and that, if you've got your health and the kind of fluctuating bank balance I enjoy, is music played by the oldest siren in the world. He didn't know it, of course, but standing there looking down at him, I'd just been presented with a lead which, the moment I could check it, might prove that Bill Dawson was really the number one, gold-plated nigger in this wood-pile. Little things tip a man's destiny. And this one was a half-folded newspaper that lay neatly to one side of his desk. Later, I learned that it was the *Sunday Ghibli*, a weekly English-language newspaper published in Tripoli. All I was concerned with was the headline. There were going to be times soon when I could have wished I had never seen it.

'So long as I keep out of your hair, that's all right?'

'Absolutely.'

'And I can stay here as long as I like?'

'I don't imagine, Mr Carver—from the information I have about you—that you will want to stay at your own expense once Mrs Stankowski terminates your assignment.'

I didn't answer.

He said, 'The police car will drive you to your hotel. As a matter of fact it is very close to the British Embassy should you want to go and see them.'

He stood up and I was surprised to see how short he was.

I said, 'Why was I picked up on the road in from the airport? All of this could have waited until tomorrow.'

He shook his head. 'It seemed to me a good thing to have it over and done with. And again I thought it might embarrass you to have a police car call for you at your hotel.'

It was weak and he knew that I knew it. A police car was going to take me back to the hotel anyway. And when the police of any country start to worry about embarrassing people like me, then it was a safe bet that the real worry in their minds was much deeper and directed elsewhere.

The Del Mehari Hotel was on the sea front to the east of the town. It was a low Moorish-style building mostly on one floor, with all the rooms set around a central hall and a couple of inner courtyards.

I took a short stroll before breakfast towards the town. Palm trees lined the long esplanade. The wide curve of the harbour was a crinkly, breeze-freshened blue. Smug-fronted Mercedes and chromium-grinning American cars made pleasant tyre noises over the tarmac. A couple of blanket-wrapped Arabs slept in a sea-front embrasure, and groups of black-dressed Arab women shuffled along in the breeze, returning from their early morning charing jobs in the government offices. The Mediterranean sky was studded with little tufts of cotton-wool cloud. Way ahead of me was the Harbour Castle and the huddle of the old Arab town. But at this end all the signals were set to GO, hell-bent into the last half of the twentieth century on the crest of the Libyan oil boom. Office and apartment blocks were reaching up to dwarf the mosques and muezzin towers, and the faithful were called to pray to Allah these days over a Tannoy system. It was about as exotic as Brighton and you could find the same things in the shops and bars but at rather higher prices. A flight of jets from the Wheelus Air Base whined through the air leaving curving vapour trails behind them. It was the same old world, distance annihilated, all services piped in, ready at the flick of a finger, and not a single real problem that had plagued the world since *homo sapiens* first planted his ugly feet on it an inch nearer being solved. Only hope can sustain a dismal record like that. Or stupidity.

I went back and had eggs and bacon and fresh rolls and coffee, and got the waiter to bring me a cable form. To Mrs Stankowski I sent the message:

Presume you have official information death brother. Cable instructions.

Knowing the efficiency of the British Post Office service, I was ready to bet that they would deliver it as a greetings telegram with a border of fluffy rabbits, song birds and nosegays.

During my second cup of coffee Wilkins and Olaf appeared. I'd met Olaf before, but he always came as a shock to me. He seemed to have put on another two inches everywhere. His pale-blue eyes sparkled with health so that I knew the tummy trouble was gone, his pale, fair hair was ruffled from the wind, and one of his great hands grabbed mine and pumped away as though he were clearing the bilges to keep the ship from sinking. He sat down and the chair just held under his weight, and he had to sit sideways because his knees would not go under the table comfortably.

'Mr Carver—you mess up our holiday. Not the first time, eh?' He grinned and the huge brown face went into a landslide of happy wrinkles.

'How's the stomach?'

'Fine. It was temporary. Some mussels we have at an Italian restaurant. Shellfish in the Mediterranean is always suspect. I should know but I never learn. You think Hilda looks well?'

Hilda, though God knows I could never think of her as anything but Wilkins, looked well, but embarrassed at the attention directed to her. She smiled at Olaf, then frowned at me, put up a hand and touched her rust-coloured hair, and said, 'What happened with the police?'

'Freeman is dead,' I said. 'They showed me his body. Fished out of the drink. So far as I am concerned it is the end of the matter. At least, almost.'

'We can go back to Cairo?' Olaf lit an Egyptian cigarette and began to fumigate the dining room.

'When a couple of small points are cleared up. Would you have any contacts with the harbour or shipping people here?'

Olaf nodded. 'Yes. Any port on the Med or the Red Sea, I know someone.'

'Good—there's a certain Leon Pelegrina who owns a steam yacht called *La Sunata*. I'd quite like to know what the movements of that boat have been lately. Say, in the last three weeks. Can do?'

'Of course.' He rose to his feet, and grabbed the table from going over. 'I go down there now. Hilda, I come back for you soon.'

He reached across for her hand, kissed it and was gone.

'Charming,' I said. 'He's mad about you. When you set up house see you get good, solid teak furniture and screw it to the floor.'

'He's a good kind man.'

'That's what I'm saying. And you're lucky—he comes in the king size.'

'Why are you interested in this steam yacht if the matter is finished?'

'I like to tie up the loose ends. But don't worry about going back to Cairo. You'll get there. But first I'd like you this morning to go into town and send a cable to a Miss Jane Judd at the Mountjoy Hotel in Dorset Square. Sign it in my name and ask for a reply Post Restante here.'

'I could do it from the hotel.'

'I know you could, but anything you send from there is probably handed first to the police.'

'Look—'

'I said I was just tying up loose ends. I am. Just say—Cable if M.F. has abdominal scar left-hand side.'

'I presume this body had?'

'Yes. It's about the only thing left for identification except the teeth.'

'I don't think I want to do this.'

'Why not?'

'Freeman is dead. Olaf and I want to go to Cairo. And you won't ever leave well alone. The police out here are very touchy about interference.'

'They are everywhere. Touchiness is essential. Even if you're the right height you can't get into the police without it. And there's something else.'

'I'm not surprised. Yov've got that look. What is it this time? Some woman—or just money?'

'Both. And in addition, a man.'

'What man?'

'Bill Dawson. Captain Asab, whom I saw at Police Headquarters, was remarkably uninterested in Dawson. No policeman can be remarkably uninterested in a man who was probably playing golf with Freeman a day or so before he was shot through the head.'

'Shot?'

'Didn't I mention that?'

She looked at me with steady blue eyes and shook her head slowly, pursing her lips. Next to Olaf, but a long way behind, I was her concern. I hoped that she wasn't going to overdo it.

'You have no intention of giving up this case, have you?'

'I don't like loose ends. I'll give it up when it's all tidy. Look at this.'

I handed over to her a copy of the *Sunday Ghibli* which I had found in the hotel lounge.

'What about it?'

'Read the headline.'

She read it. Looked at me, then read it again. I lit a cigarette.

She said, 'It's a common enough name.'

'Sure. Like Smith, Brown and Jones.'

She sniffed. 'I think you should go back to London.'

I shook my head. 'Think about Bill Dawson. William Dawson. A common enough name. Something about that keeps niggling in my mind. You could check it.'

'A call to the British Embassy would confirm it.'

'I don't want it confirmed officially yet. I just want to know privately. I thought you'd like to do it.'

'What I'd like to do is to go to Cairo, and know you were back in London. At least there your mercenary instincts are reasonably limited.' She tapped the paper. 'If what I'm thinking you're thinking is so, your plain duty would be to tell all you know to the authorities.'

'You remember the three times in the last eight years that I've done that? It did nothing for my reputation, my pocket or my comfort. Will you check it for me? I don't want to poke around. But there's a British Reading Room here. You'll probably find it full of dead-beat Libyans having a quiet snooze, but there's sure to be some gabby type in charge of the out-of-date newspapers and magazines. Turn on the charm.'

'There could be thousands of Dawsons.'

'That's it. And some of 'em get to the top. By the way, do you still remember our private code?'

'Now listen, Mr Carver!'

'All right, all right. . . .' I raised a placatory hand, my left through years of practice because you always want the right free in case it doesn't work.

Wilkins stood up and gathered herself together. She could do it better than anyone I knew. The temperature dropped and from inside the glacier she said, 'I'll do this and then Olaf and I are going back. When I joined you, you know it was agreed that I should not have to do field work.'

'You make it sound as though I'm running a cotton plantation.'

'You need,' she said, 'your head examined. And I wish I knew this time what you were after. I don't believe it's money, because you've got plenty at the moment.'

'A woman, perhaps.'

'No, because you would have been talking about her already and have that silly, self-satisfied look on your face.'

'What then?'

'I think you're just doing it for the hell of it. For excitement. In the same way that teenagers take blue pills and eventually find themselves hooked on heroin. If you can't get a kick out of chasing money or a woman, then you find something else to chase.'

I said, 'That's a very attractive straw hat you've got. The ribbon matches your eyes. And you are looking well.'

She didn't say 'pig', but she swept out.

From the Del Mehari to the British Embassy was about two or three hundred yards along the sea front towards the town. After the first fifty yards I realized that Captain Asab had put a tail on me. He was a young man in a leather jacket and tight black trousers, open-necked white shirt and a very worn round astrakhan hat. He was talking to the hotel gardener who was watering the gravel of the hotel forecourt when I came out. He drifted after me down the road and I checked him by going twice round the block in which the Embassy stood. He went round conscientiously after me and then looked a bit foolish as I stood at the foot of the Embassy steps waiting for him to come by. When he came up to me, I said, 'Is the man in the black Simca your friend?'

He looked blankly at me.

I nodded across the road. A black Simca saloon was just parking across the way.

'Your friend?' I queried him.

'*No comprendo, signore,*' he said.

'Save it,' I said. 'I shall be in here for a while, then you can give me a lift down to the Uaddan. Captain Asab won't mind.'

He gave a shy little grin, then dry-washed his chin with one hand, and said, 'The signore is talking in riddles.' He ducked his head at me and moved on. I watched him go, thinking that Captain Asab must be very hard up for trained men. Either that, or he was putting a novice on to me for the experience, knowing that I wouldn't mind.

In the Embassy hallway there was a porter in a serge suit and red fez who wanted me to fill out a memo in triplicate stating the nature of my business. Instead I wrote—Martin Freeman and William Dawson—on the back of one of my cards and handed it to him, saying, 'Ask the Ambassador if he can spare five minutes.'

He looked shocked and disappeared. I sat down and watched a girl in a white blouse and check skirt arranging a bowl of flowers on a stand further down the hall. She arranged them nicely, showing a lot of leg, one of which had a ladder in its nylon. A telephone rang twice somewhere. An Air Force officer came down the stairway and the girl moved around in her arranging so that he could see the laddered nylon. She was wasting her time. He went by her and by me and out with a glazed look in his eye as though he had just been dismissed from the service.

Five minutes later I was in a little room on the first floor talking to a secretary who had been designated to deal with me in lieu of the Ambassador Extraordinary and Plenipotentiary. There was a silver-framed photograph of a woman and two nice boys on his desk, all of them smiling. His wife and children, I presumed. It was a pity he wasn't smiling too. It spoilt the family atmosphere. He looked worried and cautious and he had the right face for it. It was clear too that he had no time for me. I was in the wrong profession and certainly wasn't wearing the right tie. His was Old Marlburian; mine was a green number with red dots on it and the silk a little frayed on the knot. Wilkins that morning had found time to give it a disapproving stare. Anxiety and caution—to them in other people I am as sensitive as a sea anemone sensing the turn of the tide.

I said, 'I just wanted to check with you whether you had had any instructions from my client about the disposal of her brother's body? Captain Asab of the police here has told me that you have already informed her of the tragedy.'

'No instructions have so far been received.'

'Will you let me know when you do receive them? I'm at the Del Mehari Hotel up the road.'

'Certainly.' He raised his bottom two inches from his chair. He couldn't wait to get rid of me.

'Dreadful thing,' I said. 'Shot through the head and then dumped in the drink. Not that he didn't have something like that coming to him by all accounts. Still—*de mortuis nil nisi bonum.*'

The tag and its sentiment didn't impress him beyond making him lower his bottom to the seat.

'I think, Mr Carver, you can safely leave everything in our hands—in co-operation with the Libyan police, that is.'

'Absolutely,' I said. 'Would you have any idea which way the sea current sets along this coast at this time of the year? East to west or the other way round?'

'I haven't the faintest idea.'

He was beginning to lift again but I stalled him.

'And what about this Bill Dawson he was last seen with?'

'How did you know—'

He broke off, not because the telephone had begun to ring on his desk, but because for a moment he had assumed that I knew something I wasn't presumed to know, and then had decided that I was probably making some kind of inspired guess. I was, of course. In fact, for inspired guessing I'm in the Olympic class. How otherwise would I make money and eat?

He picked up the phone and answered it. I sat there and listened. His eyes kept flickering towards me as he said 'Yes' and 'No,', and then once 'Would you mind repeating that?' It was a classical example of a guarded conversation and his eyes on me gave away the fact that whatever was being said to him he connected in some way with me.

He wrote something on a memo pad with a pencil, put the phone down, tore off the memo page and stood up.

'Would you please excuse me a moment?'

I nodded graciously. Why not—he was on the Queen's business. I was just on my own, but I had more than an inkling even then that the two were going to be mixed. He went out of the room, through a door behind his desk. As it closed I reached over and tore off the next page of the memo block. He had a good heavy hand with a pencil when he wrote. I didn't bother then to try and decipher the markings that had come through to the lower leaf. When he came back the memo page was neatly folded in my pocket.

I said, 'You were going to tell me something about this Bill Dawson who was with Freeman sometime shortly before his death.'

Stiffly, he said, 'I wasn't aware that I was. We know nothing of any Dawson who might have been connected with Mr Freeman.' He rose smartly, no stalling him this time, but he put a patently false note of co-operation into his voice to get me eased out of the room. 'Be assured, Mr Carver—that so long as you represent Mrs Stankowski's interests out here we shall keep you informed—so far as police protocol will allow—of all developments. The death, possible murder, indeed, of a British subject is, of course, a matter of great concern to us and the local authorities.'

He had a good platform voice when he wanted, full of the deepest insincerity, but it got me out of the room and the door closed behind me.

I stopped in the hall and took out the memo leaf. It didn't need any scientific treatment to decipher it. It read:

Manston arrives Idris 19.45 hrs. Arrange car.

At that moment there could have been a harem of naked houris arranging flowers in the hall and I wouldn't have noticed them. No wonder my secretary upstairs had itchy pants and a distant manner, no wonder Captain Asab had had me picked up on the road in from the King Idris Airport, and no wonder there was a cold feeling in the pit of my stomach and the adrenalin pump going full bore somewhere in my throat—because Bill Dawson just had to be what I had begun to suspect he must be. Once they had names like Pelham, Grenville, Perceval and Rockingham, but this is the age of the common man and in have come the Browns, the Smiths and the Dawsons to fill the high places.

I shoved the paper back into my pocket and went half-tranced out of the place. As the sea air and sunshine hit me I was telling myself that a couple of half-baked dreamy incompetents like Pelegrina and Freeman could never have dared to try and pull off something like this. Dream about it, yes. Why not, there's no law against dreams. But to try it on—and, by God, it had to be that they had . . . ! Well, they weren't even in the fourth division league for that kind of thing. In my time I'd met a few who could have tried it, even got away with it—but not those two, not unless they had all this time been hiding their real talent and brilliance.

I lit a cigarette at the bottom of the Embassy steps. For ten seconds I wondered what to do, during the next thirty I slowly

came to the decision to pack up and go home, and then in the next
ten I changed my mind. I couldn't go home. And leave all this?
Not bloody likely. This was what the doctor had ordered for my
flagging body and mind. And, anyway, leaving out health reasons,
there might be other things in it . . . like money, like women, like
kudos, like being one jump ahead of everyone else, like an M.B.E.
at the end of it . . . and like, quite possibly, a sticky end. Rex
Carver, R.I.P. But what the hell, I told myself—duck a challenge
and the dust settles thick on your shoulders like dandruff.

At my side, a real voice with a touch of Italian accent said, 'You
really like, Mr Carver, that we give you a lift to the Uaddan?'

It was my young apprentice tail, grinning.

'Why not,' I said. 'My legs feel a bit weak at the moment.'

Obligingly they brought the Simca up to the kerb for me.

They rang from the reception desk and she told them to send me
up. It was a little suite on the second floor overlooking the sea. She
came through from the bedroom wearing a cream silk dress that
showed a lot of bare brown arm. She just stood and looked me over
and I did the same for her.

She said, 'Is this business or pleasure?'

'Business first.'

She said, 'The drinks are over there. Mine is lime juice and soda
water and four lumps of ice.'

I went over to a side-table and began mixing. She dropped into
a little chair by the window, crossed her legs neatly and looked a
picture with the sun taking the whole of one side of her body.

I said, 'What do I call you? Not La Piroletta or Miss Pelegrina.'

'So long as it is business just avoid it.'

I handed her her drink and sat down opposite her holding a gin
and tonic.

I said, 'I want your help.'

'If I can. Is it this bracelet business?'

She held up her left arm; the gold python bands slid over the
warm brown skin.

'Only indirectly. I want to know your real feeling for your father.'

'Why?'

'Because I think he's heading for big trouble. May already be in
it.'

'That describes his life.'

'You like to see him in trouble?'

'No. As a matter of fact I am reasonably fond of him. But that doesn't stop me also being fed up with him. In the past I often helped him with money. But now—no more.'

'Has he tried to touch you recently?'

'Touch? Oh, you mean borrow money?'

'Yes.'

She shook her head. 'He knows better.'

'What is his financial position?'

'Rocky. He's been up and he's been down in his life. At the moment he's down. Mostly he's been in shipping or property development. There was a time when he was doing quite well. But it passed. What is he trying to do now that he shouldn't?'

'I'm not sure. He still owns a steam yacht, doesn't he?'

'*La Sunata*. Yes. But he's probably carrying some loan on it.'

'What about property?'

'He's not involved in any development scheme that I know about.'

I stood up and wandered round the room. A little wander often helps the thoughts. My back to her, I said, 'If he wanted to drop out of the public eye for a while where do you think he would go?'

'You mean if he wanted to hide?'

'Something like that. For instance, would he take off in *La Sunata* for a cruise?'

Her laugh brought me round to face her.

'That's the last thing he would do. He hates the sea. He's always sick.'

'Then where would he go? Does he own a house, villa or cottage anywhere? Particularly on this side of the Mediterranean.'

She frowned. 'Why should I help you to find my father if he's in trouble?'

'God knows. I suppose, in a way, because I'd like to help him if it isn't too late.'

'Is this something to do with Freeman too?'

'I think so. I think the two of them dreamed up something which is right outside their class. Miles outside. If I can get to your father I might be able to straighten things out for him.'

'Why on earth should you? You don't care a damn for him.'

'True. But I've often straightened things out for people I don't like.'

'On the chance that it will show a profit?' She was looking at me shrewdly. Whichever way she looked, it was good.

'Yes. Why not? Good deeds are always chalked up on the credit side either in a bank book down here or in the golden one above.'

'Perhaps you'd better tell me exactly what it is that is worrying you about my father.'

'I can't because I don't know anything definite. But you tell me where I can get in touch with him—and I promise to do all I can to help him.'

She stood up and shook her head.

'Why not?'

'Because I have to think about it.'

'That means you do know where he might be?'

'Could be.'

'Then I'd advise you not to be too long making up your mind to tell me.'

'That's what I was thinking. But one has to be sure—no?'

'Oh, yes, one has to be sure—particularly in dealing with people like me.'

She stood close to me and smiled. I really was concerned about her father, even though I guessed he was a dreamy, half-baked crook. In my book he was just pathetic. I couldn't help warm generous feelings for that type because they were all victims, reaching for the moon, eyes heavenward, and bound to walk straight over the edge of a cliff sooner or later. I put my hand on her brown arm. It felt good. Man is an ambivalent creature. I worried about her father with a small part of my mind, and at the same time wanted her with a larger part, and with the part left over hoped that if any credit was to come my way it would be in cash and not a citation in any golden book.

She raised her face a little and put her lips on mine. Gently, no fuss, nothing passionate beyond my arms going comfortably round her. Then she stepped back and said, 'My friends, real friends, call me Letta. And let's face it, there are bloody few of them because I have high standards.'

'What rating do you think I'll get?'

'Come and see me after the last show tonight and I'll have it sorted out. You—and my father. All right?'

I nodded, and she went to the door and opened it for me. I gave her a big smile and went. But only twelve paces down the carpeted corridor. Then I turned round and went back to her door. I squatted down and put my eye to the keyhole. Accurate character reading is a must in my business. Letta was no girl for letting grass grow under her feet. If she wasn't sure of somebody—me, for instance—she took her time, determined to make no mistake. But if she was sure of a thing she got on with it. She was getting on with it now. She was standing by the window table, leafing through a small notebook. She put it down and picked up the telephone. She was about to speak into it when she paused and looked straight towards the room door. She began to lower the receiver to its rest.

I moved fast, down the corridor and around the corner, to get out of the way of the little bit of her character that I had overlooked, that she had read mine more accurately than I had read hers. I kept going fast—knowing she would open the door and reassure herself that I wasn't eavesdropping—until I reached the hotel hallway. To one side of the reception desk there was a girl at the switchboard. Just beyond was a glass case full of Arab leather goods, silver brooches and bangles and fifth-rate water colours. I stood and examined the exhibits and almost immediately the exchange buzzer went. The girl plugged in a lead. I listened to her speaking. It was brief and in Italian and I didn't get much of it, certainly not the number of the call that Signorina Pelegrina was booking. But I got the exchange. It was Bizerta. Well, that was enough. All I had to do now was to get a look at her address book. There couldn't be many Bizerta numbers in it. In fact, when I did come to examine it there was only one.

Outside, I declined a lift from the apprentice tall and walked back to my hotel for lunch. The first course was some fish with cotton-wool flesh full of needle-sharp bones and then a dish of mutton and rice to apply as an inner poultice to a lacerated stomach. Afterwards I lay on my bed for a couple of hours to recover and at the same time went over the tangle of Pelegrina-Freeman loose ends to see if I could sort the mess out. I didn't have a great deal of success. That Bill Dawson had to be what I suspected him to be was reasonably certain. That Pelegrina was trying to pull off a deal far too big for him was also reasonably certain. In doing this with Freeman it could be that Freeman had either become a casualty or the body I had been shown was not Freeman's but a gruesome red herring to make everyone think that Freeman was out of the picture for good. Jane Judd would establish this for me. After all, a wife ought to know whether her husband had an abdominal scar or not, and Jane had been warned not to believe anything she heard about Freeman. Yes, Freeman could be trying to set up his future life neat and tidy and without complications. As usual he wasn't being very

efficient about it. Neither Manston nor Captain Asab would accept
a water-sodden passport as proof of identity.

But the aspect that puzzled me most was the Paulet and Robert
Duchêne angle. Just where did they feature in this, and what did
they think they were going to get out of me? Or had thought they
were going to get? I didn't know and I worried about it right
through until it was time to have a drink before dinner.

I'd got through my first whisky and soda when the reception
clerk brought me my reply from Gloriana. The cable read:

Embassy arranging all details my brother. Your services no longer
required. Appreciate efforts by you to date. G.S.

Well, it was nice to be appreciated.

Halfway through my second drink Wilkins arrived. I bought her
a Dubonnet and she handed me Jane Judd's reply which was:

M.F. abdominal scar right-hand side. Why? Judd.

Well, it might be some time before I could answer her 'Why?' All
I knew at the moment was that it was a typical piece of Freeman
carelessness to think he could get away with a slap-dash substitute
for himself.

'What about Dawson?' I asked Wilkins.

'You were right. Olaf and I are leaving for Cairo tomorrow in
the late afternoon. I suggest you get a plane back to London.'

'What did Olaf find out about the yacht, *La Sunata?*'

'It was in harbour here two weeks ago and then went up the
coast as far as Bizerta. A week ago it went across to Naples and is
now on charter doing a trip along the French coast.'

'It went just as far as Bizerta, did it? Interesting.'

'Are you going to London?'

'I'll think about it.'

'I wish you would.'

'Don't worry. I can look after myself.'

'I doubt it.'

'Examine the records—they prove it.'

'You've been lucky, that's all. What do you think has happened
to Bill Dawson?'

I gave her a smile over my whisky and shook my head. 'You're
not asking me that? Not my Wilkins? You know what's happened
to him, don't you?'

'He's been kidnapped.'

'Yes. By an incompetent couple who'll never get away with it the moment people like Manston—'

'Manston? Don't tell me—'

'I do tell you. What did you expect? This is his line of country. State security. No headlines. Just quiet blue murder the moment he and his crowd get their hands on Freeman or Pelegrina.'

'Or you—if you interfere. You fool.'

'I'm not interfering. I just want the missing piece of the jigsaw and then I can sell it to Manston. He'll be grateful and pay.'

She just looked at me and shook her head.

I was late getting down to the Uaddan that evening for the simple reason that I didn't want to take Letta out to dinner with a great rip in the front of my shirt. I had to come back to my hotel to change it.

The thing happened neatly, smoothly and was almost successful. One thing for sure was that I was taken completely off my guard.

It was a fine night, ablaze with stars. The lights of the shipping in the harbour and the great curve of esplanade lights lining the long waterfront reflected in the black sea, all made up a picture which pleased me and put me in a good mood. I like the sea and I like bright lights. The air was warm and I walked along happily, thinking about Letta and now and again getting a whiff of my own after-shave lotion and feeling that life was full of promise. The wide roadway was bathed now and then with the headlights of passing cars. A couple of Arab women passed me on the pavement. One was carrying a hand transistor set and the voices of the Beatles bounced into the night with a happy, hearty vitality. The world was good and I was in it. Four seconds later I was nearly out of it.

He came up the pavement towards me and I paid no attention. To me he was just a man in a suit, padding along enjoying the night air like myself. When he was level with me, he turned suddenly in to me and his right arm went up. I just caught the flicker of reflected light on steel and then his hand was coming down at me fast. Miggs would have given me nought out of ten for my reaction. But then a happy man is the easiest and most unsuspecting target in the world for a fast knife man. He obviously expected some fast reaction from me—somebody somewhere had given me a good build-up, briefing him about what to expect. Maybe that saved me, for he swung, expecting me to step back fast and making allowance for it. His hand came down, allowance made for my three—or four-

inch swing back, and when I didn't move he made a rapid adjust-
ment of angle and the knife caught the edge of my collar and ripped
downwards, slashing through the loose hang of my shirt front. By
some miracle the blade didn't even touch my skin. But he didn't
waste time moaning over his first botched effort. The hand swung
again and this time I did move. I threw myself sideways, slipped,
and went to the ground in the shadow of one of the esplanade trees.
He came for me and side-stepped the swing of my right foot as I
tried to take him off his feet. For a moment I saw his brown face,
serious, intent on his work, not at all perturbed by the fact that
there were a dozen people within two hundred yards' call, a work-
man's face, dedicated, content no doubt with the knowledge that
for this sudden call to night work, he was getting double rates, and
a bonus for success.

He would have got it too, except for my apprentice tail whom I
had not even bothered to look for when I left the hotel. A.T.
appeared out of the ground like a genie, not waiting for any lamp-
rubbing call from me. Suddenly he was there, between me, the man
and the knife. I heard a grunt, the clatter of the knife dropping to
the pavement and then, as I got to my feet, I saw the man running,
away from the lights up a side-street. A.T. stood and watched me
to my feet.

I took a deep breath and said, 'Thanks.'

A.T. just smiled.

I said, 'Was it anyone you knew?'

He shook his head.

I looked down at my shirt. Not even Mrs Meld was going to be
able to do anything for it. It was good, heavy silk, hand-made, one
of my recent luxuries. I went back to the hotel and changed the
shirt. When I came out the black Simca was parked in the hotel
forecourt. A.T. stood by it, talking to the driver. Seeing me, he just
held the back door open. I got in and said, 'The Uaddan.'

A.T. got in by the driver, turned to me and said, 'You were
dreaming?'

I nodded.

He shook his head disapprovingly at me. It was the same kind
of shake I had had a little while before from Wilkins.

CHAPTER 7

Of Pythons and Vintage Sardines

First there was Manston. I met him in the gaming room of the hotel. The cabaret in the dining room had just finished when I arrived and Letta sent me a message that she would be with me in half an hour. I wandered into the casino, watched some oil men playing blackjack, hung around the roulette tables for a bit, and then went over and began to feed coins into a fruit machine. The gaming room could have been anywhere in the world. All I knew at that moment was that I felt a little out of it. I was suffering. Mostly from anger with myself at being caught off guard. I was puzzled, too, trying to decide who would want to put me away and why. The only person who had tried it before was Pelegrina. If this were another of his efforts, and the quick improvisation suggested it, then I couldn't help telling myself that he must have discovered that I was in Tripoli through Letta. It was going to be interesting to hear what she had to say. But first of all I had to hear what Manston had to say.

He came up to me as I stood at the fruit machine. He was wearing a dinner jacket and looked cool, confident and in no mood for nonsense. He gave me a warm smile and a friendly nod, neither of which meant anything. With him, also in evening clothes, was an enormous man whose face was familiar. I remembered then that he had been one of the two men in Duchêne's Paris flat when I had walked in on their search. Then I had taken him for a bruiser. Now, although he was twice as big, I saw that he was out of the Manston school.

Manston looked at him and said, 'Perkins. This is Carver.'

'We've met,' I said. 'He's a dab hand with pot plants.'

'Sorry we had to be a bit rough with you, old boy.' He had a gravelly, educated voice, full of charm, reassuring. He'd probably got a blue for rugger at Cambridge. I could just see those big shoulders battering away in the scrum.

'I want you,' said Manston, 'to get out of this town.'

'I'm thinking of doing that.'

'I want you, too, to forget you ever heard of Messrs Freeman and Dawson. You know why, of course.'

I nodded. 'You've done a good job stopping any publicity.'

'There's never going to be any. Also, if you'll excuse the crudity, there are not going to be any pickings in this for you.'

'I haven't been thinking along those lines. I've got plenty of money at the moment.'

'Then live to enjoy it,' said Perkins. He slipped a coin into the machine, jerked the handle and got a bigger dividend at once than I'd had so far.

'It's like that, is it?' I looked at Manston.

'It's just like that. Take a vow of silence right now—and that includes talking in your sleep. Go away and forget.'

'Do that,' said Perkins. 'We haven't got time to be bothered with any monkey tricks. Just begin one and I'll break your neck and drop you in the sea. We'll issue a D-notice so that you don't even get four lines in the evening papers.'

'Why,' I asked Manston, 'have I never had the pleasure of meeting this number before? I should have thought he was too big and obvious for your service.'

'Far East, old boy,' said Perkins. 'Only just come back to home service.'

'Just forget Freeman and Dawson,' said Manston. 'That way we can go on being friends when we have to.'

'Charming. Okay—I won't say a word. But somebody will. You'll never keep this out of the press.'

'Our instructions are that we must. So we will. Understood?'

'Yes. And what happens to them when you catch up with them?'

Perkins winked. 'We break their necks and drop them in the sea, and then cover that with a D-notice.'

'I might be able to help.'

'We don't want it. Just go home and chase insurance cheats; live a full life and a long one,' said Manston.

'If you insist. How's the big man taking it? And I don't mean Sutcliffe.'

'Sincerely and frankly,' said Perkins, 'the big man is hopping bloody mad—and, of course, worried, as any decent parent would be.'

'As a matter of interest,' I said idly, 'where was the snatch made? Up the coast a bit at a place called Sabratha?'

Neither of them moved a muscle.

I grinned. 'You shouldn't have too much trouble. Not with a guy like Freeman. He couldn't even fake his own death convincingly. I'll bet he's biting his nails now trying to work out some foolproof method for the ransom money to be handed over. A clever man would have had that one settled before he took the first step. Yes, I can see that you don't need my help in dealing with an incompetent like that.'

'If we ever do need you,' said Perkins affably, 'don't think we won't be able to find you.'

'You will be leaving tomorrow,' said Manston. It wasn't a question. It was an order.

I nodded, always polite, and moved away because I had just seen Letta come to the door of the gaming room.

So, secondly, there was Letta. La Piroletta. Leon Pelegrina's daughter. I wondered whether Manston knew that connection. He would know about Paulet and Duchêne. He might know about the steam yacht *La Sunata*. But what he didn't know, clearly—otherwise he would never have been wasting any time here—was where Pelegrina and Freeman were at this moment. I might be a jump ahead of him there. But what could I do about it? I'd offered to help and had been told to go and chase insurance cheats. That hurt my pride. Not that I worried over that. The pain was minimal.

So, as I said, secondly there was Letta in a yellow silk gown, a scrap of mink over her shoulders, dark dusky skin making my fingers tremble to touch it and her dark, deep, brilliant eyes afire with the thought of a big plate of *pasta* and a flask of Chianti for two.

We got it at an Italian restaurant in the town, a jolly place with check tablecloths and little vases full of plastic flowers. Six men in from the desert, forgetting the sand and the oil rigs as they cut into big steaks and washed the meat down with neat whisky, stopped only for a moment to follow Letta with their eyes as we passed their table.

She ate *pasta* in a way that was right out of my class and she took more than her share of the Chianti, and she was bright with chatter and laughter and held my hand under the table when she wasn't holding a fork or glass. Anyone looking on would have thought there wasn't a cloud in her sky. Personally I wondered what the hell she was so determined to conceal. Much later I did find out—but not from her. I realized then that she was just hopping mad . . . with her father. Maybe that was why, on the swing back, she was so kind to me. All I needed was a little kindness to encourage me.

We walked back along the sea front, long after midnight. Although I was happy, and had one arm in hers, it was the left one. I wasn't going to be taken off my guard again. I didn't have to ask whether I had passed muster, all her actions indicated that I had been accepted as a custom-built job. She clearly was a quick shopper, knew what she wanted and when she found it paid cash down. It took the romance out of life a bit for me. Let's face it, I'm the kind whose performance is better if both parties subscribe a little to the illusion of love. . . . Well, it's cosier that way at the time, even if you both know that it isn't going to last.

We had a nightcap in her room, ran pleasantly through the few, obligatory preliminaries—me, wanting to linger a bit longer over them, she not indecently hasty but anxious to have them out of the way—and then she got up, said something about giving her five minutes and went into the bedroom. I was happy to give her the time. Her handbag was on the small table and I fished out her address book. It was one of those jobs with an alphabetical cut-out down the side. I tried F for father and got nothing, then P for Pelegrina or Papa and got nothing, and then found it under L for Leon. The flat in the Piazza Santo Spirito and its number was listed, and then under that came:

Villa La Sunata, Bizerta. 27.103.

I put the book back. He had a yacht called *La Sunata,* and also a villa. Obviously the name had a sentimental or pleasing meaning for him. I wondered if it had been the name of Letta's mother. I made a note to ask her at the first chance.

The thought went right out of my head when I went into the bedroom. She was sitting on the edge of the bed quite naked, her hair tied up at the back with a broad piece of red ribbon. I didn't rush things. After all, if you're being presented with something out of the *grand cru* class you don't gulp, you take it easy, missing none of the cumulative pleasures of sight, touch and taste. Her skin was an even light-biscuit colour. Her breasts had a beauty which made me feel a little heady, and she had one of those narrow little waists that flowered out to broad hips and then on to long, breathtaking legs. She sat there and gave me a little smile of delight for the wonder in my eyes.

I said, 'Don't you wear a nightdress?'

'Normally, yes,' she said. 'I'm sorry. Have I robbed you of the pleasure of taking it off?'

'No. I was just making conversation.'

'Don't bother. I'm not in the talking mood.'

She put her arms out towards me and the lift of her shoulders did things to her breasts that boosted me right off the launching pad and into orbit. We went into outer space together, and I wasn't caring if we never came back.

I woke to feel her naked body pressed close up against my back. Through drowsy eyes I could see that the room was full of half-dawn light coming through the partly drawn curtains. Outside a strong wind was making a hissing noise through the palms in the garden. There was the creak and rattle of an anchor chain coming up from one of the cargo boats in the harbour. I closed my eyes and drifted back into paradise. Behind me I felt her move to readjust our combined body contours, and dreamily I thought, Why ever wake properly, why ever bother to move out into the shoddy half-baked world? The thing to do was to turn back, away from the world, and hide oneself in the tight rosebud of drowsy pleasure; to become larvae, just the two of us, hidden forever in the dark, sweet world of the ripening apple. . . . I smiled in half-sleep, knowing that somewhere I was getting mixed in my thoughts and not caring. Behind me she stirred. I felt her arms move slowly, caressingly, over the bare warmth of my neck and then slide across my cheek, the long length of her arm running after it over my naked shoulder. Her hand and arm were cold. She must have been sleeping, I thought, with the top half of the covers off. Full of tenderness, not wanting her to be cold, I began a lazy turn that would bring her into my arms and let me pull the sheet up around her bare shoulder. My eyes opened slightly in the move and I found myself looking into a small, wedge-shaped head, flat and—although much thicker—about the size of an axe-head. From low on the crown a pair of yellow-brown eyes watched me coldly. A little red, delicately forked tongue flicked the tip of my nose and then the head moved with a little curving movement away and over me and I felt the dry, relaxing and then muscular constricting of the long scaly body across my bare chest.

As my hair stood on end and my body stiffened, a detached part
of my mind was wondering at the association of ideas that could
go on in the brain while the body slept. Paradise, the sweet ripe
apple . . . me and Letta in the garden of Eden and here, to complete
it, was the snake. And a damned great thing at that. Just feeling it
move across my chest told me that it wasn't an inch under ten feet.
It dropped off the bed with a clumsy thump—I learned later that
pythons have that in common with Siamese cats, an arrogance
which makes them clumsy, just going their own sweet way across
tables or furniture, knocking over anything that gets in their path.

I sat up in bed with a jerk and cursed myself for not retrieving
my gun from Wilkins. The python was rippling away across the
room with a nice easy flowing movement. It did a figure of eight
round the legs of a chair and then, unhurried, spiralled up a tall
lamp standard to check that the bulb was a 120-watt.

I said with a terminal hiss that any snake could have been proud
of, 'Holy Moses!'

The sound and the proceeding jerk of my body made Letta roll
over.

'Whassa?' she asked sleepily.

I looked down at her. She was naked almost to the waist and her
position flattened her beautiful breasts a little. The areola around
each nipple was a dark, crushed-grape colour. Even with your hair
standing on end you notice things like that.

I said, 'There's a bloody great snake in the room.'

She opened her eyes and smiled at me. 'There always is,
darling—of one kind or another.'

'But this—' I gagged for a moment because my throat was
dry—'is a damned great python affair. You could make a pair of
shoes and a couple of handbags out of it.'

She sat up, running her hands through her disordered hair. She
looked across the room where the python was doing a complicated
backward slide down the lamp standard.

'That's Lilith,' she said.

'What's she doing here?'

'She lives in that hamper over in the corner. She always comes
out in the morning for a little exercise. She worries you?'

'Not really. It's just my hair I'm thinking about. I'll never get it
to lie down again.'

She giggled, a rich, warm, early morning, dark-brown sound, and
then climbed across me, almost making me forget the snake. She

padded across the room, picked up Lilith by a convenient loop, draped her across her shoulders, faced me and sketched a quick bump and grind. As a cabaret act it would have given a Freudian scholar stuff for two or three chapters, and then a hefty footnote on symbolism.

She kissed the beast on the nose and said, 'You are happier if I put her away?'

'Definitely. And see the catch is secure.'

She padded to the hamper, folded Lilith away with a bending rump-and-buttock exhibition that made me reach for the water carafe to slake my snake-parched mouth.

She came back, took a flying leap into bed and lay back laughing. Then she grabbed for me and, in the few moments before speech became impossible, said, 'I will make you unafraid again. One man once, you know, had the same experience and had a bad heart attack. There was a lot of explaining to do.'

Later, lying relaxed, hearing Lilith curl and knot in the hamper, I said, 'You use her in your act?'

'Didn't you see it last night?'

'I was late getting here. But it doesn't say anything about it on the showcards in the hotel hall.'

'It is only a small part of the act. I use it as a surprise. And anyway, Lilith is sometimes in a bad temper and won't act nicely.'

'What gets her steamed up? Nostalgia for the past?'

'Guinea pigs. They are her exclusive diet. Sometimes it is difficult to get them. Then, when she is hungry, she gets temperamental.'

That wasn't hard to believe. I know a lot of people who get bad tempered if they don't get their food regularly.

'I see now,' I said, 'why Freeman had no trouble selling you that python bracelet. Is Lilith an Indian python too?'

'Yes.'

I lit a cigarette. She took it from me, had a couple of draws and then handed it back. Staring up at the ceiling, she said, 'Something else. I don't want you to worry about my father any more.'

'Why not?'

'I telephoned him yesterday.'

'Where?'

'In the Florence flat. He had returned. He swore to me he was not at the moment engaged in any business enterprise. Nor was he in any kind of trouble.'

'You believed him?'

'Absolutely.'

I said nothing. One thing was certain, however; I didn't believe her. She'd telephoned him all right. But not in Florence. He was somewhere near Bizerta. But I was prepared to believe that he had reassured her about his business enterprises at the moment. He would have to. And I guessed that she must have mentioned my name and whereabouts to him. That's why—from a piece of quick telephoning on his part—I'd had my shirt front ripped last night.

I said, 'Why did your father call his boat *La Sunata?*'

'Because of my sister. She died when she was sixteen. She was very beautiful. More than me. Also she was his favourite.'

Moving over on to one elbow, looking into her dark eyes, I said, 'I'm leaving for London today. What am I going to do about that bracelet?'

'What I said. She can have it for three thousand pounds. Make her pay—and I will give you two hundred pounds commission—perhaps.'

I grinned. 'Cutting me in, eh? You really do like me, don't you?'

She put her arms round my neck.

'I like you more than you know. You must not be upset that I show my love shamelessly. I am a very direct person. When do I see you again?'

'I don't know.'

She pouted. 'It must not be too long.'

'I'd join the act—as snake feeder—if I didn't have to go back to London. Where are you going to be?'

'I am in Cairo next week. Then I go back to Europe. I will give you a list of my bookings for the next month and the name of my agent in Paris—so you will know how to get in touch with me.' She smiled. 'Maybe I will change one of the bookings and get a London date—you'd like that?'

'Very much.'

'Then give me a nice kiss and maybe I will arrange it.'

She got her kiss and, before I left, I got the list from her.

Unshaven, and without breakfast, I walked down to the B.E.A. offices and booked on a flight out after lunch. Then I took a taxi up to the Libya Palace Hotel. I borrowed Olaf's electric razor and joined him and Wilkins for breakfast.

'You will be delighted to hear,' I told Wilkins, 'that I am leaving for London after lunch. I have recovered Mrs Stankowski's bracelet. Her money, I'm afraid, is gone for good. Approve?'

She dug her spoon into a large grapefruit and looked sceptical.

'We,' said Olaf, beginning on the first of five boiled eggs, 'leave for Cairo tomorrow.'

'I thought you were going today?'

'We have met here a nice man, a countryman of mine—he comes from a town called Kalmar which I know well. He insists on taking us out today to see the Roman remains at Leptis Magna. Already she has seen the Pyramids. Hilda is much interested in such antiquities.'

'Are you?'

'Yes,' said Wilkins.

'Well, I never knew that.'

'There are a lot of things about me you don't know. For instance, I belong to a poetry society and a jigsaw puzzle club. I collect match-box covers and I don't care for modern art.' She jabbed the grapefruit as though she were going over a battlefield bayoneting the doubtful dead.

'You're in a bad temper too.'

'Naturally,' said Olaf. 'She does not trust you.'

'Why ever not?' I asked, wide-eyed, forcing a little resentment to make it good.

Olaf grinned and scalped an egg. 'Because you are a devious man, Mr Carver. I could not say not a good one. But devious, Hilda worries over you. Too much, I think. If she did not worry so much about you she would have married me long ago. I should be angry. Perhaps one day I will be.'

'Just give me warning, Olaf—and I'll put a lot of ground between us.' Then to Wilkins, I said, 'Don't worry. I'm going to London. By the way, I'd like to have my gun back.'

Wilkins stood up quickly. 'I knew it.' She stalked off.

I looked at Olaf, wider-eyed now, and spread my hands, puzzled.

'It is the maternal instinct,' said Olaf seriously. 'I work hard to overcome this. But it is not my forte. By nature I am the passionate, romantic type. All Swedes are, fundamentally.' He gutted a great spoonful of egg from its shell and sighed before shovelling it away.

I got my gun, and a low-pitched lecture from Wilkins in the hotel hallway as she said goodbye to me.

'Stop being maternal,' I told her. 'I'm grown up now.'

'I'll believe that when I get a cable from London saying you're there. And just for the record, don't think that Mr Manston hasn't been to see me and told me to forget all about Mr Freeman and Mr Dawson.'

'Which you will.'

'Which I shall. And so should you—unless you're a bigger damn fool than even I imagine.'

I held out my hand, Continental fashion, to shake hands with her. She ignored it.

'The gun,' I said. 'I thought the handshake would cover the handover.'

'It's already in your jacket pocket,' she said.

I looked at her, pop-eyed. I knew only one person who could have done that without my knowing, and that was Manston.

Coming out of the hotel to take my taxi to the airport, I found my A.T. and his chum waiting by their Simca. I strolled over to them.

'My compliments to Captain Asab, boys—but you can knock off now. I'm London bound.'

'It is hoped that you have enjoyed your stay in this country,' said A.T. He was a good-looking youth with a nice warm smile.

'Thanks to you, yes.' I held out a bottle of Black and White whisky which I had bought in the supermarket round the corner from the Uaddan. 'I hope police regulations won't make it difficult for you to deal with this.'

A.T.'s hand was round it so fast there was no need for words. I left them, genuinely grateful for their help and care. Boy, how wrong can you be when you fall into the trap of taking people at their face value. Olaf had called me devious. What he didn't know—and I should have done—was that there were people about who just weren't happy unless they lived in a labyrinth with a fresh peril around each corner. As some people need drink, others need deceit.

At the airport, as I came out of the ticket office with my boarding card, I found Captain Asab waiting for me. It was a blazing hot morning and he wore a heavy overcoat and a light grey astrakhan cap. His brown face was smooth with years of calm, reflective living.

He shook hands with me and said, 'I was out here on other business, so I thought I would wish you *bon voyage*.'

'Thank you. I'm off to London.'

'I am not interested in your destination, so long as you are leaving Libya. I like a reasonably quiet life, Mr Carver; just straightforward murders, smuggling, theft and assault. But you strike me as the kind of man who attracts—could we say encourages?—unusual complications.'

'It's a dull world. I do my best. By the way, thank you for the two men you've had following me. The young one, I thought at first, was a novice in training. He's better than that. I recommend him to your notice.'

He smiled. 'You've made a mistake. I have had no one following you.'

'No?'

'No. But it could have been your Embassy, of course. After all, they have to look after their nationals.'

'Maybe.'

I gave him a big smile and moved off. But I didn't even mean 'Maybe'. The Embassy didn't give a damn about me. They went along with the Perkins theory. The sooner I had my neck broken and was dropped in the sea the better.

The aircraft was scheduled to stop at Malta and Rome on the way back. At Malta I got off and bought myself a flight on Swissair to Tunis. I got in at six o'clock that evening and had a taxi drive me up to Bizerta. I found myself a cheap hotel and lay back on a lumpy bed staring at the ceiling for about an hour before I turned out the light and tried to sleep. I didn't sleep much, but in between staving off dive-bombing mosquito attacks I did a lot of thinking. My chief worry was, who the hell had put the Apprentice Tail on me? I didn't come up with any answer and, anyway, I still thought that he had rated the bottle of whisky.

The next morning I bought myself a map and made an enquiry at the *Poste et Telegraphe* office. From the sea at Bizerta there is a narrow cut—La Goulette—that runs back inland and opens out into a wide lake. Most of Bizerta is on the westward side of this lake. You can cross this cut by a ferry and, if you're lucky, get a taxi on the other side. The Villa La Sunata was about two miles down the coast to the east.

I didn't bother with a taxi. I walked, with my jacket slung over my arm, the pocket with my gun in it thumping against my thigh bone. It was a tourist brochure day. Blue sky, sun blazing, cicadas sawing away in the umbrella pines, Arab women squatting amongst the myrtle and shrub watching their goats feed, a great yellow run of beach below the coast road, handfuls of terns dive-fishing in the shallow water off the sands, God in His heaven, and nothing much right with the world. You could have it all in a package tour, thirteen days, air travel included, for under forty pounds.

Personally, I'd decided what I wanted. I didn't want money, I didn't want a woman, I didn't even particularly want excitement—I was in good health now—but I thought it might be fun to have some kudos. Also it would be nice to teach Manston a lesson. I'd offered to help and been turned down. Good—I'd show him the mistake he had made, and maybe I'd collect an Order of the British Empire from a grateful government for services rendered. Possibly, too, I might be able to do something for those two incompetents, Freeman and Pelegrina. I did the last half-mile wondering why I had a soft spot for them. Perhaps it was the sheer audacity of their act which appealed. It is not every day you run into a couple of incompetent dreamers who have kidnapped the son of a British Prime Minister. Not that I go for kidnapping, of course. Who does?

Mind you, if it had been the father and not the son who had been kidnapped, I couldn't have cared less—such is the strength of political passion. They could have cut off his ears one by one and sent them to show they meant business, and slit his throat finally when they despaired of getting ransom money. Well, why not? I'm from the west of England and have been a Liberal all my life. And, anyway, if I hadn't been from the West Country I would still have been a Liberal because I just naturally gravitate to lost causes.

The villa stood up on a rising bluff of hillside surrounded by pines, scrub oak and thickets of oleanders. The driveway was barred with a wooden gate and there was a little wooden chalet lodge with an Arab custodian sitting on the ground outside it, his back to the wall, his eyes closed and a festoon of flies at each corner of his mouth. He didn't move as I tramped by. I got a glimpse of the villa about two hundred yards back up the drive. It faced the sea. Behind it the land would slope down to the lake, and the lake was big enough to take shipping. Some night recently *La Sunata* had slipped in there and Bill Dawson had been off-loaded.

Along the road side of the property was a fence—stout posts and four wire strands. When I was out of sight of the lodge I went up the sandy bank and had a look at it. The top wire strand was about five feet from the ground. The other strands were spaced evenly down from it. The lower two strands were newer and of a different gauge from the top two. I smiled at the naivety of Freeman and Pelegrina.

I didn't touch either of the two lower wires because I guessed that somewhere up in the villa a bell would ring. In their time they must have had quite a few heart-thumping false alarms from wandering goats and sheep.

I followed the fence along until I came to a spot where it was screened from the road by a clump of hibiscus bushes, covered with brilliant flame-coloured blooms that would have made my sister in Honiton itch with envy.

I squatted down and began to scoop away at the loose sandy soil. A green lizard watched me from the top of a fence post and remained frozen until I had made a depression deep enough to allow me to crawl underneath without touching the wire. As I stood up on the other side, the lizard flirted its tail and was away down the post. I went forward through the pines. A squirrel chattered briefly at me, not enquiring but damning my business there. A yellow-and-blue bee-eater swooped from a tree and took a butterfly on the wing just for a change of diet. I took off my tie and stuffed it in my trouser pocket and put on my jacket to have my hands free. The day, I thought, that Carver won himself a decoration. I could hear the booming voice of the toast-master at the Savoy at the next annual dinner of the Association of Enquiry Agents and Private Detectives, announcing, 'Pray silence for Mr Rex Carver, O.B.E.' And I could see the seedy company in their rented tails, nudging one another and the whispers, 'You know why he got it. That business of the Prime Minister's son. Actually, I'm told he made a complete balls of it.' Well, there are always the envious few who try to dim your glory. I went forward in a quiet and cautious state of euphoria, which isn't easy because some kinds of euphoria have the kick of four large whiskies.

The villa was stone-built with a wooden roof. It was all over the place in little turrets and outside balconies, and the main windows on the ground floor were a curious kind of triple-pointed African Gothic with stained glass in their upper sections. From the cover of a reed-thatched gardener's shed I saw a dust-covered Humber station wagon standing below the front steps. In the cover of the encroaching trees I went in a half-circle round the place. At the back was a modern, flat-roofed addition with a wide run of french windows facing down through the trees to the lake. Green curtains had been drawn across most of the run of the windows to keep out the blazing morning sun. A door in the window entrance was half open.

I stood there watching the door and then, in a momentary lull in the cicada chorus, I caught the sound of a man's voice. It sounded like Pelegrina's. I pulled the gun from my pocket. It was the .380 Model F, MAB *breveté*, which I had taken from Pelegrina's thug in Florence.

I went across the soft, pine-needle-strewn sand to the window, then moved along it, crouching low so that the sun would not throw my shadow against the green curtains. I reached the door on my hunkers and got a look at part of the room through the small gap the open door made above its lower hinge.

They looked as comfortable as all get-out. Freeman was lying in a cane chair which had a hole in its right arm in which rested a glass of beer. His feet were up on a small stool. I recognized him at once from his photograph. Opposite him, across a small table, was Leon Pelegrina in the same kind of cane chair, a glass of beer in his arm-hole and his feet up on the table. He was gazing at the ceiling through his monocle, his face, red and weather-tanned, screwed up as though he were searching for the answer to some quiz question. They both wore white linen suits, Freeman's neat and well pressed, Pelegrina's rumpled and a little too small for him. It was hard to believe that these two between them had done something which, if it were known, would have set the press of the world immediately rearranging its front-page spread, had radio and T.V. announcers breaking in on 'Housewives' Choice' and the morning schools programme for a special announcement, and made No. 10 Downing Street the genuine focus of world attention for the first time since Churchill left it.

There they were, potential news dynamite, men of destiny—though perhaps not the kind they thought—relaxing before the next stage of the operation, cool beer to hand, pine-bowered sanctuary for quiet, meticulous planning—and they were talking about sardines.

At least Freeman was.

'The real difference between the French and the Portuguese sardine,' he was saying, 'is in the preparation before canning. The French always oven-grill theirs in olive oil before canning. The Portuguese just steam-cook theirs and then pack 'em in oil. There's no doubt about the superiority of the French. They use a lighter type of olive oil too. This old boy I knew in Fleet Street had a vintage sardine cellar. Laid 'em down in cases. Turned the cases over every six months to get an even spread of oil. The great vintage year was 1959. And of 'em all, the French *Rodel* sardine is the king.

Cost you something like eight bob for a tin. *Marie Elisabeth*, that's Portuguese, cost less than two bob. Main thing is, there isn't a sardine fit to eat unless it's been in the can for at least twelve months.'

'You think,' asked Pelegrina, 'that there will be a reply in *The Times* today?'

'We'll know when Bou-Bou gets back from Bizerta this evening. The airmail edition will be in by then. Of course, if you don't want to spring eight bob for *Rodels*, you can go for the *Amieux, Larzul* and *Cassegrain* types. They come out at somewhere under four bob a tin. I could eat some on toast now. Go well with beer.'

I stepped through the door, gun in hand.

'How do you like them on toast?' I asked. 'Just cold, straight from the tin—or grilled hot?'

Pelegrina jerked forward and knocked over his beer. Freeman didn't stir a muscle, except to turn his head slightly and eye me. He was a pleasant enough looking type, fair brown hair, a rather long evenly tanned face, and friendly brown eyes overhung with bushy eyebrows that went up slightly at the outer corners.

'And who the hell,' he asked, 'are you?'

'Carver, Rex.'

'Oh.'

There was a silence while the penny went on dropping. I moved up to the table and sat down on an upright chair, holding the MAB *breveté* comfortably poised on one knee. There were some bottles of beer on the table and a bottle opener.

I said to Pelegrina, 'You've spilled your beer. Better have another. You can open a bottle for me too. I've had a long walk. Don't bother about a glass for me. I'll drink from the bottle.'

Pelegrina just stared at me as though I were a snake and he a mesmerized bird.

Freeman said, 'Allow me.'

He reached out for the bottle opener and began to dispense beer for Pelegrina and myself. He was cool and capable in a crisis clearly. It was a pity he hadn't the same qualities when it came to planning.

To Pelegrina I said, 'This gun belonged to your man who visited me in Florence. Don't think I won't use it. Not to kill—but just to make a nasty mess of an arm or a leg. Your knife man from Tripoli sends his regrets at having botched up his assignment.'

With my free hand I took the bottle which Freeman had opened and helped myself to a good pull. It was delicious, ice-cold.

Very slowly Pelegrina spoke. He said, '*Porca miseria!*'

I said, 'Well, that disposes of the preliminaries. Now let's get down to the real business.'

'Which is?' Freeman cocked one of his bushy eyebrows at me.

'All our cards on the table. I'll put mine down first.'

'How,' said Pelegrina, beginning to function late, 'did you get in here?'

'Under your nice new wire. Happy? All right—let's get on. You two have cooked up one of the clumsiest kidnapping jobs imaginable. You've left a trail behind you three feet wide and painted red. Coming along that trail is a certain Mr Manston and a few of his friends from the dark depths of British Security, M.I.6, the Special Branch and God knows what other organizations. Don't expect any mercy from that bunch. Their orders are—no headlines, get Mr William Dawson, son of the Right Honourable Henry Dawson, Prime Minister of the United Kingdom, back, and liquidate the kidnappers in such a way that they disappear without trace. That won't give them any trouble. Particularly for you, Freeman, since you're already dead and, even though the stomach scar on your body has slipped from right to left during immersion, they're not going to fuss with a little detail like that. Am I going too fast?'

Freeman smiled, but it didn't have a lot of heart in it. 'Not for me,' he said.

'Your trouble,' I said, 'is that you go too fast, without enough thought. Bill Dawson was your friend, working with an oil company in Libya as a geologist. Did you think when he disappeared that you'd get away with that phoney death trick of yours? And heaven help you if any harm has been done to him.'

'He's in first-class shape,' said Freeman.

'That's more than you're going to be—unless you listen to me.'

'What do you want?' asked Pelegrina. I could see that with him I was dealing with a slow-paced thinker and not a subtle one.

'To help you. But I want a few questions answered first.'

Freeman wriggled his bottom against the cane seat and began to light a cigarette. 'Ask away—if you think it's necessary.'

'I do. Because when I get in touch with Manston—and heaven knows why he hasn't got here ahead of me, except that even the brightest of us have dull patches and this must be his first in ten years—then he's going to ask me a lot of questions when I hand Bill Dawson over and suggest a grateful government make me an O.B.E.'

'You go for that kind of crap?' Freeman asked.

'That noun reminds me of your sister. It's one of her favourites. So—first—you steal from her to set up this kidnapping, yes?'

'It has cost us much money,' said Pelegrina. 'Expense all along the line.'

'It could cost you your necks unless you take my advice. Where did you get that phoney body?'

'From a medical friend of mine in Athens,' said Pelegrina.

'So that Bill Dawson should think Freeman here had been kidnapped with him and then killed, so that Freeman here would then—ransom money collected—be free to go off to a happy new life with Jane Judd?'

Freeman sat up at this.

I went on, 'It's obvious that you, Pelegrina, have never shown your face to Dawson so that, when free, he can't throw anything back at you. That means that the only person he's ever seen is some hireling who services him first on *La Sunata*—whose name he's never known—and then here in some handy cellar in a villa he's never seen and will never see. Let's face it, except for the wrong belly scar and a few other blemishes, it's all almost reasonably neat and tidy—but how the bloody hell did you ever think you were going to collect the ransom money?'

'It's given us a lot of trouble, that,' said Freeman.

'Believe me, it's the only trouble about kidnapping. That's why there isn't much of it around. What's all this about an advertisement in *The Times?* Some cryptic message in the Personal Column to indicate that the authorities are willing to parley with you?'

'Roughly, yes,' said Freeman.

'Roughly is the word. How did you get in touch with the authorities? Send a private letter to the P.M. at 10 Downing Street?'

'Just that,' said Pelegrina.

'If they agree to our terms,' said Freeman, 'they put a reply in *The Times* saying "Python Project accepted".'

I went wide-eyed. 'You called it that—and you'd pinched a python bracelet from your sister to help finance it! I'm surprised Manston isn't here already!'

'It had to have some name,' said Pelegrina.

I shook my head. They both looked at me and I could see that they were chastened. I really felt sorry for them.

'A man,' I said to Freeman, 'was found dead in your Kent cottage. Strangled. You have anything to do with that?'

'No.'

I grinned. 'Not that you're against murder. You tried it on me.'

'You worried us,' said Pelegrina.

'Fair enough. If you have a worry, eliminate it. You're a right couple. But don't begin to cry about it. We might make something out of this mess yet—not much, but just something that will leave you with your skins whole so long as you start running fast and don't stop for a long time. Tell me, where does Monsieur Robert Duchêne figure in all this?'

They just looked at me blankly.

I tipped my head at Freeman. 'You're supposed to have stolen antique coins of great value from him.'

'I never heard of anyone of that name.'

'All right, we'll skip it. Here's the deal. You walk out of this villa and leave me here with Dawson. I'll give you forty-eight hours to disappear. Then I'll call up Manston and give him a cover story which he'll not believe for one moment, but which for policy reasons he'll accept. But don't think he won't be after both of you for quite a while. It's up to you to keep out of his way—for good. Seem fair?'

Freeman shook his head. 'Give it all up now! Do you know how long I've been planning and dreaming about this thing? Over two years!'

'Write it off as a bad dream. Cut your losses and run.'

Pelegrina let his monocle drop from his eye and shook his head. 'But we have invested so much money in this. You have no idea of the expense, the incidentals. Even I have to charter my own yacht under another name. Every time you turn it is money to be paid out. And that body, that was very expensive! Anyway—' there was a sudden spurt of spirit in him—'what are we doing sitting here listening to you? Who the hell do you think you are?'

'Well, I was beginning to think I was some kind of Sir Galahad. But okay, don't listen to me. If you like I'll just get up and back out and you'll never see me again, and I won't mention a word of anything to the authorities. That'll just leave you here or wherever you choose to move to, waiting for the moment when you'll have to deal with Mr Bloody Manston. Believe me—you'd far better let me handle that for you.'

'You must have some reason other than a tinpot honour for suggesting this,' said Freeman.

'True. I'd just like to be one up on Manston and his crew for a change. And also I've a soft spot for La Piroletta, Jane Judd and

Gloriana Stankowski, whom God bless for having dragged me into this quite innocently on her part. Okay? Now, why don't you pack your bags and go fast?'

'But we might get the ransom money—we'd even give you a share,' said Pelegrina.

I shook my head. 'Tainted money, I'll be frank, I often take—but only if I know there's not going to be a kickback. Grow up—you'll never get any ransom money. You haven't even got a water-tight handover arrangement worked out. You've blundered through all the preliminaries, ignoring the big problem—and when it's the only problem left you sit down to work it out and it's so much too big for you. Your minds reject it and you end up nattering about vintage sardines.'

They looked at me. They looked at the gun in my hand. And they looked at one another. I took another pull at my beer and waited. Neither of them would have admitted it, of course, but they were both in a state of shock. They didn't have a hope. They'd both stepped into a cloud cuckoo land and they were stuck there for just so long as they could keep out of Manston's way. Once he laid hands on them life would become real and life would become earnest—and of a brief span only.

To help them along, I said, 'Don't waste your time on frivolities like wondering if you can jump me, finish me off and bury me in the backyard sand. I'm not the one you have to worry about. Keep Manston in your mind. I got the address of this place out of Letta's notebook. He'll get it too, some way or other. And forget about the money you've invested—let's face it, most of it was probably not honestly come by. All right?'

They looked at me, Pelegrina picking at his fat chin nervously, his head sunk lower between his shoulders than I had ever seen it, and Freeman tugging at one bushy eyebrow, his forehead lined with thought, not hard firm lines, but wavy uncertain ones. I was suddenly impatient with them. Damn it, I was sticking my neck out quite a bit on their behalf.

'Pack your bags and go,' I said. ''You're never going to make a cent out of Bill Dawson!'

From behind me a familiar, clipped voice said, 'That, of course, is not true.'

I began to turn quickly in my chair and then slowed up as my eyes found the doorway in the french windows and I saw that any impetuous movement might bring trouble for me.

Dark against the brilliant sunlight outside, I saw the tall form of Monsieur Robert Duchêne, flanked on the left by Paulet and on the right by my Apprentice Tail. Each one had a gun in his hand. Somewhere behind them I caught the head and shoulders of another man. For the first time ever I saw Paulet smiling broadly, a real fat blooming beam of a smile. Even Duchêne's thin lips had a little curl at the ends. Surprisingly, my A.T. looked a little sad—probably on my account, that I should have had such a touching faith in the goodness of human nature.

I dropped my gun to the floor and kicked it across to them. They let it lie at their feet.

'Don't tell me,' I said. 'Just let me guess. You're from a rival firm—and you want to make a take-over bid?'

'Exactly.' Duchêne gave me a brief nod.

Behind me I heard Pelegrina groan, and then came Freeman's voice. 'For God's sake—what a bloody morning this is turning out to be!'

Silently I seconded the sentiment.

CHAPTER 8

Saraband Two

I was not present at the take-over discussions. I was taken away to a little room at the front of the house where, if it hadn't been for the bulk of A.T. standing guard outside, I could have had a good view of the sandy drive. In the room with me was a fourth man, whose face was vaguely familiar.

He sat by the door on the edge of a hard chair, a fidgety, nervous little man who looked as though he were waiting his turn to go into the dentist. One thin, almost feminine, hand held a big Colt Service revolver which he kept directed at me. I only hoped that the safety was on. He kept flicking his eyes at me and running the edge of his tongue between his thin lips. One of his socks had been put on inside out. I guessed that he was the talkative type. Conversation would be a way of easing his nervousness. Let him sweat, I decided. I'd got myself into this by trying to do good to those who didn't deserve it, which confirmed that there was a basic flaw in the Christian ethic. I lit a cigarette and considered the Duchêne angle. It didn't need much considering. When you look back over events from some crisis point a lot of things become clear. Being wise after the event comes easy. Duchêne had wanted to muscle in on the Dawson kidnapping. And he had let me do all the leg-work for him. That annoyed me. At least, it rated a fee. I had a feeling that I would never get one. But more important, how, I asked myself, had Duchêne or Paulet ever come to know that Dawson had been kidnapped? How had they ever come to know that Freeman was involved? I could think of two or three answers to that, but I decided to reserve judgment until I knew whether they—like Pelegrina and Freeman—were just working for their private interests or, as I suspected, representing a far from private interest.

I smoked another cigarette, and studied the one picture on the wall of the room. It showed a group of Roman matrons in and around a wide marble bath, being toileted by half a dozen handmaidens. They were having a jolly time splashing water at one another. The artist must have been Victorian because their poses were so arranged that there were no *pudenda* in the slightest bit exposed. Not that it would have cheered me up if there had been.

My guard coughed dryly and put his left hand around his right wrist to help support the big Colt.

I took pity on him.

'I've seen you before, haven't I?'

The thin face broke into a happy smile to show very bad teeth. 'On the plane from Tripoli to Malta. I got off with you.'

I remembered then. He'd looked like a worried cotton-length salesman, fiddling around with his order book all through the flight, just across the aisle from me, and never once looking at me.

'You weren't on the Tunis plane?'

'No. Not yours. The early morning one today.'

'What happened to the Arab guard at the drive gate?'

'Paulet picked him up and wrapped some rope around him.' He giggled.

'Sounds like Paulet. What's the name of the nice boy outside the window?' I tipped my head backwards to indicate the A.T.

'We all call him Mimo.'

'Nice lad. Probably the best of your bunch. What do you get your pay in—converted roubles?'

He frowned. Some things you just don't joke about.

'I'm Brown. Peter Brown.' He said it amicably to counteract the frown.

'Not with your accent you aren't. Not unless some serviceman of that name did your mother in Cyprus or Aden and then, like a fool, made an honest woman of her.'

'Please not to speak like that about my mother.' Then he smiled again, not wanting to spoil the chat. 'Ah, but I remember—you are a very flippant man.'

'But clever, no?'

'Very. But you didn't see Paulet when you arrived at Tunis last night?'

'If I had I'd have broken his neck.'

'You think you could do that?'

'I would have tried.'

He shook his head. 'Many people have—but it is still sound.' He held up the Colt a little. 'If I put this down you will be reasonable?'

'Try me.'

To my surprise he laid it thankfully on a small table at his side and began to light a cigarette. Blowing a cloud of Gitane smoke, he went on, 'Your Prime Minister is not a wealthy man, is he?'

'No. He's against it on principle. Capital is a dirty word to him—at least in public. And, anyway, with your name, he's your Prime Minister as well. Or do I just say "ha-ha" to that? Further, as a matter of ethnological interest, if things keep going the way they are and all British troops are withdrawn to the other side of the English Channel, your kind is doomed. Unless the package-tour tourists take over.'

He smiled. 'You have it wrong. My mother was a Miss Sylvia Brown of Wimbledon. My father was a foreign student at London University. I took her name.'

I didn't believe a word he said. He just liked talking. But the conversation was cut off by the entry of Duchêne and Paulet. It had taken them two hours to wrap up their negotiations with Freeman and Pelegrina.

Mr Peter Brown of Wimbledon was dismissed. On a tray François Paulet had a couple of bottles of beer, a glass and a plate of sandwiches. He put them down by me and—he'd been a waiter once at the Principi di Piemonte—he opened a bottle adroitly and poured a glass of beer for me. Over his big de Gaulle nose, his close-set eyes twinkled and he smiled.

'You see how I look after an old friend?'

'If the sandwiches are cheese and tomato you can take 'em back.'

'Pâté.'

Duchêne went to the Roman picture and stared disapprovingly at it, ignoring me.

'Hardly in your class, is it, Duchêne? Not phoney enough. Like those antique coins and all that herd-returning-at-cowdust crap, straight from the Encyclopaedia Britannica. I shouldn't have thought you would have made an elementary mistake like that.'

He turned and said severely, 'I didn't. It was some fool in the Central Bureau who has never done an hour's field work in his life. But they insist that they should provide the background and cover stories.'

'He'll be shot, of course?'

'Probably. You wish to eat first, or talk business at the same time?'

Mouth full of sandwich, I said, 'Carry on.'

He adjusted his big horn-rimmed spectacles, lit himself one of his

Swiss cigar jobs, rolled it comfortably into the left corner of his mouth and said, 'May I say first of all that you have nothing to worry about. Actually we are very grateful to you.'

'So you should be. You used me to make contact with Freeman and Pelegrina—and I was fool enough not to know what was happening. But I still think you have something to worry about. By tomorrow morning anyone left in this house is going to be sitting on dynamite. Manston may have been a bit slow off the mark for once, but he'll be here.'

'I know all about Manston.'

'I'll bet you do.'

'This house will be empty by four o'clock this afternoon. Everyone except you will be moving to another and much more secure hiding place.'

'And me?' I finished the first glass of beer and Paulet poured me another.

'You like the *pâté?*'

'Excellent.' I looked at Duchêne. 'Well?'

'You are going back to London.'

'Good. I'll be glad to wash my hands of the whole affair.'

'Hardly. Though eventually you will.'

'I knew there would be a catch.'

'Please don't think we have used you without any intention of rewarding you. All you have to do is follow your instructions—simple ones—and in six months' time five thousand pounds will be deposited for you in any bank you like to nominate in any country.'

'I don't think I want your kind of money. And believe me, that's right out of character.'

'You are free to refuse it.'

'But not free to disobey my instructions?'

'No.'

'Perhaps you'd better tell me what they are.'

'You go back to London, to your office, to your home—and you wait for a telephone call or some communication arranging a meeting with someone who will identify himself as Saraband Two.'

I groaned. 'I'll bet that name was made up by your Central Bureau too.'

He nodded sympathetically.

Paulet said, 'It is always the same. The people who sit in offices, they are incurable romantics, no? We who live in the smoke of battle have a more elemental approach.'

I cocked an eye at him. 'Your approach seemed just clumsy to me. But I must say I took it for real. The world's full of clumsy people. By the way, when did you strangle our friend with the London-Scottish tie?'

'The evening before you came. He was one of Manston's men and I did not want him to have the various bits of information lying about the cottage. It was a highly regrettable thing to have to do.'

'But you gritted your teeth, said *"pour la patrie"*—or whatever the Slav equivalent is—and did it.'

Paulet looked at the stern-faced Duchêne. 'He jokes, always, Monsieur Carvay; he jokes. I like him so much for that.'

As he finished he whipped out his right hand, hit me on the side of the face and knocked me from the chair.

As I picked myself up he said very sincerely, 'There was nothing personal in that. Monsieur Duchêne just wants you to realize that this is a serious matter.'

'As indeed it is,' said Duchêne. 'And please, I wish to have no more references made to my government. Not that I am admitting that you are right as to which one it is.'

'So I go back to London, wait for a call from Saraband Two, and then do exactly as I'm told.'

'Exactly.'

'And what happens if I go back and refuse to play ball? I could go right to Manston's boss and tell him everything.'

'You are referring to Mr Sutcliffe?'

'Yes.' There was no surprise in me. The intelligence services of all countries kept directories and dossiers of the top boys on each side. I wondered sometimes why they didn't all meet once a year for a jolly reunion dinner on some neutral ground like Switzerland or San Marino. They were all inhuman bastards, anyway, and if I could have known the date and place of the next meeting I'd have put a bomb under the table and cleaned the world up a little.

'You will make no approach to anyone, nor tell anyone anything until you have spoken to Saraband Two. When you have met—you will do exactly as you are told.'

'And you think I'll do this—just because you tell me to? You're crazy. Paulet, tell him he's crazy. You know me—only wild horses can make me do anything I don't want to do, and it takes a lot of them, big, fat *percherons* weighing two and a half tons each.'

Paulet shook his head. 'They are splendid horses, but rapidly dying out. It is the growing use of tractors in my country, you know.'

Irritably Duchêne said, 'Enough of this. You will do as you are told, Monsieur Carver, because if you do not then someone very dear and near to you will be killed.'

'You must mean me.'

'No.'

'Then you're living in a dream. All my life I've avoided having anyone near and dear to me. They're always coming for loans or something.'

Duchêne rolled his cigar to the other corner of his mouth. Paulet picked up a sandwich which had fallen on the floor when he had hit me. Outside the window Mimo began to whistle gently 'Winchester Cathedral' as he watched the Arab porter, who had got his feet free of his bonds, come shuffling urgently up the drive, the rest of the cords round his body making him look like a walking mummy. Mimo fired a shot into the sand a yard to his side. The Arab sat down and stayed sat as Mimo went down to him, still whistling. You couldn't help liking Mimo, you couldn't help liking Paulet—but it was easy to dislike Duchêne.

Fishing in his jacket pocket, he pulled out a letter and handed it to me.

'Read this,' he said.

I did. It was from Wilkins:

Dear Mr Carver,

Olaf and I were stopped on the road to Leptis Magna. I am not allowed to tell you more. I do not know what has happened to Olaf—but I am being treated with every consideration.

Shocked as I am by this turn of events—the result entirely of your egotistical stupidity—I beg of you at least from now on to act as the bearer of this letter would wish.

I am told that if you do not I shall suffer some mishap.

Return to London and do as these people say. This is not a time for any of your obstinate heroics. Please be wise.

Distressed though I am about my personal predicament, I am much more concerned about Olaf's.

Tell him, if he is free, not to worry too much about me, or to blame himself for being hoodwinked by his false countryman into making the trip to Leptis Magna.

Calmly though I write, I am naturally very angry at what has happened. When I am free I shall have to consider very seriously whether I shall return to my present work.

Bluntly, do as these people request, since I am assured by them that it will not involve you in anything criminal.

Unless you do this, they have made it very, very clear that the consequences will be serious for me.

Both of us have had our disagreements in the past—and usually in your pig-headed fashion you have ignored my advice. Why is it that you have always to make a mess, not only of your own life, but of other people's? None of this would have happened if you had gone straight back to London from Libya.

No rash action on your part can help me now. Frankly my life is in your hands. For once please, please, do exactly as you are told.

Yours,

Hilda Wilkins

I read it twice. It was Wilkins's handwriting without doubt. It wasn't Wilkins's style, quite. Any communication she made to me, verbal or written, was usually briefer and quick to the point. But this time—since she was in a dangerous position and worried about her beloved Olaf—she had let herself go.

I said to Duchêne, 'If she comes to any harm, and I get the chance, I'll gut you!'

'No harm is going to come to her—so long as you act sensibly. She herself tells you to do that too.'

'You give me your word?'

'I do.'

Paulet said, 'The moment you have completed your mission, she will be set free.'

'This was your idea?'

Paulet nodded. 'Central Bureau were opposed to it until we pointed out its advantages.'

'We have got to have a go-between,' said Duchêne, 'to carry out negotiations for us. Someone who knows the other side and is trusted by them, and someone we know and can trust because he understands the consequences of keeping faith with us.'

'You've bought Freeman and Pelegrina out?'

He nodded. 'For a substantial sum. After all, they did the preliminary work, clumsily but effectively.'

'And what's happening to them?'

'That is not your affair. What good is money to them unless they have security as well? We have made an honest bargain with them. We do the same with you.'

'And Bill Dawson?'

'He is in this house. We have seen him and he is in good health.'

'I don't care so much about his health—though I'll hand the good news on to his father. What I want to know is what kind of deal you're thinking of making for his return? Not just a cash transaction, surely?'

'Clearly not, Mr Carver. Equally clearly, your curiosity will have to wait until you meet Saraband Two. Only one point remains to be stressed. So far the British authorities have kept this whole matter a secret. The press and the public have no idea he has been kidnapped. For our purposes it must remain that way. If you say or do anything which will bring this affair into the open—then you know what will happen to Miss Wilkins and to yourself.'

He didn't have to stress that to me. It was obvious. And there were two or three kinds of deals he could make over Bill Dawson. What I wanted to know—but wasn't going to ask him because I didn't want him to realize the point had occurred to me—was how, if the affair had been kept quiet so far, he had come to know about it and had decided to take advantage of it, staying in the background until the last moment and using me hard all the time. There was something very fishy there.

'Where's Olaf?'

'We held him for a while after we took Miss Wilkins, then we released him on the coast road some miles from Tripoli.'

'What, to go back to the police and make a stink about it all?'

'He won't get far with Captain Asab. The Libyan authorities have instructions to keep this quiet.'

'Olaf isn't the kind to stay quiet. And, by God, if he gets near you he's capable of doing things to you which would make any efforts of mine seem charitable.'

Duchêne shrugged his shoulders.

Paulet said, 'All you have to do is be sensible and wait for Saraband Two. If Manston gets in touch with you when you return to London, you know nothing. Nothing until you receive your instructions from Saraband Two. You can say that you were late getting back to London because you broke your journey in Rome for a day or so.'

'You think I can get away with that—or with not telling him about you?'

Duchêne shrugged. 'Who cares? You will get instructions on those points from Saraband Two. You will not, I imagine, be asked to perform too complicated a dance.'

I stared at him. For the first time since I had known him he had allowed himself a touch of humour. Not that there was any hint of it on his face. But he had to be feeling good to have gone so far out of character.

'Ha-ha,' I said flatly.

It was practically the last thing I said to them. I was kept another half-hour in the room. I didn't see Freeman or Pelegrina. Finally Mimo and Peter Brown of Wimbledon drove me back to Tunis to catch a plane to London. They had colected my cases from the Bizerta hotel and had paid my bill. Decent of them.

It was a hard drive for both of them. By nature they were affable souls who liked nothing better than a little light gossip to make the miles spin by without tedium. But Duchêne must have given them instructions not to talk. Maybe he thought they might let something slip, something which I could use. If one thing was for sure, it was that Duchêne was not trusting me an inch. The only hold he had over me was Wilkins—and it was a sound one. When Wilkins came out of this one safe and well, I knew that I was in for the worst half-hour of my life. Worse still, long before she got at me I knew that I was going to have Olaf to deal with. All I could hope was that he would leave me sufficiently in one piece to be able to deal with Saraband Two and then the Sutcliffe-Manston outfit. I had a dark future ahead and my face must have shown it, because as Mimo and Peter Brown left me at the airport, Mimo patted me on the arm and said, 'Do not worry too much. Everything will be all right. One day you tell your children about this and have a big laugh.'

'Children? I'm not even married.'

'Is that necessary?'

I went into the airport buildings, tempted to phone the police, or Manston at the Tripoli Embassy, and put them on to the Villa La Sunata. Temptation lasted only a few seconds. The villa would be cleared by now and I should only be making things impossible for Wilkins. I was sitting in a big cleft stick and any move I made was just going to be from one discomfort to another.

However, on the plane I found some comfort. Not much, but

enough. I knew my Wilkins and I knew her philosophy and her literary style. To begin with she was not afraid of anything that walked on two legs, and she had a sturdy conviction that melodrama was not something that could touch her life. She didn't believe that she could be kidnapped. If it happened she would still refuse to believe it. The only real affliction in her life was a tendency to catch colds easily, a sniff her only valid protest against fate.

As for her literary style, it was anything but long-winded. Short, tart and to the point was Wilkins's style.

Eighteen thousand feet above the Gulf of Tunis I opened her letter—which Duchêne had left with me, since he knew eventually I would have to show it to Manston as part of my credentials and serious intent as a go-between—and began to work out the simple code which Wilkins and I had established long ago. I'd had the devil's own job to persuade her, years ago, that one day it might be useful. This was the first time in two years that she had ever used it. All I had to do was to list in running order the first and last letters of each paragraph. That gave me ONSHIPREDSTACK-BLUEBAND. Which gave me ON SHIP RED STACK BLUE BAND.

Clever Wilkins. Somewhere, at least to begin with, she had been held—after the hijacking on the Leptis Magna road—on a ship whose funnel was red with a blue band round it. Single funnel, probably. Probably, too, a cargo boat of some kind. Well, probably again, that ship could have been in harbour in the last week in some port between, say, Alexandria and Sfax, maybe as far up as Tunis. If Olaf came raging after me, I could hand it to him and he could postpone killing me until he had tried to trace it.

I got in late, poached myself a couple of stale lion-stamped eggs and ate them on two toasted pieces of ready-sliced, untouched-by-hand, flavourless loaf. I washed it down with half a glass of milk that probably came from a cow untouched by human hand, finished up feeling slightly sick and, as a specific against indigestion and growing gloom, made myself a very strong whisky and soda.

I sat and stared at the telephone, willing it to ring and Saraband Two to announce himself. I wanted action to chase away the blues. I didn't get it.

Mrs Meld, seeing the light on when she put her cat out for the night, came in, eyes puffy from watching television, and said, 'Have a nice time then, Mr Carver?'

'Splendid.'

'That's the spirit then. I'll be in to do your breakfast in the morning per usual. See what happened to the bedroom ceiling?'

'No; I haven't been in there.'

'Part of it fell down. Just like that. While I was hoovering. Meld says he'll fix it. Save you a big builder's bill.'

'Did he say which year he would do it?'

She laughed. 'That kind of mood, is it? Well, we all feel down in the mouth after a holiday.'

She hadn't got it right by a long chalk. I wasn't down in the mouth. I was right down in my boots.

I was in the office by half past nine the next morning. In the outer office Mrs Burtenshaw put down the *Daily Telegraph* and greeted me without enthusiasm. Business was at a standstill, she said, and she had had a nice postcard from Wilkins two days ago. I didn't comment that she might never have another if I didn't play my cards right.

In my own office I had to use both hands to get the basset hound off my chair. He hit the ground with a thump and promptly went to sleep on the carpet under the desk so that I had no room to stretch my legs out.

I reached for the phone, feeling as gloomy as a Great Dane, and called Mrs Stankowski.

The glorious Gloriana answered it and seemed delighted to hear my voice. It did nothing to cheer me up. All I wanted was contact with Saraband Two and to be on my way. I told her about La Piroletta, that she had the python bracelet and was willing to sell it back. I gave her the name and address of Letta's Paris agents so that she could get in touch with her. Gloriana said she would consider what to do about the bracelet, and then asked me to come and have dinner with her that evening in her flat. I said I would, forcing some enthusiasm into my voice out of politeness.

I put the receiver down and sat there wondering if they had tapped my phone, and, if they had, how long it would be before somebody was around to see me.

It took an hour, actually. Mrs Burtenshaw rang through and said there was a Mr Vickers to see me. I told her to send him in. I knew Mr Edwin Vickers and where he came from—and I knew now that they were running a tap on my phone.

He came in fish-faced, drifting like a dried leaf in an idle breeze, eyes mournful, mouth turned down, and his suit needing a good brush and pressing, a troglodyte from the submerged two-thirds of Whitehall.

He took the chair across the desk and competed with me and the basset hound for leg room under the desk.

'The last time I saw you,' I said, 'you were going to retire and help your brother-in-law run a hotel in Scotland.'

'Brother. He decided he didn't want me. We never got on, anyway. And anyway, they held over my retirement date. Shortage of trained operators.'

He was flattering himself. He could have fallen down a drain opposite the Cenotaph and nobody would ever have missed him.

'What's the big message this morning?'

'I'm requested—by you-know-who—to check your itinerary back from Tripoli. Seems to have taken you a day or so longer than it should.'

'I stopped off in Rome for a night. Eden Hotel. Had a customer I thought I might sell the Coliseum to.

'Keep the hotel bill?'

'No.'

'Why not? You were on expenses, weren't you?'

'No, I wasn't. My services were terminated in Tripoli by my client. Anyway, what's the big interest?'

'I wouldn't know. Check your movements, they said.'

'Well, you've checked them. Anything else?'

He nodded. 'They want you to sit tight in London. If you try to leave the country you'll be stopped.'

'I could write to my M.P. about that.'

He stood up and helped himself to a cigarette from my desk box. 'Do that—if you know who he is. That your dog?'

The basset had come out from under and was rolling leisurely on his back in a patch of sunlight by the window.

'No. He just appears every morning in early spring—and then suddenly he's gone for another year. Away mating, I suppose.'

He bent down and rubbed the back of his hand along the length of the basset's tummy. It was a long rub.

'I'm fond of animals,' he said.

'How do they feel about you?'

He straightened up, gave me a sad look, shook his head and backed to the door as though he feared either the dog or myself would go for his lean throat. At the door he said, 'They said to keep your nose clean for once if you know what is good for you.'

'In those words?'

'No. I colloquialized them.'

Colloquially, I told him to get out. He did, looking a little shocked. He was too meek, that was the trouble. His kind might eventually inherit the earth but before they did people would always be trampling on them.

After he'd gone I sat there for a long time worrying about Wilkins. Yes, worrying. It was no good not admitting it. I was worrying about her. I'd got her involved in this and although I'd been told she would be safe as long as I played ball there were certain aspects of the situation that nagged at me. This had gone from a simple kidnapping-for-cash case right up to the high levels of security double-dealing and ice-cold bargaining where ordinary mortals begin to gasp for oxygen.

Half an hour before midday Olaf burst in—straight from the airport. He hadn't shaved and his eyes had a murderous glare in them. His pilot's pea-jacket swung open over his barrel chest and he thumped it with one big fist as he came up to the desk.

'I want Hilda,' he said. There was a faint odour of rum on his breath.

'So do I,' I said, 'but shouting won't get her back.'

'She not come back and I break your neck and all the necks I can find.'

'Sit down and stop behaving like a walking volcano.'

'Something is to be done right away. The police in Tripoli are useless. Polite but useless. Everyone is useless. I am looking forward to the Roman antiquities at Leptis Magna and so is Hilda. This worm who says he is from Kalmar—his neck, too, I break eventually.'

'Sit down.'

Surprisingly, he did. I got up and went to the special clients' cupboard and came back with a bottle of Bacardi and a glass.

'Carry on the treatment and listen.'

He poured himself a liberal glass and drained it before I had even got under way. I didn't worry about his drinking (though Wilkins would have given him hell had she been there) because he was clearly the type who could drink rum as though it were milk—and did, when he had to keep up his strength.

Before I could get going he helped himself to another glass and said, 'In five years we are to be married. By then I have saved ten thousand pounds. This holiday it was all arranged. We looked forward to great happienss to come—and now, what?'

'Just listen,' I said patiently, 'and when you've listened don't ever repeat a word of what I've said to anyone under any conditions. Okay?'

'I should trust you, is that it?'

'It may be hard, but try. In fact, you've got to if we're going to get Wilkins back.'

'Why you call her Wilkins always? Her name is Hilda. It is not right to make a woman sound like a man.'

I sighed. Love and anxiety were mixing up his thought processes. 'You call her Hilda,' I said, 'because you love her and she loves you. But to me she is Wilkins, because I have a great respect and affection for her and she is my business partner. Carver and Wilkins. And, for God's sake, let's stop quibbling over points of chivalry. Now just throttle back on the rum intake and listen.'

He did both. I gave it to him straight. The full and complete story. I didn't keep a thing back from him and that was paying him a compliment which I handed out to very few in my life. Always I had found it paid to keep a little back as a form of insurance, but with Olaf glaring at me from his red-rimmed blue eyes I dished out the full truth, and I finished, 'The first thing you have to do is to try and trace that ship. Red funnel, blue band. I've a friend at Lloyds and I'll make an appointment for you. He'll fix it so that you can see the shipping movement lists for the last two weeks. From your own sources you can find out what shipping lines operating in the Med carry those funnel markings. Can you do that?'

'Yes, possibly. Yes, certainly.'

'Even if it's an Iron Curtain vessel?'

'They are all registered.'

'Good. Let me know where you are staying and don't ever telephone me—and don't telephone anyone else unless you do it from a call box.' I flicked my hand to the desk phone. 'That's tapped.'

'It's not possible! In a democratic country?'

I didn't answer because both statements were wrong and there's something touching about the naivety of nice people who think they live in the best of all possible worlds.

I got rid of him at the cost of half a bottle of rum and told him to come and see me the next day if he had anything to tell me.

When he had gone I went out, exhausted, bound for Miggs's

place and a quiet glass of Guinness. In the outer office Mrs Burtenshaw said, 'That was Olaf, wasn't it?'

'You know him?'

'Hilda has shown me photographs. What is he doing here, and
where is Hilda?'

I didn't feel up to another involvement, so I said, 'He had to
make a flying visit to London on business. Something extremely
important. Hilda's waiting for him in Cairo.'

'That sounds very odd.'

I knew it did. It was the first time I'd ever called Wilkins Hilda
in front of her sister or anyone else.

'He's going back, probably tomorrow. I think it's something to
do with him trying to get a job in this country with the Port of
London Authority—he couldn't ignore it. If he gets it and can live
here . . . well, that would be fine, wouldn't it?'

She looked at me doubtfully, and then said, 'Hilda never told me
he was a drinking man. I'm rather surprised.'

'He's not usually. It's just that he's come from the heat of Africa
and needs a little rum to keep out the cold in England.'

It was the best I could do. I went out before she could develop
any further lines of enquiry.

I fell into the battered cane chair in Miggs's office over the garage
and gymnasium and, limp as a rag, said, 'I've changed my mind.
Fix me a stiff whisky and soda, and don't ask a lot of awkward
questions. Just let's have a little normal chit-chat about the market
price of hot cars and the current rate for heroin.'

Miggs grinned and began to set out the drinks.

'You look flaked,' he said as he put a drink in my hand.

'I am.'

'I'll give you an hour's work-out after lunch.'

'You won't.'

He sat down opposite me, his big red face like a fat autumnal
sun, and fished in one of his waistcoat pockets.

'Got a message for you. Someone phoned here, yesterday. Didn't
know you were interested in cage birds.'

'I'm not. Though I did once look after Mrs Meld's canary for
two weeks while they went to Southend.'

'Ankers, his name is. Keeps a pet shop up near St Giles's Circus.
The address is there.' He handed me the slip of paper.

It just had the name and the address on it.

'He must have got me mixed up with someone else.'

'No. He said he had a new consignment of African finches and other stuff in and thought you'd like first look at them.'

'He's mad. I don't know any Ankers, and I don't want any birds, caged or otherwise.'

'Come off it—you don't have to let me in on your secrets. You must know him. He said he'd got a copy of that book you wanted too.'

'What bloody book?'

'Wrote it down on the back of the paper.'

I turned the paper over. Written on the back was 'Saraband Two by R. Duchêne'.

I sat up smartly and said, 'Well, I'm damned!'

Miggs grinned even wider. 'He said you would be pleased. What is it—some dirty piece of work, guaranteed to rouse the dullest appetite?'

'Something like that,' I said.

'Any time between two and three of an afternoon, he said.'

'Thanks.'

'When you've finished with it I'll borrow it.'

'You won't.'

He reached for my glass which, to my surprise, was already empty. I was getting Olaf's complaint—but I made no struggle against it. A little Dutch courage was just what I needed at this moment.

CHAPTER 9

Blowing Hot and Cold

I was there at fifteen minutes past two—and left at fifteen minutes past three. In that time I had been given my instructions by Saraband Two, and also had been forced into buying an African parrot for the knock-down price of ten pounds. Its vocabulary was knock-down too; limited but forceful. I gave it to Miggs on my way home.

The pet shop had two dirty bow-fronted windows, and inside it was as dark as a cave and smelt like a kennel. The doorbell rang as I went in and closed the door behind me.

A raucous voice screamed, 'Shut it! Bloody shut it!'

I said into the gloom, 'If you use your eyes you'll see I've shut it.'

'Sad thing! Bloody sad thing!' the voice screamed.

I saw then that the owner was a parrot in a large and tarnished cage hanging just inside the door. In a tall, wire-framed enclosure that ran down the middle of the shop five or six dozen small tropical birds huddled together in groups, swopping chirping, nostalgic memories of their homelands. Bags of hound meal, fish and bird food were stacked on the floor and dusty shelves. Dog leads and collars, rubber bones and poodle jackets hung from the ceiling. On either side of the door at the back of the shop were cages with long-haired rabbits and short-haired guinea pigs. In a long glass tank a shoal of goldfish moved slowly round and round in an endless gavotte.

The parrot yelled, 'Get that hair cut! Get that bloody hair cut!'

For want of company, I said, 'I like it this way.'

For answer it blew me a raspberry. At this moment a man about three foot six high, bald as an egg, with a badly coloured shell, shuffled out of the gloom to one corner of the far end of the shop, and blinked at me through steel-framed glasses. He might have been for sale himself. Genuine dwarf, hardly used, look lovely in any front garden. He wore a green baize apron of the kind that went out with butlers' pantries, a wool cap, khaki-coloured, that went out with the First World War, and a collarless shirt that had once been white. He could have been any age from seventy up.

He squinted at me, and then at the parrot, and said, 'Dirty-mouthed little sod, ain't he?'

'Company to have around, though.'

'Come off an Esso oil tanker. Second cook 'ad 'im. Been all over the world, 'e 'as, and talks like it.'

The parrot, knowing he held the centre of the stage, said sadly, 'Nellie . . . Bloody Nellie . . .'

'Are you Mr Ankers?' I asked the dwarf.

'Unhappily, yes.' He had a gulping kind of voice, as though he were holding back a sob all the time.

'I'm Carver. You left a message with a friend of mine.'

'Ah, yes. In that case you won't want to be bothered with small stuff like Zebra finches or black-headed mannikins, will you. Not even a Spreo starling or a Shama. Right?'

'Right.'

'No. The one for you is Alfred there. Genuine African, five years Esso-cook trained, live to be a 'undred. Company for yer old age. Gentle in 'is ways, too. Only bites when 'ungry. Fifteen pounds knock-down price.'

'I don't want a parrot. You know what I want. I'm Carver.'

'I know you don't want a parrot, but you got to 'ave one or you don't get through that back door. I 'as to 'ave my perks, don't I?'

'Do you? I'm here by invitation.'

'Makes no odds.' He switched from a sob to a sigh, shook his head, and went on, 'It's an understandin' I 'ave with 'em. Got into trouble, I did, years ago with 'em. 'Ad a 'old over me since and used me. Used me cruel. But I said that's all right—just so long as I get me cut off that kind of visitor. So don't ask any that won't act straight and upcoming about buying. Fifteen pounds. Last a lifetime. Give all your friends a good belly laugh.'

'I should buy a parrot when I don't want one? Just to get through a door to see someone I don't want to see?'

'That's the long and short of it, mate. Anyway, what's wrong? You taken against Alfred?'

I looked at Alfred. He pulled the skin down over one eye in the lewdest leer I've ever seen.

'I think he's charming. You take a cheque?'

'Cash.'

'You guarantee if he bites I don't get psittacosis?'
'If he bites it'll be bleedin' painful—that's all I guarantee.'
I handed him two fivers.
'Fifteen,' he said.
'Ten is what you get. You've led me enough of a dance.'
For a moment his eyes came up to me, the glance shrewd, calculating and a little unsettling—and at that moment it wasn't taking much to unsettle me. Then he shrugged his shoulders.
'All right. Bloody soft-hearted I am. Through the door, up the stairs, first door on the right.' He put a hand on my arm. 'Listen, you look a spunky kind. Cheeky, sort of. Don't try nuffin'. Saraband's very high up, and they got ways. Nasty ways if you come the old acid. I know.'
'Thanks.'
I made for the door.
From behind me Alfred shouted, 'So long, old cock!'
'Don't worry,' I called, 'I'll be back—I hope.'
I went up a stairway lit by one bulb. The wall on my left was covered with graffiti which normally I would have spent some time over. All I got was one gem—*The Pope is the secret head of the Mafia.*
Two flights up, a radio was going full blast. Clear above it a voice yelled, 'Charlie! Bloody Charlie—where are you?' It could have been another parrot.
I found the first door on the right, adjusted my tie nervously, took a deep breath and went in without knocking.
The room was neat and tidy; just two chairs and a kitchen table. Anyone could keep a room like that ship-shape. There was a window that looked out to a blank wall three feet away. Sitting behind the table was a grey-haired woman who must have been in her sixties. She wore a neat blue suit and a tan-coloured blouse and there was a small blue hat on the table in front of her. She had one of those healthy, wise, happy faces that belong to favourite aunts, and on one hand I saw a nice dress ring, blue-enamel set with a cluster of pearls. Her earrings matched the ring. A wealthy favourite aunt who didn't neglect her looks and spent freely on clothes. She gave me a charming smile and put her cigarette down on the ashtray in front of her.
'Mr Carver?'
'Yes.'
'Do please sit down—and get over your surprise.'
I sat down on the other chair and began to get over my surprise.

'Did that horrible Ankers make you buy something?' Her voice was strictly Cheltenham and Girton and stands-the-clock-still-at-ten-to-three-and-will-there-be-honey-or -something-for-tea. Maybe, I thought, I am dreaming and back to the age of fourteen and she's going to take me out to a matinée of *The Sound of Music,* and then tea at Fortnum's afterwards.

'A parrot,' I said. 'Called Alfred. Ten pounds.'

'He's incorrigible. If you wish we'll refund the money. We're glad to always . . . that is, with our more indigent callers.'

'Don't bother. I'll send the parrot to Mr V. E. Semichastny. Its language should be useful in brushing up the idiomatic English of his K.G.B. boys.'

'And girls.' She gave a clear tinkle of laughter—bright, and even a little coquettish, the way aunts are with favourite, and fast-growing nephews. Damn it, I was beginning to like her. To keep things in perspective, I deliberately thought of poor old strangled London-Scottish tie, and of Wilkins. My frown showed.

Full of understanding, she said, 'Now the surprise is over and you want to get down to business?'

'That's why I'm here. For instructions. Though personally I can't see why one of your Embassy people from Kensington Palace Gardens couldn't have gone straight to Sutcliffe with whatever proposition you have to make.'

'No? It's simple. If anything goes wrong we wish to be able to say truthfully that there has been no official contact at any state department level. And anyway, most successful diplomatic matters are usually initiated by an unofficial, private approach.'

'Since when was kidnapping classified as a diplomatic move?'

'Since, I suppose, Mr Carver, Helen of Troy's time—or well before, no doubt. Do I detect a note of antagonism in your voice?'

'I'm trying to get it there. I think this whole business stinks.'

'Naturally. But that's another argument. However, let me assure you that as long as you do as you are told, no harm will come to your secretary. You have a deep feeling of affection and loyalty to her. That's nice to find these days—'

'And very convenient for you.'

'Naturally. One must make the most of the means at one's disposal. Do smoke if you wish.'

I lit a cigarette. As I did so she reached down to the side of her chair and brought up a blue suède handbag and opened it. She pulled out an envelope and slid it across to me. I saw that it was unsealed.

'Are these the instructions?'

'Those are the terms of the settlement which we wish to make with your Mr Sutcliffe.'

'He's not my Mr Sutcliffe. I like people who find they can only function if they have hearts.'

She smiled, and nodded indulgently.

'You can read them at your leisure. Of course, you won't show them to anyone else except Mr Sutcliffe. I'd like you to deliver them within the next twenty-four hours.'

'And when I see him—how much am I supposed to know? I mean about Duchêne and the other people involved? He's quite capable of putting me under the lights and beating the facts out of me. I might have to tell him about this place and you.'

'Yes, I understand that. I suggest you tell him all you know. There's no need for deceit—and Mr Sutcliffe well understands the conventions which have to be observed. He is not going to do anything that will put William Dawson in jeopardy. This affair has now gone far above any cloak-and-dagger level. I rely not only on your good sense, but on that of Mr Sutcliffe as well. And believe me, Mr Carver, we have made a close study of both of you.'

'Anybody who thinks he understands Sutcliffe is in for a shock. For instance, from what I tell him he might pick you up and make you say where Dawson is being held.'

'It would be a waste of his time, because I don't know where Dawson is—yet.'

'I'll bet.'

She gave a graceful little shrug of her shoulders and stood up. 'You're from Devon, aren't you?'

'Yes.' I was on my feet for a lady, a nephew well aunt-trained. 'Honiton.'

'Ah, yes—that's where they make that lovely lace. Daddy used to take us to Devon for holidays when we were young. Torquay. They were wonderful days.'

'Aren't they now?'

She gave me almost a roguish look. 'Oh, yes, indeed.'

I moved to the door to open it for her. 'How did it go?' I asked. 'Cheltenham? Girton? Nice upper-class family?'

'Yes.'

'And how the jump from there to the K.G.B.?'

'It was a personal matter—and a painful one at first.'

'But not now?'

'No. I thoroughly enjoy it.'

'Even though you go round carrying a spray gas gun in your handbag?'

She laughed. 'You have quick eyes, Mr Carver. Yes, even though I do that. After all, you might have turned out to be an unpleasant customer.'

'I might still.'

She looked hard at me then, and something was touched off within which wasn't often allowed to show in her face, but for a moment it was there, and it was something I'd seen before in Sutcliffe and Manston, something that gave one the feeling of standing naked, half-dead with fatigue, looking down into some greeny-blue ice gorge which just offered coldness while you fought off vertigo, and death when it overcame you. . . . They all came from the same mould.

I opened the door for her and as she moved the look was gone. She gave me a charming, polite inclination of the head so that I almost put my hand out to thank her for a pleasant time.

She said, 'If you wish, you can stay up here and read the contents of the envelope. No one will disturb you.'

'Thank you.'

She went and I closed the door on her. I stuffed the envelope in my pocket, gave her three minutes and then went out myself. In the shop I collected Alfred. Outside the shop I picked up a taxi. As usual I got a talkative driver.

'Where to, sailor boy?'

He got more than he bargained for because Alfred took my side and suddenly began to scream at the top of his voice, 'Bloody! Bloody! Bloody! Bloody!'

He kept it up at intervals all the way to Miggs's place. Happily Miggs was out, so I left Alfred for him with a note. As I went out, shutting the door behind me, I heard Alfred scream, 'Shut that door. Shut that bloody door!'

I went weakly to the tube station. Alfred and Saraband Two and Ankers in one afternoon were proving that I didn't have the stamina I thought I had. And, to cap it all, there was Sutcliffe to come. The cup of life was fairly brimming over with dirty water.

It was half past four. I kicked off my shoes and flopped on the bed with Saraband Two's letter in my hand. I stared at the ceiling, knowing that I didn't want to open the letter, knowing that I wished now that I had never got myself and Wilkins involved in this, knowing that this time I had really gone too far—and couldn't now avoid going further, right out of the daylight into the jungle gloom and menace of Sutcliffe's world. Frankly, Sutcliffe frightened me. Manston I could take. But Sutcliffe, no.

The plaster that had fallen off the ceiling had left a lath-striped patch the shape of Australia. That's where I should be, I thought. Somewhere in the outback, safe. But not even that would be far enough away.

I stacked the pillows up, propped myself against them, lit a cigarette and opened the letter. It was typed on foolscap sheets of paper, watermarked *Abermill Bond. Made in Gt. Britain.* And it read:

For the attention of Robert Cledwyn Sutcliffe, O.B.E., M.C.

(Well, that was something. I'd never known his second name. The bastard was Welsh. Not that all Welsh are bastards. And he was an O.B.E. I could think of lots of other orders he merited, none of them likely to appeal to his vanity because, of course, he was vain. It was the odd quality that supported his ruthlessness, efficiency and labyrinthian thinking. Military Cross too. Well, he could bring that out for an airing on St David's day and parade it around Whitehall with a leek stuck in his hat. Shut up, I told myself. You're only going on at him because you're scared stiff of him.)

I read on:

1. The bearer of this communication is well known to you. He will explain his participation in this matter, and that he is acting under duress.

2. It is requested that you bring the following information and suggestions to the attention of the Prime Minister and First Lord of the Treasury, The Rt. Hon. James Freemantle Dawson, O.B.E., M.P.

3. The Prime Minister already knows that his son, William Freemantle Dawson, has been kidnapped. This was done, purely for monetary gain, by two private individuals. These individuals have now sold out their interest in this operation to another party, who now wishes to open negotiations for the return of William Dawson, subject to suitable exchange arrangements being concluded. These will not, of course, involve any financial payments.

4. At the moment the Prime Minister's son is in good health, being well cared for and allowed reasonable facilities for exercise and recreation. It is hoped that no cause will be given for this state of affairs to be changed.

5. At the moment the following individuals, of special interest to the party who has now taken over the care and custody of William Dawson, are held in one or other of Her Majesty's prisons.

(a)   Henry Houghton, Admiralty clerk. 15-year sentence. 1961.

(b)   William Vassall, Admiralty clerk. 18-year sentence. 1962.

(c)   Frank Bossard, Guided missile researcher. 21-year sentence. 1965.

(d)   Peter Kroger, Bookseller. 20-year sentence. 1961.

(e)   Helen Kroger, Wife of above. 20-year sentence. 1961.

6. The safe return of William Dawson is proposed on the basis of the following conditions:

(a)   Any exchange would include the automatic return of Gerald Brooke, British subject, now held in the labour camp at Mordva since his removal from the Lubyanka prison, Moscow.

(b)   Any exchange must, from your side, include two of the persons listed under para. 5 above, one of whom must be one of the Krogers.

7. In order to maintain security, and avoid damaging publicity for either side, it is essential that the Prime Minister's personal interest in this matter be kept strictly secret and that no leakage should ever be allowed of the fact that his son was kidnapped.

Further, to avoid public agitation over the exchange of one of the Krogers, it is suggested that a well-authenticated cover be arranged to show that the Kroger chosen had died in prison. A guarantee is given that this cover will be strictly honoured by the party of this side. In this manner the only public announcement necessary, and an acceptable one to the world press, will be a straightforward exchange of Gerald Brooke and whichever individual is chosen from para. 5 above in addition to the Kroger selected. This open and public exchange can be arranged along similar lines to that of the Greville Wynn-Gordon Lonsdale affair of 1964.

8. A reply to this proposition can be made through the bearer of this communication. Or, if it is considered politic that he should have no further part in this proceeding, then an advertisement should be inserted in the Personal Column of *The Times* to read: 'Saraband Two: Come Home'—followed by a telephone number.

The party of this side will establish *bona fides* when answering by announcing himself as Mr Wakefield.

(That gave me a dry laugh. Wakefield was the prison in which Peter Kroger was being held.)

9. In the event of these exchange proposals being rejected out of hand, the party of this side—on receipt of such positive refusal—will allow a grace period of ten days before the regrettable elimination of William Freemantle Dawson. On the other hand, in the event of agreement being reached for an exchange, it is stipulated that all arrangements shall be completed for the necessary hand-overs within thirty days of final agreement of details.

And that was it. And I was sweating. Lots of side-issues had occurred to me as I read it through—and they were all unpleasant so far as Wilkins and myself were concerned. And Sutcliffe! He'd go up in smoke. The party of this side had him on toast . . . unless the Prime Minister was prepared to sacrifice his son. Well, he might be a tough cookie as a politician—how else can you be one unless you are?—but, as a father, he would feel the same as any other father. Why, just to get Wilkins back I would have handed over the whole of M.I.6 and the C.I.A. if I could.

I rolled off the bed and stuffed the letter into my pocket. It was still early but a drink was essential.

Before I could get to a drink the telephone rang. It was a telegram for me from Letta. She was going to be in Paris the next week and looking forward to a happy reunion. The telegram gave the address of the apartment where she would be staying, and finished 'Love from Lilith too'.

I went gloomily to the decanter. I couldn't see happy reunions being part of my lot for a while.

I was putting soda in the whisky when there was a knock at the flat door. I finished the soda job, took a deep swig, and then went to the door and jerked it open with a touch of bad temper, the kind that comes from having that little-boy-lost feeling and knowing that all the world is against you.

Standing outside was Jane Judd, looking full of the joys of spring, dark-haired, dark-eyed, wearing a black tailor-made and a daffodil-yellow blouse.

'What the hell do you want?'

'To see you—even if you are going to be damned bad-tempered about it.'

She moved past me into the room. She moved nicely and dispensed a passing whiff of perfume, but neither did anything for me.

'How did you know I was back?'

'I rang your office.'

'All right—let's have it.'

'I want to know what your cable about belly scars was all about.'

I picked up the whisky glass and gave her a pugnacious, Churchillian scowl over the top.

'Has anybody been asking you questions about Freeman?'

'No. Like who? What are you so bad-tempered about?'

'I've just been elected patsy of the year.'

'Good. You shouldn't have any difficutly holding the title for quite a while. Why the cable?'

'Because your precious Martin Freeman—whatever he was or is up to—tried to fake his death. As usual it was a pretty poor effort. So no need for tears. You're not a widow—yet. When did you hear from him?'

'How do you know I've heard from him?'

'Inspired guess. Also, you've got an enquiring mind. You're trying to figure him out. You want to know what he's up to. You want to know what you might be getting into. You're uncertain. You don't want trouble. You just want marriage and security. You've got my sympathy and—come to think of it—I'll add a little good advice. Get unmarried and forget him.'

As I finished speaking I reached out and took the long slim, black patent handbag from under her arm. She made a move but I waved her back.

I opened the bag. Inside was a coloured picture postcard. There was other stuff as well, but I didn't bother with that. It was dated the day I had left the Villa La Sunata. It had a Bizerta postmark, and showed a nice view of a mountain called the Jebel Something-or-Other. It was addressed to her at the Mountjoy Hotel and an unsigned message read: 'From July 1, book one week Doré Hotel, Barcelona. Will contact you there.'

'How do you know it's from Freeman?' I asked.

'I know his handwriting.'

'My advice to you is to ignore it. It's a pretty ordinary hotel, anyway. No bridal suite. Not even a restaurant of its own.'

'God, you are in a mood.'

'I am. You sure no one's been asking you questions about him?'

'Absolutely.'

I handed her back the bag but kept the postcard.

'What are you going to do with that?'

'Burn it,' I said, and got out my lighter.

'But it's mine!'

'You can remember it. July 1, one week, Doré Hotel, Barcelona. Take my advice, don't go.'

I lit the edge of the card and carried it to the fireplace. I dropped it in and watched it flame away. One thing I was pretty certain about was that Saraband Two and company were never going to let Freeman reach Barcelona. Or Pelegrina reach wherever he wanted to reach.

They might be jollied along for a while: but in the end they would be eliminated. No publicity, no leaks . . . these were the essentials of the exchange deal. The professionals involved had to be trusted, but outsiders were unnecessary risks. That's why I was scared stiff for Wilkins—and myself.

Jane's eyes came back from the fireplace to me. From the look on her face there was no doubt now that she knew she was in something big.

'It's as serious as all that?' she asked.

'More than that. I suggest you forget all about Freeman.'

She began to move to the door, then paused and looked back at me. 'You're involved, too?'

'A little—but on the right side. By the way, if he does get in touch with you again, let me know. But come here. Don't use the phone.'

She nodded and went out, no longer full of the joys of spring. I was sorry for her, but I couldn't waste much time on it. The best I could do for her was not to tell her the truth.

I went to the phone and dialled a Covent Garden number. It wasn't listed in the directory, but it was a number I was never likely to forget.

A voice at the other end said, 'Yes?'

'Carver here.'

'Yes?'

'I've got to see him. Urgently, importantly and vitally.'

'Tell me where you can be reached in the next six hours.'

I gave my phone number and the number of Gloriana Stankow-ski's flat.

I had a bath and changed, drank two more whiskies and then walked down to the corner of the street to the Embankment and got a taxi. Any other time going to have dinner with Gloriana would have been a pleasure that would have driven all gloom from my mind. Tonight gloom was four lengths ahead of pleasure and going well on its second wind.

Gloriana opened the door to me herself, gave me a neat little kiss on the side of the cheek which surprised me, explained that the Scots maid was out—her evening at the cinema—ushered me through the narrow hall and settled me under one of the porcelain lemon trees in the sitting room, and quickly had a large drink in my hand, all with the charming expertise of a hostess anxious to please a favourite guest. I wondered what favour she was going to ask me. It wasn't a big one, and it came almost at once.

She settled on the monster divan across the way from me, wearing a crushed-raspberry silk blouse and dark, Victoria-plum-coloured trousers, stuck an elegant finger in a large glass of gin and campari and twiddled the ice cubes around so that they chinked musically against the fine crystal. Three block-busting drinks like that, I thought, and she would be flat on her back—and I too gloomy to take advantage of it. Her hair was spun red-gold and her lips were as pretty and knowing as a Cupid's. There was a little dimple on her chin. I took a good pull at the whisky. It was strong and it hit me, as drink always does when the mind is unsettled. Maybe, I thought, she'd been playing cards with some Cupid for kisses and won the coral of his lips, the rose of his cheek and the crystal of his brow. 'O Love! has she done this to thee? What shall, alas! become of me?' Maudlin, too—that's how drink takes the enfeebled spirit.

She said, 'You look scared to death.'

I said, 'I am.'

She said, 'Tell me, what is all this secret service crap?'

'Tell me,' I said, 'what anyone has said to you.'

'The man I know in the Treasury has told me that any communi-cation I get from Martin must be passed on to him, and that I am to inform him of anyone who comes asking questions about him. Including you. What the hell has that bloody brother of mine been up to?'

'That's no way to speak of the dead.'

'Dead?' She laughed, a silvery sound that rivalled the ice music

against her crystal glass. 'Martin's kind don't die. They go on into
their nineties, still making a nuisance of themselves.'

'Sure?'

'Dead men don't repay a ten-thousand-pound theft in notes,
delivered anonymously in a brown-paper parcel.'

'You told the Treasury boy this?'

'Yes. But he won't tell me anything, except to forget Martin for
quite a while. That's why I asked you here—surely you can tell me
something? If you don't you don't get any damned dinner; oysters
and a beautiful salmon trout and a bottle of Montrachet between
us. Come on, give. One thing I can't stand is mysteries. Certainly
not the kind you stupid men cook up between you. What's that
bastard Martin up to?'

'I don't know. He tried to fake his own death in Tripoli. Don't
ask me why. Anyway, he's paid you back the money he took and,
as I said, if you get in touch with this dusky number—' I got up,
went and sat by her and took out one of La Piroletta's business
cards—'you can buy the python bracelet back. She bought it off
Martin for two thousand quid. You'll have to make your own price
with her.' I wrote the Paris address of Letta on the card and handed
it to her. 'She's going to be in Paris next week.'

'Why should I have to pay anything?'

'Because La Piroletta is that kind.'

'Was she kind to you too?'

'I'm giving a strictly professional report.'

'Then tell me what all the mystery about my brother is.'

'If I knew—'

'You know—'

'I still wouldn't tell.'

'Go to hell.'

'I'm halfway there. Any messages?'

'Yes. When you meet my old man tell him he didn't beat Martin
hard or often enough.'

'Does this mean I don't get dinner?'

'It depends on whether I can manage three dozen oysters by
myself.'

'I'll have another drink while you're making up your mind.'

I leant over and kissed her gently on the coral pink lips, briefly,
and wondered if they were soft with promise or disinterest. Then I
went over to the bar.

My back to her, I said, 'Has your only contact with the authorities been this guy in the Treasury?'

There was a little pause, and she said, 'Yes.'

I said, 'I'll send my account in to you tomorrow—if I live that long.'

She said, 'You'll live. You've got the same survival factor that Martin has. What have you told this Jane Judd?'

I turned, fat drink in hand. 'To forget him. Approve?'

She nodded.

At that moment the telephone rang. I reached out for it, looked at her and said, '*Permesso?*'

She nodded.

I picked up the receiver.

A voice at the other end said, 'Mr Carver?'

'Yes.'

'Mr Rex Carver?'

'You don't have to be so formal, you know it bloody is.'

'Report here immediately.'

'Can't I finish my drink?'

There was a click at the other end.

I looked at Gloriana and she looked at me.

'The dark clouds might,' I said, 'have rolled away and it could have turned out to be a wonderful evening. As it is, you're stuck with three dozen oysters and a bottle of Montrachet.'

'Where are you going?'

'To the Inquisitors. To the dark shrine of Security. To the devildom of men without hearts. Into the *crêpe*-festooned shadows of the underworld, where all is cold and bleak and there is a human sacrifice every hour on the hour.'

'You're tight, love.' She sounded genuinely sympathetic.

'I know. But the moment their door closes on me, the cold inside will shrive every particle of alcoholic warmth from my blood, every soft and comforting whisky fume from my brain.'

She giggled, stood up and came and took the glass from me. 'Don't have that. You don't need it. Certainly not for yourself. You're not even worried about yourself. I know you well enough by now. Who is it? Who is it you're really worried about?'

'Certainly not your bloody brother.'

'That's good, because he wouldn't be damned well worth it.'

I took the glass from her and drained it.

'Don't worry,' I said. 'It could be my last.'

She took the empty glass from me, put it down, and then reached her arms around me and gave me a hug.

'You're nice,' she said, and kissed me, good and hard and lovingly. Then, releasing me, she added, 'But too damned dramatic.'

'We can only be what we are, only do what we have to do, only end as it is foreordained.'

'Crap. And if you get away before midnight come back.'

She kissed me again and then I tore myself away and stumbled out into the night.

I got the taxi to drop me on the corner by Moss Bros, and then walked through into Covent Garden. Having a taxi right up to the door would have been *lèse-majesté* and bad security. Anyway, one had to approach as a penitent on foot; barefoot, if the weather were right. The door to Robert Cledwyn Sutcliffe's flat looked like the entrance to some seedy publisher's offices.

I rang the bell and after an interval Hackett, his man-servant, opened it. Before he did so I knew that he would have checked me over the monitoring system from inside.

'Hullo there, Mr Carver,' he said cheerfully. In itself a bad sign.

'Hullo there, Hackett, old cock,' I said, following him in.

He turned from shutting the door, and said, 'You've bin drinking.' It was a statement, not a question.

'Yes, I bin drinking, Hackett. What you bin doing? Getting the torture chamber ready?'

Hackett shook his head. 'We're in that kind of mood, are we, Mr Carver? I don't think he'll like it. He's been off his food for three weeks.'

'Good. Let's hope he keeps it up and starves to death.'

'Oh dear, Mr Carver, I would advise you to take a brace.'

'Give me a stiff one, neat, before I go up then. Who's with him?'

'Mr Manston and Mr Perkins.'

'The unholy trinity.'

He winked and nodded me up the stairs on my own. I took a three seconds' brace outside the door, knocked and walked in.

The only light in the room came from the brackets over his half a dozen paintings. They were always modern and were always different each time I came. Facing me on the far wall was a red-and-blue Francis Bacon job of a nude man who looked the way I felt, all twisted up. To one side of it stood Manston; tall, well-built, in evening dress, a red carnation in his buttonhole, his face tanned and giving me a mild smile. He looked disgustingly healthy. Perkins, in a stiff Donegal tweed suit, had his great bulk collapsed into a leather armchair. He had a fat cigar in his mouth, jutted his chin at me like the prow of a cruiser in welcome, and reached an arm about five feet long out to a side-table to retrieve his glass.

Sutcliffe was sitting in another armchair, a plump, dumpy man, face big and bland like a Buddha's. A blue smoking jacket was rumpled up over his shoulders and his small legs were thrust out for his tiny feet to rest on a footstool. He looked at me with calm, cool, grey eyes that had behind them over fifty years' experience of not being fooled or ever indulging in the stupidity of being warm-hearted. He went on looking. Nobody said a word. I shuffled my feet and looked at the sideboard. There was a lot of bracing material there. In the past they'd indulged me with the odd glass of Glenlivet—when they had wanted me to feel at home. There were no signs of real welcome now.

I said, 'It's pretty cold in here for the time of the year.' I pulled Saraband Two's letter from my pocket.

'We're in no mood for any of your low-level social chat,' said Sutcliffe. He said it quietly, but each word had a vibrant core of ferocity.

'Well, here's something on a very high level for you to get your teeth into.'

I handed him the letter. He looked at the letter, and then at me, pursed his plump lips in a prissy little movement and then said, 'God help you, Carver, if you're up to any of your old tricks.'

'I'm as pure as driven snow. And driven is the word. Read this after you've read that.' I handed over Wilkins's letter. I glanced at Manston. 'You're reasonably fond of me. Don't I get a drink?'

Perkins said, 'Just be content with breathing.'

Sutcliffe sunk his head into his shoulders and began to read. I watched his face. It showed no emotion whatever. It wouldn't. He had been training it that way for over fifty years.

Tired of Perkins and Manston, I stared at one of the modern paintings beyond Sutcliffe. The canvas was covered with irregular coloured squares and triangles, and in the top right-hand corner was the word *Hommes* and in the diagonally opposite corner the word *Femmes*. I didn't try to work it out. I was just content to be a bloody-minded Philistine.

Sutcliffe read through the two epistles, held the various sheets up to the light, squinted at them, fingered their texture and then read them all through again. This done, he said to no one in particular, 'Get Hackett up.'

Perkins reached out a long left arm and thumbed a bell push in the wall. Ten seconds later Hackett came in without knocking.

'Sir?'

Sutcliffe swung his head round slowly and gave Hackett a smile. 'Take Mr Carver down to the waiting room and make him comfortable.'

'Yes, sir.'

'And see that he doesn't panic.'

'Yes, sir.'

Hackett came over to me. An automatic had suddenly sprouted out of his right hand. With his left he ran expertly over my jacket and trousers.

'Nothing lethal,' I said. 'Except a nail-file in my ticket pocket.'

Hackett led me out and shut the door.

'They must be cross with you, Mr Carver. Never sent you down to the waiting room before, have they?'

'No.'

But I knew all about the waiting room from hearsay. Personally I would have been glad to leave it that way.

We went down into the basement. Hackett unlocked a green baize door at the end of a little corridor and waved me in. He did it with the automatic, so I had to obey.

The door closed behind me and I was alone. It was a big room without windows. The floor was tiled, plain white tiles. The walls were sound-proofed, leather panels covering whatever they had used for insulation. When you touched the stuff it gave gently. In a recess at the far end of the room was a bunk, screwed to floor and wall. At its foot a little washbasin was set in the wall. Behind a plastic curtain in the right-hand wall was a recessed toilet. A plain wooden table and a kitchen chair stood in the middle of the room. Set in the ceiling behind an iron grille was a light. Above the doorway almost at ceiling height was a row of small portholes, some glass-covered and some covered with perforated brass discs. From one of them now was coming the gentle hiss of air being forced into the room. Looking up at it, I caught the blast of hot draught funnelling down at me. As I stood there the noise of the hissing increased.

I went over to the bunk and sat down on the low pile of folded army blankets. I've lived in some odd rooms in my time, most of them crummy hotel rooms, and generally managed to make myself comfortable. In this room I knew I was never going to be comfortable. Nothing would ever make it sing for me—and why should it? The purpose of this room was to make people sing loud and clear if they had any sins or deceits to be purged.

Within five minutes the temperature had gone up to tropical level and I had my jacket off and my collar loosened. Within the next ten it went down to freezing point so that I had the blankets huddled round me and my breath hanging in cold clouds before my face. This hot and cold sequence went on for about an hour. It was nothing serious. It was just annoying. But I knew that it was no more than a mild foretaste of unpleasantness to come unless I decided to behave myself. They needn't have bothered. Within reasonable limits I had already decided to behave myself. Like Martin Freeman, I had a high survival factor and meant to protect myself.

From a loudspeaker in one of the portholes over the door Sutcliffe's voice suddenly came out cold and clear into the room.

'We'll be down later, Carver. Don't rely on any sentiment about the help you've given us in the past—almost outweighed, of course, by the trouble you've given us too. You don't come out of that room alive until we have the last scrap of truth out of you about this business. Think about it and prepare yourself for confession.'

I said, 'Can you hear me?'

He said, 'Yes. Why?'

'Because in that case I won't speak my deepest thoughts about you out loud. I'll just be polite and say, "Drop dead, you stinking bastard!" '

I heard someone laugh. It could have been Perkins or Manston. It certainly wasn't Sutcliffe.

CHAPTER 10

Next Stop Hades

At no time were they all three in the room together. Sometimes there were two, usually only one, while the others, I guessed, watched and listened on the closed-circuit screen in Sutcliffe's room. Or, if they had any sense, took a nap . . . because what was there to get from me?

But they obviously thought that there was something.

Manston, alone, started the ball rolling. About four hours after my being shown into the room, Hackett let him in. From the moment of his arrival the air-conditioning went back to normal.

He sat on the kitchen chair while I lay on the bunk.

'All right,' he said, no emotion in his voice, no encouraging look on his face, 'just tell your story from start to finish—and omit nothing.'

I sat upright and told him. It took quite a while and when I had finished he said, 'That's all?'

'Yes.'

He shook his head. 'You mean to say it was just pure chance that you were given a commission by the London Fraternal Insurance Society to recover Mrs Stankowski's property—and this led you, again by chance, into this Freeman business?'

'Yes.'

'And it was just some little bell ringing at the back of your mind that began to warn you that Bill Dawson might be the Prime Minister's son?'

'Yes. The name worried me. Then in Tripoli I saw a newspaper headline about his father. In Captain Asab's office, actually. I got Wilkins to check. Dawson isn't interested in politics. He's an oil geologist or whatever you call it and he was employed by an oil exploration company in Libya. It had been in the press at some time.'

'Why didn't you come to me with the information you had about the Villa La Sunata? We could have had Dawson back home by now.'

'I didn't know about the villa when I met you. And you made it clear you needed no help from me. When I did know . . . well, let's say I was silent out of pique, or vanity—'

'Not cupidity?'

'I've often wondered if that word had anything to do with cupid.'

He got up slowly and came towards me.

'It has. From the Latin *cupere,* desire. It's a capsule description of your basic motives—money and sex.'

'So, I suffer from a common disease.'

'How much did Saraband Two say would be put in your bank account?'

'Five thousand pounds. But it was Duchêne who said it. I refused.'

'Sure it wasn't fifty thousand—and you haven't refused?'

Light dawned.

'You think I'm in on this job?'

He reached down and got me by the shirt front. He was nothing like as big as Perkins. He wasn't much bigger than me. But I was moved, jerked up, swung round and then thrown to slam up against a wall, my head thudding against it. I lay where I had fallen.

'That's what we think,' he said. 'We're just waiting for you to confirm it.'

He moved to the door, paused by it, and said, 'By the way, there's nothing personal in my actions. I just want you in the right frame of mind.'

'That's what Paulet said. Thanks. It's nice to know this isn't going to spoil a beautiful friendship.'

He went out. I went back to the bunk. In the next hour they rang the changes between equatorial and arctic temperatures until my body responses would have sent a Pavlov off his head with delight. I swear to God they got me so mixed up that sometimes I sweated when it was freezing and shivered when the place was like a bakehouse.

Then Perkins came, big, bluff and genial.

He lit a cigarette and sat on the edge of the table.

'All right,' he said, 'just tell your story from start to finish—and omit nothing.'

I told him. It took quite a while, and when I had finished he said, 'That's all?'

'Yes.'

He shook his head.

'Jane Judd visited you because she was worried about Freeman and wanted to know if you knew what was happening?'

'Yes. And I told her I didn't know what it was all about.'

'Why didn't you tell us about the postcard you took from her bag?'

While I was down here they were obviously doing some fast checking outside.

'I didn't think it was important. You don't want Freeman. You want Dawson. They won't be in the same place. Freeman and Pelegrina have sold out to the K.G.B. boys.'

He moved fast and sledge-hammered me on the chin with his right fist. I went to the floor and stayed there.

He went to the door.

'Think the story over again and try to remember *all* the details.'

He went out. I got up. The temperature changes started again and this time went on for two hours. I thought over the details between shivering with heat and sweating with cold. Surely, I told myself, a man must be allowed to retain something, just something, which he could use in a *cupere* way.

The next time it was Sutcliffe. He had changed into a neat blue suit and wore his Old Etonian tie. He sat on the kitchen chair and pouted his plump little lips at me.

'All right,' I said, 'I will now tell you my story from start to finish—and omit nothing.'

'Good.'

I went to the little washbasin to get a drink.

He said, 'The water's cut off. It won't come on again for some time.'

I told my story with a dry mouth. When I had finished, he said, 'That's all?'

'Yes.'

He said, 'You were at Gloriana Stankowski's yesterday evening?'

'Is it tomorrow already?' I looked at my watch. It was.

'She told you that she had received anonymously ten thousand pounds in notes from Freeman. Why haven't you mentioned that?'

'Because you bloody well already know.' I could afford to lose my temper with him. At least he wouldn't try any strong-arm stuff on me. 'You've got a Treasury hyena on her tail and he knows.'

Sutcliffe shook his head. 'You must try and understand. When we ask *you* for *your* full story we mean the full story—even if some details of it are already known to us.' He stood up. 'By the way, I made a mistake about the water not being on. You can have a drink if you wish.'

I went to the basin, grabbed a glass—plastic—and held it under the tap. As my right hand closed over the metal tap to turn it I got a shock up my arm that jolted me three feet backwards. I lay on the floor and wasn't aware of Sutcliffe going out.

When I found the strength to get up I flopped on to the bunk.

For the next three hours I did the arctic-tropical trip so many times that I lost count. But that didn't matter. From the moment of Sutcliffe's going a brass band had started to play over the loud-speaker. It was a good band—mad about Sousa—and played at top volume for the full three hours. Heat, cold and sound. Simple little things. They kept them going. I slowly began to go mad. I put it off for a while by chewing up medicated toilet paper from the loo and wadding the wet pads into my ears. They finished the recital with 'Sussex by the Sea', and then a slow funeral march.

I lay on the bunk like a piece of chewed string.

Manston and Perkins came in together and propped me up.

'Shall we,' said Perkins, 'go through your story again?'

I looked at him with a limp smile. 'Do we have to? I was just beginning to enjoy the music.'

Manston said, 'The general opinion is, Carver, that while you may be holding back a few details . . . you know, magpie stuff, little bright bits that you can't bear to part with . . . the serious aspect is that you are refusing to admit the overall truth. You can keep your little bits. But you must give us the basic truth.'

'You've had it.'

'No. I'll admit the truth of your story, right up to the time you went to Tripoli and discovered that the Dawson who had been kidnapped was the Prime Minister's son.'

'Thanks. Can I get a drink now without electrocuting myself?'

Perkins, a true white man, got up and filled the plastic tumbler for me. Then he drank it himself and leaned back against the edge of the basin.

'When you learnt that, you realized why Duchêne and Paulet were stringing you along with a phoney story, and you made a good guess as to their interest. So—'

'Let me tell it, please.' I got up and went to the basin. I looked at Manston. 'Tell this gorilla to get out of the way. I want a drink and if I don't get one I'll tear his stupid Anglo-Saxon head off his over-muscled rowing shoulders.'

Manston looked at Perkins, and Perkins stepped away. I drank like a camel. I probably sounded like one as well.

Bloated, I turned. 'So,' I said, 'the moment I'd got the dope about the Villa La Sunata from La Piroletta, I did a deal with Duchêne and we all went up there together. Right?'

'Right.' Manston nodded. The carnation in his buttonhole was wilted. Not so much as I was.

'And we worked out a plan to keep me in the clear. A phoney kidnapping of Wilkins and so on. And me to come back here and play the man under duress to you. And eventually the prisoner exchange deal would go through and I'd get a whacking great secret payment for my services and Wilkins would come home, safe and sound, and never know what a triple-crossing, corkscrew-minded man she had for a boss. Is that it?'

'Precisely,' said Perkins.

'You believe that?' I asked Manston.

He nodded. 'Knowing you, yes. It measures up to your kind of morality.'

'Oh, sure. No real harm is done to Dawson or Wilkins. Brooke comes back from Russia, and the British tax-payer is saved the expense of keeping two people in prison here, and by now anyway they have no vital information to hand over to Mr V. Semichastny—he only wants them as a matter of face. So what harm is done to anyone? And I get fifty thousand pounds in a numbered Swiss account. It's all been good clean fun. You believe that?'

'It's the truth, isn't it?' said Perkins. 'And, now that you've got it off your chest, why don't we go on to the main point? Where is Dawson? Don't tell us you don't know that.'

Standing there by the bunk, I raised my eyes to heaven and clamped my hands to my brow in a gesture of despair. The trouble was, I was so fatigued that the movement made me collapse on the bunk. Leaning back against the wall, I said, 'This government spends eight million pounds a year, openly acknowledged, under State Expenditure, Class XI, Miscellaneous, for its Secret Service—and you two morons draw part of it in salary. Stick with it. Don't go out into the big, hard world of industry and commerce. You'd never survive. You've got to have intelligence and common sense to hold down a pay-packet out there. Go away, you bother me.' I rolled over and lay down. I was tired, too tired even to be angry. Too tired even to be afraid. Heat and cold and brass-band music can do that to you.

Manston said, 'All right, Perkins. He's yours for five minutes. Don't mark his face, that's all.'

He didn't. I tried to kick him in the groin as he came for me, but he grabbed my ankle and damned near broke my leg as he jerked me off the bunk. Then he worked me over, strictly for five minutes, which is a long time when you are being bounced from wall to floor. It might even have been from wall to floor to ceiling towards the end. I wouldn't have known, because I passed out without a mark on my face.

When I came round my watch said twelve o'clock, but whether it was midday or midnight I had no idea. Hackett appeared with a tray and no consolation. On the tray was a glass of milk and three very dry cheese biscuits.

I stood up from the bunk as he put the tray on the table. My body was so stiff and bruised that I functioned like a badly manipulated puppet. Hackett waved me back with one hand.

'Don't try nothing like jumping me, Mr Carver. There's someone outside the door.'

'Don't worry,' I said. 'I couldn't jump over a matchstick.'

'That's what you get for being difficult. You really ought to understand, Mr Carver, that you're in deep. The boss is still off his food. Not like him a bit.'

He came over and handed me the glass of milk.

'Why don't you be a good boy and tell'em what they want to know?'

'They've had the truth. Why can't they be content with that?'

'There's truth and truth. Mind you, I got to say that whichever one you stick with it won't do you any good. The boss, he's always had it in for you because you would never come and work for him. And because the times you have come in on a part-time basis you've always played it your own way. Bad, that. He likes things done proper even by temporary staff.'

I said, 'Is it day or night outside?'

'Midday. Lovely day, warm and bright. All the girls with skirts right up above their knees, birds singing and even the cab-drivers with grins on their faces. Pity you'll never see any of it again.'

He meant it. A cold spasm wriggled through my guts.

'Cut it out,' I said angrily.

'It's the truth. Yours won't be the first body I've carried out of 'ere. Proper routine we got. No trouble. Just a quick injection and you're out like a light. No trouble about disposal, neither. Ambulance waiting at the back, nice little drive down to just below Greenwich and you get dumped in the tide. Nice pub in Greenwich, The Ship, 'spects you know it. We always stop there on the way back for a couple of quick ones. Let's see, be three weeks since I was there last.'

'Go to hell.'

'Frightening you, am I?'

'Of course you are, you bastard.'

He chuckled and went, and I sat and munched the dry biscuits. Before I had finished they started up the tropical-arctic treatment again and after an hour a colliery brass band came on, blaring away at Colonel Bogey for a start and carrying on with a two-hour repertoire. And after that it all started again, the full story and omit no details. First with Sutcliffe, whose fat lips had started to be a little twitchy, then Perkins, who picked out a few spots on my body not already bruised and made a tidy job of filling in. I slugged him once when he got a bit careless, but my fist bounced off his jaw as though it had been made of india-rubber. Then Manston came, wearing a neatly pressed, Savile-Row, grey-flannel suit and smelling of Tabac after-shave lotion.

He was sad and gentle, but adamant; the full story and omit no details.

Lying on the bunk, chewed up, battered up, heated up, cooled down, eardrums aching from brass-band music, I said, 'For God's sake, you're a reasonable guy, you know me. I'm not part of the Saraband Two set-up. If I had been I'd have admitted it ages ago. I'm no hero. I want to get out of here.'

He said, 'We've had people in here who've said just that. Little shrimpy types, hardly any blood in their veins, skinny types, fat types, tough types and angel-faced, wide-eyed innocent types. All sorts, and you could have got lovely odds that they were innocent—but they weren't. Any more than you are.'

'Just assume I am.'

'Makes no difference. The innocent have got to suffer with the guilty in this. Get it into your head—this is a State affair of the highest secrecy. It's the Prime Minister who is involved personally. Already his bottom is itchy with anxiety because one slip-up, one

line of publicity, could blow this thing open. Can't you see that?
He wants his son back. That means a deal with the other side. Let
that story break and God knows where the consequences would
end. So . . .'

'So what?'

'So, it's obvious—whether you tell us the truth or not, you're not
going out of this room alive. Do you think Sutcliffe would let you
wander around with a scoop like this in your hands? In a year's
time you'd be turning it into cash some way.'

'You really mean that?'

'Yes. And if I didn't, I couldn't help you.'

'Why not?'

With all the cold calmness in the world, he said, 'Because we've
already made preliminary contact with your Saraband Two crowd.
They insist—for the common good—that a rider be added to the
exchange agreement. We have to eliminate you—and they will
eventually do the same for your Wilkins.'

'The bastards! You're not taking that, surely?'

'Why not? We don't want publicity, now or later. Anyway, it's
now part of the deal for Dawson's return.'

'And you're accepting it?'

'Of course, and the P.M. wants his son back. Naturally, he won't
be bothered with *all* the details.'

I was silent for a long time, largely because my throat was too
dry to let me say anything and my heart was pumping away so
loudly that I doubt whether he could have heard anything I said.

Finally I said in a very small voice, 'Can't you do something
about Wilkins? She knows how to keep her mouth shut.'

He shrugged. 'No. It would be the same for Olaf, Gloriana Stankowski and Jane Judd, if you'd told them the real facts. I tell you
the lid's going to be put on this pot for good. You think, for instance,
that Saraband Two and that lot will ever let Freeman or Pelegrina
go free?'

'No.'

'Of course not. They're giving them that impression right now,
even letting them pay back money, send postcards and so on—but
they won't ever get away. Now do you get some idea of the kind of
fix you're in? Once this exchange goes through, both sides have
every reason in the world to eliminate all the fringe types who know
anything about it. Certain professionals are going to know—but

then they're professionals, trained not to open their mouths. Pity
you didn't join us years ago—we might have treated you differently.'

I stood up. I hated his guts. I hated Sutcliffe, Perkins and the
whole cold-blooded lot of them—and I was scared stiff for myself.

'Don't try anything,' he said.

'I'm not, not for myself. But do one thing for me—try and work
it for Wilkins. She's a professional, all right. You tell her to keep
her mouth shut, and shut it will be for the rest of her life. Do that
for me, you high-class, ice-cold security bastard. Just one favour.'

He stood up and moved to the door. 'I'll put it to Sutcliffe—he's
listening now, anyway—but it will be entirely his decision.'

He went. The brass band came on. The heat and the cold started
up, and eventually they came again, by themselves, in twos, in
threes, pumping away, the whole story, omit nothing, not even the
smallest detail this time—if it had not been for Manston's talk about
Wilkins and what would happen to her, I might have disgorged the
few tiny details that I had been keeping back. Not that they would
have helped much. But now they were unimportant. I was going
and so was Wilkins, so what was the good of saying anything? Let
them rot.

Then I was left alone. My watch said seven o'clock. The girl
secretaries home from work would be taking their geyser-fed baths
in Notting Hill Gate, the chaps from Lloyds, the Stock Exchange
and the City offices would be suburb-bound through all points of
the compass to their mock-Tudor villas and Kent farms, or be in
their London clubs, hot hands already round their third whisky,
Miggs would be in his office, feet up, listening to Alfred's scurrilities,
Mrs Meld would be leaning over the gate waiting for Meld to come
back with the evening Guinness, Olaf, tired from badgering Mrs
Burtenshaw for news of me, would be sunk in a rum depression,
the Prime Minister would be struggling with his dress studs before
going to a City Livery dinner, and clouds of starlings and pigeons
would have settled around Trafalgar Square to unload another
night's guano harvest, and the world would go on turning, slowing
down a little each minute but not really worried about deceleration.
That was my worry, unique and unavoidable, I was decelerating
fast. I would never sleep with another woman, never have a drop
too much to drink again, never take that first morning draw on a
cigarette and lie coughing happily in bed listening to Mrs Meld
giving out with 'Old Man River'—I suppose I should have been
preparing my soul for the final fence. I even considered it, and then

said, What the hell? My soul had been a non-runner for too long to think it could start steeple-chasing at this late hour. I turned over and went to sleep . . . sleep . . . chief nourisher in life's feast. Well, tomorrow I would be absent from the board.

They woke me at nine o'clock. Four of them, Manston, Perkins, Hackett and a bloke I'd never seen before who had a long, drawn, hanging face and bad teeth. Sutcliffe no doubt was watching over the closed-circuit television.

Hackett and the strange man had me flat on my bunk the moment I made a move. Perkins stood by with a hypodermic syringe while Manston slowly rolled up my right shirt sleeve.

'Usual disposal, Mr Manston?' said Hackett.

'No.' Manston shook his head. 'We've used Greenwich enough lately. Take him up river. Above Richmond.'

Hackett beamed. 'Right you are, Mr Manston. Make a nice change. Jim and I can have a drink at Kew Green on the way back.'

I started to fight but they held me down. I started to shout and they let me. Alfred would have been proud of me. Perkins leaned over and jabbed the syringe in my arm. The fighting and the shouting died—and so did I—amazed how quick and painless it all was, and with no time to speculate on my destination.

It was the wink that did it. A little muscular flick of the eyelid that briefly spelled hope, a tiny signal picked up and registered within a tenth of a second.

Rooks were cawing. there was the noise of a tractor, distant, ploughing the Elysian fields or more likely carting away clinker from the great fires of Hades. Water was splashing somewhere, but was probably unreachable, a diabolical tantalization. Warmth and comfort. Maybe a gentle initiation that would rise to red-hot discomfort. Naked, of course. Naked ye come and naked ye go. Music, too. Organ music, deep, welling up, fading, a long slow monotony of sound. No brass bands, thank God or, more probably, the Devil. Voices, too. Probably the central bureau of registration, manned by trusties, privileged types who were allowed a long drink once every decade. Church bells, distant, subtle torture since to have heeded their call in the old days would have changed one's ultimate destination. A dog barked, a long, fierce, gritty sound prefacing the biting of some toiling buttock, some pain-wracked body.

I lay there, eyes shut and in no hurry to open them. I considered the wink, that last-moment act, obscured from all the others, as Manston leaned over, watching me. It had to mean something, surely? Or had it just been a nervous tic? I didn't want to open my eyes in case it had been. The beds in the place were comfortable anyway, even if they did tuck you in without pyjamas. I felt well, but bruised, rested but not eager for action. A telephone rang, distantly. That didn't surprise me. From the tractor I knew that the place was modernized.

I stretched, took a deep breath and got a whiff of tobacco in the air. Snout. That meant I would have to get on the right side of the barons.

A voice said, 'Why he so long?'

Nobody answered. The voice was familiar. I ignored it. I was comfortable.

There was the chink of a glass and then the long, slow hissing of a siphon. A delicious sound. Not to be ignored. I opened my eyes and sat up, naked.

It was a nice bedroom, diamond-paned windows, a candlewick bedcover, white carpet, a bow-fronted Sheraton chest of drawers, some tapestry-covered chairs and a little Regency desk by the window. From a transistor set on the desk came the sound of organ music. Through the window I could see a row of elms, rooks flying around their crests, and a stretch of hop garden with the bines well up the wires.

Olaf was standing by the window. He reached out and switched off the set. He looked absolutely miserable. Manston was sitting in a chair by the desk. He had a glass in his hand. Close to him was a low table, sunlight streaked across it, sparkling on crystal of decanters and glasses. A silver-meshed siphon stood on a silver coaster.

I said, 'Is it Sunday?'

'Yes,' said Manston. 'The bells are from Sissinghurst church. Wind's in the west. Morning service.'

'It's a bit early for a drink, isn't it?'

'If you lead a conventional life, yes.'

He reached out for a decanter of whisky.

'Three-quarters of the way up the glass. The rest soda. Lazarus special.'

He fixed the drink for me and brought it over.

'How was it down there?' he asked.

'They all sent messages. Freeman's father runs a tobacco ring. He's disappointed in his son, but looks forward to seeing him soon and expressing his displeasure in person.'

I drank. It was a real corpse-reviver. I shivered with the shock, looked down at my naked, bruised torso, and said, 'Why naked?'

'Because,' said Manston, 'all your clothes were put on another cadaver, now going up and down with the tide somewhere between Richmond and Westminster Bridge.'

I said, 'You did wink, didn't you?'

'I did. It was the one moment when I could risk spoiling authenticity. I felt you merited it.'

'Big of you.'

I took another drink. It was good, but I had it tamed this time.

'You did well,' said Manston. 'I was afraid you might ask the one question which would have spoiled it all.'

'How did Duchêne and Paulet, in the first place, ever get on to the fact that Freeman was mixed up in the kidnapping? How, in fact, did they ever know there was a kidnapping?'

'Yes. They knew long before you did.'

'How did they know?'

'From someone in our department—we think. Not sure, though. Freeman sent a letter to the P.M. It was opened by his personal secretary. The letter, of course, was not signed by Freeman. It just stated the facts and gave instructions for a code advertisement to be inserted in *The Times*. The letter was handed to Sutcliffe by the P.M. Five people only knew the facts right up to the time that one of our agents was murdered in Freeman's cottage. Five. The P.M., his secretary, Sutcliffe, myself and Perkins.'

'But there was a leak.'

'Clearly.'

'Perkins?'

'Who can tell?'

'It could have come through Captain Asab or one of his men in Tripoli.'

'No. Duchêne was operating before Captain Asab knew.'

'How did you know it was Freeman?'

'Through a letter that Bill Dawson sent his father—unknown to Freeman, obviously. He said that Freeman was coming out to spend some time with him. He'd got leave from his oil company and they were going to do a tour of the Roman antiquities in Libya ... Leptis Magna, Sabratha and so on. Freeman has a record. We checked him and it seemed likely that he was the man. Perkins, in fact, did the checking.'

'You were a bit late getting on to his country cottage, weren't you?'

'That's the way Perkins—if he's the one—would have worked it, giving it to us late, and having Paulet there to put the clamp on our man.'

I looked at Olaf, big, moon-faced, standing unhappily by the window. 'Why don't you say something?'

'My heart is choked. I think only of Hilda.'

I looked at Manston. 'I've an idea that we're going to do something about that, aren't we?'

Manston stood up and smiled. 'You'll find a complete change of clothes in the bathroom. We'll talk it over before lunch.' He looked at his watch. 'You're due at Lympne at three to catch a plane to Paris. You can't stay in this country —since you're supposed to be dead.'

Showered, shaved, dressed, resuscitated, I sat on the loggia of Manston's country house and watched the year's first swallows dipping over the swimming pool while Manston laid it on the line for me. His analysis of the situation was clear, but bleak, and very direct.

First, Perkins. He was only a few months back from a Far East tour. He might or might not be a double agent. Lacking proof yet, it was assumed that he was. Even so, it had been decided to let him run for a while. If he were a traitor, then through him they could be sure that the Saraband Two crowd would have written me off for dead. He, himself, had administered the injection of poison to me—only it had been, unknown to him, a nicely judged dose of pentothal, and Hackett and his friend had whisked me away before Perkins could become suspicious. The rest had been easy; another body in the river with my clothes on, and it might be some time before the body was found.

Secondly, Saraband Two had been contacted through a *Times* advertisement and Perkins was acting as the link man. Saraband Two had been told that the exchange deal was on, and that I had been eliminated, as requested, because it was vital that no outsider should be allowed to wander around with such high State secrets as I knew.

'In fact,' said Manston coolly, 'Sutcliffe was actually rather in favour of killing you.'

'He always was fond of me.'

'But I persuaded him that you might have a use.'

'Well, he can always kill me if it turns out you're wrong.'

Thirdly, they had picked up Olaf—unknown to Perkins—just after I had gone to them, and he had stubbornly insisted that all he knew was that Wilkins had been kidnapped and that I had asked him to trace a certain ship.

'Just as you never let on that you had told him about the kidnapping of Dawson, so he never admitted that he knew. In fact—' Manston glanced across at Olaf—'his mind has room for only one thought at the moment, Wilkins.'

'What about her?'

Manston considered this. 'At the moment there are thirty days in which to arrange the exchanges. I don't think they will start wiping out Freeman, Pelegrina or Wilkins until they are absolutely certain that it is going through. They don't present any security risk at the moment because they are being held.'

'Which brings us to the real reason why you didn't kill me. No?'

He nodded, and explained, 'The Prime Minister has agreed to the exchange. He wants his son back. Nothing must go wrong and there mustn't be even a rumour about the affair. You can imagine Sutcliffe's private reaction to that one. His hands are tied officially. You know how big a part pride plays in an organization like ours. We don't like to be outmanoeuvred by another organization. It hurts. We'd like to go on with the exchange arrangements, but also in the thirty days do our damnedest to find Dawson and upset Saraband Two's apple cart. But if we do that and anything goes wrong—then the P.M. will have heads rolling. You get the dilemma?'

I not only got it. I could imagine how Sutcliffe was squirming. He had been outsmarted by Saraband Two. It was a rare discomfort for him—and I couldn't shed a tear about it. Wilkins was the only person on my mind.

'So what's the score with me? Your hands are tied. And I'm back from the dead.'

'With a new identity.' Manston flipped a passport across to me. I opened it. There was the usual bad passport photograph of me, and I had become Duncan Hilton.

'I don't care for the Duncan,' I said.

'You're on your own,' said Manston. He handed me a sheet of paper. 'Olaf traced the ship for you. There's a list there of her ports of call and route over the last two weeks. At the moment she's coaling in Algiers. My bet is that Dawson and company have already been shipped ashore somewhere. If we can arrange it, we're going to get a customs or quarantine check on her in Algiers—but it won't be easy because our hands are tied officially. Meanwhile, as I say, you're on your own.'

'And what the hell do you think I can do?'

'You want Wilkins back—'

'She must come back or I kill someone,' said Olaf in an angry-bear tone. We both ignored him.

'Think of something,' said Manston. 'There's money waiting for you in Paris. Crédit Lyonnais, Place de l'Opéra. You've got a little under thirty days. Get to work. You're an enquiry agent, aren't you? And we're employing you on this job—it took me a long time to get Sutcliffe to accept that. Find something, anything, any lead. The moment you can finger where Dawson is—then let us know. The moment you have anything get on to me, or the nearest British consulate, and give the code word "Python" and he'll pass the message. That's the most we can do for you.'

'And if it comes to nothing?'

'Then it comes to nothing.'

He looked uncomfortable, and I knew why, but I saw no reason to spare him. All right, in his way he liked me, even regarded me as a friend of a kind, but his true love was the damned service he worked for. That, first, second, third and always.

'Let's get it straight,' I said. 'I'm a big boy and used to hard facts. If I fail, the only person who's going to come back and keep a shut mouth forever is Dawson. Right?'

'I'm afraid so. It's no good trying to make any deal about Wilkins. You know that.'

'Come on, Manston. Spill it all. If I don't find Dawson for you, then pretty soon after the thirty-day limit Olaf and I will go too—won't we?'

He looked at me, tight-mouthed, but he said nothing. He didn't have to. We would go, in a car accident, somehow, somewhere. And he was tight-mouthed because it wasn't his decision—but Sutcliffe's.

'Remember one thing,' he said. 'It's vital that the Saraband Two people get no idea you're alive. You go to Paris this afternoon by yourself. Olaf can join you tomorrow. You've both got rooms at the Hotel Balzac. Know where that is?'

'Yes. And blast you and Sutcliffe.'

I stood up and did a bit of angry pacing. Manston watched me. Olaf sat with his big head hanging down, staring at the pavings. A wagtail flirted along the edge of the pool and a few busy bees mined away at a row of tulips. A warm, late spring day, birds fidgeting on their eggs, water beetles skating on the swimming pool, church service just over, and a thousand Dads putting their two thousand feet up with the *News of the World* while Mum sweated over a hot stove . . . and Carver sweated over an impossible job. Oh, I knew how the minds of men like Sutcliffe worked. He didn't think I had a ghost of a chance. But he was prepared, just prepared, to give me any kind of chance if by a long shot it would save his departmental pride. But if it didn't come off—then he would want all record of that long chance expunged from the book. The last bell would ring for me. Hear it not, Duncan, I told myself, for it is a knell that summons thee to heaven or hell—and when that came there wouldn't be any reassuring wink.

Olaf stood up. He glowered at the both of us and then said, 'I think I go back to London and see the Swedish Embassy. Maybe they can do something. After all, Hilda is my fiancée.'

I went over to the cane drink table that had been wheeled out, poured him a stiff rum, and handed it to him.

'Just drink that, Olaf. And do exactly as you're told. Wilkins is coming back—and you're going to help me get her.'

'I suppose,' said Manston, 'that after all that treatment at Sutcliffe's place, there isn't anything you're holding back. Anything vital?'

'If there is,' I said, 'I can't think of it. But there is one thing which hasn't been settled.'

'Oh?'

'Sutcliffe is employing me. We haven't discussed terms.'

Manston smiled. 'You must be feeling better. Anyway, you know the usual rates. Plus expenses, of course.'

'Stuff the usual rates. This is an unusual job. If I don't pull it off . . . well, there won't be any question of payment.'

'And if you do?'

'Five thousand pounds and an Order of the British Empire.'

Manston's mouth gaped, which was unlike him, for he was a well-brought-up chap.

'You mean that?'

'I do—and you're going to fix it. Five thousand pounds for me—and the O.B.E. for Wilkins. Right?'

He paused, tickled his chin with the tips of his well-manicured fingers, and then said, 'Yes. My personal promise.'

CHAPTER 11

Sic Transit Gloriana

A hired car from a local garage took me to Lympne, and from there I got a plane to Paris—only it didn't go to Paris, it went to Beauvais, and then there was a long coach ride in.

A fourteen-year-old boy sat alongside me in the plane, going through a pile of Batman comics. He passed a couple over to me and I leafed through them. They didn't give me any ideas that I thought would work.

I got into the hotel around seven, and flopped on the bed with my shoes on, too tired and depressed to order myself a drink. I pulled the list of ship details from my pocket and went over it again. It wasn't any more helpful than staring at the ceiling but it made a change.

Olaf had done a good job. The ship was the *Sveti*, cargo boat, timber trade from Odessa, Russian owned. She did a regular route to Istanbul, Athens and through the Mediterranean to Algiers, where she now was. Olaf had made a note that she had arrived two days over normal schedule at Algiers. In the coach air terminal in Paris I had picked up a B.E.A. red-white-and-blue flight brochure—About your flight, *votre vol, ihr Flug*—which was full of good maps. From Athens through the Mediterranean the *Sveti* had to pass between Sicily and North Africa. That brought her route very close to Bizerta, close enough for Duchêne to have quietly slipped his party aboard. The run from Bizerta along the coast to Algiers was straightforward, but somewhere along it I guessed that the *Sveti* had made a two-day diversion. That put within her range Sicily, Corsica, Sardinia, Majorca and the rest of the Balearic Islands, even Spain itself—though I had an idea that the U.S.S.R. did not trade with Spain. Even so, that would not have stopped the *Sveti* heaving to at night off the coast while a party went ashore. I dropped the brochure and asked the ceiling how in hell one man, and a love-stricken Swede, could cover that area of possibilities?

Looking for a needle in a haystack was easier. At least you only
had the stack to deal with. The Prime Minister's son could be in
any of dozens of haystacks. I settled back on the bed and considered
praying for the miracle of second sight. I even considered taking a
pin and trying a jab over the map. In fact I did it. The oracle
announced that Dawson was a hundred miles south of Rome in the
middle of the Tyrrhenian Sea. Rome made me think of Duchêne.
Duchêne made me think of Paulet. Clever Paulet, who kindly
brought me beer, sandwiches and a backhander—yet still I liked
him. Not that that was going to stop me breaking his neck or
putting a bullet into him if it would get Wilkins out of her jam. A
dead Paulet would upset his girl friend Thérèse. *To lose you, my
darling, would make life empty for me. A thousand embraces.* That's what
she'd written to him.

I sat up suddenly. Manston had asked me if there was any detail
I had not mentioned. Well, there was—because I had forgotten it
myself until now. Paulet's office address I'd kicked over—they knew
it, anyway. And they knew his real wife's address. But only I knew
Thérèse's address.

I got a cab to the top of the Avenue Wagram, and then walked
down to the Place des Ternes. I went into a bar and had two
pernods. Suddenly I was feeling good and hopeful for no reason at
all.

I went out into the velvety, spring warm, Gauloise-flavoured
Paris evening. It was an old house on the Avenue des Ternes,
turned into apartments. There was no concierge. Just a row of name
plates in the hallway with bell pushes alongside them. Mademoiselle
Thérèse Diotel was apartment Number 3. I went up two floors.
There was one door on the landing with Thérèse's card slipped into
a brass holder. There was a fanlight over the door. No light showed
through it. That didn't mean she was not in. She didn't know
me—but she was a clever girl, would have to be to be hitched up
with Paulet. Any excuse I made would have to be a good one. The
trouble was I couldn't think of a good one. Nobody comes to sell
Larousse dictionaries on a Sunday evening, and I couldn't say I
was an old friend of Paulet's from the K.G.B. training school in
Moscow. So I did something which I hadn't done since my small-
boy days. I rang the bell good and hard and ran away. Up the next
flight of steps to the turn where I could just hang my head down
and watch the door. Nothing happened. I went down and repeated
the performance just to be sure. She could have been taking a bath

or even entertaining a lover—after all, Paulet had been away some time. Nothing happened.

I went back and did the door lock with a piece of perspex. The small hallway was in darkness. I let it stay that way and went through into the main room, after checking a kitchen to the left of the hall and a bathroom to the right. The main room was in darkness. I pulled the curtains and switched on the light. A door across the room led into a bedroom. I could see the end of the bed, and a red dress draped over a small chair. I went in, pulled the curtains and switched on the light. The bed was made and had a frilly sort of canopy over the top end. There were frills like candy floss over the dressing table, and a yellow-and-black stuffed Esso tiger sprawled over a little sofa. Everything was neat and tidy. I did a quick tour again of the kitchen and bathroom and main room. The whole place was neat and tidy, and with the feeling of not having been used for some time. No washing-up left, no evidence of meals, nothing in the kitchen bin, half a carton of sour milk in the fridge and a packet of sausages; no cigarette stubs in the ashtrays, no newspapers; on the table in the main room a vase held an arrangement of wilted mimosa. I had the conviction that Thérèse was away and had been for some days. So I took a good look around. One of the things I enjoy is going over other people's rooms. In ten minutes you can often learn more about them than they could tell you themselves in an hour.

She was a great one for Colette, had all her books in paperback. Her favourite aperitif was something called Ambassadeur—three bottles in the sideboard. There was whisky as well, half a bottle. I made myself a drink and carried it with me on the tour of inspection. She used Jolie Madame scent, favoured short nightdresses, one of them a rather nice number in blue and white spotted silk. She kept Paulet's love letters—about twenty of them—in a bureau drawer, tied up with a red ribbon that had Galerie Lafayette printed on it in gold. I struggled through them; they were dated from long before the Dawson affair and were mostly repetitious—Paulet, even my bad French told me, had no literary style or true lover's felicity of expression. In fact he was mostly quite earthy and direct about his need and feeling for her. There was only one thing of interest in them. It was in a letter just over eighteen months old, written from Rome. Just one sentence which read, translated, 'J. has died suddenly so the whole D. business has been cancelled'.

I stood there, pondering this. D. could, of course, have stood for Dawson. Who was J.?

I put the letters back. Under them, wrapped in a yellow duster, was a 9 mm Browning pistol—obviously a spare to the one Paulet carried—and some ammunition. I took the gift without leaving a thank-you card.

I washed my whisky glass in the kitchen and put it back in place and made for the flat door, head down with the dejection of failure. It was just as well, otherwise I might not have seen it. On entering, the opening door had pushed it back far to one side from where it had fallen through the letter box on to the thick carpet. It was a confirmatory cablegram in a little envelope—the kind they always send you the next day to confirm a telegram which has been passed over the phone.

I opened it. It was in French. Translated, it read: *We need a good cook at V.V. immediately. Meet Mimo, Tristan's Bar, any midday next three days.* It was signed François, and had been sent from Bizerta the day they had released me. Thérèse had received it—over the phone—late the same day, and had been away early the next morning before the postman had dropped the confirmation through the letter box. But where the devil were V.V. and Tristan's Bar? I went to the flat telephone and called Directory Enquiries. There was no Tristan's Bar or Bar Tristan listed in the Paris area.

I went back to the hotel and to bed, but not to sleep. I stared at the ceiling and kept saying to myself, 'J. has died suddenly so the whole D. business has been cancelled.' If D. stood for Dawson, could it have been that Saraband Two and company had had this affair lined up—maybe a straightforward job they were going to do themselves—nearly two years ago? And if so, why was J. so important that his or her death had made them cancel the deal?

The next morning—Olaf wasn't arriving until after midday —I went round to see Letta. I needed company and also I hoped that I would get some information. All right, so I was breaking a Manston rule not to let anyone know that I was alive. But I was prepared to break all the rules in the book if it would give me a chance of getting Wilkins back. And, anyway, if I told Letta to keep her mouth shut she would.

She was having breakfast near a wide window, the sunlight gold-leafing her skin, her dark hair piled up close around her head in some morning coiffure that made it look as though she were wearing a cossack hat. She wore a loose morning coat, red and white stripes, had her legs up on a stool and her feet were bare. She looked so good to me that I wished this were just a social call and that I had all the time in the world and no worries and could start off on a little interregnum of pleasure and dalliance such as a man must have now and again to rejuvenate the mind and the spirit.

It was clear, too, that she felt the same way. She came out of her chair in one long graceful movement and her arms went round me in a warm tackle. It was nice to know that I meant so much to her. I just let the mutual disentanglement come gently and in its own sweet time. Then I sat down on a chair and lit a cigarette. She sat on the arm and with the tips of her fingers did things to the top of my head. It was pleasant but made thought difficult.

I said, 'Can we talk frankly or are there any snakes around?'

She nodded towards the top of the window. Lilith was up there, coiled around a fat transverse curtain pole.

'Poor Lilith,' said Letta. 'At the moment, you know, she is not well. She won't eat and is so irritable. She is all nervous and tensed up and I cannot use her in my act. Last night she kept me awake for hours, twisting and rattling in her basket. Why should she be off her food—the guinea pigs in Paris are very good? And now she won't come down from there.'

She leaned over and kissed me on the cheek. The housecoat flapped open and I put a hand on the golden brown curve of one of her breasts to steady her from falling into my lap.

Her flesh warm under my palm, I said, 'Officially I'm supposed to be dead. You haven't seen me. You won't say anything to anyone about me. Okay?'

'For a dead man, you look very healthy.'

'Tell me,' I said, 'have you heard from your father recently?'

'No. You are still playing around with that old business?'

'Yes, I am.'

I was disappointed. Freeman had got in touch with Jane Judd, and had paid Gloriana back and out of it had come Barcelona. I had hoped that Pelegrina might have made some semi-revealing communication to Letta.

She kissed me again and this time slid into my lap. 'Tonight, after I come back from the Scherezade, I make you come alive again and forget all this business. I give you a key so that you can come in and wait for me, yes?'

With an effort I came back to the business in hand. 'But you did lend money to your father for his last venture, didn't you?' I asked.

'Yes, and positively for the last time. I made that clear. He's a man who can complicate people's lives. I like mine straightforward. Just like now. You and me.'

'You called him on the phone from Tripoli at the Villa La Sunata, didn't you?'

'Yes, to ask him what the hell he was up to. You went there?'

'Yes.'

'And he is in trouble?'

'Bad trouble.'

'Something you can do nothing about?'

'Would you want me to?'

'Yes, if you could. After all, I am his daughter and, although he is such a stupid old fool, I have some feeling for him.'

'You ever heard of a place called Tristan's Bar or the Bar Tristan? Your father ever mentioned it? Or a place . . . house or something . . . whose initials might be V.V.?'

'No. Such mystery. This, for you, is life, no? Always mysteries?'

'It could be my death.'

I said it lightly, but I don't think if I said it seriously it would have got through to her. Her lips were nuzzling the side of my neck and I needed all my willpower to keep my natural anxiety in the foreground. Up above the window Lilith lazily adjusted a couple of coils and eyed me biliously.

She didn't know it but there was a prize guinea pig sitting down below her. Me. Manston had turned me loose, a human guinea pig, into an experiment which didn't seem to have a hope of succeeding. And when it failed the chopping block would be waiting. It was this kind of thought that made it difficult for me to go along with Letta's present mood. There's nothing like worry to inhibit a man.

Before I left, she gave me a key to the apartment. I took it. Why not? I might feel a different man by the evening.

'You come and sit and have a drink,' she said. 'Always I am back by half past one.' She had her hand on the door when she turned back and went to a bureau.

She came back and held out the gold python bracelet.

'You do me a favour?'

'Of course.'

'I have had a telephone call from your Mrs Stankowski. She is staying at the Georges Cinq. We talk about the price for the bracelet but do not agree. You go and see her and get for me three thousand pounds. Then I give you 10 per cent. She is fond of you, no? She will not haggle with you—' she smiled—'and I do not mind if you humour her a little to get the right price.'

I nodded and sighed. Women.

Letta laughed, reached forward, kissed me and said, 'But you do not humour her too much. She likes you, I know. When we talk over the phone she asked if I had seen you. She sounded worried about you.'

So she might be. I had walked out of her flat, away from cold salmon, oysters, Montrachet and what could have been a pleasant aftermath, into limbo.

The thing about my kind of job which makes for the occasional success is the inability of the most intelligent human being, the Sutcliffe or Manston or Saraband Two types, to control or foresee every little circumstance that lurks on the fringe of a complicated affair. Somewhere somebody is going to make a mistake, and somewhere somebody is going to take advantage of it. Small things in the right place can have big potentials. Take a beer bottle, for instance; full of beer it has no room for anything else. Empty, well, it can be packed with all sorts of things. And master minds, thank the Lord, have occasional moods of uncritical acceptance like normal, uncomplicated people.

I didn't indulge in this piece of pretty ordinary philosophy as I was going to see Gloriana. It came afterwards. If I'd had any sense I'd have taken it a step or two further—but I suppose at that time, after leaving her, I mean, I was in a deep state of uncritical acceptance of life.

Why I went to see her I don't really know. I had time to waste until Olaf got in, and with time to waste I felt life was a vacuum unless I filled it. Though what I was going to do when Olaf got in I couldn't think—except that I didn't mean to hold his hand through any maudlin rum-drinking bout. I suppose, fundamentally, being a great believer in survival, I went to Gloriana to tidy up the python bracelet deal and make sure of my 10 per cent commission. Thinking about money, though it wasn't any great sum, kept me from thinking about other things.

At the Georges Cinq the reception clerk rang through and asked Mrs Stankowski if she could see a Mr Duncan Hilton about her brother. Mrs Stankowski said she would and up I went.

Was she surprised to see me! Her beautiful cornflower blue eyes popped and she nearly dropped the dry martini she had just mixed for herself. We just stood there looking at one another. After the dusky, Oriental charm of Letta, she was the fresh, pink and white, red-gold and blue of frank, Anglo-Saxon womanhood, and I wondered what it was about me that, even in this present crisis, could always be happy with either, were the other dear charmer away.

'You bastard—what happened to you!'

She came to me, arms outstretched, making me feel like the sailor home from the sea and the hunter home from the hill. Her arms went round my neck and she kissed me, spilling dry martini down the back of my jacket. I didn't mind. It was nice to be wanted. We let the kiss run for a bit and I smoothed the hollow of her back, appreciating the high-quality silk of the little shantung jacket she wore. After all, I had permission from Letta to humour her a little.

Stepping back, I said, 'I'm dead. This is Duncan Hilton. You never saw Rex Carver again after he left your apartment. Just be content with the new persona—and ask no questions.'

She nodded, content for the moment, but in time I knew that the questions would come. I went over to the cocktail shaker, added more gin and poured myself a drink.

She sat back on the settee, curled her legs under her and watched me. I had a curious feeling that she was waiting for something—perhaps for me to get a drink inside me before she felt ready to hand me whatever there was to hand.

'This whole affair,' she said, 'is really something stinking big, isn't it?'

'Yes. What are you doing over here—apart from getting your bracelet back from Letta?'

'My Treasury friend advised me to get out of England for a while. Go somewhere quiet and rest, he said.'

'Paris is hardly quiet and rest.'

'I'm going to Cannes.'

That hardly qualified either, I thought, but I didn't bother to say so.

'What is it all about?' she asked. 'Something quite out of the ordinary? And that damned brother of mine mixed up in it. Though he's a complete fool, he's still my brother and I'm beginning to get very worried about him.'

I sat beside her and smoothed the back of her hand. 'Gentling' they call it with animals. I had a feeling she needed it. She was all worked up. I pulled the python bracelet from my pocket and handed it to her.

'Give me a cheque for three thousand pounds and it is yours. Letta won't take a penny less.'

'You've seen her?'

'I had to. I'm her business agent.'

She fingered the bracelet and then slipped it on her arm. 'I'll give you a cheque before you go.'

That was unusual. No haggling. She clearly had something else on her mind.

'What's bothering you?' I asked.

'I don't know what you mean.'

'Come on, yes, you do. You're as nervous as a kitten.'

'Crap!' She smiled.

'Even that doesn't sound as authentic as it used to.'

'They gave you a rough time, didn't they?'

'The bruises don't show when I'm dressed. What's the matter with you?'

'I suppose it's because they wouldn't tell me a damned thing about what's behind all this. Go away and forget, they said.'

'Then do it. Head for the sunshine at Cannes. The peace and calm of the five-star Carlton and the healing solitude of the Boulevard Croisette.'

She sipped at what was left of her martini, eyeing me over the glass.

'Tell me,' she said, 'have you heard from your secretary, Miss Wilkins?'

I just stared at her.

'Have you?' she asked.

'Why on earth should I? Heard from her from where? What's Wilkins got to do with anything?'

'That's what I've been trying to make up my mind about, ever since you walked in here. You see, I was told to pass anything I got straight to them. You see . . . I only got it this morning. It was sent on with other mail from my London apartment. By the maid. Oh, hell . . . perhaps I oughtn't to—'

I took her glass from her and put it on a small table. Then I grabbed her arm.

'Try starting at the beginning. And get this straight. You can trust me. You won't be disobeying any order. I'm working for them.

They've given me just a handful of days to bring home the bacon. If I don't, then leaving aside my funeral arrangements, there's going to be a lot of other work for the undertaker.' I shook her arm. Putting it in words had brought a quick freeze in my stomach. 'I'm in a fix. If you've got anything that will help—let's hear it.'

She got up, retrieved her glass, sipped, then walked away from me and stared at a Corot reproduction on the wall. Without looking at me, she said, 'I'll give you a cheque for the bracelet.'

'I want more than that from you. If I have to squeeze it from you. Come on now."

Turning, her face worried, she said, 'They were most emphatic about anything I got going straight to them.'

'You're scared of them. I don't blame you. They scare me. But if you know anything it ought to come to me first. Hell, I'm the one who has been turned loose to do their work for them. Now tell me what all this is about Wilkins.'

She came back, stood above me, and took the plunge. 'I've had a letter from her,' she said.

I just looked at her.

Then I heard myself say, 'You've had a what?'

'A letter. It's on the desk over there. I was just going to send it off to them.'

I got up, and as I walked to the desk, she said, 'I got it this morning forwarded with the rest of my mail.'

I went to the desk. There was an opened envelope lying on it. As I picked it up, I heard Gloriana pouring herself another drink behind me.

It was a long envelope, foolscap size, addressed to her and marked *Confidential,* and it had a fancy Spanish stamp on it. Inside were two sheets of paper. One was ordinary cheap letter paper, and the other was a large piece of brown wrapping paper, torn off rough around two edges. I tackled the brown paper first, carrying it to the light of a table lamp. On it was written in block capitals:

TO WHOEVER FINDS THIS—

YOU WILL GET FIFTY POUNDS—8500 PESETAS —IF YOU SEND THIS LETTER TO MRS J. STANKOWSKI, EATON HOUSE, UPPER GROSVENOR STREET, LONDON, ENGLAND.

YOU MUST TELL HER EXACTLY HOW AND WHERE YOU FOUND IT AND WHEN.
MRS STANKOWSKI: WHEN YOU RECEIVE THIS AND ITS COVERING LETTER PLEASE GET IN TOUCH WITH MR CARVER. I AM DOING THE SAME THING IN BEER BOTTLES FOR HIM.

WE ARE NOT NOW ALLOWED OUTSIDE, BUT THIS HOUSE IS ISOLATED AND NEAR THE SEA, EITHER SPAIN OR ONE OF THE SPANISH ISLANDS. B.D. IS HERE. TREATED WELL. I SEE ONLY A MAN CALLED PAULET AND A WOMAN —THERESE.

TO WHOEVER FINDS THIS I SAY THIS IS NOT A JOKE. IT IS A VERY SERIOUS MATTER AND YOU WILL GET FIFTY POUNDS IF YOU SEND THIS TO MRS STANKOWSKI.

It was signed, in her ordinary hand—Hilda Wilkins.

The other letter, written in rather a schoolboyish hand, was also in English, and the address at the head was 7 Paseo Maritimo, San Antonio Abad, Ibiza, Islas de Baleares.

Dear Lady,

Very much I hope this no joke because I can be very useful for fifty pounds but would like it in the pesetas. I am student but work evenings in the San Antonio supermarket, chiefly washing bottles and opening crates. This letter I almost do not see, but am curious when I do. It is in a beer bottle, a large one, in two dozen returned for the consignment. Only we take back the bottles which are from us and they are for beer, mineral acqua and wines. It is good I find it because I am study the English language because there is so much tourism here and should hope one day to be in the hotel trade, not as waiter, but at the reception, perhaps rising to manager. So I hope this is serious about the fifty pounds (8500 pts). This I find yesterdays ago at 1800 hrs. Also, I find same kind of letter for Mr Carver and write him, also in London. This way, perhaps, it is permitted I get 17,000 pesetas?

        Your obedient servant, esteemed lady,
José Bonifaz.

The date on the letter was four days old.

I sat back and lit a cigarette. Gloriana came and put a fresh martini alongside me but said nothing. She was still probably wondering whether she had done the right thing. I was way past worrying about that. I had a nice warm feeling about Wilkins. What a girl. I could see her. Wilkins cooped up a prisoner. That was enough to make her mad anyway. She'd be in a filthy temper, but that wouldn't stop her thinking and scheming. It would only put an edge on her brain. It would be hot and the prisoners would be supplied with beer. Big fat brown bottles that when empty would be cleared away, and finally carted back to the supermarket for a fresh supply; big, fat, empty beer bottles going back so that the *consigne* could be allowed on them. And they'd be brown bottles. Wilkins had used brown paper so that it wouldn't show up when Paulet or Thérèse collected them. Oh, yes, she was my girl, all right. Tough, capable, bad-tempered Wilkins who never let anything in life get on top of her but a cold. Block letters to make her letter easy to read for a foreigner. And no wonder José Bonifaz preferred to be paid in pesetas—they would come to more than fifty pounds. . . . The other letter from Bonifaz to me was probably on my desk in London now. Since it would be marked 'Confidential' Mrs Burtenshaw would not have opened it. Everyone, Manston, Sutcliffe and myself, working from the outside in, and suddenly Wilkins coming up trumps, working from the inside out.

Gloriana sat on the arm of my chair, and said, 'Does it help?'

'It's going to. It's got to.'

She gave me a quizzical look. 'You didn't get a letter from Wilkins also? This José says he has written to you.'

'It's probably lying on my office desk unopened.'

'Are you going to let them know?'

'Them?'

'You know. The Treasury man.'

I stood up. 'To hell with them. I'm not going to shout for them until I really have something to shout for. Do you know Ibiza?'

'Yes.'

'San Antonio?'

'Yes. It's a nice place spoiled by tourists. Jan and I spent a week there once. Don't you think you ought to tell them? I mean, if it's all so serious?'

'Forget them.'

She looked doubtful but she kept at it.

'Is this Miss Wilkins being kept there . . . you know, against her wishes?'

'Yes.'

'And who's B.D.?'

I put my hands on her shoulders and looked straight into her blue eyes. 'Look, I don't want you to ask questions. The less you know, the better for you.'

'You're not going to keep me out of it—are you forgetting my brother is probably there, in danger?'

'You don't care a damn for your brother.'

'Not for some of the things he's done. But I do care for him as a brother.'

I shook my head. 'I don't want you mixed up in this. They've told you to go away and forget it all. Do that.'

She shook her head. 'You ought to tell them if it's so serious.'

'I'm going to—in good time. But first I want a chat with José Bonifaz, and I want to find out if there's a Bar Tristan in San Antonio. Is there?'

'I wouldn't know.'

I said, 'I'll keep these letters. You forget about them. And if I can possibly do anything about your brother I will.' I put the letters in my pocket. 'You've never received them. Your conscience is clear.'

'And you're going to Ibiza?'

'As soon as I can get a flight. No hope today. But I ought to get off tomorrow.'

I went up to her and gave her a light kiss on the cheek.

'Don't worry. You're doing the right thing. As soon as I have any positive information I'll let the right people know about it.'

If I told them too soon I knew what might happen. Somebody might try to put a stopper on it. The P.M. might not want to take any risks with his son. But if I wanted Wilkins back I had to take risks. By shouting for Manston now there was too much chance of some high-level decision blocking any further action.

I began to move to the door.

Gloriana said, 'Don't forget the cheque.'

'What cheque?'

'For that mercenary snake-charmer of yours. Don't you want an excuse to go and see her again before you take off tomorrow?'

'Well . . . I suppose it will help fill in time. I'll give it to her this evening.'

She grinned at me, raised a hand to touch her red-gold hair, and said, 'Just try and keep things on a purely business level, otherwise you'll spoil our beautiful friendship.'

She moved to the bureau to write the cheque. As she wrote she said, 'If you get any news about my brother, let me know. I'll be at Cannes. Not at the Carlton—but the Réserve Miramar. Jan and I always stayed there.'

In my business one should always listen carefully to what people say. Very carefully. I didn't know it then, but I was going to make this mistake twice. Listen, don't interrupt, and then do a lot of careful thinking. After all, I wasn't selling soap or potatoes—I was selling expertise. Now, hours later, seeing this same woman sitting opposite me, I had the tardy conviction that maybe I would have done better with soap and potatoes. She had her hands cocked up on her crossed legs, and the right hand held a gun—a gas gun; no noise, deadly effective within two yards and we were less than that apart. 'Life is very sweet, brother; who would wish to die?' And, to continue with the borrowing, it was no consolation to think that while 'every dog has his day, and mine has been a fine one', I was content for it all to end then and there. And all for the want of a little thoughtful listening.

But first there had been Olaf at the airport. I didn't tell him about Wilkins's letter. There would have been no holding him. We got bookings on a direct jet flight to Ibiza for early the next morning. Normally one had to go to Palma, Majorca, and make a change to a local flight to the island, but now the airfield on Ibiza had been lengthened and strengthened to take jets. That suited me; every hour saved could be important. Olaf stormed a bit about the mystery, but I told him that I would put him in the picture on the plane. Until then he was to go to our hotel and keep sober for the next day's trip.

'Just tell me there is some hope for us to get Hilda—then I'm content.'

'There is some hope. All you have to do is to stay in your room and don't drink more than half a bottle of rum.'

I had dinner with him, and left him about half past nine and went along to Letta's flat, deep in thought, but all along the wrong lines. I had decided that I would put a call through to Manston from the airport the next morning just before we took off. I wasn't going to run the risk of any of his Paris men blocking me from getting on that Caravelle.

I fixed myself a whisky and sat in a chair near the window and planned what I would do. It was simple. The moment I had established where V.V. was—and I was sure that Wilkins and Bill Dawson would be there—then I would call up the cavalry. I was really quite happy and pleased with myself, and full of admiration for Wilkins's cleverness. What the hell would I do without her if she ever got round to marrying Olaf?

And now here, sitting in a chair a few feet from me, was Gloriana Stankowski smiling, self-composed and dedicated to the business in hand . . . her right hand.

I'd left the apartment door unlocked and she had walked in and taken a seat opposite me. She was wearing a smart black tailor-made, with black velvet trimmings on cuffs and neck and a white silk blouse with an antique silver brooch of some Indian god with about six arms—Siva, probably, representing the destructive principle in life. She was always very studied in her dress. And she'd fooled me completely.

I said, 'I presume whatever that thing in your hand holds, you mean business with it?'

'Unfortunately, yes, but—'

'Please,' I interrupted, 'don't say you hope I won't take it personally.'

'I don't care how you take it. I'm only thinking of myself. I was given a promise that I wouldn't have to take part in active operations of this kind. The promise has been broken twice since Jan died. Now, because of Wilkins's letter and the fact that you are still alive when you should be dead, they say—'

'Saraband Two or Duchêne?'

'Does it matter?'

'Not really. I'm beginning to see light.'

J. was Jan, of course.

She shifted her hand a little, and said, 'I don't even know what chemical it contains. But it's effective. I've used it before. I had to do a course after I married Jan.'

She must have known damn well what was in the pistol. You don't take courses without being told. It was probably potassium cyanide. Maybe she just didn't want to confuse me with science. Maybe she just didn't want to think too much about what she was going to do.

I said, 'Was Jan very fond of your brother Martin?'

'Yes—oddly enough. Although Martin never knew the truth

behind it, they had this thing to kidnap Dawson fixed up over two years ago. There was no Pelegrina in the picture then. Jan saw it as a way of fixing up Martin with some money. They would do the kidnapping between them—it arose because Martin was so friendly with Dawson and had the opportunities—and then Jan's real lot, mine, too, of course by then, would take over. Martin would think the take-over genuine and would go off happy with his money. Unhappily Jan died."

'Martin had no idea that you and Jan worked for Saraband Two?'

'No. Nor does now. You like her? She gives me the creeps. In fact, I've wanted to get out of the whole thing since Jan's death, but I wasn't allowed. Anyway, you can see that you have to go. It's most important that this deal goes through on the terms already agreed.'

I moved one hand, just a fraction, hoping I might be allowed a last cigarette. She stopped me with a gesture of her hand and a shake of the head.

I said, 'But your brother, after Jan's death, still nursed the idea of kidnapping Dawson, said nothing to you about it—because right from the start he had never known that you were in on the original idea, or even that you and Jan were agents?'

'That's right. The whole thing was called off officially. But Martin went on nursing it. When he disappeared, stealing from me, I knew what he was after. I went down to his cottage—oh, I knew about that—and saw the letter from Dawson inviting him to Tripoli. So I was instructed to make a fuss with the insurance company, knowing you would be called in. They were very clever. They thought Martin would try and set it up some time on his own, so they made me transfer my insurance to the London Fraternal—just so that it would be you on the job.'

'Flattering.'

She shrugged her shoulders. 'All they wanted was for you to do their work—that's all they ever want. Somebody to do their work . . . somebody expendable or docile. I'm fed up with it. I only went in because Jan persuaded me, and with him it was fun. Nothing's been fun since. I really loved him.'

'You're breaking my heart.'

She gave a ghost of a smile. 'I like you. But you don't begin to compare with Jan. Nevertheless, I like you . . . I suppose that's why I'm talking so much, working myself up to it. The other two times I really disliked the people involved.'

I said, 'Why ever did you show me Wilkins's letter?'

'They said I was to make sure you hadn't received one and passed it on. I knew you wouldn't tell me if you had unless I showed you mine. And now—I've got to kill you.'

I said, 'Why not put that stupid thing away and have a drink? Maybe we could work something out? Why not?'

She shook her head.

'Jan's gone, but I still like living. If I disobeyed, I wouldn't live long.'

'Maybe we could fix something up. Look, other people are involved. Wilkins—and, could be, your brother. They might not let him off the hook. You wouldn't like to see him go under.'

Her face stiffened. 'I don't care what happens to him. He was worse to me than my father when I was young. He did some terrible things . . . a really terrible thing when I was fifteen, so terrible that nothing was ever right afterwards until I met Jan, and he was so sweet and understanding and then, thank the Lord, it all came right. . . .'

Believe it or not, there was the wet glint of a tear in one of her eyes. But it wasn't breaking my heart that her brother had messed about with her as a girl. I wanted to get out of this room alive. Wanted to—but how? One move from me and that thing in her hand would go off in my face, and that would be the end of me and Wilkins. I cursed myself then for not telling Olaf about the letter. At least he could have carried on. Thank God, she didn't know about Olaf or she would be leaving here to finish him off in his rum-sodden sleep at the hotel.

She stood up suddenly and stepped sideways to the window.

'I'm sorry,' she said contritely, and she stretched her right arm out, taking aim, an awkward yet very feminine movement that possesses them all when they aim a gun or shape up to throw a ball. If there had been bullets in the gun I would have taken a chance on her aiming badly and missing me as I jumped for her. But this stuff would spray wide, enveloping me as I moved.

Her lips firmed up, there was still the glint of a tear in her cornflower blue eyes, and she was all set to kill me. Vaguely, for there is no controlling the mind at such moments, I wondered who the other two had been, wondered why I hadn't paid more attention to Miggs once telling me that her husband had been as bent as a bedspring, and wondered why I'd been so dumb as to miss that J. could have stood for Jan.

Vaguely, too, I thought I ought to say something, something significant to haunt her for the rest of her life, some last, dying words; Anaxagoras, the old schoolmaster-philosopher saying, 'Give the boys a holiday'; Rabelais with his 'Let down the curtain, the farce is over'.

Well, the curtain had something to do with it. From high above her head at that moment came the faint jingle of brass curtain rings. I glanced up and saw, too, the faint movement of her head following mine. Lilith was up there still, from this morning, and finally bored with sulking. I saw the slow movement of her grey-silver coils and then she dropped in the lazy, clumsy Siamese cat way, aiming for the chair below.

She missed it, struck Gloriana on the shoulder, and knocked her back into the chair, the twelve-foot length of the python sprawling over her like a hose pipe. Gloriana screamed, then kicked and beat at the snake with her arms and legs. Suddenly Lilith wasn't sulking and bored; she was irritated, nervous and angry at the treatment, and with smooth swiftness the coils went round an arm, the flat axe-shaped head weaved upwards and, before I could do anything, the long length of her body was coiling and constricting around Gloriana's neck. If she had stayed still, fought down her panic, Lilith would have eased up, lost her fear at the threshing movement of Gloriana, and slid away.

I ran to the sideboard and picked up a bottle for a weapon and charged back to the sprawling mass of woman and snake in the chair, but Gloriana's right hand came up, holding the spray gun, and it was pointed at me. I backed off, and then saw that it had only momentarily been aimed at me. She was choking and breathing hard, trying to locate Lilith's head. She grabbed at it with her left hand and brought the right round but as she fired—a long, soft hiss of sound—the python's head jerked, forcing her hand aside and I saw the quick spread of vapour envelop the tousled red-gold hair and obscure her face.

They went, both of them, woman and snake, within three seconds, collapsing, both of them, into the chair, and perhaps for another five seconds there was a slow dying ripple of movement along the length of Lilith's coils, but no movement from Gloriana. She lay there with her blue eyes seeing nothing.

I got a taxi and went to Letta's club and met her. I took her back to my hotel and got a room for her. She wanted more explanations than I was prepared to give but in the end—knowing about Gloriana lying dead in her apartment —agreed not to go back until Manston got in touch with her at the hotel. Manston had people in Paris who would clear up the situation smoothly and without publicity.

CHAPTER 12

Trio in a Flat

I told Olaf the full story on the plane—and then it took me an hour to convince him that the best way for him to help Wilkins was to stand by at Ibiza airport as a contact for Manston when he arrived.

His parting words to me were, 'You make a mess of this, Mr Carver, and I break your neck. Hilda is the world to me.'

I took a taxi from the airport to San Antonio. It was about a twenty-mile drive from the airport. It was hot with the promise of real baking summer days to come. Old ladies in black sat under the olive trees, knitting, and keeping an eye on their goats and sheep. The earth had that dry, reddish colour and was the kind that the wind breaks down to fine dust and spreads over everything. The hills were green with scrub and, here and there, a pair of buzzards circled high in some air current over the crests. I didn't look at the scenery much. I kept telling myself that what I was doing was right. I had to get more definite information. I wanted to have enough information to be sure that Manston would have to take action on it. Bill Dawson was going to be returned anyway. But I wanted Wilkins back.

San Antonio was spread around the shores of a wide lagoon on the north-west of the island. One side was packed with new hotels for the tourist trade, and the other side held the old town, sloping gently uphill from the waterfront, a maze of narrow alleys and streets. It was all pink and white and ochre, and fast being spoiled and modernized. Buildings were going up everywhere, and every other shop was a tourist trap—postcards, beach hats, sandals, sunglasses, pottery and trashy jewellery. It was a miniature Brighton or Blackpool under a hot sun. Every holiday resort in Europe was getting to look more and more alike, a babel with a twenty-four-hour developing service, fish-and-chips and beefsteak and middle-aged mums wearing shorts or holiday outfits that they wouldn't have dared to sport at home. Well, good for them.

The taxi took me into the town, up the hillside through a maze of crowded little streets, and finally dropped me at the end of the Paseo Maritimo. It was a narrow passageway running parallel to the hillside. Number 7 was wedged in between a butcher's shop and a carpenter's workshop. An old man in faded blue shirt and trousers, barefooted, was sitting on the doorstep contemplating his dirty toes.

I said, '*Por favor, José Bonifaz?*' That practically exhausted my Spanish.

He jerked his thumb over his shoulder at the hallway and stairs behind him. I went into a gloom that smelled of frying fish and tobacco smoke. At the top of the first flight of stairs a small girl was sitting, cuddling a doll and crooning to it. I gave her a big smile and repeated my Spanish. She got up, still crooning, and went along the landing to one of three doors and knocked on it for me. I heard a voice say something inside and I went in.

José Bonifaz may have been a student but he certainly wasn't studying. The place, I realized now, was some sort of pension. This was a bed-sitting room. There was a table, crowded with books, under a small window, a chair with an opened can of peaches on it, a wardrobe with a cracked mirror front, and an iron bed with José Bonifaz on it. He was reading an English paperback with a lurid cover and, although it was long past midday, was still wearing pyjamas, the jacket open to show a thin chest as brown as a berry from the sun. His hair was as black as coal and needed cutting, his eyes were almost as dark and were the twitchy kind, never still for a moment in their sockets. He had a thin, birdy little face with a tiny tuft of baby beard right on the end of his chin. My first sight of him didn't warm me to him.

He rolled slowly off the bed to a sitting position and said, 'Senhor?' Then before I could answer, he called something in Spanish to the small girl who was standing in the open door behind me. She answered. He put out his tongue and she retreated, leaving the door open. I shut the door with my foot and said, 'I'm from Mrs Stankowski.'

He didn't get it at first. He just looked at me, puzzled.

'Mrs Stankowski,' I said. 'You wrote to her sending the letter you found in a beer bottle.' I put my hand in my pocket and brought out a pile of Spanish notes and tossed them to him. I'd got them at the airport exchange bureau.

He caught them and the dark eyes flickered with sudden interest

and understanding. He sat there, staring at the notes as though
they had just fallen out of the blue into his hands, which in a way
they had, and I knew that he was having a struggle not to start
counting them. Some lingering trace of Spanish courtesy made him
decide against it.

He said slowly, 'But it is unbelievable. I think it all a joke.'

'It's no joke,' I said. 'Apart from the one for Mr Carver—have
you found any other letters like it since?'

He stood up. 'No, sir.' He looked at me and then at the notes in
his hands and shook his head.

'You can count them later. Tell me, would you have any idea
who had returned the beer bottles?'

'No, sir. I am not in the shop when they come in. Only the
evenings I am working to wash them.'

It looked as though I wasn't going to get much from him.

I said, 'Is there a Bar Tristan in this town?''

He sat down on the bed, put the notes at his side and then looked
at me, cocking his head like a thrush listening for a worm, and it
was a good ten seconds before he said, 'Yes, sir.'

I thought it was a bit too long for such a simple answer.

'Where?'

'It is around the corner from the supermarket. I shall show you.'

He began to fish under the bed for his shoes. When he came up
with them he said, 'You stay somewhere in this town, senhor?'

I didn't like that. I was the one who had come to ask questions,
and I didn't think he was just making polite conversation. José
Bonifaz had something on his mind.

I said, 'We'll leave that for a bit. Tell me—have you mentioned
this letter business to anyone else? Your mother or father, for
instance.'

'No, sir. I live alone here. They are out in the country. A farm,
you understand? I am here for my studies and to work.'

'What about your friends? You tell them?'

'No, sir.'

'Sure?'

'Yes, sir.' He stood up and wiggled his feet into his loose sandals.
'If you like I show you the Bar Tristan now.'

I moved a little nearer him, and I could see that he was nervous
about something. His eyes were flicking as though they were full of
grit.

I said, 'You usually walk around the town in your pyjamas?'

He looked down at his pyjama trousers and was genuinely surprised. Then he gave a nervous laugh and began to move towards the wardrobe.

I put a hand on his shoulder and stopped him.

'Tell me,' I said, 'who have you talked about it to?'

'But senhor—'

'No buts, José—this is a serious matter. You have talked to someone, haven't you?'

He drew away from me. 'No, sir. Not me. I write to Mrs Stankowski and Mr Carver and I say nothing to anyone.'

For all I knew I could be on a wrong tack, but I had to take a chance on it. Something really was worrying José.

I said, 'You ever been in trouble with the police, José?'

'No, sir.' It was quite definite.

'You might be if you don't tell me the truth. This is a serious matter. After I've finished here I am going to the police. Once they know about it it won't be good for you if you haven't told the truth.'

I had him hooked and wriggling. Getting mixed up with the police had his black eyes blinking fast and his birdy head bobbing about with apprehension.

'You have talked to someone, haven't you?'

'No, sir. Not me. That is . . . well, someone talked to me.' Then cupidity came in with a rush. 'If I say, it is still mine, the pesetas?'

'If you say, you might get some more. As much, for instance, as anyone else has promised you.'

The relief on his face was like sunrise.

He ran the edge of his tongue round his lips and said, 'He say that I get five thousand pesetas.'

'Who did?'

'This man. He comes to the supermarket one evening, two-three days ago and ask me if I find anything in beer bottles. I tell him about the letters. I get five thousand pesetas if I let him know if anyone comes to talk about it. He was here again yesterday to see if I hear something.'

'Who was he? Did he give a name?'

I could see what had happened. Some time—wherever Wilkins was being held—Thérèse or Paulet had discovered one of her letters in a bottle. She would never have been content with writing two. It was common sense to run a check at the supermarket to see if any previous letters had got through. At the moment, now that they knew about the letters, they could be very worried—maybe even thinking of moving on. The Stankowski one they could discount, but not mine altogether.

'He is a young man called Mimo. Just Mimo. Five thousand pesetas he promised to let him know—'

'How were you to let him know?' My dislike for José was thickening. He worried too much about pesetas.

'At midday always he is in the Bar Tristan. But any other time, if anyone comes enquiring I let him know by going to his flat or phoning—'

'Where's the flat? Here, in San Antonio?'

'Yes. I shall show you, no?''

'No—just give me the address and tell me how to get there.'

He did, explaining that it was only a few minutes walk away. I didn't think that Duchêne would risk holding Dawson and Wilkins in a town flat. They were probably out in the country somewhere. Mimo would be the anchor man at the town end. I couldn't wait to have a chat with Mimo and I was glad that I had the 9 mm Browning in my pocket.

José said, 'What about the pesetas, senhor?'

'You'll get them—just so long as you keep your mouth shut. You haven't seen me. Is that clear?'

'Yes, sir. But you come back with the pesetas. This other man I don't like. His promises I don't trust. For that I tell you all this gladly.'

If it were just a question of money sense, the boy would go far. 'Somebody will be back,' I said.

I turned and went and he was counting the wad of notes before I reached the door.

The small girl was still crooning over her doll on the stairs. I gave her a friendly pat on the head, happy at the thought of seeing Mimo, hoping that this was the break I wanted to lead me to Dawson and Wilkins. The old man was still sitting on the doorstep, but he didn't get a pat. After the gloom of the house the sunlight hit me like a photo-flash and I damned nearly tripped over him.

I went up the street, blinking like an owl. Flat six, Casa Alcina, Mimo. For a while I wondered if I ought to go and get Olaf to help me. Then I decided against it. They might be pulling out fast, at this moment even. They must have had a bad moment when they found out about the letters. Suddenly, the cold thought hit me that they might have done something about Wilkins there and then. I pushed it from my mind.

Casa Alcina was in a small square on the hill at the north end of the town. The square was like so many squares in booming Mediterranean towns, new apartment blocks were going up and old houses were coming down and the air was gritty with cement and plaster dust. Casa Alcina was an old block, probably due to come down soon. There were a couple of small vans parked outside. The hallway was bare of any furnishing, and there was an ancient self-service lift that creaked upwards, protesting. I got out on a small stone landing which had two doors. One was half open to show a collection of buckets and brooms. The other door was shut. The number '6' was painted on it in white. I took out the Browning and listened against the door. There was no sound from inside. It was getting on for three o'clock. Mimo would not be in the Bar Tristan. He might be having a quiet siesta; though I didn't see Mimo as the siesta type. I put my fingers on the door handle and tried it gently. The door was unlocked.

I went in quietly, slipping round the door, gun and shoulder first.

It was a big room, with wide windows on the far side that opened to a narrow, railed balcony. There was a big settee against one wall, a couple of armchairs, and a low table against another wall with glasses and bottles on it. An open door to the side of the table showed a small corridor with two doors opening off it, probably bedrooms. The air was thick with tobacco smoke and there was another smell, too, familiar to me, mixed up with it. And the reason for the other smell was clear before my eyes.

I just stood inside the door and stared. It wasn't the kind of scene you want to walk into more than once in your life. Pelegrina was lying on the settee in his shirt and trousers and his big head was lolling awkwardly towards me. There was a bullet wound just above his right temple. Never again in his life would he try and touch his daughter for money. On the floor, a little way from the settee, was Mimo. He was lying flat on his face and I couldn't see any mark on him. But blood had seeped on to the polished boards near his right shoulder and from the way he lay I knew that he would never whistle 'Winchester Cathedral' happily to himself again.

Sitting in an armchair by the low table was Freeman. He was wearing a grey linen suit. He had his legs crossed and was resting his arms on them and supporting his head in the pose of Rodin's 'The Thinker'. He was thinking too. So absorbed was he that he took no notice of me. A cigarette burned in the corner of his mouth and there was an ashtray full of stubs on the arm of the chair. On the floor at his feet lay an automatic pistol fitted with a silencer.

Keeping him covered I pushed the door shut behind me. The noise made him look round. He stared at me blankly. Then he frowned, ran his hand through his brown hair and shook his head. All the colour had gone from his tanned face and he looked about ten years older.

I said, 'Just sit where you are.'

I crossed the room and picked up the automatic pistol from the floor. It was a .22 Star, made in Spain. Freeman made no move to stir from his chair. But his head followed me round, the brown eyes dull under their shaggy brows. I felt sorry for him, but I felt sorrier for poor old Pelegrina. From the thin black cord round his neck I saw his monocle dangling over the side of the settee. I found a bottle of gin, poured a fat slug into a glass, and took it to Freeman. He took it into his hands but didn't drink. Clearly he was in a state of shock and had been for some time. He was a dreamer all right, but this time he had dreamed himself into a nightmare. He and Pelegrina, a couple of ambitious incompetents, who between them had dreamed up a lot of trouble for a lot of people. When something went wrong, they went to pieces. Pelegrina had gone for good. I started to try and put Freeman together again.

'Is there anyone else in this flat?'

He shook his head. He raised the glass and drank, shivered against the raw spirit and then fetched a big sigh.

'When did it happen?' I asked.

I could see him pulling himself together. He wasn't alone now. He had company. Even sympathy. Perhaps a shoulder to cry on. In trouble, that's what his kind always needed.

'When?' I repeated.

'About an hour ago . . . that bastard . . .' he broke off, nodding at Mimo.

I began to take him along gently.

'Is this where you've been hiding up all the time?'

'Yes.'

'Where are the others, Dawson and Wilkins?'

He straightened up, stubbed out his cigarette and began to fiddle for another in a crumpled packet.

'I don't know. Somewhere out in the country. Mimo knew, but we didn't. God, this is a mess. What am I to do?'

Good form. He was coming back fast enough to start thinking about himself.

'We'll fix that later. What happened here?'

He looked at me. 'You think you can fix something?'

I held down my anger. Some people! José with his mind only on pesetas. And now Freeman full of pity for himself and wanting an out.

'Could be,' I said. 'But what happened?'

'It was all so bloody fast. Leon and I were sitting here. We haven't been out much . . . not together ever. We were waiting for Mimo to come back.'

'From the Bar Tristan?'

'No, no—from wherever they are. He's got a little van, takes supplies out. There'd been some talk of our moving on—'

'Just you and Pelegrina?'

'Yes.' He finished what was left of the gin. I went and sat on the edge of the other armchair. 'They were fixing us with passports and making all the final credit arrangements for the rest of our money. Then this swine walks in. Grinning, he was. The bastard, grinning. And he let Pelegrina have it without a word, and then he turned on me. I was sitting here. He just stood there and grinned. I couldn't move and he just grinned and took his time and then he fired. By some damned miracle he missed me. Right by my cheek and that made me jump. I went for him, full length for his legs, and I got the swine. . . . I don't know what happened then. We were all over the place. . . . I never did get the gun from him but I got my hand on it, over his, and then suddenly it went off and he flopped out . . . like he is now. Hell, what a mess! What a terrible mess!'

I said, 'You were both fools ever to think they'd let you off the hook on this kind of deal. The only reason they didn't finish you off at the Villa La Sunata was that it would have caused publicity and that they don't want. But now they're really worried and have to move fast. They don't want you around any longer.'

"But they paid me some money and let me write to Jane.'

'Of course they did. That was to keep you sweet, suspecting nothing until they were ready to deal with you. Do you think ten thousand pounds meant anything to them? How often did Mimo go out to that place?'

'Every other day. Look, what am I going to do? It's lucky no one heard the rumpus up here. Poor old Leon . . . God . . . But what am I going to do? I haven't got a passport or any money and I—'

'Can you walk?'

He looked at me blankly.

'What do you mean?'

'Find yourself a taxi and go to Ibiza airport. In the bar there you'll find a big Swede—Olaf. Tell him the score and then do exactly as he says. I'll be back there later. Is there a woman or anyone who comes in to clean this place?'

'No.'

'Then leave the door-key. Go on, get moving, the fresh air will do you good.'

He stood up, took a couple of weak steps as though he had been in bed for a month and then stopped. 'You really think something can be fixed up for me?'

I was angry then. 'Look, you started all this. A lot of nasty things have happened. And a lot more could happen. Pelegrina's dead. You're breathing and standing. Just be bloody well content with that for the moment.'

He went and I didn't feel sorry for him, but I knew that if I could I would fix something up for him, but the fixing would depend on Sutcliffe and very much on what happened about Dawson and Wilkins. If Wilkins didn't come out of this walking, then I wouldn't be caring a damn about fixing anyone up, least of all Freeman.

I turned Mimo over and went through his clothes. He had nothing on him that helped me . . . just money, cigarettes and a bunch of keys. I went through the three bedrooms. There was nothing there. Nothing anywhere.

I came back into the room and, although it was the wrong time of day, made myself a stiff drink and I sat in Freeman's chair and did a Rodin thinking act for myself. Mimo had a van outside, obviously one of the two which I had seen parked there. He made a trip every other day out into the country with supplies. Today he had come back with orders to polish off Freeman and Pelegrina and to abandon the flat. He wasn't going to go on living here with a couple of bodies. He would have turned the key on them and it might have been a week before they were discovered. It all might have worked, too, if he hadn't spent just a few seconds too long gloating over the pleasure of having Freeman at his mercy. Gloating had made his hand shake a little.

I wondered what other orders he had had. To return to the place in the country, or to take off on his own? Maybe even to run a final check on José Bonifaz to see whether anyone had turned up. They

weren't going to risk that lead in to them not being covered. José
had been given the promise of five thousand pesetas if the moment
anyone turned up he got in touch with Mimo either at the Bar
Tristan or the flat or . . . something cut into my thoughts sharply.
I stared at the dead Mimo, frowning. What was it? Something was
asking to be recognized. José had been told . . . José had to be able
to get on to Mimo the moment anyone turned up, either at the Bar
Tristan, or at the flat, or . . . what about if he were away on one
of his supply visits? Freeman or Pelegrina at the flat would be no
help. They probably hadn't known about the beer-bottle messages.
If Mimo were away a lot of valuable time could be lost. . . . Then
it came. I saw José standing in front of me, restless dark eyes full
of their peseta look . . . I stood up quickly. One should listen
carefully to what people say. Certainly in my profession. A quick,
impatient interruption could kill valuable information. I should
have learned that lesson by now.

I went back and checked the bedrooms, the kitchen, the bathroom
and then the big room. I didn't find what I was looking for.

I went out, locked the flat door and ran down the stairs. It was
quicker than the creaking old lift. With me I had Mimo's bunch of
keys. Only one van was standing outside now. It was a little grey
Fiat, covered in dust. I slipped into the driving seat and tried
Mimo's keys. The car ignition key on the ring fitted. I glanced in
the back. It was empty. There was nothing in the dash pockets
either.

I started the motor, fiddled with the gear, stalled the engine first
time, and then got away. I was full of impatience and went down
a one-way street against the traffic to a chorus of horns and shouts.
A few minutes later I pulled up outside the butcher's shop in the
Paseo Maritimo.

The old man was still sitting on the doorstep of No. 7, but he
had slid two feet to the right to catch the moving shade. The little
girl had gone from the top of the stairs. I hoped that José had not
gone from his room. Chasing José around San Antonio at this
moment would send up my blood pressure.

José was still there, knees up, reading on the bed. The can of
peaches, now empty, lay on its side by the bed. As I shut the door,
he sat up quickly and gave me a big, hungry smile.

'You bring the other pesetas, sir?'

'They're coming,' I said, "in a special gift wallet, red morocco leather with gold edges. Just repeat to me the instructions this man Mimo gave you.'

'But I tell you, senhor, already.'

'Tell me again. The moment anyone came here about the letters, what were you to do?'

'I was to let this man know. Either to find him at midday in the Bar Tristan, or other time at his flat.'

'But you said something about telephoning. I'm sure you did.'

'Yes, sir. This he told me yesterday. If he's not at flat I am to telephone.'

'Since there's no telephone in the flat, it must be somewhere else you had to telephone.'

He looked puzzled. 'Yes, I suppose so. I not think about it much. Just he gives me the number.'

'Fish it out.'

'Please?'"

'Let's have it, the number.'

He stood up and went to the book-crowded table by the window and came back with a piece of paper. On it was written *San José* 21.

'Where's San José?'

'It's a little town, village . . . about six miles from here, sir.'

'José,' I said, 'you get dressed and come down to the Post Office with me. I want the address that belongs to that telephone number. It'll be a farm or a villa of some kind. You get that, and then show me on the map where it is and we'll make it five thousand five hundred pesetas.'

He was at the wardrobe for his clothes almost before I had finished speaking.

I waited impatiently. But at the same time I was dead against impatience. I had almost missed this vital piece of information in my earlier impatience to get to Mimo's telephoneless flat.

I must say that, with the firm promise of pesetas behind him, José was a quick worker. I dropped him at the Post Office parked the car and went for a beer in a café a few doors down. Before I had finished it he was back. But before he was back I had done some hard worrying about Mimo and the telephone number. He hadn't given it to José until yesterday. That could have meant that up till then it was a number which Duchêne would not have wanted José to have, but would want him to have to cover a minimum period

of emergency. Once they knew the letters had gone off I was certain
they would take no risks, certain that they would immediately set
about changing their hiding place. It was my guess that now, with
all arrangements poised for a move, with Mimo coming back this
day to tidy up the Freeman-Pelegrina embarrassment, that the
number had been given to José so that he could send a direct
warning to them even while they were on the brink of a move.
Wilkins getting the letters out had really put them in a spot. And
now I was in a spot because the last thing I wanted was for them
to move until I could get Manston and company on to them.

José came back, armed with a map of the island. San José 21
was the number of the Villa Las Vedras, listed under the name of
Barja—that could have been a long-standing cover for Duchêne or
the name of an owner that they had rented the place from. José
knew the villa. It was in the south-west corner of the island, about
half a mile from the sea. It was about eight miles from San José
along a dirt road that ran through pine woods. Beyond the villa
was a headland and just off shore from it a group of conical-shaped
islands known as the Vedras, from which the villa took its name. I
made him draw me a sketch map of the road out and also of the
layout of the villa and the ground around it as far as he could
remember these. By the time this was done I knew what I was
going to do. I got some notepaper from the café and wrote a letter
to Olaf which José was to take to the airport. José was to tell Olaf
all he had told me. In the letter I gave Olaf Sutcliffe's unlisted
London number and told him to put a call through to him, if
Manston hadn't arrived, and give him the facts. He was also to get
in touch with the British Consul in Ibiza and pass him the code
word Python and any information he asked for which he could give.
He was also—though I didn't say anything about this to José—to
keep José with him. It was just possible that José, peseta-lust in his
heart, might take it into his head to phone the Villa Las Vedras
and make a little extra for himself. For myself, I said I was going
out to have a look at the villa and to keep an eye on things. At
least if they did move while I was around, I might have a chance
to follow them or even whip Wilkins, if not Dawson, away. All I
knew was that I had to get out there. I had a feeling that time was
running out fast. Wilkins's letter had helped me, but it had also,
for certain, decided Duchêne upon a fast move.

It didnt take me long to get to San José. The road went inland,
rising all the time until it reached the village that lay in a saddle

between two hills. It was the usual affair, a church, a bar, a few shops, a tourist place for buying pottery and iron work, and a lot of old men sitting around watching time and the traffic pass.

I had José's sketch map on the seat alongside me. Just beyond the village I found the turning off to the right. A main sign read Cabo Llentrisca—that was the headland José had mentioned—and nailed under it were the name boards of the various houses and farms along the route. One of them read—Villa Las Vedras.

It was a dirt road, built on a switchback pattern and, although I had to go slowly, I raised a great trail of dust behind me. I wasn't pleased about that. Once I was in sight of the house it might attract attention. Duchêne wasn't the kind not to have someone watching the road up to the villa. At first the road was bordered with little patches of maize, tomatoes, red fields of olive and almond trees, with here and there a peasant's single-floored house. After about a couple of miles it began to rise slowly, through pine woods and hillside covered in tall, dark-green scrub. Now and again there would be a turning to left or right with a house sign on it. After a while the turnings grew less frequent until finally the only sign left on the direct road was that of the Villa Las Vedras. I stopped and consulted José's map. A mile before the villa was reached he had said there was a small cottage. Half a mile after the cottage I would find a gate across the road, which marked the beginning of the Las Vedras property. From just beyond the cottage I meant to make the rest of the journey on foot. Anyone who wanted to come out of the villa had three routes. Either along this road, or out along the headland and down to the sea—or by an airlift. To a man like Duchêne any of these could be arranged. He had behind him any facility he liked to call on.

I found the cottage. It stood up off the road, door shut, windows boarded up. Behind it ran the telephone wire for the villa, strung out on short poles through the pine trees. I went about four hundred yards past it and then, as the ground began to rise sharply, I pulled off the road and ran the van into the cover of some scrub.

As I got out the air was full of the crazy fiddling of cicadas and the whine of a jet making a half-circle overhead to go in to land at Ibiza airport twenty miles away. I set out through the trees, keeping away from the road, but following the line of telegraph poles. After fifteen minutes I was running with sweat and half-deafened by cicadas. Twenty minutes after that I came panting up a hillside and out on to the edge of a small bluff that gave me a view which would have sent a tourist reaching for his Instamatic.

Ahead of me the ground sloped down gently through scrub, umbrella pine and low oaks to a long hollow into which snaked the dirt road to end at the Villa Las Vedras. It was a long, low white building with flat roofs that looked as though it might have been converted from an old farm or group of cottages. Beyond the villa the ground rose to the beginning of the Cabo Llentrisca, a great block of headland thrusting out to the sea. Beyond that was a wide sun-dazzle of sea with away to the right the sharp, green sugar-loaf shapes of the Vedras lying about a mile off shore. To the left, just a hazy outline on the horizon, was the island of Formentera. Further left, almost lost in the haze, I could see the houses clustered on the Citadel hill in Ibiza itself. I gave the view little attention. The villa held all my interest.

I worked around the side of the bluff for a while, keeping in the cover of the trees, then sat down, lit a cigarette to parch up my throat more, and studied it. There was a courtyard in front of the house and what looked like a wellhead to one side. Near this stood a large black saloon car. At a guess I thought it might be a Merc-edes. I wished I had provided myself with field glasses. I wished so even more a few moments later because two men—I couldn't identify them—came out of the house and got into the car. It swung round and came back along the dirt road. For a moment I panicked, wondering if Wilkins and Dawson (or just Dawson) were already in the car and this was the take-off. The road was away to my right. I got up and raced through the trees and came out just above the road in time to see the dust cloud trailing behind the car as it came slowly up the climb towards me. I threw myself down behind a myrtle bush.

The car came by me and I had a clear view of the two men in it. There was no one else. One was Paulet and the other was Duchêne. They went by me and I lay there and let their dust settle on me. At that moment I didn't realize how true that comment was to be. You should never let anybody's dust settle on you.

CHAPTER 13

The Door is Closed

Life is full of unpleasant surprises. Half of them, with a little concentrated thought and circumspection, need never arise. But some there is just no way of avoiding unless you are the absolute master of circumstance—which, unfortunately, no man is. Some people, of course, just ask for it because right from the start they are underequipped. Like Freeman and Pelegrina. It was all very well for Browning to preach that 'a man's reach should exceed his grasp, or what's a heaven for?' Most of us are short-armed and have weak fingers, and the minds to match. Some of us, to stir up the metaphors a bit, just see only the wood and not the trees. That was me.

But long before I came to give myself this homily, I had had another crisis of thought. Seeing Duchêne and Paulet motoring away down the road, chatting away and smoking, Duchêne still favouring his Swedish cigar jobs, gave the feeling that clearly they were not evacuating the villa . . . certainly not for some hours. Dawson, certainly, and, I prayed, Wilkins too, would be there. Well guarded. But I had a dirty feeling that Duchêne and Paulet might be on their way to San Antonio—maybe because they hadn't had any message from Mimo confirming he had wiped out Freeman and Pelegrina, or maybe alarmed because he had not returned. I had a lot of thoughts along these lines and none of them were very comforting. It all boiled down to what I should do. I could either go ahead to the villa and do a one-man rescuing job against whatever odds there were there, or I could go back and get Olaf and we could tackle it together, or I could go back and rely on Manston arriving before nightfall. He mightn't be able to get here himself but he would certainly have all the weight in the world to get Madrid on the phone and have the Spanish police in Ibiza and San Antonio under instructions in a very short time. In fact that was what he would have to do. Unless something went wrong between Sutcliffe and the Prime Minister and a change of policy was vetoed.

My interest was Wilkins, then Dawson. What was the best thing
to do? In the end I decided to go back, get Olaf and go to the
Spanish police. If they hadn't received instructions I hoped that,
with José as interpreter, and with a backing from the British Consul,
I could get some action within the next six hours. I still think it
was the right decision. In fact it was. But it didn't turn out like
that. That's what I mean about life being full of unpleasant
surprises. Seeing Paulet and Duchêne go by together, I
should—Browning again—have been 'stung by the splendour of a
sudden thought'. I was just stung.

I went back to the van, hidden in the scrub off the road, determined in my mind what to do. I got in, mopped my sweating face
with my handkerchief, and then half-twisted to get my hand in my
trouser pocket for Mimo's keys. The movement made me cock my
head to one side so that I could see, sitting in the shadowed back
of the van, François Paulet. He had a Colt.45 levelled at me, and
he was smiling.

I said, 'Hell!'

He reached over with his free hand and took my Browning from
the pocket of my jacket which I had slung over the back of the
spare seat. At that moment I saw Duchêne coming down through
the pines. He, too, was carrying a gun.

Sadness in his voice, but a twinkle in his eye, Paulet said, 'It is
a pity that one cannot think of everything, no?'

"It's the climate," I said. 'The brain goes soft with the heat.'

'The little cottage back along the road, *mon ami*, is not empty.
Peter Brown is there, and he reports anything that passes by telephone to the villa. *Ça vous explique tous?*'

'We all make our mistakes. But just tell me, is Wilkins up there
with Dawson?'

He nodded and grinned. "She is. She has been a lot of trouble.
Quelle femme! In our organization we could have made a great
operator of her—once her brain had been washed clear of moral
scruples."

At the window Duchêne said, 'Get out, and behave yourself."

I did as I was told. They marched me back through the trees to
the cottage. The black saloon was there. It was a Mercedes. Peter
Brown, in blue canvas trousers, a white shirt and silk scarf at his
neck, opened the back door for me.

'Mr Carver. Nice to see you again.'

'I wish you hadn't.'

'I'm sure you do.'

Duchêne said nothing. He got in alongside of me and Paulet drove. Within five minutes or so we were at the villa.

The front was covered with plumbago and bougainvillaea and there were large red earthenware urns full of geraniums and petunias, flourishing in a way that would have delighted my sister. I was greeted by Saraband Two. She stood on the low patio by the front door, wearing gardening gloves and holding a watering can. She had a wide-brimmed straw hat, a bit like the jobs they used to put on horses, a floppy blue dress and rope-soled alpagatas. Her pleasant aunty face warmed at the sight of me and she didn't look as though she had a worry in the world except greenfly and drought.

'Mr Carver,' she said, 'how nice. We thought you were dead.'

'That was the official bulletin.'

'It just proves,' she said, standing aside for me to pass, 'that you can't believe everything you read in newspapers. But I mean the second time.'

'Your girl Gloriana made a mess of it.'

'Indeed.'

I couldn't tell whether she was surprised or not.

They took me through a cool, stone-flagged passage into a wide, long room with a wooden floor and a wooden ceiling. Clearly it had been an old farmhouse. The furniture was mostly cane stuff for coolness and there were gay green, gold and red tiles let into the walls. Through the window, between a clump of cactus, I could see the beginning of the rise to the headland. I flopped into a chair. Duchêne shut the door. Paulet went to a sideboard and said, 'Beer?'

I nodded.

Aunt Saraband took off her gloves and her hat, patted her neat greyish hair tidy and then brought a cigarette box and offered it to me. I lit up and said nothing.

Paulet brought me a glass of beer. It was all very friendly and controlled and I wondered how the real business would be.

Aunt Saraband, who clearly outranked Duchêne, opened the proceedings.

'Would you like to tell the story freely or do we have to be unpleasant, Mr Carver?'

She said it with her back to me, as she fussed at a vase of some short-stemmed lily flowers on a table.

'I hate unpleasantness.'

'Good.'

'Monsieur Carvay is always reasonable,' said Paulet. Trust him to put in a good word for me.

Aunt Saraband turned and smiled. I was being a good nephew.

'I suppose it started with the beer bottles?'

'Yes.' I'd decided to stick to truth as far as I could. They could be told a lot of things which were no longer important.

She sat down, crossed her legs and pulled her dress down. There was no need, it was already only a foot from the ground. 'Your Miss Wilkins is a very fine and determined character. Too much so.'

'She's an excellent secretary too—and is very much missed at the office.'

'We shall miss her too. She has kept everyone on their toes here. She has twice tried to escape. That was after we found out about the beer bottles.'

'When I gave her exercise one day,' said Paulet, without rancour, 'she hit me with a large stone and ran. You know she is a fast runner. *Mon Dieu,* we had trouble with her. Since then she has no exercise.'

'Perhaps,' said Aunt Saraband, 'we should let Mr Carver get on with his story, step by step.'

Looking at the table with the flower vase, I said, 'Those are new to me, those flowers.'

'Sand lilies,' said Aunt Saraband. 'And don't change the subject. I presume you received the letter from José Bonifaz?'

'There's a lad who should go far. Show him a peseta—'

Paulet moved, with that swiftness some big men have, and the flat of his hand slammed across my face. I blinked and my eyes watered.

'Of course, there's nothing personal in that,' I said.

'No, *mon ami,*' he said, as he stood over me, and he slammed me again.

'Enough, François,' said Aunt Saraband. He went back to his chair. She looked speculatively at me for a moment or two and then said, 'Mr Carver, we haven't much time to bother about you or Miss Wilkins. I am sure you realize that we are not staying here. In fact we leave at six o'clock tomorrow morning. You, of course, and Miss Wilkins, will be left behind.'

'In no state to talk,' said Duchêne with his prim, irritable voice.

'I don't feel like talking now,' I said. 'But perhaps if you gave me a whisky—' I looked at my watch, it was half past six—'I might open up a bit.'

To my surprise Aunt Saraband nodded at Paulet and he got up to do the necessary. I saw the bottle. It was a cheap Spanish whisky fake. Surprisingly it didn't taste too bad, if you didn't think of it as whisky.

'What happened to Mimo?' asked Duchêne.

'José gave me his flat address. I walked in on a pretty tableau. Mimo standing over two dead bodies. He tried to make mine the third. I had to shoot him.'

Not on any of the three faces watching me was there a flicker of doubt, surprise or even disapproval. They just looked at me and showed nothing.

'I locked the door,' I said, 'and left them for the charlady to find sometime. I found this place, of course, from the telephone number that Mimo gave José. It cost me five thousand pesetas. I hope it's going to be worth it. And thinking it over, why the hell should I tell you anything? You're not going to do anything for me and Wilkins in return except put us out of circulation. I call that a no-deal.' I took a gulp of the whisky. It tasted worse the second time.

'We would make a deal gladly with you, Mr Carver,' said Duchêne, 'if you had anything to offer.'

'Haven't I?'

'What?' It was Aunt Saraband.

'You want to know how close on your heels Sutcliffe and his merry men are. For all you know he may be coming up the dirt track now—or he may know nothing.' I smiled, though it took a little effort with my sore cheek. 'You really are in a spot. You're going to have to worry through life until six o'clock tomorrow morning, nearly twelve hours. And don't try to tell me you could go now, because if you could you wouldn't be wasting time on me at this moment. You'd be packing. What are you doing—going over the cliffside at dawn to make a rendezvous at sea with some Baltic or Black Sea timber boat? Or perhaps a quick helicopter lift out to sea to meet the *Sveti* on her way back—detouring, of course—from Algiers? So, you've got twelve hours to pass, worrying. Either I've passed the word to Manston or I haven't. What am I offered to tell you the truth?'

I looked around at them. They looked back at me. They didn't have a thing to offer and they knew it. They weren't going to let Wilkins go and they weren't going to let me go.

Aunt Saraband stood up. 'You're quite right, Mr Carver. There is no offer. There is no need of one.'

'I could get the truth out of him,' said Paulet.

'It would take some time,' I said, 'and you would still have no guarantee that it was the truth.'

'We don't need any guarantee, Mr Carver,' said Aunt Saraband. 'In a situation like this the obvious line to take is that you have passed all or some of your information back. And—there's no point in denying it—since we cannot leave here until tomorrow, we must take the obvious precautions.'

'To stop anyone coming to the house?"

'Quite. We can hold out here for more than twelve hours if necessary, particularly as most of that time it will be dark. At first light we shall be lifted out by helicopter.' She spoke calmly, but underneath she had to be worried. The helicopter lift was all laid on and they clearly had no way of communication that would bring it earlier than first light. But her biggest worry was that if things did go wrong the really big boys of her service would be handing out painful demerit marks.

She moved to the door, paused and looked back at me. It was the sad, hurt look of an aunt whose nephew, loved and spoiled, had wounded her by stealing from her purse.

'We entered,' she said, 'into an honourable contract with your government. They have broken the contract. It could have very serious consequences, particularly for young Mr Dawson.'

'People,' I said, 'are always letting other people down. I gave up crying about it long ago. Anyway, a contract is only as honourable as the people who make it. In my book you and Sutcliffe are non-starters.'

She smiled then. 'Considering your position, you are remarkably provocative.'

'You've only got to shoot me to make an end of it.'

But I knew she wouldn't. Not yet. If a posse of tricorn-hatted Spanish police came roaring up in the night she wanted to have hostages, a couple of good cards in her hand to play with until the helicopter came. I knew it, and she knew that I knew it. Aunt Saraband was no fool.

'Put him up with the others,' she said, and she went out. Paulet and Duchêne moved towards me and formed a prisoner's escort.

They were in a long upstairs room, directly over, I judged, the room in which I had been interviewed. It had two camp beds in it, discreetly screened from one another by a couple of sheets hung on a wire. There was a table and a few odd chairs, and some gay rugs on the bare wood plank floor. Against the far wall was an old-fashioned wash-hand stand. There was a small window, set low in the wall, but no light came through it because it had been boarded up outside, and there were bars—their ends set in the stone—on the inside. The light in the room came from two oil lamps. The atmosphere was warm and thick.

Bill Dawson sat on the end of one bed. He was in shirt sleeves and trousers. He had a square, freckled face and a mouth that smiled easily, and he wore thick, horn-rimmed glasses. He might have been a first-class geologist, but it soon became clear that he was a young man who took people on trust too easily. He had to be to be where he was. The first thing he said, after the introductions, was, 'Have you got a British cigarette on you?'

I tossed him my packet. He was easily satisfied. Wilkins less so. She stood by the table, rusty hair a little untidy, a cold glint in her blue eyes, and marked the silence between us with an occasional sniff.

"You've caught another cold,' I said sympathetically.

'It's the same one,' she said, and fished in the pocket of her cardigan for a handkerchief.

'Hilda's like me,' said Dawson. "Once I get one it takes ages to go.'

I looked around. 'Do you think theyll bring another bed up for me?"

'It's the least of our problems,' said Wilkins. She sat down on a chair, and went on, 'I might have known that you would make a mess of things. We don't want you here. You're just another complication.'

'Nice welcome for a rescuing knight.'

'What Hilda means,' said Dawson, 'is that there's a motor scooter in their garage. But it only takes two. One pillion.'

'You've got it all fixed?' I really was surprised.

'Hilda,' said Dawson, 'has been wonderful.'

'She always is.' I turned to her and, believe me, I really was anxious to get back into her favour. 'Your beer-bottle message worked. But they got wise to it.'

'And naturally,' said Wilkins stiffly, 'you didn't go straight to a set of responsible people—but you had to come here on your own.'

'There were complications.'

'There always are with you.'

'You want to hear the form or just go on grumbling?'

'The form is all fixed,' said Dawson. 'By the way, what happened to old Freeman? They really killed him, did they? Such a nice chap.'

I said, 'Don't let's bother about Freeman. We have to think about us.'

'He was my friend,' said Dawson. 'We had some good times together.'

I made no comment.

Wilkins said, 'Where's Olaf?'

'At the airport. You're on Ibiza.'

'Does he know you're out here? I mean, does he know about this place?'

'By now, yes.'

She sighed. 'That means he'll come charging out and upset things more. You shouldn't have let him know. He might get hurt.'

I said, 'For two people in deep trouble, you're not exactly wild about being rescued, it seems.'

'We've got it all arranged,' said Dawson. 'We could have managed nicely on our own.'

'You've only got until six tomorrow morning—and then you'll be lifted out of here by helicopter. You will. Wilkins and I will stay.' I gave her a straight look. She sniffed. But she knew what I meant. She was too intelligent not to be way ahead of me all the time.

Dawson, taking a deep draw at his first British cigarette for days, said, 'We can get out of here the moment they go to bed.'

'They won't go to bed tonight. They're not sure whether they're going to have a police visit. They'll be on guard all night.'

'You see,' said Wilkins, 'how you've messed things up. We were going tonight.'

I sat down on a chair by the boarded window. I don't often feel chastened but I was now. A man works his fingers to the bone trying to set something up and when he's finished, or failed, he gets no thanks or sympathy.

'Perhaps,' I said, 'you would tell me how you propose to get out? I know I've got no standing, of course, but it would be nice to know that you might let me follow you and run along behind this motor scooter.'

'Just try and take this seriously,' said Wilkins primly.

'A wonderful girl,' said Dawson. 'She's been a tower of strength. This I say sincerely.'

'Reminds me of your old dad,' I said. 'But let's have the facts.'

'How is my father?' asked Dawson. 'How's he taking all this?'

A little exasperated now because there seemed no way of pinning these two down to a straight line of talk, I said, 'He's reacted as any father would, and also with true British phlegm. For your safe return, he's agreed—no publicity, mind you—to a highly one-sided exchange of political prisoners between London and Moscow.'

His eyes popped. 'You mean we're being held by the Russians? I thought it was just for money. Didn't you, Hilda?'

She shifted uncomfortably. 'No, I didn't,' she said. 'But I didn't see that there was any point in bothering you with my conclusions. You've had a bad enough time.'

Firmly, I said, 'Just tell me, for God's sake, how you propose to get out of here?'

'There is,' said Wilkins, 'no need to blaspheme.'

'It was Hilda's idea,' said Dawson. 'You see, when we first came here, they used to take us separately for exercise in the courtyard. Hilda saw this motor scooter in the garage, and she saw one of them use it once. The cars were no good because we guessed that they'd never leave the ignition keys in at night. So, one morning, Hilda hit the big French chap with a stone and ran.'

'It wasn't a very big stone,' said Wilkins.

'They chased after her,' said Dawson, 'but she got into the garage and shut herself in. It took them a little while to break down the door and get her out. That was clever of her, wasn't it? You see, they smashed up the bolts so that the door can't now be shut up at night. That means we can always get at the scooter.'   .

'Clever,' I said. And it was. I should have taken over the secretarial work long ago and let Wilkins do my job. 'But what good is access to the scooter out there if you can't get out of here?'

'Two birds with one stone,' said Dawson, beaming at Wilkins. 'You tell him, Hilda.'

'While I was in the garage,' said Wilkins, 'I took a pair of pliers from the work bench and hid them on me. They didn't search me when they brought me back here.'

I didn't ask her where she had hidden them on her because I didn't want more trouble from her. Instead, I said, 'He's right. You are wonderful. But don't forget I've been saying it for years.'

Dawson stood up, and pulled back one of the floor rugs. 'These boards, you see, are in short lengths and they're nailed to the rafter of the ceiling below. We've been working with the pliers for three days taking out the nails. All we have to do now is to lift out three boards and we can drop through into the room below.' He beamed at Wilkins and then at me. 'She thought of it all,' he said, replacing the rug.

At that moment the door opened and Paulet, gun in hand, came into the room, standing aside to let a woman with a tray pass him. I didn't have to be told that it was Thérèse. She was a neat, trim, dark-haired number of about forty, in a linen frock. She put the tray on the table, gave us a smile all round, held it a bit longer for me as she studied me and then said, '*Bon appétit*.'

She went out. Paulet gave us a nod and followed. The door was locked and bolted from the outside. I looked at the tray. There was a plate of cold meats and some salad stuff. I suddenly remembered that I had not eaten since early that morning and, instinctively, I said, 'Lord, am I hungry.'

Wilkins gave me a disapproving look.

The first part was easy. We waited until about half past four in the morning. In another hour it would begin to be light. During the night there had been a lot of movement and voices from the room below us. But now everything had been quiet for over an hour.

We pulled the rug back and Dawson and I between us carefully and quietly lifted out the first board. In our room we had put out the lamps so that no light would shine through into the room below. I put my head into the board space and looked down. The room below was in darkness.

We lifted out three more boards and then I went through, hanging by my hands and then dropping little more than a couple of feet to the floor below. Wilkins came next. I reached up and got her by the waist and eased her gently to the ground. Dawson followed.

We all three stood there in the darkness, listening.

There was no need for talk because we knew exactly what we were going to do. It was too risky to go out through the front of the house into the courtyard. We were going to climb out of the room window, circle around the house towards the headland and come down to the back of the garage. There was a longish slope down the entrance road from the garage until it started to rise towards the bluff where I had hidden. Dawson was to ride the scooter, Wilkins on the back, and free wheel away down the slope, not starting the engine until he was almost at the bottom. Once they were away I was going to take off into the scrub and pine woods and make my way back, staying clear of the road. But first of all I was going to climb one of the short telegraph poles and cut the line so that the party in the house could not get in touch with Peter Brown if he were still in the cottage on watch. Simple, straightforward, and it should have worked. Would have done with most people, even with someone like Aunt Saraband—if it had not been for the beer-bottle episode. They had slipped up on that one. Aunt Saraband and Duchêne never made the same kind of mistake twice. From that moment they had upped Wilkins's I.Q. rating to a level which would have made her president of Mensa for life.

I went towards the window, Wilkins and Dawson following. I was still four feet from it when two torches came on, pinning us where we stood.

Aunt Saraband's voice said quietly, 'Please don't move.'

For a moment I was tempted to ignore this and rush the window. But another voice, Paulet's, said, 'If you do, *mon ami*, Miss Wilkins will get the first shot.'

We stayed where we were. There was movement at the far end of the room, a match was struck, and suddenly the oil lamp flared. I saw that it was Duchêne lighting it. He turned away from the lamp after adjusting the wick and made a motion with his hand to us. 'Just come back into the centre of the room.'

We moved back, controlled by his hand which had a gun in it, shepherded, too, by the automatics that Aunt Saraband and Paulet held.

Aunt Saraband shook her head sadly at Wilkins.

'If we could have had you ten years ago, Miss Wilkins, and you'd been willing, we could have made you a great operator.'

I began to reach for my cigarettes.

'No, Mr Carver,' she went on, 'just keep your hands where we can see them.'

Paulet winked an eye at me over his big de Gaulle nose. 'You had a treasure there, Monsieur Carvay. Not until yesterday did it strike us. A woman, an ordinary woman, hits a man with a rock and runs . . . just runs.'

'But Miss Wilkins ran into the garage,' said Aunt Saraband. 'Why?'

'The answer comes,' said Paulet, 'when there is wood dust on the table there each morning, fallen from ceiling boards. Thérèse, you know, is good housewife and very observant. So.'

Duchêne, who had been standing by almost, I thought from his face, disapproving of this exchange, said sharply, 'I think I hear it.'

They were all silent, listening. Far away I thought I could hear the sound of an engine.

'If it is,' said Aunt Saraband, 'Peter will put on the car lights.'

The noise grew louder, and then unmistakable. The helicopter was coming, coming in at the first faint streak of morning light. Another day was beginning—badly. I looked at Wilkins. Her face was expressionless. I wondered what she was thinking about? Her father in Greenwich, the socks she would not darn any more? Olaf, wanting to marry her, and she reluctant to leave her father? I knew what I was thinking . . . not of a hundred lost opportunities, the small, but bright change of life . . . not of never again the amber circle of whisky in a glass and the comforting hiss of the first siphon squirt of the day . . . no, I was just wondering how the hell I could get something into my hands that I could sling at the oil lamp. How do you get something into your hands when you have to keep them still and in the open?

Outside the helicopter racket increased. It was overhead now, circling. Peter Brown would have the Mercedes' lights on to monitor the pilot down to the courtyard. There would be a fast take-off with Dawson and Aunt Saraband's party—and Wilkins and I would be left. Either here, in this room, or in the courtyard. No formalities, no bandage round the eyes, no last requests.

Of course, I'd made a mistake about Wilkins. She might have been thinking about her father and Olaf, but she was also thinking way above them, had to in the circumstances because the instinct for survival runs strong in all of us at such times, and in Wilkins probably stronger than most because it was backed by a natural obstinacy of character. She was to one side of me and a little ahead, a wing of rusty hair untidy over one ear, sensible old cardigan creased, sensible tweed skirt drooping a little unevenly to one side. To survive, risks had to be taken. Her hand came down sharply into the front pocket of her skirt. She whipped out the pliers she carried there and threw them awkwardly at the lamp.

She missed by a foot, but she hit the vase of sand lilies and the whole lot went crashing to the ground. Outside, the helicopter was down. The engine note had changed.

Aunt Saraband's face showed her anger.

'You really are a dangerous woman.'

Wilkins looked at me. 'I'm sorry,' she said.

'Never mind,' I said. 'You tried. It's a good thought to go out on.'

Dawson said, 'It's funny about women not being able to throw straight.' Then to Aunt Saraband he went on, 'Look—I know now you're not going to do anything to me. But do you really have to . . . well, do anything to these two? It doesn't serve any useful purpose and I'm sure they would keep the secret. Please . . . why do something so unnecessary?'

Duchêne said, 'It has been decided not by us. We have orders.'

Aunt Saraband said, 'François, you take him out. Duchêne and I will do what is necessary here.' She looked at Wilkins. 'I am sorry. Personally I consider it unnecessary. I would trust you both, but unfortunately my employers haven't the first-hand field knowledge of you that I have. To them you are just two people who could talk loosely and ruin this thing by creating publicity . . . bad publicity, for both sides.'

It was then that the oil lamp was shattered. Olaf did it. Though it was some time before the thing was sorted out in my mind because I was too busy going into action on the heels of a miracle.

There was the sound of a shot, the window glass crashed, and the oil lamp exploded in a brief flare of flame and then there was a grey gloom in the room, and the sound of a window being kicked in, frame shattered, as Olaf, a dark mountainous bulk, burst through.

I didn't wait to congratulate him. The edge of my right hand was already hitting out for the spot where I took Aunt Saraband's wrist to be. I got her inner elbow and heard the gun go to the floor. I heard Dawson shout, heard Olaf bellow, 'Hilda, this way!'

For a moment or two the room was a grey tangle of movements, noisy, with chairs going over and the sound of two shots. One of them fanned my neck and then I heard Duchêne roar, 'Stop shooting!' He was right. It was dangerous for both sides.

'I've got him!'

It was Paulet and briefly I saw him hurl himself at Olaf. Paulet, big, competent and dangerous. Not the kind of man I would want hurled on me. But he had met his match. Olaf stretched out his giant arms, embraced him, crushed him, spun him round, picked him up and threw him. Paulet hit the wall and dropped to the floor with a crash that shook the house.

I saw Olaf spin round and grab Wilkins. I kicked out at Aunt Saraband who was coming at me like a Kilkenny cat who was going to knock the English stuffing out of a London tom. I got her legs and she went down.

I picked up a gun from the floor and the next moment I was at the window with Dawson. We went through after Olaf and Wilkins in another minor explosion of glass and wood. Dawson fell and rolled over on the hard-baked ground. I jerked him up and we ran. I heard him sobbing and cursing to himself and he pulled back from me. I grabbed harder and kept him going. In the fall he had ricked his left ankle. Ahead of us in the growing dawn I saw Olaf running, pulling Wilkins along, heading up a small path that led to the headland.

As we crested the rise to the top of the headland plateau the sun began to lip the eastern edge of the sea away to our left. It was a good sunrise, as sunrises go, a fancy affair of orange and tangerine flame, with a high wash of slowly fading pearliness in the upper sky, and we had time to admire it because Dawson really had done something to his ankle. He could only just limp along.

Olaf said, 'We've got a mile and over to the end of the headland. Then a path to the beach. I've got a motorboat standing off.' He looked at Dawson. 'I carry you?'

Dawson shook his head.

'We've got to do something,' I said. 'Here comes the helicopter.'

It came up the wind, rising, crabbed around in a circle and found us. It came down to about two hundred feet and hung above us, the racket deafening.

Olaf fired a shot at it.

I said, 'Don't waste your shots.'

We made about two hundred yards as fast as we could with Dawson, the helicopter hanging over us. I couldn't see who was in it, but it was a Westland Whirlwind.

Wilkins looked back and said, 'They're coming.'

I looked round. Topping the headland crest now were Duchêne and Paulet and Peter Brown, running hard along the scrub-lined path towards us.

The path ahead of us twisted into a wide patch of scrub oak and pines, the trunks of the trees hidden some way up by a thick undergrowth of heath and myrtle. We were fifty yards into the trees when Dawson fell, pulling away from Olaf's great hand that held him.

'I carry him,' said Olaf. 'You cover us.'

He picked Dawson up and slung him over his big shoulders in a fireman's lift. I was puffed and blown. At the side of the path was a big notice on a pole. The best thing for me to do, I thought, was to get behind it and cover the path. I couldn't hold them up for long.

Ahead Olaf was trotting along slowly with Dawson. Wilkins stayed with me. 'Get going,' I said.

Overhead the helicopter clattered away like a crazy washing machine. She looked at me, tight-mouthed, eyes bright with anger at the indignity of it all. She shook her head.

'Have you got any matches on you?' she asked.

'No. A lighter. Don't tell me you're taking up smoking? Now get moving.'

She shook her head. Two hundred yards away I could see Paulet lumbering along.

'Look at the notice,' she said.

I did. It was Spanish and not much help to me. Something about *Cigarillos . . . Cuidado...*

'Lighter,' she insisted.

I fished in my pocket and gave it to her. She turned and ran along the path after Olaf and Dawson.

I got behind the notice and let off a warning shot at Paulet. I couldn't hit him at the range but I could stop his headlong rush. I did. He went off the path and I saw Duchêne and Peter Brown do the same behind him.

I fired another shot in their direction and then left the notice and sprinted up the path. As I did so the first acrid breath of smoke came wafting down on the wind to me. Then there was a spurt of flame ahead and just off the path. I got it then; the notice had been a fire warning.

I found Wilkins moving through the trees at right angles to the path, scrabbling up bunches of dried grass and scrub and lighting them from my lighter.

I didn't stop to tell her what a treasure she was. I was in there, grabbing tufts of last year's bracken and grass and helping to spread the line of flame. For a few moments the whole thing sulked and then suddenly there was a small whoof and the fire went away, racing and crackling down through the trees towards our pursuers.

On the path in the middle of the trees I saw Paulet suddenly stop. Then a great coil of smoke obscured him. A small pine suddenly went up like a Roman candle.

I swung round and made for Wilkins who was still spreading the line of fire.

'Enough,' I shouted, and grabbed her. We turned and ran, and the noise of the spreading fire behind us was music. If you really want a good blaze there is nothing like a sun-baked, scrub-and-pine-and-heath-packed Mediterranean headland ... a pyromaniac's dream. In a few minutes the whole headland behind us was ablaze, leaping flames and great clouds of smoke barring the way against pursuit. Two days later, I was told, it was still smouldering.

And that was that. Except for a few minor details.

Duchêne, Paulet and Peter Brown couldn't face it. But Aunt Saraband had a go. She was in the helicopter. It came down to fifty feet above us, and she hung out, gun in hand. I knew that now, knowing there was nothing to be saved of the grand design, she had to be full of old-maidish spite. She just wanted to hurt someone because she knew that when she reported back to Mr Semichastny she was going to be hurt.

She would have hurt someone, too, if it had not been for Freeman, coming fast up over the top of the cliff from the beach, hunting rifle in hand. He stopped and took a couple of pot shots. However bad he was at other things, he could shoot. One of the shots must have got the helicopter in a non-vulnerable spot. But it was enough. The pilot suddenly opted for discretion. The machine lifted, wheeled and circled away.

After that there was the beach path down to the sea, and waiting a few yards out a motorboat with José Bonifaz at the tiller.

There were a few high points after that. I remember particularly Manston's fury because he had arrived at the airport to find no one there. No Olaf, no Freeman, no José.

It was José's lust for pesetas, of course, linked with Olaf's rum-whipped impatience to come to grips with the people who were holding his precious Wilkins, that had left Manston and company high and dry, without a single shred of information to work on.

José's parents lived in a small fishing village called Purriog, up the coast from the airport. One could go by sea to the Villa Las Vedras and his father would gladly hire Olaf a motorboat, and, yes, a hunting rifle. Olaf didn't stop to count the cost. They were off, Freeman dragged with them.

'Charging in,' said Manston, 'like a bull in a china shop. They could have spoiled everything.'

'They didn't,' I said. 'Anyway, don't let's argue about the way it should or should not have been handled. A man in love can only do what at the moment he thinks is the right thing. And don't forget Wilkins's M.B.E. or O.B.E. or whatever it is.'

He didn't.

José, not caring what it had all been about, went happily back to San Antonio, loaded with pesetas. Spain will be hearing from him, I'm sure.

Freeman got a discreet pardon and was ordered to leave the country for good. I heard later that Jane Judd had joined him. Some women are gluttons for punishment.

There was never any publicity, of course.

But there was Sutcliffe in his London flat, mild-mannered but still disapproving of me. He handed me a letter from the Prime Minister which thanked me for my services, but didn't invite me down to Chequers for the weekend. Sutcliffe took the letter back and destroyed it.

I said, 'There's still the cheque for my services.'

'You'll get it.'

He pressed a wall switch and one of his modern paintings slid aside and on a twenty-one-inch screen I had a view of Paulet and Duchêne in the waiting room, shivering on the camp bed and looking miserable. They were the only two they had managed to pick up.

'No music?' I asked. 'No brass bands?'

'Wagner. They hate it. But the sound is switched off up here. I hate it too.'

I said, 'It's a pity Perkins turned out not to be a traitor. I'd like to see him down there.'

And then it was back to work—without Wilkins because she was still off with Olaf catching up on her holiday.

Some days later, going back to my flat, after a hard day repeatedly turning the basset hound off my desk chair, I found Mrs Meld hanging over the gate enjoying the summer evening.

'Nice evening, Mr Carver.'

'Splendid, Mrs Meld.'

'You look a bit baggy under the eyes these days.'

'I have worries at the office.'

'You got one waiting for you up in the flat.'

I went up and into the flat. As I stood at the door, a voice shrieked, 'Shut that bloody door! Shut that bloody door!'

It was Alfred in his cage on the table, a note from Miggs pinned to it: 'This bastard is losing me business, so back to you. M.'

Alfred carolled, 'Bloody! Bloody!'

I ignored him and went into the bedroom. Letta was lying on the bed reading *Vogue*.

I said, 'I thought you were in Athens?'

She smiled and said, 'I was. But now I've got two free weeks. If I stay here, though, you'll have to choose between me and that bird.'

I said, 'Friend of mine keeps a pub round the corner. He'll love him.'

'Good.'

She sat up, her dark hair taking the evening sun through the window in a hundred burnished points.

I said, 'Isn't it a bit early in the evening only to be wearing a copy of *Vogue*?'

She dropped it to the floor.

Outside, Alfred cried, 'Shut that bloody door!'

I did.

A Delivery of Furies

Contents

CHAPTER 1

I came in from the hard sunlight and paused for a moment on the edge of the great, cool pool of the hotel lobby. The pause was less for my eyes to settle to a new focus after the brilliance outside than for my mind to brace itself, without hurry, to the pleasure in this moment of coming back.

Dropping my battered leather suitcase to the tiles that spread away to the reception desk in great whorls of blue, yellow and green, I lit a cigarette slowly. Shadows passed across the gloom and, somewhere up in the roof, a great fan sucked soothingly at the air. Outside was the heat and the sunbite, the blare of horns and voices, the rattle of the trade winds in the palms, the smells of hot, dungy dust and the stale headiness of flowers and river mud; everything lush, everything bursting with life and growth and noise. . . .

I picked up my bag and went slowly across to the desk. *Hotel Polo Norte,* Barranquilla. That was the latest name for home. The clerk on the desk was new and from his face I could see that he didn't think much of me. I didn't blame him. I could see myself in the long mirror on the wall at the side of the desk. I looked like hell. My suit was water-stained and shrunk, making me look taller and leaner than I really was; a hard-looking, sun-burnt number whose brown hair needed cutting and whose chin bore a two days' growth of stubble. As I turned to the clerk I knew that he was preparing to say that there were no rooms.

'Señor?'

'Marchant.' Nodding at the pigeon holes behind the boy I added, 'Number 37.'

The frost went from his eyes. A black hand went up for the key which had rested in its slot now for three weeks. He passed it over and raised a hand to ring for a boy to take my case. As the bell pinged, he said in proud English:

'Very welcome back, señor.'

'Thank you. I want *La Prensa* and *El Nacional* for the last three days. And some soda and ice.'

The entrance to the bar was flanked by two lemon trees in large marble urns. The fruit, so symmetrically poised amongst the dark green leaves, glowed with a fine polish; the polish that was over everything in the place. This was another world from the one I had just left. The last bar I had been in had been a *cantina* five hundred miles south, with the Indian proprietor asleep on the dirt floor, chicken pecking round him, the counter sour-smelling and stained with *aguardiente,* and a radio pumping out a *paso doble* that lifted the tin roof. *My Sweet Love Returns* had been the name of the bar. It was a good name, a good thought.

I moved to the doorway. From a small group around a table at the far end of the room there came a little burst of a woman's laughter. She had her back to me. I paid no attention to the others, saw no one for a while but her. Her head moved with laughter and subdued lights ran across the heavy chestnut hair. She raised an arm and the movement had all the lithe grace that took her easily through the neon-lit, martini-watered jungle of hotel bars and restaurants. The man next to her had his arm along the back of her chair. His hand touched her shoulder, rested there a moment and then drew back. I gave myself the pleasure of imagining one good firm stroke with a machete that would take it off at the wrist.

I didn't go in, not looking as I was, not wanting to meet her in a crowd. At the lift, Felipe, the attendant, gave me a nod as though I had only gone out that morning.

As he closed the door, I said, 'The desk clerk is new. What happened to Fico?'

'Gone down to Puerto Colombia for better job in the *Pradomar.*'

'Any other changes?'

'No, señor. Except for new mosquito nets in all rooms. Shall I send a girl along for your things?' The old man's eyes went slowly over my battered linen suit. It had been small for me when I borrowed it. Water hadn't improved the fit.

'Don't bother, Felipe. It's going into the waste-paper basket.' I didn't offer it to him. Felipe had his pride. But I knew he would fish it out, clean it and sell it.

'You treat clothes very hard, señor.' He looked down with pride at the shining brass buttons on his white drill suit, at the sharp creases of the trouser lengths. 'This uniform belong to me for five years.'

'Maybe I should get a job in a lift.'

'Why not, señor? No troubles in a lift.'

It was an optimistic statement. There were troubles everywhere. The only thing that mattered was how you took them . . . thinking that, I knew I would have to be careful with Drea. Like all women she was inclined to fuss a bit when things went wrong.

The lift stopped with a sigh. The door slid back. Sunlight came through the green shutters at the end of the corridor, striping the carpet as I went along to my room.

My bag was in the room. In the bathroom, I stripped off and took a shower and then shaved, padding about the place naked, except for the bandage around the top of my right arm. The wound was a little sore still, but I couldn't be bothered to change the dressing. I put on clean pyjamas and a dressing-gown, adjusted the blinds at the window so that the room was shadowed, and then stretched out on the bed. The papers, the ice and the soda had come while I was showering. I reached out to the bedside table and filled a glass with ice and soda. The whiskey was in the cupboard by the door but I couldn't be bothered to get it. That was something I could take or leave at least, something I liked but didn't have to have. In fact, practically everything in my life was like that—except Drea. Without her when a thing was done, I could file it away into the folder marked *Experience*, strike a cash balance, sometimes red, sometimes black, and be left with the pleasure of anticipating the next thing. Happy-go-lucky. That was the way to be, committing yourself to no false stability.

Drea didn't like my way of life. There'd be trouble this time, for instance, not because the job had turned out profitless, but because of the wound in my arm. She worried about risks, about me. If she found out, I'd just have to sit tight and let her have time for her anger to blow over. We loved one another; but with Drea there was no question that *she loved me for the dangers I had passed*. Or because I was happy-go-lucky. Some other witchcraft held our love.

I lay there thinking first of her, and then, because of the echoes of Shakespeare in my mind, of my father, dead now, a parson . . . and always tolerant of the break I had made from everything which had been expected of me. A shilling for every time you could cap one of his quotations. Drea and my father, both, in their own ways, disapproving. . . . But both so close.

Two hours later the door opened. There was the small click of the lock, a rapid filtering of light from the corridor, and then gloom as the door closed. I lay in the shadows and said nothing. It was dusk outside now. The taxis were hooting as they climbed the hill from the port, and, distantly, came the thump of a stern paddler beating up the Magdalena river. Or it might have been my heart. Knowing that Drea was standing just inside the door, listening for the sound of my breathing, I was filled with a swift affection for the river. The first time I'd seen Drea—five years ago—had been on a river boat, a shabby old tub with tall twin smokestacks, curtained decks, and the great paddle wheels going *flop, flop* at the back.

From the door she said, 'Keith . . . I know you're awake.'

Her voice had a vibrancy which after absence always hit me afresh.

'Who told you I was back? Felipe?'

'No. I saw you as you came into the bar door.'

'You had your back to me. A man had his hand on your shoulder. Remind me to cut it off when I go down.'

I heard her come forward slowly. In the darkness I reached up and found her hand, knowing it would be there in the darkness, waiting for mine. It was a cool hand, long and firm, a hand that could be commanded only at her own will.

'I saw you,' she said, 'in the mirror on the back wall. You looked like hell.'

'I flew into Soledad, and then on by car. Quite a nice trip.' When things hadn't gone well, I made a point of avoiding details with her if I could. Once the first half-hour of being together was past she let her worries for me slide. My fingers left her hand and were on the warm flesh of her wrist and arm under the loose blouse sleeve. 'So you let me sleep?'

'That's what you wanted or you would have come into the bar.'

'Yes,' I lied, 'that's what I wanted.'

'Bastard. . . .'

The breath from the word moved over my face as she came swiftly down to me. She slid on to the bed at my side and my arms were round her and my lips on hers and everything was as it always had been . . . no thoughts, no questions so long as her lips were on mine.

I felt her stir and lift her hand. She kissed me on the cheek, and then said, 'You're all right. . . . Everything was all right?'

'I'm all right,' I said lightly. 'In one piece. And wanting nothing in the whole world but you—but this—'

She came back gently in my arms and I could feel the touch of her hair against my cheek. Time meant nothing. There was just Drea. Her hand came out of the darkness and moved gently across my cheek and neck, tracing with light fingers the angle of my jaw.

'Drea. . . . Wonderful Drea.' I don't know whether I said it aloud. I just wanted to mark the long contentment of the darkness with her name.

Her hand moved down to my arm, moulding my flesh gently through the silk of my dressing-gown. The ceiling was suddenly faintly marked by the purple blur of light from some neon light filtering through the blinds.

I felt her hand stop, resting over the bandage under the silk. Slowly she sat up and slid off the bed and switched on the table lamp. I watched her . . . her movements full of firm, incisive grace. The light burnished her chestnut hair and up-shadowed the fine line of her cheek bones, the puma-strong loveliness.

'Take off your dressing-gown and that pyjama jacket,' she said sharply.

I was back at school with the matron bawling me out.

'Why the hell should I?'

'Take them off, you hare-brained idiot.' She turned away from the bed, swearing at me in Spanish, as she always did when roused.

She opened the cupboard by the door and came back with the whiskey. She poured two drinks, watching me slip out of my gown and jacket.

'You miss nothing,' I said.

'Drink with your left hand.' Handing me the whiskey, she sat down at my side and began to unfasten the bandage from the top of my right arm. Her fingers trembled.

'It's filthy.'

'It's a strip off an underskirt.'

'Who did it?'

'An Antiquenos woman. She was about ninety. A dear old soul. Wouldn't take anything for the damage to her skirt. You'd have liked her.'

'Not the bandage—the wound? Hold still!'

She leaned over me, frowning as she peeled back the cloth and exposed the wound.

'It's only a bite. A mosquito bite. Don't fuss.'

'A funny kind of mosquito.'

'You haven't seen them all. There are eight different kinds in Colombia.'

'This one was made of lead.' As she bent closer to examine the wound I kissed the side of her arched neck. She shook her head impatiently, and went on, 'It's clean, anyway. I'll get a fresh bandage and stuff from my office.'

'Don't bother. There's all you want in the cupboard. Forget it. It's just a graze.'

She stood up and swore at me again in Spanish, and then, her back to me on the way to the cupboard, finished, 'God, Keith, why do you have to do this? Six inches the other way and it could have killed you!'

I tried to jolly her out of it, saying, 'Six inches the other way and it would have missed me altogether. I don't try to interfere with the little chaps sitting on clouds who decide these things. They don't like it.' I tried to keep it light because I hated to see her angry.

'Lord, will you ever learn? Ever be different?'

She came back, cleaned the wound and started to put on a fresh bandage. I tried to kiss her but she avoided me. But I didn't mind. I knew it would pass.

When she had finished she took her glass of whiskey and walked towards the window. Her hand went up and jerked at the blind cord. The shutters gaped and the neon light glowed on her face.

'I suppose this was Barrau?' she asked tersely.

'Yes. Straightforward job—but it turned out a shade tough.'

'One day they'll carry you home.'

'I could just as easily be hit by a street car.'

She held the whiskey glass close to her breasts. She looked beautiful and I could see the green light flecks in her eyes, the powder brown bloom of her skin and the pull of her breasts against her blouse as she breathed hard. She had all the magic of Cleopatra for me . . . me, a third-rate Antony, but a happy one. I wanted her to be happy too. I heaved myself up half-way, wanting to go to her but she shook her head and said:

'Stay where you are. I don't want to be smoothed down. And don't talk to me about street cars. One day some damn fool may press the button by mistake and we'll all go up. But you—you go out of your way to invite things.'

'Drea—cut it out. What on earth's all this in aid of? Just a scratch on the arm. No more.'

She laughed dryly. 'And was the scratch worth it? What did you get out of it?'

'What do you mean?'

'You know damn well what I mean, Keith. How much did you get for the job?'

'Well . . .'

'I see, one of those. You come back here, looking as though you've swum down the river. And not a cent to show for it. And you don't care. You put yourself in jeopardy. Get nothing out of it. And you don't care.'

'It's the way I live. You know that. Oh, Drea, be sensible. Forget this.' I touched my bandaged arm. 'Have another drink and stop looking at me like a mountain cat that's about to go for my throat.'

She shook her head angrily, 'You're not going to put me off.'

Just then the telephone by the bed rang and I reached out for it. 'I'm not trying to put you off,' I said. 'I just want you to relax.'

Over the telephone came Barrau's voice, Spanish, rich with a rummy burr. 'Is that my good friend Squadron-Leader Marchant?'

The last person I wanted then was Barrau and I said sharply, 'This is nobody's friend and stop calling me Squadron-Leader. And go to hell, Barrau.'

I heard him laugh at the other end of the line.

Drea came forward and said, 'It's a pity you don't mean it. Hang up on him. Tell him you're too old for his rackets.'

I grinned at her. 'Thirty-odd summers. Not all of them golden of course.'

'Oh, for God's sake—what's the use of talking to you?'

At the other end of the line patient Barrau said pleasantly, 'Who's with you? Drea?'

'Yes.'

'I hear her voice. She is angry?'

'You could call it that.'

'Tell her not to worry. This time things went a little wrong. But there is always the next time.'

As he spoke I saw Drea, with a fierce shrug of her shoulders, go over to the door and put her glass down on the cupboard top. As she reached for the door handle, I called, 'Hang on, Drea.'

She went out without a word, slamming the door.

Barrau said, 'What was that?'

I lay back against the pillows. When I saw her later she would have calmed down.

To Barrau I said, 'That was Drea, giving me hell. She doesn't like me having bullets flying around my ears and nothing to show for it. Frankly, neither do I.'

'Yes, yes,' said Barrau soothingly. 'It was a little unfortunate, that affair. But we both knew it might be. If it had come off, she could have had a new mink.'

'Barrau, she doesn't want mink. Not that much. Now, what the hell do you want?'

He was silent, but I could hear his breathing at the other end and I could imagine the heaving of his silk waistcoat.

'Nothing,' he said finally. 'Nothing, except that I'd like you to call by and have a chat. Say before dinner if you can manage it.'

Barrau was my business and I said, 'All right. If I can manage it.' I put down the receiver, and I lay back, wishing that Drea hadn't stormed out.

I picked up the telephone again and called the Boutique Ballaya in town. They had a topaz brooch that Drea had once admired. It was to have been my coming-back present, if I'd come back with money. They still had it and I told them to send it to her with some flowers. It was no good worrying about money just because you didn't for the moment have it.

'No message, señor?'

'No, no message.'

CHAPTER 2

I looked in at Drea's office on the way through to the lobby, but she wasn't there. I wanted to ask her to have dinner with me. She was the assistant to the hotel manager, and she'd worked in hotels for a long time and knew the business backwards. I left a message for her and went out.

A coloured boy in red vest, white slacks, his skin grained like sandalwood, brought the car round from the garage. From the neatly trained pergola at the side of the door I snapped off a sprig of plumbago and stuck it in the lapel of my suit. It was pleasant to be wearing a suit that fitted. Beyond the drive, through the dark frieze of oleanders and palms, there was a blue upwash of radiance from the underwater lighting of the *Polo Norte*'s swimming pool. Voices and the sound of splashing came subdued across the heat-heavy evening. On the terrace away to my right a few people were already dining early. The boy descended from the seat of the car with the dignity of a Haile Selassie and the grin of a Louis Armstrong and held the door for me.

I went down the hill to the river and the port, driving easily and without hurry. The traffic thickened up as I skirted the Parque II de Noviembre. I had the top down and the air that came back into my face was warm and steamy, beating down as though the sky were a great damp electric blanket turned on full blast. The skirts and dresses of the women on the pavements were humid-draped about them and the men's shirts were marked with dark patches of sweat.

I came out of the Paseo Bolivar and around the Plaza by the Cathedral. A bunch of noisy youths and girls at the foot of the Columbus statue were being hustled away into the main stream of pedestrian movement by two policemen.

Barrau's place was a few blocks east of the Cathedral. How many statues of Columbus, I wondered, were there around the great blue

bowl of the Caribbean? He'd certainly started something over this
side. Not so long ago, this had been mud-swamp, silted, lazy river-
land that suited the Indians. Now industry and its hangers-on had
taken over Philip the Second's dream. Not gold and silver ingots
now, but textile mills, perfumes, soaps, beers, oil and hats, flour
mills, saw mills, shipyards and paint and plastics. Well, all cities
were much the same to me as long as they gave me a living, and
if my jobs and working hours were irregular that was the way I
liked it. Drea worried over what might happen to me. So did I,
sometimes. But usually I didn't give the future much thought. Why
bother these days? Enjoy things while you could. And if you couldn't
be lucky, at least be happy. Not that I wasn't sure that somewhere
along the line my luck would change.

Barrau's offices were set in some old colonial type buildings
overlooking a small yard. The flanks of the yard were sheds, garages
and three or four small hovels. An old woman sitting on a stool
outside a lighted room looked up as I parked alongside her. She
had a lapful of Lima beans and from the room behind her came
the hot smell of tamales.

I picked out the biggest boy from the children playing in the yard
and gave him a ten centavo piece to look after the car.

'Another ten when I come out,' I said. 'You knock the head off
anyone who tries to touch the car.' These children could wreck a
car in a few minutes.

He nodded gravely and got into the driving seat. As I went to
Barrau's stairway I heard him noisily electing lieutenants at two
centavos each to walk around the car on guard duty while he lolled
back against the leather.

A painted board, among others, at the bottom of the stairs
announced—*L. Garcia Barrau. Importadora y Exportadora de la Barranquilla.* Just below the boards the wall was covered with *graffiti.* At
the first turn of the stairs two little girls were playing with a doll.
Above them in a glass-fronted wall niche was a painted plaster
figure of the Madonna lit by a weak electric light bulb. Another
two floors up was Barrau's brightly painted green door.

The outer office was empty, but the door to Barrau's room was
half open and he called me to come in. He had his bottom in a
deep leather chair and his feet on his desk. He was a big, fat sealion
of a man wearing an expensive American suit of bronze silk. The
stuff was like a pelt on him, as slick as though he had just come

out of the sea. He rubbed his three chins with a pudgy hand and beamed a smile of welcome.

'Amigo—it is good to see you. How is the arm?'

'It's O.K.'

'You are angry with me?'

'No. Things just went wrong. Nobody cheated me—unless you've become really clever.'

His face saddened. 'I lost money. You lost money. We close the books on it. You are sure about your arm?'

'Forget my arm. What do you want me for?'

He got up and walked to the office door, closing it with a push of his foot. 'A job. Tricky, maybe. When I was asked to find someone who could set it up I naturally thought of you.'

'Naturally.'

He came back and sat down and began to prepare himself a cigar. 'You know,' he said, 'that here in Colombia—by agreement with the American and British governments—the Air Force is just taking delivery of twelve new Hunter jet fighters?'

'I was reading something about it in *La Prensa*.' Britain and, more particularly, America were very touchy about the increment of new weapons and military aircraft in the Caribbean area. Not that there weren't ways of getting around their embargoes. Civil aircraft, crop sprayers, helicopters and transport planes could be bought and converted. Also when British fighters were made abroad under licence in places like Sweden and Italy the British Government did not always retain rights restricting their ultimate disposal. This was the kind of business world Barrau and I could move about in blindfold.

'Well, because of the American touchiness over Castro in Cuba, and President Trujillo in Dominica, both governments made it a condition of the sale to Colombia that the existing fighter planes here—which the jets would displace—must be handed back and sold only to a country which had the approval of Whitehall and Washington.'

'That's the usual form.' It was the old, old game. The papers were always full of the possible threats to Caribbean peace from the delivery of arms and planes to Cuba and the Dominican Republic. Behind it all, of course, was the big money, the American and British business interests and concessions. The Caribbean was the Mediterranean of the New World . . . there wasn't a situation which had plagued Europe for hundreds of years which wasn't

inevitably duplicating itself under these sunny skies. In a way that
was why I and hundreds like me were here. There were always
eager hands around a melting pot, waiting to take a dip.

I said, 'What are the planes, the ones they're kicking over to get
the jets?'

'Hawker Sea Furies. Piston-engined. You know these?'

'I've flown them. Not officially.' There had been some in Korea.
'Even now they'd be good for a lot of work. Two 20 mm British
Hispano cannons in each wing. A 2,550 horse-power Bristol
Centaurus eighteen-cylinder engine. You'd probably get about 450
miles an hour out of them around twenty thousand feet.'

'You remember all these things?'

'You remember the women you've slept with?'

'*Ciertamente!*'

'It's the same thing.' For a moment I forgot Barrau. I was off
the deck and up into the wide blue and the rolling clouds. *Oh, for
a horse with wings* . . . sleeve-valved, air-cooled, and fifteen hundred
miles of heaven in the tanks.

Barrau said, 'Six of them are being shipped next week to Caramanga for the Republic of Cordillo. It is all approved by the Americans and the British. But not by other people.'

I came back to the rat race.

'Other people,' I said. 'You mean Angelo Libertad and his revolutionary boys stuck away in their little corner of Cordillo?'

'It's more than a corner,' said Barrau. 'They've got nearly half
of the island. It's a simple matter of switching these planes two
hundred miles from Caramanga to the revolutionary port of Acaibo
at the other end of the island.'

'Very simple,' I said ironically.

'It would be done at sea. While the planes are being shipped. It
could be worked out.'

'How? Bribery, or do you know a captain who's prepared to go
in for barratry?'

'Nothing like that. The captain of this boat can't be got at. No,
it would just be a straightforward take-over by you.'

'By me?'

'Why not? Libertad's agent is in Barranquilla at the moment.
You could fix the details with him.'

I stood up and went to the window. My lieutenant was sitting
comfortably in the car and boys and girls had joined hands and
were circling around it, chanting derisively.

'You must be off your head, Barrau. You're talking about piracy.'

'I suppose you could call it that,' Barrau agreed.

'You can't call it anything else. Just plain piracy. The moment it was done I'd have to go well away from here, and lie low for a hell of a time. No thanks. I'm hard up and I want to be able to go on working. Lord knows, I don't make a fortune out of your jobs. But they all have some appearance of honesty. You go find yourself another pirate.'

'I can do, I suppose. But I naturally give you first chance. The money is very good, you know. Ten thousand American dollars now. Forty thousand more in Acaibo when you deliver. It is a lot of money.'

'And I'd be a marked man for a long time. No thank you.'

Barrau pursed his fat lips and blew gently as though he were fanning embers that needed careful coaxing. 'Think it over. There's no need to decide for a couple of days. Even if you know you are going to say No—just think it over.' He stood up, smiling. 'You want the beach house again?'

He had a small cottage down at Puerto and usually he lent it to Drea and myself when I came back from a job. She could always get away from the hotel for a few days so that we could be on our own.

'I suppose so. But you can scrub this other thing.'

'Maybe. But it is so much money, I thought I should give you the chance. You will, of course, understand that all I have said to you is in confidence.'

I grinned. 'Everything you say to me in this office is in confidence.' I turned towards the door. 'But you're way off this time.'

'You may change your mind.'

'Not over this.'

Back at the hotel I was heading for the bar when Drea came through from the dining-room which overlooked the terrace. She was wearing a white dress and I was relieved to see my topaz brooch pinned under one shoulder.

I smiled at her and said, 'Are you still slamming doors on me? Or can I say how beautiful you look?'

'I'm not sure.'

'Then I must do something about it. Did you get my note?'

'Yes.'

'I thought we might have a bite down at Puerto. We can stay

down there in Barrau's beach hut. Can you manage that, or are
you too busy here?'

For a moment I thought I caught some hesitation in her. Then
she said, 'No, I can get away. An hour from now?'

'Fine.'

She put up a hand and touched the brooch. 'Thank you for this.
How the hell are you going to pay for it?'

I smiled. 'Name anything you want and I'll get it—and worry
about payment afterwards.'

'Miracle man—that's your trouble. You've been down to see
Barrau?'

'Had to clear up a few odds and ends.'

'I can imagine.'

'Barrau's all right. He's just doing his best in a difficult world.
Out of his office he's just a happy family man, four lovely children
and a wife who adores him. Just as I adore you.'

'His third wife—and strictly for kitchen work.' But she smiled
and I felt forgiven.

'An hour from now, then. I'll 'phone Puerto and order a table
and afterwards we'll sit and watch the sea and listen to what the
wild waves have to say.'

I took her hand and kissed it. Her anger was gone. That was a
good thing. Puerto was our special place and not built for
arguments.

We drove down to Puerto and had dinner and then danced for a
while. Then we drove out along the beach road towards Barrau's
place. Somewhere along the road we drew in and stopped under a
clump of palms. We sat there watching the knee-high drift of fireflies
under the trees and the faint stippling of phosphorescence where
the water touched the white shell beach. Drea was alongside me,
happy and relaxed, and everything was perfect. I leaned over and
kissed her. When, after a while, she drew her head back I saw the
starlight touch her eyes, tiny points of diamond brilliance. I lit a
cigarette for her and put it between her lips. She drew at it and
then let the smoke go with a long sigh.

I said lazily, 'This is really us. This is how it should be always.
No slamming doors, no scoldings.'

She nodded. 'This is how it could be always if you'd be different.
But you like trouble. You like uncertainty. Like living on hope.'

'You mean I'm an optimist?'

'Yes. And the trouble with optimists is that they won't face facts. They're convinced that somewhere along the line a miracle is going to happen which will put everything right.'

'What's all this in aid of?'

I leaned forward and kissed the sweet curve of her throat. She gave a shrug of her shoulders.

'Nothing, just talk.'

I gave a little laugh and put my arm around her.

'You're not still worrying about me? I'm here, look. Right alongside you.'

I reached out for her. For a moment she hung back, looking at me with an expression I couldn't quite place. Then with a sigh, as she slid into my arms, she said, 'Yes, here we are. The golden moment that shuts out the future. So the world's all right and must go on that way. Oh, Keith, darling, you're impossible. What the hell do I do about you?'

I didn't try to answer that one, because it didn't seem to need an answer. Somewhere on the highway behind us a car went by with its horn blaring and its headlights probing along the low run of sand dunes. My body was suddenly hard against hers and my lips on hers and there was nothing in existence except the surrender to the golden moment. What was there to worry about? People worried too much and too often, racking themselves with cares that passed, that would have passed quicker if only they hadn't clung to them. Feeling the movement of her body against mine and her arms about me, I was content with the only miracle which a man and a woman could truly know.

She eased away from me and looking down at her I bent and kissed her cheeks, her eyebrows and her lips with tenderness. She reached up gently with her fingers and touched my chin. It was a gesture so familiar . . . the feather tap of her fingers acknowledging love.

Very softly she said, 'Why did you have to be on that river boat . . . Why?'

I didn't have to answer that one either. I had been. That old river boat, stern wheeling up to Bogota five years ago. . . .

Our lips came together and there were no more words.

Barrau's cottage was at the head of a small cove that looked northwest to the sea and to the dark line of the Isla Verde. There was a chain link fence round the property, shutting off about three acres and the beach. The cottage had a large living-room opening to a verandah that overlooked the sands, a couple of bedrooms and a kitchen. We had it all to ourselves for two days, with the world safely on the other side of the fence. Two blissful days and nights.

Drea was wonderful. She made no more reference to the trouble I had got into on my last trip. The brief storm was over and the sun shone. We kept no time-table; we bathed and ate and drank when we felt like it. Just Drea and myself, and if I was happy I also knew that I was lucky because Drea was the only woman I wanted and I blessed the moment when I had walked aboard that river boat. A man could go a lifetime and not find what I had found. When the thing happens there is no questioning it. Everything you share together takes on a beauty and rareness which makes you both unique, which shuts out everyone and everything else.

In the mornings she was lazy about getting up, and I would go down for a swim by myself and come back and make coffee to wake her. I would sit by her bed and kiss her and sleepily she would laugh at the taste of brine on my lips, and during the long day we would lie on the sand letting the sun beat at us and now and again her hand would reach across for mine and we would lie there in silence, utterly content.

On our last morning I was up early as usual and went down to have a swim, and as I came back up the beach the low sun threw long black shadows across the sand. To my surprise when I got back, Drea was up and dressed and in the kitchen making coffee.

'Good Lord, what's the matter with you?' I caught her by the shoulders and spun her round and, laughing, kissed her. 'Where's my old slug-a-bed, this morning?'

She smiled and said, 'I felt like getting up.' Then she turned from me and went on preparing the coffee. I carried the tray out on to the verandah for her and we sat with our hands cupped round the coffee mugs, watching the day warm up.

Usually over our coffee she chatted away but this morning she was silent, just staring out to sea. I thought that perhaps she was hating the thought of going back to Barranquilla. Myself I could have stayed on the beach for ever.

I said, 'Why don't you 'phone the hotel? Tell 'em you'd like to take a couple more days. They wouldn't mind.'

She turned and looked at me and I caught a suggestion of her lips trembling. I put my mug down and moved to take her by the arm, but she stood up and walked a few steps up the verandah. I would have followed her, but she said:

'Stay where you are, Keith.'

Puzzled, I asked, 'What's the matter?'

She was silent for a while and then with an odd sort of forced calmness in her voice, she said, 'There's something I've got to say to you, Keith. And I'm going to hate saying it.'

I looked across at her, not understanding. Then lightly, I said, 'Well let's have it then. Get it off your chest.'

After a moment's hesitation she said, 'Well, it's nothing very new really. It's just—'

I got it then and broke in quickly, 'Oh, Drea—not that. Not on our last morning. You're not going to start fussing about this bullet business.'

'That's part of it.'

'But that's nonsense. We've had all that. This is our last morning here. Forget it.'

She turned then and faced me squarely and her face was serious. She said firmly, 'That's just it, Keith. This is our last morning here or anywhere. Keith . . .' I saw the rise of her lovely shoulders as she breathed. 'Keith . . . unless you change your way of life, I'm leaving you for good.'

I sat there, wondering if I'd heard her aright. Leave me for good?

Sharply, I said, 'What the hell are you talking about?'

She shook her head. 'You know, only you won't face it. I should have made this stand years ago. I tried to once but you came after me and I wasn't strong enough to go through with it. But I am now. No matter how much I love you, I'm leaving you unless you alter.'

It was a quick outburst and it brought me to my feet, moving towards her, but she waved me away.

'No, don't come near me. Stay there.'

I stood looking at her, my hands going automatically for a cigarette.

'Drea. . . . What's got into you? What's wrong with me? What's all this about change?'

'You really don't know? You really don't?' For a moment a tired smile touched her lips.

'No, I don't,' I said. 'I've never known a piddling little bullet scrape upset you as much as this before. It can't be that. But whatever it is, you'd better let me have it straight. What's so wrong with me?'

Her head came up, her chin firming. 'Everything's wrong. The way you live, and the way you expect me to fit into the pattern. God knows, I've tried. But I can't go on like it. For five years I've been wondering what was happening to you while you were away. And when you're back, it's spoiled because I'm wondering when you will be off again. The only time I've ever been free from anxiety was after we first met and we had that holiday in St. Thomas. I've told you all this before, but you've never taken any notice. Or you haven't believed me. Keith . . .' she paused, looking frankly at me, 'you've got to change. Otherwise, I'm leaving you.'

'Change? But how can I? I can't be dishonest with you. People can't suddenly start being different because they're in love.'

'Why can't they? That's something you can expect from love. I'm not what I was at eighteen. I'm changing all the time. Why can't you? Aren't I worth the effort?'

'Drea, you know it isn't that. I'd do anything I could for you.'

'Then why should it be so difficult for you to be a little more like other men?'

A little sourly, I said, 'Other men? You want a man who comes home every day from some office. Steady, reliable?'

'Why not?'

'So that's it.'

I went and sat on the verandah steps, digging my toes into the loose sand at the bottom. I'd never seen Drea like this before. She'd blown me up many times. But this was different. Her mind was made up and she wasn't going to change it. Somehow I knew that even if I got near her, got my arms around her, it would mean nothing this time. She was armoured against me. And the hell of it was that I didn't really have any way in words of explaining to her why I couldn't be like other men. . . . I just didn't see life in terms of any routine, clock watching, settling down into a steady groove, putting myself into a cage where I could only prowl four steps up and four back. I hadn't thought that she honestly minded so much how I lived. I hadn't thought that her anxiety for me was more than passing, storm and then sunshine. You had to be what you were, you had to find the way which was your way. . . . I had to be on my own, indifferent honest, maybe, but my own master. But now here was Drea wanting me to be a different person. If I didn't she would go. The last time I'd been lucky, I'd got her back.

Supposing I wasn't so lucky again. But the thought of Drea leaving me was like a black cloud over the morning sun.

I looked up at her. She was keeping her eyes off me, her attention on the stretch of beach and the far run of sea.

I said, stalling, 'You really mean this?'

'I do . . . God, I do. And, Keith, don't try and pretend that I don't mean it. I love you, but I can't take the waiting and wondering any longer. Do anything but these Barrau kind of jobs and I'll be with you always and through everything. But not this way. Never again.'

'God, I don't know what to say to you! How can anything break us up? We'd be lost without each other.'

'That's what's made it so hard for me. But my mind's made up. Don't fool yourself, Keith. I mean it. We're wonderfully in love. It's all I've ever wanted. But I can't live with it any more your way. It's up to you, Keith.'

She turned slowly and came down the verandah towards me. The morning breeze teased the edge of her dress, and caught lightly at her hair. I loved her more in that moment than I had ever done before or ever thought possible. She came and sat by me and her arms were wrapped tightly across her breasts, almost as though she were cold. She was holding herself in, showing me that all the hunger of love in her, all that was between us, couldn't break out and make a nonsense of what had been said. She meant every word and wasn't going to weaken.

I put my hands on her shoulders, leaned forward and kissed her gently. But she was armed against any kind of magic.

I said, 'O.K. You put it squarely. I'm not losing you. I'll just have to look round.'

It sounded lame. It was lame. I was coming down with all the engines gone and the wings shaking themselves to hell. . . .

She said, 'I must go and pack. I've got to be back at the hotel by mid-day.'

She got up and just for a moment her hand touched the side of my cheek. I put up my own hand to catch at hers, but it was gone and I heard the verandah boards creak as she went away from me.

CHAPTER 3

That afternoon I went down to the hotel swimming pool to cool off. I was feeling pretty low. I'd gone gaily along without once stopping to think about what was happening to Drea. I really had thought that she hadn't minded, that her outbursts of concern on my return from various jobs had been no more than temporary displays . . . not meaning much, just unloading the kind of tension which women so easily build up. But I couldn't believe that any longer. She really had suffered and would go on suffering. I ought to have seen that. Selfish, unobservant and taking too much for granted. . . . I lay there calling myself quite a few names.

I sprawled in a deck chair and held a magazine in front of my face to ward off any social chat from the few other people using the pool. I didn't read. I was thinking about Drea. I remembered our first meeting on the river boat . . . and later at Bogota. Almost from the start she must have been seeing just what kind of relationship she was letting herself in for. She had kept pushing the truth away, but gradually it had caught up with her until she could no longer ignore it. The first moment of hesitation, I saw now, had been in the hotel at Bogota. But then it had been no more than an instinct . . . giving out some feeble unheeded warning.

I'd made a nice little packet from my job at Bogota and had been ready to splash it. Her hotel appointment there hadn't turned out well and I knew that she was ready to leave it.

I walked into her bedroom one evening and handed her a bunch of tickets.

'I'm flying to St. Thomas tomorrow. A month's holiday.' I nodded at the tickets. 'There's everything there you need. The plane leaves at nine tomorrow.'

She looked from the tickets to me and then walked away and fixed a couple of drinks. My heart was in my mouth. Despite all that had happened between us so far we were both unsure, both maybe still a little shy. For the last four days I'd felt that from now on everything I wanted to be and to do was linked with her. She came back and handed me my drink. I didn't touch her. We didn't kiss one another as we usually did over the first evening drink. A custom only a few days old but already a part of the thing which was building in us.

She leafed through the wad of tickets.

'St. Thomas? That's in the Virgin Islands?'

'Yes.'

'You sure you've got the right girl?' She said it with a hint of a smile and her green eyes narrowed.

'Two seats. For tomorrow at nine. I know a chap up there who runs a small hotel.'

She handed me back the tickets, shaking her head. 'One seat. You can get a refund on the other.'

I didn't argue. And she didn't turn up. But before I took off I scribbled her a note and enclosed her tickets.

The man I knew was called Marty James, an Englishman, who owned this rather run-down hotel on the eastern end of a little offshore island. He had a wife, a palish, washed-out creature. They were both good-natured, charming and inefficient. The place was no more than a comfortable, easygoing shambles which would have made a first-class tourist shudder.

Drea turned up two days later. There were no explanations. We were both committed. And for a month we lived in our own world.

At the end of the month I had a cable from Barrau. He wanted me for a job. I told Drea about it while we were having drinks on the beach below the hotel.

Drea said, 'I don't want you to go.'

I laughed. 'Do you think I want to go? But money runs out and I've got to work to get more.'

'What kind of work?'

'It's just a commission job for Barrau. Wants me to handle the sale of some lorries in Venezuela.' They weren't lorries but there was no point in Drea knowing that.

Some children were splashing about at the water's edge and their shouts were bright, echoing over the sands. A launch went by a couple of hundred yards out with a fat man in a red shirt sitting in the fishing chair.

Drea was so silent that I put my hand on her arm and said,

'Cheer up. I'll do the job. It won't take long and we'll come back if you like. Or find somewhere else.'

She turned to me then, giving me a long look.

'Do you remember what Marty said the other evening?'

'He says so many things.'

'About the hotel, I mean.'

I remembered then. Marty usually joined us for a drink at the bar before dinner. His wife didn't like the place much and he'd said that if he could get a cash offer he'd sell up and go back to England.

I said to Drea, 'You know why he said that? He wants to get back to England. He knows you're in the hotel world. Probably thinks you could find him a buyer.'

Drea leaned forward. 'Maybe I could. This place could be a goldmine.'

'You think so? Looks pretty run-down to me.'

'That could be changed.'

I was silent for a moment as a thought struck me, then I said excitedly: 'But why not? Why don't we take it? Between us we could get it going. You could run the hotel side. And it needs a launch or a small schooner to take guests offshore fishing, charter parties to the other islands. I could do that.'

'Oh, Keith . . .' the eagerness came bursting from her. 'Do you mean it? Do you really think we could?'

'Sure, why not. It's the kind of job for both of us.'

Enthusiastically she said, 'Then why don't we go ahead, Keith? Oh, Lord—we could do it. You wouldn't know this place.'

I laughed. 'Must be fun to run your own show. But there's always the one snag.'

'What?'

'Money. Marty wants cash. Twenty thousand dollars. I've got two hundred dollars in the world.'

'I've got four thousand.'

'It wouldn't stretch.'

'Not at the moment. But Marty isn't going to sell this place quickly. If we saved for the next six months we could make half of it and get the rest on mortgage. Put the money you earn away, and we could do it. . . .'

We got quite excited and we decided to do it. But it faded. A couple more jobs for Barrau that didn't quite come off, and then a couple more, and then the whole business was forgotten. That had been five years ago.

Lying there in the sun, I heard Drea's voice from that morning saying, "The only time I've been free from anxiety was after we first met and had that holiday at St. Thomas." It was a hell of a thing to say. But I could see now that it was true. I'd forgotten all about the hotel. But I knew Marty was still there.

Remembering our past excitement it was hard to realise that I'd forgotten all that until now. If I'd really stuck into some lousy job and saved we could have had the hotel years ago. If I'd even saved some of the big money I'd earned with Barrau we could have had it. The thing had gone from my mind completely. I wondered if Marty was still there. God, what a fool I'd been.

I got up, took a plunge to cool off, and then went back to the hotel.

As I went by the desk I found myself turning aside. I went up to it and asked for a cable form. I filled it up and gave it to the clerk.

Three hours later a boy brought the reply up to my room where I was changing.

Still for sale. Twenty-five thousand. Give you a two month option for two thousand dollars. How are things? Long time no see. Marty.

I sat by the window with a whiskey and thought it over. Twenty-five thousand. I couldn't even have done it in matchsticks. Two thousand option. I had about two hundred dollars to my name.

The answer was obvious. There was one quick, direct way to what I had to have. I fenced with myself for about half an hour and then I telephoned Barrau and told him I was coming down to see him. There was no harm, anyway, in getting a little more information.

Barrau didn't show any surprise. He didn't ask any questions either about my reasons for coming back to him after turning the job down originally.

He said, 'It's fifty thousand dollars gross. Ten thousand now and the rest in Acaibo. You should clear thirty thousand, at least. If you want to do it you must see Libertad's agent who is in Barranquilla at the moment.'

'Where?'

'At the *Polo Norte*. It is convenient for you, no? I will give you the introduction and then I am out of it.'

'Except for your commission?'

'It is small. I am just finding and introducing you.'

'And the introduction at the hotel?'

'You simply write *Amairi* on the back of your card and send it up to Room 15. The rest will follow.'

'What the hell does *Amairi* mean?'

Barrau gave a fat giggle. 'It is the agreed code word. For use on the telephone for reference and so on. It's an anagram of *Mara II*, which is the name of the ship which carries the planes. I thought it was good.'

'I'm mad about it.' Barrau had a passion for mystery, code words, and the secret rendezvous. Underneath his mountain of flesh was a romantic small boy delighting in a complete spy's outfit. He'd called our last operation *Salvavidas*, which was Spanish for lifebelt. I'd finished up swimming three miles down river without one and with a bullet wound in the right arm.

'These precautions are necessary,' said Barrau firmly.

I said, 'If I do this, everything would be in my hands? Right down to the last screw? And the people I pick?'

'Everything.'

I took a cigarette from his desk box and blew a smoke screen between us.

'About your commission. I pay you?'

'Yes.'

'How much?'

'Fifteen per cent.'

I blew the smoke away so that he could see my face clearly. 'Think again.'

'Not fifteen on the whole sum—but on what you make. Your expenses then are commission free. It is generous.'

'Five,' I said firmly. The expenses would be high and with what was left I wanted Marty's place and a small schooner or launch, and there would be other things, too.

Barrau exploded. 'But this is ridiculous! Amigo, you make me angry.'

I gave him a smile. We always had this pantomime.

'Five,' I repeated. 'Or find someone else. This isn't a job you can farm out easily. I'm taking all the risk. You just sit here.'

'You are wrong,' said Barrau. 'There are plenty of others.'

'Then you'd better find someone else.' I turned and went towards the door. But I knew he would never let me get outside.

With my hand going out for the door knob he said, 'All right. Seven and a half.'

I turned and shook my head. 'Five.'

He gave in then, his plump shoulders slowly collapsing in resignation.

'As you say. Five. But this is not like you to be so hard. Think of my expenses, too.'

'I daren't. It would break my heart. I'll give you a ring after I've been to Room 15. You get your commission after the job is done. If it goes wrong, we're both out.'

He nodded.

I went down to my car, knowing that if I did it and it went wrong I would certainly be out. Even before I could begin I had Drea to face. Back at the hotel I checked on Room 15. It had been taken two weeks previously by a Señor Gracioso Fondes from Puerto Rico. I wondered how true that was. He probably had a choice of passports. I wrote Barrau's childish code word on the back of my card and gave it to the boy to take up.

Five minutes later the boy found me in the bar and asked me to go up to Room 15.

I knocked and the door was opened. A girl stood back to let me enter. It was the sitting-room of the suite and the only light came from a table lamp by the curved settee near the window. There were some bottles and glasses on a tray on the centre table.

The door closed behind me and the girl came round the far side of the table. She stood there and fidgeted nervously.

'Señor Fondes?'

'He's not here at the moment. You are Mr. Marchant?' She spoke English and there was no mistaking the American accent.

'I am. Where is he?'

'He's out. But it is all right. You can talk to me. Señor Barrau has already telephoned me.'

'Who are you?'

'I'm sorry. Katrina Davia. You would like a drink? Whiskey?'

I nodded and watched her as she took the bottle. She wasn't used to whiskey, that was clear—or maybe she'd got the wrong impression of me. She almost filled a tumbler and hesitated with her hand on the siphon. I gave her a smile and moving forward took the tumbler and poured half of the whiskey into another glass and then filled my own with soda. 'I put too much? It is not a drink I understand.'

'It's fine,' I said. 'When will Señor Fondes be back?'

She didn't say anything for a moment. She just stood there and looked at me over the table lamp. She was, I supposed, about twenty, a tall, slim girl with dark, smooth hair tied back loosely on the nape of her neck. She was a bit coltish, but she held herself well and the green linen dress was well-cut. There was a little gold chain around her neck, dropping into the top of her dress. And she was good-looking. Not in the way that did anything for me, but in a quiet, dark, almost gentle way, like any one of a hundred girls you could see every night in any city making the walk round the plaza with their parents, eyes down, subdued, afraid to look at life until Mama told them it was safe, everything arranged for them through confirmation up to marriage.

She took the other tumbler in which half of my whiskey rested and filled it with soda. She let it swirl in too fast and some of the liquid splashed on to her hand.

'You can talk to me,' she said firmly. 'My name is Katrina—but not really Davia. I am the sister of Angelo Libertad.' She took a sip at the whiskey and then, motioning to the settee, added, 'Won't you sit down?'

I sat down and she took a chair by the table.

I said, 'You speak English well.' I wanted a little time. I wasn't used to doing business with madonna-eyed innocents.

'I haven't been back to Cordillo for eight years. I've been in New York. You can talk to me. It is perfectly safe.'

'And Señor Fondes?'

'He went back to Acaibo three days ago. He is a cousin of mine. I have been staying here with him, but my brother needed him back. He's a captain in the People's Democratic Army.'

I smiled. It was a good title for an army. The people, democracy . . . just like having a good address to impress the suckers.

I reached out for the telephone and said, 'Do you mind if I make a call?'

'Please do.'

I rang Barrau's number and was lucky to find him still at his office.

When he answered I said, 'Barrau—you know the person I'm supposed to be meeting?'

'Of course. You refer to *Amairi*?'

'What else? Give me a description.'

I heard him chuckle at the end of the line, and then he said, 'She is charming. Not your type, of course. But if you look closely you will see that she has a tiny mole underneath her right ear.'

I put the receiver down and said to her, 'I hope you will forgive that but I have been in this business much longer than you.' The mole was there.

She flushed a little and there was the hint of annoyance in her eyes.

'I told you that you could talk to me.'

'I can now.'

Calmly but with a hint still of nervousness she said, 'You are a very suspicious person.'

'Careful is the word. You have to be if you're contemplating piracy. You realise that that is what it is?'

'I want to help my brother. I realise that. Only that.'

'Why did they send you? This is a man's job.'

'Gracioso Fondes was going to do it. I met him here from New York with the money I've been collecting.'

'Fifty thousand dollars?'

'No. Just over ten thousand. Ten is to be paid here for expenses and the rest in Acaibo. You need not worry about that. It is there waiting.'

'You've thought about this thing? You know what it involves?' It was strange talking to her. All wrong. You didn't do this kind of deal with a girl who obviously was as nervous as a kitten underneath.

'It is for you to arrange. That is why you will be paid. The planes are being shipped on the *Mara II* in the next few days. All my brother requires is that the ship should be taken over when it is nearing Caramanga and then diverted to Acaibo. He is prepared to send a boat of some kind out to meet you when you are near Acaibo.'

'What line is the *Mara*?'

'She belongs to the *Flota Mercante Interoceanica*. She carries cargo and a few passengers.'

'I should need three men besides myself. We must go as passengers and unless we can get bookings there's no point in going on with this.'

'Gracioso thought of that. There is already a block booking of three cabins. Two of them are double-berth.'

'Well, good for Gracioso. Are you going to be on the boat?'

'Of course. I shall give all the help I can.'

258 A DELIVERY OF FURIES

'And when we get to Acaibo—what happens to the ship and the rest of the passengers?'

'The ship will be allowed to proceed when the planes have been taken off. I don't think there will be any other passengers, except the mechanic who travels with the planes. If there are they will go away with the ship. My brother is only interested in the planes.'

'Who's doing the shipping over here? The Republic of Cordillo will have sent more than a mechanic.'

'They have one of their Army officers, a pilot. His name is John MacIntyre Albano and he's the son of their Defence Minister.'

'It's a fine name.' But not unusual. I'd met this Scots-Spanish combination all over South America. 'If he's on the boat I can't see your brother letting him go. He'd be too valuable.'

'He won't be on it. He's flying back to Caramanga. Gracioso found this out.'

And was probably disappointed, I thought. There was nothing like an important hostage in these affairs. However, I was glad he was flying. I didn't want to hand anyone over to Angelo Libertad.

I said, 'You know him, this John MacIntyre Albano?'

'I have met him. Many, many years ago when I was young. He would not recognise me now.'

Many, many years ago when I was young. I wondered what kind of man Angelo Libertad was to let her get involved in a business like this. I realised then why Barrau had picked me. Any other of his men would have been unable to resist some kind of double-cross. She would have had her money taken and nothing done for it. And Barrau would have lost his commission.

She said, 'You will do it, won't you?'

'All right,' I said. 'Pay me over the ten thousand dollars and I'll give you a receipt.'

'You want the money now?'

It was a silly question but I humoured her.

'The moment I walk out of here the expenses start. There isn't a lot of time. The men I engage won't wait for their money. And there are things to be bought. Do I pay for the passages, for instance?'

'I don't know.'

I smiled. 'Well, I suppose I do—unless Gracioso has already done that.' I discovered later he'd only put down a booking fee.

She got up and went out of the room into a bedroom. I sat and sipped my whiskey and after a while she came back carrying an envelope. She'd probably had to fish her travelling case out and unlock it. The envelope was one of those tough, yellow-looking jobs in which they mail the *National Geographical Magazine*. She handed it to me and I counted it. If she was going to be in this business she must start to learn it thoroughly. Always count the money. It was fifty dollars short of ten thousand and when I told her so she looked worried and flustered in the way women do when they go through their purses after shopping and can't make out why they are short.

'I'll get the rest from my purse,' she said.

'Don't bother.'

I wrote her out a receipt for nine thousand nine hundred and fifty.

As I stood up I said, 'If you could, why don't you go back to Acaibo some other way? I shan't really need you.'

'Oh, no. . . . No, I couldn't do that.'

'O.K.' I reached down and picked up my glass, raising it a little to her. 'Well, here's to us.'

She took her own glass and drank with me and I could see the quick little wrinkle of her nose as she swallowed.

I said, 'You don't like whiskey? You're not used to it?'

She smiled, a sudden frank and warming smile. 'It's horrid.'

'Stick to orange juice then. You don't have to drink it to impress me. You must be very fond of your brother?'

'I am. Also I believe in what he is doing.'

I didn't want to argue about that. He was running a revolution in Cordillo which wasn't going any too well. There was someone who could fill me in on the details with far more accuracy than she could.

I said, 'I'm staying at this hotel. I'll get in touch with you tomorrow. But for the time being if you see me around I should pretend that we have never met.'

She saw me to the door, a nice, well-brought up girl who would have resented any suggestion that she wasn't capable of looking after herself, that she hadn't begun to know her way around . . . but that was what she was. She'd probably shared a flat with two other girls in New York, had a job in a shop or an office, and at night had mixed with the Cordillo expatriates, holding meetings and collecting money for her brother. She saw herself as an hardened revolutionary, with the usual rosy ideas of liberty, equality and fraternity. They were growths that didn't flourish too well under the Caribbean sun. She'd find that out in time. And because she seemed a nice creature and there was something about her that I liked, I hoped that the process wouldn't be too hard.

I went down to the hotel lobby and wrote a cable to Marty, taking an option on his place. I might have been blind about some aspects of Drea's character, but at least I knew that my only chance of going through with this was to present her with facts. Hard facts from which she couldn't escape. An option taken, and a job accepted that would bring in the money. I was doing the one thing she hated me to do, but I was going to do it for the last time.

CHAPTER 4

I went down early the next morning to see Monk Sandoz. As I crossed the hallway a woman came out of one of the adjoining doors and stood at the foot of the stairs blocking my way. She was new to me, which wasn't any surprise because I hadn't seen Monk for about three months. She was one of his usual waifs and I could see that the old Monk magic was working. I could not get up the stairs until she was certain that I meant him no harm. I could think of very few people who would want to harm Monk—but all his waifs went this way, fiercely protective after a few weeks of his help . . . stray dog, mangy kinkajou rescued from some miserable side-show, parrot with a broken wing, or a girl like this whom he'd probably picked up broke in a bar, they all finished up by fancying that he needed more protection than they did. Which he didn't, of course. He sent them all on their way when they were mended or they drifted away on their own without his noticing it. I don't think he ever slept with any of the girls he helped. He probably meant to but never got round to it because somewhere on the way he was side-tracked by something that really interested him.

'It's all right,' I said in Spanish. 'I'm a friend of his. Is he in?'

'He sleeps.'

'I'll wake him.'

She shook her head.

I smiled. 'I've known him years. I've lived in this house.' As I spoke I went to the side of the stairs and looking up shouted, 'Monk!'

I had to shout twice and then heard a door open at the top of the stairs.

'Who is it?' His voice boomed down.

'Marchant. Call off your bloodhound so that I can come up.'

I heard him laugh. Then he called, 'Let him come, Valda.'

She stepped aside and watched me go up the first flight of stairs.

At the top of the stairs part of the landing wall had been knocked away and he'd fitted up a small aviary that looked out to the yard beyond. It had two rather sick looking Guatemala king birds in it. A sailing dinghy's mast lay up the length of the next flight of stairs and a blue sail was draped over the banisters, neatly patched in three places. Without looking I knew that the stitches would be his, small and neat like all his work; that he could be so precise with his great banana fingers always amazed me.

The door of his room was open. He was standing at a wall mirror, wrapped up in an old brown dressing-gown, and shaving with a cut-throat, his face lathered up to his ears. He grinned at me in the mirror and, screwing up his mouth sideways as he scraped away, said:

'Coffee on the table there. Help yourself. Use my cup. She brings it up every morning. Never touch the stuff as you know. But I dirty the cup to please her. You can do it for me. How are you? Lovely day. Heard you were dead. The land of rumours.'

Pouring myself some coffee, I said, 'She's new.'

'Is she? She's from Cartagena way. Her uncle threw her out. Uncle . . .' he laughed. 'The world's full of wicked uncles. Nice kid, but a hell of a cook. Thank God I don't eat at home much. Come to think of it, I don't eat much. Never got over the bottle stage.'

I lit a cigarette. The coffee was bitter and strong. 'When did you come out of the last one?'

He took a final flick at his face and then examined the ridge of soap-sud along the razor. 'About two weeks ago. Don't drink that if you don't like it. She can't make coffee, either. Just dirty the cup. Would you believe it? In this country. Can't make coffee. Maybe that's why uncle threw her out. Poor kid. She's nice though. Sings like a canary when there's no one around.'

As he spoke I was thinking that if the last drinking bout had been two weeks since, then he would be all right for my job. There were usually five or six weeks between his sprees. This job would be over in about six or seven days. Not drinking he was utterly reliable.

'Does it fit in?' he asked, watching me for a moment in the mirror and then plunging his face into the hand-basin. I didn't answer while he snorted and blew like a grampus, showering water everywhere. I wasn't surprised that he had taken the point so quickly either. The longer you knew Monk the less susceptible to surprise about him you became. He was a big, bluff-faced man, bald except for a narrow tonsure of hair which had given him the name Monk. I didn't know his real name. Even Sandoz, I suspected, wasn't accurate. I didn't even know his nationality, though it must have been some European mixture, or his history. Sometimes he said that he'd been a cashier of a store in the Bahamas and had money trouble, sometimes that he'd been a dentist and had got into customer trouble, and sometimes that he'd been a tug-boat master who got mixed up in the illegal shipping of narcotics. His best one which he swore to when he was drunk was that he'd been a curator at a Zoo and had, through negligence, been responsible for the death of an old man who'd fallen into the bear pit. Maybe they were all right because in his fifty odd years he'd been everywhere and was still travelling. Some things about him, however, were certain. He was usually two jumps ahead of anything you were going to think. Sober there wasn't a mean streak in him and, drunk or sober, he'd never harmed anyone without due cause. His definition of 'cause,' though, wasn't orthodox.

He turned to me, wrapping his face in a towel and repeated, 'Does it fit?'

I nodded and said, 'Yes, but it could mean you won't be able to come back here.'

He waved a big hand and his dressing-gown fell apart to show a gorilla-haired chest. 'Pooh! Nothing. I can open a boarding house anywhere.' Seeing his open gown he stared down at his nakedness and then patted his paunch. 'Filling up. I need exercise. Thought of taking up golf again. Know I was once runner-up in the Dutch open? Fact. Haven't touched a club since. . . .' He paused and then gave a little shrug of his big shoulders. 'Well, tell me about it while I dress.'

I told him what the proposition was and roughly how I thought we should handle it. All the time I was talking he was wandering round the room collecting his clothes and dressing. It was the untidiest room in the world. It gave you the impression that at some time or other he expected to be isolated here by some cosmic catastrophe and that he had gathered up all the odds and ends he felt might be useful for survival. There were no food stores, of course, for he wouldn't need any food. But there were a couple of crates of whiskey and a shelf full of brandy bottles. He jerked aside the bed covers looking for a neck-scarf which he had draped over the end of the bed. A cat with one battle-scarred ear drooping

crawled out from the foot of the bed and, arching its back and
purring loudly, began to sharpen its claws on the sheets.

'Sarah,' he said, 'a real old Madam.'

'You can see,' I pointed out to him, 'that you can't come back
here. Not for a long time, anyway. What about all this stuff and
this house?'

'Don't worry. I'm due for a move. Valda can take over here.
How much do I get?'

'You name it.' I wouldn't argue with Monk over money.

'Let's see?' He picked up the cat and ran a hand over its muzzle
affectionately. 'Fifty thousand dollars. . . . You'll need two other
people, some kind of arms, possibly the passages and Barrau's
commission. Normally I'd say five thousand dollars. But this time
I'll settle for two thousand now.'

'What do you mean, this time?'

He dropped the cat gently to the bed and began to pull on a
linen jacket over his sky blue shirt.

'You need the money more than I do. You wouldn't have
accepted this otherwise. We won't argue about it. The man who's
coming out best is Angelo Libertad. For fifty thousand he's getting
six planes worth a damned sight more than that.'

I pulled out the yellow envelope from my pocket and began to
count out dollars. 'Two now,' I said, 'and another three thousand
when I collect in Acaibo. No argument. What about the other two
men? They've got to take orders and work fast, and they've got to
look as though they're passengers. Just a couple of toughs that every
shipmaster knows won't do.'

He went towards the door. 'I'll get the Hueica brothers. They've
just sold up their taxi business and want to get back to Guatemala.
They could use five thousand between them. Tomez is the brains
and the mouth. Sardi is the body, the hands. They'd kill their
grandmother if the price were right. But if you say go gentle, then
they'll go gentle.'

'I want it gentle. That way the thing will blow over quicker
afterwards.'

He opened the door to call for Valda but she was already coming
across the landing with a cup and saucer in her hand.

'I bring a cup for your friend for coffee.'

'Good girl.' He took the cup and saucer and patted her on the
cheek in the same way that he had fondled the cat. 'Now go and
tell the Hueica brothers to come up here.'

'Hueica?'

'The little dark ones. Room with the broken wash-basin.'

He shut the door and turned back to me.

'Another one to dirty.' He filled the cup with cold coffee, swilled it round and jerked the liquid into the basin. Then seeing the yellow envelope in my hands he went on, 'Count out their five thousand now and then put that away. Don't let 'em ever see your accounts.' He sat down on a whiskey crate and began to roll a cigarette, doing it deftly with one hand while he looked up at me and said:

'You know the Cordillo set-up?'

'Only roughly.'

'That's the word—rough. Angelo's been at it for a couple of years. It's the usual stuff. Land reform, a better deal for the peasants, abolition of privileges, Cordillo for the Cordillans. He's got some points. So have the other side. But he's too much of an idealist. That's what makes it tough for him. He's doing this on a shoestring. If he wanted to, he could have had a dozen backers with plenty of cash—as long as he paid them off afterwards with concessions, oil rights, transport agreements and exploitation grants. Plenty of pickings in Cordillo. But he won't do it. He's not selling out to the oil, fruit or mineral people.'

'He's getting money, though.'

'Sure. From the workers. Collections all over the place. But there's a bottom to that kind of well. As for the military position—'

He broke off as there was a knock on the door.

'Come in,' he called.

The door opened and shut and they were in; the Hueica brothers, two small, dark-skinned little men in white suits and flowered American ties topped by neat, friendly smiles. They looked very much alike, except—as I learned when Monk introduced them—Sardi was the one with a thin pencil line of moustache. They were Guatemalan born and clearly had a lot of Indian blood. I explained to them what I wanted and that I would pay them five thousand dollars between them. Sardi said nothing and Tomez in a gentle little voice said, 'Yes, señor.' He took the money, counted it carefully, and then split it, handing Sardi his share. I told them to stay on tap in the house and that Monk would give them their instructions.

I finished, 'From Acaibo, you find your own way home. That understood?'

Tomez nodded and said, 'Yes, señor.'

When they were gone, I told Monk that I would fix the passages. He could go aboard the *Mara II* tomorrow and look over the lay-out. We would make our final plan on board. It was a three-day trip to Caramanga. We wanted to take over on the second night out. That meant we could get the *Mara II* into Acaibo late the following night. The four of us could hold the ship for twenty-four hours. And it could possibly be less if Angelo sent out a boat to meet us.

When I left Monk I went to the shipping office and took up the reservations for the four of us. Señor Fondes had paid a hundred dollars deposit. I had the passage bookings for Monk and myself made out under false names. Smith for myself and Grusman for Monk. It wasn't the first time that Monk and I had travelled under false names. Barrau would fix the passports. There was sure to be a lot of stir when this job was done, though I guessed it would quickly die away, particularly when Angelo Libertad's people took over and Cordillo became respectable. Anyway, I didn't want the police to be looking for Keith Marchant. Mr. Smith they could chase for ever. I asked the clerk who else was on the passenger list and he pushed it across for me to see. Señorita Katrina Davia and a Señor H. Parkes were the only other two.

'Six, is that all she'll take?'

'No, señor. Twelve. But from here there are never many. She picks up more at Caramanga.'

After the shipping office I went along to Barrau and found him with his bottom still in his chair and his feet on the desk.

He gave me a warm, commission-flushed smile and said, 'How do you find the little señorita?'

'She's a child. Angelo wants his head examined.'

'He's not such a fool. No one knows the family connection. Any of his men over here would cause comment. It was unwise for Fondes to come. Maybe that's why he changed his mind and went back. You have found the people to go with you?'

'Yes. Monk Sandoz, and a couple of brothers Hueica.'

'Ah, Monk. Yes, he is all right. And the little taxi-men. They had to sell up because the big boys don't like these little operators. Don't be taken in by their smiles . . . Sardi especially. He can be very fast, like a *fer-de-lance*. And now?'

'I want false passports for Monk and myself, and arms. No revolvers. They don't impress on this kind of affair. Four sub-machine guns, not too heavy. I want them aboard in a suitcase in my cabin tomorrow evening. Locked. The key to me at the hotel. And fifty rounds for each. You can manage that?'

He nodded. 'Expensive, though. One hundred dollars each. The passports come free—for you.'

'Four hundred dollars? Are you mad?'

'I have to get them aboard past the customs. You know how to do that without money? Besides, why should you worry? When you get to Acaibo, you can flog them to Angelo's people at a profit. The current rate for what you want is about a hundred and twenty dollars a gun over there.'

I paid him four hundred dollars. By the time I had paid the hotel option, and a few other debts, including Drea's topaz brooch, I was going to step aboard the *Mara II* with very few dollars in my pocket. However, once in Acaibo things would be different.

As I was about to leave, Barrau said, 'Where do you go after this is all over?'

'I can't come back here, and I don't want to. From Cordillo I shall go on to Haiti—it's less than a hundred miles north. I'll work something out from there. I'll send you your commission.'

'This I know . . .' He stared at the end of his pointed black crocodile skin shoes on the desk. 'You need this money bad, eh?'

'Why do you say that? I always need money.'

'But not so bad that you beat me down so much on commission. That is not like you.'

'Times are hard,' I said.

He shook his head, his chins flopping loosely. But he said no more.

I went down the stairs past the poorly lit Madonna and out into the yard. There were no children about and the heat came up off the stones full of smells. The old woman of the Lima beans stood in the doorway of her hut and watched me climb into the car. She came slowly over and held out her hand. I gave her twenty centavos, but I wasn't sure whether it was just charity or whether she felt there had been an unspoken agreement between us for looking after the car.

I drove slowly down to the docks and found the *Mara II*. I didn't want to go aboard yet. I just wanted to have a look at her. I parked alongside a warehouse and then strolled across the rail tracks.

She was a biggish cargo boat. By the look of her she hadn't long had a repaint and her single stack was banded with the house colours of blue and maroon. The bridge and cabin superstructures

were set well aft to accommodate a long foredeck and cargo well.
Her bows went up high and sheer, giving her a racy, thrusting look.

There was an officer out on the starboard bridge wing directing
loading operations. Alongside there was a lorry, just a cab with a
long, articulated chassis, and squatting on it, wings dismantled,
was a Hawker Sea Fury. It looked like some stranded, mutilated
insect. Slings were coming down from the derricks. There was the
usual shouting match between deck and quay parties, the officer on
the bridge cutting in now and then with a sharp blast on a whistle.
The lorry driver was in the cab, smoking and reading a newspaper.

As I went across a bunch of five or six men came from the left
of the lorry and walked slowly the length of the tender, keeping
about ten yards away. Two of them carried a banner supported on
a couple of poles and the rest trailed behind like a church procession.
The banner proclaimed—*Viva Angelo Libertad*. One of the men
moved out of the file and thrust a sheet of printed paper into my
hand.

I looked it over quickly. It was the usual stuff . . . the workers of
Colombia protesting over the sale of planes to the Republic of
Cordillo . . . planes that would be used against Angelo Libertad
and the workers of Cordillo. None of the men in the procession
looked as though he cared a damn about it either way and I guessed
they were hired for a few centavos a day to march up and down.
They went the length of the *Mara II*, then the pole bearers were
relieved by two others. They turned and came back again. They
made a sad little procession and no one was taking any notice of
them. In this and all the other countries out here few workers cared
a button about other workers. If you had a job, you stuck to it
because there were plenty of others waiting to take your place. No
revolutionary movement stood a chance unless the big boys—the
generals, the business men and the politicians—were behind it.

The procession came back past me and, to avoid them, I went
forward a few steps. As I did so a man came round the lorry cab
and danced up to me, frowning, and growled in English, 'Get back
there, you! If you want to start bloody agitating, bloody agitate
somewhere else. I've got enough on my hands without having to
be pestered by you bastards. Workers! Hell's bells, I thought the
English workers were bad enough—but this lot!'

He was a short, square-faced man, restless as a pug-dog, and
with bushy, sandy eyebrows, and he wore a shiny navy blue serge
suit which must have been as hot as hell in this heat. I stood there,

the leaflet in my hand, and tried to place his accent. It was that flat, anywhere west of London voice . . . Middlesex, Surrey.

He came up closer to me and made an angry sound, and then, flapping his hands at me, said, 'O.K. O.K. So you don't understand my lingo. Scarper! Vamos! And if you want to know what to do with that bit of paper in your hand I'll tell you. Bloody politics!' He looked away from me briefly as the dockhands on the lorry began to pass a sling under the tail end of the Fury's fuselage and he clucked to himself just like an old hen.

I said, 'I understand the lingo all right. It's my own. And you needn't tell me what to do with the paper.' I screwed it up and tossed it away.

He looked at me without saying anything. Then he shook his head and for a moment the square, wrinkled face broke into a smile.

'Sorry, guv'nor. Thought you was one of them. They get on my nerves. They've got 'em up at Soledad, too.'

'The airport?'

'Yes. We're bringing this lot down from there. What a job! Excuse me—' He moved away from me and climbed up on to the lorry and pushed his way between the three men who were fiddling with the sling. Someone shouted down from the deck and the officer's whistle blew. I saw the back of his blue serge suit heave up from amongst the men and he shouted, 'Hold it! What do you think you're slinging—a crate of bloody oranges? Tell that bastard not to blow his whistle until I give the sign or I'll . . .' The rest was lost as he went to examine the sling fixing.

I went back to the car, smiling. Señor Parkes, without a doubt. How was he going to feel when I took his beloved planes from him? I'd met his kind many times amongst ground staff. They were the ones who really kept you aloft. Though never flying, they had more love for the machine than anyone else, ready to swear at any ignorant who didn't respect the beauty of their charges.

I watched the operation for a while. It looked to me as though they might get perhaps four of the planes below deck. They were just under forty feet long. Some would clearly have to be deck cargo.

That evening I took Drea to a place down the river for dinner. You could sit on a balcony, hung with vines, overlooking the Magdalena. The darkness over the water was studded with the lights of small craft and now and again there was the slow, brilliantly lit crawl of big stuff coming in from the sea. In the room behind the balcony

was a band and we had a couple of drinks and danced for a
while before eating. We didn't talk much. Since she had issued her
ultimatum we had never referred to it, but it was with us both.
Quite frankly I didn't know how to get things started. I'd well
committed myself now. All that remained was to get her agreement.

In the end, over our coffee and liqueurs, I said bluntly, 'I'm
sailing for Caramanga in a couple of days.'

She watched me across the table, one hand playing with her little
silver cigarette lighter. She said nothing, so I went on, 'I've got a
job there, and I want to talk to you about it seriously, Drea.'

Smiling, she said, 'It'll be a change for you to be serious. And
you know how I feel about your jobs. I hope it's the right kind.'

I said quickly, 'Let's skip that for the moment. You remember
Marty's place at St. Thomas? You know, that scheme we had for
taking it over . . . you doing the hotel and me running charter trips,
fishing cruises?'

'I remember.'

'We're as good as there. I've got a two month option on it.'

Her eyes came up quickly. 'It's still for sale?'

'Yes. I paid two thousand dollars for the option. It's going for
twenty-five thousand. For thirty odd thousand we can fix up a
schooner or launch as well.'

'I'm sure we could. But where do you get that kind of money,
Keith? Another miracle?'

I shook my head. 'Not this time. Look, everything you've said
about these Barrau jobs is right. I'll do what you say. But you've
got to face the fact that places like the hotel at St. Thomas, something that we know is absolutely right for both of us, don't come
along so often.'

She said quickly, 'Why don't you come to the real point?'

'I am.'

'No, you're not. You're going round it. Keith, I'm not a fool.
You hate the thought of settling down for years and working for
something. Marty's place would suit us both, and you want it right
away. A lovely short-cut. So how do you get the money?'

'I just want you to give me a chance. St. Thomas would be our
place and we'd be together and you wouldn't have any more waiting
around worrying while I was away.'

'You're talking too fast, Keith! Where and how are you going to
get all that money so quickly?'

'Barrau's got a job for me that would bring in all we needed.'

She was about to speak, but I went on quickly: 'It's a simple job, too. No great risk attached to it. All I ask is that you let our old contract run for a couple more weeks. You've stood it for five years. Just let me do this one job—another two weeks at the most. It's a really big chance.'

For a moment I thought she was going to stand up and walk away, but I put my hand on hers and she stayed where she was. I saw her breathe deeply, the line of her lips tightening. Then she relaxed, and her free hand went up to her cheek as though she were soothing some sudden spasm of pain.

'Keith,' she said, 'haven't you really got it into your head that I'm serious? Hasn't it got through to you that you can't go on relying on our love? I meant what I said the other evening. And now here you come back asking for one more mad chance to make a killing. Say I give it to you—and then it fails? I'll have had another spell of anxiety. And up you'll come again asking for another chance, and then another chance, and so it will go on.'

'It won't be like that. This time nothing will go wrong. I'm just asking you to give me this one last chance.'

She didn't answer for a moment. In the room behind us the band began to play a tango. A man and a woman came along the balcony, his arm around the woman's waist, and they were laughing.

Drea said, 'I'm in love with you, God knows. But I'm still learning about you. The trouble is, you never learn about yourself. If you fail this time, you'll want another chance. I could want to give it to you. After all why should I try and tell you how to live? But I'm not going to let myself do it.'

'You mean you won't give me this chance? You don't want me to try and get this hotel?'

'Of course I do. But not so much that I'd let you take on some job where you might be killed—'

'That's nonsense!'

'Is it? What kind of job is it? I want the truth, Keith.'

'Barrau and I have fixed up an armaments deal and I've got to run the stuff into Cordillo.'

'Armaments?'

'For the revolutionaries. The only snag is that there will be some temporary political repercussions. I shouldn't be able to come back to Barranquilla. But then I won't need to. We shall have the hotel. You could meet me somewhere in a week or so.' I didn't want to go into details of the job. Even so she was ahead of me on that.

She got up from the table and went slowly along the balcony. I followed her, my hand on her elbow. We went down a flight of steps to a small concrete pierhead by the river where there were a few boats tied up. The dank river smell was strong on the air and I found myself thinking of the old river boat going up to Bogota where I had first met her. I had to have this chance. We had to go on being together.

Without looking at me she said, 'I can see you don't want to tell me what the job really is. All right, I don't want to know. But there's something you've got to know. Something which I know about you and which you won't ever believe about yourself.'

'Just give me this chance,' I said.

'If I do it's for the last time. If it doesn't come off it will be the end. I shall go and you won't be able to stop me.'

I put my arm around her, drawing her close to me. 'Nothing will go wrong,' I said tenderly. 'It's a simple job. We're heading straight for that place up in the islands.'

She trembled against me and then said, 'But have you got it, Keith? Do you really understand? If this chance goes wrong, I'm not going to give you other chances. If this affair goes wrong—then you've lost me, Keith.'

I walked her gently towards the end of the pier. 'Of course I understand. But frankly, I'm not going to worry about it because nothing will go wrong. And when I'm away don't go working yourself up. . . . There's nothing to it.'

She turned then, facing me, standing close to me within my arms.

'You're a liar, Keith, aren't you?' she said softly. 'For so much money, this job must be dangerous. Whether I know what it is or not, I shall worry. But it's for the last time. Where do you want me to meet you?'

'In eight or nine days after I leave. I thought Port-au-Prince would be a good place. I can get there easily.'

'Port-au-Prince?'

'It just happens to be the most convenient place.' I knew what she was thinking. We'd been there three years before when there had been trouble between us . . . the only time until now. Our hotel room had been like an eagle's perch above the town, looking down on the blue bay of Gonave and the green and yellow plains backed by the Boutillier mountains.

'The Hotel Montana,' I said. 'You may have to wait around for

A DELIVERY OF FURIES 273

a few days because I'll have to get a passage from Cordillo. But I'll turn up.'

She came close to me, her face hidden. 'I've hated saying this to you, Keith. It makes me feel bitchy and hard, but I had to make you understand that no matter how much I love you I have to have something else from our love than the things I've had so far.'

I put my arms around her and kissed her.

'Darling, don't worry. Everything is going to be all right.' I kissed her again and then seeing how miserable she looked, I went on, laughing, 'Come on, we'll open a bottle of champagne to the future and dance all night. . . .'

With a little cry she came to me then, collapsing into a fierce hungry embrace, her arms and hands hard and binding round my body. Everything was going to be all right. I was going to make it all right. I loved her and she loved me. She wasn't going to have to refuse me other chances because this was going to be a success.

The next two days passed quickly enough. On the first of them I telephoned Katrina Davia in her room and we had lunch in the town and I gave her a progress report. I asked her if she had any means of communicating with Acaibo and when she said she had—there was a radio ham just outside Soledad who worked for Angelo—I gave her the position and time for a meeting off Acaibo. Monk had worked this out for me. He was the man who knew all about navigation and the likely speed to be logged by the *Mara II*. I told her, too, about Monk and the Hueica boys, but that as far as she was concerned they were to remain strangers except for the normal sea-passage exchanges one couldn't avoid on a boat. As for me, there was no harm in knowing me since we were from the same hotel.

'If anything goes wrong, don't get yourself involved. You know nothing about me, except that you met me at the *Polo Norte*. Monk knows who you are, but the Hueica boys will have no idea you are anything to do with us. They'd sell you off in Caramanga to save their own hides. You've got that? If anything goes wrong—keep out of it.'

She nodded a little primly and sat there as though she were being given instructions for a Sunday School treat and what to do if she got lost. There wasn't any job comparable to this one even in a small way which I'd ever done when at some very early point I hadn't got butterflies in the stomach. She was so raw at this kind of thing that, I could swear, she hadn't even got as far as that. Which was reasonable, I suppose. It's not until you hear your first blast of machine gun fire, or the first dull smack of a bullet meant for you behind your head that you acquire the grace to be scared.

But she did ask, 'Will there be any shooting?'

'If there is it won't be at anyone, I hope. Just a rat-tat or two to keep people in their places. That's all that's needed.' I hoped that this would be strictly true, but there was no need for her to have any doubts.

We had a bottle of wine with lunch and towards the end it loosened her up a little—or maybe she was beginning to lose her strangeness with me and to see me as a personality not just as a name among others in a plan—for she said:

'I suppose it doesn't matter to you which side you work for as long as you get paid? You'd have done this the other way round, say?'

'I would. I'm for hire. I don't involve myself in issues. But once the contract is signed you don't have to worry. I'll honour it.'

'I don't understand. You don't seem like that at all.'

'You'd like me to do it for love? The love of an idea? Take sides?' I shook my head and beckoned the waiter over to order brandy and coffee. 'Not me. I stopped doing that years ago.'

For a moment I thought she was going to go on with her questions. She thought better of it—but only for a few moments—because after she'd refused a brandy and while I was taking my first sip of mine she said:

'But there are some things you wouldn't do for money?'

Momentarily I felt I might be a man from Mars being questioned about his general ethics. Then I realised that she was—for all her involvement in her brother's affairs—really new to my world and my kind of men. She had no idea how we ticked.

Patiently, I said, 'Well, let me think, what wouldn't I do for money? Not murder, ill treat babies or animals, steal from those who would really miss it . . . quite a few things I suppose. And now, if you've finished your coffee I'll drop you back at the hotel.'

There was a note from Barrau waiting for me in my room. In it was the key to the suitcase he was going to have smuggled aboard for me. The note said that he had put in three or four tear-gas grenades as a bonus, and added that he couldn't accept responsibility for their effectiveness if used because they were very old American stock, police issue from the Panama Zone.

I spent the last afternoon packing for the boat and going around town paying off my bills. I finished up at Monk's place for a final word with him. He'd been aboard the *Mara II* and had a look round. She had a Costa Rica registration and most of the crew were Costa Ricans, but the captain was a Greek, and the first mate a French-Canadian. I had a couple of drinks with him and then went back to the hotel and showered and changed.

Drea and I went down to Puerto for dinner and although we both knew that this evening was different from all the others we had spent together we made no reference to it. We laughed and drank and danced, making a hedge around these few remaining hours, looking neither forward nor back. Afterwards we drove along to Barrau's cottage and she made coffee and then we lay on the beach mattresses on the verandah. For a little while as she rested in my arms I could feel her trembling, feel something of the apprehension for us both which was awake in her. And her weakness gave me a sense of strength and almost angry determination. Nothing was ever going to part us. Nothing was going to stop me giving her the future she wanted from me . . .

Before midnight we drove back to the *Polo Norte* and she sat in the car while I got my cases. Then she drove me down to the dock. She kissed me before I got out of the car.

'Keith, oh Keith, look after yourself.'

'I'll be all right. Hang on here and I'll fix it so that you can come aboard for a last drink.'

I carried my cases up the gangway to the deck and was met by a steward. I was about to ask him to bring some drinks to my cabin and for permission for Drea to come aboard when I heard the sound of a car driving off. It was Drea going. I stood there and watched the car bump across the tracks, then turn a warehouse corner and disappear.

I didn't mind. This was the way she wanted it. Hating the dragging out of goodbyes. But I would see her again in Haiti. She would always be with me. I could feel the strong chain around my heart. . . .

CHAPTER 5

It was a long time before I went to sleep that night. I had a double-berth cabin to myself on the port side. I lay in the top bunk with the light off and listened to the deck noises. We pulled out about an hour after midnight and went down river. I liked moving off. I liked starting something anew. That had been my trouble. I liked new routes and a flexible time-table. I didn't want to stay on one road and pass the same places, the same people each time, every day. There was nothing you could do about it if you were really like that. I'd tried in the past. A man, everyone said, must make something of himself, carve a niche for himself, settle down and prosper. After Korea I'd flown for a time with *Aerovias Brasil,* and then with the *Rutas Aereas Nacionales, S.A.,* in Venezuela. But in the end the routine had got me down and I'd given up fighting the nomad instinct. And now, when I should have been looking forward to this trip . . . yes, looking forward, since whatever I did I had to enjoy otherwise there was no point in it . . . it was to know that too much depended on it. If I failed Drea she would go. Life without Drea. . . . Well, there had been a life without her up to five years ago. I tried to remember back past that, to the girls I'd known and loved. They were just a lot of grey shapes. What is it that one woman has, only one woman in any man's life, the woman who comes early or late and is there for ever?

I went to sleep before I got too morbid. I woke early and, locking the cabin door, I checked the arms in the suitcase. They had seen some use but I worked them over, bolt and trigger action, and they were all right. I slipped a full magazine on each one and then locked them back in the case.

When I went on deck there was no land to be seen, just a smooth run of sea and a few puffs of idle cloud high up. Although I was early into breakfast the Hueica brothers were already there. The dining-saloon was small and narrow with one long run of table down it and a small cross-table at the top for the captain and his officers. The Hueica brothers sat side by side half-way down the table, looking very subdued, neat and, I felt, very much aware that they had to show their best party manners. I gave them a nod and sat down at the near end of the table. They bent over their grape-fruit, two quiet little men in linen suits and flowered ties, their dark hair plastered tightly over their heads. They looked just like some brother-act, acrobats, jugglers, heading for their next booking.

The steward brought me coffee and toast and as he went away from me I heard him greet someone with '*Buenos dias, señor.*'

I looked up as a young fair-haired man began to take a place opposite me. He gave me a smile as he sat down. I saw the Hueica brothers' heads swivel round for a moment to take him in and then go back like marionettes. He was in his twenties, a tall, well-set up figure in white trousers and a blue blazer with some motif on the silver buttons which I did not recognise. He looked well-tubbed and shaved, and was good-looking in an athletic way, with a squarish, well-marked face. In England I would have put him down as public school, then one of the services, or perhaps a young city type, stockbroker, Lloyds. But his speech as he ordered his breakfast from the steward marked him as good-class Spanish. Since I had seen the passenger list and knew everyone who was to be on the *Mara II*, I decided that he was a late booking. Well, he didn't know it, but he was in for a little excitement.

And then, as I was lighting a cigarette a few minutes later to finish off my coffee, Señor Parkes came into the saloon. He still wore his navy serge suit, but as some sort of concession for being on shipboard he had white deck shoes and carried a panama hat. He sat down alongside the young man who turned to him and said in English:

'Everything all right, Henry?'

'Yes, Mr. Albano. Everything's O.K.'

'Good. Now you can relax for a couple of days.'

'I'll say. What a caper, eh?' He turned to the steward who had come up and went on, 'Tea—and make it strong. And eggs and bacon.' He glanced at the other's grapefruit. 'That stuff goes sour in my stomach.'

I got up to go. What was John MacIntyre Albano, son of the Minister of Defence for the Republic of Cordillo, doing on board?

As I moved, Parkes looked across to me and gave a quick, friendly nod.

'Seen you before, haven't I? Yes, of course.'

'Briefly. I was on the dockside.'

'That's it. Took you for one of those Libertad agitators.'

The young man looked quickly up at me. I laughed. 'Don't worry. Agitation's not my line.' I introduced myself as Mr. Smith and he half rose and held out his hand.

'Albano,' he said. 'Parkes here is my right-hand man. You're English?'

'Yes.'

'That's nice. I was in England for a spell, at Cranwell. We must have a chat sometime.'

'I'd be glad to.'

The steward came back and put a plate of bacon and eggs in front of Parkes. As I moved away I heard him saying, 'Why do they have to fry 'em in this bloody olive oil? Did the same thing in Yugoslavia when I was there.'

I went on deck and walked along under the bridge wing and leaned over the rail, finishing my cigarette. On the cargo deck below me were three Sea Furies, swaddled up in tarpaulins, wings gone, propellers off, looking like enormous mummies in their wrappings. They were roped down to stanchions and one of the crew was swabbing the decks between them.

John MacIntyre Albano, a nice-looking young man, a touch of Scots in him still from some distant marriage . . . the blue eyes, maybe; the square line to the top of his cheek bones. . . . And he was heading straight for Acaibo and Angelo Libertad. I didn't feel at all good about that.

I flipped my cigarette end into the sea and turned away. Katrina had the cabin opposite mine. I hesitated for a moment outside the door. They were going to pay me a great deal of money for this job. Not more than it was worth, but it could be that they were, with my help, taking a quiet bonus for themselves in the shape of Albano. Perhaps I'd made a mistake about Katrina. Perhaps she wasn't as raw to this kind of thing as I imagined. I could feel my anger coming up. I knocked and she called, 'Who is it?'

'Marchant.'

'Come in.'

She was standing by the wash-basin on the far side of the cabin, one foot up on a small stool, and she was painting her toe nails. She looked round and up to me and smiled. She made a pretty picture, young and nice looking, a pleasant girl with her pleated white skirt falling in a graceful line from the angle of her poised knee, the dark hair neatly tied back into a short tail of hair at the back of her neck.

I said, 'John MacIntyre Albano is on this boat.'

Her foot came down from the stool and she turned to face me, one hand going back and placing the bottle of nail polish on the edge of the basin behind her.

'He can't be. He's flying.'

I went across to her and took her firmly by the arm.

'He's on board. I've just had breakfast with him. Did you know this was going to happen?'

'Of course not.'

Her face was close to mine and I could see the firming of her mouth, the little movement of her chin.

'He's here. And he's going to finish up in Acaibo. You may not have known it was going to happen. But what about Fondes?'

'He didn't know, either. He expressly said that Albano was going to fly.'

'I wonder. I've a damned good mind to call the whole thing off.'

'But you can't do that.'

'I can. Listen,' I let go of her arm; 'this job is big enough by itself. If it comes off I'm going to have to tuck myself away for quite a while until it blows over. But if anything happens to Albano it will take ages to blow over. You don't think your brother is just going to let Albano go . . . sail out in the *Mara II* when he's taken the planes?'

She moved away from me, her hands fiddling with one another, long hands with a fresh coat of pale pink varnish on the nails. Then she turned back and her chin tilted up as she looked squarely at me.

'Which are you worried about? Yourself or Albano?'

'Both. I want this thing to go through smoothly and be quickly forgotten. That's for me. And I'm not in any kind of business which goes around body-snatching for a lot of lousy revolutionaries—'

'Don't talk like that!' she said sharply. 'My brother is a man of the highest principles.'

'Look, let's not argue that one. Albano's here, aboard. What do you think your brother will do with him at Acaibo?'

'I don't know.'

'I do. He'll hold him. He's the son of the Defence Minister. That's a good card to have. More than that he's organising the Republic's

half-pint air force. There are six more Sea Furies to come from
Colombia. Can you see your brother letting him go off to get on
with that job?'

I moved away and lit a cigarette. I was pretty sure that she
hadn't expected Albano to be aboard. But that didn't help me or
Albano. The only thing I could do to help him was to call the whole
thing off. But I couldn't do that. Maybe it was what I should have
done, but I couldn't. Drea was going to be sitting in Haiti waiting
for me. She meant more to me than all the Albanos in the world.
I had a bad case right then of uneasy conscience. I turned back to
her. A tiny edge of little teeth was biting at her lower lip and her
dark eyes watched every movement I made.

I said, 'How close are you to your brother?'

'Close?'

'Yes. To what lengths would he go for you?'

'He's . . . Well, he's got no one else. And neither have I. He
brought me up, saw me educated in America. Did everything for
me.'

'And you'd do anything for him?'

'Yes.'

'How long since you last saw him?'

'Why do you ask that?'

'Just answer,' I said impatiently. 'How long?'

'Five years.'

'And this affair has been going on actively for two years. He's
been under a lot of pressure for a long time.'

'Nothing could change him. He's absolutely honest and decent.'
There was no doubting her belief.

'He wants these planes badly. They're vital, aren't they?'

'Yes.'

'O.K., then. So if you make a promise on his behalf which will
get him the planes, he'll keep it?'

She saw what was coming then and just for a moment I caught
the change in her face and knew what it meant. She was young and
untouched, but she was learning fast. I knew exactly the doubt in
her mind because I had put it there. Two years of fighting, hiding
and running in the mountains, can change a man, sour him up and
knock the shine off his ideals.

'He wants these planes. He must have them. What promise do
you want from me?'

'I'll do this job still, if you promise on your brother's behalf to let Albano go.'

I was fighting to get some kind of break for Albano so that I could go on with this and get my money. I'd go on anyway, but she wasn't to know this. Barrau, Drea, a hundred other people would have seen through me right away, but not this girl, not yet. A few more years and she'd be wiser. I could see the hesitation in her.

I went on, 'He never expected—according to you—to collect Albano with the planes. It won't be any hardship to let him go.'

She didn't hesitate then. She said almost curtly, 'I have absolute faith in my brother. And I promise. Does that satisfy you?'

'Yes.'

'Good. And now I think I'll go and have some breakfast.'

She went out quickly, leaving me standing there. But I knew she wasn't going to eat any breakfast. She just wanted to get away by herself on deck and get used to the idea of doubting for the first time someone she loved and trusted. I wasn't happy that I'd given her a push towards reality. She was out on deck now wondering whether her brother would stand by her. She would be telling herself that he would, that she had faith in him, but she wouldn't know for certain. Yesterday, she would have staked her life on it. *An unlesson'd girl, unschool'd, unpractis'd; happy in this, she is not yet so old but she may learn...*Happy? Unhappy, I'd say.

I went to find Monk, not feeling that I liked myself much, and wondering just what sort of a chance Albano had. I'd done all I could for him.

Going out of the cabin I almost bumped into Katrina coming back.

'That was a quick breakfast.'

For a moment I thought she was going to snap some remark at me, angry with me for making her uncomfortable, but she suddenly smiled and gave a little laugh.

'It was silly of me. I went out without any shoes on.'

She looked down at her bare feet and the gleam of fresh paint on her toe nails.

I put a hand gently on her arm and said, 'Don't worry. I'm sure it'll be O.K. I only wanted to get things straight.'

With Monk it was different. He was lying on his bunk, smoking a cigar and reading. When I came in he rolled off the bunk and took off his glasses which were steel rimmed and repaired on one wing with a neat binding of thin copper wire. I told him about Albano and he rubbed a hand over his bald head and said:

'Changed his mind about flying. Couldn't bear to leave his babies. But he's in the soup now. Why'd they take the propellers off those jobs?'

'For slinging 'em aboard, I imagine. You can smash a propeller easily.'

'Why didn't they fly them over?'

'Red tape. Barrau said the Colombian authorities wouldn't admit members of the Republic's armed forces to the country. Albano got in as a civilian member of the Ministry of Defence. I don't like this at all. Do you think Katrina will have any pull with her brother?'

'Could have. My guess is they'll do a deal. Albano goes back in exchange for one of Angelo's men. Caramanga jail is full of prisoners they've pulled in. Anyway, it's not your worry. You start that kind of thing and you'll never get anywhere. Albano's father will take care of it. A straight deal.'

'I don't like him aboard, and I don't like her aboard.'

I said it almost to myself but I saw his head come up sharply and he gave me a quizzical look.

'Since when have you started kicking against facts? Hold an umbrella over someone in a storm. Act of kindness. Lightning strikes the brolly and away you both go.'

'That's good, coming from you. You're always hoisting umbrellas.'

'Sure, but I accept the risks. You'd be surprised how many times I've had my wallet lifted. Albano's not your pigeon. Let's go over this job and settle it.'

We got down to it, but all the time we were talking I was seeing that first moment of doubt take Katrina's face. I didn't think I was a sentimental type. I'd have betted against it, but there had been something in that moment which had hit me. It was going to take me a little while to push it out of my mind. Monk must have guessed it was with me for he broke off in the middle of our plans once and said:

'The trouble with you is that you've never had any children.'

'What the hell's that got to do with anything? Anyway, what do you know about children?'

'Damned sight more than you. I've had four. They're great educators for an adult. Watch them grow. You see life taking over. See 'em making their own discoveries. You've pushed Katrina into making a promise for her brother which you don't think he'll honour. Probably can't because other people won't let him. He'll give her all sorts of excuses, except the real one. So a little bit of her faith in him is whittled away. So what? When you've been a parent you can watch the whittling go on day after day. And again, so what? That's how life is. Now, stick your nose into this and let's get it sorted out. You'd better have Sardi with you. He enjoys a bit of violence but you can keep him on a tight rein.'

The plan we'd worked out didn't have any obvious snags. We only had to hold the *Mara II* for something less than twenty-four hours and during that time we should be in control of the bridge and the engine room. With any luck there wouldn't be need to fire a single shot in real earnest. I spent most of the morning on deck, going over all the details in my mind. Nothing must go wrong. I had too much at stake. Normally, I suppose, I would have been confident of my own planning, but then, normally, I wasn't personally so much committed. At the back of this was Drea, the hotel, our future. . . . Everything would be all right, I told myself. But it isn't what you tell yourself that counts. It's what you feel.

Here was the *Mara II* lifting and dropping her nose gently as she cut through a sunlit sea, everything going like clockwork, and me—with an empty feeling in the pit of my stomach, because this job meant more to me in terms of my own ultimate happiness than any other.

After lunch I took a stroll along the foredeck where the planes were lashed down. I met Parkes there. He was seldom very far from the planes. We chatted for a while and I learned that he had been sent out by the Hawker people to supervise the servicing of the planes before they were handed over to the Republic of Cordillo and then to help in their shipment and assembly when they reached Caramanga. He'd been all over the world doing similar jobs for his firm. But he made it quite clear that he hadn't much time for any place that was farther than fifty miles from London, and that for his money a plane was infinitely more complicated and precious than any human being. But that didn't mean that he was unaware of people. If they didn't have wings that was a pity but he had a shrewd eye and he surprised me after a while by saying:

'What lot was you with, sir?'

With a smile, I said, 'How on earth did you know?'

He grinned, taking off his panama and wiping his forehead with

a handkerchief. There was little breeze down on the deck and the
sun was striking hard down at us.

'You can tell always and no bloody mistake. Just a word here,
or the way a man looks at 'em. Way a bloke's hands go out sometimes when he wants to make a point. You got it. Mr. Albano's got
it, too. But not as much as you. He's young yet.'

I told him the name of a squadron—not my own—and he nodded
and then he turned his sharp blue eyes on me steadily and said,
'You like it out here? You're out here all the time?'

'More or less. My business is here.'

I wouldn't have liked to guess how much weight he gave to the
word business.

'Dunno how you stand it. They're a funny lot. Never know when
they're going to boil over. Even Mr. Albano, and he's got a lot of
Scots in him, he tells me, even he . . .' He laughed quietly. 'I seen
him go up in the air once at Soledad over a small thing one of the
men did! All he needed was a knife and the bloke would have had
it. Then the next minute he's as nice as pie. Suppose that's why
they have all these revolutions. Gets it out of their system for a
while. What's your business?'

'I'm a coffee broker.'

'You are? Well that's something. It's about the only thing they
know how to make. Though I'm a tea man, myself.'

When I left him I knew that in addition to the six Sea Furies,
the *Mara II* was carrying ten thousand rounds of 20 mm. ammunition for the Mark 5 cannons with which the planes were armed.
That was a nice little bonus for Angelo Libertad which hadn't been
mentioned to me.

He must have told Albano about my service, for the young man
invited me to have a drink with him after dinner that night. We
talked the kind of mess talk which had filled so many of my nights
in the past. He was a nice young fellow, keen and full of go. Up
until now the Republic of Cordillo had been without planes and
this was one of the reasons why Angelo had been able to hang on
to the far eastern tip of the island. Planes were needed to help blast
a way through the two mountain passes that guarded the way to
Acaibo. I didn't say so, but I knew that the blasting could be
done the other way round . . . out of the mountains and towards
Caramanga.

'Angelo's been at this for two years, hasn't he?' I asked.

'Yes. Two years open fighting.'

'What's he after?'

He had a habit of reaching up with his right hand and twisting at a stray piece of his fair hair. When his hand came down it hung for a moment in a tight ringlet and then slowly straightened out.

'Just whatever he can make for himself. He's a fake. There's a lot of talk about land reform, confiscation of sugar refineries and so on . . . Everything to be run for the people.'

'Some people must believe him. He's kept going for two years.'

'That's partly the terrain, of course. But he has support, I can't deny it. Plantation workers and that kind. He's got a way with him. And I don't say that our people haven't helped. No government is perfect. There are a lot of things that need changing in the Republic. You should hear my father on the subject! But they've got to be done slowly and sensibly—'

'So that no one who matters gets really upset or suffers?'

His hand went up nervously to his curl again but he took the remark with a smile.

'You know the world. There's no such thing as a simple problem with a simple solution. But violence and revolution never help. Libertad may have started out with all sincerity. But after a few years . . . Well, you can't avoid change. And you have to pay for the support you get.'

I said, 'Eventually you're going to fly these planes. Shoot up those passes so your troops can go through.'

'Yes,' he said firmly. 'Because I think it's the only thing to do if Cordillo is to have a real future.'

'How long has your family been in Cordillo?'

'Oh, a long time. My great-great-grandfather was a Scot. He married in Caramanga, a Spanish girl. We've been there ever since. But all the boys, you know—my father, myself and brothers, have been educated in England.'

At that moment Katrina came through the small lounge, searched for a moment until she found a book she had been reading and then went out. I saw Albano's eyes following her and I wondered what he would have said had he known who she was. Certainly not what he did say.

He turned to me and said, 'That's the kind I like. Dark, and quiet. Wonder who she is? Davia, the passenger list says, and she's getting off at Caramanga. I don't know any Davias there. Pity it's such a short trip, I might have got to know her.'

'You've still got forty-eight hours or more. Why did you come on

this boat, anyway? I should have thought you would have preferred
to fly?'

'Oh, I would. But the old man wired at the last moment and
said he thought I should stick with the planes all the way.' He
laughed. 'Parkes didn't like it. Thought I didn't trust him.'

Going back to my cabin, although I was glad to know that the
change in his plans came from his father, that Fondes and Angelo
hadn't been pulling a fast one on me, I was aware of a premonition
of trouble.

I hadn't been in my cabin long before there was a knock on the
door and in answer to my call Katrina came in.

I said, 'What have you come for? A whiskey night-cap before
turning in?'

She shook her head, smiling, and said, 'I just wanted to ask you
if everything was all right?'

'Yes, it's all fixed.'

'For when?'

'Tomorrow night.'

'But when? What time?'

'Look—it's much better that you don't know. You're a passenger.
You're going to be surprised by it, too. It's safer like that. Just in
case.'

She had the book she had been reading in her hands still and I
could see the nervous fiddle of her fingers, riffling the pages.

'Forget all about it. Until it happens,' I said.

'I know.' She nodded and the cabin lights streaked the black hair
with gold. 'It's just that I'm a little nervous. Well, not a little. Just
plain nervous. After all—'

'I know. After all, you've never done anything like this before.
Never been mixed up in this sort of thing. Well, if it's any comfort,
I can tell you that I'm a bit nervous, too. That's how it always is.
Monk's nervous and so are the Hueica brothers. We all are until
the starter's bell goes. Now go and get some beauty sleep.'

For a moment I thought she was going to turn docilely away.
But in her movement towards the door she hesitated and her face
turned back to me.

She said, 'I won't be any trouble. It's just . . .' One hand made
a little flutter like a bird going up and then back from a false alarm,
' . . . just that I find it hard to accept that it's me here. Involved
in all this.'

I went over to her and put my arm round her shoulder like an old uncle.

'I know. That's part of it, too.'

'You know that feeling?'

'I did, years ago. But I've grown up now.' I opened the door and shook my head as she made to answer. I gave her shoulder a squeeze and steered her out into the companionway and watched her walk across to her cabin door.

CHAPTER 6

It had been arranged that Monk and the two Hueica brothers
should come to my cabin at half-past ten the next night to collect
their arms. Monk and Tomez were to go to the engine room which
was entered by a small doorway leading off the main deck. Inside
the doorway a steel ladder dropped sheer to the engine room and
they could cover everyone there and also part of the deck through
the doorway behind them. Sardi and myself were to go up to the
bridge. On the way we would deal with the radio operator and
smash up his apparatus. From the bridge we could cover the full
run of the cargo deck and the bow space which held the crew's
quarters. Once we were in possession we could hold the ship until
Angelo's men met us.

At half-past nine that evening I was in my cabin waiting when
there was a knock on the door. I glanced at my wristwatch. Momentarily I fancied that Monk had made a mistake in the time. But
there it was, half-past nine.

'Who is it?' I called.

'Steward, señor.'

'Come in.'

The door opened and he came a little way in. He was the cabin
steward, not the dining-saloon man. He gave me a nervous nod of
his head, his hands burying themselves in the sleeves of his white
jacket, a small birdy man with a skin the colour of cinnamon bark.

'What is it?'

'Many apologies, señor. But here is first mate like to talk to you.'

I rolled off my bunk where I had been sprawling. The first mate
came into the cabin, past the steward who backed away a little,
holding the door half-closed. I'd seen him around, on the bridge
and in the dining-saloon. According to Monk he was a French-
Canadian. Just one look at him told me that he was a man who
had no fears about being able to look after himself. He had a big,

horsey face, and was tall with narrow, stooping shoulders. I didn't like the look of him and it was clear that he didn't like the look of me. He stood there with his peaked cap on still, his shirt open to show a streaking of grey hairs running up to his throat. His white trousers hadn't seen a crease for weeks.

'Monsieur Smith?' His eyes went from me and around the cabin. I nodded. 'What is it you want?'

He came forward a step so that I was almost crowded back against the bunk and said:

'The steward is going to search your cabin.'

'What did you say?'

'The steward,' he repeated, 'is going to search your cabin.'

He gave it to me bluntly: a dark, sour-looking man who acted as though he'd long ago been convinced that there was no need to be pleasant with people.

'Why should he want to do that?'

He gave an impatient grunt, and said, 'Hand over your luggage keys.'

'No "please"?' I said. 'No "do you mind"? I'm not one of your crew.'

'The keys.' There was no shaking him.

I sat down on the edge of the bunk and said, 'Look, I don't know what all this is about, but aren't you getting out of line? I'm a passenger on this ship. Even if there were a reason for searching my cases, it would take the captain personally to make me hand over my keys. Now I suggest that you get out of here.'

'I'm a ship's officer. I'm acting with the captain's authority.' He said it over my head, his black eyes flicking round the place.

I stood up, impatient and showing my anger, and he moved back from me, watching me, giving himself room now in case I made some move. He was wise. If he'd been alone I would have gone for him, but I knew that if I tried anything now the steward would be quickly out of the door and calling for help. I couldn't risk that. But I think my move induced him to be a little more reasonable.

He said, 'We've had a radio message from Barranquilla. From the police. It states that it is thought you might have smuggled arms aboard.'

'What damned nonsense.'

'Let us hope so, monsieur. But we can only tell if you hand over the keys.'

'And if I don't?'

A small, grey smile touched his lips. He knew I was stalling. He shrugged his shoulders and said, 'I shall have to call for a couple of the crew and do it by force. Please give me the keys and if you have no arms, I apologise in advance for myself and the captain, and trust you will accept.'

I was wondering what leak there had been in Barranquilla. You never could tell. Possibly Barrau had got on the wrong side of someone, or the man who had brought the case aboard had taken his money from Barrau and then, opportunist, had doubled it by going to the police.

I moved slowly away towards the far end of the cabin. My back to him, I reached up and took down my jacket that was hanging on the side of the cabin cupboard. I took the keys out of the pocket, and, turning, jerked them across to the first mate. His eyes never leaving me he reached back and handed them to the steward.

'The cases.'

They were piled on the floor, three of them, at the foot of my bunk. The steward went to them and lifted the top one on to the bunk. It was unlocked and contained my clothes. He ferreted through it. The second one went on to the bunk. It was locked and held the rest of the stuff which had accumulated in my room at the *Polo Norte*. The first mate backed away casually so that he had me and the steward now in his vision. The steward unlocked the second case, examined the contents and then lifted it on to the first case. He turned and picked up the last case. I heard him grunt a little and wasn't surprised. It was heavier than all the rest. He found the key on my ring and opened it. It was a great moment.

The first mate cocked his head to one side, gave the case a glance and said:

'*Eh bien*, so it is true.'

I shrugged my shoulders and said nothing.

'Lock it and bring it along,' he said to the steward, and then to me he added, 'You will come with me to the captain.'

As the steward lifted the case, the first mate jerked his head at me and said sardonically, 'You go out first.' There was the gentle movement of his left thumb massaging the palm of his right hand as he flexed his knuckles. Come on, he was saying to himself, out of the door or make your bid.

This was the moment. I tensed myself to go for him. As I did so, stopping me, a voice from the partly open doorway to my right said, 'Drop that case.'

For a split second the tableau was arrested, me leaning forward on my toes, the first mate's right hand half-raised.

And then Katrina came through the doorway, pushing it closed behind her.

She must have been walking on deck before turning in because she wore a light coat, loosely open, and a yellow silk scarf was tied about her throat. Her right hand was thrust forward awkwardly and I saw the clumsy bunching of her fingers round a tiny automatic. It was the smallest thing I'd ever seen, a handbag toy . . . and, for a second or two, while we stood there immobile, I wondered if it *were* a toy, if she were taking some wild chance; wondered, too, whether she had the faintest idea how to use it.

'Drop the case,' she said again and there was no mistaking the nervous shake in her voice.

The steward half bent to obey her, beginning to lower the case when the first mate said, 'Hold on to it.' All the sourness of his character was in his voice. He cocked his head towards Katrina and went on, 'Hand over that gun and get out of our way.'

I was two yards from her and I wanted the gun, but I knew that if I moved he would move too.

Katrina said, 'Put down the case and both of you go over there.' Her right hand jerked towards the far end of the cabin. There was a break in her voice, and I knew she was fighting to preserve a fading resolution.

He didn't believe her. He had all my experience and more, maybe, and he knew how she stood.

He said, his voice searing with contempt, 'Get out of my way, you stupid bitch!' He moved forward to her, to brush her away.

She fired. Once, and then again. Two sounds, surprising and incongruous in the small cabin; two sounds like the quick slap a salmon makes when it jumps and smacks its tail against the water.

I saw the red stain on the dirty white trousers at the top of his right leg. She'd missed with her first shot and deliberately fired again. He stood looking stupidly at her, his mouth open, and then he toppled sideways and collapsed on the floor, half-sitting, and leaning forward to press his hands to the wound.

The steward dropped the case and ran for the door. I jumped past Katrina, caught his shoulder and swung him round and then hit him hard. He went spreadeagling backwards and his head got the corner of my bunk and he slid to the floor and lay there. I spun round and took the automatic from Katrina's hand. The first mate

straightened up and began to pull himself towards me. I showed
him the gun and shook my head. His face winced with his pain and
he stopped moving, leaning forward again over his wounded leg
and grunting to himself.

'Don't make any noise,' I said to the top of his head. His cap
had come off and there was a tiny patch of baldness, scurf-flaked,
right at the tip of the crown. 'If you do I'll treat you like the
steward.'

Maybe he didn't hear. He just kept his head down and I saw the
blood coming slowly out over his fingers on the crumpled white
drill.

I turned to Katrina. 'Go and get Monk. Get him here right away.
And act naturally outside. Walk, don't run.' I was pretty sure that
the couple of pip-squeak shots would not have been heard.

Katrina, shaken and white, said, 'I was coming down the corridor
and I heard them here . . . I heard them.' She looked down at the
first mate in horror.

'Get Monk,' I said.

But she stood there and stared at me and I knew I had to rush
her. I put my free hand on her shoulder and shook her hard.

'Get Monk! Get him!' I snapped and I pushed her towards the
door.

She looked at me, and then slowly nodded her head. I slipped
the door open and she went out as though she were passing from
a dream.

I turned, put my back against the shut door when she had gone,
and pulled my handkerchief from my pocket. I tossed it down to
the first mate.

'Plug it with that. You won't die.'

He took the handkerchief, made a rough pad and pressed it over
his leg.

'Bastard, you! Bastard!'

I didn't answer. We had nothing to say to one another. The
steward was snoring on the floor as though sleeping off a long
drunk.

There was no real trouble after that. Just a routine job, running a
little ahead of schedule, and with all the advantages on our side.
You must have the advantages, otherwise you get stuck with heroics.
Bravery is all right kept in its place, but I would rather have the
help of two cowards and the advantage of surprise.

Monk came back with the Hueica brothers and the cabin became an emergency ward. The Hueica brothers stripped my sheets into lengths and without a word gagged the recovering steward and bound him hands and feet, Sardi's fingers flicking the white lengths round and jerking them tight with quick little tugs, enjoying himself.

Monk slit the first mate's trouser leg and bandaged him, the big hands, slow and deft in their work, and the cigar still in his mouth which he had been smoking when Katrina called him. And the first mate said nothing because he couldn't, because Monk had gagged his mouth before he concerned himself with his wound. He was tied like the steward and lifted to my bunk. When it was done and I went to open the case I saw Katrina standing inside the door still, watching it all.

I went over to her and for a second caught her chin between my finger and thumb. I tilted her head up and saw from her eyes that she was all right now. This was just curiosity . . . the trance of watching the second act, the theatre all illusion.

I said, 'You go to your cabin and lock yourself in. Stay there until I send for you. We're all right now. Thanks to you.'

She went out and I opened the case.

Sardi and I left Monk and Tomez on the lower deck at the entrance to the engine room. We went up to the boat deck and the bridge. The *Mara II* was running sweetly into a gentle swell, just lifting and shouldering a little, on good terms with the sea. There was a moon and a sky full of stars almost as bright as a holiday poster. A yard from the door of the radio room I stopped Sardi, putting a hand on his arm. He stood by me, whippet small and breathing easily, his moustache a charcoal brush across the moonlit face.

'Remember these . . .' I lifted my sub-machine gun, ' . . . these we don't use. Unless. But a big unless.'

He nodded.

I opened the door of the radio cabin and stood aside, letting Sardi go in. I stood there, watching the light up on the bridge a few yards away and the indigo and grey sweeps of the deck below and the wingless moth shapes of the Sea Furies echeloned along the cargo well. A man began to say something inside the cabin, his voice edged with surprise and then abruptly cut away. There was a sound like a woman thumping up cushions into shape on a settee. Then a few sharp crashes and cracks and the noise of glass breaking thinly. Sardi came back. His breathing was only a few points above normal. He closed the door and we went towards the bridge.

There was no trouble with the captain. He was alone on the bridge with the wheelman.

I pushed open the half-glass door and stepped into the bridge house. The captain was leaning over a chart table on the far side of the wheel. He was a Humpty-Dumpty of a man with heavily bagged eyes and a little black mourning strip of silk in the lapel of his white jacket. He straightened up and looked at me curiously, frowning.

'Passengers are not allowed up here, señor. Will you please—'

He stopped short as I slid the sub-machine gun round to cover him. Sardi went by me and a little wide to cover the wheelman.

'I am not a passenger any longer, captain. I'm taking over this ship. I have two men in control of your engine room, your radio has gone, and your first mate is a prisoner in my cabin. All I need from you is sensible co-operation for twenty-four hours. That way neither you, nor the ship, nor the rest of the passengers will come to any harm.'

It was a long speech but I wanted to make all my points at once and he listened, still half erect, one hand on the chart table. He looked at me, lips pursing, deliberating, and his eyes on my gun. Then he straightened up and gave a fat shrug of his shoulders. Clearly he was a sensible man who knew his own limitations. Maybe in his own mind he had already made the hopeful reservation that '*the whirligig of time brings in his revenges.*' He was prepared to wait.

'You're Señor Smith?' he said.

I nodded.

'You will permit me to check what you have just said?'

'On the bridge 'phone. But move gently.'

He stepped back to the telephone and gave the handle a couple of twists.

'Speak in Spanish or English,' I said.

He rang again but there was no reply and I knew that he had been trying the radio operator. He rang again, three times. This time there was a reply from the engine room.

He said, 'You have the same trouble down there that I have here?'

I could hear the engineer officer's voice, thin and nagging like a mosquito whine. It went on for some time.

The captain said, 'Do nothing. Cause no trouble and obey all the bridge signals.'

The voice whined and hummed again and then was cut short by the captain.

'Those are my orders.'

He put the telephone back and as he did so the wheelman turned and jumped for Sardi. My eyes came back from the captain to see the wheel spin unattended and the wheelman almost on top of Sardi, a long brown hand striking downwards with a knife in it. Most other men would have been taken by surprise, even in their watchfulness, but not Sardi. *Fer-de-lance.* Barrau had said that. He melted sideways and the wheelman stumbled full length and finished up on his hands and knees. Sardi jumped behind him as he sprawled on the boards and the sub-machine gun was pointing at the back of the man's skull.

Sardi waited for the word from me.

I said, 'Stand back and let him get up.' I took a step forward and kicked the knife from the man's hand. 'Get up.'

He pulled himself up and I nodded towards the bridge door.

The captain said, 'Go forward to the crew's quarters and tell them what has happened. Tell them to do nothing.'

'Tell them also,' I added, 'that any man who shows himself on deck will get this.' I tapped the stock of the gun.

When he was gone, I said to the captain, 'Take the wheel. This is the course.' I laid Monk's bearing written on a piece of paper by him on the chart table and watched as he retrieved the wheel and brought the *Mara II* on to her new course. Then standing behind him I said, 'I want the keys of your armoury.'

He gave them to me.

'Where?'

'In the locker below the telephone.'

I opened the locker. There were three revolvers, a twelve-bore shot gun, and two .303 Lee Enfield rifles. I had Sardi carry them outside and to the far end of the open bridge wing and toss them into the sea. Then I told Sardi to go down to the deck and watch the entrance to the cabin accommodations and the crew's quarters forward. No one was to be allowed out on deck. It was late and no one was likely to try to come out. They would all be sleeping now. Every fifteen minutes he was to check with the engine room and then with me.

I was left alone on the bridge with the captain at the wheel.

He said, 'Where do we go?'

'Acaibo. To unload the Sea Furies.'

He slewed his head at me. I liked him for his self-control.

'Libertad?'

'Yes.'

'This is piracy.'

'I suppose so.'

'You must be mad.'

I didn't answer. Though I could have repeated myself and said,
I suppose so. But I didn't want to go into my form of madness, the
kind of inflexible madness which seems saner than sanity . . . Drea
waiting for me in Haiti.

He said, 'Acaibo is more than twenty-four hours. What about
the change of the deck and engine room watches?'

'Nobody changes.'

'And here? You expect me to man this wheel for twenty-four
hours?'

'At daybreak you can have the same wheelman back. He's learnt
his lesson.'

He looked at me, his thick neck creasing with the turn of his
head, and said, 'He's an honest man who tried to do his duty.'

'I know. But they learn like all the other kinds.'

He didn't say any more. He just kept his hands lightly, expertly
on the wheel, looking straight ahead of him, out to the starlit night.
Now and again I moved behind him and checked that he was still
on the same bearing. And once every fifteen minutes Sardi came
up, quiet, puppet-faced, and moving like a shadow.

By mid-day we should be met. All that remained now was to sit
out the hours. The hours to being met, the hours to reaching Acaibo
and being paid, and the hours until I could make Port-au-Prince.

CHAPTER 7

Just before daybreak when Sardi came up I made him go forward and fetch the wheelman. When the two came back, the wheelman took over from the captain and I left Sardi to watch him.

I went down and along to the cabins, making the captain go before me. There was a smudgy blur of light creeping over the eastern horizon and the deck lights were beginning to have a dissipated look as the darkness went, like creatures caught out long after the magic hour had struck.

We went first to Albano's cabin. It was unlocked and when I switched the light on he sat up in his bunk, fair hair ruffled, the front of his silk pyjamas unbuttoned to show a brown chest.

With the captain standing between us I gave him the straight facts. He didn't get what I was talking about for a while. When he did, he exploded like a rocket and was off the bunk with his feet on the ground before the quick lift of my gun restrained him. He wasn't scared, but he had enough common-sense to hold back. He stood there with his nice, young man's face working with anger, his eyes moving from me, around the cabin, to the captain, searching for something, some way to break through. He was the other side of the coin which carried Katrina's head on the reverse. They were both idealists, both dedicated to a cause . . . both the kind who could start trouble without caring what happened to themselves.

I said, 'I want your cabin key. You'll stay here until you're let out. That'll be mid-day. You won't starve.'

He was silent for a moment, and the captain said, 'I'm sorry, señor. You will be wise to do as you're told. There is nothing I can do.'

He spoke, ignoring the captain, whipping his words at me venomously. 'You swine! You dirty English swine! If you were a Libertad man I'd have some respect for you. But you're not that. You're just a rat! A money rat! So much for the planes and so much for me!'

I took it because I had to take it. All the arguments against it would have wasted too much time to set out. But I said, 'I didn't know you were going to be aboard. You were supposed to fly. You should stick to your arrangements.' I didn't say anything about the promise Katrina had made to me about him. He wouldn't believe it. I didn't have much faith in it myself. 'Calm down and behave yourself.'

'Go to fiery hell!'

'Get his key,' I said to the captain.

He kept his eyes on me as the captain went to the dressing table for the key. It lay there with his loose change, a cigarette case and a lighter. 'Wherever you go after this,' he said, 'I'll see you're found. You won't get anything out of this. Libertad's no fool. We hold many of his people. People he wants back. They'll exchange me for one of them, and one day I'll be after you. . . .' He broke off and slowly threw his head back and put his hands wearily to his forehead as though he'd been struck by some tremendous pain. And I knew he had. He had just thought of the planes and of their enormous importance to his side. He didn't look at me again. He stood there with his hands knuckled against his eyes in an anguish which had nothing to do with any anxiety for himself.

I took the key brusquely from the captain and backed out of the cabin quickly, and because I didn't want to think I just kept repeating to myself . . . Drea in Port-au-Prince. Drea in Port-au-Prince. It worked. I didn't care a damn for Albano or the tin-pot politics and struggles of Cordillo. And who the hell was Albano, anyway, to be so high and moral? If the planes had been going to Acaibo, to Angelo Libertad, then Albano would have employed me to do the job in reverse for him without a scruple. *He's an honest man who tried to do his duty.* That's how they all thought of themselves at the beginning, but once they surrendered themselves to a party, to an ambition, then the pace became too hot for them. They changed. Even his anger would change in a few months, that young man's dedicating anger to follow me and find me wherever I went. Too many things would get in the way.

I locked the door on him and we went along to Parkes.

He was up and fully dressed and was writing a letter with a pencil. To his wife, maybe? He was the kind who would use a stubby pencil, distrustful of the vagaries of fountain pens. He sat there, one hand over the sheet of notepaper to protect its privacy.

As I talked, he slowly licked the end of the pencil, watching me from under his bushy eyebrows.

I finished, 'I'm keeping your boss locked up for a while. He's the kind that needs to cool down. But if you give me your promise to try nothing you have the freedom of the deck and holds to keep an eye on the planes. I know you check over the holding ropes each morning.'

He nodded calmly, and then said, 'Coffee merchant, eh? Somehow I didn't believe that. Or the Mr. Smith. I even told Mr. Albano so. You're the other kind we used to get. Plenty of guts while they were in, but when they went out . . . Itchy bottoms, keep on the move, and sticky fingers. I'm sorry for you, mister. Now get the hell out of here and let me finish my letter.'

I went and there was no pretending that he hadn't got under my skin far more than Albano. Those hard blue eyes on me, unwavering from under the sandy brows, weren't easy to forget. Outside, as I turned back towards the deck, the captain said, 'What about Señorita Davia?'

'We needn't bother about her. She's free to go where she wants.'

I didn't explain why and he didn't ask. I stopped at the door to my cabin and unlocked it. He went in and freed the steward and then we left him to look after the first mate, locking them in again.

By mid-day we were at our rendezvous. Monk had come on to the bridge with me during the morning and the two Hueica brothers had taken over the engine room. Monk was in a good mood, a cigar sticking out of the corner of his mouth, his large face dark stubbled. He took over from the wheelman, who was sent back to the crew's quarters.

The escort from Acaibo was waiting for us. It was an old three-masted motor-schooner running under a jib and a foresail and with the motor going. We hove-to and she came alongside. Tomez Hueica dropped a rope ladder over and ten men came aboard. Three of them were West Indian negroes and the others lighter-skinned Cordilleans. They all wore green shirts and American-pattern army trousers, carried rifles, and had bandoliers slung over their shoulders. Their leader, wearing a peaked officer's cap, came up to the bridge and introduced himself to me as Lieutenant Ocampo. He was a stiff, rather jerky little figure, very correct and curt from the importance of his mission. He saluted me with a snap that must have made his wrist ache and informed me that he was

now taking over command of the ship in the name of the Democratic
Army of Cordillo. I let him get on with it. Monk and I stayed on
the bridge and watched the pantomime. Four machine guns were
slung up from the schooner and mounted strategically about the
Mara II. There was a great deal of shouting and one of the guns
was almost dropped into the sea. Half an hour later we were on
our way with the schooner some distance astern of us. I left Monk
with the captain on the bridge and went down to the cabins. The
first mate and the steward had been taken from my cabin. Albano
and Parkes were under guard in the saloon.

I shaved and put on a clean shirt and then went across to
Katrina's cabin. There was a negro guard on the door and he
wouldn't let me in. He just shook his head and said that it was the
lieutenant's orders.

I went out on deck and found the lieutenant.

'Why is there a guard on Señorita Davia's door?'

He stiffened his thin shoulders and said curtly, 'I have strict
orders, señor, from the Generalissimo that she is to be given every
protection.'

'The Generalissimo? You mean her brother?'

'No, señor. The Liberator is at the front. I speak of Generalissimo
Lemaza—her brother-in-law. He is responsible for her to her great
brother. It is my responsibility also. It is safer for her to stay where
she is.'

'Then tell your guard that I can see her.'

I saw his prim mouth work a little at the suggestion of an order
from me, but I didn't care a damn for his brief authority. As he
hesitated, I said sharply, 'I'm not going to do her any harm. I've
just handed the damn ship over to you, haven't I? I've taken the
planes for you. Besides, she's my friend. She can do with some
company. Ask her.'

'Very good, señor.' But instead of moving, he hesitated again and
I could see that something was worrying him. He swallowed a little,
making his adam's apple wobble in his thin neck, and then said,
'You did not inform me that we had Señor Albano aboard.'

'You didn't ask me.'

'You should have said. He is a most important prisoner. This I
might not have known. I should have been made to look foolish.'

'How did you find out anyway?'

'From his passport. I am careful always to check everything.'

'Well, good for you.' With any luck, if the revolution lasted long enough, he'd make captain one day. 'Now be kind enough to ask the señorita if she would see me.'

He wasn't ever going to take a liking to me, I could see that. Eventually I was allowed in to Katrina.

She had just finished a cold lunch which had been brought to her. She looked tired and I guessed that she had not slept much.

'You're hard to see,' I said. 'The full V.I.P. treatment.'

She gave a little laugh. 'It is my brother. He treats me like a baby. I must be looked after.'

'I don't get it. He lets you take on this job which is dangerous. But when it's over he puts a guard on you.'

'No, it is logical. Before, the risk had to be taken. He could do nothing about it. But now, the moment he can do something, he does.'

'Who's Generalissimo Lemaza?'

'He is my brother-in-law.'

'Everything in the family.'

'He married my sister. But she is long dead. She was the next after Angelo. Without Lemaza my brother would have found things difficult. Lemaza has the kind of brain for facts and figures, for supplies.'

'Paymaster and Quartermaster-General. Is he the chap who will pay me off?'

'I imagine so.'

'I can't wait to get to him.'

I saw then that she was looking at me with the same kind of look the lieutenant had had, a question poised, waiting to be asked.

I said, 'Go on. What's on your mind?'

'It is just for money? Nothing else? You do all this just to be paid? Oh, yes, I know you have said you do before. But I cannot believe it. There are other moments when it is not a part of you.' She dropped her eyes from me, embarrassed by her own frankness, and touched a fork on the tray.

'Just money,' I said. 'It's a portmanteau word. It wraps up everything.'

'Or everybody?'

'Why do you say that?'

She shrugged her shoulders, looking up at me, and said, 'I know you think I am young. No experience. But I am not so young. People don't do things for things. They do them for other people,

and I am sure that if you need money you do not need it for
yourself.'

'I need it. Let's leave it like that.'

'If you say so. But I should like to have heard about it. You see
I am learning fast. Last night. All this business. Learning about
myself. It was me who stood in your cabin and shot at a man. I
have learnt that I could do that. I have learnt how strongly I feel.
I have also learnt that there are some people to whom I can speak
like this. To you, for instance. But there is much more to know.'

'Why?'

She turned away a little and caught gently at the end of her bunk
curtain. 'Because I wish to grow up, quickly.'

I laughed gently. 'Don't force the pace. It will all come in its
own good time. What you want is some fresh air, some exercise.
Shall I go and twist the lieutenant's arm and get permission.'

'No, thank you.'

Her face came back to me, but it was no longer the young,
unmarked Madonna face, the chaperon-shadowed demureness of
the evening stroll round the town square. Something had happened
to her. She was waking up fast, she was finding she had a tongue
to speak more than common-places, a mind that forced curiosity
on herself, and emotions which she had to learn to handle.

I said, 'If I were you I'd take three aspirins and turn in. You've
had a basinful.'

The age-old prescription that no one ever takes. Go to sleep and
forget it.

I went up on to the bridge to join Monk. He pointed to a long
green smudge away to the north.

'Cordillo. It'll be dark by the time we get there. We'll have to
lay off tonight. Can't take her in at night. It's too tricky. How long
do you reckon to stay in Acaibo?'

'Just as long as it takes me to collect my money.'

It was dark when we got to Acaibo. The *Mara II* dropped anchor
off the mouth of the harbour to wait for daylight to get into her
berth. A couple of motor boats manned by Democractic Army
soldiers came out to us after about half an hour. Lieutenant
Ocampo, in full and brisk command, had the companion steps
lowered over the side and a little later Albano and Parkes were
taken off with their luggage. I was with Monk on the bridge and

heard Parkes cursing stolidly to himself. The second motor-boat took off Lieutenant Ocampo and Katrina.

I went down to the deck and met them as they were at the head of the steps.

'Am I free to go ashore?' I asked the lieutenant.

'In the morning, señor. There are rooms for you and your friends in the hotel. I go to report to the Generalissimo and then I shall be back. Señorita. . . .' He stood aside for Katrina to pass to the steps.

She looked at me and smiled and said, 'I shall see you in Acaibo?'

'You're staying at the hotel?'

She shook her head. 'No. I shall be with my brother. He has a house just outside.'

'Señorita, please. . . .' Ocampo made a fussy movement with his arms.

I leaned over the rail and watched the smudge of wake from the motor-boat fade creamily against the dark water. A few lights showed from Acaibo and distantly I heard the sound of a car revving up and a sudden burst of shouts and laughter.

Monk and I went down to the little bar at the back of the dining-saloon and sat there drinking leisurely until it was time to go to bed. Every so often we heard a motor-boat coming out and then going back, and orders being shouted on deck. Just before we were ready to turn in an Indian came into the bar and asked for a limejuice from the steward.

He was a doctor from Acaibo and had come out to attend the first mate.

When I asked him, he said, 'It is a fracture. Not so bad, señor. The bullet I have taken out. Tomorrow he shall be plastered.'

They'd moved him from my cabin and the place had been tidied up. Ocampo was efficient.

The next morning Monk and I went ashore. We went off in a motor-boat while the *Mara II* was being got under way to enter. The harbour was a large semi-circular bay about half a mile across and enclosed by two encircling horns of land. On the eastern horn, at its tip, was a grey stone citadel, El Castro, which had been built in the nineteenth century. Its gun emplacements covered the harbour and the town. Acaibo itself was a straggle of houses and buildings, white, pink and brightly shuttered, that sprawled along the water front. The main plaza lay behind the houses and was dominated by an eighteenth-century church, its baroque façade flaking with old plaster. Beyond the town were foothills rising to the great mountain chain, in places five thousand feet high, that ran westwards for about fifty miles. A long, rugged, tree-covered spine which, so Monk told me, dropped away eventually to the flat savannah lands of the western part of the island which stretched another hundred and fifty miles to Caramanga. Angelo's people held a line across the mountains about thirty miles from Acaibo at a place called San Pedro de Rabosa, a small mountain town at the end of a narrow pass through which the main road ran to Caramanga. It was this pass which formed the focal point of the present fighting. Both sides had been sitting at either end of it now for over six months.

Cordillo itself had been Spanish for about four hundred years up until the Spanish-American war. When the Spaniards went out of the Colonial business it had become a Republic. Its history had followed the usual West Indian pattern; Columbus, the Spanish greed and concern for gold and harbours rather than sugar cane and tobacco; massacre and counter-massacre of the original Caribs and Spanish garrisons, the influx of Negro slaves, the mixing of blood and the more recent, less apparent, infiltration of Indian and Chinese traders . . . it was a hotch-potch, but a valuable one, even apart from its sugar and tobacco, because in the last five years offshore oil had been discovered on the north coast above Caramanga and was being worked under a concession to an American company. Monk gave me a lecture on it all the way in and he finished, 'Whatever happens, it's like all the others, a sugar pot with flies crowding round the brim. From time to time a different lot of flies take over. But they're flies just the same. Sucking away and paddling their dirty feet over everything.'

I said, 'I just want to take my little bag of sugar and get away.' The far side of the harbour under the lee of the eastern horn was crowded with schooners, motor launches and a few paint-weary yachts . . . all the night-running stuff that a place like Acaibo and a cause like Angelo's attracted. It shouldn't be hard to get a passage out.

Monk said, 'Maybe I'll stay a while. History in the making. Perhaps I'd like to see that.'

The hotel was in the main square opposite the church. It was called *Hotel de la Reina* and its pink façade with green shutters sloped out at an alarming angle from the flanking buildings. It looked as though it only needed someone to move impetuously in one of the fourth-floor bedrooms to send the whole affair topping forward on its face. Across the square which was littered with market stalls, with only a narrow passage through them for cars and donkey carts, the sun was full and blinding on the ornate face of the church to the rails of which chicken were strung up by the legs for sale. A square, unadorned bell tower rose at once side of the church with two bells, one above the other, showing in the open bell turrets. Below them was a clock which had one hand only that pointed to four stubbornly unmoving. Acaibo had nothing I hadn't seen before. And even the smells were the same.

Monk and I got two rooms, vacated about an hour earlier by a couple of Democratic Army officers, leave expired, who were going back to San Pedro de Rabosa. The one from my room, which overlooked the square, had left a pile of empty crab shells and claws in the waste-paper basket, and an earlier occupant, I imagine, had pencilled an obscene drawing on the back of the door. I shoved the waste-paper basket into the corridor and hung my jacket over the drawing. The Hueica boys hadn't come ashore with us. They were waiting for the *Mara II* to berth, and had said they didn't want hotel rooms. They'd find something for themselves which was cheaper.

It was hot in the room, but I kept the window and the shutters drawn against the market noise outside and I stretched out on the iron bed. So far as I was concerned there was nothing to do until I had collected my money and could arrange to get away. Lieutenant Ocampo had said nothing to me about it. I didn't really expect anything to be done about it that day. The Generalissimo and Ocampo would be busy enough. I decided to give it a day. Tomorrow I would get busy.

That night, after dinner, I went into the bar for a drink. The bar was perched up on a bamboo pallisaded platform overlooking a long room which ran out at the back of the hotel. At the far end of the room was a three-piece band, a piano, saxophone and a guitar. Now and again a coloured woman with thin shoulders and long hands, in a black dress which she kept kicking irritably with a backward flick of one heel, came to the microphone and sang the same dreary sort of song which was no doubt being sung in a thousand other similar places at that very moment, tropical nights, silver sands, holding hands, palm trees over us, love, love until we die. . . . And about four couples danced.

'Is it always like this?' I asked the barman.

'No, señor. This is between leaves. The officers and men went

back this morning. Another lot come day after this. Then you see
life.'

I couldn't wait.

He looked at me as he polished a glass and went on, 'For you,
it is better company at the *Cantina del Morro*.'

'Where's that?'

'By the harbour. Plenty of men from the boats, and also some
men who come to fly. Up here is only Army, and they get wild.'

It was the place, I thought, to arrange a passage. Later I'd have
a look at it.

Someone came up to the bar behind me and I turned and saw
Parkes. He was still in his tight blue suit, sweating hard, and
mopping his face. He looked tired and grim. I waited, saying
nothing, not knowing how he was going to take me. But he gave
me a nod as though nothing had happened between us and said,
'The lassie back there would do a damned sight better if she had
a voice and a body to fill her gown. Whiskey. Double, and no ice.'

'There is no ice, señor,' said the barman.

I let him get his drink and put half of it away, and then I said,
'What's happened to you, and Señor Albano?'

He cocked his head at me and the blue, steady eyes were on me
unblinking.

'Do you care?'

'As a matter of fact, yes.'

He breathed hard and then let his shoulders slump.

'I've got a room here. The boss is being held by them. Army
headquarters. Big sugar mill place outside the town. I've had a
day, I can tell you. I didn't take to that bastard at all.'

'What bastard?'

'General whatever his bloody name is. Dressed up like a Christmas tree and giving his orders. You're welcome to him.'

'I don't know him.'

'Then you've got a pleasure to come, I don't think! I don't think
much of the food here, either. All fish stuff. Can't stand that fish
soup.'

'What's the position . . . about you?'

He began to pack a pipe that looked as though it had been buried
ten years. 'Simple, according to His Nibs. They're beginning to
unload the planes tomorrow. They've got a strip bulldozed out of the
palms, over the hill from here on the coast. I supervise everything.
Unloading, assembly and tests. When that's done I can go. With

a bonus if I like to take it. Told him what he could do with the bonus. My firm would play hell, and I don't want his dirty money.' He looked frankly at me as he said this, and I realised that although he was prepared to talk, prepared to have me even buy him a drink, he still held to his opinion of me.

'And if you don't do this?'

'Simple. They shoot young Mr. Albano.'

'So you're doing it?'

'What do you think? Of course I am. I don't want people shot. Besides if anyone's going to touch them planes it's going to be me. They've got a shower of mechanics up there that I wouldn't trust with a kid's sewing machine. You should have seen that strip they'd bulldozed. About six hundred feet long. I asked them what the hell's good they thought that was. Six hundred feet! You could do it, just about, from the deck of a carrier. Fifteen hundred feet, I said. Not a foot less. That gives a nice safety factor. Silly bastards. Now they've got to send up to the front to get the bulldozer back. One bulldozer. A bloody Fred Karno outfit. Blimey, listen to her.'

The singer was murdering a Cole Porter tune.

I said, 'I hear they've got some flyers here.'

'So I'm told. I can guess the type, too. Ex-Nazi boys beyond the age limit, the boozy-fingered types no airline would look at. Can't hold a glass without spilling it.' He looked at my hands on the bar counter and then shook his head. 'You beat me. Still, it ain't my worry.'

He put his glass down and went out without saying a word. Of all the people I'd known in my years out here he was the only one with the blunt gift of being able to make me think about myself from a different viewpoint. I didn't care for it. He couldn't have made it more plain that, like Orlando, he did *desire we may be better strangers.*

But, despite him, I couldn't really feel upset. There was a fine elation in me, running sweetly and powerfully like a dynamo. I'd succeeded. I was going to have the money I needed. Drea and I were going to have the hotel. We were going to be together. I kept coming back to that thought and it was like champagne in me.

Monk came in after a while and as we stood at the bar the singer came up from the dance floor. She was a light-coloured girl, nose a little flat and a big gamin mouth. She couldn't have been twenty. Monk bought her a drink and she sighed over it with resigned, dark spaniel eyes. She'd been caught at this end of the island when the trouble started five years before, visiting her brother. He was with the Democratic Army now. She wanted to get to Caramanga and have a job in one of the real night clubs, improve herself. . . . I saw the old, paternal look coming over Monk's face as she talked to him. It was always to Monk that the waifs turned, the beaten-down ones, the hopeless, the ones who were never even going to catch the tail of their phantom ambitions. Eglantina her name was. Singing and dancing. And some of the officers were nice. But it was usually a rough crowd. . . . I left Monk talking with her and went to bed. But I lay for a long time, thinking about Drea . . . seeing us together . . . together always.

CHAPTER 8

By mid-day I had heard nothing from Army Headquarters and I decided that I'd given them all the grace which could be decently allowed. I went down to the *Mara II* to find Lieutenant Ocampo. The harbour and dockside were the only places where there were any signs of Army activity. Trucks were unloading petrol from a couple of schooners. The stuff was in old American army four-gallon jerry-cans and the work was being done by a negro gang.

I met the Hueica brothers coming from the *Mara II*. Sardi gave me a solemn little nod, and Tomez beamed a smile. They'd found themselves a couple of rooms in some house up by the church, so Tomez said, and hadn't decided whether to hang on here in the hope of finding some kind of job or to look for a passage out right away. I watched them go off in their neat suits, walking as though they were hand in hand. They were no longer anything to do with me. They'd been paid and they'd done their job. That's how I wanted it to be with me, too.

There was a large, open, six-wheeled lorry alongside the *Mara II*, and they were preparing to swing off the first of the Sea Furies. Parkes was there in the thick of the operations. At the bottom of the gangplank was a sentry and I noticed three others along the length of the ship. Lieutenant Ocampo was a stickler for military precautions. I had a little trouble getting by the sentry. He conducted me to the top of the gangplank and then made me stay there while he sent a message to the lieutenant. Finally I was taken to him. He'd made temporary headquarters in the saloon and already army-style, he had his table covered with papers, a couple of trays for files, and a field telephone with nice new blue and yellow wires trailing away and out of a porthole on the harbour side. An orderly was smacking away with intense one-finger concentration at a typewriter on a small table by the bar. On one of the saloon pillars a sheet of foolscap was stuck with scotch tape. A glance at

it as I waited for Ocampo to look up from his table showed me that
it was the standing orders for the ship's company while under
detention in Acaibo, written in Spanish and English.

He looked up, gave a stiff, curt little sigh to indicate how busy
he was, and said, 'Well, señor?'

'Have you had any instructions from Generalissimo Lemaza
about me?'

'No, señor. Should I?'

There was no doubt that we didn't like one another.

I said, 'I have an urgent business matter to settle with him. I
don't regard Acaibo as a health resort. I want to get away.'

'So?'

'I'd be glad if you would telephone him and ask him to make an
appointment with me.'

For a moment I thought he was going to make an issue of this,
but he gave that quick, bony shrug of his and reached for the
telephone. While he talked I studied the standing orders. No officers
were allowed ashore. All crew would be in their quarters by ten
o'clock at night and must remain there until six the next morning
unless they were detailed members of working parties. An efficient
little man, Ocampo.

He spoke in Spanish and was having a huffy argument with
someone at the other end of the line. Then there was a long silence
while he waited. Another outbreak of speech from him and then he
put the telephone down. I turned back to him.

'Well?'

'You are at the *Hotel de la Reina*?'

'You know I am.'

'I will pick you up there at five o'clock this afternoon and conduct
you to the Generalissimo.'

'Good. Thank you.'

I left him and went over to the *Cantina del Morro* for a drink. You
went down six steps from the dockside level, through a double
arched doorway and into what had obviously once been a rum or
molasses store. The smell was still there, thick and strong. There
was a high bar pushed to one end with a juke box close to it. The
glass of the juke box had been broken. There were no records to
be seen but a ginger jar full of pomegranate blossoms stood on the
turn-table. Fishing nets were strung along the roof and bits of
seaweed and glass float-balls hung from it. There were four long
tables with benches on either side and each table held a pot of

flowers. The owner was a big, fleshy man in red trousers and a
white silk shirt, with a large, colourless, epicene face. He looked
German to me but everyone in the place called him Tino.

Monk and Eglantina were sitting by themselves at one bench.
The bench nearer the bar had four men around it. One look showed
me that they were the types Parkes had referred to. For a moment
I went over their faces. But there was no one I knew. One wore a
thick brown leather American flying jacket. They were playing
cards with a quiet concentration. I knew the kind. I'd just missed
being one of them. They only had two lives, one when they were
aloft, and the other when the evening closed around them and they
began to feel the liquor in them. Otherwise they just sat out time,
waiting. Life became hell when they could no longer take-off.

Monk said, 'How goes it?'

'I'm seeing the General this evening.'

I ordered a rum and when Tino brought it he said, 'Velcome.'

'Thank you.'

'You bring the planes in?'

'Yes.'

'The boys are glad for you.'

The boys went on playing cards.

Eglantina said, 'The Generalissimo is very handsome man. But
no good. Particularly with women.' She'd got her hair screwed up
into a bun right on top of her head and was wearing a green dress
with yellow bamboo stripes across it. She had a ten-cent brooch of
some blue stuff shaped like a butterfly at the neck of her dress.

I said to Monk, 'When I've collected are you coming out with
me?'

He leaned back against the wall lazily and jerked his cigar so
that it almost burnt his left eye.

'Dunno. Think I like it here. Besides, sure to be a fuss outside
about this business. Stay here and let it blow.'

I looked from him to Eglantina. He saw the look and grinned.

'When you go,' he said, 'I'll move out of *la Reina*. Child here says
her brother's got a cabin up in the hills. Sit on my bottom and
watch the melons grow for a while. She wants me to train her voice.'

'Her voice? What do you know about singing?'

'Ran the biggest choir you ever saw once. True, she doesn't have
much of a voice. But you don't need one for night clubs. Just a
manner. I can give her that.'

'Well, the best of luck to you.'

'Brother's got a boat, too. Needs a bit of work on it. You know me and boats. When she's trained I'll take her out. None of the regulars here are allowed out. Officially.'

I saw then how it was. It was Monk all over. He hadn't the least interest in her as a woman. To him she was a child who wanted a toy, the smoky tawdry glitter of a night club, wanted to get out of Acaibo. And because she wanted it he couldn't stop himself from helping her.

'He's a good man,' said Eglantina.

'Too good,' I said.

She put her hand on Monk's arm. A simple gesture but there are about five hundred different meanings to be got into it. Hers was clear.

'Already I do anything for Mister Monk.' She smiled, everything on her face breaking up into a monkey wrinkle. She really was the plainest thing I'd seen, but I liked her. If it had been left to her kind he would have been canonised long ago.

Lieutenant Ocampo picked me up at five o'clock on the dot. He had an old, but clean and well-maintained red Ford convertible with an Army sign on one of the wings. I'd already seen it on some of the trucks. A Picasso kind of bird with a rifle in its claws. Later I learned that it was meant to be an eagle.

We sat together in the back and were driven by a soldier in a smart green tunic who kept up a steady forty irrespective of the pot holes in the road. There was little conversation between Ocampo and myself for we were bouncing up and down like sacks most of the way. We went out through the square with the horn blowing and took the slope towards the far side of the island. All the way up the bluff, on either side of the road, were little checker-board patches of cultivated ground, maize, tomato, pimento and melon. On the far side the road dipped to the sea and a long stretch of curving white sand flanked by tall palms and groves of ragged looking sea grape. The ground here was flatter than around Acaibo, running back in a small coastal plain to the foothills. A couple of miles ahead I could see a block of grey and white buildings, but before we got to them the car turned off to the left and passed through the gateway of a private drive. A sentry at the gate saluted us. A few minutes later we drew up at a large wooden house, two storied and built in colonial style, a long verandah running down one side of it and fronting an overgrown garden full of poinsettias, oleanders and stubby palms. There was another sentry at the foot of the verandah.

When we got out of the car Lieutenant Ocampo said, 'You will excuse me, señor.'

He stepped up to me and ran his hands quickly over my clothes feeling for arms.

'Don't worry,' I said. 'I'm not in the assassination business. And come to think of it, I've got four sub-machine guns and a handful of grenades back at my hotel which I'd be glad to sell to the Democratic Army.'

We went up the steps of the verandah into a large hall. As we entered a man came across the hall and out past us. I looked at him and he looked at me. For a moment some dusty memory shook itself. I hesitated and I saw the same hesitation in him, the beginning of a recognition which neither of us could place. Then he was past me, down the steps and into a jeep which was parked on the gravel. I went on, seeing his face, greyish and tired with a cynical droop to one corner of his mouth. From somewhere I knew him but I couldn't place him.

I said to Ocampo, 'Who's that?'

'I do not know, señor.' Maybe he didn't. Sometime, I knew, the memory would come back.

A few minutes later I was with Generalissimo Lemaza.

He was sitting at a large mahogany desk. Ocampo introduced me and then retired. Lemaza placed a pair of big hands widespread on the edges of the desk, half rose and half nodded and gave me a beaming man-to-man smile. Within a few moments he'd left me in no doubt of the way in which he wanted the world to regard him . . . big, bluff and frank, an honest turn of speech, and a giant's amused, but still concerned, occupation with the complexities of the world. A giant who had taken a bunch of pygmies under his fatherly control. . . . Father Lemaza who was going to be really sorry if he had to punish anyone because it would hurt him more than them. . . . He fixed me a drink and gave me a cigarette. He neither smoked nor drank himself. He smiled as he explained, and his big teeth flashed. I had learned from Monk that he had been a dentist in Caramanga before the revolution, and a good one. Maybe all this bluff, jolly-you-along act, bags of confidence and nothing to worry about attitude, was a hang-over from those days. Just lean back, señor, open your mouth and I'll take your teeth out before you can say *Ave Maria*.

Having fixed me a drink he stood by the window and, speaking in Spanish, said, 'We are grateful to you, Señor Marchant, grateful, grateful. . . . A fine job. The sinews of war. That is my concern, that was your concern. Up there—' he gestured vaguely out of the window, 'they fight. Heroes everyone, but fighting is not enough. Arms are not enough, nor ammunition. They must eat, they must drink, they must be clothed, trucks must have petrol and oil, and orders are non-existent without telephones, without wires, without pen and ink.' He beamed at me. 'Back here, the non-combatants, the seat-polishers work and there is no glory. You agree?' He jerked the last sentence at me.

'I agree.'

'Of course you agree. You are a man of sense. And there are other worries too. War is a business, revolution is a business. Money and thought, money and thought. While the campaign is being fought the political future must be planned. And let's face it, señor . . . most soldiers are children, children politically. They never grow up. But a new society does not grow up on its own like a coral reef. It needs planning.' He smiled again, but shadowed the smile with a little concern. The confident planner not under-estimating anything, confident but not optimistic. On a political platform, letting fly at the plantation workers under a ceiba tree, he would have been irresistible, I could see that.

But to show him that I was no sugar worker, no peasant hungry for land he would probably never get, I said, 'I've brought your planes in. I've been paid ten thousand dollars on account. There's forty thousand to come.'

He came back to the desk, nodding wisely. He was quite something to look at. He wore a coffee-coloured tunic—much the same style as a British officer's dress tunic—in some soft shantung and it sparkled with silver cuff and breast buttons. The flying eagle with its rifle was on each shoulder with two stars above it. A couple of rings winked richly from one hand. From the crest of a high forehead his hair went back, short and stiff, en brosse, and the skin of his face was like pale, walnut-coloured pigskin. He lifted the lid of a fruit box which stood on the desk and put an Elvas plum into his mouth. A sweet-tooth, that was bad for a dentist.

He sat down at his desk and said, 'You have never met our Leader?'

'No.'

'You will. And you will make no mistake about him, Señor

Marchant. You will recognise the man of destiny. Look around you in Acaibo, in the bars and on the streets, look around you here, and you ask yourself "What is it I do not see? What is it which is missing?" Something which is to be found everywhere else in the world where men fight for liberty?'

'What is it?'

'His photograph, señor. His face. Those posters with the monster face looking down at you. But not here. And why not? Because Angelo Libertad is not a face, or a figure. He is a voice and an ideal. A Power for good. The symbol of justice. Why should our men need his face on every wall? Already they carry him in their hearts. In their hearts, here.' He smacked his large chest as though I might be in doubt of the exact position of the heart. As far as he was concerned I was. He had no heart, only a great bag of wind in its place. But he had a brain and I had no doubt that as Quartermaster-General he was in the top class. He could get what had to be got, and he wouldn't waste a penny over it. This show was being run on a shoe string.

I said, 'Once these planes are in the air, your troubles will be over. You'll break out to Caramanga; three months from now and you'll be lords of the island, master of Cordillo. . . .' I found myself talking like him. 'Even if you could have bought those planes they would have cost you the earth. I'm a business man, General, and so are you.'

He took another plum, nodded, and leaned back in his chair.

'Señor Marchant,' he said, mumbling it a bit because of the plum in his mouth, 'as well as a business man, you are, so I'm told, a flyer. Squadron Leader?'

'I was.'

'For these planes, we have at the moment four pilots. But these men are just flyers. They have no character. They fly because they know nothing else. As a business man I would like to make you a proposition.' When he got down to business the bonhomie went from his voice and there was no rebel rousing grandiloquence in his speech. Hard facts.

'What proposition?'

'I will give you command of the planes. Full command. Training, operations, and so on. You fly with them. For this you would be paid five hundred dollars a month, with a bonus of five thousand when we enter Caramanga. Wait—' He raised his ringed hand as I moved to speak. 'In addition, as you are a business man, I will

be frank with you. As frank as though you were my own brother
. . .' he smiled as he lapsed back into rhetoric for a moment, 'for
between us already I have seen that nothing but the truth can
stand. We owe you forty thousand dollars. Invest them in this
struggle which is on the lip of success. I personally guarantee you
that you will receive your money back, doubled, when we reach
Caramanga. Let us see, that would give you eighty-five thousand
dollars in three months. How could any business man treat such a
proposition lightly?'

'I'm not treating it lightly,' I said. 'Any other time and I might
have accepted. But not this time. I just want to be paid and to
leave.'

'So you shall be.'

'Good.' I waited for him to make some move.

'Unfortunately, however, I cannot pay you until Angelo Libertad
returns tomorrow. I need his authority—'

'Look General Lemaza, I've done this job for you. I hope you're
not going to keep me hanging around.'

He smiled, ignoring the irritation in my voice. 'Tomorrow you
will be paid. There is no question of it. Meanwhile, it won't hurt
to consider my alternative offer. It merits thought. Angelo Libertad
returns to Acaibo tomorrow. It would be our pleasure if you came
here tomorrow evening and had dinner with us.' He stood up and
reached behind him for his cap, a peaked affair with the old eagle
on its front, and moved towards a door on the other side of the
room. 'Senorita Katrina has said she would like to see you. You
will find her through here. I myself must go.'

And he went, leaving me high and dry and with no option but
to wait until the next evening for my money. I was full of irritation
over the delay. I wanted to be away as fast as I could.

The room had a large window looking out over the garden. There
were green and white tiles on the floor and the furniture was all
cane, cane chairs, cane table, and the place looked bare. There was
a large radio set in one corner with a great jar of canna lilies on
top of it.

Katrina turned from the window as I came in. With an impulsive
movement which surprised me she came quickly towards me and
took my hands.

'It's nice to see you again.'

'It's nice to see you.' Somehow she made me feel that it had been a long time since I had seen her last.

'Can I get you a drink?'

'No thank you.' I moved towards the window with her. She looked fresh and young and there was the scent of some perfume about her which was new to me. It was light and faint, retiring . . . not the kind of thing Drea would have used.

I said, 'I've just had a basinful of Brother Lemaza.'

She laughed. 'He's a bit overpowering, isn't he? Angelo has to have someone like that. Angelo just goes ahead and does the thing which has to be done. He's no good at detail. Siles worries about that.'

'He certainly does. I hope I'm not going to have trouble getting my money from him.'

She turned sharply towards me. 'Oh, no. No, there won't be any trouble about that.'

'I'm glad to hear it.'

'Angelo has promised it. That is all that is needed.' She paused for a moment and then went on. 'But didn't he ask you to stay on, and make you a much better offer?'

'Yes. Supreme Commander of the Air Force.'

'And you're going to?'

There was no missing the enthusiasm in her voice. She wanted me to stay on.

'You knew he was going to ask me?'

'Of course. I think it's a wonderful idea. Don't you?'

'No, I don't.'

'But why not?' she said, puzzled. 'But you must. It's such a good offer.'

'Maybe, but I've got other plans. I just want to get away as soon as possible.'

'Oh. . . .' Her disappointment was obvious. 'But I thought you'd be glad. It's far more money.'

'I'm going to have all I need. Remember, too . . .' I gave her a smile. 'I don't have the same interest in Cordillo as you. My interests are miles away from here.'

She stepped back from me a pace and I saw her mouth tremble. Then she said, 'Is it for someone else? For a woman, for someone you—' She went to the window and with her back to me played absently with the cord of the blinds. 'I'm sorry. It is none of my business.'

I would have avoided it if I could but since I couldn't I decided
that it was as well to have the thing in the open. I liked her and I
thought I understood exactly what had happened. She'd only just
come into this new world; mine and her brother's and the General's.
Everything in this new world seemed exciting, romantic, razor-
edged with risk. It was new and the men in it new. No matter how
hard the reality of that world was, it also bred romance for the
young. It wasn't my fault if she'd taken a fancy to me.

'You needn't be sorry,' I said gently. 'It's a woman. I love her
and she loves me. And we need money to make the thing stick.
Love by itself doesn't pay any bills.'

Without looking at me, she said, 'Who is it?'

I told her and she nodded.

'I remember seeing her.'

Remember. . . . She was always there, walking with me . . . tawny
hair, that movement of her body and arms which was her alone,
that voice, nothing but Drea. . . .

I put a hand on her arm and turned her gently towards me.

'It was nice of you to think of me. About the job. If I were on
my own I'd probably take it. But it can't be done.'

To my surprise she double-backed on me and said, 'Does she
know you're doing this?'

'She does,' I said. 'But she didn't want me to do it. I had to . . .
for reasons.'

'She means so much to you?'

'So much, and much more.' I laughed quietly. 'Don't look so
gloomy. You're home, you're with your brother, and he's going to
get to Caramanga. You've got the whole world in front of you. You
don't want to waste time on hard-bitten types like me. . . . No, no.'
I stopped her as she stirred to speak. 'Let's have a drink together.
To the future. Yours as the mistress of Cordillo.'

'And yours?' She was recovering and there was a smile in her
eyes.

'Just the future.'

She went over to a table by the radio which was full of bottles and
glasses. She fixed me a whiskey and this time she did it properly.
Just the right amount, but it had to be cut with water not soda.
Generalissimo Lemaza didn't have soda siphons on his list of stores.

Lieutenant Ocampo had gone off with the Generalissimo, but he
had left his car and driver for me. The man took me back to Acaibo

through the swiftly gathering darkness. In a few hours Acaibo had changed. Four lorries with men and officers on leave from San Pedro had arrived and the square and the hotel were full of them. Some of them were already well on the way to being drunk. They seemed a tough but good-natured lot and most of them carried arms. After dinner I went along to the bar. The dance floor was crowded and a bunch of girls had appeared from somewhere. Just inside the bar door was a pile of rifles against the wall with a hotel servant looking after them and on a shelf behind him an odd selection of revolvers and automatic pistols was laid out. The band had been augmented and music was pumping through the room.

Monk was sitting at a little table at the edge of the floor near the bar. I joined him.

'How did it go with the General?' he asked.

'He's going to need watching. He offered me command of the Air Force.'

'You told him what to do with it?'

'Not yet.'

He looked around the room. 'They're really letting go, aren't they? The radio's just broken the news about the planes. All the world knows now. For these lads it's only a matter of time before they hit Caramanga. When do you get your money?'

'Tomorrow.'

An officer with his shirt front unbuttoned came up to the table holding a glass and swaying. He beamed at us and said, 'You bring the planes. Gracioso. . . . Soon we go forward to Caramanga, to glory. . . .' He lurched sideways, spilt his drink and was swallowed in the crowd of dancers.

I looked at Monk and smiled. ' "We go to gain a little patch of ground, That hath in it no profit but the name." '

'That's about right, too, as far as the little boys are concerned. They'll get nothing. Should read their revolutionary histories. First duty of any revolutionary leader is to destroy the political force that brought him to power. Castro did it. Angelo Libertad will. They'll get nothing. No one ever learns.'

The floor trembled with the stamp of dancers, the air pulsed with the music and somewhere, far away in the smoky haze over the heads of the dancers, I heard the thin voice of Eglantina trying to sing with the band. Give me my money, I thought. Give me my money and let me get out of here.

I left Monk to keep an eye on Eglantina and went down to the

Cantina del Morro where it was quieter. The arc lights of the *Mara II* were on and a squad of labourers was still at it, unloading the Sea Furies. I saw a bulky wingless body swing over and drop slowly towards the waiting lorry platform. In a couple of weeks, maybe sooner, the Sea Furies would be over San Pedro. The pilots in the *cantina* would be alive again. They'd be right with themselves again, doing the one thing they knew . . . coming down out of the sun with their cannons going and the earth sweeping back past them in a green, brown and yellow blur, the figures of men and vehicles coming up from insignificance to the sudden, gesturing, frantic clarity of helplessness. . . .

The flyers were still in the *cantina,* still playing cards but with more animation now that the evening and the liquor had gathered about them. Also there was the man I had passed coming out of the General's house. A small, neat looking man, Latin-American, with that tired, cynical droop to one corner of his mouth. He looked up at me and then gave a little nod. I went and sat down by him.

'It was somewhere,' I said. 'But I can't place it.'

'Marchant?'

I nodded.

'Da Silva,' he said politely. 'It was two years ago in Barrau's office. There was a little trouble with a firm called *Industrias Reunidas J. da Luz.*' He had a quiet, unemphatic voice, and went on, reinforcing my memory. 'Manufacturers of medicinal and industrial castor oil, glycerine, linseed . . . all the usual stuff. Labour trouble.'

I remembered then. Our meeting had been brief and I hadn't been involved in the trouble. But I remembered now the things Barrau had told me about Da Silva. His easy, neat and tranquil appearance had all the deception of a shark basking in the sun.

I said, 'There's no industrial or commercial trouble here.'

He shrugged his shoulders. 'There is trouble everywhere. My employers like to help people out of trouble. So long as they make a profit. Since you brought the planes in this could be a good investment.'

'What did you think of the General?'

He didn't answer the question. He just smiled at me and said, 'Let me buy you a drink.'

When I got back to the *Hotel de la Reina* the door of my room was open and a drunken officer with a black eye was snoring, fully dressed, on the floor by the window. I dragged him out on to the landing. The dancing was still going on down below.

I lay in bed before sleeping, thinking about Drea. And when I slept I dreamt about her.

CHAPTER 9

I had time to kill the next day. Now that a fresh batch of soldiers was on leave a couple of taxis had appeared in Acaibo. They stood outside the church, two old Chevrolets with canvas awnings in the place of hoods. The awnings were striped in red and gold—the revolutionary colours—and fringed with little red tassels. Ribbons of the same colour ran from the windscreen ends down to the radiator tip. Along the body each one had a name painted in Spanish; the *Singing Heart that Never Tires,* and the *Space Sputnik Special.* Philosophy and Science parked side by side. I chose the *Singing Heart.* It was driven by an enormous negro, his face broadly divided by a smile. We took the slope out of Acaibo in a mad, honking rush through the morning market crowd, but long before we were at the crest the pace had dropped to a wheezing, thrombosis-threatened crawl.

We passed the drive turning to Angelo Libertad's headquarters and a little further on skirted the block of cane-milling buildings which had now been turned into a barracks. The dusty enclosure before it was wired in and there was a little guard house at the entrance. Some soldiers were drilling in squads on the far side of the enclosure, and I saw two groups of men about instructors and machine guns. The eagle flag flew from the top of the building. The sentry at the gate waved to my driver.

He turned to me and said, 'That's Ernesto. We work here once. Start as cane cutters. But I get more brain, sir. I get job in distillery here. He still cut cane. I still get more brain, sir. He soldier, me owner-driver of *Singing Heart.* I call that upward progress, sir.'

'You should go far,' I said.

'Yes, boss!' He nodded happily.

A couple of miles beyond the sugar-mills the road curved back, following the shore line and meeting the long, gentle slope of the foothills. There was a little group of houses by the sea edge and beyond them a small stone jetty. Back from the houses and running into a thickness of bushes and palms was the landing strip which had been made for the Sea Furies. A bulldozer was still working at the far end of it, lengthening the run. At this end, near the houses, a long, tall Nissen hut with a semi-circular roof had been erected. As a workshop, I guessed. Outside it, four of the dismantled Sea Furies stood in the strong sunlight and there was a working party around one of them. But I saw no sign of Parkes. He was probably down at the harbour superintending the offloading of the last planes. I got the driver to pull up opposite the little jetty. The strip hadn't been too well planned. For take-off it meant taxiing to the far end and then making a run out to sea. It would have been dangerous to take off towards the slope of the foothills and the tall crests of the palms and trees. Just for a moment I wondered whether—if there had been no Drea—I would have got more brain and gone in for some upward progress, too.

From the air strip he took me around the northern sweep of coast, following a cliff road that dipped and soared. After about ten miles we came to a junction with a sign in English and Spanish. *No Civilian vehicles beyond this point.*

'Sometimes from here, sir, when wind right you can hear guns at San Pedro.'

We couldn't hear any that day. We went away lefthanded and circled back to Acaibo through the mountains, eventually coming into the town by a road that brought us to the harbour.

I had lunch with Monk, whom I hadn't seen so far that day.

He had a cut over his right eye with a piece of sticking plaster over it.

'How did you get that?'

He grinned, wrinkling his big, easy, brown face.

'The dancing got a bit rough. High spirits. Even on leave they like to fight. I got mixed up.'

'You had to pull Eglantina out, you mean.'

'No girl likes her dress ripped off her back.'

I saw then that the knuckles of his right hand were sore and cut. I'd seen him in a fight more than once. It was an uncomfortable business unless you were on his side.

'Galahad.'

He smiled. 'That's me. Galahad without hair.'

'Why'd you do it?'

'You're too old to begin asking *why*. Just get *why* right back. Why

do you do what you do? Why'd you take this job? Ten steps out of
your line. But I don't badger for reasons. You took it. Good enough
for me. Reason is just a string of decoys. Compulsion is the hunter.
Anyway we all finished up friends. Nice chap really. Just likes to
tear dresses when he's drunk. Put him in your room to sleep it off.
He wasn't in any shape to make the barracks.'

'I put him on the landing. He was snoring like hell.'

I slept most of the afternoon and just after six Ocampo's driver
called for me to take me out to the villa. On the way out we passed
the *Singing Heart* and the *Space Sputnik Special* and three army trucks
coming in with their evening load of mischief. They went by in a
roar of shouting and singing. Ocampo's driver turned and said, 'All
very happy. Soon we go to Caramanga. Soon I get sixty-six acres
good land. Same for each man. Viva Libertad.'

'Viva Libertad,' I said. It seemed expected of me. If he ever saw
his land he would be lucky. Land hunger. One of the oldest wants.
One of the easiest and most effective promises to make. You shall
have land if you fight for it. Usually they finished up with co-
operative farms, and militant youth organisations. Co-operation and
organisation; maybe, subconsciously, that was what we all wanted.
Anything that would dispel the loneliness of being an individual.
You lived under the shadow of the Bomb always—it was easier to
face the threat as one of a group. Us, not me. There was an illusion
of security if you were in a crowd.

I went into the hall and an orderly showed me into the room
where I had met Katrina. There was no one there. I waited, staring
out of the window for a few moments. As I did so, I became
aware of voices coming from behind the door that led into General
Lemaza's room. I couldn't catch any of the words but there was
no doubt that the General was excited and doing most of the talking.
Just now and again I caught the lower pitch and brief interjection
of the other person. The whole thing had the feeling to me of
someone making a plea, arguing some point and not getting very
far with it. There was a moment when the General's voice faded
into silence and then suddenly came back sharp and strong, almost
angry, only to be cut off by some quiet dismissal. The room went
silent and I heard a door open away to my left.

I turned and saw Katrina coming in. She wore a cool green dress
with white collar and cuffs and she came smiling across to me. This
time I was ready for her outstretched hands, catching them briefly
and returning her smile.

'Drink?'

'Thank you.'

'I'm sorry I wasn't here. But at the last moment I had trouble.' She half turned to me. 'The hooky things on the back of this dress. You need to be a contortionist.'

'You haven't got them all now,' I said.

I stepped up to her and began to fix the lowest of four hooks on the back of her dress. I could see the nape of her brown neck and the fine peak line of dark hair running up into the smooth sweep of her head. . . . Just for a moment I had a swift impulse to lean forward and kiss the back of her neck . . . for no reason at all. Out of affection, because she was a nice girl, because that little piece of exposed flesh was so womanly . . . God knows. No reason. Just a compulsion which I killed rapidly.

A few minutes later General Lemaza came into the room from his office and with him was the great Angelo Libertad. I don't know what I had expected. What I saw was someone who was the complete opposite of Lemaza, Lemaza who was dressed to kill in his silver-buttoned tunic, fresh-shaved, confident with men's cosmetics and his padding of rodomontade.

Angelo Libertad was about forty-five, lean and tall, his skin and the rather stiff, unbending movement of body and limbs giving the impression of a piece of sea-weathered drift oak. You could have knocked a nail into this man and got no sound of pain from him. He wore a khaki shirt buttoned at the neck without a tie and khaki drill trousers held by a simple brown belt. His hair was as dark as Katrina's and parted in the middle, spread away in two wings to give him an old-fashioned look. He had a short dark beard into which disappeared the deep clefts that marked either cheek. He had the trick of seeming to be always still, waiting, except for his eyes which were grey, curiously light coloured and which took in everything with a warm curiosity. He carried a cheap cane walking stick, the kind you could buy in any bazaar for a few cents, and he used it when he moved to offset a stiff left leg. The result, I learned, of a badly treated bullet wound in his early days as a revolutionary. His voice was quiet, and when he spoke English, which out of courtesy he did most of the evening, it had that singing touch, almost Welsh in its inflexion which I had noticed before in educated West Indians.

He was no self-flagellating prophet squatting on a barren mountain top. He smoked and drank and laughed, but all the same there was no mistaking his hardness, his force and determination. General Lemaza's windiness would just blow past him.

At dinner he said, 'I must thank you for looking after my sister on the *Mara II*. It was not a position in which I would have willingly placed her. Let me say, though, that it might have been hard to stop her from doing it . . . she feels as I do.' He smiled at her.

I've no very clear recollection of the way the dinner talk went, except that it went the way he wanted it. But very early on he said, 'I understand that General Lemaza has made a proposition to you?'

'That's so.'

He looked at me, put one finger on the edge of his glass and said, 'Do you wish to accept it?'

'Not so bluntly, Angelo,' said the General. 'It's an excellent proposition for Señor Marchant. You will give him the impression that we do not want him to accept. We do, of course. He is just the man to take charge—'

Angelo shook his head. 'Señor Marchant understands bluntness. Does he look like a man who would be undecided after twenty-four hours? Am I right?' He looked at me.

'Yes, you're right,' I said. 'To be equally blunt, I just want to be paid and to leave. I'm not interested in flying or fighting. I've had my share of both.'

'And, of course, this is not your country. Why should you? Still, the General did wisely to ask you. He has his problems . . . chiefly money and supplies. You see,' he smiled, 'he does not have my faith. With faith all things can be accomplished.'

'It doesn't buy petrol or arms, Angelo. These are the sinews of war, these are the materials of victory.'

'Victory is here or it is not here.' Angelo to my surprise tapped his head and not his heart. His style, verbal and gesticulatory, was quite different from Lemaza's. He looked at me and went on, 'The General would finance a revolution in the same way as you float a company. Issue a prospectus, underline the prospects of future developments, and make a share issue. It is on this that we part company, because I know that the seeds of true defeat, the coming death of ideals, is in that way. This is a democratic movement, not a company. When we enter Caramanga it must be free of all debts, tied by no promises except the ones already made to our people. It is, I believe, forty thousand dollars we owe you?'

'That is so.'

I saw Katrina watching me.

'Before you leave here the General will pay you the money.'

'Thank you.'

'You have earned it. The planes are all we need.'

I said, a little stupidly maybe, but I was in the clear now and the money was coming to me so I felt I had to say it, 'I never meant to bring in Albano with the planes. Quite frankly, I wouldn't have settled for that if I'd known.'

'I can believe that. But there is nothing to be done about it. It was just an unexpected turn of fate. Fate must be accepted.'

'You're going to exchange him?'

'I think so, eventually. But it does not concern you.' And in the last sentence there was dismissal, unmistakable. I was to be paid, but beyond that I had no privileges. A few minutes later he was talking about Cuba, and the mistakes which had been made there by Fidel Castro since the end of the revolt, of how Castro had smashed his own movement, supported originally by moderates, and handed over Cuba's political and economical future to the extremists. He spoke with a quiet bitterness about the way the land reform law and the expropriation of land holdings had been abused by the National Institute of Agrarian Reform . . . I could see that there was no question in Angelo's mind of what should happen when they got to Caramanga. He would be master. Cordillo was going to get a new deal. Anyone who was hanging on in the hope of getting a bigger slice of victory than anyone else was in for disappointment. But even as he spoke I was thinking of dark, neat little Da Silva in the *Cantina del Morro*. Da Silva wouldn't be over here wasting his time. And looking across at General Lemaza, I didn't need to be told that just because the General had married the now dead sister of Katrina there was any deep family bond between them all. I didn't need to be told, either, that paying out my dollars was going to hurt the General. There were a hundred better ways of spending it he could think of. . . .

We went into the other room for coffee and after a little while Angelo excused himself and left us. A few minutes later the General went back to his room to work. He said, 'When you are ready to leave, the car is waiting. Come to see me first.'

Left alone with Katrina, I said, vaguely aware of uneasiness in me, still seeing Da Silva sitting in the *Cantina del Morro*, remembering more about him now, 'Just how well do those two get on?'

'Much better than it seems. Siles worries about the small things.

He needs to. My brother thinks only of the big thing. They need one another.'

'And when you get to Caramanga?'

'What do you mean?'

'You heard your brother talking about Cuba. Things went wrong there. Precious little land has been distributed. But the boys behind INRA are filling their wallets. And Castro is President of the National Institute of Agrarian Reform. How many men are incorruptible?'

Sharply, she said, 'My brother is.'

I nodded. 'Yes, I think he is, more than most. I get that feeling. . . . But people aren't comfortable with men like that.'

'What do you mean?'

'I'm not sure. Yes, I am. I mean that people like General Lemaza can't live with people like your brother. Only during the emergency of a revolution, of fighting. Afterwards something has to blow.'

'You're wrong,' she said. 'I know Siles isn't a man who appeals to you. Just as I know that my brother is. But Siles is the same as everyone else in this fight. They would die for Angelo.'

I said, 'I don't doubt it.' And when it was all over, I wondered just how different things would be—and just how many, like my driver, would go on with the 'upward progress'. You had to be smart to keep on the band-wagon, and ruthless. Anyway, the only thing I was concerned with was my own 'upward progress'. I wanted to have my money and be away. I said, 'Well, I think it's time I went. I've still got some business with General Lemaza.' I stood up.

She stood beside me. There was just one table lamp alight in the room and a mosquito was singing about it.

'When are you leaving Acaibo?'

'Tomorrow. There are one or two boats going out.'

'I shan't see you again?'

'It's unlikely.' This was going to be difficult and I wasn't sure how to handle it.

'I shall miss you.'

She said it simply, and before I could help myself I had put out my hand and taken hers gently.

'I'll think of you,' I said, 'and I hope all goes well for your brother.'

She slipped her hand out of mine and smiled and said, 'It's embarrassing for you, isn't it? You must have had it happen before,

surely?' The more she said the more confident she became. 'I know
it doesn't mean anything to you. But it does to me. You'd call it
part of growing up, wouldn't you, Keith?'

It was the first time she'd ever used my name. I couldn't escape
her, she didn't mean me to have an easy exit so I decided to be
frank, too.

'You're dead right,' I said. 'It's all part of growing up. You've
fallen in love with me because I happened to be around at the right
moment. It could easily have been someone else.' I put my arm
round her shoulders and pulled her slowly towards me. I kissed
her, feeling her eyelids flutter against the top of my cheek. I took
my lips from hers and put my hand against the smooth run of her
cheek and looked into her dark eyes.

She stepped back from me and her face was suddenly awake and
she said breathlessly, 'Stay here in Acaibo.'

I shook my head. 'I'm going.' I raised her hand to my lips and
kissed it. 'Good luck,' I said. 'And thank you for trying to make
me Supreme Commander of the Air Force. I could have got myself
a fancy uniform like Lemaza. Ten years ago just the thought of the
uniform might have decided me.'

She laughed, but I could see that there was no real laughter in
her. This was another moment of learning about herself; one of the
romantic growing pains we all have to face. I went across to the
door of the General's room, knocked and entered when he called.

General Lemaza pointed to a box file on his desk. There was no
need of words. I opened it. Inside the dollar bills were neatly stacked
and banded with slips of brown paper. There they were. I held
down the elation and excitement in me. Drea . . . waiting in Haiti.
The thing was done. No more Barrau jobs. Everything plain sailing.
It was a great moment. I took the stacks out and carefully counted
them. The notes were new, clean and crisp, and the flutter of their
edges was the only sound in the room. When I had finished I
snapped the spring-loaded lid of the box back and put it under my
arm.

General Lemaza leaned back in his chair, chewing on one of his
preserved plums, and said affably, 'As a business man you are
making a mistake. There's a fortune to be made in this country for
the wise investor.'

'I don't wish to speculate.'

He smiled and rubbed a hand over his broad chin and then slid it up and back over his stiff brosse. 'It is a pity you would not stay. We could have worked together so well, I think.'

I didn't. But I didn't say so. He held out his hand to me and then walked to the door. Before he opened it, he half turned and said, 'I watched you at dinner tonight. Oh, yes, I watched. It is mostly all I can do when Angelo is present. I know your thoughts, the contrast you make between us. Even, I guess, you imagine some antagonism. That would be wrong. We are just different parts of the same symbol. He is the flag that flies at the masthead, and I am that mast, that stout pole which must be there, always there if the flag is to fly. The flag of liberty and promise.'

I could have clapped I suppose at this parting oration, but I didn't. I was wondering what kind of liberty it would be. The promise I didn't even consider.

Ocampo's driver was waiting with the car. It was dark, no moon, but a sky full of bright stars that seemed too close to the earth to be comfortable. One of those tropical nights which overdid everything, too hot, the air too thick with flower scents, and the fireflies around the oleander bushes too brilliant. I sat in the back of the car with the box tucked under my arm. It was going to be under my arm or I was going to be sitting or sleeping on it until I got out of Acaibo.

As the car turned out of the drive and bumped along the road to Acaibo I was thinking of Drea. By now she was probably on the point of leaving for Haiti. She'd fly. She hated the sea. Sometime or other, I supposed, I would tell her about Katrina. She had all a woman's interest in another women's emotions. And for awhile, because I was relaxed now, and could detach myself to some extent from myself, I tried to imagine what it might have been like if there had been no Drea. Maybe I wouldn't have been so avuncularly amused by Katrina. The fondness in me for her, which must have been maddening because she didn't want such an innocuous response, might have been passed over quickly. She was quite unlike Drea. Drea, out of her love, demanded. In a way she led me and I followed. But Katrina would have followed because she couldn't escape her own nature. No matter what I did or where I went she would have followed. . . .

Half-way up the slope to the hill above Acaibo the car began to splutter, spitting back through the carburettor and finally stopped. The driver got out and fiddled around under the bonnet for a while and I sat in the back smoking. He made a few adjustments and tried to start her again. She refused to come to life. I got out.

'What's the trouble?'

He turned his hands slowly palm upwards.

'It is always happening, señor. The petrol they bring in. God knows from where. Sometimes it has water in it. Sometimes there are whole tins which are nothing but water. Thus they cheat the Movement.'

I got him to hold a torch while I unshipped part of the carburettor and worked the priming lever of the petrol pump. Petrol flowed out into my hand and in the light of the torch I saw that it was half water.

'You'll never get this thing started until you drain the tank and put in fresh petrol.'

'But what do I do, señor? I have to take you to the hotel?'

He was a good soldier. He had orders and wanted to carry them out. Now, in an emergency he wanted fresh orders. The Movement had need of his kind. No resource. Just order-followers.

I said, 'You hang on here. The *Singing Heart* or the *Sputnik Special* will be taking leave parties back later. You can get a tow. I can walk to Acaibo. It's only a couple of miles.'

I left him there and went on up the hill. At the top there was a large saman tree. I stopped under it and lit a cigarette. Below me were the lights of Acaibo.

I went down the roadslope. It was hot walking in the still air and after a few hundred yards, where the road took a turn to the left through a small cutting in the hillside, I came to one of those stone troughs let into the side of the road. A thin trickle of water came from an iron pipe above it. I went over to it to take a drink. The water came straight down from the hills. I bent over the trough to get my mouth under the pipe, the box file under my arm. As I bent I heard a movement from the road behind me; a swift shuffling sound, not more perhaps than a fast-moving snake might have made in the dust, but it was enough. I began to straighten up and saw on the star-reflected water of the trough the dark loom of a figure behind me. I turned and met the full force of a blow on the side of the head. I went down, crashing backwards against the stone edge of the water trough.

CHAPTER 10

When I came round the negro driver of the *Singing Heart that Never Tires* was crouched over me, splashing water in my face. My left temple throbbed viciously and I could feel the whole of the left side of my face stiffened up as though with frost-bite. I pushed myself up a little and he helped me to sit on the edge of the stone trough. My trousers were wet through from the overseep to the ground from the trough. I waved a feeble hand at him to stop him from splashing more water over me.

'You mus' sure be drunk, boss, to get right up here in this fix. Man, you sure want to see your face . . . !'

I couldn't answer him. It was coming back now fast. I groped in my pockets for a cigarette. The packet came out damp and sodden.

He fixed me with one of his own cigarettes, even lit it for me.

'You mus' been here when I take early leave party back. Didn't see you, though. Lights only hit this bit of road coming back. You all right . . . ? Here, take little more pain killer.'

He pulled a bottle from his pocket and offered it to me. It was rum, strong hard rum, and it burnt me all the way down, but it pulled me round.

I stood up and swayed a little.

I said, 'What time is it?'

'Just after midnight.'

I must have been there about two hours.

'You got a torch?'

He went over to his taxi and came back with a torch. I flicked it around on the ground by the trough. I knew I wasn't going to find anything, but I had to do it. A black desperation was building slowly in me. There was nothing to be seen except the damp ground and a confusion of foot prints. No sign of the box file. I was still silly in the head from the blow. I could kiss that goodbye, I thought.

Kiss forty thousand goodbye and with it all the other goodbyes. . . .
The pain behind my eyeballs was suddenly shot with red streaks.
I swayed and he held me.

'You lose wallet or somethin', boss?'

'Something,' I mumbled. 'Get me back to the hotel.'

He helped me across to the taxi and eased me into the back. I
flopped out against the leather like a sack of wet rice.

'Here.' He had the rum bottle at my mouth but I shook my head.
Rum was no good. Already I could see Drea looking up at me as
I crossed the terrace of the Hotel Montana; knowing at once that
I was returning empty-handed—no hotel, no future in St. Thomas.
I cried out inside myself, fiercely, murderously against the
vision. . . . He offered me the rum bottle again and this time I took
it. It wasn't going to happen . . . I'd tear this island apart first.

He began to drive me back and I lay there, coming and going in
waves of brief clarity and then long troughs of confusion. Half-way
down the hill I made him stop and I vomited over the side. When
we went on I lay there with my body shivering violently for a while
until I got angry at myself for being all body. The anger did more
for me than the rum but as we reached the hotel I was still in a
bad way. I had a recollection of three or four officers playing some
drunken wrestling game in the hotel hall, and a bottle being slung
between them. In the dance room the music was pumping away.

Singing Heart was a good boy. He stuck with me all up the stairs,
taking my weight and clucking like an old rooster.

I found my room and flopped on to the bed.

'I get your friend, Miss Eglantina's man.'

He went out and I lay there in the darkness, coming back fast,
and trying to sort it out, and with the coming back I could feel
myself hardening up, not just in the mind but in the body as well.
Whatever slack there was in me was being taken up, sweated right
up taut, and it was like a kind of medicine, no cure for the real ill,
but bringing me back into shape.

Monk came in after about five minutes. Eglantina was with him.
He switched on the bedside light and stood over me.

He just stood there looking down at me without speaking for
some time. He didn't really need to be told. He said to Eglantina
without turning, 'Get some hot water and some plaster.'

She went out and I could see the thin shoulder blades working
in the deep vee of the back of her red dress. Monk bent over me
and his fingers turned my head gently sideways.

'Christ, what a bruise. Not badly cut though. Fix you up all right. Drink?'

I shook my head. He lit a cigarette for me and put it between my lips. Everything was going through my mind, everything that hinged on the loss of my money. Already I had murder and God knows what else planned.

Eglantina came back with a bowl of water and other stuff. She stood behind him while he fixed me up expertly. And it was expert. The real Monk touch. I'd never thought that I would become one of his waifs . . . but I was at that moment. A waif, and well astray. Eglantina stared down at me with eyes as big as eggcups.

Monk, easing plaster over the temple cut, said, 'You were paid tonight?'

'I was.'

'No trouble?'

'Not to begin with. The car broke down outside town. I walked.'

'Into trouble.'

'For me, and a lot of other people.'

'Who was it?'

I didn't answer, my eyes on the scared, fascinated face of Eglantina.

'In my room you'll find a clean shirt or two. Bring one here,' he said to her.

She went.

I sat up and rolled my legs off the bed. The damp linen clung to me.

'Who?' he asked.

'Sardi. He was quick but not quick enough.'

'Sardi, eh? But he couldn't work this on his own.'

'I'm damned sure he didn't. He's just hired.'

Eglantina came in with the shirt. As the door opened music pumped in and I heard the officers shouting below. Outside in the square a drunken handful of soldiers were murdering some song and the church bell gave a cracked boom to mark the half-hour. I stood up and stripped off my shirt. Eglantina held the clean one for me like a jacket. She gave me a timid little smile as she slid around me.

Monk said, 'What do you think you're going to do?'

'I'm going out.' Eglantina had slipped back in front of me and was doing up the shirt buttons. With everything I had on my plate now, the really big stuff, I couldn't help noticing small things. She'd

painted her nails silver and her hands worked neatly. She belonged
to Monk and now, since I was part of Monk, she belonged to me.
If I'd let her she would have tucked the shirt into the top of my
trousers. I put my hands on her shoulders and eased her away.

'Eglantina,' I said, 'get downstairs and fetch me some cigarettes
and a bottle of whiskey.'

She looked at Monk and he nodded. She went.

'Where are they?' I asked him. 'They didn't check in here.'

'They got rooms in a house by the church. But if they did this
job they won't be there.'

'They might. If they thought I hadn't seen them. Anyway I've
got to try it first.' I walked over to the window, tucking my shirt
in. I was easing up now, my body was coming back under control.

Monk said, 'Hang on here a moment.'

He went out and I waited. Eglantina came back with the cigarettes and the whiskey.

She said, 'You better now, boss.'

I nodded. 'Too much drink. Slipped and cracked my head.'

She didn't question me.

Monk came back after a while and said, 'Okay, let's go. And
you—' he patted Eglantina on the bottom, 'get back to your singing.
Just going to walk Señor Marchant for some fresh air. And
remember with that blues number, keep your eyes down. Till the
last chord and then give it this—' He did an exaggerated impression,
throwing his arms wide and flinging up his head. She giggled and
went out ahead of us.

Outside the hotel he handed me a revolver and a handful of
shells.

'It's loaded. I swopped two from the dance hall shelf and left a
couple of our sub-machine guns in exchange. They'll sort it out.'

The house was only fifty yards away across the square. We went
in without meeting anyone and up to the third floor to a room
overlooking the square. We didn't stand on ceremony. Just pushed
the door open and went in with our revolvers ready, snapping on
the light.

The room was empty. Two little folding cot beds, American army
pattern, stood one against each wall. Everything was neat and tidy
and unlived in.

We went downstairs and got hold of the *portera*. She was a big,
sleepy-faced negress in a stained old wrap and her hair done up in

twists of newspaper. The Hueica brothers had paid their rent and left early that morning. She didn't know where they had gone.

Monk said, 'How did they go? Just walk out carrying their cases?'

On the *Mara II* they had each had a couple of cases, carrying their fortune and their furnishings with them, working their way back to Guatemala, to be big shots when they got back to Guadaloupe, or wherever it was. I could see them for the rest of their lives sitting around in some *cantina*, shuffling their feet on the pine-needle stewn floor as a juke-box thundered out its endless *pasos dobles* and the tide went lower and lower in the bottle of *aguardiente*. In luxury for the rest of their lives on some substantial cut from my money.

The negress said, 'They go by car, boss.' She couldn't keep her eyes off my face and the sticking plaster.

'One of the taxis?' I asked.

'No, boss. In Lieutenant Ocampo's car. This mawnin'.'

Outside, unsurprised, I said to Monk, 'They must have been pretty sure they weren't going to be spotted. Or else General Lemaza didn't care a damn if they were. He never intended me to have that money.' I laughed. 'Except one way. I could have invested it in the revolution. I think he was honest about that. The bastard!'

Back in my room Monk poured some whiskey for us. I sat on the bed and he stood by the window, a big, bulky figure whose simple presence there was a great comfort to me.

He said, 'Got to handle this carefully. No good steaming up to Lemaza with a revolver in your hand.'

'I don't mean to. I'll tackle him through Katrina and Angelo. Damn it, the thing's so obvious. He's employed the Hueica brothers to rob me. I'll swear it. They must be on the island still. God, if I ever get hold of that Sardi—'

'Sardi, and Lemaza particularly, will deny everything. You were robbed by one of your own men. That's Lemaza's line.'

'He won't be able to make that stick with Angelo. He's no fool. And he's honest.' I finished my whiskey and slapped the glass down hard on the bedside table. 'To think I fell for that petrol-water trick!'

Monk came across to me. He had the whiskey bottle in his hand and he filled his own glass. He held the bottle towards mine but I shook my head.

'Got to face one thing. You may never get this money back. What then?'

I stood up and began to unbutton my shirt front.

'That isn't going to happen, Monk. No bloody tin-pot dentist jumped up to Generalissimo is going to do that to me.'

'Be careful.'

'I'm going to get it. One way or another.'

'Better have another whiskey. You won't sleep.'

I didn't have more whiskey. But he was right. I didn't sleep. I lay there hearing the church bells ping out the hours and half-hours and I went over the whole thing, over and over again. I worked at it in the darkness and played it in my mind all the ways I could imagine it might go and I found an answer for them all, an answer that would put me back to the point where I was walking again with the money under my arm and Drea on her way to meet me in Haiti. It had to be like that. Just had to be.

My face wasn't so bad the next morning. There was a big bruise running out from under the plaster to the top of my left cheek bone and the ache in my head was no more than a man might have from a mild hangover. I shaved and put on a clean shirt and suit and went out into the square.

The market stalls were up, brightening the morning with their reds, yellows and greens of tomatoes, maize and beans. An old man came through the crowd, whacking at the rump of a donkey piled high with bundles of cut bamboo, and a couple of old girls on a hardware stall shouted some good-natured obscenity to me as I passed. Yes, the world was stirring and full of vigour and happiness. Caramanaga would soon fall and the future was bright with the prospect of free land and easy hours.

The *Singing Heart that Never Tires* was parked by the church and Singing Heart himself was asleep in the back. I woke him and told him I wanted to go to General Lemaza's headquarters.

'Man,' he said, 'you sure look fresh again. Powers of resistance. You sure got that. Yes, boss, you sure got to have that in this world. Now me, when I'm drunk, I'm drunk, man. Two, three days.'

I got in the back. He went on talking most of the way but I didn't listen.

When we got to the gateway of the drive to the villa the sentry stopped the taxi. Unless I was in a military car with a military driver he couldn't let me through without a pass. I argued for a while but he was adamant. He did, however, tell me that the General was not up at the villa. He had driven out a little while before and gone towards the barracks. We went down there and this time I got Singing Heart to go and talk to the sentry at the entrance to the enclosure. He came back and told me that the General had been at the barracks for a while but had now gone up the road towards the air strip.

We motored up to the little group of huts by the stone jetty and I told Singing Heart to wait for me. I got out and walked towards the Nissen hut at the end of the strip. The six Furies were all up there now, wingless, propeller-less, and with a bunch of mechanics working around one of them. A sentry stopped me short of the hut, but I saw Parkes by the hut and shouted to him. He wasn't glad to see me, but he did as I asked, and ushered me past the sentry, biting the man's head off when he began to make a protest.

I asked him how things were and he said, 'Not bad, not bad. But they're slow and you have to watch every move. What happened to your face?'

'I fell down the stairs.'

He gave me an old-fashioned look but didn't pursue the subject. When we got to the hut he nodded inside. I'd told him what I wanted and he said, 'You'll find His Nibs in there. Counting the screws and the spare parts.'

I went into the great hut. At the far end, past the work benches and the piles of stores was a small glass-partitioned office. General-issimo Lemaza was inside with Lieutenant Ocampo. They saw me coming; the General himself came out to meet me when I was about three-quarters of the way down the hut.

I gave him a good-morning and didn't waste words with him. I told him exactly what had happened, except that I didn't say that I had recognised Sardi. That was something I was keeping for Katrina and Angelo. He listened to me with patience and when I had finished he said—

'So, señor, I am sorry. . . . But what is there I can do? You have no description of the man. If you had I could have a search made for him. But it could be anyone. A Movement like this attracts all types . . . adventurers, the scum of the world. They are good fighters but when they are not fighting they are what they have always been . . . thieves, murderers. . . . But I feel for you. It is an unfortunate thing to happen.'

Unfortunate, I thought, was a mild word.

I said, 'I need that money. I mean to get it back.'

'Naturally, señor, you feel like that. But what can I do?'

'There's one thing. I want to see Señorita Katrina. But I can't

get by the sentry at the villa without a pass. You could give me
that.'

'But of course.'

He turned, leaving me there and walked to the little office. A few
moments later Lieutenant Ocampo came out and over to me. He
handed me a pass, admitting me to the villa. General Lemaza was
in the office, bending over a table. He didn't give a glance in my
direction.

Ocampo said, 'Your pass, señor.'

His neat, dark little face showed nothing.

I went out and heard Parkes roaring at one of his men for smoking
near a large dump of petrol cans on the runway.

Back at the taxi Singing Heart was standing on the jetty talking
to a fisherman who had just come in with a motorboat and had
thrown him a rope to make fast.

I gave him a shout and we started for the villa. I sat brooding
in the back.

The sentry let us through this time and Singing Heart took me
up to the front of the villa. There was an orderly at a small table
in the hall and I went straight in to him.

'I'd like to see Señorita Katrina,' I said.

He stood up politely.

'I'm sorry, señor. She is not here.'

'Where is she?'

'She went early this morning to San Pedro.'

'San Pedro?'

'Yes, señor. With her brother, the Leader Libertad.'

The cunning bastard. No wonder he'd given me the pass so
easily.

'When will they be back?'

'I don't know, señor. Two, three days. Is there anything I can
do?'

'No . . . it's nothing. I was here to dinner last night and I left
my cigarette lighter. If it's all right with you I'll go through and
get it. I think I know where I left it.'

'Certainly, señor.'

He sat down and I went over to the door of the large lounge. I
shut the door behind me but I didn't waste any time in the lounge.
The door of the General's office was unlocked and I went in. There
was a safe in the wall opposite the window but it would have taken
a better man than me and the right tools to get it open. Anyway

that wasn't the way to do things. I wanted a case against the General that I could put before Angelo. Something that couldn't be ignored.

His desk was neat, both his In and his Out baskets empty. A half-empty box of Elvas plums stood by the telephone. The waste-paper basket was empty. Sometime last night I was sure either Sardi, but more likely Ocampo, had come into this room with my box file. The dollars would be in the safe. But the box file might not be. It wasn't, however, anywhere in the room.

I went back into the hall through the lounge, held up my lighter to the orderly with a smile and then walked out to Singing Heart.

I leaned on the door and said, 'You know this house well, Singing Heart?'

'Yes, boss. Owner of sugar plantations live here before. I done jobs around this place when I was a boy. Before I got up and coming and get brain. What for, boss?'

'What do they do with the junk they throw out?'

'What you want that for, boss?'

I pulled out a ten-dollar bill.

'Just answer the questions, Singing Heart, and then forget they were ever asked. You'd do that for me?'

He grinned. 'For any man with a ten-dollar bill in his hand, boss.' He took the bill and said, 'Get in, boss.'

A hundred yards down the drive he stopped the car.

'Over there. Behind them bushes.'

To the left of the drive was a large growth of bamboo flanked by two or three oleander bushes. Behind them I found a small gardener's shed and to one side of it a brick-sided incinerator with a tin top punched with ragged holes. A couple of cans of wet rubbish stood alongside and two sacks of old paper and cartons. I lifted the lid of the incinerator. It was empty except for a few black ashes at the bottom. No fire had been lit there that morning. I went through the first sack of papers without any luck. Half-way down the second sack I found my box file. It was dry but stained with mud where it had fallen on the ground by the trough. It was empty, too. I took it and went into the shed which was full of hoes and long-handled spades. I pushed the box right up under the thatch where it was out of sight.

Singing Heart was a good boy but General Lemaza had more ten-dollar bills than I had. Sometime during the day the rubbish would be burnt. I wanted the General to think the file had been burnt, too. It was tucked away where I could find it when the moment came.

I went back to Singing Heart and he looked at me puzzled.

'You all that interested in trash, boss?'

'Sure, some people have made a fortune collecting rubbish. I knew a man once who made himself an aeroplane, just out of stuff he picked up from dumps.'

He laughed. 'That's for me.'

We went back to Acaibo and I was feeling better. I was going to get the General up against a wall, squirming in front of Angelo and Katrina.

There was a little telephone booth at the back of the hotel hall. There was no directory or instructions on how to make calls. I picked up the receiver and after a while a man's voice answered. I told him that I wanted to make a call to Army Headquarters at San Pedro. Privately, I didn't expect to be able to get hold of Angelo, but there was a fair chance that I might get Katrina.

The operator said, 'Who is this calling?'

'Señor Marchant at the *Hotel de la Reina.*'

'Ha. . . .' I could hear the sigh of recognition and he went on amicably. 'The señor who brought in the planes?'

'That's it.'

'I am sorry, señor. Maybe you do not know the rules? Calls from civilians are restricted to a radius of five miles of Acaibo. It is an Army Order. For a civilian to speak outside that radius he must have Army authority and use an Army telephone. Application for this may be made to Lieutenant Ocampo, the town commandant. In your case, señor, I should think that there would be no difficulty after all you have done for us.'

'Thank you.'

I put the receiver down. In my case there would be every difficulty. I didn't mean even to try. They would have to come back. Singing Heart had told me that in a few days' time the People's Democratic Movement would be celebrating the fifth anniversary of the outbreak of the revolution. Angelo Libertad was due in Acaibo for this. Apparently there was a review of troops in the town square and a blessing of colours service in the church. Not once in five years had he missed this, for it was in Acaibo that the fight had started originally. All I had to do was to sit time out patiently. It meant that I would be later than I had anticipated getting to Drea.

I picked up Monk and told him what had happened and then we walked down to the harbour for a drink at the *Cantina del Morro* before lunch. We got there just in time to see the *Mara II* going out.

We watched her go and I could see the small figure of the captain on one of the bridge wings.

In the *cantina*, Da Silva was playing cards with the flyers. He gave me a brief nod over their heads. If they thought they'd enticed a sucker into their school they were mistaken.

I said to Monk, 'Where does Da Silva hang out?'

'Tino's given him a room over this place, I believe.'

'I'd like to know what he's after.'

'That's easy. These people have got planes. Success around the corner. The big boys want to invest. Da Silva comes from them.'

'The General would go along with that. But not Angelo. Not if they promised him a dozen Sherman tanks and two cruisers. He's doing this on his own.'

'Da Silva wouldn't be staying if it were all that hopeless.'

Tino brought us our drinks. He looked at my piece of plaster and clucked his tongue. 'It is a bad place that *la Reina*. Always fighting.'

'I slipped on a banana skin.'

He smiled and on his way back to the bar stopped to fiddle for a moment with the vase of flowers in the broken juke-box. Today there were white marguerites.

We drank and Monk was quiet, rolling a cigarette.

After a time I said, 'I've been thinking of that place you said Eglantina's brother had.'

'Why?'

'Because of Lemaza. He must know I'm waiting for Angelo to come back. He's no fool. Something could happen to me. I could slip and go over the harbour side. An Army truck could side-swipe me. I could make a list a page long. Both of us should get away.'

Monk nodded. 'Good idea. Eglantina's brother's place is on the north side. We could go there tonight and keep low. Walk it. No trusting *Singing Hearts* or *Space Sputnik Specials*.'

'That's what I think.' General Lemaza was king around here. Anything could happen.

Monk fished in his back pocket for his notebook and with his pencil drew a little sketch of the north coast. I could follow it because I'd driven along the road with Singing Heart.

'I was up there yesterday with Eglantina for a drive,' he said. 'We'll go tonight.'

Somewhere out at the mouth of the bay the *Mara II* suddenly sounded her siren . . . a long, derisive hooting that came wailing back to us as she hit the open sea.

CHAPTER 11

After lunch I went up to my room and had an hour's sleep. It was the best time to sleep really. The heat cleared the square and Acaibo dropped off into the quiet of a long siesta. At night the place was full of noise from the leave parties that came swarming in after six o'clock. It was nothing to have drunken officers or men blundering into your room at two and three in the morning. You couldn't stop them because all the bolts and locks on the doors had long been broken from constant battering. And even when the leave parties cleared off the radio was usually left on in the hall, nattering away all night.

When I woke it was about three o'clock. I lay on the bed and gradually became aware that something was different. A truck rumbled through the square and I heard men shouting. There was silence for a while, and then another truck came roaring into the square and pulled up with a screech of brakes somewhere near the church. I heard the clatter of heavy boots as men jumped down from it. Orders were shouted and there was the sound of running footsteps. House doors slammed. Another truck burst through the square and I heard it revving away on the hill beyond the harbour.

I got up and went to the window. There was an open army truck by the church. Two men squatted behind a machine gun which was mounted on it. At intervals around the square soldiers were posted, carrying their rifles at the ready. A squad of four men came out of the house where the Hueica brothers had lodged and went into the next house. Further up the square I could see another party working from house to house.

From the hallway of the hotel I heard voices and the clatter of feet. I leaned out of the window and saw that there was a soldier on guard at the hotel entrance. As I drew back from the window the door of my room was pushed open. A soldier came in while another one stood in the doorway and covered me and the room with his rifle.

'What the hell—' I began.

The soldier in the room said curtly, 'Just stay where you are, señor.'

I stood where I was.

The soldier went over to my bed and looked under it. He went then to the small curtained recess that hid a hand washbasin. He jerked the curtain aside. He turned back to the door.

'Nothing,' he said to the other soldier. They went, slamming the door after them. I heard them working their way through the other rooms on the floor.

A little later I saw them come out of the front of the hotel and disappear down the square. I went along to Monk's room to see if he knew what all the fuss was about.

Eglantina was sitting on Monk's bed. She was wearing a loose yellow silk wrapper and underneath was stripped to her bust bodice and pants against the sticky heat. She pulled the wrapper close to make herself decent. The movement sent two or three shirts balanced on her knees to the floor. A tobacco tin full of odd buttons was on the bed at her side and she had a needle and thread in one hand. She gave me a grin and said:

'Every time this man put on shirt he busts off buttons like shelling peas.'

'Where is he?'

'Harbour. Every afternoon he plays 'bout with that motor-boat of my brother. Gonna fix it so one day we make trip to Caramanga. . . .' She glanced at the open door and shrugged her shoulders. 'Like things go now, though, maybe we won't need it. Go there by road in one, two months' time.'

'What's all the fuss about outside? And these soldiers? Were they here?'

'Sure. They didn't tell you?'

'No.'

'Them soldiers looking for that one you bring in. That John MacIntyre Albano man. He done a skip from the barracks. They look all over for him.'

'He's out?'

'Sure, he's out. One of those soldiers is friend of my brother. Tell me 'bout it. Got away two hours since. Hit the guard over head

when his food is brought, take his clothes and walk straight out
pass all them sentries.'

'Well, good for him. But General Lemaza will have someone's
head for this.'

'Could be. You need anything fixing, buttons or something, while
I got steam up?'

'No thanks, Eglantina.'

I went out and downstairs, thinking I'd go and find Monk, but
I wasn't allowed to leave the hotel. There was a sentry outside and
nobody moved anywhere until they had finished their searching.
The way they were going about it I didn't think Albano would have
much chance—unless he'd got smartly into the hills behind Acaibo.
Once there he might have a chance. . . . I had my own troubles
and they didn't leave any room for his. It was a pretty selfish
attitude, but then I was in no mood to think about other people
except the ones who were making it difficult for me to get what I
wanted. Concentrating on one thing can give you a narrow view of
life, like walking along with blinkers and only seeing right ahead of
your nose. That may be all right for a horse in shafts, but it doesn't
help any man. In my business you don't want any blind areas. To
keep healthy you need a hundred and eighty degree arc of fire. This
job had me committed right up to the neck. It just couldn't be
allowed to flop. It had to be successful because I had the biggest
stake in its success. I couldn't pay enough attention to all the little
straws that were being blown in the wind. A straw at the right
moment can trip a man as surely as a tautly stretched wire. Placed
as I was I needed the kind of vision which could 'look into the
seeds of time and say which grain will grow and which will not.'
Nothing was going to stop me from getting my money and meeting
Drea in Haiti.

Meeting Drea in Haiti. That was my future. Towards that one
point I lived. Back in my room, lying on my bed and listening to the
noises from the square, I thought about her and our first meeting, of
the first moment when I had seen her on the deck of the old stern
paddler going up to Bogota. It was the rainy season and the river
was in yellow flood. She'd come past me, wearing a white mackintosh, her chestnut hair free to the wind, and my eyes had followed
her, but right from that moment it had not been the idle compulsion
of watching an attractive woman. I watched her go by to the stern
and then come back, walking with that grace which was peculiarly
hers, and I don't think she even saw me. Later that day the steamer

had broken down. It was always breaking down and usually at well-regulated calls in some river port where the captain could spend a pleasant three hours drinking while his engineer sweated. This time it broke down in mid-stream and there were a few minutes of panic while we drifted on the flood into the bank, crashing into the overhanging trees, and then were finally made fast. After six hours the captain announced that no repair could be made until he sent up-stream for spares. The steamer would be delayed for at least twenty-four hours. Most of the passengers, country people for whom time meant nothing, elected to stay on board. Bogota was two days upstream. What did it matter if it took four days? Or six days? It mattered to me. I wanted to get to Bogota in a hurry. I knew this part of the country, so I decided to go ashore to walk to a village a couple of miles inland where I thought I could get a car.

As I was going off the steamer Drea came up to me.

'That captain tells me that you want to get to Bogota in a hurry and you're going to hire a car?'

'I think I can get one in San Juan—that's a couple of miles away.' It was the first time I had heard her speak and there was a slight huskiness in the voice somehow so right with that controlled puma-like grace of her body.

'Can I share it? I don't want to be stuck here a couple of days. I know these boats.'

'If you don't mind the walk. It's rough going.'

She got her case and she came with me. We didn't speak much, and a few minutes after we left the steamer it began to rain. It took us an hour to make San Juan and we were wet and muddy when we reached it. It was almost dark and we went to the one hotel, little more than a *cantina*. I asked the proprietor about a car and he said that there was one. His brother drove it, but he was away with a wedding party and wouldn't be back until the early morning.

I turned to Drea and said, 'There's nothing we can do. It's this or back to the steamer, and frankly this is no night for walking. The car will be here in the morning and we can make Bogota by tomorrow evening.'

'This,' she said.

I asked the proprietor if he had room for us and he nodded. He took our cases off and we dried ourselves in front of the fire. There was a kind of stiffness, almost shyness, between us which made talk difficult. It was as though we were both waiting for the other to say something pertinent and revealing which would allow us to be easy with one another. The place was dead, the bar empty and the proprietor's wife killed a couple of small chicken and made supper for us. The chicken was the toughest I'd ever had. We had a couple of drinks and a bottle of wine, but they did nothing for us. I had the feeling all the time, that much as she attracted me, we could easily finish up by disliking one another. One or other of us only had to say the wrong word. The right word didn't seem to exist.

Later, when we decided to go up to our rooms, we discovered that the proprietor had taken us for man and wife. He only had one room and he showed us into it. It had a big double bed with a crumpled blue silk spread. We stood in the doorway looking at it and I think the proprietor took our silence for admiration, for he nodded at the bed and said, 'Very beautiful, no? I am married in it. Anita has all our children there. Seven, señor. All married now.'

I told him that we weren't married, but if he could find a couple of blankets I'd sleep by the fire in the bar.

He was embarrassed about his mistake and spent a long time apologising. Drea said nothing but I noticed that she was smiling.

I said good night to her and went back to the bar. I had a last drink and the proprietor's wife brought me in some blankets and cushions and I made myself comfortable. I lay there by myself in the glow of the fire, far from sleep and thinking about Drea. I was puzzled by the barrier to even the most ordinary conversation between us. And then after an hour she came down in her dressing-gown.

I sat up as she came over to the fire.

'What's the matter?' I asked. The fire gleams on her hair caught my eyes and I could feel my heart beginning to pump rapidly.

'Bed bugs,' she said. 'They came out of the mattress like an army. I couldn't cope with them. Have you had trouble?'

'None.'

She stood over me and said, 'Do you mind if I share the fire with you?'

'Of course not.'

She lay down on the blankets beside me and put her hands behind her head, staring up at the smoke-brown ceiling. For a long time she was silent and then, suddenly, without looking at me she said, 'We don't seem to have much to say to one another. Why?'

'I don't know. There's a lot I want to say. I think I'm scared . . . of saying the wrong thing. It must be something new.'

'Is there anything new?'

'I think so. . . .'

She half-turned her head and looked at me. Her eyes were very close to mine. Then she nodded her head and said, 'Yes, I think there is. I think so.'

I moved enough to reach her and put my lips on hers. She let me kiss her, but it was cool and unrevealing and after a second or two she lay back and stared at the ceiling again, smiling. I put out a hand, to find hers. She shook her head.

'Not yet,' she said. 'There's lots of time ahead.'

I relaxed, not looking at her, but knowing she was there and that slowly the right words would come, that no matter now what we said or did it would be beyond our power to escape. And it had been like that. Not that night. Not the next day when we got to Bogota. But it had come and there was no more that I wanted. Nowhere else in the world was there anything that I wanted more than Drea and our love.

It was two hours before they took the guards off the square and we could move about freely. Eglantina had found a couple of light bags for us and we planned just to take these with a few necessities and leave the rest of our stuff in our cases at the hotel. I kept my revolver out handy. Of the four sub-machine guns we had brought (the Hueica brothers had handed theirs over to us when the *Mara II* had docked) two had already gone in exchange for revolvers. Of the others Monk and I had one each. I packed mine in the bottom of the case I was going to leave at the hotel, together with the tear-gas grenades. We planned to leave about an hour after darkness. The place then would be jumping with parties and no one would pay any attention to us. When I was all ready to go, I sat down and wrote a letter to Drea. I kept it short, merely explaining that the job was going well but that I might be delayed a few days before getting out. Then I walked down to the *Cantina del Morro* and gave it to Tino. He knew all the skippers who came in and out. If he could find one going to Haiti so much the better, but anywhere with a postal system would do. He just looked at the address, Hotel Montana, Port-au-Prince, Haiti, and said, 'Nice place. If you can afford it.'

With luck, I thought, as I walked back through the thick swift-gathering dusk, I might be there before the letter. Monk was in the bar and we had a drink together.

I said, 'You heard Albano's out?'

'Yes. They were down at the harbour. Going over all the boats. He knows this country. He'll be up in the mountains. They're offering a reward for him—alive. If he weren't the son of the Minister of Defence it would be dead or alive. Lemaza doesn't want any assets spoiled.'

I said, 'I wonder where Lemaza laid up the Hueica brothers?'

'In the barracks would be my guess.'

'I'd like just ten minutes alone with Sardi. My God, I would.'

'If you get it, make sure he hasn't a knife in his hand.' He looked at his watch. 'Another half hour and we should push off. I've fixed the motor-boat up. Could have taken that and had a nice trip round. But with this Albano business they've got their eye on all the boats.' He patted his belly. 'Walk'll take this down. Nice night for it too.'

We passed the half hour in the bar and then Monk said, 'Time to start. I'll go first. Meet you by the water trough on the hill. From there we'll start being careful.'

He went out and I stayed, finishing my drink. Eglantina was singing her blues number. I couldn't see or hear any improvement in her act. There were quite a few dancers but the place hadn't started to warm up yet. I gave Monk ten minutes and then I went up to my room to get my bag.

I pushed open my door and went in. The light was on. Lieutenant Ocampo was standing by the window. There was a soldier standing just inside the door and another bending over my bed and on the point of closing the lid of my case.

Lieutenant Ocampo said, 'Good evening, Señor Marchant.'

The soldier by the door slid behind me and blocked the way out. On the top of the dressing-table close to Ocampo were four grenades, the sub-machine gun, my revolver and a pile of ammunition.

'What the devil are you doing here?' I demanded.

Ocampo gave a neat little shrug of his shoulders and he pursed his lips primly before answering. He looked too damn satisfied with himself.

He said, 'The standing orders for civilians in Acaibo are posted in the hotel lobby, señor. You have read them?'

'No, I haven't. The whole place is crummy with notices for this and that. Anyway, what's it got to do with me? You don't consider me a civilian, do you?'

'Why not, señor? While you worked for us, no. But your work is finished. The standing orders state that all civilians must hand over their arms to the Town Commandant. These'—he jerked his head towards the dressing-table—'I shall have to confiscate. Ordinarily there would be a fine for the breach. But in the circumstances, I think we can dispense with that, señor.'

'I should damn well hope so, after what I've done for you. Now, do you mind getting the hell out of here?'

He didn't like my attitude and I didn't mean him to like it. But he didn't rise to it.

He said to the soldier by the bed, 'Corporal, search him.'

The soldier came over to me. He had a revolver in his right hand. With his other hand he felt over my clothes, and then stepped back, shaking his head.

'Good,' said Lieutenant Ocampo. 'Then let us go.'

'That's all right with me,' I said angrily. This jumped-up popinjay was getting under my skin; the whole place was getting under my skin. I'd done a job for them and they'd welshed on me. I had to be careful to keep my thinking about it within limits otherwise I knew I should start breaking something. 'The sooner you get out the better.'

The Corporal went to the dressing-table and packed the arms and ammunition into a small canvas bag. Then he stood smartly alongside Ocampo. The soldier at the door opened it and stood to one side.

I waited for them to go. But none of them made any move.

Ocampo motioned towards the bed, on which lay my case and the light back packed for my trip with Monk.

'You will want those, señor?'

I stared at him.

'What are you talking about?'

He gave a sigh then as though he were losing patience with some dumbwitted child.

'Since you are leaving, señor, you will naturally want to take your things.'

'But I'm not going anywhere. Look, what is all this?'

He raised his hands slightly and rubbed the palms on the smooth leather of his belt. He had rather a fancy revolver holster studded with brass rivets in the shape of his initials, A. O.

He said in his patient-parent voice, 'Señor, my instructions from General Lemaza were to make this as least embarrassing to you as possible. After all we are grateful for what you have done. It is for this that I did not come to you in the bar, where the scene would have been too public. My instructions are to see you aboard with every courtesy.'

'Aboard!'

'Yes, señor. Those are the instructions from the General.' A hand slid up to his tunic breast pocket, and he began to fiddle with the button to bring out his instructions.

'Don't bother,' I snapped. 'Let me get this straight. You're going to see me aboard? I'm being kicked out?'

'If you put it that way, señor.'

There were a lot of ways I could put it. I didn't need it in words of two syllables. I wondered if it were worth-while trying to make a break for the door. I stood there, seething with frustration and anger. If Ocampo had come half an hour later I would have been away.

I said, 'I want to see the General.'

Ocampo gave his neat shrug. 'It is impossible, señor. He has gone up to San Pedro this evening. My instructions are to put you aboard the *Aciano,* which is leaving tonight. Your case, señor.' He waved his hand towards the bed.

I said, 'What about the rest of my party?'

Ocampo said, 'My instructions concern you only, señor.' He gave me a brief smile which was about as warming as a cold draught.

Sandwiched between the two soldiers I went down the stairs. It was on the stairs that I'd already decided to take my chance, drop my cases and jump for it. If I could reach the square I might get away. But Ocampo's instructions covered the possibility that I might try to escape. There were two more soldiers in the hotel hallway, just by the door. I went down, deciding to do nothing.

Outside the hotel his car was waiting. I was put in the back between the soldiers and he sat in front with the driver. The two soldiers from the hall stood, one on each running-board. No chances were going to be given to me. A few people outside watched us curiously, and I saw Singing Heart standing by his cab near the church. Up at the water trough Monk would be waiting for me and wondering what had happened. . . . I owed Monk three thousand dollars for his work. Forty thousand dollars. And Drea in Haiti. Inside me there was a volcano waiting to blow its head off. I thought of the letter I had written to Drea. It looked as though I were going to beat it to Haiti . . . I'd walk in to the hotel and there would be Drea waiting. She'd take one look at me and she would know.

The warm night air pressed against my face as the car swept

around the curve of the harbour, past the row of red bulbs over the door of the *Cantina del Morro,* out towards the dark plug of the Citadel. There was a length of quayside there where the schooners and motor-craft of the gunrunners, the petrol carriers and all the other black-market stores came in.

The *Aciano* was a refurbished torpedo boat, low and squat and painted a pale sky blue. Three men leaned over the starboard rail and watched our little procession. One of them was wearing a high-crowned Mexican hat and had a guitar in his hand. The other two were in dirty singlets and greasy trousers. One of them had a long, naked woman tattooed the length of his right arm. I was taken forward to the old ward-room, which was about the size of a good hen hut. A young man with a pink and white face and a yachting cap at an angle opened the door and I was invited to step in.

I had the place to myself and one glance showed me that the ports were too small to let me out. Ocampo stood at the door and rubbed his palms again on his leather belt.

'This boat sails in an hour,' he said. 'There will be a guard on the door until she sails. You will be confined here until she is outside the three-mile limit.'

He was about to close the door on me when the pink-and-white-faced youngster said cheerfully in English, 'There's whiskey and cigarettes on the side there, chum. Help yourself. Don't try anything because these bastards mean business.'

The door closed and I had the place to myself and my luggage.

There were a couple of bottles of Four Roses on the sideboard. I helped myself to a large whiskey, neat, and flopped into a cane chair, my feet and legs sprawled out, and let the savageness in me run free. It took a long time and I had to keep telling myself to stop thinking about what had happened, stop killing Lemaza and Ocampo in my mind, but to chuck away the past and get down to the future. I had to have my forty thousand. Some way I had to have it. . . .

An hour later I heard the engines start up, heard men call and move about the deck. By that time I'd calmed down a bit and was beginning to think. To think ahead.

The *Aciano* moved away from the quayside and a little later I felt her begin to lift and swing as she met the sea outside the shelter of the harbour. She was running easily, not pressing her motors. After about half an hour the door was unlocked. The young man with the yachting cap came in and gave me a grin.

'Rimmy will be down in a minute,' he said.

'Who's Rimmy?'

'The captain.' His grin broadened. 'You're taking it very well. Not nice to be kicked out. I'd be out for blood.'

'I'm saving that,' I said. 'Marchant's the name.'

'Yes, I know. Sea Furies.'

He went to the sideboard and helped himself to a drink, saying over his shoulder, 'I'm Foxton. You must have stepped on someone's toes. Big three-star toes. The higher the rank the bigger the bastard. Brief military service taught me that one.'

'You're English?'

'No. Everyone thinks so. Swedish. The name isn't, but then it isn't my name. If they think you're English,' he gave a shrug, 'might as well go along with it.'

He came back with a glass of whiskey so full that it reminded me of the one Katrina had first poured for me. He knocked back half of it in a couple of swallows and smacked his lips. Seeing me watching him, he said:

'No drinking in port. Rimmy's orders. Sound, too. Mostly we're at sea. Get drunk in joints like Acaibo and there's always some bastard trouble.'

'Where are you heading?'

He shrugged. 'Don't know until Rimmy says. Last time it was Curaçao. Help yourself to a drink.' He took another pull at his whiskey, and went on, 'Where do you want?'

I got up and helped myself to a whiskey.

'I want Acaibo,' I said.

He shook his head. 'Rimmy would never wear that one. . . .' He tipped his chair back and switched on a radio on a shelf above his head. Some American station flooded the ward-room with dance music. He relaxed with his glass cuddled on his belt and began to sing the words gently.

I sat and waited for Rimmy.

He came down a little later. His procedure was the same as Foxton's. He went straight to the sideboard and poured himself a whiskey. He took a swig at it as he stood there, back to me, and then turned.

'Sorry about this. Don't hold it against us. If I hadn't taken you the General would have made trouble for us. We've got all we need of that.' He spoke English, but it was much more accented than Foxton's. He was a big man, well in his fifties, with short blond hair going a little white over the ears, a big, bushy beard, and a fine, strong body showing no signs of flabbiness. He looked the hard, carefree type who could float happily on a balsa raft for half a year to prove something about sea currents. He wore a lightweight, highnecked blue jersey and white trousers. Big toes stuck out through the open ends of leather sandals.

I said, 'What are they paying you to take me?'

'Two hundred dollars. It's not a long trip so you can't eat or drink into too much of that. Hundred and eighty left by the time I land you.' He came over, flopped into a chair by the table, and reached back and turned the radio down to a whisper.

'They paid me forty thousand dollars for bringing in the Sea Furies, paid it, and then hit me over the head and took it back.'

He shook his head sadly. 'What is it they say? When you sup with the devil use a long spoon? Lemaza is a sharp business man. Me, I never unload until the money has been paid.' He nodded at a safe in the corner of the ward-room. 'Lock it in there before the hatches come off. Don't deal with him much, though. Only our second run here . . . iodine, sulpha drugs, bandages, quinine. Could have a red cross painted on the deck, eh?' He laughed gently to himself.

I said, 'I've got to get back there. I need that money and I know how to get it.'

He looked at Foxton, who held up his whiskey glass and squinted through it.

Rimmy said, 'It would mean we couldn't come back here again.'

Foxton said, 'Plenty of other markets, Rimmy. He's in our league. We ought to help, what?' He got up and went to fill his glass. Over his shoulder he said, 'Who's got the wheel?'

'Joey. There isn't a rock between here and South America he doesn't know. Sure,' he put his glass down on the table, 'we ought to help. But what is help?'

I said, 'Two hundred and fifty dollars. Take me up to the north coast and put me over in a dinghy half a mile from shore. Just before dawn tomorrow.'

'Dinghies cost money. We wouldn't see ours back.'

'Three hundred.' I had just about that in my wallet.

'Not just the money, Foxton knows that. It's you, brother-worker. You'd only get yourself in a mess and still no money.'

'It's his neck,' said Foxton. He'd drawn a whiskey to match Rimmy's this time, right to the brim of a tumbler. He was a nice lad, but even though he was on my side I knew that I had been landed with a couple of soakers. I wanted to get things fixed while they could still give the crew a few orders. Foxton took a pull at his glass to prevent it slopping as he walked. He went back to his seat carrying the second bottle with him and put it by Rimmy's glass. Rimmy topped his glass up and poured a healthy shot into mine.

'It's his neck,' said Rimmy. 'But I don't like people getting into that kind of mess. Quixotic. What chance have you got?'

'I just want five minutes with Angelo Libertad. He's due back tomorrow or the next day. A few words with him or his sister who came over with me on the *Mara II* and I can have the pressure put on Lemaza. I've got a friend ashore, waiting for me in a hiding-place.'

Rimmy cocked an eye at Foxton.

Foxton said, 'His neck. But he's got it worked out. I think we should for two-fifty.'

'Three hundred,' said Rimmy, grinning. 'It's a beautiful dinghy. Mahogany fittings, clinker built, silver rowlocks and a built-in radio. Couldn't replace it for a hundred.'

They both laughed together and I could tell that the drink was working fast. I took a sip at my own glass. Heavy drinkers don't like to see you hanging back and I needed all their goodwill.

'Three hundred,' I said. 'And I can look after myself.'

'Can you?' Rimmy scratched at his blond beard. 'You've already looked after yourself forty-thousand dollars down. Maybe you need protection. I don't like people I like to get messed up.'

'I was day-dreaming before. Now I'm awake and coming back fast. Let me worry about myself.' I had to get him soon because there would be no shaking him in fifteen minutes. He'd be full of drunken philanthropy and father-love for me, determined to save my neck.

Neither of them said anything for a while. They took their whiskey glasses down to well below the plimsoll line, topped them up before they hit bottom, and considered the situation in silence. I'd met some heavy drinkers before, but these two were all-time champions and they had the champions' knack of never letting the bottom of the glass dry out. Curious thing was, they both looked so damned healthy on it.

'Where'd we take the next cargo?' asked Rimmy out of the blue. 'No welcome at Acaibo.'

'Heard Batista's boys were starting up in Cuba and places. Could try that,' said Foxton.

I said, 'Where are you heading now?'

'Curaçao,' said Foxton.

'Aruba,' said Rimmy.

'Both Dutch,' said Foxton. 'Nice, clean Dutch. Eat off the floors.'

'Wherever it is,' I said, pulling out my notebook, 'ring this number in Barranquilla and speak to Señor Barrau.' I scribbled his number as I spoke and tore out the page. 'He's got a stake in the forty thousand. He'll fix your next cargo.'

'Barrau?' Rimmy took the paper.

'Yes. He does your kind of business.'

'Barranquilla?' Foxton leaned back and put the radio up a shade. 'Wha's like?' It was the first shade of slipping I'd heard from either of them.

'A paradise,' I said.

'A paradise on earth, eh?' Rimmy nodded to himself. 'I'd like that.'

'We'll go there,' said Foxton. 'Yes?'

'Yes,' said Rimmy, and looking at me, he went on, 'You come along, too. Can't miss a paradise.'

Foxton, on my side still but fast easing off, said, 'He wants Acaibo. Remember?'

'So?' Rimmy's hand went out for the bottle.

Foxton was silent for a moment and then with a sudden spurt of brightness he said, 'Know what? Let's put it to the vote. Acaibo or not for him. Eh?'

'Good idea,' said Rimmy. He was smiling gently at his half-full glass. 'All those in favour of Acaibo for the señor raise right hand.'

Foxton put up his hand and Rimmy kept his down. I raised my right hand. Rimmy looked around at us and then said, 'O.K. Carried two to one. Democratic decision.'

I raised my glass and drank to them and they acknowledged the toast, and while the goodwill stirred strongly in them I said, 'Maybe you should get your helmsman Jocy down and give him instructions now.'

'Okay. Okay,' said Rimmy.

Foxton leaned back and pressed a push-button switch close to the radio. A horn sounded on deck. A few minutes later the man I had seen with the High Mexican hat on deck came into the ward-room. It took about ten minutes for him to get his instructions from the two of them, but he showed no surprise or concern at their state, and he was dead sober.

When he went Foxton said, 'First-class chap, Joey.'

'First-class,' said Rimmy.

'Officers drink at sea. Crew drink in port. Excellent system,' said Foxton.

Half an hour later they were both as drunk as I'd seen anyone for a long time. But they were still sitting up and taking it, talking now to one another in Swedish. I left them and went on deck and they didn't know that I was gone.

Two hours before dawn I went down to the ward-room. The radio was going full blast. There were three empty whiskey bottles rolling gently about on the floor, clinking now and again with the odd glass. Rimmy was asleep in a cane chair, snoring hard. Foxton was lying on the floor with his head pillowed on a pile of old magazines. He was breathing evenly and looked the picture of health. I counted out three hundred dollars from my wallet and left them on the table with a scribbled note of thanks. I picked up my case and light bag and went on deck.

Joey was in the wheelhouse, his face just touched with the light from the binnacle. He pointed away to the port hand and said:

'Red light. That's on palm tree at air strip.'

I could see it dimly, losing it now and again and we swung in a swell that was coming in from the north-west. We were around the eastern tip of Cordillo and running steadily up the north shore. But I couldn't see any land. The night was overcast. We were running without lights except the one in the wheelhouse over the binnacle.

Joey said, 'Captain sleep?'

I nodded.

'Good man, captain.'

'Is he always drunk at sea?'

'No. Only first three days. Señor Foxton two days. Not so tough.'

'How long have you been with them?'

'Five year. Everyone here five, four year. Not same boat though. You got trouble in Acaibo?'

'Yes.'

Up forward I could see the shapes of two men getting the lashings off the dinghy. Now and again a lick of spray came back over the bows, flecking the deck briefly with dying phosphorescence.

'I had trouble in Mexico once. That's why I leave. You got gun?' He looked down at my cases.

'No.'

'Need gun? German Mauser pistol. Twenty-six rounds. Always keep clean since Mexico but never use. Fifteen dollars.'

I bought it. It would make me feel more comfortable when I got ashore.

We ran for another half hour and then I told him to take the *Aciano* in. We stood in for about a mile and then he cut the motors down so that we just held our way against the run of the sea.

'No farther, señor. Bad coast.' He nodded to the foredeck where the two men were waiting. '*Adios...*'

They lowered the dinghy and held it while I went over. My case and bag were handed down. The man with the tattooed woman on his arm pointed obliquely to the south-east. 'Keep her heading that way. The wind and tide will take you, señor.'

They let go and the dinghy slid down the port side and in a few moments was astern of the *Aciano*. As I unshipped the oars the motors roared and there was the quick white creaming of foam above the *Aciano*'s screws as she turned away and went out to sea.

I didn't hurry. I had plenty of time and darkness and I wanted the light to be just breaking as I closed in to the cliffs. I rowed easily for half an hour, and then the first grey loom of light began to ease up like a long bruise along the eastern horizon. A little later I could make out the low line of cliffs, their tops fringed by tall palms. Once I saw the headlights of a truck or car come snaking along the cliff-road making for Acaibo.

I found a small V-shaped beach running sharply back into the cliffs and put the dinghy ashore on hard white sand. She hadn't got the *Aciano's* name painted on her. I pulled her up the sands and dragged her into a rock cleft. The beach didn't look as though it were used much. In fact, at its head there was no path up to the cliff top. I had a fairly easy climb up through shrub and rocks. Half-way up I hid my case under a rock and piled dead palm fronds over it. I wanted to travel light and my bag was enough. The sun lipped the eastern sea as I reached the top. The coast road was about fifty yards away through a grove of king palms. I sat down and had a look at Monk's map. So far as I could make out I had to go about three miles westwards along the road and then take a

small path up into the mountain country. About a mile off the road
Eglantina's brother had a small plantain holding which hadn't been
worked for three years. Whether Monk would be there or not I
couldn't know. He would have waited for me at the trough for a
while and then certainly have gone back to find out what had
happened. If he had stayed in Acaibo I would have to get in touch
with him.

CHAPTER 12

The path ran up into the mountains, following a steep valley which had been cut into terraces in the usual *barranco* fashion to make small plots of ground for cultivation. It was obvious that there had been no work on the terraces since the beginning of the revolution. Everything was overgrown. I passed a couple of drum-shaped concrete water reservoirs. They were empty and given over to lizards and ghekkos. The hut was about a thousand feet up and built of timber and bamboos, the palm thatch gone in places. It sat back squatly against the mountainside, screened by shrubs and backed by a clump of immortelle trees, their flaming blossoms vivid against the blue sky.

Monk wasn't there. It was just one large room and then a sort of lean-to construction at the back which housed the cooking quarters. Against one wall of the main room was a rough wooden bunk with a mildewed canvas mattress.

I fetched some water from a small trickle that came down the hillside not far from the house, made a fire, and gave myself a shave and a swab down. Afterwards, I sat at the hut door and smoked, watching the path. Now and again, very faintly, I thought I could catch the rumble of distant artillery fire up towards San Pedro. I sat there for a couple of hours and it began to be clear to me that Monk wasn't coming. Once he had heard what had happened to me there would be no reason to come out here. He had far too much sense to go and make trouble with Ocampo about my deport-ation. He might even begin to question his own safety in Acaibo. More than likely he would decide that it was time for Eglantina and himself to clear out and would be working hard to get the motor-boat fixed up. I decided to give him until mid-day. I sat there and watched the sun climb higher. The heat increased and my only company came from a couple of fork-tailed kites that circled in the air currents high above the valley.

By now, I thought, Drea was on her way to Port-au-Prince, could be there even. It was curious that it should have been Port-au-Prince and the Hotel Montana again. Once before she'd walked out on me; not being able to say then what she had said this time. I'd been frantic, not understanding, knowing only that I had to find her. I had caught up with her there. It had taken me a month to find her. As I had got out of my taxi, she had come down the steps. There was a tall, a little too-plumpish blond man with her, wearing a flowered shirt and beautifully creased lavender slacks, and a Cadillac was parked just ahead of my taxi.

She saw me, but she said nothing. Neither did I. They went past me to the Cadillac. I followed and the man in the flowered shirt had turned and said, 'You want something?' He was holding the door of the car for her.

I said, 'Yes.' I looked at her, at the open door of the car. All she had to do was to get into the car. She knew it, and I knew it. Then she turned away from the car and came towards me. For a moment I thought he was going to take it badly. Then he saw her face as she came to me and with a sudden shrug of his shoulders he got into the car. We never saw him again. What would it be like, I wondered, this time? Just wanting her wouldn't be magic enough this time.

At mid-day there was still no Monk, so I decided to move. There was an old straw sun hat on the wall of the hut. I put this on. I had a blue shirt in my bag. I ripped it here and there and rubbed some dirt into my drill trousers and turned them up a few inches at the cuffs. I was brown enough to pass for a near-white if no one looked too closely. My shoes were too good, so I changed them for a pair of white canvas shoes from my light bag. I went on up the valley, hoping to strike across and meet the San Pedro road which would take me down into Acaibo on the harbour side. I was in no hurry because I didn't want to reach Acaibo until it was dark. I carried my Mauser in my bag, right at the top where I could get at it quickly. My one anxiety was that there might be parties of soldiers out in the hills still looking for Albano. I didn't want to get mixed up with them.

It took three hours to reach the San Pedro road, three hours of hard gruelling going. I needn't have bothered to mess myself up before starting because the climb up the valley and down to the road achieved the tatterdemalion effect I needed. There was a certain amount of traffic on the road, mostly lorries going up to San Pedro. I headed for Acaibo, shuffling along in the roadside dust and keeping my head down, giving a very good imitation of a work-worn peon. Two miles down the road I had luck. Just off the road under a group of tall palms was a long tin-roofed cabin with a couple of trucks pulled up outside it. A green-and-white board over the door said—*Cantina de las Fuerzas Armadas Libertad*. I could see that this complimentary gesture to the Armed Forces of the Revolution had been painted crudely over some previous name. But the thing that interested me more than my thirst for a drink was the fact that a set of telephone wires ran up from insulators at the side of the cabin to join the wires that were slung down the roadway on poles.

There were four soldiers drinking beer at a table just inside the door, and a black-faced mountain of woman behind the bar with her head wrapped in a yellow handkerchief. Talking a bastard Spanish I ordered a bottle of beer and, after a bit of trouble, managed to get some bread and a tin of sardines. The Armed Forces weren't interested in food. No one took any notice of me as I sat at a table at the far end of the counter and waited for the soldiers to go. The telephone was on the wall by the door. I was pretty sure that the place was well within the five-mile radius of Acaibo. After the beer and the sardines I felt better. Since leaving the hut I had moved in a dull, unthinking mood; not concerning myself much with any problem except the immediate one of contacting Monk. I had plans for the future beyond that but I kept them stowed well away.

The soldiers went and I bought another bottle of beer and got some coins for the telephone. The woman sat behind her counter and closed her eyes against the heat, which was almost unbearable because of the tin roof.

She looked up briefly as I went to the telephone and then relapsed into her dozing.

I called the *Hotel de la Reina* and got through without any trouble. I asked for Eglantina. She was usually around the place most of the day. I had to wait five minutes before she came.

I said, 'Eglantina, is Monk there?'

She was a bright girl. I heard her breath go and she gave a little 'Oh, Lordy,' as she recognised my voice.

'Tell him,' I said, 'that I'll be in Acaibo at eight tonight. I'll be in the church. Just inside.' I rang off without giving her time to say anything.

I went down the road about a couple of miles until from a high bluff I could see Acaibo at the foot of the hills. I turned off the road and found a spot overlooking the sea. I slept in the shelter of a cane break, content to wait until the daylight went. I only had an hour's walk to Acaibo.

I slept like a log, a thick, dreamless sleep. When I woke the light was going fast. I started for Acaibo, feeling stiff. As I hit the outskirts I heard the church bell strike the half-hour. Lights were showing from the houses and from the few craft at moorings in the harbour. People were sitting outside their doors catching the coolness after the heat of the day. I moved along, head down. A party of soldiers came up the harbour side with a couple of girls between them. I stepped out of their way.

A few moments later I was in the square. There was the usual noisy evening parade going on with the leave parties. Both taxis had gone from the front of the church. I went in and slid into a seat just inside the door. The place was in gloom except for a few lights over the figures of saints in the side chapels. Four great candles flickered in the draught at the altar at the far end of the church. I tucked my hat on my knees and half bent in a devotional attitude. There were two figures in similar attitudes close up to the altar and a woman, her head black-shawled, came down past me, her lips moving noiselessly. As I sat there, waiting for Monk, I thought of my parson father. Right up until the time I had left England I had gone to church regularly, without question. In the last five years I could count the times on the fingers of one hand. He wouldn't have approved of this occasion. With a little bit of shock I realised how far away I'd slipped, not just from him, but from a lot of things which had been me. All that business of the body renewing itself completely in seven years was nothing compared with the change that went on in the mind, in one's real self. Little by little one changed and woke up to find oneself a different character. Here I was in Acaibo, determined to get my money, thinking of nothing else. If there had been no Drea, I would probably have cut my losses and gone. Five years ago I would have done this. But not now. The money was vital because of Drea. And Drea, without question, was vital for me. There was no questioning that. We had come together and the thing was complete. Unanswer-

able. Changing us both. She was for me, and I was for her. Only
now, some growing, irrefutable sense of self-preservation, fatigue,
if you like, from the forces holding us, had made her impose a
condition.

Alongside of me Monk said in a whisper, 'You're a damned fool,
but I'm glad to see you. Excuse me.' He leant forward and I knew
that he was praying. I'd have given a lot to know what he said in
those few moments.

His head came up after a while and he said, 'We can't talk here.
I've got lodgings for you. Eglantina's outside. Go with her. I'll be
along.'

I got up and went out.

Eglantina was outside, a large silk scarf draped over her shoulders, a high comb in her hair, and the edges of a white gown held
up daintily in one hand. She looked very conspicuous.

'Mr. Keith, you come my place. No trouble there.'

She began to walk up the side of the square. A few doors beyond
the house where the Hueica brothers had lodged we turned into a
dark doorway. She stopped and handed me a key.

'Top floor,' she said. 'The door with three brass monkeys. Go in.
There's candles on the wash-basin. Don't run to 'lectricity here.
Here—' From under her shawl her hand came out holding half a
bottle of whiskey.

I said, 'What if I meet anyone going up?'

She chuckled. 'You won't. But if you do nobody's goin' to be
nosey about a man going to my room. Only wish I could get Mr.
Monk up there. Seems he don't like a girl to say thank you no way.'

She went. The stairs were in pitch darkness and I went up until
I could find no more stairs. I struck a match and found a door with
a small brass knocker in the shape of the three wise monkeys. See
all, hear all, say nothing. That suited me. I went in.

I struck a match and found the candles on the wash-basin. It
was a small, rather long room, and one could only stand upright
well away from the window because of the slope of the roof pent.
By the window was a bed with a patchwork quilt, the brass head-
rail hung with a collection of gaily coloured tourist dolls. A white
plaster figure of the Madonna was on a bracket against the wall
over the bedhead. A radio and a record player stood on a table
behind the door and there was a coloured photograph, taken from
some magazine, of Ella Fitzgerald stuck above the wash-basin. Two

chairs were piled untidily high with clothes. I fixed myself a whiskey and sat down on the bed.

Monk came in after about fifteen minutes. He stood just inside the door, pursing his thick lips and frowning at me, a big, unshakeable-looking man. It was good to have him there.

He said, 'You must want those dollars bad. I'd written mine off.'

'You don't have to. They owe us the money. I got the chaps who took me out to put me over the side in a dinghy. Went up to Eglantina's brother's hut to look for you.'

He went to the wash-basin and rinsed out a glass and then reached for the whiskey bottle. 'What do you plan to do?'

'Wait for Angelo and Katrina to come back. Then I'll give them the whole story.'

'Katrina's back. Came into town this afternoon. Not her brother, though. He's up at San Pedro still with Lemaza. They come back tomorrow afternoon. Some big parade in the square here.'

'The anniversary of the start of the Revolution. It's going to be an anniversary day for Lemaza, too. I'll tackle Angelo when the parade's over.'

'How are you going to get to him?'

'I don't know. Go up there at night. The only sentry is at the drive gate. I could go in the back way, across the fields.'

'Just walk in?'

'Why not? With Angelo and Katrina there Lemaza could do nothing. I don't have to think about his feelings.'

'He'll deny everything. You were robbed. Period. You started to be a nuisance so he kicked you out. Period. He'll stick to that.'

'I've got the box file. Can he talk himself out of that?'

'He'll try.'

'It won't come off. Angelo knows him too well.'

Monk picked up a pile of clothes from a chair and dumped them on the bed.

'Girl's as untidy as hell. Like me.' He tossed the whiskey back and reached for the bottle. He saw me look from the bottle in his hand to him and grinned.

'Don't worry. I was beginning to feel like it. But now you're back I'll hold it. They haven't picked up Albano yet.'

'He's well away by now.'

'Won't make Lemaza any sweeter.'

'Who cares? I can't wait until tomorrow evening.'

'You've got to up here.'

'What about Eglantina?'

Monk smiled and stood up. 'She has the bed and you have the loft. Unless you come to some other arrangement.'

He got up on the chair and pushed up a wooden trap in the slope of the ceiling. His head out of sight through the trap his voice came to me muffled. 'We've stuck a palliasse up here. Couple of blankets. You can use the room during the day.' His head came into sight and he got down from the chair. 'She'll see you get food. There's a way on to the roof at the end of the loft. You can sun yourself out there, but keep out of sight. Anything you want?'

I shook my head. I just wanted tomorrow evening to come quickly.

He went to the door. Standing there, he said, 'I met Parkes today. He was clearing his stuff out of the hotel. He was erupting. When Albano slipped away he refused to go on with his work. Ocampo gave him two hours to decide whether he'd go on or stand against a wall and be shot. Parkes voted for work. He's living up at the strip now.'

'We've all got our troubles.'

Monk grinned. 'I'll tell him that. Should make a big difference.'

A couple of hours after he was gone I climbed up through the trap and bedded down for the night. It was hot with the accumulation of the day's heat under the roof, so I pushed open a small square door at the end of the loft and had a view of the sky and an angle of chimney pots silhouetted against it as I lay on a hard palliasse. I woke once, around three o'clock, to hear Eglantina come in. She was singing to herself and clattered between bed and wash-basin for what seemed hours. Then I heard the springs of her bed go and there was silence.

I was awakened the next morning by Eglantina. Her head came through the trap and she pushed a cup of coffee to me across the joists.

'You sure sleep well,' she said. 'Snorin' hearty. I lay there for half an hour listening. Sounded good to have a man almost in the room again. What you care for to eat?'

'Some rolls and butter?'

'I'll get that.' Her brown face smiled at me from floor level. 'Yes, Mr. Keith, is very good to have a man about. 'Fore Mr. Monk came was always a man up here with me usually. But since he come I sort of lost the habit. Just happy to go to bed to sleep at nights. Don't make so much money, of course, but I sure feel brighter in the mornings.'

She withdrew and began to sing about the room below. I lay there and drank my coffee, watching the morning sky through the roof door. Later the rolls came up with more coffee, and after that Eglantina said she was clearing out and it was all mine for washing and shaving. I took my time over it because I had nothing else to do. While I was shaving I switched on the radio and got the Caramanga station. There was a long military bulletin, mostly about the fighting in the San Pedro area, but it didn't amount to anything. There was a brief mention of the fact that the *Mara II* had docked at Caramanga the previous day. I imagined that the station had instructions to play this down. There was no point in reminding people that Angelo Libertad now had their planes. Neither was there any mention of Albano. Which meant that he probably hadn't made his way through the lines yet. I shut the set off when it started to play dance music. That wasn't my mood. And anyway Eglantina kept me going with all the song I could take.

I went up on the roof for about an hour, but it got too hot up there so I came down. I'd just pulled the cover over the roof trap and had stepped down from the chair when there came a light knock at the door. No one knew I was back in Acaibo, so I was not worried about search parties. But I wasn't keen to be seen in Eglantina's room by any stranger. I took no notice of the knock and began to move quietly towards the curtain of the hanging cupboard in the far corner of the room.

Before I could reach it the door was pushed open. Katrina came in. I stood there like a fool, wondering where in hell she had sprung from. For a few seconds we faced one another without movement or words. Then she came flying across to me and was in my arms and her head against my shoulder, calling my name, and her hands on my back shaking me gently. I don't know why it should have been so, but it seemed the most natural thing in the world for her to do. I held her close to me and kissed the top of her head gently. For more than one selfish reason I was glad to see her, but to my surprise I was also just glad . . . in the way, I supposed, that a brother might be glad to welcome a favourite sister after a long absence. She was a nice girl and I was very fond of her, and there was something about the spontaneous way in which she had come to me that touched me. She leaned back from me and her eyes were shining and there was a curious pleasure in me as I held her weight. She had a slip of a summer dress on, and she was warm and soft and unexpected. But for all her knee-length dress and long arms, the nearness of being a young girl still in all her movements, she was a woman. My salad days were over and at this moment I couldn't afford to be green in judgment. I kissed her lightly on the cheek, which wasn't at all what she wanted, and I released her.

'Keith,' she said, not managing her breathing very well, 'I never thought I'd see you again.'

'You can thank your brother-in-law for that. How did you know I was here?'

'Monk told me.'

I gave her a cigarette and watched her hands shake a little as she held it.

'When did you see him?'

'Just now. I came in to do some shopping and he was in the square.'

'He told you why I'm here?'

'No. Just that you were here and wanted to see me. What is it all about?'

'Someone may have seen you come up here.'

'No, I just slipped in. Anyway I'm told Eglantina does a little dress-making at times. I could be coming to see her. What's happened, Keith? Why are you hiding here?'

'Because,' I said bluntly, 'General Lemaza robbed me of my money the night I left you. Within an hour.'

'I can't believe it!'

'It's true. Why do you think I'm up here, hiding? He arranged it neatly. Couldn't bear to part with all those lovely dollars.—'

'But you should have come to me, to Angelo. Oh, it's not possible!'

'The next day I did try to get in touch with you or your brother, but he fixed that. And then he shipped me out.'

'And you came back.'

'Of course. I need forty thousand dollars. Remember?'

She was silent for a moment, then nodded and said, 'For her.'

'For me. This evening after the parade I'm coming up to see your brother. He's getting the full story.'

She walked away towards the bed and her hand went out absently and played with one of the toy dolls.

'Lemaza,' I said, 'is one kind of man. Your brother's another. In a way, I can even sympathise with Lemaza's point of view. He's got to find the cash and the supplies. He must have plenty of headaches.'

She turned and said firmly, 'There's no doubt you'll get your money when my brother hears.'

'I'm sure of it. But it won't improve things between the two of them. However . . . for the time being you haven't seen me and you know nothing of this affair. Don't go talking to your brother. Let me do that. You promise?'

She nodded and then went on, 'No matter how difficult money matters are, Siles shouldn't have done it. Angelo will be furious. A bargain is a bargain . . .'

I didn't say anything. There was no point in making trouble for her by saying that in my opinion Angelo would always have difficulties with Lemaza. The two just couldn't pull in harness together. Even less would they be able to do so when they got to Caramanga. Señor Da Silva wasn't sitting in Acaibo for nothing. Apart from my trouble, I was sure that some deal had been made by Lemaza for the future. . . .

'This is the first time you've been with your brother for some years, isn't it?'

'Yes. Why?'

'Do you think he's changed at all?'

She looked at me, just the edge of her teeth biting gently at her lower lip as she thought it over. 'Yes, he has. But not in the way you imagine. Oh, I know you're cynical about ideals and the men who live for them. But that hasn't changed. He's just the same. But he's older, inside, simply because of fighting for what he believes in. I suppose if you live with a burning truth, and for it . . . well, it makes its mark on you. He's the noblest man I've ever met. . . .'

She waited for me to say something, to disagree, to argue, but I didn't want to do any of those things. From the way she said it there was nothing one could do but accept it.

'You don't believe it. You think there's something of Lemaza about him?'

'No. I believe it. It just is, and you must see this, that noble men make all the others uncomfortable.'

'Oh, no. I've just come back from San Pedro and I've seen how the men up there worship him. In a way it was quite frightening. They look up to him, he's everything they believe in. Having to carry all that is a tremendous strain. That's why—whatever you and I may think about Lemaza—he has to have other people to take the smaller things off his shoulders. And, of course, they take advantage of him—but only in small ways. Nobody can touch what he really is. You know. . . .' She came back to me and I was seeing now no girl, but a woman, shaped and impressed and accepting a whole new world of experiences. 'You know, there were times when it was hard to believe that he was my brother. . . . He seemed to have gone beyond any relationship like that. To have become what he believed in. Just a force. Does that sound far-fetched?'

'No . . . I suppose not.'

'He doesn't think of himself. He doesn't even look after himself. He wouldn't let me go anywhere where it was dangerous. But he goes everywhere, just carrying that stick of his. No one up there can stop him. . . .'

Somewhere, flickering in my memory, came up a shadowy lithograph of General Gordon at Khartoum facing death at the top of the steps, cane in hand. I wouldn't disillusion her about her brother, because I couldn't, and didn't, in fact, have anything to disillusion her with. Maybe he was right out there in front, in the Gordon class. But if he were then I knew that somewhere in the men around him there must be those who would hate him simply because they couldn't stand the sight of a goodness they could never emulate, couldn't live with his kind of shining truth . . . not in this day and age.

I put my arm around her shoulders and began to lead her towards the door.

'You look after him all you can,' I said. 'When you find someone who means so much to you, hang on. Don't argue with yourself about it, just hang on. In a way I envy you.'

She turned, lifting her small nicely ovalled face to me, and said, 'Do you? I thought you had someone like that. Isn't that why you're still here?'

I laughed. 'Drea . . . ? Yes, I suppose she is. But I wouldn't put her in Angelo's class. She's the other thing that men are ready to die for.'

'Die?'

'It's a figure of speech. Now remember, you know nothing about me until I turn up tonight.'

'All right. I'm sorry, I shouldn't have said anything about her. It's just that I'm jealous. I can say that quite frankly. I'm jealous.'

She gave a little laugh. 'And I won't say anything. About the other thing.'

Just for a moment her hand touched mine and then she went. From the window, I watched her come out and cross the square towards the harbour entrance. She looked very small, a girl walking slowly, her dress a bright splash of colour against the dusty stones of the square.

I went to the wash-basin and got a glass and poured myself a bottle of beer. A few minutes later Eglantina came singing up the stairs with a straw bag full of tomatoes in one hand and a bowl of dressed crab in the other.

CHAPTER 13

I watched the anniversary parade from the roof top. During the morning working parties had strung lines of bunting and the revolutionary flags along the fronts of the houses. Everywhere you looked was the yellow and scarlet blazonry of the eagle carrying its rifle. Most of the housewives had left their coloured bed covers hanging from their balconies. A platform of wooden planks had been erected on timber baulks just in front of the *Hotel de la Reina* and the front of the stand had been decorated with great swags of poinscttias and stiff bunches of wild arum lilies. There was a microphone on the stand and a couple of amplifiers were slung on a wire across the square. From just after mid-day an army truck with a broadcasting system relayed gramophone records at full volume. The whole square was vivid and shrieking with colour and noise. By two o'clock the square was packed with people who were held back four and five deep against the houses by a cordon of soldiers.

It was hot on the roof, but not so hot as it was in Eglantina's room. Seeking for shade I moved along to the right about fifty yards, scrambling over a couple of low parapets until I found a tall clump of chimney pots. I sat down with my back against the brickwork and had a fine angled view of the square. Monk and Eglantina were keeping away from me that afternoon, but I could see them with some other people on one of the hotel balconies across the square.

I don't know who was responsible for the show, probably Ocampo, I guessed, since he was Town Commandant, but it was done with great precision and smoothness. It didn't surprise me for there was nothing the Latin-American liked better than a good, colourful show. Their fighting was mostly guerilla and mountain warfare, so they jumped at the chance of formal parades.

Two companies of infantry marched in and formed up in front of the church and facing the platform. Then came a couple of staff cars and I saw Angelo Libertad, Generalissimo Lemaza, and three other high-ranking officers get out and take their places on the stand. A great cheer from troops and the crowd greeted Angelo. From the other staff car came Katrina, Lieutenant Ocampo and two more officers. Katrina went to the back of the stand, a little to the left of her brother.

When the cheers had subsided General Lemaza came forward to the microphone and began to speak. He really let himself go, for this was the kind of occasion he was born to enjoy. Above the square the amplifiers cracked and spat and whistled and it was hard to catch what he was saying. Not that there was any need to know because it had to be, coming from him, a paraphrase of everything martial which had been said before and so much better. . . . *Now thrive the armourers, and honour's thought reigns solely in the breast of every man.* . . . *He which hath no stomach to this fight, let him depart.* . . . But one thing was certain with Lemaza running things, the departing would get no passport, and no crowns for convoy would be put into his purse. He went on and on, ten minutes too long by my reckoning, and the cheers of the crowd which had punctuated his speech, strophe, and antistrophe, weakened and lost gusto.

Lemaza stopped at last, but Angelo did not come forward. From the far end of the square a convoy of six armoured cars rumbled through and Angelo raised his hand to take the salute from them. Following the armoured cars came a couple of bren gun carriers, freshly painted, a troop of twenty-five pounders, lorry after lorry, canopies stripped, full of erect, green-bereted soldiers, three tanks which I could not identify, a truck towing a water tank which had been decorated with yellow and scarlet flowers and had a papier mâché figure of the revolutionary eagle perched on it . . . on and on, men, vehicles, roaring and stamping across the square . . . And most of them, I guessed, would be on their way back to San Pedro that evening.

More troops marched into the square, darkening the yellow dust. The packed crowd on the church steps parted to let through a priest in full canonical dress. With him went four boys in white surplices swinging censers. After Angelo had spoken the troops were to be blessed. There it all was below me, the world in little . . . the soldiers, their guns, the Church, its blessing, the people, their betrayals. . . . Only one type was missing. . . . I wondered where Señor Da Silva was passing the afternoon. Taking a siesta, probably;

lying on his bed working out the swift moves that must follow victory, for victory in any revolution is a sitting duck for a shot from the curtained East or the debentured West.

I moved along a little to follow the shade and lit myself a cigarette. As I did so I happened to look sideways, further along the run of roof tops with their crumbly parapets and shabby, paint-blistered pents and gables. On the roof of the house which formed the far corner of the square on my side, I saw a man come through the doorway of a penthouse. He was about a hundred yards away. His back was to me and he was bending down, dragging out something which was masked from me by a run of parapet. As he came into the sunlight another man followed him, bending also and helping with the load they were managing. They dragged whatever it was to the edge of their roof parapet, then straightened up and went back to the doorway. They stood just inside it, the sun striking down at them.

There was no mistaking them . . . the neat linen suits, the splash of flowered ties, and the dark, smoothly greased hair. Not more than a hundred yards from me were the Hueica brothers. If they could see me it would be no more than my head and I was wearing my old straw hat so they would have taken me for a spectator of the scene below. I sat there, wondering what I should do. Pretty obviously Ocampo had kept them hidden up since robbing me. My whole instinct was to go over and grab Sardi . . . but a few moments' thought showed me that this would serve nothing. I could have the satisfaction of beating him up . . . but that would ruin everything. I edged back a little to be less in their view. The Hueica brothers would keep until after I'd had my interview with Angelo.

It was at this moment that I heard the noise from the north. It was thin at first, then beat up against the hot blue sky into a familiar pulse. All the heads in the square below swivelled upwards. I looked up, too. It came in over the town from the direction of the air strip, flying too damned low, and its new roundels of scarlet and gold flashed in the sun. It went over with a mighty throaty scream. Above the harbour it climbed, much too steeply for its age and performance, rolled at the top as it turned, and came back again in another shattering explosion of speed and sound. As it flattened away out of sight, the crowd in the square became one mouth and throat, one pulsating roar of approval and delight. The first of their Sea Furies was in the air. It didn't come back again. I could guess why. Up at the strip Parkes and his men must have worked like

beavers to get it in trim for this celebration flight. This must have
been its first time off the deck. No test flights. Parkes would have
fought every inch of the way against such a dangerous first demonstration. Lemaza and Ocampo would have over-ridden him. They
needed the sign of victory in the air.

Angelo was waiting for this moment. The noise echoed away in
the square and I saw him step forward to the microphone. The
priest was on his right now and Katrina was half-hidden by the
boys in their white surplices. I saw, too, that at some moment she
had been presented with flowers for she stood, holding to her bosom,
a great sheaf of the wild arum lilies. This was a great moment for
her, to stand behind her brother and watch the adoration in the
eyes of the crowd, to be near him, and to see his work after the
years of separation. Maybe I was wrong, I thought. Maybe he
would turn out to be different. Maybe he would know how to handle
peace and to plan prosperity. Maybe he was one of the few who
knew the right moment to shave off the mountain beard and to
make guerillas become good neighbours . . . maybe. For her sake I
hoped it.

He began to speak, not raising his voice, giving the amplifiers a
chance . . . a tall, thin figure, dressed in green trousers and a khaki
shirt, his body a little stooped on one side as he rested a hand on
the thin rattan cane . . . and he spoke without any pomp, without
any flourish, a quiet voice that drew the square and its people and
its soldiers in to him, the voice of a brother and a good husbandman
giving his report.

'Five years ago, the struggle for freedom began in this square.
Since then we have all fought and made our sacrifices. Today I do
not mean to go back, to recall our triumphs or our bitterness. You
have all seen—' his hand went up to the sky briefly, 'the token of
our coming victory. It is certain. It is waiting for us within the next
few weeks.'

The crowd roared and he waited for them to quieten down.

'Today, I want us all to think of what victory is going to mean.
When the fighting finishes, the work begins. Victory must be turned
into peace, and peace must be turned into order, prosperity and
justice. To do this will take longer than all the fighting we have
known; to make the name of Cordillo respected will mean more
sacrifices, more struggles, and all the good will and good sense that
are ours because we are human beings and wish to live with one
another as human beings, in faith, in love, and in pride of our

country. It is useless to call for a blessing on our arms if that blessing does not touch our hearts. Victory will bring no exaggerated rewards. Our house has been shattered. We must mend the walls and the roof before we think of luxuries. . . .'

He meant what he said. He stood there and in their taste of coming triumph he had the courage to point to the future and its hard promise of labour and sacrifice. Nobody was going to get an unfair share of the cake. There would be no cake. Bread and sweat. He meant it.

He stood there on the platform, well out in front of the others, a quiet man, talking firmly to his people. I wondered what Lemaza and Ocampo and the others grouped at the back of the platform were thinking. After victory the loot. After war the feast.

Angelo raised a hand, pausing in his speech, and for a moment the square was so still that I could hear the gulls crying out over the harbour and the bickering of sparrows on the roof tiles behind me.

Then he cried with a sudden passion, his voice full of command, 'Take this then to your hearts, people and soldiers of Cordillo! No matter what lies in the future, no matter what happens to us as individuals, we are one body, one mind, one heart and one resolution—'

They were the last words he spoke. From my right I heard the single crack of a rifle shot. So absorbed was I in Angelo and the square below that for a moment there was no awareness in me of what had happened. I saw Angelo stagger, almost fall, and then steady himself on his cane. His head came up and he shook it as though he were shaking off some unexpected dizziness. The rifle was fired again and this time he dropped, falling forward on his knees, smashing into the microphone stand and finishing with his head lost in the bank of flowers along the front of the platform.

Away to my right, the figure of Sardi with a rifle rose from where he had been crouching by his roof parapet. In the doorway behind him was Tomez. Sardi turned and he dropped the rifle to the ground at the foot of the parapet and then went quickly back and through the doorway. I jumped to my feet, pulled myself round the chimney pot so that I was out of sight of the square and began to run across the roof flats. As I did so, from the square, as though some anguished animal were trapped down there, came a great howl of despair. I ran, not thinking, not planning anything, following the simple instinct to get hold of Sardi before he got away. I went over the dividing parapets, round the junky penthouses and stucco-walled water tanks and finally reached the doorway through which the Hueica brothers had disappeared. As I came up to it, I saw the rifle lying over by the far parapet, and close to the rifle the recumbent figure of a man.

I pulled up then. With an icy suddenness thought and common-sense gripped me hard. The man was lying on his side with his face towards me. It was a face which I recognised immediately, athletic, fresh, squarish, with a tiny scar at one corner of the mouth. His fair, sun-bleached hair fell forward over his forehead. It was John MacIntyre Albano in a crumpled blue blazer with silver buttons and dirty white trousers and many days' growth of beard on his face. I saw him stir a little and heard a faint groan.

I didn't wait for more. Understanding, if not complete, at least enough to put me on my guard, was coming to me. Through the doorway I caught the sound of footsteps and men's voices. I swung away from the door, away from the square and raced around behind the penthouse and to the far side of the roof. Below me was a stretch of waste ground and then the backs of the buildings which faced the harbour. Away to the left the ground rose steeply to one shoulder of the headland which guarded the eastern edge of the bay. There was no way down and no way back to my room which I could take before people would be on the roof. But in the far corner of the roof was a decrepit pigeon loft, wire-netting over wooden frames, empty of birds now, and the floor strewn with boxes. I ran into it and threw myself on the ground behind a couple of low boxes. I just had time to pull one of the boxes in front of me for better cover, and then a bunch of men came through the penthouse door.

I lay there, holding my breathing down, and watched them through the thin gap between the two boxes in front of me. All hell had broken out in the square. I could hear men shouting, women screaming, and now the quick revving up of vehicles, and above it all somebody was roaring unintelligible orders over the amplifiers.

There were five men on the roof. It didn't surprise me to see who they were. I was gone a long way past surprise now. I was beginning to understand Lemaza more than ever before and I had no more curiosity about Da Silva. And though I had always considered myself hard-boiled enough for most things, this was making me feel sick.

Lieutenant Ocampo, two soldiers, and the two Hueica brothers were on the roof. The Hueica brothers kept well back out of sight on the square. Ocampo gave no orders. The pantomime had been well rehearsed. The two soldiers went over to Albano and lifted him to his feet. They lifted him and held him so that he could be seen by all the people in the square below. Holding him they shook him, gripping his arms and shoulders as though he were struggling with them. He had no more struggle in him than a mouse long paralysed by a cat's play. A great roar of anger billowed up from the square at the sight of Albano.

The men turned and dragged him, upright still, towards the door. As they disappeared through the door Ocampo turned towards the Hueica brothers. He smiled at them and nodded. They faced him, their backs to me, two neat, tidy figures, not a crease out of place on them, efficient, obedient Tweedledum and Tweedledee. . . . Oh, they were going to be big shots when they got back to Guatemala, men full of the profit from darkness, their hiring days over, nothing to do but sit in the sun and blink and drink the hours away. I had my Mauser in my pocket and, against all thought for my own self-preservation, it was hard not to let them have it from where I lay hidden.

But I didn't have to do it. That equally efficient couple Lemaza and Ocampo had got it all arranged. As Ocampo smiled at them, the brown warm smile of commendation for filthy work well done, his right hand which held his revolver came up swiftly and he gave them their reward. He fired four times, twice at Tomcz, dropping him where he stood, and twice at Sardi as the little man turned and began to run. He hit him twice; once as he ran and once as he stumbled. Sardi skidded on his chest across the roof and finished with his head not three feet from the loft where I lay.

A soldier came through the doorway and I heard him say:

'Shall we take them down, lieutenant?'

'Leave them until the square is quieter. Vermin. We have the one who really counts. Keep a guard on the house door and come up for them later.'

He went through the door and out of sight. The soldier stood there for a moment, lit himself a cigarette, and then went to Tomez. He rolled him over with his foot and I saw the blood patterning the flowery tie. The soldier went through Tomez' pockets and then stole his wristlet watch. He came over to Sardi and did the same for him, humming gently to himself. Then he went back to the penthouse and disappeared, closing the door behind him.

I gave him two minutes; two minutes during which I lay there with Sardi's face a few feet from mine. He was on his side now, facing me, his dark eyes wide open, his mouth slack in death, and even in death he didn't look any different . . . just a dark, quiet, intent little man who had nothing to say, no thoughts which could be trusted to the world. But there was nothing he needed to say to me.

Five minutes later I was back in Eglantina's attic. There was no one in the room below. I dropped through the ceiling trap and fixed myself a drink. My hand shook as I held it and walked to the window. Outside, the square had been cleared and a cordon of soldiers was posted at intervals all the way around. The platform was empty. So long as the square was guarded neither Monk nor Eglantina could get up to me. I lay down on Eglantina's bed with my drink. This was the kind of thing which went on everywhere, part of the cynicism which kept me the way I was. I lay there while the afternoon died, while the soldiers patrolled the streets, while the lorries and armoured cars rolled back through the square, while somewhere Katrina sat mourning, and somewhere Lemaza and Ocampo toasted themselves in private triumph that out of a live and dedicated Leader they now had created a martyr, a figure of legend for whom every soldier would fight harder than before in order to bring them the victory and the fruits which were to be piled high into only a few chosen bowls.

And then, over the other thoughts, came sweeping in the picture of Drea waiting in Haiti. A little while ago I'd been confident of getting my money. Now Angelo was dead. Lemaza was king, and in one stroke I was out in the wilderness . . . a couple of rifle shots had killed Angelo—but they had also taken Drea from me, robbed me and committed her. It was a bonus result which would have made Lemaza smile. It filled me with a heavy, murderous blackness.

Just as it was getting dark the soldiers were withdrawn from the square. Life came back to it slowly. I stood at the window, waiting for Monk and Eglantina, and watched. *The Singing Heart that Never Tires* and the *Space Sputnik Special* came back to their stands by the church. The church bells began to beat out a long-paused note and a queue of people, marshalled by a couple of soldiers, began to form outside the church, stretching away around the corner into the harbour. Angelo, I guessed, had been taken into the church, was now laid out, and the people of Acaibo were moving past him to pay him their last respects. Lemaza was wasting no time.

Eglantina came up first.

She stood just inside the doorway and said, 'Oh, Mister ... ! Oh, Mister ... !' I could see she had been crying. 'He was a good man.'

'Sure. He was a good man. Where's Monk?'

'Come in a minute. You want some food?'

'No, thanks.'

She went over to her hanging cupboard affair and began to ferret amongst a pile of stuff on the floor. Finally she came up with a black headshawl.

'No dancing or music this night.'

As she draped the shawl over her head and turned back towards the door, I said, 'After you've been to the church, Eglantina, keep away from here for a while. I've got to talk privately to Monk.'

'Yes, Mr. Keith.'

'And when you do come back, I want to know if Miss Katrina is in church and whereabouts.'

'Yes, Mr. Keith. You sure you don't want food?'

'No.'

Not long after she had gone Monk came in. He went over to the bed and sat down, resting his great head on his hands.

'Christ, what a thing!'

'There's a damned sight more to it than you know.'

'Not that I can guess. I wasn't born yesterday. You should have seen that poor Albano bastard when they brought him down. Took them all their time to stop the crowd from ripping him to pieces. Saw that happen to a man once. Bloody crowd went over him like swarming bees. When they cleared off there was nothing left ...'

He got up and went and helped himself to whiskey. He took a large shot but I didn't say anything even though I knew from the moment he came into the room that he had been drinking.

'I was on the roof. I saw it all ...'

He came back to the bed with his drink and sat silently while I told him all I had seen.

I finished, 'Albano was framed. They had him lined up for this from the moment I brought him in. He was a gift, my gift to them,' I said bitterly.

'And the escape from prison?'

'They just took him out and cached him away in that house. Said he'd escaped. Up there he was lying drugged or something. He couldn't have had any idea of what was going on. God, you've got to hand it to Lemaza. The Hueica brothers pinch my money and hand it back to him. Then he gets rid of me. Then he frames Albano to assassinate Angelo—and the Hueica brothers get paid off. Two bullets each instead of the handful of cash they looked for. Not even Sardi was expecting that. Not even his dark mind could place Lemaza with that stroke.'

'Poor old Tomez. I liked him.'

'You're wasting your sympathy.'

'Maybe. But I've got plenty to waste . . .' He looked up. 'You had the radio on? No. Well, it's started already. Blasting away. Lemaza is taking over. Everything Angelo stood for will be accomplished. That'll keep 'em going until they reach Caramanga. Nobody like a martyr to stir the troops to fighting pitch. Angelo's worth as much dead as alive. And now they know it was Albano who did it—son of the Minister of Defence on the other side! He's in the soup.'

'They won't touch him yet,' I said. 'He's too good a pawn to wipe out quickly. They'll go through all the rigmarole of a People's Court and wring every drop of propaganda from it they can first. Meanwhile . . .'

Monk levered himself up from the bed and went for more whiskey. I still said nothing.

'Meanwhile, what?' he asked.

'We've got to do something.'

'You're crazy! There's nothing you can do. Nothing. Angelo was your trump card. He's gone, Keith, boy, you're in a situation familiar to us both. One that is always liable to happen. Everything's blown up in your face. *Stay Quiet* and *Get Out*. They're two good hounds for this hunt.'

'Not for me,' I said grimly. It was there inside me, the hardness which had been forming for hours in this room. 'That bastard Lemaza has too much owing on his slate.'

Monk drank, shook his big head, and said, 'Forget your dollars. I've got the motor-boat fixed up. We can get out.'

I shook my head. 'I'm staying. There are things to do.'

Monk frowned. 'For God's sake, know when to quit. You can't touch this man. Cut your losses and go. Lemaza is going on. The race has been rigged. He'll have Cordillo. He's too big for you to handle. Only Da Silva's people can do that—and they will if he doesn't play ball.' His hand went out for the whiskey bottle.

I went across to him and I took the bottle from him. He let me without any protest. I knew my Monk and he knew me. He knew, too, what was going on inside me.

I said, 'Listen, for a lot of reasons that seem good to me, though I can't line them up nicely, I'm going on. I can try it by myself, but I'd rather have you with me. If you want to be with me, you've got to knock this off. I know the way you're heading.' I held up the bottle between us. 'You just say if you want it back.'

For some time he didn't say anything. He leaned back, his large, brown, capable hands spread on the wash-basin for support. He watched me, rubbing his thick lips together as though he had a sour taste in his mouth. Maybe he had . . . the bitterness that comes with a conflict between friendship and common-sense. I wouldn't force him.

Finally he said, 'You're a stubborn bastard.'

'Call it that.'

'Have you got any ideas?'

'A few.'

'Could they work?'

'With a bit of luck.'

'That's a great comfort. Got to have luck.'

'It can be promoted. With good planning. Do you want this?' I offered him the bottle.

He straightened up and took the bottle from me. Then he tossed it gently on to the bed. 'Let Eglantina have it as a night-cap. Okay—what do we do?'

'We go to see Parkes,' I said. 'But it might be a rough visit. Can you get the motor-boat out of the harbour?'

He looked at his watch. 'Yes. There are four or five fishing boats go out each night. In another hour. I can go out with them.'

'Bring it round the headland. There's a beach where the headland tails away into the long straight stretch up to the barracks. I'll be there at midnight.'

'No more than that?'

'Not for the moment. I've got some thinking to do.'

'Okay, you do that. Think. I'll concentrate on the luck. Whatever you've got in mind we're going to need it, and I can't think why the hell I've agreed.'

'Put aboard all the spare petrol you can. How big's the boat?'

'Take four or five. Small cabin.'

'Can you get enough petrol to make Haiti?'

'I guess so—if the north-east trades aren't too strong. Why Haiti?'

'We've got to go somewhere.'

'Sure. Anything else?'

'Yes, a spare anchor, plenty of rope, a block and tackle and a small marker buoy. Something that looks like a lobster pot marker.'

'What do you want that for?'

'It's the beginning of an idea. Depends on Parkes. But get it, anyway.'

He spread his arms and rolled his eyes and then said humorously, 'Why should I worry? I was forgetting. I'm not going anywhere. Nobody's waiting. It's better to do something crazy than nothing at all.'

He went and half an hour later Eglantina came in.

'Miss Katrina's still in church, Mr. Keith. Way at the back on the left. There's a pillar with some flags hanging on it.'

'Good.'

'You hungry now?'

I was going to say no, but I changed my mind. 'You make up some food, Eglantina. Take it down to Monk. He's with the boat. Be quick.'

'You leaving?' Her small face came up to mine, suddenly shadowed with anxiety.

'Not without you. Take some things with you and tell Monk I said you were to go out in the boat with him.'

'You mean take my things for going away?'

'Sure—and not a trunkful, either. One small bag.'

'Oh, Lordy!' Her face broke into a smile. 'All I want of this place could go in one pocket, Mr. Keith.'

CHAPTER 14

There I was in my old straw hat, ragged shirt and trousers, shuffling along in my canvas shoes down the side of the square to the church. Just beyond the church steps I saw Ocampo's car parked, the driver sitting on the running board. Two soldiers stood guard at the top of the steps, but the queue had thinned now to just a trickle of people moving quietly in and out of the church. There was some wind going, hot and filling the air with whipped-up dust. The platform was still standing outside the *Hotel de la Reina* and groups of people were clustered about it, talking and moving slowly, held by it, describing no doubt to one another that moment of death under the bright sun. I could see the white trumpets of the lilies against the dark boards.

My head low I shuffled up the steps past the two sentries and went into the church. Hat in hand I stood just inside the entrance, dipped my fingers in the holy water and crossed myself.

Right up by the altar was a catafalque on which Angelo Libertad lay. It was guarded by four soldiers, their arms reversed, and six tall candles stood around it, their flames burning stiff and straight in the still air. People were filing by slowly and there was a sprinkling of men and women sitting in the nave, heads bowed. From one of the side chapels came the sound of a priest praying, his voice a low, broken, almost querulous mutter that went on and on. I went slowly up to the catafalque, keeping my head low, and joined the slow file about the body. Only for a moment or two did I raise my head and then it was to see Angelo Libertad's face.

He lay under the scarlet and gold of the Army flag, just his face visible. He lay there as though sleeping, his face relaxed and expressionless, no sign on it of the way of his death, no shadow of any last thought or emotion. Had he known in those last few seconds of the treachery around him? Had he had time to take the bitterness fully to his heart? Maybe he had known for years that it could always happen and so could never surprise him. He was as Katrina believed him to be . . . *not for the fashion of these times where none will sweat but for promotion.* I had long been out of touch with such men, but that did not now prevent me from taking some of the bitterness of his end and cherishing it as an anger in me. It was a new kind of anger for my kind. But it was there and I knew that I was going to have to follow it. And if in doing this I served my own interests, too—and I meant too—then that would only be more humiliation and bitterness for Lemaza. I could have been paid and gone days ago with my forty thousand dollars. Now, forty thousand dollars would be the symbol in his mind for as long as he lived . . . the symbol, maybe, of a lost kingdom. For the want of a nail, of a shoe, of a horse . . . the kingdom was lost. For a few hours of scheming to cheat me, one of Lemaza's own kind, one of the sweaters after promotion and money like him, he was going to have his own bitterness to live with.

I went shuffling down the far side and found the pillar which Eglantina had mentioned. Halfway up it was hung with duty banners. Katrina was sitting on a chair a few yards in from it. She wore a black dress and there was a black shawl pulled over her bowed head and shoulders. There were a few other people sitting on the benches and chairs, but they were well away from her. She sat alone with her grief and everyone respected it.

I stood by the pillar in the gloom. Up by the altar the candles threw a pale wash of yellow against the grey stone vault of the nave and transept arches. I stood there and watched her and I knew that in a little while she would know that she was being watched. And after a time she did. Her head came up and slowly round. She saw me. I made no sign but I stepped back from the pillar and into the semi-darkness of one of the side chapels.

It was so dark that when she came to me I could hardly see her face. I put out a hand and took hers. We said nothing. But her hand was there in mine and I held it and knew that for the moment it was all she wanted. After a moment she said, 'Keith, you shouldn't be here. . . .'

'I know,' I said. And then, inadequately, as it must always be, I went on, 'I'm sorry about Angelo . . .'

She raised her head a little, but didn't trust herself to words.

'Listen,' I said, 'I've got a lot of things I must tell you. But I can't stay here with you now. Can you meet me tomorrow? As it gets dark?'

She nodded.

'Good. There's an old plantation reservoir on the hill behind your villa. I'll meet you there.'

'Keith . . .'

'Don't say anything about me. Just be there.'

I let go of her hand and I left her. As I got to the church door Ocampo came through, short and dapper in uniform. I stepped back to let him pass, my head going down, my body cringing in an anonymous movement of deference to the Army, my straw hat pressed against my chest, the upper rim over my chin and mouth. He went by without seeing me.

I passed down the church steps and walked away from the harbour, across the square and towards the road that led up the hill past the water trough where I had been robbed.

The wind was fresh from the north-east, slapping a choppy run of waves against our starboard bow as we went up to the air strip. We carried no lights and kept well out. She was a solid boat, tubby, and high decked with one small cabin forward and the wheel just aft of the cabin break. Not built for speed, but a good plugger. Away on our left a few lights showed from the barrack buildings and against the night sky I could see the high loom of the mountain inland. Eglantina was in the cabin to escape the occasional wave crest that broke aboard. Monk had the wheel.

As we drew level with the barrack lights Monk said, 'Why do you need Parkes?'

'I need his advice.'

'He doesn't love you. Not to distraction. Maybe he won't give it.'

'I think he will. If he won't I'll work it out myself.'

'Work what out?'

'Forty thousand dollars.'

Monk laughed gently and then after a little silence said, 'You don't have to do it, you know. You could cut your losses and go. Drea wouldn't want you to go on.'

'I've got to go on. I need that money.'

'Because you think it's going to solve everything? Maybe it is. But is the risk worth it? Why don't you chuck it in?'

I wasn't really listening to him. He wanted to help me, genuinely—but he didn't know everything. I had to have the money. He thought that Drea would change her mind. Women did.

I said, 'I've got to have that money. I know how Drea feels . . .
I know exactly where I stand.'

Monk shrugged his shoulders, and said, 'Then you're unique.
Most of us know what we want. But few of us know what we are.
That's the thing that counts.'

I shook my head. 'I know what you're after, Monk. But it's too
late. I'm going through with this. I've got to. Nothing can stop me
from trying. Don't waste your breath.'

Monk said no more.

A little later, as a few lights began to show from the group of
houses at the small harbour by the air strip, I said, 'Beach her on
the sand just the other side of the strip. And keep it quiet.'

We ran in with the engine cut down and I could hear the wash
of the waves creaming over the sand. To our left was the sharp
silhouette of the houses. An oblique rectangle of light came from
the open doorway of a small *cantina* and I began to catch the sound
of a radio, a man's voice going on and on . . . *propaganda, Cordillo,
the death of kings and dictators, the martyrdom of innocents, we must, you
will, victory, defeat* . . . pounding away through the air, the sky
charged with it all, and no truth, no truth that wouldn't need
dynamite to blast it out. Just at that moment I envied Monk.
He wanted nothing. He asked for nothing. He was just himself,
untouchable . . . needing no one. Then I saw Drea, walking like a
puma, saw the shift of light on her tawny hair and heard the rough-
touched voice, and had more strongly than I had ever had the
aching fierceness for her, the thirst and the hunger and the need
for possessing.

Eglantina's head came out of the cabin and she said softly, 'You
boys wan' anything I can get? Drink? Food?'

I said, 'No. You stay here while we're gone. In the cabin.'

I went forward and took the small anchor on its rope. When the
launch hit sand in about two feet of water I jumped down and
waded to the beach. A few yards up I drove one of the flukes deep
into the sand.

When Monk joined me, I said, 'How's the tide?'

'Coming, for another two hours. She'll be all right. Eglantina
knows how to handle her.'

We went up over the lip of the sand dunes to the end of the air
strip. The nissen hut was about two hundred yards away. Farther
on, at the far end of the strip, I could see the red light burning,
marking the edge of the palms.

We moved off, across the strip and then along a little path that ran towards the nissen. As we got closer to it I saw that there was a light showing through the window of a little lean-to affair at the back of the hut. I left Monk and went on alone.

Avoiding the light cast from the window, I went round to the narrow wooden door. I tried the handle and it moved easily under my hand. I pushed it open enough for me to slide in and then closed it behind me.

Parkes was lying on a wooden bunk that ran along the far wall. He was half-sitting up, reading, a pair of spectacles perched on the end of his nose. He was wearing thick blue and white striped pyjamas. He looked across at me and said nothing. A pressure lamp on a packing case a yard from the bunk hissed quietly. Parkes just cocked his head in my direction, his sandy hair tousled, bright eyes considering me deliberately.

Then he said, 'You might have knocked.' He put the book down flat on his chest.

'This is a private visit. I apologise.'

'Private? I see. What the bloody hell do you want? I thought you'd left Acaibo.'

'I came back.'

'I can't think why.'

'We won't go into all the reasons. Just a few of them.'

'Which ones?' He was very self-possessed, neither hostile nor friendly to me.

'The ones that concern you and Albano—and General Lemaza.'

'That bastard.'

'It's an accurate description. Do you believe that Albano shot Libertad?'

'He might have done. Depends whether his Spanish blood had the upper hand.'

'He didn't do it. I was up on the roof and saw it happen. Albano was rigged. General Lemaza arranged everything very neatly.'

'Maybe you did it,' said Parkes coldly. 'For money, I guess.'

'I'm not in that class yet. Give me time.'

'What are you after? Out with it.'

'I'm arranging for Albano to get out of prison and off this island. I thought you might like to leave at the same time.'

He didn't say anything for a while. He just looked at me, his weight now on one elbow and one hand rubbing at his stubbly chin. Then with a gruff little chuckle that had no real humour in it, he said, 'You thought I might like to go, too. Did you now? And so I would. But Mr. Bloody Marchant I think you expect me to pay for my passage. Eh?'

'Naturally. But the price isn't high. I don't want to upset you, but unless we all co-operate a little Albano's going to be stood against a wall and shot for something he didn't do. He's a nice lad. I don't think that should happen to him.'

'Neither do I. But let's face it, he's where he is because of you. You beginning to have a conscience?'

'Call it that if you like. But to do anything for Albano, I've got to have a few cards up my sleeve before I go and see General Lemaza.'

'Do that and he'll have you smartly up against a wall, my lad.'

'Not if it's handled properly. How are the planes going?'

'Another week. They made me rush one for the parade today. I didn't expect to see it come back in one piece.'

'He did a half loop and a roll over the harbour.'

'The bastard.'

'General Lemaza has got to have those planes in the air. All I want from you is the key of the nissen hut. You just tell me what parts to take away—parts that can't be replaced—to keep the planes on the ground.'

He lifted the book and closed it with a snap.

'So that's it. You're going to bargain with him. Parts against Albano. That it?'

'That's it.'

'Anything else.'

For a moment I hesitated. Then I let him have it straight because there was no hope of deceiving him.

'He still owes me money. That comes with Albano, too.'

'We're frank, aren't we? And tomorrow when the balloon goes up how do I explain that my key was used?'

'You don't have to. You can come with us now. There's a launch at the bottom of the air strip. We can make Haiti in a couple of days. You can fly home from there. Your company wouldn't expect you to stay, in the circumstances.'

He considered this for a while. Then he said, 'Nobody's going to touch me. I shall get away in time. What happens if I tell you to scarper off.'

'I'd go. But first I'd have to give you a crack over the head to keep you quiet while I took your key. The parts I'd have to figure out for myself. I know something about aero engines. You just say the word which way it is to be.'

He shook his head like a man tired of arguing with some childish demand.

'You're mad to try it—one way or the other. There's four crates of spare parts in that shed. You'd never sort them out. Still . . .' he paused, a crinkled grin slowly spreading over his face, 'I don't altogether dislike you. Don't altogether blame you. Seen too many of your kind—from the moment they begin to take too much gin in the mess until they start forging cheques. I suppose it's something about bein' up there that gives a man different ideas. Big ideas. Some can handle 'em. Some can't. Anyway, you needn't worry about me. Or my key.'

'What do you mean?'

'That you don't need my key. There's a sentry round the front of the hut. He's got a key. He'll be sitting in his box smoking if I know him. And as for the parts to take, you'll fall over them—just inside the door on the right. Only things we haven't got spares of. Typical. But you'll have trouble carting and hiding them.'

'Leave that to me.'

'I am. I'm going to finish my chapter and have a good night's sleep. Just where do I meet this boat of yours and when?'

'Tomorrow night. You be in this hut from the moment it's dark and I'll send someone for you. And thank you.'

'For what? I'm doing nothing. We just had a little chat. Just is, that since you're in the mood for cracking heads I don't see why it should be mine. He's the only sentry there is. The relief comes on in about three hours.'

We had no trouble with the sentry. Parkes had been right. He was sitting in his sentry box smoking. He looked up as I moved quietly around and in front of him. I hit him hard with the butt of my Mauser on the side of the head. He slipped sideways, grunted, and then tried to come up at me. I hit him again and the second time he went down and stayed down. We took the hut key from him and opened up the door. Just inside on the right I found the parts which Parkes had mentioned.

Monk flashed his torch on them and said, 'They'll take some carrying and hiding.' Laid out on the floor were the five propellers from the Sea Furies which still awaited complete assembly. Spare parts of practically everything else, but no spare propellers. I could see the flicker of disgust on Parkes' face as he had mouthed the word—typical.

Using our block and tackle and a low transport trolley from the sled, it took us five trips to get them down to the beach. We went across the strip, past the still shapes of the Sea Furies, and into the bushes on the far side. The sentry showed signs of coming round when we had cleared the third propeller so we hauled him into the nissen, and roped and gagged him. When we came back for the fifth propeller he lay there, his dark eyes flickering at us anxiously.

Within an hour and a half of my leaving Parkes the launch was heading out to sea to round the north-east tip of the island. Clear of the land we turned westwards and began to run up the coast. After about a quarter of an hour I picked up the shape of the island off which I had been dropped from the *Aciano*. A hundred yards east of the island we roped the propellers with a twenty foot gap between them and, moving gently, lowered them by block and tackle hoist over the side into about two fathoms of water. The last one went over and I paid out on the rope and finally cast it off with a lobster pot float.

We went round to the north of the island and ran into a small cover with bamboo and palms growing right down to the water edge. We took the launch in as close as we could get her to the rocks at the head of the cove. Monk and I went ashore and brought back bundles of dead palm fronds and branches which we spread over the decks and superstructure for camouflage. By the time we had finished the dawn was beginning to show signs and Eglantina had coffee ready. When we had finished we all went ashore and lay down under the palms to get some sleep.

CHAPTER 15

It was a long day, hot and breathless as the sea wind dropped. We kept away from the launch, sticking to the cover of the trees on the island. For a time, around mid-day, I walked across to the landward side of the island. I could see parts of the coast road up to San Pedro, but nothing of the air strip which was masked by a rising bluff of ground some miles away to my left. A few lorries went by on the coast road, but there were no signs of any special activity. Parkes would have kept his mouth shut I was sure, but by now the propellers would have been long missed and the sentry would have identified myself and Monk. Ocampo would be working hard going through Acaibo. If the launch were missed then Ocampo's men would certainly begin to comb the coast-line. But there was a lot of it to search. And anyway, for all they knew, we had headed right out to sea with the propellers without any intention of ever coming back. Just south of Acaibo, about a couple of miles offshore there was a small group of islands and sand cays which it would take half a day to search thoroughly. I hoped Ocampo would be concentrating on them first. I sat under a palm by myself and watched the dust trails rise as the occasional lorry went along the road. Lemaza wouldn't advertise the loss of the propellers. The search parties would be at work but the public wouldn't know what they were looking for . . . and sometime during the afternoon there would be Angelo's funeral. Lemaza and Ocampo were going to have a busy and disturbing day. I could imagine them both. . . . Ocampo snapping around like a terrier, and Lemaza big and full of outward confidence, but inwardly knowing that the props, if they weren't found, meant the end of his ambitions. I wondered how long it would be before Da Silva, sitting quietly in the *Cantina del Morro*, found out. No props, no triumphal entry into Caramanga, and no support from Da Silva's employers. It was going to be a bad day for Lemaza, a long bad day and if I could have made it a forty-eight hour one for him I would.

And well within forty-eight hours, I thought, I would be at sea and on my way to Haiti, to Drea. . . . All I had to have was a little luck, no more than any man could reasonably count on, and to keep my head. By now, Drea must be long in Haiti, and getting anxious. I leaned back against the tree and thought about her. Once in the past she'd walked out. Once in the past we'd come together again. I imagined her waiting for me now, sitting at this very moment possibly on the hotel terrace, looking down over Port-au-Prince. I saw myself walking on to that terrace when the moment came. She would turn and watch me and she would know right away. If I had failed she'd go because she had more courage than I had; a courage that made her face facts, let her see clearly how the future would be. And I would deserve to lose her because I saw now how obsessed I had been with my own selfish view of our love.

I stood up, disturbed by my thoughts, my feet making the dead palm litter crackle. Suddenly, I heard away to my right the sound of a plane. It was low at first, mosquito thin, and then welled up into that big, throaty roaring, into that scream and shriek of wings and propellers which had always been music to me. . . .

It was the one Sea Fury which remained operational. It came low over the far bluff that hid the air strip three miles away, climbed steeply and then levelled out and flew up the coast. I watched it. It flew at about four hundred feet, following the coast line and in a few seconds was gone out of sight to the west. But almost as soon as the noise had died, it began to grow again. The plane came back and this time it was flying low, no more than fifty feet above the water and retracing the line of the coast. It flashed by the island, a half a mile away.

I ran through the trees and joined Monk and Eglantina.

'Hide,' I called. 'Get down in the bushes. He's sure to come out here.'

As I finished speaking I heard him coming back. We crouched in the undergrowth, deep in the trees. He went over so low that the wind of his passing shook the top hamper of the palms. He came back in another pass over the island, low again, too low, I thought, and I prayed that the camouflage we had piled on the launch would fool him. I would soon know. It was not easy to make up your mind at the speed he was going that you really had seen something. If I'd been up there and fancied I'd seen a camouflaged launch, I would have come back for another, and then, maybe, even another look.

We waited as the noise died, waited for it to well up again. But it thinned away and there was only the sound of the sea lapping gently on the rocks. For the rest of the afternoon Monk and I kept watch on the landward side of the island, watching the coast road and the beaches for any sign of movement. But the day passed uneventfully.

When it was dark enough we went aboard the launch, took her around the island and straight across to the coast. We hove-to about twenty yards offshore. It was a calm night with a great blaze of stars above, so still that I could hear the occasional crackle of bursting seed pods in the shrubs on the cliff side. The three of us were in the well behind the cabin.

Monk said, 'I don't like this at all. You can't manage it by yourself.'

During the afternoon I had told him what I intended to do and he had been arguing about it ever since.

I said, 'I've got to manage it. And I think I can. I need you with the launch more than with me.' I patted my pocket in which I carried a torch that came from the launch. 'I'll signal with this from the beach below the air strip. You've got to be standing off there all night. If you don't get a signal by an hour before dawn you know what to do.'

All he had to do was to go back to the propellers. He and Eglantina could haul them up between them on the tackle hoist, and head out to sea. Far out, they could dump them where there would be no hope of finding them. I wasn't being heroic. It was just common-sense. If anything went wrong then I would be the only one to suffer. And Albano—but he had to take his chance of standing against the same wall with me and facing a firing squad. Parkes and Katrina would have no connection with me that Lemaza could trace.

'Eglantina could handle this boat easily,' he persisted.

'But she couldn't pull up the props by herself.'

'She could cut the buoy. Nobody would ever find them.'

'They would if we didn't come back. They'd make us speak. Given time. No, you stay here.'

He didn't argue after that. He took the launch in a little closer and I dropped overboard into about two feet of water and waded ashore with the phosphorescence creaming around my legs. On the beach I turned and watched the launch go out. A few minutes later I was up the cliff and over the road, breasting the climb to the top of the long bluff that hid the air strip away to the left. Once over this all I had to do was to follow the line of the foot of the hills that stretched away towards Acaibo. I reckoned that it would take me about an hour of cross-country going to reach the reservoir above the villa.

I passed through the trees about two hundred yards up the slope from the red warning light at the end of the air strip. Over the bluffs the ground was badly broken with rocks and thick shrub and it was hard going. It was a warm night and in no time I was sweating all over. The only company I had were the mosquitoes that rose around me from every shrub I brushed.

After a while, I had to work up the hill slope to avoid the broken run of a small gorge. I caught a glimpse of the harbour lights at Acaibo. I couldn't be far from the villa now. I skirted the gorge and then came down, low enough to be free of the shrubs and trees, and found the edge of the old cane plantations. An overgrown path ran along their top side and I followed this. After a while I saw the rounded edge of the old water reservoir come up sharply against the blaze of stars some way ahead of me. I slowed up and went cautiously. Down to the left a light shone in one of the windows of the villa. Along the road beyond it a car beetle-crawled, its headlights probing through the night. It went up over the hill and disappeared on the dip to Acaibo.

Ten yards from the reservoir I stopped. The path ran around the lower side of it through a clump of trees. Nearer me I could make out the tufted crests of a patch of bamboo. I stood there listening. This was the true beginning of the night's work. From now on I was going to walk on edge and there had to be no slip.

I moved quietly towards the bamboos. It was an hour and a half after darkness now and Katrina, if she were here, must have been waiting some time. A mosquito whined close to my face and I brushed it away with a slow movement of my hand. As I did so something moved in the darkness at the base of the bamboo clump. I dropped my hand towards my pockets and the Mauser but I did not more than touch the cloth of my jacket.

She came out of the darkness, swiftly and silently to me and it was exactly the same as it had been in Eglantina's room. Her arms went round me and her head was against my chest. I could feel her hands gripping the looseness of my jacket shoulders. She didn't say anything; she just held to me and I wrapped my arms about her to still the shaking of her body. After a moment she raised her head and I had the paleness of her face below mine and the soft dark line of her lips. Without thought I kissed her as a man kisses a woman who offers herself to him. Then I held her away from me. I had no wish to offer even the edge of any promise. I concentrated on what had to be done. But perhaps there was an unnatural harshness in my voice which went on misleading her though it rose from a desperate need to ensure that she came to no harm. Time had a wallet at his back all right. . . . *Wherein he puts alms for oblivion.* Well, these few moments had to go in and *be forgot as soon as done.*

I said, 'You've got to make me a promise. And you've got to keep it. Whether you like it or not.'

I still had my hands on her arms and for a while I don't think she really took in what I had said. She leaned back a little from me, looking at me. Through the darkness I could see her eyes shining and catch the sound of her breathing, a sound that still carried the pulse of her exaltation and wonder.

'Promise,' I said. I gave her a little shake.

'Anything.'

'You'll do exactly as I say, even if what I'm going to tell you makes you feel you must disobey me.'

'I promise, Keith. Oh, Keith. . . .'

I shook her again gently, ignoring all she wanted to say. Cursing myself for those few moments. Right now I was going to drive her hard. She had the spirit and fire of her race and there would be murder in her when she learned what Lemaza had done to her brother. Her hand would reach for knife or revolver. It had the instinct worked into it now. She would go to him with the cold passion of a woman who is possessed by revenge.

'You'll go down to the villa before me.'

'You're going there?'

'Yes. But don't worry about me. You'll go quietly. Pack yourself a small bag and then slip away. Go up to the beach below the air strip. Don't let anyone see you. Are you taking this in?'

'Yes, yes, of course. But Keith—'

'Go up to the beach. Take a torch with you. If I'm not there three hours after midnight you flash it on and off three times . . .'
I went on, telling her what to do to get Monk, what to do to get

herself away from this island, and all the time her hands were on
my arms, not wanting to break the contact with me.

I finished, 'Is Lemaza in the villa?'

'Yes. But why are you going there? What do you want from him?'
Katrina was hanging on my arms, her face tilted so that I could
catch the small points of star reflection in them.

I moved, releasing one of her arms, but still holding her with one
hand, and began to walk her towards the trees below the reservoir.
I said, 'I want my money. But there's something else. You're leaving
this place with me and Monk. There's nothing here for you now
that your brother has gone. General Lemaza will take Caramanga
and from then on everything will be different. . . . You wouldn't
want to be here to see it. You, particularly, since you are his sister.'

'Why should it be different? Angelo's gone . . . but his work
remains. Every soldier now is more determined. Cordillo, the new
Cordillo, is going to be his monument. . . . In the church today one
only had to see their faces . . .' She broke off and I felt her hand
grasp mine more tightly.

I said, 'I was up on the roof of Eglantina's place when your
brother was shot. I saw everything. I saw how it was done and who
did it. I saw Albano—'

'Keith, please. I don't want to talk about it.'

'But I must. You've got to understand.'

'Understand what?'

'That Albano didn't shoot your brother.'

'Albano didn't shoot my brother?' It came flatly.

'No.'

'Who did?'

I said: 'The whole thing was arranged. Albano was framed.
Lemaza was behind it. He betrayed your brother, had him
assassinated—'

'Lemaza!'

I nodded.

'Oh no! I can't believe it.'

'I was there—'

Before I could say anything more four shadows rose out of the
periphery of gloom that held us beneath the trees. A carbine was
jabbed into my back and my arms were seized. A familiar face came
between me and Katrina. Two men pulled her back, wordless and
shrinking with them into the darkness, the only sound the reluctant
scuffle of feet as they went. Lieutenant Ocampo's hands went over

my body and I was relieved of my torch and my Mauser. And for
good measure as he stood in front of me with his trophies, he raised
the Mauser and whipped me across the side of the face with it. I
raised my right foot and kicked him in the groin. He doubled up
for a moment, groaned, and then slowly straightened, coughing,
while the two soldiers held me from behind. He moved safely to
one side of me and hit me again.

I didn't see Katrina. They must have taken her down ahead of me.
They tied my hands behind my back and I was marched down to
the villa between the two soldiers. Ocampo came behind me and I
could hear him coughing and spitting occasionally from the blow I
had given him. Ocampo's car was in the driveway and his driver
beside it. The man came to attention as we passed. My head was
still muzzy from the two blows I had received and I walked, awake,
but as though still half held by some recent dream. An outside light
was on over the door at the top of the house steps and a scattering
of moths fluttered around it like snow flakes. An orderly opened the
door to us and we went across the hall. The orderly, after a knock,
opened the door of the Generalissimo's room.

   I was marched in and halted a few feet from his desk. The two
soldiers were dismissed. Ocampo went past me and placed on the
desk my Mauser and my torch. General Lemaza, who was sitting
behind the desk, looked at them briefly and then ignored them. No
word passed between him and Ocampo. I had the impression that
they too were all part of a wordless dream. In a moment they would
come into the realm of sound and reality.

   General Lemaza looked up at me and he smiled; a smile of
genuine welcome and pleasure, I decided. He had been looking
forward to this moment, had played some slender hunch in the hope
of picking me up, not expecting it to work, maybe, but delighted now
at his combination of luck and perspicacity. There he was, the bluff
Father Lemaza, showing me his tartar-free dentist's smile, confident
and beautifully dressed as usual in his coffee-coloured shantung
tunic, the room lights winking on the silver buttons with their flying
rifle-carrying eagle, the close-grained walnut pigskin of his face,
lotion fresh, and one big, ringed hand, lightly touching the top of
a box of Elvas plums. I waited for him to take one, but he held
himself back, promising himself one, no doubt, as a reward after
he had finished his business with me.

   The General got up from his desk and walked around to stand

in front of me. He hawked a little in his throat, like an amplifier crackling, and then the sound came on.

'Señor Marchant, you have been very unwise. Tenacious, admirably tenacious, but wholly unwise.'

It was a good beginning. Nice rounded phrases.

Lemaza's right hand came up and he hit me. It was a powerful hand and I went over and backwards to the floor and lay there for a moment dazed by the brutal shock.

Ocampo came to me and kicked me hard in the ribs.

'Get up,' he said calmly.

I saw no point in it so I stayed where I was.

'Get up,' repeated Ocampo and he kicked me again.

I lay where I was, breathing hard, so hard that it sounded to me as though I were sobbing.

General Lemaza pulled a chair forward.

'We should be a little more polite, perhaps?'

He bent down and with Ocampo's help lifted me into the chair. He made me comfortable with another blow alongside the face, nicely calculated so that it did not knock me off the chair. I saw his face smiling at me through a blood-shot haze and I licked at the corner of my mouth to taste the seaweed tang of blood running from some cut on my face.

'Unwise,' he said with parental concern. 'But not unintelligent. Intelligent people learn quickly.'

I was sagging a little sideways in the chair and he hit me on the side of the face to correct the sag and save me from falling. He was all consideration and I was beginning now to be ready to shut my eyes as the blow came and take the shock.

He stepped back a little and examined the knuckles of his right hand, brushing them lightly with the finger tips of his left hand. A dentist, I suppose, must look after his hands, and that was all the future he could hope for—to go back to dentistry. He reached back to the desk and picked up a long, black circular-sectioned ruler. He stood in front of me and tapped the end of it into a palm which he intended to have well greased for the rest of his life.

I said, 'You've had enough exercise.'

'Ha. . . .' Lemaza's face beamed. 'You wish to talk. That is an excellent decision. Force is repugnant to me. You realise that? It is peasant's work. You and I are reasonable men, though occasionally you have curious lapses into indiscretions. However, Señor Marchant, we shall be delighted to listen to you. You know, of course, why you are here? The sentry at the air strip recognised you. Let us confine our talk purely to the subject of propellers.'

'It's not as simple as that—'

The ruler flashed out and cracked me over the shoulder, jarring my collar bone.

'It must be as simple as that, Señor Marchant. The propellers.'

'I've got them,' I said. 'If you want them, you've got to pay for them.'

General Lemaza rested his bullock-sized backside against the edge of the desk. He said to Ocampo, 'Get Señor Marchant a drink. The best business is done over a drink.'

Ocampo went to a wall cupboard. He came back and held a glass to my lips. It was brandy and I took it. I was in no position to refuse hospitality.

'You will, of course, be paid,' said Lemaza. 'We both appreciate the enormous importance of these propellers. Normally, after you had told me where they are, I would have you shot. But I have no personal animosity, and you did bring the planes in originally. In view of all these circumstances, you shall be paid. The price is your freedom. You will be put on the first boat leaving Acaibo. Whichever way you consider it, a handsome arrangement.'

'It stinks,' I said quietly. And then as he moved the ruler I went on quickly, 'Lay off that for the moment. I'm not in a position to run away. But you've got to know the facts.'

'And what are the facts? Simple. You came back to Acaibo because of your money—taken from you through no fault of ours. You steal our propellers so openly that it was clear you would come to me with some kind of blackmail offer, Señor Marchant . . .' He paused for a moment, smiling, and then went on: 'In all fairness I must give Lieutenant Ocampo full credit for your present position. He suggested that before you got in touch with me, you might try to contact Katrina. . . . You would want to know where to find me, to be sure of a word with me. So, all day we have watched her. I never believed it would be successful.' He half-turned to Ocampo. 'My congratulations, Lieutenant Ocampo.'

Ocampo's dark face creamed with a happy smile.

'You should make him a captain.'

Lemaza chuckled. 'It is already in hand. Let us get down to these facts of yours.'

I said, 'If I tell you where these propellers are you won't let me go. We must be realistic about that. Don't bother me with it again.

And get this straight. They're hidden and there are two people with them. If I don't return to them by dawn the propellers will be destroyed. You'll never have them.' I looked up then, directly at him and the smile was gone from his face. 'Whether you believe it or not, General, I can hang on until dawn.'

It shook him. There was no doubt about it. He leaned back against the desk, frowning at me and then his hand went back and he put the ruler down and absently reached for the box of Elvas plums. He put one in his mouth and sucked on it and then began to chew.

Then he said sharply, 'Maybe we can't get you to talk in time. That's possible. But we can still find these people and get the propellers.'

'You can't find them before dawn. By then they'll be away. And they're taking something with them, General—not only the propellers. But a story the press of the world would like to hear. A story that unless you get to Caramanga and become President or whatever it is you want—you'll never be big enough to deny. A story that will make Da Silva's people pull out, money bags and all.'

'What is this story?' he asked.

'I was on the roof top the day of the anniversary parade. I saw Angelo Libertad shot dead. I saw Tomez and Sardi Hueica shot. And I saw Albano too drugged to know what was happening. It's a hell of a story. My friends know it. You can never handle it unless you get to Caramanga. And you can't get there without planes. One isn't enough.'

I leaned back then, letting my head drop away on my shoulders, feeling the brandy inside me fighting against the bruising ache in my body. I didn't care a damn for him because I knew he had to make a bargain with me.

He straightened up, rubbing one hand over his smooth chin. Ocampo stood to his side like a dark whippet.

'This is a fantastic story. Completely and scurrilously un-true.'

His emotions worked in clichés too, but they couldn't help him.

'Save that stuff for your victory speech in Caramanga. Your troops won't believe it here. The only thing that can save you is having planes in the air. I'm willing to trade in those propellers—for a few considerations. It's your choice.'

It was some time before he said anything. He walked around and sat at his desk and took another plum. He sat there, looking across at me, chewing the cud like a cow and I knew that underneath his fine uniform he was giving house-room to a flock of private agonies. Fame may be the spur, but the steed is ambition and it's a horse that takes a lot of handling . . . but he had capable hands, dentist's hands, and he knew when to rein in for a spell.

He said bluntly, 'What do you want?'

I said, 'My hands untied first. I can't bargain in the attitude of a trussed fowl.'

He considered this for a moment and then he picked up my Mauser from the desk in front of him and slipped it into his pocket.

'Ocampo.'

Ocampo came over and behind me, looking like a man well out of his depths.

CHAPTER 16

Ocampo cut the cord from my hands. It was a bad moment for me. Until then the cords and the pull of my bound hands behind me had given me a tension and restriction which had acted as a support. As I brought my hands in front of me I could feel my aching body crying out to be allowed to relax. I bowed my head forward as I chafed at my wrists, giving my body a few moments' grace. Then I pulled out my handkerchief. It was damp with salt water which had seeped up my trouser legs from wading ashore. I wiped my face and stood up.

They said nothing. But they watched me, Lemaza behind the desk and Ocampo standing now by the drink cupboard. I fished for my cigarettes. They were damp, too, and I threw the packet into a waste paper basket by the desk.

'Ocampo.'

The little dark lieutenant, soon to be captain, took a packet from his pocket, came forward a couple of steps and handed them to me. He stood there with his lighter posed.

The first hungry draught at the cigarette made me feel better.

Lemaza said bluntly, 'What do you want?'

'Two things to begin with. Forty thousand dollars from that safe behind you.'

Lemaza smiled sourly. The situation had changed and he was accepting it.

'I have them,' he said. 'It was purely a matter of good business. Revolutionary house-keeping. You shall have them. The second thing?'

'Albano,' I said. 'I brought him here. I'm taking him out with me. You can always pretend he escaped again.' I nodded to the telephone on his desk. 'Ring the barracks and have him sent here.'

I saw Ocampo stir, rather like a fussy woman wishing she could dare to butt in on some bold policy of a determined husband.

It was some time before Lemaza said anything. He was marching step by step with me. I knew that with every yard he went he was searching around for some tripping point, some unwariness on my part which would give him the advantage.

He said, 'It could be done. And in return?'

'In return you get your propellers.'

'How, Señor Marchant?'

'Albano comes here. You dismiss his guard. You give me my money—and then we all walk out. You, Ocampo, the whole bunch of us. We take Ocampo's car and drive to the coast. You won't know where until we reach the place. A boat will pick us up and take us away. As I leave the beach I'll tell you how to find the propellers. The moment we leave this place, of course, you will hand over any arms you carry.'

'I see. I am to hand over the money, and Albano. Give you a safe conduct—and then trust you at the last moment to tell me what I want to know.'

'What you must know if you want to get to Caramanga.'

'Why should I trust you to tell me where the propellers are hidden?'

'Because you damned well have to.'

He eased himself back a little in his chair and then looked from me to Ocampo. Almost casually he said:

'Captain Ocampo, what would you do in my place?'

Ocampo wasn't a man for this kind of decision. He shuffled uncomfortably.

He plunged, 'In a few hours we could make him speak, Generalissimo. Why should he tell you where the propellers are when he's free to go?'

Lemaza's eyes came back to me. 'He's a fool,' he said quietly. 'A good officer, but a fool when it comes to matters like this.' He reached out for the telephone.

I said, 'Say one word more than is necessary and the bargain is dead.'

He just looked at me without bothering to reply. He got through to the barracks commander and instructed him curtly that he wanted Albano brought to the villa under the guard of one officer and one private. 'He must be here within fifteen minutes.' He put the telephone down.

'When they come, dismiss the officer and the soldier back to the barracks.'

Lemaza smiled. 'You should have taken command of our air strength. It is a pity there is something in you which only lets you go so far. The remnant of a conscience, maybe?'

'Anything you said about my teeth I'd believe,' I said, 'but leave my conscience alone. It's outside your field.'

He laughed then, though I didn't expect him to laugh. Maybe it was his way of riding an insult.

'The dollars,' I said.

He got up and went to the safe.

He brought out a shabby brown brief-case and put it on the desk.

'They're all there. Just as I took them out of the box file when they were brought to me.' It was his first open admission of the theft, and the fact that he made it without emphasis or excuse showed me that the game was really running now, high-staked, and wide open. I only had to make one slip and he would have me up against a wall with six carbine mouths ready to roar a quick farewell.

I went forward to the desk and opened the bag. I tipped the money out and counted it. Then I put it back and lifted the case over to the chair on which I had been sitting.

Watching me do it, he said reflectively, 'Angelo was right. I should have paid you. He was always so right. You can go on being right for just so long as discretion demands. If you take it too far people end up by hating you. There was always a bullet waiting for him in the years ahead. I did him a favour. He died with everyone loving and respecting him. Not with everyone hating and fearing him because he wouldn't give them what they wanted.'

I said, 'You don't have to make two funeral orations in one day for my benefit.'

It was then that I realised that he was looking right past me.

I spun round.

The side door in the main sitting room had opened quietly while I had been talking. Katrina stood just inside the room. She wore a black dress with a large shawl over her shoulders. Against her bosom I saw the length of chain with its gold cross. In her right hand she held the small automatic which I had first seen on the *Mara II*.

'Katrina!'

I made a move towards her but she brought the gun up a little and for a moment it included me as she shook her head.

'Stay where you are, Keith. Stay where you are. He had my

brother killed.' She broke off and came forward a little into the room. Out of the corner of my eye I saw Ocampo's hands poised against his hips. A quick move would put his hand on his holster. Lemaza stood behind the desk, his finger tips resting on his blotter.

Keeping my voice calm, I said, 'Katrina, if you kill him now you'll—'

'Don't talk to me, Keith. He killed Angelo. He knows I'm going to kill him.'

I didn't say anything. She was going to kill him. She was going to walk a few more paces towards the desk so that she couldn't miss, and when she fired she was going to bring everything down in a great crash around us. Albano would get his bullet, so would I, and so would she.

She wasn't watching me. Her eyes were on the silent Lemaza. I reached back behind me slowly and felt for the brief-case on the chair. I got one of the handle loops and I slung it out from me and towards her. She had a lot to learn still and I hated teaching her.

The case caught her on the right hip and jolted up her right elbow. I jumped for her and got her wrist and the impetus took us to the floor. When I stood up the automatic was in my hand.

I reached down and helped her up and she stood in front of me, dazed. Suddenly her head dropped and she began to sob.

Lemaza dropped back into his chair and I saw his big shoulders collapse.

'Thank you, Señor Marchant,' he said.

'Don't thank me. You've got a bullet coming to you one day. And now, just to show how much you trust me I'll have the rest of the armament. My Mauser and Ocampo's revolver.'

They handed them over. I kept my Mauser and dropped the other two into the case. A simple movement. But then they always are, the little movements eating up only a few seconds of time, but loaded, loaded down to the gunwales, with the freight of the future.

There was a knock on the door. I looked at Lemaza.

'That'll be Albano. Let me do the talking.'

Katrina's head came up and I saw the tightening of her lips, the flash of returning spirit in her eyes. She was coming out of her trance fast.

'For this,' she said bitterly, 'I'll never forgive you. Never.'

The knock came on the door again. I nodded to Ocampo and he went over.

A captain brought him in while the soldier escort stood at the open door. Albano came into the middle of the room. His blazer was ripped and dirty and he hadn't shaved for many days. He looked around him suspiciously. They had been keeping him without adequate toilet facilities. The dirtier and more disreputable he looked the better showing it would have been at his trial . . . a young desperado. His face was puffy and cut below the right eye. It looked as though they were still keeping him drugged. If they were I might have trouble getting through to him.

Lemaza said, 'All right, captain. You can go back to the barracks. I will telephone you when you are needed.'

The captain saluted and turned away to the door.

As the door closed I said, 'What have you been doing to him? Softening him up with rifle butts so that he'll remember his lines for the trial?'

Lemaza stood up and the muscles of his face tightened.

'I've put myself in your hands, Señor Marchant. I don't want this business prolonged by any discussion of our prison methods.'

And then, astutely, beginning already to hedge the future, prompted to it by the knowledge that the captain would go back to the barracks and talk and set people wondering, he went on, turning towards Katrina:

'This man killed your brother. The rest is lies. I am being forced into a bargain by Señor Marchant which I must accept.'

Katrina said nothing.

Albano moved and looked at me and then he said slowly as though each word were an effort, 'What is he talking about?'

I said, 'I'll explain later. You're coming with me. Away from Acaibo. It is part of a bargain.'

'Bargain?'

I nodded.

He shrugged his shoulders, awake but not really with us. And I was glad that I didn't have to go into the details of the bargain with him. Even in his present state he would have resisted any bargain that put the Sea Furies into the air against his side. I went over to the cupboard and poured him a glass of brandy. He took it and held it cupped against his chest.

'Drink it,' I said.

He drank obediently.

As he did so I turned to Katrina.

'We're going now,' I said. 'You're free to stay here or come with us.'

'She will stay here, of course,' said Lemaza quickly.

'There is no reason for her to go. Katrina—'

'Let her speak for herself.'

She looked from me to Lemaza and then at Albano. Then she said to me, 'What do you want me to do?'

'It's your decision. Not mine. You know the facts.'

She shook her head. 'What do you want me to do?'

If only I could I would have wiped out those few moments at the reservoir. Already they had put on me a weight I didn't want to carry.

I said, 'You must come with us.'

'With you?'

'With us,' I repeated firmly. 'I'm not going to be alone in the boat.'

'All right.'

At once, Lemaza said, 'I can't allow this.'

'She's coming with us,' I said. 'You don't start giving orders again until the bargain is completed.'

Albano said, 'I don't understand any of this at all.'

I didn't bother to help him. I turned to Ocampo who had been standing in shocked silence at Lemaza's impotence, and I said, 'Go and clear the orderly from the hall and then stand by the car. If there are any of your men outside clear them off. And, remember, don't try anything. I'm going to be right behind your General . . .' I lifted my Mauser.

Lemaza said, 'Captain Ocampo, you will do exactly as Señor Marchant orders.' And then as Ocampo moved towards the door, Lemaza turned to Katrina, 'Katrina, I beg of you to reconsider this most hasty—'

'Skip it,' I said. 'Her mind's made up, and you haven't got a cliché in you that will change it.'

CHAPTER 17

We went across the hall and out to the car. Ocampo was the only person in sight.

I made Ocampo drive and the General sat alongside him. The rest of us got into the back of the car and I sat directly behind the General.

'To the air strip,' I told Ocampo.

At the end of the drive the sentry on duty saluted smartly and then we turned north. Away on our right I could see the pale line of wash from the waves rolling up the beaches. The wind had got up a little and there were patches of small cloud racing across the star-loaded sky. It wasn't midnight yet. I was glad of that because the more hours of darkness we had at sea for a start the safer we would be. Once Lemaza knew where his propellers were he would send a boat out from Acaibo after us. I couldn't stop that, but I reckoned that two or three hours' grace would be as much as we needed in the launch, for no one would know which course we had taken.

Katrina sat alongside me and, knowing the emotional burden that hung between us, knowing, too, that the longer I let it rest there the harder it would be to support it, I said easily, 'What happened to you after we were caught?'

She was staring straight ahead of her and for a moment I thought she wasn't going to reply.

'What happened?' I asked.

'I was locked in my room,' she said. 'Lemaza was to see me later. They didn't know you'd already told me. Keith—' Her head came round and I could tell she was going to change the subject.

I put my free hand on hers and said quickly, 'It's all right. You don't have to say anything. How did you get out?'

'On to the verandah through the window and then back into the house through my . . . through his room . . .' Her head turned away from me and her hand tensed under mine.

The lights of the barracks came up on our right and as we passed the entrance I saw the *Singing Heart that Never Tires* drawn up and some leave men getting out. I don't know why but the sight of the taxi, reminding me of my first days in Acaibo, served to point the fact that now, very soon now, I would be getting out, and taking with me the money I had earned . . . not honourably, maybe, but certainly earned. And I was going, too, without leaving any responsibilities behind me. It wasn't often that life handed you a nice profit and also left your conscience untroubled. . . . The weight of the brief-case on my knees was pleasant and I think I should have been completely happy had it not been for Katrina at my side. She was in love with me. She was going to have to work it out for herself, gain a little more experience. . . .

But although I was beginning to feel easier I didn't let that tempt me into any carelessness. Lemaza would be watching for the slightest advantage.

The barracks dropped behind us and then I saw the red light of the air strip. I told Ocampo to run the car up to the large nissen and round to Parkes' hut. There were two sentries at the hut now but Ocampo dealt with them.

As the car drew up Parkes came out of his hut. He had his panama hat on, a light overcoat and was carrying a small grip. Somehow the sight of him turned the whole affair into a commonplace departure. Mr. Henry Parkes all ready to leave for Balham or Tooting or wherever he lived . . . spare socks and shirt in his grip, passport and wallet tucked away in his jacket.

He came over to the car and looked at Albano. Although Albano was brightening up he still had a long way to go. Parkes must have appreciated at once what had been happening. He put a big hand out and gripped Albano's arm.

'Nice to see you, Mr. Albano, sir.' And then to Lemaza he said roughly, 'I'm leaving. What there is to do here can be done by your chaps. Also I won't tell you what I think of you. It would take too long and there's a lady present.'

Lemaza said nothing.

Albano said, 'You're coming with us?'

'Yes, sir,' said Parkes. 'We'll be all right.' He stood on the running-board of the car for the short ride down to the beach and

as he did so Albano said, 'But what about the planes. Are they
going to be in the air for him?'

Parkes said, 'I don't know. That depends on Mr. Marchant here.'

Albano turned towards me. 'What about the planes?'

He was coming back fast and I didn't want any trouble with
him.

'Sit tight,' I said. 'And be glad you're getting out. There's no
future in facing a firing party.' To Ocampo I said, 'Run down the
strip to the beach.'

'But I want to know,' Albano insisted.

'Sit tight,' I said sharply.

A little later we were on the beach. I took the torch out of my
brief-case and signalled. It was a good ten minutes before I heard
the sound of the launch's engines. Soon afterwards her bulk rose
against the night sky. She came into the beach and her bows grated
on the sand about three yards out from the water's edge. Monk
called gently to me from the bows.

'Hold her there,' I said.

I stood at the back of the group, brief-case in one hand and my
revolver in the other.

Parkes and Albano waded out and I watched Monk help them
over the side. Katrina followed them. She ignored Lemaza altogether and he made no move or sound. He and Ocampo stood there
with the waves fading up towards them and they watched me. I
waited until Katrina was safely aboard and then I went down to
the water, keeping the two covered.

It must have been an anxious moment or two for Lemaza. I
could break my bargain easily. The water came up around my feet
and Lemaza's eyes were on me.

He didn't say anything. He just waited, a big, smartly dressed
man, his peaked cap tilted just slightly at an angle, the starlight
glinting on his silver buttons. He was going to remember this
moment and I didn't hurry to relieve his agony of mind. I waded
back until the water was up to my calves.

It was too much for him then.

He said hoarsely, 'I have kept my side of the bargain, Señor
Marchant.'

'Because you had to. Don't worry. I'm going to keep mine. Along
the coast from here about four miles, there's a small island. The
propellers have been roped together and sunk about a hundred
yards east of the island. They're buoyed. You'll find 'em.'

I think then, if he had thought it would be successful, he would have come for me. I could see the swift reassumption of command in him, bracing his body. But the Mauser kept him off. I stepped backwards, facing them all the time. But Lemaza didn't wait for me to reach the launch. He turned sharply, snapped something at Ocampo, and the two of them began to run up the beach, back to their car.

Above me Monk said, 'Come on.'

I turned and climbed aboard, holding the brief-case firmly. I found myself facing Albano. His damaged face was creased with anger.

'What you've just done, I'll never forget. You've given him those planes back, haven't you?'

'Yes.' I was suddenly tired and near to losing my temper with him. 'If you want to, you can go back and do something about it. Go on, if you want to.'

I went by him and aft and found Eglantina.

'We could all do with a drink, sweetheart,' I said.

We went north all night with a fresh trade wind slapping the occasional wave over our starboard bow. Some of the party slept, but I stayed with Monk beside the wheel and now and then Eglantina came up from the cabin with a mug of coffee. Towards dawn the sky clouded right over and when daylight came the sea was running grey and there was a sporadic sweep of rain squall at times, hissing across the dull waters. The clouds were down to about three or four hundred feet. I didn't mind the dullness of the day. It cut the visibility down and that was a help if anyone was searching for us.

Just after daybreak Katrina came up from the cabin and stood beside us. She looked pale.

'How are they down there?' I asked.

'Albano is sleeping. He had three glasses of whiskey and in his condition they've sent him off.'

'He'll feel fine when he wakes. I shall have trouble with him.' I gave her a grin. 'He's another who isn't going to forgive me.'

She shook her head. 'We all say things we don't mean at times.'

Monk nodded. 'The hardest thing at any time is to say the thing you mean. Even when you know someone well you're always having to hide things from them.'

'He's always like this in the early morning,' I said to Katrina. I was feeling good and I didn't want to think about anything but Haiti and Drea ahead of us.

An hour later Parkes and Albano came on deck. Parkes gave us all a good morning, but Albano said nothing. He went and sat in the stern and Parkes kept him company. They didn't talk much. Albano was young, too, like Katrina. He was learning all the time.

Eglantina fixed up some breakfast and I took over the wheel from Monk while he went down to eat with the others.

Katrina kept me company. My hands on the wheel, I whistled gently to myself. I was happy, elation running firmly in me. I had my money and Drea was waiting for me. I wanted nothing else.

Alongside of me Katrina said suddenly, 'You're thinking about her?'

I nodded.

She said, 'I wish she didn't exist!'

I smiled. 'I'm glad she does.' And then, because I liked her so much and knew how she was feeling, I went on, 'Don't look so glum. In six months you'll be in love with someone else. Someone far more worthy than me.'

She made an impatient movement of her head. I said no more. There was nothing I could say.

Parkes came up to us and said, 'What's that?'

'What's what?'

'Listen.'

He cocked his head, cupping one ear in his hand.

I listened.

It came up then, growing stronger every second; the sound of a plane's engine.

'Hell!'

Parkes' bright blue eyes were on me and then went up to the grey clouds. A few seconds later we saw it, skimming through the lower layers of cloud away to the east. It was the one Sea Fury which General Lemaza had in operation. It was about a mile away and there was a chance it might not see us. The sound of its engine brought the others on deck.

I grabbed Parkes' arm and swung him round to me. 'Did you get as far as fitting the armament?'

'Ay, we did.'

Two 22-mm. Bristol Hispano cannons in each wing. They could make a mess of this launch in no time.

I said, 'Everybody keep down. No movement. He may not see us.'

'And if he does?' It was Albano.

I said, 'You know what those cannons can do. If he comes for us our only hope is to go over the side. Swim away and spread the target.'

I put a hand out and took Katrina's shoulder. 'If we go over, stick with me.' I cut the engine dead. We didn't want to advertise ourselves with a wake.

The noise of the plane died and it was swallowed in a far bank of cloud. Then a little later it swelled up again and Monk said, 'There he is.'

He'd gone round to the north and was now coming back on a course to the west of us. I watched him. He came down a bit to be free of the cloud cover and I wondered which of the *Cantina del Morro* boys it was. They'd had him out of bed, out of drunken sleep and waiting on the air strip for first light. I watched him away on our left now. He took the Sea Fury down almost to wave level and then brought her back in a climb that carried him into the clouds. The bowl of sky above us echoed with the roar of the engine. General Lemaza had his propellers by now. General Lemaza was going to wipe us out, but not just us. He was going to wipe out a story, wipe out the need for any denials of the truth about Angelo Libertad. . . . And I'd had all the time in the world last night to remember the one good Sea Fury.

The noise above us deepened. He broke cloud about a quarter of a mile astern and came down in a long shallow dive. He was down and over us with a great screech, clearing us by about fifty feet, the wind of his passing battering down on us. As he went away he waggled his wings, and I could imagine him, laughing to himself, sure of his identification as he swept up into the low cloud again.

'Get over,' I said. 'The next time he'll go into business.'

I heard Eglantina say, 'Mr. Monk, you can swim?'

'Not as far as Haiti,' he said.

'You stay around me. . . .' Out of the corner of my eye I saw her strip off her dress. If she had to she would swim all the way to Haiti dragging him.

I pulled off my jacket and picked up the brief-case and jumped over. At the stern I heard the splashes as Parkes and Albano went. I trod water, waiting for Katrina. She followed Eglantina's example and pulled off her dress. She jumped in and we swam quickly away from the boat. A hundred yards from the launch I stopped swimming and Katrina came close to me. The others were spread away on the far side of the launch. There was no sign nor sound of the Sea Fury.

Katrina's hand came out and touched my shoulder gently. I saw the run of her long brown arm, the water shine on her brown shoulders and a wet wing of dark hair clinging to her cheek. . . . She looked like a child then, like the girl I had first met.

'Stick by me,' I said. 'And if he comes our way, dive under.'

The first time he came down out of the clouds about half a mile ahead of the launch. I watched him level out, hearing the scream of the engine, knowing in a quick turn of memory just how he must be feeling, remembering the times I myself had come down like that with a thumb ready on the button. . . .

Two hundred yards from the launch he let go and the air shuddered with the sudden wicked punch of his guns. He was a good boy and knew his stuff. He was back in his element with all the night's hangover dissipated, eyes clear, brain and body one. He came in slightly at an angle to widen his target and I saw the sea swiftly ripped into ragged white tears that flashed from fifty yards out right up to the launch and over it. He roared past and the launch jumped like some sluggish animal and the air was briefly slashed and dirtied around it with splintering wood and debris.

He did a long, lazy turn under cloud level and came back. This time he took the launch full on the beam. He was down and over chattering and roaring and the cannons tore furrows away to our left as he passed. I went under with Katrina, clasping the brief-case to my chest. When I came up the launch had lost its high cabin forestructure and was afire. A thin plume of smoke rose from it and tailed away in the wind.

I began to swim away from it further and Katrina went with me. There was water in the brief-case now, sogging through it and weighing it down in my hand. But I hung on to it. Wet notes could be dried.

He came back again, well away from us and this time he must have hit the petrol tanks. There was a mighty double pulse of explosion, beating for release against the surrounding atmosphere and then the boat blew up, bursting into an untidy flower of wreckage. And as he went what was left of the launch settled swiftly and then disappeared, leaving for a moment or two a spreading flare of burning petrol on the surface.

He came back again, over the spot where the launch had been and then turned in a tight circle. But his guns were silent. I watched him finish his turn a quarter of a mile away and then head back to us. We were well spread now. As he came I wondered . . . the launch was fair game and, if we'd stayed in it, so would we have been. When you've got a target nothing can keep your finger off the button as you come in . . . when you've got a target. But people struggling in the water weren't targets. When you ride high and fast on wings like a god then you have to act like a god . . . use your power to destroy or to spare . . .

He went over us again and his guns were silent. He went over and up into the clouds and I trod water with Katrina's hand on my shoulder and knew that he was deciding. Up there above the grey pall, clear in the morning sunshine, with the cloud tops bright and floss-whipped, he was deciding still.

He came down from the east, faster than ever before, screaming towards us and flattening out until he was no more than twenty feet above the sea. Away ahead of me I could see the black spots of the heads of Parkes and Albano. A hundred yards before he reached them he suddenly pulled up steeply, dangerously, practically standing on his tail and then was over, streaking up and away from us into the clouds without firing. The noise of the plane died away and he didn't come back. He didn't have to come back. Our launch was gone and we could drown at our leisure.

But it had been decided somewhere that we had no drowning mark upon us. I remember thinking sometime during the long hours that perhaps my complexion was, indeed, perfect gallows.

With the going of the plane we all came together. But it was hard work staying that way. Different bodies drift at different speeds. Now and again I lost my temper, shouting at Monk and Eglantina to keep close. We drifted in our three double-headed groups, Parkes and Albano, Monk and Eglantina, and Katrina and myself.

Towards the afternoon, I saw that Katrina was weakening. She didn't speak, but her head kept dropping and her hand on my shoulder began to lose grip and now and again slipped from me. When it happened I grabbed at her with my free hand and helped her to catch hold of me again. I kept talking to her, because I could see that she was at the point of being really scared. From the moment she had come aboard the *Mara II* she had been changing and learning all the time. It had been all a bit too fast, too violent, too crowded. Experience wants to come slowly. For a while she responded to my talk and then I saw that she wasn't with me. Fatigue was now swamping her fears. . . .

An hour later Katrina gave a little cry and her hand left me and she went under. One moment her face was close to me and the next moment she was gone. The going struck a jolt of panic through me. I kicked round and porpoised after her. Somewhere in the green fog of water I found her, caught her by the shoulders and brought her up. She lay back weakly, her shoulders against my chest and I got both my hands under her armpits to hold her while I lay back supporting her.

I can remember talking to her. God knows what nonsense. Telling her to take it easy, to relax, let herself float while my hands kept her shoulders up. And sometime in the talk and the unreal passage of time I realised that in diving for her I had let go of the brief-case. I even looked around for it, wondering if it would float and then remembered that inside it with the money were her automatic and Ocampo's revolver. *A thousand furlongs of sea for an acre of barren ground.* Well, I'd made my payment. It was then that depression came down on me. I'd lost everything. After all I'd gone through, I'd lost everything. I didn't care then what happened to me. Nothing mattered because nothing worth having lay ahead for me.

At ten minutes past four that afternoon a Puerto Rican schooner picked us up. She was on the run from Jamaica. As soon as we were aboard Albano demanded that the captain should arrest me. Personally, I didn't care a damn what he did. I think the skipper thought Albano was delirious. Anyway, he refused to involve himself in the charges.

It was Monk who arranged things. The next morning he got the captain to go off course northwards to the Baie des Cayes on the south coast of Haiti. We lay off Cayes and got a passing fishing boat to take us in.

Parkes and Albano, leaning over the rail, watched us go. Parkes raised a hand in farewell, a short, solid figure, heading for Balham. Albano at his side gave no farewell gesture.

In the boat I said to Monk, 'How did you fix it? Albano could have made trouble for me in Jamaica.'

Monk smiled. 'I talked to Albano. Just talked to him and he saw reason.'

'You must have had something pretty powerful to say.'

'I did.'

'What?'

'I'll tell you later. He just saw reason.'

We had to do a little fast talking with the harbour officials when we got in, but we had no trouble with them and by mid-day we were in a small hotel in the town. I had a few dollars from my wallet which I had carried in the back pocket of my trousers. I dried this out on the window seat of my room. Monk I knew had some money, too.

As I was laying it out Katrina came into my room. She was still wearing a jersey and canvas trousers she had been given on the schooner.

She stood inside the door and watched me. From the moment we had been picked up she had made no mention of my brief-case. But I didn't have to be told that she knew what had happened to it.

I straightened up and looked down at the money.

'It's not much,' I said wryly. 'But it's enough to keep going on for a week or two.'

'What are you going to do?' she asked. Her voice was gentle, uncertain.

'Do?'

'You know what I mean.'

'Yes, I know. I'm going to hire a car and go over to Port-au-Prince. It's only about ninety miles.'

She came over to the window by me and looked out over the houses to the sea and the tufted crests of the palms along the coast. An old man in a straw hat and blue shirt was pushing a handcart up the rough roadway. The wheels, unoiled, creaked and sang.

She said, 'The money meant everything, didn't it?'

'Yes,' I said.

'Then why go?'

'Because I've got to go.'

'Will you come back?'

I shrugged my shoulders. 'I don't know.'

She turned and left the room.

I let her go and then went along to Monk's room.

Monk was lying back on his bed in his underpants, smoking, while Eglantina was busy washing shirt and trousers in the hand-basin.

I said, 'Eglantina, go and see the clerk downstairs. Fix me up a hire car for Port-au-Prince right away.'

She reached for a towel and began to dry her hands.

'Sure, Mr. Keith.' She gave me her brown smile and went out singing gently to herself.

Monk scratched the top of his head. 'Something I ought to tell you. About the propellers. While you were ashore, Eglantina and I lifted 'em all. Hell of a job, but we did it. Dropped 'em, unbuoyed, a mile out at sea. That bastard Lemaza will never find 'em.'

'Why did you do that?'

'Frankly, I didn't think you'd carry things off. Anyway—it was a trump card with Albano. He could have made real trouble for you. Now the whole thing will be forgotten.'

'I've got other trouble.'

'I know. But there's nothing I can do about that. Wish there was.'

'To think that I had it all in my hands. I could see the future . . . all beautiful. Well, there it is.'

'You don't have to go to Port-au-Prince.'

'No, but I'm going.'

'I know that. Maybe it's as well. Anyway, I'll be here. I've got a little cash. You need any?'

'No thanks, Monk.'

Eglantina came back.

'Car right away, Mr. Keith.'

'Thank you, Eglantina.'

I went out of the hotel into the sunshine and to the car. The boy who was driving it was the dead spit of *Singing Heart*.

As I got into the car he gave a melon grin and let in the gear. We were off and before we had cleared the town he switched on the car radio and a thumping calypso began to shock the sunlit air.

We had two punctures on the way, and the engine gave trouble. I began to think that the delays were deliberate.

We got there just before six and the beginning was just as I had imagined it might be. She was sitting at a table on the terrace, close up against a wall covered with bougainvillaea. The canopy over the table was tipped to let the westering sun strike across her hair and I saw the reddish lights slide over it as she turned and watched me coming. She was wearing a white dress and my topaz brooch . . . Drea. There was no one else in the world for me. No world for me without her. But I was coming back with a broken lance and without the garlands of victory.

She knew that before I had reached her and sat down.

Her hand came across the table and took mine.

'Keith . . .' The rough-touched, beloved voice.

'Drea . . .'

We sat looking at each other silently.

Her hand left mine and she said, 'It didn't come off?'

'No.'

'Your face is awful. What happened?'

I said, 'Forget that. Stick to us. All you have to say is Yes or No.'

'What happened?' she repeated firmly.

'I was in a car accident. The driver called his cab the *Singing Heart that Never Tires*. Nice name.'

But she didn't smile. She said, 'You had the money?'

'I had it. In my hand. Then I dropped it.'

'Why?'

'I was in the sea. I needed both hands.'

Her eyes came down from my face to where my hands rested on the edge of the table. I saw the tiny movement of her shoulders as though she felt suddenly cold. Then her hands came out and took mine, holding them, gripping at them and without looking at me she said with a rush of words, her fingers tight over mine, 'Blast you! Oh blast you . . . !'

I dropped to my chair and put my lips to her hands, and catching at any hope I began to beg . . . 'Anything. Blast me . . . Anything. But don't go . . .' Her face came up towards me and I stopped for I could see that there was no need to beg. The Drea who was holding my hands was my Drea. The truth was then sharp and inevitable between us; try as we might to escape it, or put conditions to it, we were its creatures, bound to it irrevocably. We had to go on together, knowing that nothing could be settled in advance, that love changes its course from moment to moment, and that we had to follow because we weren't just lovers, but a part of love itself, for better or for worse.

The Melting Man

Contents

CHAPTER 1

'O, how that glittering taketh me!'
(Robert Herrick)

I had my feet up on the window sill, watching the pageantry of
life outside. It didn't amount to much. The cab driver at the head
of the rank was reading the morning edition of the *Evening Standard*
and smoking a cheroot. A handful of early fallen leaves from the
plane trees did a little dervish dance in the wind. A coloured gent
went by in a big, blue bedspread. He had a beaming 250-watt smile
on his large face that could only have come from transcendental
meditation or a new and satisfactory addition to his harem. A traffic
warden was booking a Mini-Austin for parking on a yellow curb
line. Two girls went by on the far pavement; one had blonde hair
and a face that would have made Botticelli's eyes pop, the other
carried a transistor set and sucked at an ice-lolly. A porter polished
a brass plate. A pigeon bullied a couple of sparrows in the gutter.
Two businessmen hurried towards Trafalgar Square, bowlers set,
brief-cases and umbrellas at the ready.

I got tired of the pageant and looked at my feet. The suède shoes
wanted a good going over with a wire brush. My green socks didn't
look good with a dark suit. I didn't care much. At this time of the
year lethargy and sloppiness always seemed to set in. In another
five days I would be off on holiday. The battery wanted recharging.
Pretty soon, I thought, I must decide where I was going.

The office door opened behind me. I didn't turn. I knew it was
Wilkins: Hilda Wilkins, thirty-five, spinster, rusty red hair, honest
blue eyes (too honest), thick tweed skirt, plain white blouse, sloppy
grey cardigan – no oil painting, my partner, and the bond between
us unshakable. There was little about me that she approved of. I
sometimes wondered why she stayed. Certainly not for the salary.

She said, 'I'm going to the bank.'

I turned.

'Put or take?'

'Take,' she said. 'I've switched the office phone through here.'

I said, 'I didn't think there was any to take.'

'A little. Have you decided where you're going?'

'No. Nor who I'm going with. Or should it be whom?'

She sniffed, and backed for the door. She had no opinion of my morals or my grammar.

I said, 'I thought about the Gritti Palace in Venice.'

She said, 'Why not – if you're only staying one night? You'd do better with your sister in Honiton. You'd eat free.'

'It's a point. Devonshire cream and cider, great rashers of bacon, fried eggs, chitterlings, black puddings, roast pork, boiled beef and dumplings . . . Yes, I need feeding up.'

She looked pointedly at my lowest waistcoat button and said, 'That's not the impression I get."

She went, and I looked down. Maybe she was right. Life had been sedentary lately. I looked at the calendar on the wall opposite and because I had nothing else to do I wondered how many more shopping days there were to Christmas. I couldn't bother to work it out.

The telephone rang. I let it ring a while and then picked it up.

I said, 'Carver and Wilkins. Can I help you?'

A man's voice said primly, 'I wish to speak to Mr Rex Carver.'

I said, 'Hold on a moment, I'll see if he's in.'

I put the phone down and lit a cigarette. It was a small office, just Wilkins and myself and a little outside help when we were pressed. It didn't hurt, though, to give the impression of a big organization. And, anyway, years of experience had given me a sixth sense that could always pick a new client on the line. I was going on holiday, somewhere, and I didn't want to be tied up just then with some crummy recovery job or an insurance fiddle or wearing my feet out looking for some man or woman who didn't want to be found.

I picked up the phone.

'I'm sorry, Mr Carver is not available at the moment.'

'You mean he's not there?' He sounded as though he weren't used to people not being there when he wanted them.

'I'm afraid not. He's out.'

'Then would you take a message?'

'Certainly.'

'Tell him it's from Mr Cavan O'Dowda's secretary. Mr O'Dowda's car will call for him at three today. I think it would be advisable if he brought an overnight bag.'

I said, 'Does Mr Carver know about this appointment?'

A little irritated, the voice said, 'Of course he knows. I wouldn't be phoning to confirm it otherwise. The car will be there at three o'clock. Thank you.'

There was a click and he was gone.

Interesting. But not enough to make me get up and check the O'Dowdas in the London telephone directory. I needed a holiday, not work. Mind you, I needed money too. I always needed it, and sometimes when the need was great I wasn't too fussy how I got it. But just now – so long as there was a little in the bank – I needed complete rest and relaxation. I sat there and thought of all the places I could go to. I had a friend who'd retired to Malta to beat the tax game – but that would mean sailing and I hated pulling away at sheets, the kind you find on yachts, anyway. The Costa Brava? Fish and chips, ghastly *gazpacho,* and even ghastlier flamenco singing. Biarritz? Quiet, Edwardian – only it wasn't any longer. Just big, bustling and noisy, the streets full of Citroens and the Atlantic filling your face full of wind-blown spume and sand the moment you went over the dunes. Somewhere quiet, way up at the back of Cannes? Well, I might find that; peace, solitude and relaxation under some grape-festooned arbour, swigging *vin rosé* in the morning to taper off from the previous night's Pernod. Fine, all except the solitude. I'd have to have company to beat that. I'd almost worked up enough energy to reach for my address book in the desk drawer when the phone rang. I changed my hand direction and picked it up.

Wilkins said, 'I'm back.'

'Good. The office wasn't the same without you.' When she didn't reply, I said, 'Did you make an appointment for me with a Mr O'Dowda?'

'No.'

'That's good then.'

I put the receiver down and forgot about my address book. They'd all have some excuse, anyway. I could break fresh ground, of course. Perhaps a cruise, if I could get a booking. No, they were all so damned hearty, betting on the day's run, deck quoits, table-tennis and that bloody fancy dress thing, and, anyway, all the unattached girls were too soon swiped by the officers. You can't compete with a uniform and that deep sea-tan.

My private outside line rang. I got the receiver to my ear with an effort.

'Carver here.'

Miggs's breezy, booming ploughman's voice made me wince.

'How are we, me old cock? Haven't had you here for a work-out in a month. I'll bet you can't see your Poupart's ligament for fat and if there's a depression over your great trochanter I'm a Dutchman.'

'Go away and carry on with your drinking.'

'Stone sober. Have to be in this job. But come round and we'll have a couple. Also, I've got something for you.'

'Anything you've got you can keep. But I'll come for the drink – that's if my rectus muscles can make it.'

In the outer office Wilkins was knitting something in a bilious yellow wool and doing the *Daily Telegraph* crossword.

'Going to see Miggs,' I said.

She gave me a look and said, 'Don't forget to have some lunch. And why did you ask me about Cavan O'Dowda?'

'I didn't say his name was Cavan.'

She nodded to the equipment panel on her desk. 'I left the recorder on.'

'Know him?'

'I've heard of him. He's—'

'Don't bother to tell me. I've only one problem at the moment. Where to go for a holiday.'

I flexed my legs and went out.

I went down the stairs and stood in the doorway, looking out into Northumberland Avenue. Away up to my left Nelson was standing on his column turning a blind eye to the assault of pigeons and starlings. To my right the brass plate which said *Carver and Wilkins* wanted polishing. It had just been *Carver,* until in a more than usually bad year Wilkins had insisted on emptying the old tea-caddy on the mantelshelf at home (where she lived with her father, a retired ship's steward and an indefatigable but not very successful player of the horses) and coming to the rescue—with a look in her eyes which dared me to show even a two-second flash of gratitude. Without saying anything to her I had had the plate changed. From its present state I knew that somebody soon was going to get hell about it.

I went down to Miggs's place. It was hard work for a man in my lackadaisical state but I stuck to it, the whole of four hundred yards.

Behind his garage Miggs had a gymnasium. His charges were salty, but his appointment book was always full. Miggs had once been a sergeant in the Commandos. After a work-out with him, a really fit man would discover he was aching in about a dozen muscles he never knew he had. For special clients – and he had quite a few of them – he ran a course in unarmed combat which comprised some very fancy ways of killing a man swiftly and silently.

He was finishing a session when I got there, so I went and sat quietly in his office. He came in, his red face shining from a shower, took one look at me and said, 'My God – a young man in an old man's body. You'd better let me book you in for a dozen sessions. Special price for you.'

'I'm happy the way I am. I like to put it on around September. Live off my fat during the winter. Bears do it. What about a drink?'

He opened a cupboard and brought out the whiskey.

We sat and drank and he shook his head sadly at me, his eyes running disappointedly over me as though he were a sculptor and I his first clay mock-up for a Greek athlete which had gone wrong everywhere it possibly could.

'A job is just what you need. But before you get stuck into it, you report here for a few days.'

'A holiday is what I need – and what I'm having.'

'A holiday can wait – but good money can't. You take the job. There could be a lot to make on the side, too. That's what you like, isn't it? Anyway, the cropped-headed bastard has got more than he knows what to do with – not that he throws it around without being sure of a return. These millionaires never do.'

'What I like,' I said, 'is someone who doesn't talk in riddles, and a higher percentage of whiskey to my soda.' I pushed my glass towards him and he obliged.

'Didn't you get my message?'

'No.'

'I phoned your Mrs Meld last night and gave it to her.'

'Today is Monday. I spent the weekend at Brighton and came straight into the office this morning off the train. Do I gather you've been trying to fix me up with a job?'

'Have done. He said he'd send a car for you at three today.'

'Presumptuous.'

'Not when it's a millionaire. His son was killed alongside me in Italy. He's always had a soft spot for me and gives me all his car business. Makes Jack Barclay and those types mad because it's all Rolls and Bentley stuff and he changes on whim four or five times a year sometimes. I delivered a Facel Vega to him yesterday – he's giving it to his daughter as a birthday present.'

'I always wanted a millionaire daddy. What do you think of Ireland for a holiday?'

'Nothing. All those bars they call Select which turn out to be a table and three chairs in half a grocer's shop. And then their screwy attitude to the weather. You step out of your hotel into driving rain and wind and the doorman says, "It's a grand day, sor." In addition I don't like Guinness or John Jameson.'

'Ireland's out then.'

'So take the job. I gave you a good write-up. Honest, reliable, intrepid and the soul of discretion. Quick in a tight corner, resourceful, and a contempt for all hazards.'

'Nice. Add a pair of wings and I'd be Batman. I presume you're talking about Mr Cavan O'Dowda?'

'Didn't I say?'

'No. But don't bother. I don't want any job. I'm going on holiday.'

'You take the job.'

'Which is?'

'Somebody stole one of his cars.'

I laughed. Anyone at Scotland Yard would have done, too. By now it would have been cannibalized – number filed off the engine block and restamped, gear-box changed, number on the chassis plate changed – resprayed and up for auction with a phoney log-book in some car mart, or sitting abandoned around Hackney after a couple of villains had used it for a job.

I said, 'Let the police worry. Not that they will.'

'There's more to it than that. It wasn't stolen in England.'

'Where?'

'Abroad somewhere. He didn't say. And I don't think it's the car he's really worried about, though he pretended it was.'

'I don't want a job. September I always take a holiday.'

'Just go and see him. After all, I said you would, and if I let him down he might take his business from me.'

'I'd weep if I didn't know you were lying.'

'Just see him. If you turn him down, that's okay. But I gave you the build-up of all time. The daughter was there, the Facel Vega one – you should have seen her eyes shining as I painted your picture. Though I must say, I thought you were in better shape than you are. Still . . . '

'Thanks for the drink.' I reached for the door.

'You're going?'

'To have lunch. I've been instructed not to miss it.'

'You disappoint me.'

'I disappoint me, sometimes. But I need a holiday. Sometimes a man has got to get away."

'What for?'

'I'll send you a postcard and let you know.'

I went.

And there it was. A man should always know what he wants to do and, if he can, why he wants to do it. And what I didn't want to do was to chase some stolen car. Let O'Dowda buy another car. And if there was more to it than just a stolen car, well, let someone else worry about it. That's what Scotland Yard, Interpol, the Deuxième Bureau, and the Garda Civile were for. Yes, eleven months of the year I worked, if it was there to work at, but come September, season of mists and mellow fruitfulness, I took a holiday.

But not this September.

At four o'clock that afternoon I was sitting in a Rolls-Royce going like a hot knife through butter along the A 21, heading down into Sussex.

The explanation was very simple and touchingly human. Herrick had the lines for it of course, not only because he had her name right, but because he was a Devonshire man like me and, contrary to the ploughboy school of thought, Devonshire men are great romantics, particularly when as in silks a woman goes and all that about how sweetly flows the liquefaction of her clothes to finish with the real punch line—'O, how that glittering taketh me!'' It took me, in twenty seconds dead.

At two minutes to three I had my heels up on the desk and was reading for light relief the August copy of *The Criminologist* – for some reason the Forensic Publishing Co. Ltd always sent me complimentary copies. I was well into an article on 'The Forensic

Aspects of Dust' when the intercom buzzed like a tired hornet and
Wilkins came on.

'Mr Cavan O'Dowda's car has arrived for you.'

'Send it away.' I switched off.

Analyses of ordinary household dusts, I read, show a fine line-
up of materials like silica, oxides of aluminium and iron, magnesia,
lime, titanium oxide, alkalis—

The buzz came again.

Wilkins said, 'Mr O'Dowda's driver would like to see you.'

'Tell Mr O'Dowda's driver,' I said, 'that I made no appointment
to go to his employer. Tell him – if he's interested in personal details
– that I don't want a job. I want a holiday. Tell him—'

Wilkins cut me off, fearing no doubt some more telling expression.

Three seconds later the door of my office opened. I looked up,
and of course that was fatal. I was hit straight between the eyes.

She looked at me for a moment or two in silence while I blinked
to get the glittering out of my eyes. Then she closed the door and
came slowly across to the desk. It was pure liquefaction with even
a little sweet disorder in the dress. Not much, just a hint of it. It
was a grey silk dress shot with tiny gold and silver threads that
helped to roll the light over each moving swing and curve and
stretch. If you can imagine a dress that might have been made out
of water with gold and silver sun-ripples on it then I needn't say
more. There was a jaunty little bow at the lowish vee of the neck,
like some butterfly poised for flight. If it took off, I thought, it would
kindle in her clothes a wantonness.

She said, 'What is all this? I've come all the way up to London
for you.'

With an effort I said, 'If you're Mr O'Dowda's chauffeur, that's
a wonderful uniform you're wearing.'

'Dont be an ass. I'm his daughter, Julia.'

I stood up. I wouldn't have done it for a chauffeur, but a millionaire's daughter was different. And even if she hadn't been a millionaire's daughter I would have done it. She was in her early twenties
and her hair was as dark as a raven's wings and her lips cherry
bright. Her face was tanned, her dark eyes had a what-the-hell look,
and there was a suggestion of stubbornness about the nicely pointed
chin. Her face was beautiful, a bit gipsyish, but full of self-confident
sparkle. Angry or excited, I decided, she would be hard to handle.

She was taller than I, but I didn't mind. You can't have too much of a good thing. I just stood there, quivering finely like a pointer, waiting for the command to flush game.

She said, 'It's a nice dress, isn't it? Jacques Fath.'

I said, 'I can't keep my eyes off it. I'm Rex Carver.'

With a little lift of her eyes for my persisting stupidity, she said, 'I know you are. But you don't come up to the description Miggs gave of you. Sort of blurred around the edges somewhere.'

'Come autumn,' I said, 'I begin to disintegrate a little. My best month is May.'

She looked at her watch – I caught the faint sparkle of a diamond setting – and said, 'I can't wait until then, neither can my father. Are you coming or not?'

'I was thinking,' I mumbled, 'of taking a holiday.'

'You look,' she said, 'as though you could do with one. I'll tell my father you're not available.' She turned for the door.

I went across the room and picked up my weekend case.

'You're bullying me,' I said. 'But I don't mind. For you I would go anywhere.' I gave her a big smile. It was an effort, but I thought it worth it. 'Julia O'Dowda. It's a wonderful name. Wild Irish, a strong Connemara wind whistling through your hair and—'

She moved to the door, saying, 'I'm his stepdaughter. The name's Julia Yunge-Brown. And on the way down you'll sit in the back. I don't like a hand on my knee as I drive. Okay?' The dark eyes, faintly smiling, fixed me.

'Okay,' I said.

Obediently I followed her through into the office. Wilkins looked up at me woodenly.

I said, 'The next time you use the word "driver" over the phone, qualify the sex. I'm being led into captivity.'

Julia, ahead of me, giggled. It was a nice sound, like a fast brook tumbling over stones.

Wilkins said, 'I'll phone Mrs Meld to say you won't be back tonight.'

It wasn't the Facel Vega, but a big black Rolls, looking a bit like a hearse and as quiet in the back as a funeral parlour. Clipped into a silver holder alongside me was a speaking horn.

Going over Westminster Bridge, I whistled down it and then said, 'What happened to the regular chauffeur?'

Horn to my ear, I got the reply: 'Tich? He's gone fishing with my father. Stepfather.'

I said, 'What's all this about a stolen car?'

'Something to do with Zelia. She's always messing things up.'

'Zelia?'

You had to be quick with the trumpet thing, but it was fun for a long journey.

'My sister. You'll get all the details.'

'Where are we going?"

'Sussex. Near Sedlescombe. You'll be just in time for the evening rise.'

'Evening what?"

She nipped between a bus and a petrol tanker, and then said, 'Stop talking. There are magazines in the rack in front of you.'

I fiddled for a bit and got the rack down. It held the latest numbers of *Vogue, The Field, Illustrated London News, Playboy and Reveille*. And also a half-empty box of cigars, Bolivar Petit Coronas. I lit one and settled back with *Playboy*.

Once we were clear of London she drove the car as though she wished to God it had wings, half-hoping, maybe, that if she did go fast enough it would take off. Anyone riding in it might not have been able to hear the clock ticking in the silence, but they would have heard my heart going *bump, bump* against the roof of my mouth. I began to regret my hasty impulse. A good-looking gipsy girl walks into your office, wearing a Fath number that would cost more than your cigarette bill for a year, gives you a what-the-hell look and there you are – every good resolution gone, back at work again when you should be on holiday.

I didn't try to keep track of where we were going, but it took us an hour and a half. Finally we turned in through lodge gates, the pillars ornamented with stone greyhounds, each holding a shield. I couldn't see the device on the shields because we went by too quickly. We then did a half mile of drive through parkland. Up ahead I saw the big bulk of a country mansion, but I didn't get a long look at it because we turned off, away from the drive and down a long slope through beech and fir trees with dirty, dank-looking rhododendron growths under them.

We came through the trees and the side drive ended in a wide circular turning space below a high grass bank. Julia swung the car round and stopped. She sat in the driving seat while I got out and went up to her.

'Stimulating drive,' I said. 'Tonic for the nerves. When you get her back in the stables, give her a good rub down and a handful of oats. But don't let her drink for a while. Sometime you can take me out in the Facel Vega and we'll really enjoy ourselves.'

She looked at me thoughtfully, up and down and then down and up, as though I were a piece of antique furniture, a tallboy or something she fancied she might fancy, and then she said, 'You've got something. Just something – but I suspect you're trying too hard with it.''

'Or just out of practice. All I need is a few days' country air. Where's daddy?'

'Daddy is someone you want to be bloody polite with.'

I knew then what it was that had boosted me off my office cushion. She was a border-line girl. Somebody you could go either way with. Get her wrong, rub the knap the reverse way, and you had, not an enemy for life (there's always hope there), but someone who just obliterated you from her memory. But get her right, handle her with the capable, finessing touch of a master, and you had a star-spangled carnival stretching ahead of you. But there wasn't any hope of that unless you were at the top of your form.

I winked at her. 'I've dealt with millionaires before. They handle easily so long as you let them know it's their money you're after. Where is he?'

'Up over the bank. Just ring for him. You can leave your bag. I'll take it up to the house.'

She started the engine.

Before she could move off, I said. 'What is it about step-daddy that you don't like?'

I got it then, full and square for the first time; a cold, dark stare that came from surprise she was not quite able to hide. She put her foot down and the Rolls swung away from me and back into the beech trees.

I lit a cigarette and climbed a flight of stone steps to the top of the grass bank. It was a dam, grassed on this side and faced with concrete slabs on the other. Along the top of it ran a grass walk, mowed tight. Stretching away from it was an artificial lake of about thirty acres. It was fringed with pine woods and backed at the far end by a hill studded with great oaks. On the far bank, away to my left at the end of the dam, was a boat-house and a landing pier that projected twenty yards into the water. Way out in the centre of the lake I could see a rowing boat with two men in it.

I walked along the dam towards the landing pier. A couple of pigeons came over the pines, a pheasant called from somewhere back in the beeches and a flight of duck got up from shallows at the far side of the lake. It was a good spot and, from the state of the damworks, the boat-house and pier, I guessed that it hadn't long been constructed. It must have cost O'Dowda a packet. Nice, I thought, when you couldn't get away to Ireland or Scotland, to have your own fishing on the doorstep.

I made my way past the boat-house on to the pier. A fibre-glass hull with an outboard was tied up alongside. At the end of the pier was a vertical wooden post, rather like a small gallows, with a big brass bell hanging from it. I gave the tongue of the bell a whang or two. The noise rolled out across the water and I sat down, legs dangling over the edge of the pier, to wait for the rowing boat to come in.

The men in the boat took no notice of me, though they must have heard the bell. I sat where I was, content to finish my cigarette. They'd heard. They would come when they were ready. One thing you can't do is to hurry a millionaire. If I took the job, I decided, I'd add 5 per cent for being kept waiting. A water-rat swam leisurely out from under the pier and headed for the iris beds up the bank. A swallow dipped near the dam and made a ring like a trout rising. A hundred feet up a heron went over the pines, legs trailing, unhurried, a real dowager of a bird. There was sun and some cloud, a little ripple on the water from a faint breeze, a perfect day. Out on the lake I caught the sudden shine of sun on wet lines as one of the men false-casted. I didn't mind waiting. It suited my mood. I was almost at peace with the world.

The next moment I was almost right out of it.

Two things happened, simultaneously it seemed to me. First the crack of a rifle, and then the thud of a bullet smacking into the bell-post three inches above my head. A chip of wood flipped by me and curved out over the water. Before it hit the surface I was on my feet, running for the shelter of the boat-house.

CHAPTER 2

'A bright torch, and a casement ope at night, To let the warm Love in.'
(John Keats)

Whoever it was took another shot at me just before I reached the boat-house. The bullet whined overhead, too close for comfort. Angry, frightened and short of breath, I reached the shelter of the side of the boat-house.

I looked back along the pier. The two men were fishing on the lake, not even looking in my direction. There's nothing like a fisherman for being truly absorbed in his sport.

I poked my head round the far side of the boat-house and eyed the near pines. To my surprise a man in jeans and a Windbreaker came out of the cover of the trees and began to run up the side of them. In his hand he carried a rifle.

Sportingly, I gave him fifty yards' start and then went after him, doing a zig-zag along the outer row of pines so that I had cover most of the way. The ground sloped gently upwards and where the pines finished was a five-barred gate.

The man with the rifle vaulted it and stopped to pick something out of the grass near the hedge on the other side. It was a motor scooter. He slung the rifle over his back by the sling. Seeing this, I sprinted. I saw the movement of his right leg as he kicked the engine start.

I reached the gate just as he drove away fast down a rough lane. I leaned on the gate and watched him, making a mental note of the number of the scooter. JN 4839. Twenty yards from me, he twisted his head back over his shoulder to look at me. I gave him a wave and the bastard briefly waved back. His face was coal-black.

I went slowly back to the pier wondering what I had done to incur the wrath of the coloured races. Nothing as far as I knew, recently. As I reached the end of the pier the boat was just pulling in.

It was being rowed by a little jockey of a man with a face like a shrivelled lemon. Round his neck was a pair of field-glasses. This, I guessed, was Tich, the chauffeur. He was in shirt and trousers and had a big cigar clamped into the corner of his mouth and on his head was an old cloth cap stuck about with trout-flies. Sitting in the stern, on a comfortable chair-arrangement which had been fitted, was Cavan O'Dowda.

While they made the last twenty yards I had time to get a good look at him. Standing, I reckoned he would go about six feet six, and he had more than the girth to go with it. He would have had trouble packing himself into any overnight sleeper. When he'd been made there must have been a lot of spare material lying around which they'd decided to get rid of. I put him at somewhere around sixty. He was wearing a light blue siren-suit and gum-boots. His head was pumpkin-shaped and large enough, if it had been one, to take a prize anywhere. So far as I could see he had no neck and his hair was so close-cropped that it looked like a faint powdering of red-brown dust. He was wearing dark Polaroid glasses and had a cigar clamped into the corner of his mouth. His hands were huge, backed with a faint down of ginger hair – but they were good hands, capable and sensitive, as I saw when he began to fish later.

As the boat steadied at the bottom of the pier steps, O'Dowda said, "You Mr Carver?'

'Just.'

He gave no sign of being aware of the irony.

'Get in,' he said.

As I went down the steps, he took off his glasses to rub his eyes and I saw that they were light blue, much too small for his face, and embedded in a puffy setting of fat wrinkles. He was not only the most unwholesome-looking millionaire I'd ever seen, he was the biggest as well.

I settled myself in the bow.

'Take her out again, Kermode.'

Tich began to pull away from the pier and I watched O'Dowda over the back of his head.

'Nice of you to come,' said O'Dowda. 'Good of Miggs to recommend you. He must make a couple of thousand every year out of me. Welcome, of course. Real character, Miggs. Thought we heard a shot back there just now.'

'Two,' I said. 'Somebody using your bell-post or me for target practice. I followed him up to the edge of the wood and he rode away on a scooter.'

The big face showed no surprise.

He just said, 'Kermode,' and nodded at a basket at the chauffeur's feet. Tich stopped rowing, dug in the basket and handed a flask over his shoulder to me. I unscrewed and swallowed. It could have been Courvoisier V.S.O.P. I handed the flask back. Tich took it with one hand and held the other out to me with a cigar in it. I lit up as he began rowing.

'Ever fished?' Irish his name might be but I couldn't hear a spot of accent. It was a big, resonant voice. If anything there was a transatlantic touch to it – Canadian, maybe.

'My father, rest his soul,' I said, 'taught me how to tie a turle knot when I was five."

'And damn right he was. More fish have been lost from a boshed-up half-blood than most people know. Take Kermode's rod."

The rod was at my side, half over the bows. It was a Hardy job and Tich had got a Bloody Butcher on the point and a couple of Invictas as droppers.

I said, 'What have you got in here?'

O'Dowda, beginning to fish, said, 'Rainbow and brown. And a few gillaroo. Know them?'

'No.'

'Irish. Find 'em in Lough Melvin and Erne. They don't do so well.'

I worked out some line, false-casted once or twice to get the feel of the rod – it was a beauty – and then made a cast of about twenty yards. It wasn't bad, considering I hadn't touched a rod for a year. I knew O'Dowda was watching me. O'Dowda, I reckoned, was a man who watched everything and everybody around him.

Tich held us in the wind-drift and we wet-fly-fished down the length of the lake. Halfway down I saw the quick water-bulge out by my flies and the sharp knock of a take. I struck, the line sang, and the rod-tip bowed. I played him for about five minutes and then he came in, tired, flashing his flanks, and Tich put the net under him. It was a rainbow on one of the Invicta droppers. A nice fish, just over two pounds, I guessed. I unhooked him and tapped his nose with the priest. He lay on the boards, the sunlight bringing up boldly the broad carmine band down his side, the bright colour that fades so soon with death. I looked at the bordering pine woods. The black bastard could easily come back.

'Not bad,' said O'Dowda. 'You can have him for dinner. The chef has a way of grilling 'em with a Parmesan cheese flavouring that's out of this world. Not enough to kill the flavour of the fish. Just enough to bring it up. Did you get any kind of look at the man who shot at you?'

'No. Not really. He was away before I was close enough. It has occurred to me, though, that he might come back.'

'He won't.'

'I'm glad to hear it.'

'Anyway, he wasn't after you. He was after me. Just made a target mistake. Badly briefed.'

We were in close to the tree-linked bank now. O'Dowda did a neat switch-cast and dropped his flies just off a clump of lily-pads. A moment later he was into a fish and Tich finally netted a big brown trout for him. Watching O'Dowda, I was wondering how badly briefed a man had to be to mistake me for him. If I took this job, I was thinking, there would have to be substantial danger money.

We fished for an hour. O'Dowda got three brace of brown trout. I got a brown and then hooked something that finally smashed my trace and got away.

'Must have been a big one,' I said.

'You rushed him a bit,' said Kermode.

'Out of practice,' said O'Dowda. Then he slewed his head at me and gave me a Polaroid look. 'Little fish land easy. Big fish . . . well, the time element is in geometric not arithmetic proportion. For big fish, you need time and patience. That's why I'm a million-aire.' He laughed and it was a sound like flood water rising rapidly in an underground tunnel. I didn't like the sound and – I had a strong feeling – I didn't like him.

O'Dowda looked at his watch and gave Kermode a nod. Kermode reached into the hamper at his feet and pulled out a hand micro-phone on a flex. He spoke into it.

'Mr O'Dowda's car. Five minutes.'

He replaced the microphone and we began to row back to the landing stage.

O'Dowda saw me looking at the hamper, and said, 'Time and patience, Mr Carver. And always keep in contact with the outside world. Life is full of sudden emergencies.'

I said nothing. I had no real quarrel with his philosophy. But you had to be a millionaire to be able to afford it.

There was a big navy blue Ford Zephyr station wagon waiting for us in the turning space when we arrived. In the driving seat was a small, neat-looking man of about forty. He had a bristly little toothbrush moustache, large teeth and hard agate-coloured eyes which he kept moist by constant blinking. I wasn't introduced to him but from the conversation I gathered that he was called Durnford and was O'Dowda's secretary.

The only item of conversational interest on the way to the house was O'Dowda saying, 'I want a full report on how that fellow got in, Durnford.'

'It's the public bridle path, sir,' His voice, even to O'Dowda, was clipped, sharp, just as he had been to me on the phone. 'We've got no legal right to close it.'

'Then find some other way.'

That was all. The millionaire's solution. No legal right – then find some other way.

The house was a great square construction of rag stone. You went through a small archway into an inner courtyard that was flagged with great paving stones and lined with a small raised walk, the balustrade of which was marked every few yards by nude classical statues, mostly of women with expressionless faces and large thighs. The entrance hall was small and one entered through mahogany doors which, I later learned, were steel-lined. O'Dowda and I got into a lift, went up two floors and stepped out into a long picture gallery. A manservant was waiting and O'Dowda instructed him to take me to my room. O'Dowda then gave me a nod and disappeared in one direction while I followed the manservant in the other, walking gingerly on the highly polished floor-boards to avoid slipping.

'Dinner,' said the servant as he left me, 'will be in one hour.'

'You'd better leave me a map of the place. Otherwise I'll get lost.'

'It won't be necessary, sir.' He went.

I had a bedroom and a bathroom. From the bedroom window I could see the park. Outside the window was a small balcony, big enough to take a deck-chair. Standing on it, I could see that all the other rooms on this side of the wing had similar balconies.

My Brighton pyjamas and dressing gown had been laid out on the downturned bed. There were cigarettes and a glass, siphon, water-jug, ice and four bottles on a silver tray on top of a low dressing table. The carpet gave little wheezy gasps as I trod on it. There were two water-colours of the fishing lake, and there wasn't a piece of furniture which didn't have the shining, well-kept patina of age. The bathroom was chrome and marble and the toilet flushed with just the hint of a faint sigh. The bath-towel was so big it really needed two men to handle it. I finished my inspection of the luxuries and went back to the silver tray to fix myself a whiskey and soda. Underneath the soda siphon was a little piece of pasteboard with a message in ink on it.

I want to come and talk to you late tonight.
So don't scream when I arrive.
Julia.

I sipped my drink, staring out at the now darkening parkland. Tich Kermode wore field-glasses. He could have seen the man run out of the woods. They would be good glasses and they could have seen as much as I saw. And clearly, from O'Dowda's remark to Durnford, the incident had been reported over the radio to the house. If the two bullets had been meant for O'Dowda then he was being remarkably calm about it. If they were meant for me, then he was being remarkably cavalier about his concern for a guest. But, as he was a millionaire, I suppose he'd long ago given up having a normal person's reaction to abnormal events. Not that that made me any happier. And what the hell did Julia want?

I finished my drink and picked up the telephone by the bed. It was a house-phone and somewhere, probably in some basement office, a girl asked if she could help me. I gave her Miggs's number. She said she'd call me, and I went and got another drink.

Miggs came through in about three minutes. He started his usual jossing act, but I cut through it and he knew at once that it wasn't the time or place. I was willing to bet that every phone call that went out of the house was monitored, or would be for a guest of my standing.

I said, 'See if you can get me a line on a motor scooter, don't know the make, number JN 4839. Gubby at the Yard will do it for you, and you can let Wilkins know.'

'Okay. Will do.'

I put the phone down, and went through for a bath. The cabinet held a wide range of bath essences. I chose Floris, No. 89, and soaked for half an hour.

He was wearing a green smoking jacket, a loose white silk shirt open at the neck, tartan trousers and black patent leather slippers. He had a glass of brandy in one hand and a cigar in the other. I sat opposite him, similarly armoured, except that my cigar wasn't as big as his – my choice – and I hadn't been poured – his doing – so much brandy as he had given himself.

The manservant had come for me and escorted me to the dining room, a small private one off his study, where we had dined alone; a clear soup and sherry, the trout, lightly flavoured with Parmesan cheese and a good Mersault, and then fillet of beef, spinach *en branche,* roast potatoes and a claret that was nameless to me, out of the decanter, but which was so good that we had finished it between us. Overall he ate and drank twice as much as me, but I suppose given his size it was reasonable. Apart from that it was evident that he enjoyed the delights of the board for their own sake. In fact, I was sure that he was a man who enjoyed most of the world's delights for their own sake, which, of course, would make him dangerous if anyone got in the way of his getting what he wanted. Through dinner he had talked of fishing and his various houses. I didn't have to say anything. I just listened, and wondered when he would get around to business. Okay, he had this house, a London house, another in Cannes, a château just outside Evian, a flat in Paris, the fishing rights on an Irish river, the shooting over a few thousand acres of Scotland – oh, and an estate in the Bahamas where he went for the golf and big-game fishing – and, boy, wasn't it good to be alive and have all that. Not that he said that, but it was there. Naturally, as the claret mellowed me, I felt jealous. Why not? I've got nothing against wealth. I would have settled for a third of what he had and been happy for life. Not that I wasn't happy as I was, but a little more cash to go with it would have taken the greyness out of Monday mornings. I should add that somewhere in the catalogue he mentioned that he had six cars in the garage at this place, and quite a few in other places – so why was he concerned about the loss of a Mercedes 250SL? To him that was like losing a bicycle.

He fixed me now with his tiny, fat-set blue eyes, all comfortable in his chair, his tarten trews wrinkled up a little to show two inches of big, pale leg above his wrinkled black silk socks, and said, 'You don't seem to be in any hurry to talk business?'

I said, 'I haven't got any business with you. You have business with me. If it's urgent you'd have got it off your chest on the lake.'

He considered this to see whether he liked it then decided he had
no feeling either way, and said, 'Miggs gave you a good write-up.'

I said, 'That's what friends are for. But sometimes they
exaggerate.'

'How much do you make a year?'

It's funny. They can't keep away from it.

'Less than you spend on fishing and shooting – but if you're
going to be a client I'm hoping this is going to be a big year.'

He considered that, too, fractionally, before he laughed. Then,
rather surprisingly, he said in a friendly voice, 'You've got the
usual conventional idea about millionaires, haven't you? And you've
picked one of the two conventional responses. Truculent, to-hell-
with-you. The other is an anxious subservience. I get tired of both.
Why not just be natural?'

'You're asking for the impossible. But I apologise if I sound
truculent. Why not just tell me what the job is and let me get on
with it – if I take it.'

'You'll take it – otherwise you wouldn't be here. Anyway, the job
is simple. I've lost a motor car. To be exact a Mercedes-Benz
250SL. The registration is 828 Z-9626. It's red, hard-top, 1966
model . . .'

As he was talking I was thinking that I wouldn't have minded
one myself. They sold in England at around three thousand pounds
. . . elegant, distinctive lines, a car designed for zestful driving,
modern without being tied to short-lived fashion, bold design and
technical perfection . . . I could hear Miggs giving that patter if he
were trying to sell one.

'It was lost, somewhere between Evian and Cannes. My stepdaughter Zelia was driving it. This was two weeks ago.'

He paused and blew a cloud of cigar smoke.

'You notified the police?'

'Yes. But I have no faith in them. They have their hands full of
other stuff. They'll be content to wait until it turns up – or if it
doesn't, well . . .'

He shrugged his shoulders.

'If it doesn't, will it break your heart? You're insured against
theft, I presume?'

'Yes.'

'Then why do you particularly want this car back?'

'Let's say I do. I don't like losing things. I want it back and I
want to know who's had it and where it has been. Every detail.'

We faced one another across almost immobile layers of cigar smoke.

I said, 'You want more than that.'

He smiled at me, cradling the brandy-glass in his big palms.

'Could be.'

'You want something that was in it.'

'Obviously.'

'Hidden in it?'

'Yes. Miggs was right about you.'

'Forget Miggs. A child could read the message. Did your daughter know that something was hidden in it?'

'No.'

'Does she now?'

'No.'

'Or your other daughter?'

'No. And I don't wish it to be known to either of them. Not that it concerns them in any way.'

'And am I to know what is hidden in it?'

'Not unless it becomes absolutely essential for the recovery of the car. Now ask the other question, Mr Carver.

'Which is?'

'Is whatever is in it something illegal, something prohibited by law, say, drugs, gold bullion, diamonds and so on.'

'Well?'

'It is nothing that would interest the police at all. Something purely private. Let's just say papers.'

'Did you inform the police of these hidden papers?'

'No.'

'Why not?'

'Because, admirable though police organizations are, if they knew I wanted the car because of the hidden papers in it, then the fact might leak out in their enquiries – and I don't want it to be known that I don't care a damn about the car, but only what is in it. The fewer people who know, the better. More brandy?'

I shook my head. He refilled his glass.

'Where,' I asked, 'did all this happen?'

'Some place on the way down to Cannes. Durnford will give you what details he has. But to get the full facts you will have to see Zelia. I'm hoping that you will get more out of her than I have been able to.'

'Why do you say that?'

'Although I'm very fond of her, she is very unsympathetic towards me. But the fact is that she stayed at a hotel on the way to Cannes. Next day she drove off. . . . Forty-eight hours later she turned up at Cannes without the car.'

'And what was her story?'

'She hasn't got one.'

'She's got a tongue. She's got to have a story.'

'Not Zelia. Her memory is a complete blank for those forty-eight hours.'

'You believe this?'

'I've had her examined by two of the best amnesia specialists in France. They confirm that she is suffering from loss of memory.'

'People sometimes forget because the truth is too unpleasant to remember.'

'Exactly.'

'And why would you think she'd open up for me?'

'I don't know that she will. In that case your job is so much harder. But if she hasn't lost her memory, then she might let something slip that will help. I want the car back. I want you to get it. I think you're the man to do it.'

'Because Miggs recommended me?'

'Originally, yes. Since then I've made other enquiries. They confirm Miggs entirely. You have weaknesses – some of which I share, I may say – but if you take a job you don't go back on it. Correct?'

'If the money is right.'

'You can write your own terms. See Durnford about that. You have *carte blanche* for all expenses while you work for me. Everything. That includes any temporary relaxation or pleasure calculated to keep you going in full trim on this job. Over and above all, I'll add a bonus of one thousand pounds if you find the car and the papers.'

'Even though they may not now be in the car?'

'Quite so. But I think they are. No one could find them accidentally.'

I said, 'Why travel important papers in a car driven by your daughter who knew nothing about them?'

He smiled. 'Because they were important.'

'You could have mailed them from Evian to Cannes, registered.'

His smile broadened. 'Come, Mr Carver. Don't tell me you've never heard of mail being lost in transit?'

'And a car can be stolen.'

'Life is full of uncertainties. Can you think of a foolproof way of moving a valuable object from one point to another?'

'No. Not if somebody else wants that valuable object or bunch of papers.'

'Exactly.'

I stood up.

'How many people knew that you were going to ask me down here?'

He stood up too.

'Myself, Julia, Tich Kermode, Durnford, some of the household staff, and Miggs, of course. And the two or three people from whom I made enquiries about you. Why?'

'Because I have a feeling that those two bullets today were meant for me.'

'I assure you they weren't.'

'Why are you so sure?'

'Because in the last month I have had three telephone calls, threatening my life. And this evening, just after we got back, there was another. It was a man. If I remember the phrasing correctly it went: *You were lucky today. But I'll get you, you bastard.*'

He gave me a fat smile. He could have been lying, of course.

'You don't seem worried.'

'I may not show it, Mr Carver, but I am. I like living. But anyway, the attempt on my life has nothing to do with this business. Do you want to see Durnford now, or in the morning?'

I looked at my watch. It was past twelve.

'He'll be in bed.'

'I can always get him up.'

Sure, if you're a millionaire what does another man's sleep mean? But I didn't feel like dealing with those blinking agate eyes tonight.

'The morning will do.'

'All right. And before you leave, get a list from Durnford of my movements during the next week or so. I want you to report progress to me as often as you can.' He drained his brandy-glass and winked at me. 'I'm a big man, Mr Carver. I've got big appetites. I like life and I'm prepared to like people. But I'm a millionaire. Nobody really likes me.'

'I shouldn't think that thought keeps you awake at night.'

For the first time using a thick Irish accent, he said, 'You're bloody right, boyo.'

The moment my head hit the pillow I was away. It was two hours later when I woke. I lay there for a while trying to place myself and wondering what had wakened me. Then there came a flicker of torchlight on the balcony outside my open window. It flicked off and, against the pale night sky, I saw a shape move to the window and into the room. Almost immediately I heard the quick scrape of a chair. A woman's voice said, 'Damn the blasted thing.'

I remembered Julia's note, sat up in bed and switched on the bedside light.

She was standing just in the room, one hand on the back of a chair, the other stretched down to rub her left ankle. She was in a short evening dress and her dark hair was ruffled.

She looked at me crossly and said, 'You knew I was coming. Why did you leave that damned chair there?'

'It was there when I came. What was the balcony crossing like tonight, rough?'

'Keep your voice down.'

She turned and pulled the curtains across the window. Then she came and sat on the end of the bed. Even with my eyes still full of sleep she looked good. She curled up her left leg and went on rubbing her ankle. It was a nice leg.

I said, 'Can I do that for you?'

'You stay where you are.'

I said, ' "A bright torch, and a casement ope at night, to let the warm Love in." '

'What the hell's that?'

'Keats. I've got a weakness for him and quite a few others. And when I'm embarrassed I always fall back on poetry.'

'Just fall back on your pillow and don't move.'

I did, and lit a cigarette, then tossed the packet and lighter down to her.

It was a pleasure just to look at her. The thing she had which had hit me in the office was still there, and I knew there was no fighting against it. She was in the *grand luxe* class compared with most other girls I had known – ones who had merited a detour only; but this one, if I could find the energy, was well worth a special journey.

As she lit up I said, 'Why this secret, nocturnal visit?'

'You don't know this house. It's like a prison. Modern. Every security device. Walk down a corridor and a television eye or whatever picks you up. Open a door and a red light flicks on in the basement ops room. Nobody can get above the ground floor at night without a special lift key.'

'Millionaires have feudal habits. You wouldn't be a damsel in distress, would you?'

'I want to talk to you – sensibly.'

'Go ahead.'

'Why did you ask what it was about step-daddy that I didn't like?'

'I was just making conversation.'

'Liar.'

'What have you got against him?'

'Nothing. He's generous and kind.'

'Well, that's that. Can I go back to sleep now?'

She went over to the dresser and got herself an ashtray and then settled on the end of the bed, legs curled up underneath her.

'Why,' she asked, 'is he so keen to get his Mercedes back? He's insured – and God knows, we've got enough cars.'

'He wants it back. That's enough for me – so long as he pays the rate for the job.'

She stretched one leg out, and wiggled her toes inside the nylon.

'Meaning you don't intend to discuss the matter in detail?'

'Yes.'

'Because he asked you not to?'

To change the subject, and still far from sure why she had made this visit, I said, 'Tell me about Zelia.'

'Why?'

'I'm going to see her. I want to get details of how and where and, maybe, why she lost the car. So far, I'm told, she hasn't come across with much. Loss of memory, she says.'

'That's right. She's had treatment for it, but it hasn't helped.'

'It never does if people don't want to remember.'

'Why the devil do you say that?' There was a high-voltage flash of anger in her eyes.

'It was just a kind of general observation. Is she younger than you?'

'Almost two years.'

'What about your mother – can't she get anything out of her?'

'Mother died a few years ago.'

'I see. You're fond of Zelia, aren't you?'

'Of course I am. She's my sister.' There was no doubting her sincerity. On the other hand, there was no doubting the fierce, almost passionate, protective feeling that was coming from her as she talked about her sister.

I said, 'Before we get to the real reason for your coming here, do you think you could answer a few questions about Zelia and so on without biting my head off if I touch you on a sore spot?'

She gave me an obstinate little look, then softened it and said, 'I'll try.'

'Good. You know Zelia well, you're very close to her?'

'Yes.'

'She lost this car and her memory. Do you think she really knows what happened but is clamming up just to annoy O'Dowda . . . say, to get back at him for something?'

I wasn't there, but I was near it. I could tell from the movement of her body, the lift of her chin, as she considered it.

'Neither of us get on too well with our stepfather, but I'm sure that's not the reason. She really has lost her memory and. . . . All right, I'll admit it – I don't think she wants to remember.'

I could have gone in straight away from there but I didn't think it was wise because I knew that once I did I might not get any more from her – and there was a lot more I wanted if eventually I was going to get my hands on O'Dowda's thousand-pound bonus. Mercenary, but there it is. I was in business for money.

I said, 'How many times has O'Dowda been married?'

'Twice. He married his first wife in 1926. They had a son. She died ten years later.'

'The son was the one killed alongside Miggs?'

She nodded. 'He was nineteen. He got into the army early by faking his age. I think he was the only person that O'Dowda really loved.'

I made no open comment that she, too, had now called him O'Dowda.

'After that?'

'He married my mother in 1955. She was a widow. Zelia was twelve and I was fourteen at the time.'

She looked at me, waiting for my next question. I didn't put it. I just contented myself with looking. She sat there, her dark hair a little disordered, gipsy eyes deep and large, and posed in a way that would have made a Goya want to strip and paint her, and I knew that she was reluctant to come to the real point of her visit.

I said, 'What kind of social life does Zelia have? I mean, is she a friendly, out-putting type? Does she get on well with men? Lots of friends?'

She shook her head. 'She keeps herself to herself. She's very lovely, but men don't interest her.'

I said,'Then what's the problem? What are you doing here?'

She frowned. 'I don't get you.'

'Oh, yes you do – you've been making the signals for a long time. Maybe you don't want to put it in words. You'd like it to come from me, perhaps. Look, she's mislaid a car. It could have been stolen from her. She could have sold it. . . . Oh, there are lots of things that could have happened. But none of them would have inhibited her from telling O'Dowda about it – except one. And that one thing would have to be something to do with Zelia, something that happened to *her* that she doesn't want anyone to know about. Not even you – though I've an idea you can guess at it. Right?'

'How can you possibly know that?'

I shrugged. 'I've been digging dirt professionally for a long time. I know the form. Millionaires' daughters don't have anything to worry about. Money can fix anything. Except one – their personal pride, shame, anguish, or whatever. So what is it you want to ask me to do?'

She was silent for a while, and then she said, 'I think, maybe, I was wrong about you. I don't see how you could have known all this, but you do. Yes, there is something I want you to do. That's why I'm here and why I came this way. I wouldn't want him to know. For Zelia's sake, I just want you to say you can't do this job. I just want her left alone. This job doesn't matter to you. You can get another. But I don't want Zelia hurt—'

'And particularly you don't want me to find out what happened and hand the information on to O'Dowda.'

'Of course I don't. It would kill Zelia.'

I lit myself another cigarette.

'You'd even pay me something for chucking the job in?'

'Of course. That's what you're interested in, isn't it? Money.'

'Show me someone who isn't. But I'm also interested in logic.'

'What do you mean?'

'If I kick this job in, then O'Dowda will hire someone else. When he wants something he gets it, doesn't he?'

'If money could buy it, he'd organize the weather the way he wants it, and the crops could go to hell.'

She slid off the bed with an angry movement, and began to grope for her shoes.

'Then you'd have someone else to deal with. O'Dowda wants that car. You might find yourself landed with someone who lacked my sense of discretion. Someone who wouldn't care a damn about Zelia. Might even get a big laugh from it all.'

'You're just saying that you're not going to give up a good job.'

'Could be. And it's no good you being indignant about it. I'm going to find his car for him. That means I may have to find out about Zelia's missing forty-eight hours. But it doesn't mean I have to tell anyone else about it. Not you, not O'Dowda. My contract is to find the car. The small print at the bottom of the form has a clause which says that I don't have to supply details of all my operations or betray any confidential information or sources. That suit you?'

She looked down at me, worked up, not sure whether to let it all slide and ignore me, or give me a blasting. Not because she had so much against me, but because she was worrying about Zelia, as maybe she had always worried about her, fighting for her, as maybe she had always fought her battles, and yet wanting to clear the load of her emotions with a first-class row with someone so that she would feel better afterwards.

'I don't have much choice, do I?'

'As a matter of fact, you do. I pointed it out to you just now – and you can make it. Either you settle for me, or for the next chap that comes along to take my place. Well?'

From somewhere outside a little owl screeched, and I kept an Indian expression of graven nothingness on my face while the night breeze flapped the curtains and this gorgeous wind-on-the-heath girl looked down at me as though she couldn't make up her mind which dagger to stick in my heart.

Then she said, 'You do anything to hurt Zelia, and I'll make it my business to find some way of hurting you.'

I gave her a big, boyish grin. 'Fair enough. And thanks for the vote of confidence.'

She moved to the window, picking up her torch. I liked the way she moved. In fact, I liked the way she did everything, even when she got angry with me, but from a personal point of view I couldn't kid myself that I had made a good start with her. Which was a pity, because not for a long time had I met anyone with whom I would have preferred to make a good start.

From the window, she said, 'Do you mind switching off the light?' Her hand was on the curtain, ready to draw it. 'Why?'

'Because there are two men who take it in turns to patrol the grounds at night. I don't want an audience for my balcony scramble.'

I switched off the bedside light, heard the curtain sing back, felt the fresh night air billow into the room, and saw her shape slide across the long rectangle of pale night sky. I lay back then and thought about millionaires, about how ready O'Dowda had been to haul Durnford out of bed after midnight, how he had poured himself a bigger brandy than the one he had given me, about the dozen or so cars and almost as many houses, about the purple grouse moors and the peaty Irish loughs and the public right of way to the lake which had to be stopped up somehow . . . and I thought how wholesome it would be to be a millionaire and not to have to go digging around in other people's dirt but to have minions ready at hand to clear up your own. And then I thought of Zelia who didn't have any time for men. That hadn't pleased old Mother Nature and I was prepared to bet that, as usual, she had chosen an awkward moment to do something about it. And then I went to sleep and dreamt of walking over MacGillicuddy's Reeks with Julia, wind and rain in our faces, and the same song in both our hearts. At least my dreams never let me down.

Breakfast was brought to me in bed by the manservant. I rolled over and sat up to find tomato juice, two poached eggs on toast, a pot of coffee, marmalade and all the trimmings under my bleary eyes.

The manservant said, 'Good morning, sir.'

I said, 'I don't think so.'

He just looked at me, puzzled.

I said, 'I've never known a good morning which began at six-thirty.'

Pompously, as though he were reading out a club rule which every member should have had at heart, he said, 'Mr O'Dowda, sir, believes in early rising. Breakfast is always served between half-past six and seven.'

I lay back and nodded at the tray. 'Take that away and bring it back at a quarter to eight. And I'd like boiled eggs, not poached. Two and a half minutes. And if Mr O'Dowda is checking the breakfast programme tell him that because of a professional ulcer I'm under doctor's orders not to rise or eat before seven-forty-five.'

I rolled over and went into a light sleep filled with unpleasant dreams about millionaires.

I got my boiled eggs on the dot.

And I was in the secretary's office just after nine. Durnford looked bad-tempered. He had probably already done a full day's work. I did my best not to look at him much because it was still too early in the morning for me to face those blinking cold agate eyes, the big teeth and the nicotine-stained wisp of moustache. If I did my best not to look at him, he did a much better best of not wasting time on me. I didn't know it then, of course, though he might have done, but time wasn't going to improve our relationship. We both knew quite instinctively that we were never going to like one another, which in many ways was a good thing. We knew exactly how we stood with one another, and weren't going to waste time over any damned nonsense about brotherly love.

He quibled over my terms and I stuck fast. He gave way.

He gave me a list of O'Dowda's movements, addresses, and so on for the next two weeks and against two of them he had made a red asterisk. They were the names of hotels, and at these, if I wanted him, I was to make personal or telephone contact before eight at night. After that hour on no account was he to be disturbed.

I said, 'Why?'

Durnford just ignored the question.

He gave me an itinerary of Zelia's movements with the Mercedes from Evian, so far as they knew it, and her present location which was on O'Dowda's yacht at Cannes.

I said, 'Do you really think she has lost her memory?'

Stiffly, he said, 'If Miss Zelia says she has, then she has. I have never had occasion to doubt her word.'

'That's good to hear. By the way – how does she get on with her stepfather?'

He considered this, then said curtly, 'Not well.'

I said, 'How did her mother get on with him?'

Something moved in him, briefly but violently, and I couldn't miss the quick tremor of control as he held it back.

'I don't see the relevance of that question. You're being hired to find a car.'

'Which includes finding a reason for Miss Zelia's loss of memory, which might arise from a lot of things. However, let's stick to the car if you don't care to discuss O'Dowda's marital relationships.'

'I don't,' he said.

He then gave me details of the Mercedes and a colour photograph of it, and a list of banks abroad which were being informed of my credentials and on whom I could call for cash. He then stood up to indicate that he was finished with me. Although I had been going to ask him some questions about O'Dowda, about his business interests and so on, I decided not to. I could get them elsewhere. So I stood up and made for the door which he showed no signs of opening for me.

From the door I said, 'What are you going to do about that public footpath?'

For the first time, and not because he was warming to me I'm sure, he showed signs of being human.

'If you think, Mr Carver, that working for a man like Mr O'Dowda is a picnic, get it out of your mind. He expects results.'

'No matter how?'

He blinked his eyes rapidly as though I had suddenly let in too much light, and said, 'Usually, yes.' He looked at his watch. 'Kermode is waiting to take you to the station. You should get the ten-ten easily.'

I half-opened the door.

'Kermode,' I said, 'will run me up to London. Otherwise the job's off. Yes, or no?'

It took him some time, and I was damned sure that the station ploy had been his idea. When you work for a millionaire it's therapeutic sometimes to pass a few of the bitchinesses off on to somebody else.

He said, 'In that case, yes.'

Kermode drove me to London in the Ford station wagon. I sat alongside him and he talked fishing, horses, shooting, women and politics all the way. Of the lot he talked fishing most, and never once said a word about O'Dowda which was other than respectful and admiring. Tich Kermode was O'Dowda's man right down to the tip of the O'Dowda cigar he smoked.

I got into the office just before twelve. I had to use my key because Wilkins was out. I didn't know where. The note in her typewriter said, *Back after lunch.*

On my desk was a quarter-sheet of paper with a typewritten message from her.

1. Message from Miggs, nine-thirty. Following information received by him from Guffy (Yard). Owner motor scooter JN 4839. Joseph Bavana. West African. Flat Two, Marshcroft Villa, Fentiman Road, S.W.8.
2. Message from Miggs, ten-thirty. Guffy reports Sussex Constabulary report. Joseph Bavana, driving motor scooter JN 4839, hit by unknown car, Uckfield-Forest Row road, 1800 hrs yesterday. No witnesses. Bavana dead when found.
3. Message from Guffy, eleven-thirty. Please call him.

I sat back and stared at the sheet. Joseph Bavana, West African. To block a public footpath could take time, even for a millionaire. But to wipe out a human being, that was easy – if you were an O'Dowda, and had two or three private guards around the estate. You just sat working a mallard and claret along the edge of the weeds for a brown trout while Kermode passed your instructions over the radio-telephone. Durnford's eye-blinking rate must have gone up as he listened to them.

The telephone rang on the outside line.

'Carver here.'

'And it's Guffy here, dear boy. Don't bother to come round here. I'll be with you in five minutes.'

He rang off, and I stared into space. It was a thing I frequently did. You just stare into it and after a little while you find yourself thinking about absolutely nothing at all, which is, while it lasts, comforting.

CHAPTER 3

'Youk'n hide de fier, but w'at you gwine do wid de smoke?'
(Joel Chandler Harris)

Guffy was for Gerald Ulster Foley. As far as anyone at the Yard could be called a near friend of mine, he was the nearest, and even that did not put us too close. However, he was – no matter how hard pressed or frustrated by any dealings with me – always pleasant and well mannered. It's nice to know someone who would put you under the lights and grill you, smiling, and murmuring apologies all the time.

Officially he was a Detective Superintendent in 'C' Department, earning around two thousand five hundred pounds a year. With his qualifications and abilities he could have got ten times that in industry – but not half the excitement and fun, I imagine. And Guffy liked excitement and variety. Just the thought of it narrowed his greeny-yellow tabby-cat eyes and made him purr. He had a lean, alley-cat look, and if his ears weren't torn and his face scarred from fights with other toms, it was because he knew how to look after himself in a scrap as well as almost any man I knew. No one that I knew at the Yard ever had cared to outline what his specific duties were. But I did know that he had done a two-year stint at No. 26, Rue Arnengaud, Saint Cloud, Paris, France, and, for all I knew, still did work for Interpol.

He sat across the desk from me, smoking one of his usual Dutch Schimmelpennincks, smiling, and looking as though he was going to believe every word I said, and in return would be equally trusting with me.

Very carefully I was outlining my interest in the defunct Joseph Bavana. I told him the whole story of my visit to O'Dowda, except that I did not mention the nature of the assignment which my client had given me, nor anything about Julia's midnight heart-to-heart talk. Also, I omitted to mention the field-glasses or the two-way radio in the row-boat on the lake. O'Dowda might have had Bavana killed, or it might have been an accident. If it hadn't been an accident, then O'Dowda was doing his warm-hearted best either to protect me or himself. Either way ethics and common sense dictated that I shouldn't indulge in speculation with a man like Guffy until my arm was forced.

When I had finished, he said affably, 'A good synopsis of the whole affair. Taut, dear chap, crisp, omitting all the relevant facts. Such as, for example, the nature of your commission for O'Dowda.'

'He wants me to find something for him. A straightforward recovery job. You feel inclined to press me on that?'

'Not immediately. Perhaps never at all. Why would you think Bavana would want to shoot you or O'Dowda?'

'No idea. Tell me about Bavana.'

'Willingly. The rifle he used was found, dismantled and packed away in one of the carriers of the scooter. He was a student over here. Not London University, but a business college. Prior to that he'd done a course in computer management. None of it meant anything. Just a cover for political activities. Any idea how many African political groups operate from London at the moment?'

'No.'

'Far more than there ever were of *émigré* Poles, Russians and all the other run-of-the-mill Europeans. Every time you move you trip over them. Fifty per cent of them are as innocuous as a Band of Hope society. Of the rest, some are intelligence organizations for African states and some are exile organizations wanting to get back into the great wind-of-change game that's going on. Some of them are operated by idealists, but most of them by chisellers. Some of their activities would make you laugh and some would make you cry – and some would curdle your blood. Overall they're a nuisance, but we have to keep an eye on them. I was naturally curious about your interest in Joseph Bavana. He was one of the blood-curdlers, a paid killer.'

'Paid by whom?'

'I don't know. That's why I'm talking to you, old boy.' He stood up. 'Logically – and I've no doubt you've got there before me – if it were you he had wanted to kill, then it must have been because someone didn't want you to carry out O'Dowda's commission for the recovery of whatever it is.'

'O'Dowda says it was a mistake. They wanted him.'

'Could be, could be. And between ourselves, old boy, I wouldn't have shed a tear. But that's off the record.'

'So what,' I said, 'are you doing here?'

He looked genuinely surprised. 'Why, just having a chat. Haven't seen you for ages. Always enjoy talking to you.'

I stood up, too, as he moved to the door.

'It hasn't occurred to you, of course, that O'Dowda might have had Bavana bumped off?'

'I'm sure he did.' He gave me a charming, disarming smile. 'And just as we can never finger the big boys behind the gold-smuggling rackets through London, Beirut and Calcutta, say, though we know them – the same applies to O'Dowda. They give orders, but the chain of command downwards is as thin and elusive as a thread of the finest gossamer.'

'Poetic.'

'Not at all, old chap. Gossamer comes from goose-summer, that's early November, when spiders' webs are most seen, and when geese are eaten. And it's always the foolish geese that get eaten. Nice parable there, somewhere.'

'In a minute you'll have me off *pâté de foie gras* for life.'

'Not you.'

I opened the door for him.

I said, 'Has O'Dowda got a record at the Yard or with Interpol?'

I saw the cat's eyes narrow, and I knew damned well that he had not come here for nothing, certainly not for a cosy chat.

'None at all. He's a respectable millionaire. All we know about him, you could read in *Who's Who* – well, almost all.'

'And you want nothing from me?'

'You sound like a guilty bloke that's been called in for questioning and is surprised to find that he's being let go, old boy.'

'I am. You don't waste your time like this normally.'

'Wish I could oblige you. But we don't want anything from you. Of course, that's not to say that if in the run of your work you came across anything which you felt was a serious police matter, well you might let me know. Or, since you will be abroad chasing this car, give Commissaire Maziol a ring at Interpol.'

'How did you know it was a car?'

'My dear old chap, Miggs said so. Just let us know if you come across anything interesting.'

'Like what?'

'Anything that strikes you. We can always do with outside help from the public. Even if it's only an anonymous letter.'

'You've had one about O'Dowda?'

'A little while ago, yes. Can't reveal the contents, naturally.'

'What was the handwriting? Male or female?'

'Couldn't say, old chap. It was typed. Unsigned. Well, keep your eyes open.'

He went.

Sometimes I thought I went a bit too far in keeping things to myself. But I was a novice compared to them. I didn't like the look of this commission at all. Right from the start it had begun to breed complications. Bavana shooting at me, Julia wanting me to chuck it, and now Guffy going away up Northumberland Avenue, laughing his head off and already knowing that he had me where he wanted me but in no hurry to let me know exactly where that was. I should have been firm and have taken my holiday. But it was too late for that.

I went over to the reference bookcase and pulled out a three-year-old copy of *Who's Who* – well, who's going to renew it each year at six quid a time? For wrist exercise I carried it back one-handed, all five pounds of it.

O'Dowda was there. Just. And it was clear that he hadn't cared a damn whether he was there or not.

The entry read:

O'DOWDA, Cavan; Chairman of Athena Holdings Ltd.; *b.* 24 Feb. 1903. *Educ.*: Dublin. Is also Director of number of public companies engaged in commercial and industrial enterprises. *Address:* Athena House, Park Street, Park Lane, W.1. *T.*: Grosvenor 21835.

There was a lot to fill in between the brief lines. And, I was sure, a lot that could never be filled in, otherwise Guffy would never have been round to see me.

I pulled out the almost as brief account, which Durnford had given me, of Zelia's trip from the château near Evian to Cannes.

On Day One she had left the château at two in the afternoon, driving by herself in the red Mercedes. On her own account she had driven south, through Geneva, Frangy and Seyssel, to a hotel on the west side of Lac Le Bourget.

I took the *Who's Who* back and found a Michelin map, 'Routes de France'. It was clear at once that a more normal route would have been to have come down through Annecy, Aix-les-Bains and

Chambéry. But she had explained that. She had plenty of time and wanted to vary her route. She had stayed the night at a hotel called the Ombremont at Le Bourget-du-Lac. From here, around nine at night, she had put in a call to her father at his Sussex country house. O'Dowda hadn't been there and Durnford had taken the call. She had told Durnford that the next day instead of going straight down to Cannes she might break her journey to stay a couple of days with some friends on the way. She hadn't said who the friends were, or where they lived, and Durnford, the perfect secretary, had not asked for information which had not been proffered.

On Day Two she had left the hotel in the morning, before nine-thirty. This had been established because Durnford, like a perfect secretary, had got in touch with O'Dowda who was in London (probably a do-not-disturb-after-eight night somewhere) and O'Dowda had instructed him to phone the hotel and tell Zelia she was to make the trip straight to Cannes without any delays. Durnford made the call at nine-thirty and Zelia had already left. From then on, through Day Two, Day Three, until the morning of Day Four (when Zelia, on her own account, had found herself at Gap, a town on the Route Napoleon, some 160-odd kilometres south from Le Bourget-du-Lac) her life was a blank. In Gap she had been minus the Mercedes, minus her luggage and minus any memory of what had happened to her since she had left the hotel. Life, since leaving the hotel, had become a void. She had the clothes she stood up in, and her handbag with money. She had hired a car and driven to Cannes and the yacht, where O'Dowda had been impatiently waiting for her. No details of the scene on her arrival, or what had happened after, had been given me – except that no one, including Zelia, could think of any friends of hers or the family who lived in the area between Le Bourget-du-Lac and Gap. Betting on probabilities: for my money, Zelia was a liar. For my money, if she wanted to she could give a blow by blow account of every minute of every missing hour. And with O'Dowda's money I'd been engaged to prove it and find the missing car.

I had trouble with Wilkins after lunch. She'd been to the dentist to have a filling renewed. It was a bit difficult to understand her when she spoke because one half of her jaw was still frozen with novocaine.

Following my usual practice, I dictated to her a simple, straight-forward account of what had happened so far for my confidential

files, and I could see that she was taking against the whole affair.
She sat there as though I were dictating the operation order for the
extermination of some mid-European ghetto.

At one stage she said, 'I don't think you should have any more
to do with O'Dowda. This Bavana man obviously was trying to kill
you.'

'For big money risks must be taken. Life is full of hazards.
Anyway, that one's been eliminated.'

I finished the dictating. She closed her notebook and got up to
go. I stopped her.

'What do you think?' I asked.

'About what?'

'Various things. Zelia first.'

'She obviously had some emotional or disturbing experience and
her subconscious mind has decided to force her to forget it. I wonder
it doesn't happen to women more often.'

'Then, if you think Zelia's an innocent mind in traumatic shock
– why shouldn't I go on with the job?'

'Because men like O'Dowda clearly aren't innocent – not when
it comes to things that matter, like business interests and rivalries.
Often there's no way of getting what they want legally. That's the
moment when men like O'Dowda begin to use people. That's why
– almost before you were on his payroll – somebody tried to kill
you. Just write and tell him you have thought the matter over and
regretfully, etcetera, etcetera. There's plenty of straightforward work
waiting for you if you take the trouble to look for it.'

It was about the longest harangue I'd ever had from her. And I
should have taken her advice. Two things stopped me. First, there
was Julia, and her anxiety over Zelia. I'd more or less promised to
handle that for her. And then there was O'Dowda. Something about
his character rubbed me the wrong way. He'd got well and truly
under my skin. I knew that most of it was pure envy. But, at least,
it was pure. I just wanted to show him that here was someone he
couldn't play around with and make dance his way at the flap of
a cheque book. Whatever was in that red car he wanted it badly.
Okay, it was my commission to find that car, and it stopped there.
When I knew what was in the car, and perhaps had it in my hands,
it would be fun to have him dancing for a while as I dangled it in
front of him. Not nice perhaps, but then we all have to have our
moments of power. Also, power meant cash, and that was something
I could always use.

I said, 'I'd like you to book me on a plane to Geneva tomorrow morning and have a self-drive car waiting for me. And then get me a reservation tomorrow night at the Ombremont Hotel, Le Bourget-du-Lac. If you have any trouble about it, use O'Dowda's name hard. It'll work.'

She just looked at me, nodded, and made for the door. As she reached it I said, and God knows what quirk of self-indulgence made me, 'About the hire car. I want a red Mercedes 250SL.'

Hand on the door knob, she jerked her head back at me. 'Why?'

'Because I've never driven one. And red is my favourite colour. Tell them I've got to have it, no matter what it costs.'

'Well, in that case, we must do our best for you, mustn't we?' She went out. It was a long time since I'd known her so icy.

By the time I went home that evening Wilkins had fixed my air travel and had an assurance that there would be a car waiting for me at Geneva and that, if it were at all possible, it would be a red Mercedes.

Home was a small flat – bedroom, sitting room, bathroom and kitchen – in a side street near the Tate Gallery. From the sitting-room window, by risking a crick in the neck, I could get a fair glimpse of the river. Mrs Meld, who lived next door and did for me, had cheerfully been fighting a losing battle against my untidiness for years. She'd put some rust-coloured chrysanthemums in a vase on the window table and propped a note against them, saying, *Left a little something for you in the oven. We're almost out of whiskey.*

The little something was a cottage pie. That meant she was in a good mood. I lit the gas oven to warm up the pie and then went back and fixed myself a whiskey. She was right. There was only three-quarters of a bottle left. I sat down, put my feet up and stared out of the window at the London dusk. Life ought to be good, I thought; a cottage pie – plenty of onion in it – warming in the oven, a glass of whiskey and my feet up, and tomorrow I would be off to foreign parts chasing a stolen motor car. Other chaps my age would be home now, cuffing their kids away from the telly to get on with their homework, hunting for a screwdriver to fix a busted plug lead on the vacuum cleaner, wifey would be in the kitchen opening cans of instant steak-and-kidney pie and rice pudding, and tomorrow would be the same old day for them. Variety is the spice of life. That was for me. Each day different. Never knowing what was coming. Never knowing when you were going to be shot at, or when a beautiful girl would come sliding into your bedroom appealing for help, never knowing when you were being used, lied to, conned or secretly laughed at and despised. A great life. The trouble was that just at that moment I didn't feel up to it. I suddenly felt moody and sour and I wondered what it was a reaction to. Something. I considered digging deep to see if I could find out, then decided against it and had another whiskey.

I'd just settled with it when the flat bell rang. I let it ring two or three times hoping whoever it was would go away. It went on ringing so I got up and went to the door.

Outside was a man in a dark blue suit and bowler hat, umbrella crooked over one arm. He had a fat cheerful face with high arched eyebrows, a squat lump of putty for a nose, lips that somehow reminded me of a duck-billed platypus, and he was wearing a big floral-pattern tie against a pink shirt. Just to top the bizarre appearance his face was coal-black with a sort of underlying purple sheen, and to bottom it he was wearing ginger-coloured suède shoes. The distance between his shoes and the top of his bowler was all of fifty-four inches. With a flash of white from teeth and eyes, he held out a slip of card to me and I could feel the cheerfulness radiating from him like a convector heater.

'Mr Carver, yes?' It was a cheerful singing voice.

I nodded and squinted at the card in the bad hall light. It wasn't easy to read because the whole thing had been done in Gothic type. He must have been used to people having trouble with it because, chuckling as a preamble, he recited to me—

'Mr Jimbo Alakwe, Esquire, Cardew Mansions, Flat Three, Tottenham Court Road, London, West One. Representations. Specialities. Accredited Courier. Imports and Exports.' He paused, and then added, 'A willing heart goes all the way, your sad tires in a mile-o.'

'Where does it say that?'

He reached up and politely turned the card over for me, and there it was printed on the back.

'A splendid sentiment, Mr Alakwe, but I don't want any representations, specialities, imports or exports, and certainly not a courier with a willing heart. Okay?'

He nodded affably. 'Okay.'

I made to shut the door and he moved in and shut it for me.

I said, 'Look, I've got a cottage pie in the oven, and I want a quiet evening. There isn't a speciality in the world you could provide that would shake me from a quiet night at home.'

He nodded, took off his bowler politely, pulled a handkerchief from inside it and gently tapped his face with it, looked at it – to see if any of the black had come off, perhaps – put it back in the bowler and put the bowler on.

'Ten minutes of your time. No more, Mr Carver. And a splendid proposition to put. You will, I think, find it to your advantage. Did I say "think"? No, I know. You need me to help you. Splendid prospects and, believe me, absolutely nothing to pay, man. The contrary.'

'You should sell insurance,' I said to his back as he went into the sitting room.

He looked around the room curiously and said, 'Did that for two years once. In Ghana. Accra, you know. It is considered a U-thing there, you know. But I prefer now more variety. Lovely flowers, dahlias, no? Ah, your autumn is a prolific time for dahlias. I have seen some once, purple with a little white zebra stripe. Most splendid.'

He sat down in my chair and looked, his face wreathed in a rapturous smile, at the whiskey bottle.

I gave up. I could have thrown him out, but it would have been an effort. And against all the *bonhomie* and cheerfulness any resentment would have been churlish. Churlishness and effort, I decided, could be postponed for ten minutes by which time my pie would be ready.

I tipped some whiskey into a glass for him.

'Water or soda, Mr Alakwe?'

'With many thanks, neither.' He took the glass from me, sipped, nodded approval, and said, 'A very nice place you have here. My own flat I share with three others. They are most uncongenial types but useful for business contacts. You have any idea how much I am authorized to offer you?' Big smile, another sip of whiskey, and a fat hand momentarily adjusting and smoothing down the floral tie. It should have had dahlias and chrysanthemums on it, but it didn't.

I sat in the other armchair and just studied him, in silence. The silence puzzled him.

He said, 'I say, Mr Carver, have you any idea how much I am authorized to offer you?'

'And I say, Mr Alakwe, Esquire, that you'd better begin at the

beginning. As a suggestion, in what role are you here? Represen-
tation? Specialities? Import and Export or—'

'I am, Mr Carver, representing.'

'Who?'

He sipped again at the glass. 'Damn fine whiskey. Would I
imagine be a good proprietary brand?' He squinted at the bottle.
'Yes. Very good mark.'

'Who?' I repeated.

'Let us say friends of friends who have friends who have very
delicate susceptibilities towards matters which affect their political,
industrial, commercial and international reputations, etcetera and
etcetera.' He smiled. 'You see I have need to be discreet. So,
naturally—'

I lay back in my chair and shut my eyes. 'Wake me,' I said,
'when you come to the point.'

He laughed.

I opened my eyes.

He winked at me, and said, 'Five hundred pounds?'

I shut my eyes.

'Guineas, Mr Carver. That would be—'

'Five hundred and twenty-five pounds.'

'Ah, then you agree? Good. Very sensible, Mr Carver. And if
you wish for some advice as to investing such a sum, I have a
proposition which would double your money in six months. After
that, another proposition that would double that amount in a
similar time, and so on ad nauseum. In some years you are a
millionaire, thanks to Jimbo Alakwe.'

'Esquire, or Mister?'

I opened my eyes.

He genuinely looked a little crestfallen but it didn't last long, the
thick lips spread, the fine teeth shone, the pudgy nose wrinkled and
the bright eyes spun in their sockets promisingly as though when
they stopped the whole jackpot would come spouting out of his
mouth. In a way, it did.

'One thousand. Not pounds, Mr Carver. Guineas. Which is one
thousand and fifty pounds.'

I stood up and said, 'The only word you've said so far which
makes sense is the word "millionaire". I suggest you take it from
there very quickly.' I moved to the door. 'Not that I want to be
rude – especially to a man of your ebullience. But I want my supper.
Okay?'

'Okay. Ebullience. Splendid word. Yes, that is me. Okay. These friends of friends, etcetera and etcetera, would like you to relinquish your commission with a certain gentleman. Then you get the money. Okay?'

He stood up, and I had no doubt that he thought that it was going to be as simple and painless as that. Only a fool would turn down one thousand guineas.

I held the door open. 'What was their top limit, Mr Alakwe? Surely more than a thousand?'

He said, 'I think I am smelling a good aroma. Your supper, no doubt? The cheque will be sent.'

I shook my head.

'Don't bother. When I take a job I stay with it.'

He was genuinely concerned for me, surprised, no doubt, at my lack of common sense.

'Please, Mr Carver, for your own sake. This is not a situation which calls for any high-mindedness or lofty idealism. Just work and money, Mr Carver. Perhaps one thousand five hundred pounds.'

'No. And don't make it guineas. Just tell them I'm not interested in their money.'

'Absolutely?'

'Absolutely.'

He came by me, as near stunned as he had ever been, I imagine. In the hall he stopped, eyed me, shook his head and said, brightening a little, 'Yes, now I understand. There can only be one explanation. You are eccentric. Very eccentric.'

'Something like that.'

'Well, Mr Carver, all I can say is that it is your privilege to be that. But it is dangerous. These people – you understand, I only act for them – please be polite they say, this man is intelligent, good-mannered and understanding. But these people may now take other action. D for drastic action, Mr Carver.'

'And you would act for them?'

'Well, naturally, if they pay me. One thousand five hundred pounds or guineas – for the first time I meet a sensible chap who says no to it. You know—' hope sprang briefly to life—'it would be arranged, the payment I mean, so that you would not have to pay tax.'

'Goodnight, Mr Alakwe.'

I opened the door for him and he went reluctantly past me and paused on the doormat, carefully scuffing his shoes on it.

'Tell me,' I said, 'in your dealings with these friends of friends, etcetera and etcetera, did you ever come across a countryman of yours called Joseph Bavana?'

'Bavana? Why of course. He is my husband-in-law.'

'Your what?'

'Well, if that is not right . . . I mean, he is married to my second wife. Who now, of course, is a widow. So now, of course, maybe, I shall take her back.'

'You know Bavana's dead? How he died?'

'Of course. I tell them not to use that way first of all. Joseph always was accident prone. This Mr Carver, I tell them from reading their first report, is not a man to deal with like that, but Joseph persuaded them.'

'And what are you going to advise them now?'

'I like you, Mr Carver. You are polite and respectable with me. I shall tell them you ask for five thousand pounds. That gives you a few days to think about it. I know them. They will say, "God man, five thousand – for doing nothing? Offer two thousand five hundred, guineas if necessary." Then I come to you. You accept—' his face began to beam—'and we shall be happy. You should expect me tomorrow. Don't worry, Mr Carver.' He thumped his chest with the handle of his umbrella. 'A willing heart is mine. For a friend I go all the way.' He tipped his bowler and turned away, borne on a euphoric cloud of human kindness.

I went back into the flat to be greeted by the smell of burning from the kitchen.

Mrs Meld woke me with a thump on the door and a few exuberant lines of *Yellow Submarine*. I'd noticed recently that she'd slowly been bringing her repertoire up to date.

'Good morning, Mr Carver. How was the pie?'

'Splendid,' I mumbled, rubbing my eyes.

'What you need,' she said, 'is a woman to look after you – not that you can't cook as well as any woman, but it's the cooking that does it. Time you've done it, as I tell Meld, it puts you right off. And then things like laundry, you never think about them. You going to stay a bachelor all your life?'

I said, 'Go away. I want two eggs, lightly fried, and some bacon, crisp.'

'Ten minutes, then. And I'll fix a nice steak and kidney for tonight.'

I got out of bed. 'Don't bother. Tonight I shall be in France, eating *omble chevalier,* straight from the lake. You know what *omble* is?'

'Well, if it ain't fish, I don't know what it would be doing in a lake. But anyway, that accounts for the spade across the road maybe. He was there when Meld went off at seven. France, is it, and more of your larrikins? You have a nice life, Mr Carver, but you need a good woman to share it with.'

I pulled on a dressing gown and went into the sitting room.

From the kitchen Mrs Meld said, 'He's in the Mini, parked by the letter box.'

From the window I couldn't see much of him, just his bulk behind the wheel and a pair of brown hands spread over the wheel rim. The bulk of his body looked too big to be my friend Jimbo. But I had no doubt that they were connected. While Jimbo Alakwe tried to negotiate new terms for me, they were keeping an eye on me.

At half past nine I dropped my travelling case out of the bathroom window at the back of the flat. Mrs Meld caught it for me from below in her garden, and then I followed, moving into her kitchen, pausing to admire the new washing-up machine that she'd finally persuaded Meld to buy for her, and then through the house and out of her side door which opened into the next street. It was a route that I'd used many times before, so many times in fact that I'd probably established a permanent right of way by now.

I took a taxi to Miggs's place and got him to send a boy up to the office to collect my air tickets and passport. If they were watching the flat they could well be watching the office. I phoned Wilkins and told her what was happening, and then asked her to have someone check at Somerset House and get all they could on Athena Holdings Ltd. Wilkins was in a better mood, and made me run over all I'd packed for my trip to make sure that I hadn't forgotten anything.

She finished, 'You're not taking a firearm?'

'No,' I said, 'I'm not taking a firearm.' Mrs Meld would call a spade a spade, but not Wilkins. 'Why? Do you think I should have a gun?'

'No, I do not. You're much too bad a shot for it to be any use.'

Well, maybe she had something there. But, now and then, they were comforting things to have to hand.

I then phoned Guffy and told him about Mr Jimbo Alakwe,

Esquire. At the moment I considered this a frank, open approach which might be useful.

'If there's anything about him or his employers which you know, which could be helpful to me, I would appreciate it. Let Wilkins know.'

He said he would consider it.

At two o'clock I was in Geneva, and there was a red Mercedes 250SL waiting for me. What it is to work for a millionaire and be able to use his name and credit rating.

I went south like a red streak on the wings of fantasy. I had fishing loughs, grouse moors, town and country houses and reserved suites where I was not to be disturbed after eight. I had a yacht and a handful of cars of which this was my favourite. I daydreamed my way down to Annecy and Aix-les-Bains along a road I knew well. My hands had a millionaire's firm grip on the steering wheel with its large, padded safety boss, and – thanks to the single joint, low-pivot swing axle, the separation of wheel mounting and wheel suspension – the car held the road like a high-speed leech, gentling down the moment I put a foot on the two-circuit servo-assisted disc brakes. Oh, I knew all the jargon. I'd done a year as a car salesman before I had moved into business on my own, chasing other people's troubles and generally ending up with a bag full of them for myself.

Below Aix-les-Bains, at the end of the lake, I swung across country and then up to the west side of the lake. The Ombremont Hotel sat on the hillside above the lake, looking across to Aix. I had a large, bright, chintzy room overlooking the water and when I phoned down for whiskey and Perrier water I got it within five minutes, which was something near a record. For records, it was going to be my lucky day. Within the next two hours I had found out something about Zelia which went a long way to convincing me that she had no more lost her memory than I had lost mine – not that there weren't a lot of things in my past that I would have liked to have forgotten. But there it is, things happen to you and things are done by you which are forever on the record.

Just before dinner I went down to the reception desk and cashed a traveller's cheque with the girl who was on duty. I didn't need the money because I had picked up cash at Geneva, but it was a way of opening a conversation and letting her get a few minutes of my warm, affable, engaging nature before I started on the small deceits and oblique questions which were part of my other, second, nature.

She was a girl of about twenty-plus with a little mole at the right corner of her mouth, a pair of dark, wise eyes that had an occasional flash of humour, and she had time on her hands, for all the evening transients had booked in. Her English was streets ahead of my French. I complimented her on it and asked her where she had learnt it. It worked, of course. It always does. There's nothing people like more than to have it acknowledged how well they speak a foreign language. In no time we'd got to the point where she asked me whether I was in France on holiday or business. I said that I was on business, that I was the private secretary of one Mr Cavan O'Dowda, and I didn't have to tell her who he was. She knew. If you're in the hotel business you probably know all the millionaires and, anyway, the French have this natural reverence for money which makes the names of the world's millionaires as familiar to them as football players are to the differently oriented Anglo-Saxons.

Confidentially, shuffling my franc notes slowly into my wallet, I said that I was making some enquiries about his stepdaughter Mademoiselle Zelia Yunge-Brown who was at this moment suffering from loss of memory which had come on at the moment she had left this hotel some weeks ago. For a moment her dark eyes were sad, at the thought of a millionaire's daughter being so afflicted – every memory must be golden, what unhappiness to lose even one.

I agreed and asked if I could see a copy of Zelia's hotel bill. I didn't think it would give me anything openly to prove a theory which I was nursing, knowing human nature, and that Zelia had been off the direct route down to Cannes. But there was no harm in checking. The girl produced a carbon copy from a file. It was for Room 15 and she had paid for the apartment and breakfast. No dinner charge. Well, she might have eaten out somewhere. I was about to hand it back when I noticed that there was no charge for an item which should have been there.

'While Mademoiselle Zelia was here she put in a call to her father in England, at about nine o'clock in the evening. There's no charge for it.'

The girl agreed that there wasn't a charge.

I said, 'Do you keep a record of phone calls?'

'From the rooms, when they are to be charged, yes.'

'Can you check the long-distance calls that evening? From all the rooms.'

'That would mean checking the copies of the accounts of all the

guests who were here that night.' There was no sadness in her dark
eyes now, just wisdom. A millionaire was fussing about his daughter
and, while anyone in their right mind would be anxious to help, it
would mean extra work.

I said, 'If it will take you a little time, then naturally Monsieur
O'Dowda would wish me to acknowledge that.' I pulled out my
wallet and handed her a hundred-franc note.

She took it with a quick, sensible nod of her head; no one in the
French hotel business is anything but sensible about money. She
said that if Monsieur would look back after dinner, no?

Monsieur went to dinner. There was no *omble*.

I made do with a *terrine de canard aux truffes*, and a *poulet aux
morilles* with a bottle of Château-Rayas.

And, after dinner, the information was waiting for me. The only
phone call to England made from the hotel that night – and it was
just before nine – had come from Room 16 which had been occupied
by a Monsieur Max Ansermoz who had booked in the same evening
and left the following morning.

Not bothering with niceties, I asked, 'Is there a communicating
door between Rooms 15 and 16.'

'Yes, monsieur. Normally it is locked but one would only have
to ask the chambermaid.'

'What address did this Monsieur Ansermoz give?'

She had done her homework. It was a Geneva hotel, the Bernina,
22 Place Cornavin. Instinct told me that it wouldn't be any good
making enquiries for Max Ansermoz there.

Quite genuinely, the girl said, 'I hope this information will not
make trouble for Mademoiselle Zelia.'

'On the contrary. I think it will help her recovery. Her father
will be most grateful to you.'

'It is a pleasure to help, monsieur. If you would wish it, some
of the hotel servants might remember this gentleman. Maybe, by
tomorrow morning, I could tell you what he looked like, no?'

I said I would be grateful for any scrap of information, no matter
what the cost of the trouble, and then I went up to my room and
sat on the little balcony, smoking, and looking across the lake to
the lights of Aix-les-Bains.

So, Zelia had met Monsieur Max Ansermoz at the hotel. It had
been careless of her to put a phone call through from his room, but
then at that time she probably had not realized that there was any
great need for care. Something had happened after leaving the hotel

which had brought dull care on to the scene. After leaving the hotel, somewhere along the line, she had started losing things, her car, her luggage, her memory, and who knew what else . . . my guess was that Max Ansermoz knew. It would be interesting to know what Zelia's present feelings towards him were. It would be even more interesting – for this was my particular baby – to know what he had done with the red Mercedes.

I went back into the room, picked up the phone and booked a call to Paris 408.8230. It came through about twenty minutes later and I was put on to a duty officer, sitting bored miles away in 26 Rue Arnengaud, Saint Cloud, who was distinctly cagey about the call. I told him he could check my credentials with Commissaire Maziol or Detective Chief Superintendent Gerald Ulster Foley, but either way I would like any information Interpol was prepared to pass on about one Max Ansermoz, if he were on their files; either here if before nine in the morning or to my office in London if later. Reluctantly he said he would see what could be done and then rang off, no doubt to go back to reading his *Paris-Match*.

I didn't get my call before nine, but for twenty francs extra I had a description of Ansermoz. The hall porter remembered him well, a tall, dark gentleman between thirty and forty who had arrived with a young lady in a red Mercedes and had departed with her in the car the following morning – and he'd had with him a dog, a white poodle. He was a very nice, pleasant gentleman and was French, or at least he thought so, but, of course, he might well have been Swiss.

I tipped and thanked him, and then headed south down the Route Napoleon.

I reached Cannes late, largely because I had stopped for a very leisurely lunch and put a call in to Wilkins afterwards, which had taken over half an hour to come through.

She had had a message for me, through Guffy from Interpol. There was no one of the name Max Ansermoz on their records, but he might easily be there under another name. Would I please supply a description if possible and any other details which might be helpful. I passed the description, the name of the Geneva hotel and the fact that he probably owned a small white poodle, for Wilkins to relay.

'And Miss Julia Yunge-Brown called on behalf of her father and

wanted to know where you would be staying in Cannes. I'm to ring
them as soon as I know.'

'Tell them the Majestic, if I can get a room there, which I ought
to do because they've got three hundred. Have you looked into the
Athena Holdings set-up yet?'

'I've got someone on it today.'

'Good. I'll phone you tomorrow about it.'

Between that moment and the time I arrived in Cannes somebody, I was to discover, had kept the wires busy. I got a room
without trouble, ran the car around the corner from the Rue des
Serbes and found a garage for it. I had two drinks, dinner, and then
a short stroll down the street on to the Boulevard de la Croisette to
get a whiff of the sea breeze and then back to bed. Somewhere in
the port was O'Dowda's yacht, the *Ferox* – which was a name that
had not surprised me, knowing his passion for fishing and knowing
also something now of the nature of the man . . . By any standards
he was a cannibal trout preying on large and small fry.

In my room I dropped into a chair, lit a last cigarette before bed
and began to think about Zelia and Max Ansermoz, and more
particularly of the combinations of human experience and passion
which, so soon after a no doubt romantic night at the Ombremont,
could have made her decide to lose her memory of the events of the
next two days and with it the red Mercedes. Somewhere along that
line somebody had had a change of heart. I didn't get far with the
obvious possibilities because the telephone rang.

There was, the desk informed me, a Mr Alakwe to see me.

It was nearly eleven o'clock and my first instinct was to tell them
to tell Mr Alakwe to go to hell. Then curiosity as to how he could
have traced me made me tell them to send him up.

He came in, dressed now for the Continent in a lightweight fawn
linen suit, smiling all over his face, snub nose creased up like a
wrinkled black plum. He carried a panama hat with an orange-
and-silver ribbon round it. His tie was pale blue with a yellow
horseshoe and hunting crop, rampant, over a bilious green shirt
with a fine yellow stripe. He still wore his ginger suède shoes. He
shook my hand and then presented me with his card.

I said, 'Don't let's go through that ritual again, Mr Jimbo
Alakwe, Esquire.'

He shook his head, his smile almost cutting his face in half, and
said, 'Not Jimbo, Mr Carver. Jimbo's my brother.'

I looked at the card. He was right. This was Mr Najib Alakwe,

Esquire – in the same line of business, but with an address in Cannes in the Rue de Mimont which, as far as I could remember, was somewhere behind the station. I turned the card over. The quotation on the back read: *Un bon ami vaut mieux que cent parents.* Well, I wasn't going to argue with that.

I handed the card back and said, 'Twins?'

'Yes, Mr Carver.'

'How the hell am I going to tell you apart?'

'Very simple. I am always in France and Jimbo is always in England.'

I wanted to ask about the ginger shoes but decided not to because it would be some simple explanation I should have thought of for myself.

I said, 'How did you know where to find me?'

'Again very simple. Jimbo telephones me with the information.'

'And how did he get it?'

'This is not for me to know. We keep our departments very separate except in peripatetic cases like yours, Mr Carver, where the subject is long-ranging. May I say already I have a great admiration for you. Man, you're a damned fast worker.'

I sat down, suddenly feeling very tired. Jimbo and Najib might look and act like a couple of clowns, but there had to be more to them than that. They had to be good for far more than a laugh. To prove it, Najib put his hand into his pocket and pulled out a gun.

I said, 'Is that really necessary?'

He said, 'Man, I hope not, because I am very bad at aiming.' He half-turned and called over his shoulder, 'Panda!'

From the little hallway outside the bedroom door, where she had been waiting, a young woman came into the room. Not that 'came' was the word. She breezed in like a whirlwind, smacked Najib on the back and waltzed up to me in a cloud of some very strong scent, ran her fingers through my hair, tugged the lobe of my right ear and said, 'Whoof! Whoof! Happy to know you, Rexy boy.'

Wearily, I said to Najib, 'She's not real, is she?''

Panda gave me a big grin. 'You betcha, daddy-ho. Every curve, every muscle, genuine human and jumping with life.'

She was over six feet tall, wearing a very short skirt and a gold lamé blouse. She was good-looking, with big, moist brown eyes and a laughing mouth full of the most splendid teeth I had ever seen, though I felt that there were too many of them. In fact there was too much of her altogether. Her legs were too long and her arms were too long, and as she pirouetted in front of me she gave off a hum as though she were driven by some high-powered dynamo. Her skin was a pleasant milky-coffee colour, and her hair was a mass of tight black curls. From her ears dangled gold ear-rings, each shaped to represent a man hanging from a gallows.

Najib said, 'My assistant, Miss Panda Bubakar. Pay no attention to her. Tonight she is full of beans.'

'Panda hungry. Panda want man,' said Panda.

'Panda search room,' said Najib, smacking her on the bottom. Standing, he could just reach it.

'Panda can search room,' I said, 'but what the hell is she looking for – apart from a man?'

'In England,' said Najib, holding the gun on me, 'you were given damned honourable offer of cash for non-cooperation with O'Dowda. Now, cash offer withdrawn. We just take the goods.'

From behind me, where Panda was turning over my bed, she said, 'Ra-ra! Ritzy pyjamas. Anytime you want those pressed, Rexy, just call for me.'

Something bit me gently on the back of the neck and I jumped.

'Leave Mr Carver alone and get on with job,' said Najib.

I slewed round, rubbing my neck and watched her. Winking at me, she started to go through the room. She did it well – not as well as some people I'd seen, but good enough to prove she was no amateur.

Some of her remarks as she went through my case and the bathroom wouldn't have gone down well at a vicarage garden party, but there was no denying her high spirits and exuberant *bonhomie*. At a distance she was – once you got used to the length of her – quite good to look at, but I didn't trust the hungry man-glint in her eyes. After mating, she was the kind that topped it off by making a meal of her consort.

She came back from the bathroom and said, 'Nothing, Najib – except he wants a new toothbrush and he's almost out of sleeping pills. You sleep bad, honey?' She kicked out a long leg. 'Whoof! Whoof! Mamma has something for that, too.'

'Give me your number,' I said. 'The next time I have insomnia I'll ring. Now will the two of you get the hell out of here?'

'If it is not here, then it must be in the car still. The key, please?' Najib held out his hand.

Panda sat on the bed behind me and wrapped her arms around my neck. 'Give the man the key, honey.'

I said, half-choked, 'What's all this about a car?'

Najib said, 'The car you find. I wait here all this evening and see you arrive, but I am not quick enough to see which garage you took it to.'

One of Panda's hands had snaked down inside my jacket and now came out, holding my car key. She slid around me and handed it to Najib.

'Okay,' I said. 'It's in the Renault Garage just up the avenue and behind the Rue d'Antibes. Just leave the key with the hall porter when you've finished. I'm going to bed.'

It was a stupid thing to say.

Panda gave a couple of barks and high kicks and said, 'Mamma stay and tuck Rexy up.'

I said, 'Take this praying mantis with you, too.'

Najib looked at the key which lay like a fat tear-drop in the palm of his black hand, and then raised a pair of puzzled eyes to me.

I went on, 'It's not the car you want, but one I hired in Geneva to drive down here. Why didn't you check the registration number when I arrived?'

'Numbers can be changed, honey,' said Panda. 'You go check, Najib.'

'You both go,' I said. 'Check the car. There's one thing will tell you whether it's the right one. The secret compartment. You know where it is supposed to be?'

Najib grinned suddenly. 'I know where it is, Mr Carver, sir. But I don't think you do. O'Dowda would never have told you. Damn right, yes?'

'Course he doesn't know,' said Panda. 'Mamma can tell from his eyes.' She made for the bathroom.

'That's not the way out,' I said.

'Man, I know that. I'm going to fix your bath and rub you down after.' She opened her mouth and snapped her fine teeth at me, her eyes rolling.

'You come with me, Panda,' said Najib. Then to me, he went on, 'I make the check and return the key. Sometime, also Mr Carver, after you have seen Miss Zelia, we must have a man-to-man talk because it could be to your profit.' He got hold of Panda's arm and began to tug her towards the door.

'Mamma stay,' she cried.

'Mamma go,' I said. There was a moment's temptation, but I put it firmly aside. I just wasn't in her league.

From the door Najib said, 'While you are in this town, if there's anything you need, just let me know.'

'Double it for me,' said Panda.

'After all—' Najib ignored her—'we are in the same line of business, so no need not to be friends unless it becomes absolutely damned necessary otherwise.'

'Nicely put,' I said.

'Sleep well, Mr Carver.'

'I don't like to think of you all lonely in this room, lover-boy,' said Panda.

'I'll survive.'

'Say, Rexy—' her eyes open wide with a thought—'you ain't discriminating about colour are you?'

I shook my head. 'I like your colour. But I need a lot of building up to deal with the size it comes in. Goodnight.'

They went. And I went to bed. Both of them were putting on a big fooling act. But neither of them were fools. And how the hell had they known that I was coming to the Majestic? Nobody had known until I told Wilkins, and she had phoned the O'Dowda place in Sussex. Within three or four hours of that time Najib had been on my trail. Somewhere in the O'Dowda *ménage* there was somebody who was tipping off the other side. Somebody in the household didn't want O'Dowda to have his Mercedes back, and they weren't being very subtle about it. My guess was that it was Durnford. Working for O'Dowda, he could be expected to have a healthy dislike for him, but this went further, this was a horse called Revenge out of Dislike by Disloyalty. Good lines but obvious breeding. As far as O'Dowda was concerned something was really burning up Durnford, and quite clearly he wasn't overworried about what the man said, that you can hide the fire, but what do you do about the smoke? When O'Dowda saw that smoke Durnford was due for trouble.

CHAPTER 4

'Fate cropped him short – for be it understood.
He would have lived much longer, if he could!'
(William Barnes Rhodes)

It was a warm, gentle, late September morning, full of soft yellow light bouncing off the sea from a golden mesh of ripples.

The *Ferox* was anchored just outside the port, floating like a fluffy white meringue, the final thread of confection piped out to a narrow prow. For ten francs, a gross overcharge, a boy of about fifteen rowed me out in a pram dinghy. He was bare to the waist and the sight of his brown, muscular torso, not a spare ounce of fat on it anywhere, made me consider the possibility of starting my early morning exercises again.

I went up the gangway to the deck and blinked my eyes at the white and gold paint, the polished brass and chromium, did a quick sum in my head of what this outfit probably cost O'Dowda a year, shuddered, and became aware of a woman sitting in a deck-chair reading a copy of *Vogue*. She had silvery hair, touched with a purple rinse, and was wearing red shorts and a red blouse. She was somewhere around thirty, had a baby face, a tiny pout to her full lips, and was smoking a long thin cigar.

I said, 'I have a kind of appointment with Miss Zelia Yunge-Brown. Carver is the name.'

She dropped the *Vogue* lazily on to the deck, studied me, and in an American accent said, 'What kind of appointment? Personal, medical, social or just hopeful?'

'Personal.'

'Well, that makes a change from head-shrinkers and social boneheads.' She looked at a small gold watch on a slender wrist and said, 'She'll be doing her jigsaw in the sun-lounge up front.' She tipped her head forward. 'Don't knock. Go straight in. If she's

in a good mood maybe she'll let you stay. Before you go, come and
have a drink with me. I might give you my autograph.'

'Is it worth anything?'

'Mercenary type, eh? On a cheque, value nil. On a photograph,
value sentimental. But come and have a drink. You'll be helping
my beat boredom campaign.'

She blew a cloud of smoke without removing the cigar, picked
up the magazine, winked at me and began reading.

I went forward along the spotless deck, under the bridge-wing
and had the run of windows of the sun-lounge on my right. They
curved round in a wide semicircle above the forward deck. A seagull
cut down through the warm air and screamed something at me in
French. A man wearing a blue singlet leaned over the bridge-rail
above me and nodded, and a Chris-Craft went by at speed, spewing
a trail of wake like a plume of ostrich feathers.

I looked through the glass of the sun-lounge door and had my
first glance of Zelia Yunge-Brown, the girl with the lost memory.
She was sitting at a table, bending over a big tray on which part
of a gigantic jigsaw was coming to life. At her right side the table
was covered with a muddle of loose jigsaw pieces. All I could see
at first was a sweep of long dark hair, the slope of a high, sun-
tanned forehead, brown arms and hands and part of a simple blue-
and-white-striped dress that looked like the stuff that butchers used
to wear for aprons. I stared at her for a while, hoping she would
become aware of me. The glass was proof against my magnetic
personality, so I went in. She made a little clicking noise with her
tongue, removed a piece from the tray and began searching in the
loose pile alongside her, ignoring me completely either from rude-
ness or absorption in her work.

I walked across the lounge and sat on the arm of a blue leather
chair. There was a bar at the back of the lounge with a chromium
grille pulled across it, through which I could see rows of glasses and
coloured bottles. Either side of the bar were a couple of paintings of
old-time tea-clippers, and above the bar in a glass case a stuffed
swordfish with a stupid grin on its chops.

I said, 'What's it going to be when it's finished? The Houses of
Parliament? George the Fifth's coronation? Or one of those old
hunting scenes with chaps in red coats drinking port while the hunt
servants pull off their boots and the inn servants are charging in
with boars' heads and poached salmon three feet long. Those were
the days. Everywhere by horse and coach. None of the roads stinked

up with motor cars. By the way, talking of cars – my name is Carver and your father has hired me to find the red Mercedes which you carelessly mislaid.'

I said it all coolly, in my best unruffled manner, but, I hoped, getting a little hint of something not quite friendly in it to show that I wasn't in the mood for moods. Halfway through she raised her head, and that made it difficult for me to maintain my even manner because she was one of the most beautiful women I had ever seen. She had this wonderful black hair, pale blue eyes, and perfect classical features, and she was as cold as ice. An ice maiden from the frozen north. There was something of Julia in her looks, but only just enough to tell they were sisters. She settled back in her chair to get a good look at me, and I saw that she was a big girl, tall, statuesque and as strong as an ox. All she needed was a winged helmet, a shield and a long boat, and Eric the Red would have gone crazy over her. Personally, she made something quietly shrivel up inside me and die.

In a voice, steely and cold, straight from the refrigerator locked somewhere inside her, she said, 'I don't care particularly for your manner, Mr Carver. And I have already given all the information I can about the car.'

I gave her a big smile, trying to get the atmosphere above zero, even feeling that maybe I had judged her a little hastily. After all she was beautiful enough to merit a second opinion. Could be I was wrong.

'So,' I said, 'you're sorry you can't help me?'

'I can't help you, Mr Carver.'

She moved forward and studied the jigsaw.

I stood up, and the movement brought her head up a little.

She said, 'I'm sorry you've had a wasted journey – but I did tell my stepfather that it was unnecessary for you to come.'

I walked round her to the bar, gave a bottle of Hines a quick, frustrated glance through the grille, and said, 'I'd like to make one thing very clear.'

She had to turn a little to get me in focus and the movement showed off the splendid shoulders and torso to more than advantage.

'Yes.'

'I've been hired to do a job of work. I like to finish what I've started. It's a kind of thing with me. Stupid pride. Professional prejudice. Call it what you like. But I'd like you to know that I am only interested in the car. I want to get it back for your stepfather.

But when I hand it over I don't have to give a blow-by-blow account of the recovery. Anything revealed to me in confidence by anyone along the line remains that way. You understand?'

'Perfectly. But I can't help you.'

She turned back and began to fiddle with the puzzle. I walked round the back of her and finished up full circle in the blue-leather chair. She glanced up briefly as I sat down.

'I would like you to go, Mr Carver.'

'I will,' I said, 'when I've done what I'm being paid to do. For some reason your stepfather sets great store by this car. As his daughter—'

'Stepdaughter.' The word was snapped at me, like icicles breaking.

'—I should have thought you would have wanted to help him.'

She gave me a cold stare, and said, 'I have every reason in the world for not caring a damn about him.'

'You can't really mean that, otherwise you wouldn't be sitting here enjoying all the luxuries he provides. No girl with any spirit would. Now, come on, what happened to the car?'

I was pushing her, hoping to break her down a little; but it didn't work.

She got up from the table and began to move towards the bar. In the woodwork at the side was a bell-push. I was so absorbed in watching her walk, this frozen, beautiful Amazon, that I almost let her reach the bell-push.

'I wouldn't do that,' I said. 'Not if you want me to help you. It won't do you any harm to listen to me for a few moments. Then, if you want to, you can push the bell.'

She was silent for a moment or two, then she said, 'Go ahead.'

I stood up and lit a cigarette. Having her towering over me made me nervous.

'I'll be frank you with. You may or may not have lost your memory. Personally, I don't think you have. But if it suits you for good and private reasons to have people think that, then that's okay by me. But one thing is for certain – you haven't been truthful about your stay at the Ombremont Hotel. If you'd known what was going to happen after you'd left it, then, of course, you'd have naturally been more . . . well, discreet.'

'I don't know what you're—'

'You do. I'm talking about Room 16.'

'I was in Room 15.'

'But you telephoned Durnford in England from Room 16.'

'I certainly did not.' Big and frozen she might be, but I didn't have to have a trained eye and ear to know that she was holding something down inside, probably a desire to shout at me to clear out and go to hell. And it wasn't something that was pleasant for me to be aware of. Quite suddenly I had become sorry for her.

I shook my head. 'There was no telephone charge on your account. On the other hand there was on Room 16's account. And the person in that room – a man – paid for it without any fuss. So where do we go from there?'

She moved back towards the table until she was almost alongside me.

'We don't go anywhere, Mr Carver. I know nothing about Room 16. If the hotel desk got their accounting mixed up and somebody paid for my telephone call because they were in too much of a hurry to check their account, I'm not interested. The only thing I'm interested in is that you get out of here and leave me alone. Go back to my stepfather and tell him to forget his car.' She paused and I could see the fine tremble all over her as she held on to her control, and I knew that she only needed a push from me – the mention of Ansermoz's name or a reference to a white poodle and her leaving in the morning, laughing and happy – to go right over the edge. With a lot of people I would have happily given the push. But I couldn't with her. Julia apart, there was some barrier in me that wouldn't let me do it. Whatever I wanted from her I would have to get some other way. This job made you think of and see people as jigsaw puzzles; you had to piece the parts together and not mind what sort of dirty or unholy picture came out. But I couldn't rush it with her. She was big and dark and as solid as an iceberg but she'd come too far south in the warm currents and was ready to topple. I didn't have to be the one to give her the final push. But now I was determined to find Ansermoz. Oh, yes, I wanted to meet him.

I moved to the door.

'All right. Just forget I ever came.' I gave her a brotherly grin. 'But if ever you want a shoulder to cry on, somebody to talk to – just get in touch.'

She dropped a hand and touched one of the loose pieces of the puzzle and, without looking at me, said, 'Thank you, Mr Carver.'

Hand on the door, I said, 'Think nothing of it. But don't forget I've got a broad pair of shoulders.' So they were, almost as broad as hers. I went out, thinking of what Robert Burns had said about waiving the quantum of the sin, the hazard of concealing. If ever a woman had hardened all within and petrified the feeling, then Zelia had done it since leaving the Ombremont Hotel. And I meant to know why.

But first I had to get by the silver-haired, purple-rinse number in the red shorts. I didn't have a hope and in the end I was glad of it, because although I couldn't use Zelia the way I ought to have done, it was easy with Mirabelle Heisenbacher, née Wright, stage-name Mirabelle Landers, age thirty-eight, friendly, bored, and all set to marry O'Dowda when she got her divorce from Mr Heisenbacher, a rot-the-bald-headed-bastard-of-a-shoe-manufacturer (her words).

As I stood by the gang ladder wondering where my boy with the pram dinghy was, she came down the deck, changed into a green silk beach-suit, cigar in one hand and the other reaching for my arm as she said, 'Unless you have a drink first, you've got to swim back. Come on.'

She led me up to the stern where, under an awning, chairs, tables and drinks waited. She was as friendly as a puppy and just as restless.

She said, 'Did you get anything out of Zelia?'

'No – she's still in some kind of personal deep freeze.'

'I can't think why Cavan is riding the child about the damned car. He's so loaded, what does a car matter?'

'He was tough with her, was he?'

'Originally. I thought he was going to go into orbit. Gave me a few moments' doubt. Such a temper. After all, he's the guy I'm going to marry. Then I thought, what the hell? All men have something and, unlike most, he's got millions so I didn't see why love's blossom should be allowed to wither. Why's he so stuck on getting the car back?'

'I wish I knew. You known him long?'

'Three, four years. Nice guy – except I don't like the side he's been showing since the car went. It's got to be more than the car. You know my theory?'

'Tell me.'

'Sometimes I think Zelia lost the car on purpose to annoy him. She must have guessed there was more to it than the car and she ditched it to get back at him. Some kind of emotional compensation for something or the other.'

'You've been talking to a psychoanalyst.'

'Not me. Any time I spend on couches is strictly for pleasure. Not that I'm like that now. I'm strictly a Cavan O'Dowda girl these days.'

'If he got that car back he'd be nicer than he is at the moment, wouldn't he?'

'Sure. And I wouldn't be stuck here, keeping an eye on Zelia. I hate boats. She wants to be out here. She hasn't been off this yacht for weeks. What are you driving at?'

'Was I?'

'Come off it, buster, I know the look in a man's eyes when he wants something and at the moment you've got that look – though it isn't asking for the usual thing which, in a way, is no damned compliment to me.'

'I just want to satisfy O'Dowda.'

'Snap. So?'

'Is there a shore-going telephone from the *Ferox*?'

'No.'

'What happens about the mail? When you write to O'Dowda, for instance?'

'Now we're getting down to business. Why not be direct? You think Zelia might want to write to someone now that you've seen her?'

I looked at her over a large gin-and-tonic she'd fixed for me. She was a woman who knew where she was going and how to handle herself. She was going to marry O'Dowda. What she didn't know about men would probably make only two dull lines of addenda to a large volume of personal reminiscences. She had to be like that because I hadn't said anything of note yet and already she was with me. I gave her a wink. She tossed the end of her cigar over the rail and winked back.

'Level,' she said, 'and Mirabelle might help – just so long as it all adds up to making O'Dowda sweet and getting Zelia out of the doldrums.'

'I've mentioned a little fact to Zelia which may make her want to write to someone. If I could have the names and addresses of all the people she writes to in the next twenty-four hours it could help a lot. Difficult?'

'No. All the ship's letters are put in the mail-box in the saloon

and one of the stewards takes them ashore late afternoon. Any name
and address in particular?'

'Not really.'

'Liar. Where are you staying?'

'The Majestic.'

'You like your kind of job?'

'I travel and meet people, and help some of them.'

'Then I wish to God you'd help Zelia to come out from under
the glacier. I'm liable to be stuck here for weeks and that adds up
to a lot of lost fun. It's a man, of course, isn't it, that she'll be
writing to?'

'I wouldn't bet on it.'

'Why not, it's an even money chance? Anyway, it's got to be.
Any girl ever needed a man, she does. My bet is she found one and
he went bad on her. For the first time in her life she went into it
starry-eyed and then – bam! the bastard ran true to form. They all
do, even the nice ones, but she didn't have any experience to help
her ride the punches. Correct?'

'You'll make a first-class stepmother.'

'Wife is all I'm interested in. I thought I had it made with
Heisenbacher, but he developed nasty habits, and when I broke
him of those he just withdrew and started collecting Japanese ivory
carvings, netsukes, and all that stuff. I gave up. You like to stay
for lunch?'

I said regretfully that I couldn't and it took me another half-hour
to get away. I was run ashore in the yacht's launch and on the
quayside waiting for me was Mr Najib Alakwe, Esquire.

He fell into step alongside me, handed me the ignition key, and
said, 'Okay, Mr Carver, wrong car. You get anything from Miss
Zelia?'

'No. But why should I keep you up to date on things?'

'Two thousand pounds, Mr Carver. Damn generous offer. Cable
from Jimbo this morning. Two thousand pounds you resign from
Mr O'Dowda's employment now, or three thousand you go on, find
car, and hand same over to us intact.'

I shook my head.

His eyes spun in just the same way as his brother's had.

'This is a serious refusal, Mr Carver?'

'Absolutely.'

He took a deep, sad breath and said, 'Then all I can indicate is
that the consequences for you, Mr Carver, may be—'

'D for drastic?'
'Absolutely.'

I had lunch at the hotel and then went up to my room and lay on
the bed and stared at the ceiling. It was a boring kind of ceiling to
stare at, not a crack or a stain on it, so I had to fall back on pure
thought. What kind of people, I asked myself, would employ the
Alakwe twins? The best answer I could come up with was probably
people of their own race. O'Dowda, for instance, would never have
employed them – except on an African assignment where they
would not be conspicuous, though I had an idea they would still
be just that even in an Accra bazaar. In Europe they stuck out like
a couple of sore black thumbs. Probably their employer or
employers didn't mind this. The Alakwes wanted whatever was
hidden in the Mercedes, and they knew that O'Dowda knew they
wanted it and – almost certainly – that O'Dowda knew who their
employers were.

Then I had a think about Zelia. I was beginning to get some
kind of picture of the nature of her amnesia. Max Ansermoz, I
hoped, if I ever reached him, could fill in the blanks.

The phone went about four o'clock and it was Wilkins, with a
list as long as my arm of companies and holding companies, subsidi-
aries, agencies and property investments which were all wrapped
up in Athena Holdings Ltd. Most of the information I knew had
never been got from Somerset House. It was the kind of stuff that
came from a good city man working the pubs around Mincing Lane
and Fleet Street. As I finished taking down the list, Wilkins said,
'Are you interested in any particular one?'

'Should I be?'

'In view of Joseph Bavana and a certain gentleman called Mr
Jimbo Alakwe who called round here for a general chat about you
this morning, I should have thought that—'

'How did you get on with him?'

'He said he could get me an electric typewriter brand new at a
discount of 50 per cent. Do you want me to get more details about
United Africa Enterprises?'

I said I did. It was on the list she had just dictated to me.

Half an hour later I had Durnford on the line. Mr O'Dowda, he
said, wanted a progress report up to date, and with particular
reference to my visit to Zelia. He assumed I had seen her.

'I've been with her, and I've got nothing from her.'

'Nothing?'

'Absolutely nothing. But I'm following a different lead which may help me.'

'Mr O'Dowda would appreciate some indication of this new line. You realize that?'

'Sure. I'll give you details very soon.'

'So, in short, you've made no real progress at all?' I could imagine his cold agate eyes blinking.

'Yes, I'd say that was a fair summary. But don't worry. I'm not downhearted. A willing heart goes all the way, your sad tires in a mile-o.'

'I beg your pardon?'

'Never mind. But you can do something for me which might help. I'd like a complete list of guests, friends, or family who might have been staying at Mr O'Dowda's Evian château for the two weeks before Zelia took off on her trip in the Mercedes. Can you let me have that?'

There was a little longer than natural silence at the other end, then he said, 'Yes, I suppose so.'

'Now?'

'No. I'd have to make enquiries.'

'Okay. I'll phone sometime tomorrow or the next day. Oh, there is one thing you can tell Mr O'Dowda. I've been offered two thousand pounds by a certain Mr Jimbo Alakwe – my secretary will give you his address – to drop this job. Interesting?'

'You refused, of course.'

'With a struggle – yes.'

Around six I was still on the bed, thinking of having a shower before going down to the bar for a drink, when the phone went. The desk said that there was a Miss Yunge-Brown wanting to see me.

I was at the door waiting to greet her. She came in with a warm, flashing smile, a passing whiff of *Jolie Madame,* and a silver mink cape draped over one arm. After staring at a bedroom ceiling all the afternoon she gave my eyes trouble in focusing for a while. She dropped into the bedroom chair, crossed two beautiful long legs, fingered the fall of her black dress smooth, and said, 'I've never seen a man's eyes look so pouchy. Drinking at lunchtime?'

'They go like that when I sleep in the afternoons. A couple of whiskeys and everything soon shakes back into place. Where shall we go for dinner?'

'We don't. Why don't you give up?'

'You've decided I'm not your type?'

'It's under review. What did you get out of Zelia?'

'Zelia,' I said, 'is a woman who needs understanding. I might make something of her if I could get her away from that jigsaw long enough.'

She gave me a cool, long look. There was in it even a hint of something a little warmer than a review-board stare. She topped the look with a little shake of her head so that one coral-pink tip of an ear showed against a raven wing of smooth, loose hair and then slid back shy as a sea anemone.

'Zelia,' she said, 'has spent most of this afternoon on her bed crying. That's something I've never known her do before. What the devil did you say to her?' The last sentence came curt and hard.

'When did you arrive?'

'Lunchtime. What have you done to Zelia?'

'Nice drive down in the Facel Vega?'

'Yes. And don't hedge. You bloody well leave Zelia alone if all you can do is to twist her up. Yes—' she eyed me with angry thoughtfulness—'maybe I am going to dislike you a lot.'

'Pity. I'd prefer it the other way. And don't get so het up about Zelia. Between ourselves she brings out the Sir Galahad in me and I'm looking forward to going into action. I like big, beautiful girls. But I don't like them frozen. They should be warm and full of bounce. So why don't you belt up and give me that envelope you're fiddling with?'

She looked down at her right hand and seemed surprised to find the envelope there which she had drawn from her handbag.

'I wish I didn't keep changing my mind about you,' she said.

'Give it time. The needle will settle down soon and show you the right course.'

She handed me the envelope.

'It's from Mirabelle. She asked me to deliver it.'

'Now there's a woman who's going full steam right ahead, armour-plated, reinforced bows and god help any pack ice that gets in the way.' I turned the envelope over. She'd made a reasonable job of it, but it was quite clear that it had been opened and then stuck down. I raised my eyebrows at her.

'I opened it,' she said. 'I couldn't imagine what Mirabelle could have to say to you.'

'You couldn't? Well, given a million pounds, I could have her lisping in my ear for the rest of my life and I wouldn't mind at all, except that she'd have to get rid of that purple hair-rinse.'

It was a half-sheet of plain notepaper and Mirabelle had written—

One letter an hour after you left. Now she's taken to her bed. Letter went ashore five o'clock with yacht's mail. Max Ansermoz, Châlet Bayard, St Bonnet, Hautes Alpes. Don't you do a damned thing to hurt the kid.
Mirabelle.

I put the letter in my pocket. Julia eyed me like a child watching a conjuror. I pulled out my cigarettes, lit one, and she watched the first curl of smoke fade away.

'Thanks for trusting me,' I said.

'What makes you think I do?'

'This.' I waved the letter. 'You'd have torn it up if you hadn't.'

'Well?'

'Well, what?' I said.

'Who is this Max Ansermoz – and what's he got to do with Zelia?'

'You've never heard the name before?'

'No.'

'Then forget it,' I said, hard. 'If you're fond of Zelia, really forget it. And when you get back to the *Ferox,* thank Mirabelle and tell her to do the same. Okay?'

'If you say so. Are you going to see him?'

'Yes.'

'When? Tomorrow?'

'Yes.'

'I'll drive you up.'

'I've got my own car and you'll stay here. I've just told you to forget Max Ansermoz.'

She stood up and came across to me, slipping the mink over her shoulders, the diamond setting of her watch pinpricks of brilliance with the movement. Mink and diamonds, Facel Vegas and yachts, Mercedes and châteaux in the Haute Savoie, *paté de foie gras,* caviare and pink champagne, dream stuff . . . but it didn't isolate her or Zelia or Mirabelle or any other woman from life . . . from the nasty little habits that some men are born with and others develop. Men were hunters and, no matter how much they kidded themselves otherwise, women were the prey. Just at that moment I didn't like the idea; wished I could be outside it, but knew I couldn't. The only consolation was that most men reluctantly observed the game laws and the close seasons. Some didn't. Max Ansermoz I was sure was one. So, I had an idea, was Cavan O'Dowda. Someday, somebody, I told myself ought to shoot the pair, stuff and mount them, and hang them above a bar.

'What on earth's got into you?' she said. 'You suddenly look as though you wanted to hit somebody.'

'Don't let these puffy old eyes fool you.'

She came closer. 'They're not as puffy as I made out. And I'm really beginning to think that they don't fool me as much as you would like. Would you like me to break my dinner date?'

'Not on my account. I'm going early to bed. I've got a busy day tomorrow.'

She wasn't fooling me. I knew exactly what was in her mind, and had been ever since she had steamed open the letter on the yacht or wherever it was.

She was as anxious to see Max Ansermoz as I was. That didn't suit me. I wanted to see him first, and alone. In fact, I was already looking forward to it.

She said, 'I really want to come with you tomorrow.'

I said, 'I'm going alone. If you queer that I'll toss in this job – and then O'Dowda will get someone else, some fast slick operator who'll probably make a juicy story out of it afterwards for all the boys in the bar to laugh at. So keep away!'

Deep and warm inside me, heating up fast every moment, was a feeling that I didn't have very often, wouldn't wish for often, but which when it came just had to be obeyed. Somebody had to be hit . . . Oh, yes, somebody had to be hit hard and the name was clicking through my brain like a ticker tape. She knew, too, what was there. Slowly she put out a hand and gently nipped the cloth of my sleeve between two fingers.

'All right,' she said. 'I won't interfere. . . . Poor Zelia.' She turned away to the door. Then, her fingers on the door handle, she turned and said, 'Do me a favour.'

'What?'

'Don't bother to be polite with him.'

She went. I gave her a few minutes, and then I called the desk. I wanted my bill made up. I was leaving right after dinner and would they send someone up to get my car key so that the Mercedes could be brought round for me. With any luck I might arrive at the Châlet Bayard just about the time Max Ansermoz got Zelia's letter. One thing that I knew for sure I wasn't going to find at the Châlet Bayard was a *chevalier sans peur et sans reproche*.

I left just after ten. There was a light drizzle falling and I could see no sign of Najib Alakwe being on the watch outside. If he had been I wasn't going to worry. In the Mercedes I was reasonably confident I could shake any trail.

St Bonnet was about twenty- or thirty-odd kilometres north of Gap, and my route was back along the road by which I had come down from Grenoble. From the map I worked out that it gave me something over seven hundred and fifty kilometres of driving. I had time on my hands and took things slowly.

I gave myself an hour's sleep, somewhere well south of Gap, and then drove on to Gap for an early breakfast, coffee laced with cognac and a couple of crisp croissants spread with apricot conserve. Fortified, I left Gap and drove up and over the Col Bayard, thinking that if I had a troubled life, the *chevalier* had had the edge on me, every head of his family for two centuries having fallen in battle, and he himself likewise in the end – to an arquebus ball, whatever that was. From the top of the pass I rolled down into St Bonnet and got directions for the Châlet Bayard. It was a small, rough road, doubling back out of the village along the course of the river for a while and then climbing steeply through pine and oak woods by way of a series of *virages* that made me keep my eyes strictly on the road and ignore the views.

It was a wooden-built chalet, fairly new, with pink-and-green shutters, and the roof barge-boards decorated with pink-and-green stripes. It stood to one side of a steep green alp, on a plateau about the size of a couple of tennis courts. There was no garden, just trees and scrub running either side of the rough drive and then spreading back from the house itself. There was a garage beyond the open space in front of the house. The doors were shut.

I parked the car close under the verandah which ran along the front of the house, and went up the steps. There were petunias and geraniums in flower-boxes all along the front of the verandah and the front door was wide open to show me a small hall of narrow, polished pine boards, the odd rug and a grandfather clock with a loud tick, announcing that it was five minutes past nine.

There was an iron bell-pull at the side of the door. I gave it a couple of jerks and way back in the house a bell clanged, loud

enough to wake the dead. But it didn't wake anyone in the house.
I tolled again and still no one came to answer it.

I went in. There were two doors off the hall. I tried them both.
The first led down a corridor to the kitchen quarters. It was a neat
bright kitchen and there were the remains of a breakfast on the
table, and a ginger cat curled in a wicker chair. The cat eyed me
for a moment, stood up, stretched its legs stiffly and then collapsed
on to the cushion, rolled itself into a turban and ignored me.

I went back and tried the other door. It led into a large lounge
which ran the full length of the far side of the house with a view
across part of the alp and away beyond to the valley peaks and
crests, some of them already smudged with a patchwork of snow.
It was a good, big comfortable room, polished pine boards, skin
rugs over them, two big settees, four large armchairs, a wide,
circular table adzed out of oak and ornamented with a bowl of
multicoloured dahlias that would have had Jimbo in ecstasies. In
one corner was a desk, and against the false wall that made part of
a staircase that ran up to an open gallery with doors along it, was
a bookcase and a long sideboard with drinks, cigarette box and a
pile of old newspapers. I lit a cigarette and went upstairs. There
were three bedrooms, all the beds neatly made, and a bathroom.
The sponge on the side of the bath was damp, and so was one of
the toothbrushes and the cake of soap. I went down to the lounge
and started a more detailed inspection. The bookcase was interesting. One shelf had as big a collection of cookery books as I had
ever seen in half a dozen languages. If Max were the cookery expert
he had something for a guest of any nationality. There were three
shelves full of thrillers, French, English, American and German. It
was nice to know that Max was multilingual. We wouldn't have
difficulty communicating.

The desk was neat and tidy, and contained very little. It was
clear that Max didn't care to leave any private papers lying around.
There were some cancelled cheques, paid bills, most of them local,
a list of shares and securities, some American, most French, which
had been added to from time to time. He didn't seem to have sold
any for there were no deletions. I didn't try to make out what they
were worth. In one of the drawers was a pile of estate agents' leaflets
and they were all concerned with restaurant and café properties as
far apart as Paris and Marseilles. Another drawer held a 9mm.
Browning pistol, the magazine full, and alongside it a box of ammu-

nition and a spare magazine. I pocketed the lot as a safety
precaution.

I went across to the window, admired the view, and wondered
how long Max would be. My guess was that he had gone off for
his morning constitutional. He was a neat orderly type, bed made
before he left the house, not a speck of dust anywhere, ashtrays
emptied. Neat and – normally – regular in his habits, fond of the
culinary arts to the point of already owning, or contemplating
owning, a restaurant or a café, kind to animals – the cat seemed well
content – and with a nice touch of expertise in flower decorations as
the bowl of dahlias testified. Turning from the window and looking
at the flowers, I noticed something I had not seen before. Lying on
this side of the bowl was an envelope.

I picked it up. It had been slit open along the top and the letter
tucked back inside. It was addressed to him and postmarked Cannes
the previous day. I had to hand it to the *Postes et Télégraphe* boys.
They had had five hours' start on me and beaten me to it.

I dropped into an armchair by the fireplace. It was so deep and
wide I wondered for a moment if I was ever going to hit bottom.
I did, bounced a bit, and then took the letter out of the envelope.
It was to him from Zelia and read without benefit of any superscrip-
tion, no glad 'Darling' or 'Dearest one'—

I had hoped that I would never have to communicate with you in
any way. Circumstances now make it necessary. For some reason
my father is highly concerned about the loss of the car and has
employed a certain Mr Rex Carver of London to trace it. This man
saw me today. Although he did not mention your name, he must
know it, because he knows that you stayed in the next room to me
at the Hotel and that I made my phone call to home from it. I
denied everything. I shall continue to deny everything. I just want
what happened to become a blank in my mind. If this man should
trace you, you will do the same. You have never known me. You
have betrayed me once. For this I do not hate you, or forgive you.
I have simply made you nothing in my mind. Betray me to this
man, or anyone else, and I swear that I will have you killed. You
have destroyed something in me. Make this in any way public and
I will destroy you.
Zelia

I put the letter back in the envelope and slipped it into my pocket.
Nothing she had said was news to me. She meant every word she

said, and I was sorry for her. That was the hell of it. I was sorry for her, but I had a job to do. If I possibly could, I wanted to do it without hurting her more. She might want what had happened to be a blank in her mind, but I had to know what had happened. Once I knew, I could pass on to my real concern, the car, I would make it a blank in my mind. I sat there, wondering how Max Ansermoz had felt when he had read the letter. Not over-much concerned, I imagined, or he would not just have chucked it across the table.

At this moment there was a yappy bark from the open door of the lounge behind me. Something white skittered around the side of the chair on the polished boards, leapt on to my knees and began to lick my face. It was a small white poodle. I'm not going to upset anyone by saying I'm no dog-lover, but I like dogs big, discriminating, and with a certain secret contempt for mankind. I was just about to chuck this one into the empty fireplace as under-sized when a breathless voice from the door called, 'Otto! Otto – *tu es fou venir ici avec cette sacrée auto? Tu voudrais que tout le monde—*'

He broke off as I stood up with the white poodle in my arms and he saw me for the first time.

I said, 'You're rushing it, Max. That's not the car Otto went off with. Same colour, different number.'

I dropped the poodle to the ground and it began to walk around on its hind legs like some circus number.

'Cute,' I said. 'How is it as a gun-dog?'

He had a shotgun under one arm and a couple of pigeons hanging from his right hand.

'Who are you and what are you doing here?' He said it in English, not much accent, and his voice under control.

'Carver,' I said. 'Rex Carver of London. I think Miss Zelia Yunge-Brown mentioned me to you in a letter.'

I had to hand it to him. He didn't faint or have palpitations or collapse into a chair. He just stood there and for the fraction of a moment his eyes glanced at the big circular table. He was taller than me, slim, not an ounce of fat on him, and he had one of those dark, unhealthy-looking tans which come from chromosomes more than the sun. He wore a loose shooting jacket with a fur collar, a black peaked cap, and black breeches tucked into the top of gum-boots. He had an intelligent, good-looking face and sparkling teeth and eye-whites. I didn't like the look of him at all, but I could see how in a bad light, after a few glasses of champagne, some women

might have called him a dreamboat. Not Zelia, I shouldn't have
thought. But there you are – when a woman finally decides to drop
the barriers you never know which way the water will flow.

Calmly, he said, 'I don't know what you're talking about. Kindly
get out of my house.'

He dropped the brace of pigeons on to a chair and eased the gun
into both of his hands, the muzzle low, pointing to the ground. He
was over his surprise now, and had me sized up. What could I do
while he had a gun in his hands? I decided to see how far he would
go.

I shrugged my shoulders, and said, 'You can take that attitude
if you like. But it won't get you far – and I'll be back.'

I moved up towards the door and he swung slightly round to
keep me fully under observation. When I was abreast of him, he
said, 'Before you go I'd like the letter which I left on the table.'

I stopped moving, eyed him as though I might be going to make
an issue of it – which I certainly wasn't while he stood at the ready
with a double barrelled twelve bore – and then with another shrug
I slipped my hand into my pocket for the letter and handed it out
to him.

He smiled, just the faintest edge of white teeth showing, and
shook his head.

'Put it on the chair there.'

I moved to the chair, put the letter on one of its arms and then
gave the chair a hard push towards him across the slippery pine
floor. The far arm caught him on the thigh, knocked him off balance
and before he could gather himself together, I jumped him. Miggs,
I'm sure, would have said I was slow, but I was fast enough for
Max Ansermoz. I chopped down at one of his wrists, broke his hold
on the gun, grabbed the barrel in my other hand and twisted the
weapon free from him. I could have stopped there, I suppose, but
a nice warm feeling flooded through me and I didn't see why I
shouldn't take the opportunity to put him in a co-operative mood.
I jabbed him hard in the stomach with the butt of the shotgun and,
as his head came forward, I slapped him sidehand across the neck
and he went down with a crash that had the fool poodle dancing
and yipping with excitement.

He was game. He came up twice at me and I put him down
each time, not bothering about the Queensberry rules, remembering
Miggs saying, 'Don't be nice, be nasty, but leave 'em so they can
talk.'

I let him crawl off his knees and into a chair. He flopped back, murdering me with his eyes, blood trickling from one corner of his mouth. I sat on the edge of the table and faced him.

I said, 'Before I begin the questions, let's get one thing clear. Everything you say to me about Miss Zelia will be in the strictest confidence. Think of me as a confessional. It comes to me – and goes no further. Okay.'

He spat something at me in a language I didn't know. To gentle him down I smacked the butt of the shotgun across the top of his kneecap, just not hard enough to break it. He gasped with pain, doubled forward and the poodle jumped up, trying to lick his face. He shoved it away roughly and dropped back into the chair.

'Bastard.'

'I don't expect you to like me. I'd take it as an insult if you did. Just answer me – or I'll break every bloody bone in your body. Ready?'

He said nothing and I took it for assent.

'Okay,' I said. 'Let's start at the end. Maybe that way we can skip some of the dirty middle. Who's Otto?'

He considered this, and he was considering more. I knew the look and that slow pulling-together movement of the body as they decide to go along with you, hoping that their co-operation will make you so pleased that you'll drop your guard for a moment.

'Otto Libsch, a friend of mine.'

'Age, nationality, description, residence and occupation.'

'Thirty-odd. Austrian. He's tall, biggish, fair hair, going slightly bald. Walks with a bit of a limp and has the lobe of his left ear missing.'

It was too glib, too fast, so I smacked him on the back of his right hand with the gun barrel. He shouted and swore with the pain.

'Try again,' I said. 'From the start.'

He sucked the blood off the back of his hand, and then, his eyes full of the comforting fantasies of what he would like to do to me, he said:

'Twenty-five. French. He's short, dark-haired, thin, weedy-looking. God knows what he does, or where he lives. He just turns up.'

'Not quite good enough. If you wanted to get in touch with him what would you do?'

He balanced that one for a moment, eyed the gun, and decided to give good measure.

'I'd ring his girl friend, Mimi Probst. Turino 56.4578. That's 17 Via Calleta.'

Keeping my eyes on him, I backed to the sideboard and picked up the telephone and carried it to him, putting it on the ground where he could just reach it.

'Ring directory enquiries and ask for the telephone number of Probst, 17 Via Calleta, Turin. Then let me have it.'

He picked up the phone and dialled, saying to me, 'I'm telling you the truth.'

'The one thing I always check is the truth.'

I waited while he put the call in. It took a little time and I lit a cigarette one-handed, keeping the other on the gun. After a time he spoke, asking for the information, then he nodded to me and put the phone with the loose receiver on the floor. I retrieved it, eyes on him all the time. After a few moments the girl at the other end came on and my French was more than good enough to follow her. He'd given me the right number.

I shoved the telephone on to the table and said, 'Otto was here when you were here with Miss Zelia, yes?'

'Yes.'

'He stole the car?'

'Yes.'

'And her luggage and any loose stuff she had lying around, watch, jewellery and so on?'

'Yes.'

'Nice man. Weren't you worried?'

'No.' There was the faintest shadow of a smile about his lips, and I was tempted to smash it off his face.

'Was he interested in this car particularly, or was it just a car like any other, fair game if he could see a way of driving off in it?'

'Otto would steal anything. He's my friend. He's amusing – but he is a born thief.'

He was coming back fast, I could sense it.

'How long had you known Zelia before you came here with her?'

'Quite a while – on and off.'

'Where?'

'Geneva. Whenever she was staying at her father's château.'

'You read her letter carefully?' I nodded to where the letter lay on the floor by the chair.

'Yes.'

'Then take my advice. She wants the time she spent here to become a blank. That's how it's going to be. You step out of line over that and I'll do the job of wiping you out for her free. Understood?'

'Don't you want to know what happened here?'

'No, I bloody well don't. I'm only interested in the car.'

He grinned and I began to see red.

'You don't want to know what she's like, this beautiful iceberg when for the first time a man gets his hands on her and warms her up? When for the first time—'

I should have sat tight and blasted his head off from a safe distance. I should have known that he was deliberately provoking me, hoping for some advantage from it. Christ, I should have known, but I didn't care. I just went for him, to stop the dirty words in his throat, and he played my own trick on me, suddenly swivelling the chair round on the polished floor so that the arm crashed into my hip as he leaped from the chair and kicked my legs from under me.

I went sliding across the floor and almost before I had finished moving, he was standing over me with the gun pointing at me.

'Just stay there,' he said. 'You move and I'll blow your head off a little quicker than I intend.'

I lay where I was, and said nothing. It was one of those times for inaction and silence. He had a finger crooked round the lead trigger and I saw his thumb slide the catch off *safety*.

'And I do intend to,' he said quietly. 'You've annoyed me, assaulted me and entered my house unbidden. I shall say that I came back, found you robbing the place, that you attacked me, and the gun went off accidentally. The police won't make any trouble about that.'

'Other people might.' I felt that I ought to make some case for myself.

'No. Not Miss Zelia, as you so nicely call her. Or her father – because she will never say a word about me.' He gave me a warm, evil grin. 'She wants to forget she ever knew me – or Otto. You know she knew Otto as well, of course? No? Well, I want you to know it. I want you to know everything before I shoot you. When I met her in Geneva she was ripe, you know. Ripe to explode – and she did, like a wild thing after a few drinks here, in this room. We all finished up together, upstairs in the one big bed: Otto, dear Zelia, and me—'

'Shut your dirty mouth!'

'Move – and I'll shoot you. It doesn't matter to me now when I do it. Yes, she was wild. She suddenly woke up and began to live and she tried to put all she'd missed in the last ten years into two days.' His eyes sparkled as he spoke. He was thoroughly enjoying himself. 'There were times when even Otto and I found it hard to handle her. But if she went up like a rocket – are you enjoying this? – the charred stick came back to earth eventually. But before it did Otto moved out with everything she had – the car, her luggage, everything. He didn't tell me he was going to do it. At six o'clock on her last morning he was gone from the communal bed. . . . No, no, hear it all. It amuses me to see you hating me and every word I say. He went and she came back to earth, back to what she'd been before I met her. And she walked out too. Just walked. I didn't mind. Except when she was wild, she was rather boring.'

I said, 'It would be a pleasure to kill you.'

'Happily you're not going to have that pleasure. Mind you, I don't want you to get the wrong idea of Zelia's character. Everything was perfectly correct, all those times in Geneva. They were just warming-up exercises. And here . . . well, just drink wouldn't have released her to such wild heights of non-inhibition. Oh, no – Otto and I doctored her drink. In a way, you could say it was an act of mercy, a form of therapy which she needed. You know, ever since she left I've been wondering whether to be content, altruistically, with having helped her to discover herself, or whether I shouldn't make a charge. Blackmail, I suppose you would call it. What do you think?'

I wasn't thinking. I was just aware of the twin muzzles of the gun a few feet from my face, and of a maddening pressure of rage inside me, mounting to a point which in a few moments would take me off the ground and at him regardless of what happened to me.

He said, 'I asked you what you think? I did it with other women before, of course – until I had enough to set myself up in business. After that I promised myself I would help the cold, frustrated ones like Zelia just for the pleasure of it. But with a millionaire's daughter, perhaps it would be silly not to make a charge—'

At this point I jerked the poodle at him. It had come dancing up on its toes to me as he talked, licked one of my ears and then he begun to worry playfully at my left hand. I grabbed it by its skinny loins and threw it, rolling sideways and jumping to my feet as he staggered back a few yards and fetched up against the table. But I wasn't quick enough to get at him. The gun barrel was out, levelled towards my face.

'Good, monsieur,' he said. 'Now I kill you. But first I tell you I have made my decision. I shall blackmail Miss Zelia. Yes, I shall make her pay, and each time she does it will be necessary for her to bring the money here in person. You understand? Part payment in money and part in—'

I began to move for him. There was no time to get at his gun in my pocket, no time or thought for anything except blind action. But as I felt my muscles contract, the hollow of my guts squeeze tight with the moment of taking off to get at him, there was a *zip* past my shoulder like the clumsy whirr of a June bug. Max's head jerked as though he had been struck violently under the chin and upwards. He stared at me stupidly, his mouth rolled open and then he fell backwards to the ground with a neat little hole drilled an inch above his nose, dead centre between his dark eyebrows.

A voice I knew said from behind me, 'Damn necessary, and no great regrets. In fact, Mr Carver, sir, no regrets at all.'

I dropped back into a armchair, shaking all over like a man with Parkinson's disease. After a moment or two a glass was put into my right hand.

'Here, lover-boy, down this and get the roses back in your cheeks.'

Panda's long fingers patted my shoulder. The glass was full to the brim.

I had to steady my wrist with my left hand to get the glass to my mouth. It was cognac and went down like lava and the shaking in my body stopped.

Mr Najib Alakwe, Esquire, stepped back from me and said, 'It is a nice little dog, but I think not right for it to lick dead master's face.'

Panda picked up the poodle and moved out of the room with it. She was wearing sky-blue ski-trousers and a short red jacket and her legs seemed to have grown in length since I had last seen them.

Najib sat on the edge of the table, one leg swinging and showing a flash of purple sock above his ginger-suede shoe.

I put the glass down, almost empty, and said, 'Thank you very much, Najib.' If any man deserved to be promoted into the first-name category he did.

He beamed at me. 'Yes. I saved your life. It is a good feeling for

me since I do not often do good deeds. But also I am sad.' He
looked down at Max. 'What good is damned dead body? You get
much information from him?'

I said, 'How did you know about him?'

Panda, coming back into the room, said, 'That is my department,
lover-boy. There is a steward on the *Ferox* who likes Mamma. I say
to like Mamma and have Mamma like him then Mamma likes
names and addresses of all people Miss Zelia sends letters to. So
everything ends up very likeable. One day soon I'll show you.' She
sat on the arm of my chair and twined a long arm around my neck.

Najib said, 'But there never are any letters until you visit Miss
Zelia. Then there is the letter to this gentleman and you are gone
from your hotel, so we come up here. We have damned fine car,
American Thunderbird, hired, you understand, because I cannot
personally afford to own such a luxury. You wish more cognac?'

'No thanks.'

Panda patted my cheek. 'Good. Complete recovery.' She looked
at Najib. 'I shall take him up to the bedroom for some liking and
then he will tell me all Mr Max tells him?'

I said, 'It's not such a complete recovery as that.'

'Nevertheless,' said Najib, 'in return for life-saving you will tell
what he said about the red Mercedes. Personal details of Miss Zelia,
of which I hear a little before I shoot, do not interest my good self.
I read between the lines why she said nothing about whereabouts
of car. But it is damned reasonable now to tell me what you know.
Yes, sir?'

He was dead right, of course. It would have been only damned
reasonable to repay him with the information he wanted. I wanted
to do it. But, like most people who have been hauled out of trouble,
once the shock of crisis has passed, I knew that life had to go on
in its same old sordid, double-crossing way. Gratitude must never
get in the way of bringing home the bacon. The best place for
sentiment was on Christmas, birthday and get-well cards. Najib
was on the other side. I wanted to help him. But I had a job to do,
fees and a bonus to collect, so there was never a moment's doubt
in my mind.

I said, 'I didn't get much out of him – and I don't know that
what I did was the truth. I think I'd have needed a few hours to
work him up into a state of frankness. You know how it is.'

Panda stood up, stepped over Max, and helped herself to a
cigarette from the box on the sideboard. She turned and winked at

me. 'Try, honey, try hard to remember all the lies he gave you. We'll sort 'em out. You want that Mamma takes you up to the bedroom and works you up to a state of frankness. Whoof! Whoof!' She did a couple of high kicks.

I said, 'The car was stolen from here by a friend of his called Otto Libsch. He's a pretty undesirable character, I gathered. If you have a way into police records, you'll probably find him there. Because of what happened here with Miss Zelia, he was pretty safe in taking the car. But he didn't have any idea – nor did Max here, I imagine – that there was anything special about the car.'

'This man, Otto – you have an address for him?' asked Najib, and I noticed that when he was getting down to facts his pidgin English slipped.

'No.' I decided to play hard to get, because if he had to drag it from me he wouldn't suspect, perhaps, that it was a false address.

Najib fingered his tie, took off his panama and laid it on the table by the bowl of flowers.

'Splendid dahlias,' he said. 'I am very fond of flowers.'

'Runs in the family.'

'Maybe,' said Panda, 'I should break the bowl over his head? Eh, honey?' She came back and sat on the arm of my chair.

Najib shook his head and smiled at me, his dark eyes full of understanding. 'You are, of course, Mr Carver, stuck on the horns of a dilemma, no? In thanks for your delivery, your heart wants to be generous. But your brain is a professional man's brain. Tell nothing, it says.'

'In my place, what would you do?'

'The same.'

'Stalemate, then.'

'But you have an adress for Otto Libsch?'

'Well . . . I've an address but I wouldn't know whether Max had just made it up.'

'That we can check. The address, please, Mr Carver.'

He produced his gun from his pocket and nodded at Panda. She slipped a long arm round me and took Max's Browning out of my pocket, kissing my left ear as she did it.

'Damned big bulge these make,' she said. 'You should have used it on the late gentleman.'

'I didn't get a chance.'

Najib said, 'You get no chances now. Personal feelings are disqualified. I want the address.'

'And if I won't give it?'

I just caught the flicker of his eye towards Panda and then it happened. She grabbed me by the wrist, hauled me up, dropping her shoulders as she did, and I went cartwheeling over her and hit the floor on my face. Her weight dropped on my back and a pair of long legs took a scissors grip round my neck, almost choking me.

'For proper likings, honey,' she said, 'we begin with gentle love play.' She twisted my right arm hard and I shouted.

'Let him up,' said Najib. There was nothing phoney about him now. He was crisp, cold and determined and there wasn't a thing wrong with his Queen's English.

Panda let me get up. Najib faced me, pulling at his pudgy nose. Panda straightened my tie for me.

'You ought to meet a friend of mine called Miggs,' I said. 'You've got a lot in common.' Then, out of sheer pique, I kicked her feet from under her and she sat on the floor with a bang. For a moment she stared, disbelieving, at me, and then she began to laugh. 'Oh, Rexy-boy,' she chuckled, 'I got you wrong. You got promise.'

Najib made an impatient movement of his gun-hand.

'Give me the address. If not I shall shoot you so that you cannot take advantage of it. The situation will then be that I still do not know the address, but you will be dead, and I shall be able to find it some other way without trouble from you.'

'That'll leave two bodies here. Could be embarrassing.'

'If you have a coloured skin like mine, Mr Carver, and live in a white man's world, then you know all about embarrassments, most of them more damned awkward than a couple of cadavers. Give me the address or it is D for drastic.'

He waggled the gun. Panda got up off the floor.

'Be reasonable, lover-boy,' she said. 'You gonna miss all them lovely things otherwise. That extra drink you shouldn't take. Lovin' arms around you in the night and the first cigarette with your hangover in the morning. Why, I just couldn't bear to see so much good manpower go down the drain.'

She was right of course. And anyway, I felt I had stalled long enough. I flapped my hands and let my shoulders collapse.

'Okay, I'd hate to arrive at the pearly gates next in the queue to Max Ansermoz.'

'Splendid.' Najib beamed. We were all friends again.

'Otto Libsch,' I said. 'The Bernina Hotel, Geneva. That's in the Place Cornavin.'

Najib beamed. 'Thank you, Mr Carver. This Max may have lied, of course. That I accept. But if I find that you have lied then you go right down the drain. Now, please, turn round.'

'Why?'

'Do like Najib says,' said Panda.

I turned.

Najib hit me on the back of the head with his gun and I went down and out.

When I came to, I was lying on the floor with my head on a cushion. My face was wet and my shirt-front was soaked with water. Sitting on a chair close to me was Julia Yunge-Brown, holding a glass jug of water in her hand. She flicked half of it into my face as my eyes blinked at the light.

I said, 'If you really want to help you might find something stronger than water.' This was my morning for girls and cognac. As she moved away I sat up and looked around.

'Where's the body?' I said.

Over her shoulder, she said, 'What body?'

I didn't answer. What a nice chap Najib was. He had carted off the body to save me embarrassment. I really felt bad about lying to him. But I knew that the next time we met he was going to be anything but nice, and would want to take all the lovely things away from me.

CHAPTER 5

'We ride, and I see her bosom heave.'
(Robert Browning)

It was a pleasant enough family scene. Ten o'clock on a Sunday morning, the sound of church bells coming through the open kitchen window, the smell of coffee from the percolator on a small electric ring, and over everything the warm, steamy smell of baby clothes half dry, strung out on a line across the top part of the window.

The man was lounging in a broken-down cane chair, nursing the baby in his arms. I couldn't tell its sex and never asked, but it had a red face, screwed up like a toothless old man's, and a fluff of soft black hair on its head that looked like the combings from a dog's coat. It was sucking away at the business end of an old fashioned feeding bottle, slipping its mouth sideways from the teat now and then to give a milky belch.

The man manoeuvred a cigarette one-handed from his shirt pocket, struck a match, one-handed, on the sole of his sandal and said, 'After the business with Otto, Mimi lost her milk. Big shock – but she's over it now. In good hands.'

Mimi Probst – I was sure about her because she had answered the door and identified herself – was ironing on the kitchen table. She wore a loose apron affair and had bare legs and bare feet. Her red hair was untidy, and her blue eyes were quiet and mild. She had a thinnish face with high cheekbones and a narrow chin. She looked about eighteen but was probably more. She gave the man an adoring look when he said 'in good hands', smiled and made a silent kissing movement with her mouth. Happy, contented, couple, baby giving no trouble for once, all Sunday, the day of rest, before them, and on her wrist she was wearing a small diamond-set watch that was right out of her class and an identical number to the one which Julia wore. When I got back to Julia I wasn't even going to ask if Zelia had a watch like hers. Cavan O'Dowda had probably unloaded a couple on the girls at some time to mark some coup he'd pulled off.

I said, 'You know who I am. And I know who Mimi is – but who are you? Otto is the man I want, and you know why.'

My card was lying on the edge of the chair he sat in. I'd just said that I was looking for Otto to try and recover a Mercedes that belonged to a client of mine. No more, no less, not even how I had come to trace Otto. Right from the start I'd been troubled by their manner. There hadn't been the slightest edge of resentment at an intrusion on their Sunday morning. Every time I'd mentioned Otto so far, they had looked at one another and giggled.

Mimi tested the flat of the iron by spitting on it, was dissatisfied with the heat and dumped it on another ring alongside the coffee. She turned back, put her hands on her hips and looked at me. Dolled up, she would never have passed unnoticed in a crowd.

She winked at the man. 'What do you think?'

His English accent would have passed, but hers was surprisingly thick. She could have had a mouth full of sticky toffee.

The man nodded, and eyed me affably as he slipped the teat from the baby's mouth, hunked the infant gently over one shoulder and began massaging its back through the shawl to ease up wind.

'He's doing a job,' he said to no one in particular. 'Been frank. Right to the point. Broad-minded, too, I should say. Would have to be in his job.' Then to me particularly he went on, 'I'm Tony Collard. You're wrong about Mimi. It ain't Probst. We were married last week. I can see you're wondering about my English. No need. My father was a Canadian, volunteered at the beginning of the war into the British Royal Artillery, came over here, changed his mind about war, deserted, settled down, married and eventually had me. He died two years back. I run the garage and repair shop that never made him a fortune.'

I said, 'You jump about a lot. And you're giving me a lot of information that I don't want. Otto is my bird. Where's he roosting now?'

At that they both gave out high squeaks of laughter. When the paroxysm was over Tony said, 'Like some coffee?'

'No thanks.'

He massaged a final burp from the baby and then stuck it back on the bottle. He had nice, easy, comfortable hands, gentle, but I had a feeling that there was far more to him than a smiling frankness of manner and an occasional mad laugh. He was about twenty, plump and big built, and with a face like a young Pickwick, made more so by the steel-rimmed glasses he wore. He had thin, blond-white hair, and would be bald before he was thirty.

'What's the score on the car?' he asked.

'My client wants it back. He's a millionaire. They get touchy about property. You and I worry over the pence. His kind worry all the way up through the cash register. That's why they're million-aires. I understood, from a gent I met recently, that Otto regarded Mimi as his girl.'

Going back to the pile of baby-clothes and diapers, iron in hand, Mimi said, 'I was. That's his baby. I had a bad time with it.'

'Caesarian,' said Tony, proudly almost, and I thought at any moment he would ask her to show me the scar. He gave her a loving look and she angled it back with that silent kissing motion of the lips. I began to feel out of place in so much domestic bliss.

'Being Otto's makes no difference to Tony,' said Mimi.

'Not a scrap,' said Tony. 'I loved Mimi long before Otto came along. Old faithful.' He chuckled. 'But then every girl's due for one stupid infatuation. Come to that, so's a man. More than one, perhaps. Eh?' He winked at Mimi and she brandished the iron, mock angry at him. I began to get the idea that they were either playing with me, or just glad to have a diversion on a warm, happy Sunday morning before they put the kid in its bassinet and wandered down the road to some *trattoria* for lunchtime *spaghetti Milanese* and a couple of glasses of Chianti.

I put some lira notes on top of the refrigerator and said, 'Don't be offended. Good information – particularly about bad characters – is worth paying for. And it isn't my money, anyway. Just tell me about Otto. Description, habits, and, maybe, present whereabouts.'

They both went into their side-splitting-giggle act, and then recovered themselves and looked a bit self-conscious.

'We don't need the money,' said Tony, 'but we'll take it on principle. Money is always something you take even if you don't need it. Money, as my old man used to say, is like music. No matter where or in what form it comes we should be glad of it. It cuts across international and cultural barriers and it is a sad person who gets no joy out of it. The other thing he used—'

'Don't start about your father,' said Mimi, shaking her head at him, smiling indulgently, and finishing again with that silent kiss.

He said something to her in rapid Italian beyond me. She blushed in a swift curtain fall from the roots of her red hair down to the point of her pert chin and said something back in Italian, and Tony squirmed in the chair and rolled his eyes behind the spectacles. It was a horrible sight. The baby burped, slipped the teat and was sick all down the front of its shawl. Tony took out his handkerchief and mopped up the mess with the loving unconcern of a devoted stepfather. In my book, there was something wrong about Tony and Mimi. I had the feeling that not only outwardly, but quietly, inwardly and even sadistically, they were laughing their heads off about me. There was, I felt, some monstrous, side-splitting joke going on so that when I left they would collapse on to the floor, rolling over and over as the pent-up mirth oozed out of them.

Tony got up and took the baby to a wicker cradle that stood on a side table. He began to tuck it away, making father noises. Without turning he said, 'What kind of car did you say?'

'I told you. A red Mercedes 250SL. Number 828 Z-9626. 1966 model.'

He turned, smiled at me and nodded.

'That's the one. Otto brought it to me almost a month ago. I did it over for him. Only an outside job, no fiddling about changing engine numbers and so on. Just a respray and new number plates. Let me see.' He screwed up his eyes in thought, staring at the ceiling. He was a big man, bigger than he'd looked in the chair. 'Yes.' He came back to earth, having remembered, walked to his chair, patted Mimi on the bottom as he passed, and collapsed into the cane chair so that it creaked like a building about to come down in a high wind. 'Yes. I did it up cream, and the new number was something like 3243 P 38. Or it may have been 3423. But it was certainly P and 38. The last tow numbers, you know, show what department a car is registered with and he particularly wanted it to be Isère – that's up around Grenoble.'

I said, 'You don't mind sitting there and telling me you did this?'

'Why should I? But you try to put it on the record – which I don't think you will – then I'd deny it. I run an almost honest business. That's as much as any garage can say.' He chuckled, and winked at Mimi. Thank God, she spared him the silent kiss on that one.

'What would he do – resell it?'

'With Otto, he could do anything. Enter it for Le Mans perhaps. Give it to his old mother for a present – if he ever knew who was his mother.'

'What does Otto look like?'

He didn't answer at once. He glanced at Mimi and I could sense the joke bubbling silently between them like a dark underground stream while their eyes lightened with merriment.

'He's four foot nothing and built like an ape. Very strong. Brown hair, long, always tossing it out of his eyes. Smart dresser. About thirty-five. Good dancer. Women fall for him, God knows why, but it never lasts because he's so selfish and unreliable with money. Still owes me for the repaint job.'

'That's all?'

'What more do you want?'

'He's got two heads,' said Mimi.

I sighed as they went into a convulsion of laughter. In fact, I was a bit annoyed. If there's a good joke going I like to be in on it.

I said, 'Anything else you've overlooked? Hare lip, forked tail, or a club foot?'

Mimi said solemnly, 'On the inside of his left thigh he's got a birthmark shaped like the cross of Lorraine.'

They both laughed again and when Tony had squeezed the last tears of delight from his eyes, he said, 'Pay no attention. Just Mimi's jokes. She's a good one for a giggle.'

I said, 'How come Otto let you walk in and take over Mimi?'

'Because he knew I was going to do it anyway, and break him in half if he made trouble. Oh, he knew it. But trust Otto to get out without trouble. A week after he took the car off he phoned, long distance somewhere, saying he was through with Mimi. Right, *cara mia*?'

'Just like that.' Mimi began to put away the ironed clothes. 'Just phoned. Everything was over. It was not unexpected. The baby was a mistake. He never loved it. Never wanted it – but I am naturally shocked until Tony comes and says marry me. Tony is a good man.'

'The best,' said Tony. 'True love triumphs. You know what we're going to do – when the baby's a little older? Sell the garage and go to Australia. No more garage. I'm going to farm. With animals, I am good. Like with children, like with women.' He reached out as Mimi passed and held her by the left knee under the apron and they both made silent kissing motions at one another as though I were not there. He let her go and she moved over to the baby.

I said, 'Any idea where Otto might be now?'

Tony choked on his mirth, pursed his lips, gave it thought, and then said, 'Sitting comfortably somewhere without a care in the world.'

I wasn't meant to see it, but there was a mirror on the wall over Tony's chair. In it I could see Mimi's back as she bent over the cradle. From the movement of her shoulders and head, I thought she was about to have a convulsion. She just stood there, holding down a great, pulsing pressure of laughter.

I was glad to get out of the place, to get away from the homely shrine they'd built to their true love. Going down the street, heading for the nearest bottle of beer, I knew that up in the flat they were letting the laughter flow like red-hot lava. I didn't believe a word they'd said about Otto. But what they hadn't said didn't make me feel sorry for him wherever he was sitting – comfortably and without a care in the world – because always at the back of my mind was the thought of Zelia with him and Max at the Châlet Bayard.

After the beer I took a taxi to the Via Sacchi and the Palace Hotel. Lying on my bed, I put in a call to Paris and got the duty man at Interpol. I had a brief up and down with him, establishing my credentials after he'd told me that Commissaire Maziol wasn't available. I threw Guffy's name at him – told him that my *bona fides* had already been checked through him once, and what was the matter, weren't they interested in suppressing crime and bringing the riff-raff of Europe to book? He said it was a beautiful day in Paris, and would I make it as brief as possible. So I said in *précis: Otto Libsch. Could be Otto Probst. Possible descriptions. Four feet high, strong as an ape, brown, floppy hair. Or, maybe, six feet high, round happy face, steel-rimmed spectacles, fair hair, going bald. Associate Max Ansermoz – enquiry already made viz same. Otto floating around possibly in cream-coloured Mercedes 250SL. Index number – 3243, 3234, or 3423 P 38 according to latest inaccurate information, probably different number altogether, possibly car not cream, but green, blue, black or maroon. But certainly Mercedes.* For a moment or two I debated dropping in the names of Mimi Probst and Tony Collard and then decided against it. They were a couple I'd like to have up my sleeve just in case anything definite came up about Otto.

Just as I was finishing, Julia came in without knocking and sat at the end of the bed. She wore a cream coloured silk dress with a little snatch of red scarf at the throat, and I could see by the set of her mouth that she was determined to have things out with me. I looked at her watch and checked it against Mimi's – they were both the same. Otto, before taking off, or Tony, before settling in, had made it a love gift.

I put the phone down and Julia said, 'I've driven you all the way down here. When do I get let into your confidence?'

I should say that Najib had taken my car. He'd left a note on Max's round table saying that Panda was driving it off, and he gave the name of a garage from which I could collect it in Geneva. That was merely to get a head start on me in the chase after Otto. At this moment he was probably a damned angry man without any doubt that I was anything but a *bon ami* of his.

So Julia had been press-ganged into driving me to Turin and no explanations. She'd been content to wait for the right moment which, as she swung her legs up on to the bed, I saw she had decided was now.

I said, 'There isn't any need for you to know anything. You want to protect Zelia. So do I. Let's leave it like that.'

'I want to know about this Max Ansermoz.'

'He's dead – and I'm heartily glad. A sort of friend of mine shot him just before he could shoot me, and then this friend conveniently carted the body off – and my car. All I need say to you is that Zelia spent a couple of nights at the chalet. Okay?'

She looked at me, head lowered a little, and then slowly nodded.

'Okay. But why are you here?'

'I've got a job to do. Remember? I have to find your father's car.'

'Can't I help you with that?'

'You have, by driving me here. But that's as far as it goes. Look your concern was Zelia. You've got my word about that. O'Dowda's not going to know anything. But there's still the car, and that's my job. It isn't a game. I'm paid to take bumps on the head and stupid risks. I've a defect of character which forces me to accept it as a way of life. I'm a hard case, hooked. I can't afford to have you along all the time. Somebody might flatten you – and then what chance would I have of a bonus from step-daddy? Business to me is money, and I don't want you involved just for the kicks. Let me finish this job and then, if you like my company, I'll give you two weeks you'll never forget.'

'God, you're impossible.'

Her bosom heaved. It was something I had never seen happen before. She almost burst.

'I dislike you,' she said, 'more than I can say.'

I said, 'The top button of your dress has popped.' It had, too.

She swung off the bed and made for the door, her hands up, buttoning her dress. Halfway there, she turned towards me.

'By the way, while you were out I phoned my father. He wants to see you at once. That's an order.'

'Where is he?'

'Evian – at the château.'

I gave her a big smile.

'You wouldn't care to drive me back as far as Geneva?'

'Not bloody likely. Remember, you don't want any help from me.'

'Okay.'

She went to the door, and then paused before opening it.

She said, 'Tell me one thing – and I'm not asking out of idle curiosity. When you talked with this Max, did he tell you how he came to know Zelia?'

'No. He just said he met her in Geneva and Evian.'

'Secretly?'

'I imagine so.'

'Poor Zelia.'

'Well, she doesn't have to worry about Max any more. And when I get hold of the other bastard I'll do something about him.'

'The other?'

'Yes it can't hurt you to know. There was another man at the chalet. He's the one who ran off with the car. I thought I might find him here, but I was unlucky.'

'What was his name?'

'Otto Libsch.'

There was a long pause, and then she went.

I didn't care for the pause. There was something unnatural about it. I had the impression that for a few seconds she was fighting within herself to decide whether she should move out at the end of the pause or say something.

Somehow I wasn't surprised when, ten minutes later, she phoned through and said that she had changed her mind and would be willing to drive me to Geneva. And that change of heart I was convinced had something to do with the name Otto Libsch.

A few minutes later my phone went again. It was a Paris call. The duty officer out at Saint Cloud was brisker this time, alive, alert, almost commanding. Somebody had not only confirmed my rating with him, but somebody clearly wanted something from me.

Where, he asked, could I be found in the next twenty-four hours?
I said that I was going to be driving through the night to Geneva,
where I should be picking my car up at the Autohall Servette in
the Rue Liotard, and then going on to Cavan O'Dowda's château
above Evian, and what was the sudden urgency about? He said it
was still a splendid day in Paris and wished me *bon voyage*.

At nine the next morning Julia dropped me in the Rue Liotard.
The night drive had been quite an experience, like being crated up
in the hold of a jet cargo plane. I croaked appropriate thanks and
crabbed my way down the street on bent legs, my eyes gritty for
sleep and my mouth dry with smoking too many cigarettes. She
swept by me with a wave, smiling and as fresh as a dew-spangled
rose.

At the entrance to the Autohall I was met by an old friend,
looking, as usual, as droopy and sun-dazzled as a day-trapped owl.
He was leaning against the wall, Gauloise dangling from the corner
of his mouth, wearing a shabby brown suit, brown shirt without
tie, and big brown shoes that turned up at the toes. Over his rusty
brown moustache he blinked upwards at me in welcome. Upwards,
because Aristide Marchissy la Dole was only just over four feet in
height. He looked at his watch and said, 'Good timing. I heard it
was a Facel Vega. I had you bracketed to the half-hour.'

I said, 'What the hell are you doing in Switzerland?'

The last time I'd met him he had been with the *Sûreté Nationale
– Office Central des Stupéfiants*. Before that with *Renseignements Généraux*.

He said, 'I've moved on to higher and no better things. Let's
have breakfast.'

He took me around the corner to a *pâtisserie* where he loaded his
plate with a large slice of *gâteau Galicien,* oozing with apricot jam
and stuck all over with pistachio nuts, ordered a large cup of hot
chocolate into which he poured cognac from his own flask and then,
butter cream fringing his moustache, asked, 'You are well?'

I was feeling sick, but said, 'Yes. And you?'

'I am in good health and appetite, despite a lack of sleep. But
sleep is for weaklings. Tell me, are we going to have the usual
trouble with you over this?'

'Probably.'

'You know what I mean by this?'

'No.'

He stoked up with more cake and through it said, 'I am very

fond of *Galicien*. It was first made in Paris at the Pâtisserie Frascati, alas no more. It stood on the corner of the Boulevard Richelieu, on the site of what was at one time one of the most famous gaming houses in the city.' He sighed, blinked, and went on, 'I wish I were back in Paris at the Sûreté. I do not like International things nor anything that begins with Inter. Despite De Gaulle I am not even in favour of the Common Market. I am parochial. And much as I like you, I am sorry even to meet you briefly on business because I know you will only give me trouble as before.'

He held a brief silence in memory of the troubled past. I lit a cigarette and, reaching for his flask, put the rest of his cognac in my coffee.

He said, 'Let us now play the frankness game. I will be frank with you.'

'And I will be frank with you.'

'Up to a point.'

'Up to a point where individual ethics, self-interest, etcetera, etcetera demand otherwise. So?'

'We have no information on one Max Ansermoz.'

I said expansively, 'Forget him. *Requiescat in pace.*'

He gave me a look and said, 'We will not pursue it unless it comes up. Without a *corpus* there in no *corpus delicti*. Something like that, no?'

'Something,' I said.

'Tell me,' he said, 'before we get down to the real business. Have you engaged yourself – on the side – in another commission which concerns O'Dowda?'

'Like what?'

'Possibly from some member of his family?'

'I've enough on my hands with his Mercedes job. I just stick to one thing at a time – and often that's too much for me.'

He nodded approvingly, and I said, 'Tell me about Otto Libsch?'

'Willingly. He is about thirty-five years old, born in Linz, Austria, of course. Passes as a Frenchman. Five foot ten, dark-haired, good physique, various prison sentences, various names, same crimes – armed robbery. From a description given, and the method used, he is now wanted for a payroll robbery which he carried out with a companion two weeks ago. It was in France and they got away with the equivalent in English money of . . .'he thought, licking the fringe of his moustache with his tongue – 'say ten thousand pounds.'

'Where did this happen exactly, and how?'

'At the moment my frankness doesn't reach that far.'

'How far does it reach?'

'Let us see. Ah, yes. A car was used in the robbery. It was a black Mercedes 250SL. Index number – different from any that you named.'

'I'm not surprised. Has the car been traced?'

'No. Nor Otto.'

'Or his companion?'

'No. He was tall, six feet, big build, round, plump face, steel-rimmed spectacles and he had fair hair. He doesn't fit anyone in our records. Naturally we are interested in anything you might have to say about any person of your acquaintance who fits this description.'

I was silent, trying to figure the best way out because I didn't want to declare as good an ace as Tony Collard yet. He got up and went over to the counter and came back with a concoction that made me feel I would never want to eat again.

Seeing my look, he said brightly, 'It is a *Saint-Honoré*. He was, you know, once Bishop of Amiens and is the patron saint of pastry-cooks for no reason that anyone has ever been able to discover. So, a big man with big face and cheap glasses – you met someone like that in Turin?'

'No. I got Otto from Max Ansermoz. He also gave me an address for Otto in Turin – but it was a phoney. Nobody knew of Otto.'

Aristide chuckled.

'You want the car,' he said. 'And we want Otto, plus friend. Please try to find a way around this which will trouble no one's ethics.'

'I'll do my best.'

He nodded. 'Of that I am sure. The trouble is that you produce such a poor best at times. Now me, for example, for a friend I always try to give of my best. Take your car in the garage around the corner. The same kind of car that your employer is so mysteri-ously worried about. You should not drive it away without having a good look under the bonnet. While waiting for you I took the trouble to inspect it only because I am interested in engines . . . purely that. How large events sometimes hang on the smallest of human curiosities.'

I stood up. 'I'm sure,' I said, 'you'd like to be left alone in peace with your *Saint-Honoré*. But thank you for everything.'

'Nothing at all. I have left my card in your car. When you are ready – just give me a call.' He raised a large round of sugar-iced *choux* to his mouth and crunched on it hungrily. Then, mouth full, he added, 'By the way, there is one other small point.'

'Nice of you to save it for last. That means it's the real point.'

'Possibly. When you locate this car – you will notify me at once, and say nothing to your employer until I give you permission.'

'And if I don't?'

He gave me a beaming smile, his mouth flecked with crumbs.

'If you don't – then many people more important than me will be angry. Very angry. Influential, official people, who could make life hard for you.'

'When has it been any other?'

He took another bite at his *Saint-Honoré* and winked, his mouth too full for words.

I went and collected my car, but before driving it away I inspected the engine as he had suggested. In the long run, professional ethics are one thing. But if there is going to be a long run there's nothing like friendship.

The Château de la Forclaz was about ten miles due south of Evian, out along the road to a place called Abondance. It had a mile of road frontage, a high wire fence studded with the usual notices, *Chasse Interdit, Défence d'Entrer, Propriété Privée*, and so on. There was a lodge, a lodge gate with a wide cattle-grid across the road, and then half a mile of private drive up through pine woods, curving and banking, and with more notices telling one to take it easy on the curves and not exceed thirty kilometres an hour. The rich are great ones for notices telling you what not to do, which is odd, really, when you consider that they take no account of warning notices themselves.

The château, with a façade almost as long as that of Buckingham Palace, was big enough to give a millionaire a feeling of not being too cramped. From the corners and roof spaces of the building – which was built of a pleasant grey-yellow stone – a series of round towers with blue slate roofs fingered their way skywards. There was a terrace along the front with wide steps leading up from either end. In the centre of the terrace a bronze fountain spouted water twenty feet high over a centrepiece of mixed-up mermen, mermaids and dolphins engaged in some nautical frolic that in real life would certainly have led to trouble. Naturally, being O'Dowda's place, there were no goldfish in the fast swirling waters of the fountain's bowl. Just brown trout.

I had a room in one of the towers with a view reaching way back to Lac Léman. I took lunch in a small, sub-guest dining room with Durnford, who was still twitching his eyes and was not particularly friendly towards me. He told me that O'Dowda was in residence and would send for me after lunch.

I said, 'Did you get that list of people in residence here at the time Miss Zelia left?'

'I am working on it.'

It occurred to me that it wasn't something that required all that much work, but I made no comment because I could see that he was in no mood for comments.

I lingered over my coffee much too long for him, so he got up and excused himself, making for the door. But from the door he did a Wilkins on me, turning and saying, 'I think I should warn you that Mr O'Dowda is in a particular mood today.'

I looked at him enquiringly.

'You care to enlarge on that?'

'No.' He opened the door. 'But I thought it only fair to warn you. His staff are used to him but it sometimes disconcerts strangers.' He went.

I sat there and, after a few moments, it occurred to me that perhaps he wasn't as unfriendly as he always appeared and sounded. If he disliked me he would have been happy for me to meet any awkward mood of O'Dowda's head on.

Half an hour later a footman in green livery, silver buttons, and with the face of a professional mourner, came to conduct me to O'Dowda. We went through and up what seemed a quarter of a mile of corridors, picture galleries and stairs and finally landed up in front of a tall pair of doors covered in red leather and ornamented with copper studs.

From a niche in the wall alongside the door he pulled out a hand microphone and announced, 'Mr Carver is here, sir.'

Almost immediately, the double-doors slid back, and the footman nodded to me to enter, looking as though he were muttering a requiem for me under his breath.

I went through the door, heard it whisper to a close behind me, and faced a long room full of people, not one of whom took the slightest notice of me.

It was an enormous room, originally intended for stately balls, masques, routs, assemblages, minor coronations or, maybe, indoor joustings. Tall mullioned windows ran along one wall, draped with heavy red velvet curtains. From the barrel-vaulted ceiling hung three Venetian glass chandeliers. The floor under my feet was polished Carrera marble, and on the wall opposite the window hung four Velasquez portraits.

Although the place was full of people there wasn't a sound to be heard. There were about fifty of them – men and women, more men than women, some black, most white and a few yellow. Their dress was everything from evening gown and tiaras, court dress, rough old working suits, shirt sleeves and denims, military uniforms to national costumes. Some of them were sitting, some standing, and one couple were down on one knee in the act of obeisance, and they were all looking towards the far end of the room. Not a muscle amongst them moved because they were all made of wax. Nearest to me was a woman in a low-cut evening gown whose shoulders wanted dusting.

At the far end of the room was a raised platform, half-crescented at each side with a pierced marble balustrade. Three low steps ran upwards to a final dais on which was an enormous throne-chair in gold stucco with a back that ran up into a kind of baldachin affair overhead from which fell silver-and-gold curtains. On either side of the throne-chair stood a pair of seven branched candelabra, all the candles lit. In the chair sat a wax figure, double life-size, of O'Dowda. The big head was decked out with a chaplet of laurel leaves, a purple toga swathed the huge body, and there were gold sandals on the big feet. One fat hand held a silver drinking goblet and the other a long roll of parchment. Take the parchment away and stick a lyre in it and you could ring the changes: Caesar or Nero, according to mood.

Just at that moment, having got over the shock of the Madame Tussaud collection in the room, I was wondering what was the particular mood of the man who sat on the edge of the platform below the effigy. Normally it might have been difficult to guess. It could have been his day to be Caesar, Nero, Hitler, Napoleon, Karl Marx, Sam Goldwyn or Kruschev. But it wasn't. He was all togged up from ankle to neck in one of those blue siren suits Winston Churchill used to wear, and there was a fat cigar stuck in his mouth and a fat scowl overhanging his eyes. In his right hand he held a whippy little cane with which he was gently smacking his right leg.

He just stared at me across a hundred yards of marble floor, waiting for me to speak, I imagined. But I knew my place. You do not speak to royalty until they speak to you first. I knew something else, too. Despite this show, he wasn't mad. He wasn't even eccentric. Everything he did, he did from reason; cold, hard, cash-registering reason. Only the failures in life go mad. It's their way of opting out of the rat-race.

He got up and slowly made his way down the room. He stopped once alongside the figure of a London policeman and gave the blue serge of the man's seat a whippy slash with the cane.

Then, coming up to me, he said, careful all the time to keep the scowl on his face, 'Know why I did that, Carver?'

I said, 'I should think because years ago he was the one who around midnight nobbled you as you came out of the neighbourhood grocer's with the contents of the till in your pocket.'

O'Dowda grinned, but he still managed somehow to keep the scowl going.

'Bad guess. Sure, before I had real hairs on my chest I knocked off a till or two. How the hell do you get capital to start otherwise? No – he nobbled me for drunken driving when I was twenty-two. Licence taken away for six months, meant I couldn't drive the van. Business kaput. They're all like that.' He waved the cane around the crowd.

'You brought me all the way up here to tell me about the people who've crossed you in your life?'

'You'll learn why I brought you up here soon enough. Sure, yes, they are all people who crossed or tried to cross me. I like to come in here sometimes and talk to them, let 'em see where I am now. You know how much one of these figures costs?'

'No.'

'Kermode does them. Clever sod, is Kermode. Used to work for Tussaud's once. Two hundred quid, he charges me.'

'You could save money by having them done in miniature. Keep 'em all in a glass case. That way the dust wouldn't settle on them.' I ran my finger down the V-back of the tiara number and showed the tip to him. 'Now stop trying to impress me.'

'You're fired, boyo.'

'Splendid.'

'You were going to cross me up.'

'You should have let me do it – then you could have stuck me in here. I'd have sent you one of my old suits to make it authentic.'

'Watch your tongue when you speak to me. You're just the hired man.'

'You fired me a moment ago. Remember? Anyway, hired or fired I speak as I find. Stop playing games, O'Dowda.'

For a moment I thought he was going to hit me with the cane. He stood there and bulged his big face at me, little blue eyes boring at me, the afternoon sun sparkling on the short copper scruff of his hair, the end of his cigar glowing like a Stop light. Then he wheeled away and went up to the figure of a coloured gent wearing a tarboosh and ten yards of white Manchester cotton robe and swiped the tarboosh off with his cane.

'What did he do?' I asked. 'Sell you a dud lot of dirty photos?'

'As a matter of fact it was a dud lot of industrial diamonds during the war. He lived to regret it. And don't think I'm trying to impress you. For me this is therapy. Every so often I like to review 'em, talk to 'em. Afterwards I feel as clean and pink inside as a baby. And when I'm not here they still have to face me.' He nodded towards the outsize Caesar figure.

I said, 'You should open it to the public. Cover your costs in a couple of years. Kermode could sell hot-dogs and ice-cream on the terrace.'

He scowled at me.

'You're fired,' he said.

I turned and made for the door. He let me reach it, and then said, 'Don't you want to know why?'

I looked at him over my shoulder. 'If you feel you've got to tell me – okay. But in that case let's do it over a drink and a smoke.' I fished out my cigarette case. 'The drink,' I said, 'is up to you.'

He gave me a grin then.

'You're a lippy bastard. But it's a change. You're still fired, though.'

He went back to the other end of the room, smacking the odd rump and shoulder here and there and stopped in front of what was probably a Louis-the-something console and produced brandy and glasses. Again, he gave himself the bigger helping. I went up and sat in an armchair with an elderly, diplomatic type in court dress resting one elbow nonchalantly on the back. (He'd probably blocked O'Dowda's bid for a knighthood.)

I breathed the brandy aroma, sipped, let the liquid roll around my mouth like a mixture of ginger and fire, swallowed it, and felt it like the beginning of a young volcano in my stomach.

I said, 'This is bloody awful stuff.'

O'Dowda said, 'You think I'd waste my best brandy on a man I've just fired?'

I said, 'Why am I fired?'

'Because, Carver, when I employ someone I demand complete loyalty for my money. Nobody has to love me for it. But they have to earn it.'

'So far as I know I haven't even got round to cheating you on a hotel bill yet. But I'll make a note to do so when you reinstate me.'

He whipped the cane through the air in front of him angrily and said, 'Bejasus, you try me hard.'

I said, 'You're the first Irishman outside of a music-hall I ever heard say Bejasus. Just let me have a few facts about my disloyalty.'

'Two days ago I had a visit from a black number called Alakwe—'

'Was this in England or over here?'

'Why?'

'Because then I'll know whether it was Jimbo Alakwe or Najib.'

'In London.'

'Good old Jimbo, still trying hard. Don't tell me – I can guess the kind of line he would take. I've taken a bribe of, say, two thousand guineas, not pounds, to double-cross you by letting him know before you where the Mercedes is when I find it? Something like that?'

'More or less. You're damned frank about it, aren't you?'

'I'll be even franker. Jimbo's the simpler of the two brothers – twins actually. God knows what the people he works for make of him. He should have known that my price for a double-cross like that would be in the region of ten thousand. I'm happy in my work with you. It gives me a change of scene, luxury living, new faces – some of 'em pretty and feminine – and a life expectancy that would have me booted out of any insurance office. Take a look at this.'

I reached into my pocket and tossed it across to him. It was the size and shape of a half grapefruit, but a good deal heavier.

He held it in one gorilla paw and said, 'What's this?'

I said, 'It's a magnetic limpet bomb, thermo-activated. There's a little sliding pointer on the side which you can set against the scale to any temperature. The temperature readings are calibrated in Fahrenheit, Centigrade and Reamur. No detail overlooked. At the moment it's set to "safe". It was stuck on the side of my car engine in Geneva, set to a reading that would have blown me sky-high after a couple of kilometres.'

'Boyo, what a damned useful gadget.'

'You can keep it. But if I'd taken cash to double-cross you, why would they want to knock me off? Waste of money. They were annoyed because I wouldn't double-cross you. I suppose you've now paid Jimbo good money to double-cross them, whoever they are?'

'Yes, I have.'

I shook my head. 'You'll have him all mixed up. He isn't the kind to carry a double disloyalty in his mind without getting the wires crossed. All right, am I back at work?'

He reached round and put the bomb on the console affair behind him. Then he slewed his big head back at me, lowering it like a bull sighting on the middle point of a matador's cummerbund, and heaved a great sniff of air out of his nostrils.

'What the hell goes on?' he said. 'I just want that car back.'

I said, 'You're going to get it. It was pinched by a crook called Otto Libsch.' I paused, watching him closely as I mentioned the name. It had, I was sure, meant something to Julia. It could mean something to him. If it did he didn't show it. I went on, 'He had a respray job done on it and some weeks after used it to carry out a payroll hold-up somewhere in France. Since then, neither he nor the car has been seen. But I'll lay you ten to one in hundreds – pounds not francs – that I find the car in the next few days. On?'

'No.'

'It's nice you have such confidence in me. Am I reinstated?'

'Temporarily, yes. But by God – you put one foot wrong and—'

'You're jumping the gun,' I said. 'If you want me back, there's a condition on this side. No, two conditions.'

'Nobody makes conditions with me.' He said it with a rumble like a runaway steamroller. As I knew better than to argue with a steamroller I began to get up to leave.

He waved me down. 'Let's hear them.'

I sat back. 'First, I don't want to be badgered with questions about how I traced Otto and the car. And I don't want your stepdaughter Zelia badgered. Like she says, she knows nothing. Secondly, I want to know what's in the secret compartment of that car and who the people are who are employing Najib and Jimbo Alakwe. This I have to know for my own protection. What do you say?'

He stood up slowly and gave me a warm smile. You wouldn't believe it possible, but suddenly that big brute of a face was transformed. He was a solid, bearlike father-figure reaching out his arms with a benign smile, ready to take and comfort the world's weary and sick at heart, the oppressed, the poor and the homeless. It didn't impress me at all, because I knew that he would take them all and make a profit out of it somehow.

'What I say, Carver, is that I've obviously been mistaken in you. Just get on with the job. I've complete trust in you, boyo. And as far as Zelia's concerned, I'll never mention the car to her again.'

'Good.'

He shook his head. 'I'll never understand why you haven't made a million for yourself already. You're got all the gall in the world.'

'What I haven't got is an answer to the second condition. What's in the car and who wants it?'

'Ah, yes, that. Well, that's a little more difficult. Delicate, in fact.'

'Try.'

He chewed the end of his cigar for a while, working up in his mind the lie he was going to tell me. After the write-up he'd just given me he knew it would have to be good. He wasn't long about it.

'In the car,' he said, 'is a very considerable parcel of bonds. Gold bonds. To be exact they're Imperial Japanese Government external loan bonds of 1930, sinking fund $5\frac{1}{2}\%$, which are due for final redemption in May 1975, but these bonds are ones that have been drawn for redemption in January of next year. Naturally no further interest accrues to them after that date, but their redemption value is around twenty thousand pounds. Originally they belonged to me. But I was passing them over to a friend in return for services rendered. You with this, so far?'

'Yes. But I shall check that there are such bonds, naturally.'

'Do that, you careful bastard.' He grinned.

'And the friend?'

'He is an important figure in the opposition party of one of the new African states. At the material time this opposition party was the ruling party. Times change. The present ruling party considers that the bonds belong to them since, they argue, the favour done for me by my friend when he was in power was done in his official, not private, capacity.'

'What do you think of that argument?'

'I don't care a damn. I promised him the bonds, and he gets them. And that's all the damned details you're going to get about it.'

I said, 'Where do these bonds have to be delivered for redemption?' It was a quick one but he was up to it, the answer rolling out smoothly.

'The Bank of Tokyo Trust Company, 100 Broadway, New York, N.Y. 10005. Naturally you'll check that, too. But do it on your own time, not mine. Now get the hell out of here and find me that Mercedes.'

I stood up. 'And where is the secret compartment in the car?'

He puffed his cheeks out like a grotesque cherub, exploded air gently, and said, 'That's no affair of yours. You're all right in my book so far, but not so far that I would trust you with twenty thousand pounds' worth of bonds.'

I looked sad, but only for the record, and I went towards the door, past the bobby who had flagged him down for drunken driving, past the Syrian diamond merchant who had switched stones on him, past a slick looking South American type who'd probably sold him a salted gold mine, past men and women who once, for a brief while, had got in his way, shaken him down, held him up, and had eventually lived or died to regret it. And not for one moment did I believe a word about the bonds . . . that is, that that was what was in the car. Imperial Japanese Bonds existed all right. He'd just used the fact to get rid of me. And I'd accepted it. Why not? A job is a job, and this one paid well, and when I got the car somebody – I wasn't sure who yet – was going to pay well for whatever was in the secret compartment.

I went back to my room, panting up the spiral stairway to my turret, anxious to pack and be away. Waiting for me was Miss Zelia Yunge-Brown.

She was sitting in a chair by the window, in a blue anorak and a blue skirt and wearing heavy walking shoes, looking as though she'd just come back from a long tramp through the pine woods.

I said, 'So you finally decided to come ashore?'

'Yes.' She put up a hand and ran it through one side of her dark hair and did a little brow-knitting act; no smile on her face, but not, I thought, as cold and glacial as she had been at our last meeting.

She stood up as I dumped my case on the bed and began to pack my pyjamas which some flunkey had already laid out.

'I was stupid about the Max Ansermoz letter. I should have guessed that was what you wanted me to do. You must have enjoyed yourself.'

I said, 'Between ourselves, Max is dead.'

'Dead?'

'Yes. You want me to look unhappy about it?'

'But you—'

'No, I didn't do it. But Max is dead and I'm dry-eyed about the whole thing. I'm only interested in a motor car. So's your father.'

'Stepfather.'

'Well, yes, if you're sticking to niceties. He knows nothing. Nobody knows anything except me – and for some things I have no memory at all. Now stop doing an ice-maiden act on me. Write it off to experience and get into gear again.'

'You have said nothing to anyone?'

'That's right.'

She was a big girl, and she was embarrassed suddenly, and she wasn't very good at carrying it off. For a moment I was afraid that she would come across and embrace me, crushing me in those lovely long strong arms. However, she got it under control and slowly held out a hand to me.

'I am very grateful to you.'

She had my hand in hers and now I was embarrassed.

'Just forget it.'

I got my hand away. She clumped to the door in her heavy shoes and paused before going out.

'I wish there was something I could do to show you how grateful I am.'

I said, 'You could try smiling again. It's a knack that comes back easily.'

'It's not easy to smile in this house. It has too many memories for me . . . of my mother. I have decided to go away and get a job.'

'I'm all for the job. You'll land one easier though with a smile on your face. Try it.'

It came back easily. She gave it to me, a slow warm smile that was followed by a little shake of her head and then a laugh. Then she went.

I snapped the lid of my case down, glad that Max was dead.

In the hallway, down a long perspective of green and white marble slabs Durnford was waiting for me. He came up to me with the practised glide of one used to walking in marble halls, and said, 'You're going?'

'Be glad,' I said. 'Besides, I don't like staying in a wax-works. I presume you've heard from the boss that I'm reinstated?'

'Yes.'

'In that case, could I have the list of people who were staying here before Miss Zelia took off with the Mercedes.'

He handed me a sheet of paper and said, 'I think you should know that I had been given strict instructions from Mr O'Dowda that I was never to make that guest-list available to anyone.'

'Then why me?'

'That's not a question I'm prepared to answer.'

I slipped the paper into my pocket and gave him a cocked-eyebrow look.

'You don't like him, do you?'

'He is my employer.'

'You'd like to see him come a cropper, a real trip-up, flat on his face?'

He gave me a thin smile then, and said, 'I'm hoping for more than that. And I've been waiting a long time. Contrary to what you imagine, I have no animosity towards you. I think you may turn out to be the *deus ex machina*.'

'What you mean is that if I find the car, you hope that I will walk off with whatever is in it. Or hand it over to someone else?'

'Possibly.'

'You really hate his guts, don't you? Tell me, have you ever written any anonymous letters about him to Interpol or Scotland Yard?'

'Why should I?' He was well in control.

'It's just a thought I had. Anyway, whatever game you are playing I think it's a dangerous one. You watch it, unless you want to end up in the waxworks with all the others.'

I picked up my case and went outside to my car. Standing alongside it was Julia.

She said, 'Was everything all right?'

'Fine. Your father almost trusts me, Zelia's grateful, and Durnford is full of hints. What are you registering?'

She said, 'Why is it that you can't talk to me without being cross or vulgar?'

'It's something you do to me. There's nothing I'd like better than a beautiful relationship but I always seem to knock on the wrong door.'

She lit a cigarette as I put my case in the car.

I paused at the door before getting in and said, 'Don't do anything stupid like trying to follow me.'

'It wasn't in my mind. Where are you going, anyway?'

'To find Otto Libsch. Any messages?'

She gave me a quick, almost apprehensive look. 'Why should there be?'

'I had the impression that you knew him, or something about him.'

'I don't know why you should think that.'

'No? I'll tell you. When you came to my room that first night, there was more on your mind than just protecting Zelia. When I mentioned his name in Turin, it was no surprise to you, and right now you haven't said you don't know him. Don't worry, I'm not going to force anything from you. I just want to find a car. That's my brief.'

'Did you mention him to Zelia?'

'No. The less said to her about either of them the better. But I mentioned him to your father, naturally, and his big happy face remained quite unchanged. Now, do you want to talk about Otto, or do I get moving?'

She blinked at me a little and bit her lip. Then she shook her head, and said, 'There's no point. Absolutely no point whatsoever . . . it couldn't change things from being what they are.' Then, her manner hardening, she went on, 'You go. Go and find your car. That is important. That's money, that's business. Things that really count in this life.'

She turned abruptly away from me and made for the house. I drove off, not pleased with myself, knowing that she needed help, and knowing too that it was no moment for me to get involved in anything else. This car business was all my hands could hold at the moment – particularly with Interpol sticking their noses in.

CHAPTER 6

'And Laughter holding both his sides.'
(Milton)

I drove without hurry south from Evian. In Grenoble I went into the Post Office and found the Botin for the Gap-St Bonnet district and turned up Max Ansermoz's number at the Châlet Bayard. I rang through – it was now about seven o'clock – and the phone rang for ten minutes without being answered. That was good enough for me. With any luck the only living thing in the house was the white poodle and by now it must be damned hungry.

I had a quick meal in Grenoble, and then went south down the N 85 towards St Bonnet and Gap. I didn't try to push it. This was my second night on the road and my eyelids had begun to feel like heavy shutters that every bump in the road brought down. I pulled up for a couple of hours' sleep somewhere around a place called Corps, and then drove on to the Châlet Bayard. I came to it at dawn with little wisps of mist lying between the trees and the air full of bird-song, which shows how isolated the place was because normally if a bird gives out with an aria anywhere in France some *chasseur* promptly blows its head off.

The front door was still open and I walked straight in and was greeted by the poodle lying curled in an armchair. A few days without food had taught it manners and it came to me, trembling and with all the bounce gone from it. I gave it some water in the kitchen – the cat had disappeared, which didn't surprise me, cats can knock spots off any dog in the independence and survival stakes – and then fed it a bowl of scraps which I had scrounged in the restaurant where I had fed. In half an hour I knew it would be its same old jaunty, face-licking self. While it was tucking in I went upstairs and had a bath and shave, and then came down and carted Max's typewriter and some of his stationery to the round table, and

wrote a letter to Otto. I had to write it in English because my
French would never have been good enough to fool anyone that it
had come from Max. And the fact that it was in English wouldn't
matter to the people who opened it because I guessed they wouldn't
know much about the way Max usually wrote to Otto.

The letter read:

My dear Otto,

Going off like that with the Mercedes almost landed me in a
great deal of trouble, and I have been very angry.

I decided to have nothing more to do with you, until yesterday
it came to my attention – through Aristide, you will remember him,
always two ears to the ground—

(That was safe enough for Mimi and Tony when they read it
because they would assume Aristide was some genuine nark known
to both Otto and Max.)

—that you in fact used the car to pull off a neat little job in your
usual line with a companion who – from Aristide's description, and
you know how reliable he is in the matter of police dossiers – sounds
just like the Turin type, Tony Collard, you were telling me about.
I presume he did the respray.

Well, dear Otto, my friend, since I virtually provided the car and
as times are never as good as they should be, I've decided that I
should have my cut. And no argument.

I shall be here for the next two days, and shall expect you. If
you don't turn up I shall let Aristide – to whom I owe a favour –
have a few details of you and this Tony Collard, and where to find
you. (My love to the delightful Mimi, by the way, though how you
stick that baby I can't think. Not your style.) I am sure Aristide
will promptly find a market for such information with the police.
So don't let me down, dear friend. I promise to be reasonable about
my share – but don't think I don't know how much you two got
away with.

Salutations,

I found a wad of cancelled cheques in the bureau and without much
care forged the signature 'Max' to the letter. I addressed it to Otto
Libsch at Mimi's flat and then drove into Gap and sent it express.
When I got back I was greeted by the poodle, all its elastic reset,
gave it a stroll through the pines and then shut it up in the kitchen.

Back in the main lounge I settled down with a large glass of

Max's brandy and pulled out Durnford's sheet of paper, which I had already glanced at, knowing that it demanded a lot of thought. Before I could start on it, the ginger cat walked in from nowhere and came and sat in the empty fireplace and stared at me, accepting a new owner without comment.

The list of guests was in Durnford's handwriting. The château had been given over to them completely for five days. Durnford commented (the list was full of little comments, as though he were aching to say more, willing to wound but afraid to strike) that O'Dowda often let business associates and friends have the use of the château. Not all the guests had stayed for the full five days. The principal guest was a General Seyfu Gonwalla. Durnford commented that he did not have to tell me who he was. He did not. The General had stayed there in strict incognito – none of the servants had known who he was. (For my money, it was probable that he had made the trip to Europe in strict incognito, too.) He had stayed four out of the five days, missing the first, when there had only been one guest, the General's aide-de-camp, who had preceded him to see that all the appropriate arrangements had been made. And, surprise, surprise, the aide-de-camp was named as Captain Najib Alakwe. (I'd chewed that one over for a long time during the night drive, and for my money again, Najib had to be a Jekyll-and-Hyde character, though at the moment I didn't know which of the two I had had dealings with.) Najib had stayed the full five days. The next guest, and she had stayed for the middle three days, was a Mrs Falia Makse (strict incognito). She was, Durnford noted, the wife of the Minister of Agriculture in General Seyfu Gonwalla's government. Also for the middle three days there had been present a Miss Panda Bubakar. There was no comment against her name – though I could have made one. For the last two days only – and no comment also – there had been present a Mr Alexi Kukarin. And that was the lot.

At the bottom of the sheet, Durnford had added a note:

You realize that in giving you this information I am very much putting myself in your hands. I do so because I flatter myself that I am a good judge of character. The secret apartment in the Mercedes is behind the large air-intake opening on the right-hand side of the facia board. You just unscrew the circular vent with an anticlockwise movement. You will, of course, destroy this communication. So far as the Press etc. are concerned, no one knew of the presence of the above guests at the château.

I destroyed it then and there, burning it in the fireplace while the cat watched without much interest. That I did destroy it didn't mean that Durnford was a good judge of character. It simply struck me as a sensible thing to do with people like the Alakwe brothers, Aristide, Tony Collard and so on around.

I sat back and gave some of my attention to the rest of the brandy. The other part I gave to O'Dowda and General Seyfu Gonwalla. If I were right, Gonwalla, as Head of State, was the guy who now thought he should have the twenty thousand pounds' worth of bonds. Odd that O'Dowda thought not, yet gladly lent him the château for a five-day conference, if that were the word for it.

I reached back and picked up the phone and booked a call to Wilkins in London. It came through much later.

Wilkins said, 'Where are you?'

'France.'

'I know that, but where?' She sounded cross and clucking like a disturbed mother hen.

'A chalet in the Haute Savoie, very comfortable, with a white poodle and a marmalade cat, well, ginger, to keep me company. No women – glad?'

She said, 'I thought you must be dead.'

'Why?'

'Because that Mr Jimbo Alakwe was here this morning offering to buy out your share in this firm.' She paused, enjoying the moment to come. 'He said that with imaginative and efficient running he could make a real success of it.'

'He's a comic – but not as much as he would like people to think. Anyway, I'm alive and kicking, and I want a *précis* of all the press comments you can get on General Seyfu Gonwalla, Mrs Falia Makse, and possibly though I doubt it, a Miss Panda Bubakar. And I particularly mean the outer-edge comments that run near libel. You know the kind of stuff, "great and good friend of". Also – I hope you're getting all this down?'

'The tape is on, naturally.'

'Also any record you can find of dealings, difficulties or troubles that any of O'Dowda's companies, especially that United Africa job, may have had, or are having, with Gonwalla's regime. Also, ring Guffy, or invite him out for a coffee and Danish cakes, and see if he'll admit that at some time or the other, meaning fairly recently, he's had some more anonymous letters suggesting that O'Dowda is worth investigating from a personal point of view, that is to say—'

'You needn't elaborate. But I doubt if Superintendent Foley would tell me anything like that.'

'You try. He goes for blue-eyed redheads. Or offer to darn his socks, the heels are always gone.'

'Is that all?' The old tartness was back.

'No.' I gave her the telephone number of the chalet, so that she could ring back, and went on, 'And don't fuss. I'm well and happy and not lonely. In fact I've an interesting guest arriving soon who will be able to tell me, possibly under duress, where the Mercedes is located. Isn't that good?'

'You sound,' she said, 'too pleased with yourself. That means you're probably up to your neck in trouble.'

'Well, so what? That's life. Didn't the O.T. expert on it say that Man is of few days, and full of trouble?'

'Or else you've been drinking. Goodbye.'

She was right, of course. It's funny how you can sit in a chair occupied with your thoughts and the brandies go down unnoticed.

I had a great night, ten hours of dreamless sleep with the poodle at the foot of the bed and the cat on the spare pillow.

The cat woke me by kneading determinedly on my chest, and when I blinked at it said it was time to let him out to forage for his breakfast which I could hear singing in the nearby scrub. The poodle slept on, knowing there was no point in moving until I was down slaving away in the kitchen at his and my breakfast.

After that it was a matter of waiting and taking what precautions I could. The moment my letter arrived in Turin I was sure that Mimi and Tony would open it. Tony would come, as fast as he could, to make sure that Max never got anywhere near grassing on him to any Aristide. If the letter arrived by first post, it meant Tony could be at the chalet by the evening. If by the afternoon post, then he could make it by midnight or early morning. Whenever he came I just couldn't afford to be sleeping and not give him a welcome.

I spent the morning making a reconnaissance of the surroundings of the chalet. At the back, which I had not noticed on my first visit, well up in the pines, was a wooden shack which held a small Volkswagen saloon, Max's. I ran it down to the front of the chalet and put my Mercedes in its place. I didn't want Tony arriving and being confused by the sight of the Mercedes. Then I went down to St Bonnet and bought some supplies, but I had to cuff the poodle out of the car – my car – because someone in the place might recognize it.

When I got back the telephone was ringing. But instead of Wilkins it was some French woman asking for Max. It took me a little while to put over to her that Max was away in Cannes on a property deal and had lent me the chalet for a few days.

We all three had lunch together, sharing everything except a bottle of Clos-du-Layon *vin rosé*. After that we took a long siesta, very long, until it was gin-and-Campari time, strictly one, because there was soon to be business ahead. Then I shut the animals in the kitchen, found a warm hunting coat of Max's, borrowed his twelve-bore and a handful of shells, and went and sat in the Mercedes where I could catch the lights of any car coming up the road to the chalet. I didn't want to be inside when Tony arrived. It wasn't going to give me any points as a host, but I felt that for this visit protocol could be dropped.

By midnight nothing had happened, except that I was colder than I thought I would be and wished I'd brought some brandy out. I sat there, thinking about a quick nip and how it was only a few yards away. The more I thought the colder I became – the chalet was up around the twelve hundred metre mark where the nights are chill at the end of September – and I was tempted to go and serve myself. It was only fifty yards to the chalet. I'm glad I didn't because Tony would have walked in on me as I had my hand on the bottle.

I had to give him full marks for his approach. Either he'd been to the chalet before or Mimi had briefed him. He must have parked his car well down the road and approached on foot. The first sign he gave me was a quick flicker of a torch away in the pines, a hundred yards to my right. I got it out of the corner of my eye, which, in my job, is what corners of eyes are for. Then there was just the darkness, the odd hoot of an owl and the noise of a plane droning overhead. The next flicker was when he hit the drive; brief, but enough to give him his surroundings.

I slipped out of the Mercedes and went cautiously down through the pines on my right. Ahead of me somewhere he had to be crossing left-handed to the chalet, even if he were going to avoid the front in favour of a side or back entrance.

Actually, he opted for the front entrance. When I was down level with the parked Volkswagen, I saw the torchlight come on and stay steady as he cowled it with one hand and examined the door. I'd locked the door and the key was in my pocket. That wasn't giving him any trouble. The torchlight went off and I could make out his bulk against the night sky as he worked on the door. He jemmied it, and well. There was just one quick scrunch of wood and steel going and then silence, and Tony standing there, waiting and listening. Nobody could tell me that this number was an amateur. I kept my fingers crossed and hoped the poodle wouldn't set up a racket inside and scare him off. The poodle was silent, stuffed with food still, and sleeping secure on that phoney reputation which dogs have conned mankind with since the first cave. Ask any T.B.N. man.

Happy in his work, Tony pushed the door open and went in. I gave him a few moments and then I went after him. I slipped through the front door and at once saw his torch doing a low sweep round in the main room, the door of which was wide open.

I went gently to the door, flicked on the lights and raised the twelve-bore, holding the sights on his head as he turned quickly.

'Just keep your hands where they are. It's not my house and I don't mind blood on the carpets.'

He blinked at me through his steel-rimmed glasses and then gave me that babyish grin of his and a fat chuckle. It didn't fool me. He had only one way of expressing any emotion.

I went up and around him carefully. He was wearing rubber-soled canvas shoes, black trousers, a thick black sweater and, for relief, a pair of white cotton gloves. From the corner of his left-hand pocket the handle of the jemmy stuck out. From behind him I reached out and retrieved it, slipping it into my coat pocket. Standing back I tapped his trouser pockets with my left hand, holding the gun in the right, barrel end pressed hard against his back. There was nothing bigger than a packet of cigarettes and a lighter in his pockets by the feel of it.

He said, 'I've got nothing but the jemmy, but I can see you're the thorough type, like my old man. Nothing on chance.'

I said, 'You can tell me about your father some other time. Turn around.'

He turned, beaming a Pickwick smile at me.

'Pull your sweater right up, but keep your hands in sight.'

He pulled his sweater up. He wore a singlet underneath and a leather belt round his trousers.

'Anyway, I've got nothing against you.'

I nodded to him to drop the sweater and said, 'Now, sit on the floor, keep your legs crossed and your hands at the back of your head. It's a tiring position but if you talk fast you won't have to hold it long.' I had memories of this room with its polished floor and sliding chairs.

He sat on the floor and I went three yards away from him and sat on the edge of the table, the shotgun cradled in my lap, covering him. Just then the poodle began to bark its head off. They time it well – the moment real trouble is over.

Tony, hands behind his head, said, 'That's a dog.'

'Don't be fooled. It's only the impression it likes to create. Now, give me the story from the moment you held up that payroll and then went away like bats out of hell in the Mercedes. I don't want any colourful matter about your emotions of the moment or unnecessary details. Just a plain unvarnished tale. I want to know what happened to the car, and what happened to Otto. Not that I care about him – the car's my concern. But it would be nice to hear that he's dead. And don't worry about my saying anything to the police. I'm in private business and I just want that car.'

'Wow! You had me fooled. That letter from Max, so-say.' He rolled his eyes in his horrible laughing manner. 'Yes, you're a number.' His face went serious. 'But you know, you got Mimi really upset with that letter. I had a terrible time with her, 'cos I didn't really want to do it. But she says if it's true bliss and a bright future we want, which it is, then there's nothing but come here and knock this Max off. I had to give in.'

I said, 'Why be squeamish about Max? You'd already got your hand in with Otto. Come on, now. Start talking.'

'But I didn't do anything to Otto. He did it to himself.' He started to chuckle. 'Yes, he did it to himself. I never laughed so much in all my life. It was real funny. Mind you, it was convenient, too. I mean, seeing that Mimi and me had decided anyway to give Otto his cards – on account of we loved one another. He was wanting out anyway, chiefly because of the baby. Even so, he'd have made trouble. But we were prepared to face that. Course of true love. Two hearts beating as one. My old man was pretty cynical about all that, of course. You'd think I'd be, too, wouldn't you? You know, just four legs in a bed, any bed, any four so long

as two of 'em are yours and the others are a nice shape. But in our
family sons must go by opposites. I'm a faithful man, you know.
One woman's all I want.'

'Congratulations. Now get on with the bloody story."

'Of course, of course.' He started to laugh, tears squeezing out
of his eyes, and there was no doubt that it was genuine. I couldn't
wait to be let in on the joke. There's nothing more annoying than
people laughing and you right out in the cold as to why. He looked
up at me, hands behind his neck, sitting there like a Buddha, and
he wobbled his big head with joy. 'He was drunk, you know. Not
stoned. But . . . well, well away. That's why it happened. Mind
you, he was always like that after a job, excited, wings on him. You
know, feet right off the ground. It takes you all ways after a job.
Me, well, I don't alter much – except I get bad heartburn. Never
anything more.'

I said firmly, 'If you don't come to the point I'll—'

'All right. All right now. Just wanted you to know how it was.
Yes, Otto was well away. That's why I never liked him driving,
but he always would. Anyway, we took off in the car. We were only
going to use it for about ten kilometres. Not safe otherwise. We had
another waiting for us up in the mountains, ready for the switch
and the ditch. The switch and the ditch!' He started to chuckle
again and it rumbled around inside his throat like a caged bear
trying to get out. I sat there and ordered myself to be patient. He
had only one way of telling a story and there was nothing I could
do about it. If it had been his gallows-side confession he would
have laughed through it in his own good time until any priest would
have wanted to crack him one and skip the final absolution.

He looked up at me, tears in his eyes, and said, 'It was the
funniest thing you've ever seen.'

'It wasn't – because I didn't see it. But come on, tell me, and
make me laugh.'

'Well . . . there was this place up in the mountains. Up a dirt
road through woods to a lake. We'd left the other car there. Otto
sang like a bird all the way there. Man, he was wild. You know, I
think when he did a job there was something sexual about it for
him. I was talking to Mimi about it—'

'Come to the point.'

For a moment he looked piqued, really hurt, like a fat, jolly boy
who'd been reprimanded unjustly.

'Well . . . the other car was there, so we off-loaded the stuff into it, and then Otto ran the Mercedes close to the edge of the lake. It was an open slope, about ten yards of it, down to the lake edge and over a ten foot drop into deep water. Nobody goes up there much. Just a few fishermen. It's a beautiful spot. A good place to spend a day . . .'He rocked with a sudden outburst of fresh giggles. 'A great place to spend the rest of your days.'

In a minute he was going to tell me what size the trout ran to and I was going to clout him over the head with the shotgun.

He saw the look in my eyes and sobered up a little.

'Well, all you had to do was let off the hand brake and start her rolling. And that's all Otto did. He opened the door, reached in and let off the brake – and the Merc started rolling. Lord, I never saw anything so funny. The car went off before he was ready for it . . . really it did. Rolled away and the door swings back a little against him and somehow his jacket or something got caught up inside so that he was dragged with it, half in half out. You've got to believe me when I say I tried to get to him. It was instinctive. You see a man in trouble and you go to help – but it was too late. The tipsy bastard lost his head and he yells and pulls his feet up, half in and half out. I think he was trying to get at the brake again to hold the Merc. Before I could do a thing, he was over the side in a damn great splash.' He looked up at me, shaking his head at the comic wonder of it all, his plump face beaming, the little eyes shining with happy tears behind his glasses.

'And what did you do?' I got to my feet. 'Just stand there and read the service for those lost at sea?'

'I couldn't do a thing. I can't swim. And the lake, right off the edge there, is about twenty feet deep. Anyway, I knew Otto could swim, so I just waited for him to come up. But he didn't. I gave him fifteen minutes, but no sign of him . . . so what would you have done? What would any man have done in the circumstances? He was out of my hair, no trouble to Mimi anymore – he really didn't like that baby, you know – and I got the full share of the payroll we'd taken. I just got into the other car and drove back to Mimi.'

'Laughing all the way.'

He grinned. 'Well, I had to chuckle now and then. Don't tell me you're upset about this? You said you hoped he was dead.'

'Frankly, I'm delighted. It's just that I'm old-fashioned enough not to show it by a good belly laugh.''

Keeping him in sight, I went to the desk and got a pencil and a sheet of paper.

Tony was a bright boy.

'You want me to draw a map?'

I dropped the paper and pencil at his feet.

'Do that. And make it accurate. If you shove me off with any phoney details, I'll laugh my way to the nearest phone and ring a friend of mine at Interpol. Play ball – and you can shove off from here and I'll forget that I ever met you. You'd be surprised how easy that will be."

'You can rely on me. Besides, I got Mimi and the baby to think about now.'

He sat on the floor and began to sketch out the details of the road and the track to the lake, giving me a running commentary as I stood behind him.

Once, he looked up and said, 'What's all the fuss about this car anyway?'

'My client wants it back.'

He shrugged. 'Why – O'Dowda could make a better deal with the insurance company?'

I went poker-faced.

'How did you know my client was called O'Dowda?"

'From Otto, of course, and the car. All the registration papers were in it when I did the respray.'

'Did Otto know O'Dowda?'

Tony shook his head at me sadly.

'You haven't done your homework. Up to about two years ago Otto was second-chauffeur at O'Dowda's place near Evian. Used to drive the wife about. News to you?'

It was news to me – and news that suddenly made sense of a lot of things that had quietly puzzled me.

I said, 'Give me the map.'

He handed it over his shoulder and I stood back from him.

'What now?' he said.

'You blow,' I said. 'I'm not having the spare bed mucked up and I'm not making breakfast for two. On your feet.'

I escorted him to the front door and covered him as he went down the steps. At the bottom he turned and beamed up at me.

'Done you a good turn, haven't I? And all for free. No charge. Just goodness of heart. Know what, too? I've complete confidence in you. About that Interpol thing, I mean. Keeping your mouth shut and so on. I'm a good judge of character. I said to Mimi after you left, "Now, there's a *buono raggazzo* who—" '

'Skip it. I've got all the character references I need.'

'Okay. And when you finally lift that car out, just say hello to Otto for me.'

He went and I could hear his rich laughter burbling all the way down the drive. Life should have more characters like him, simple, uncomplicated, always ready to look on the bright side of things, and good with children, too.

I went back in and packed up my stuff and made myself a cup of coffee against the journey ahead. I should have skipped the coffee because then I would have missed Aristide.

As I picked up my suitcase in the main room and made for the hall door, I saw the headlights of a car wheel across the window. Not knowing who it was, but having various possibilities in mind, I had only one thought. Almost any visitor at four o'clock in the morning might be interested in the location of the Mercedes. I whipped out the plan which Tony had drawn and shoved it under one of the chair cushions. Then I picked up the shotgun from the table. It was a good gun, a well-used Cogswell and Harrison hammerless ejector with nicely engraved strengthening plates on the walnut stock.

I opened the door to the hall, prepared to welcome guests.

The main house door swung back and Aristide came through. He took off a beret and gave me a half wave with it, and then stood there, shaking his head either in sadness at the sight of me or to get the sleep out of his eyes. Behind him was his driver, a big fellow in a tight blue suit and a peaked chauffeur's cap.

'The shotgun, my friend,' said Aristide, 'will not be necessary. You were just leaving?' He nodded at the suitcase inside the room door. Then he sniffed the air and said, 'Coffee?'

'In the kitchen. Help yourself.'

'You must share it with me.'

He came down the hall, took the shotgun from me and handed it to his driver.

'Have a good look round, Albert. Miss nothing.'

He took me by the arm, steered me into the main room, glanced round, nodded approvingly, and said, 'Always it has been a dream with me to have such a place. Secluded, the mountains, peace, and the air so clean you can wear a white shirt for a week without dirtying it.'

Albert clumped by us, and I led the way into the kitchen. The poodle greeted me as though I had been away for a month. The cat opened one eye, and then closed it, dismissing the interruption to its sleep.

Aristide said, 'Excuse me,' and began to make fresh coffee. I found a tin of chocolate bisuits and put them beside him. Not to get into his good books but because I knew he would have found them for himself anyway.

I said, 'How did you know I was here?'

He said, 'I didn't, but I am glad you are. I was merely informed that this was the address for Max Ansermoz and that the place might be of immediate interest. Personally, I am sure that behind it all was a desire to embarrass you. You are embarrassed?'

'No more than usual. Who informed you?'

'It was a woman – on the telephone – and she gave her name as Miss Panda Bubakar. A fictitious name, of course. It is always that, or they remain anonymous.' He gave me a warm smile, and went on. 'There is cream somewhere?'

I found him some cream.

'Did you know,' he said, 'that coffee, which is held in such high esteem in the Middle East, used once to be taken during prayers in the mosques and even before the tomb of the Prophet at Mecca? And at one time the Turks, on marrying, used to promise the woman that in addition to love, honour and a daily bastinado or whatever, she should never go short of coffee, and that we owe that filthy instant stuff to a countryman of yours called Washington who, while living in Guatemala – yes, Albert?'

Albert had appeared in the doorway.

'It is there, *monsieur*.'

'Good. Go back and stay with it. We will be with you in a little while.'

'What is where?' I asked as Albert disappeared.

Aristide stuffed a chocolate biscuit into his mouth, generously tossed one to the poodle who was walking around on its hind legs, and then said, 'You have had a visitor tonight?'

'No.'

'Then it was you who jemmied the front door? The jemmy is on the table out there.'

I said, 'Do me a favour, Aristide – don't save the main point till last. I've got a long drive ahead of me and want to get off.'

'You have found where the Mercedes is?'

'No.'

'A pity.'

'Why?'

'If you had, I might have stretched a point. The main point you were talking about. This is good coffee. Martinique. It was a great countryman of mine, one Desclieux, who under severe hardship brought the first coffee seedling to Martinique. You can always tell Martinique coffee, big grains, rounded at both ends and it is greenish in colour. Did you see Max Ansermoz at all on this visit?'

'No.'

'You are becoming monosyllabic.'

'What do you expect at this hour of the morning?'

'That you would be in bed, sleeping the sleep of the just. However, it is convenient that you are already dressed. Are you sure that you do not know where the car is?'

'Frankly, no.'

'Splendid. If you tell me where it is, you can go, and I shall ignore all that this Miss Panda has said, ignore even the evidence of Albert's and my eyes, and even the fact – which I have no doubt the laboratory experts will establish – of your fingerprints.'

I said, 'I'd better have some coffee to clear my head.'

Graciously, he poured me a cup and another one for himself. Then he gave me one of his warm, owlish smiles, and said, 'Just tell me where the car is and I will smooth away all difficulties for you. I have the power – and after all I have, too, a certain affection for you. You have had a visitor tonight – otherwise you would not be leaving at this hour. The car, *mon ami,* where is it?'

I lit a cigarette and shook my head.

'You insist?'

'I insist,' I said. 'And what is more I insist on my rights. Unless you are going to make some charge against me, I wish to leave. Okay?'

I turned to go.

Aristide said, 'I think we had better join Albert first. He is a good man, Albert. Solid, a little slow-thinking, but a first-class driver. He comes from Brittany where they make a coffee substitute out of chickpea and lupin seeds. This way.'

He held out a hand with a gun in it and pointed towards the door on the far side of the kitchen through which Albert had gone.

I went through the door and he followed me. At the end of the corridor I could see Albert waiting. I'd been down here before when I first searched the house. There were a couple of store-rooms and a cellar. Albert was standing outside the cellar door.

As we approached he turned the key in the lock and opened the door for us. They stood aside and motioned me in first, Aristide switching the light on behind me.

One wall held racks of wine bottles. There was no window and there were empty crates and cartons stacked against another wall. Along the wall that faced the door was a big deep-freeze unit. The lid was pushed back, resting against the wall, and an internal light was burning in it, throwing a soft glow up to the ceiling.

One of them prodded me gently up to the deep-freeze. Lying inside, knees bent up, head sunk between his shoulders, was Max Ansermoz. On a pile of frozen spinach cartons rested the gun with which Najib had killed him, and I didn't have to be told, because I already had been, that my fingerprints would be on it, placed there by Najib while I lay knocked out in the main room. Najib wasn't the kind of man to throw anything away that one day might come in handy.

'Well?' said Aristide at my side.

I stepped back. 'You'd better get the lid down,' I said, 'or the rest of the stuff will spoil.'

'You killed him,' said Aristide.

'I didn't – and you know it.'

'I only know it if you know where the car is. Otherwise we go to an examining magistrate. Your prints will be on the gun.'

'That won't surprise me.'

'If you know where the car is it will save endless complications . . . the slow progression of the law to establish innocence . . . the *procès-verbal*. Have you any idea how long it all takes?'

'How,' I asked, 'can I tell you where the car is if I don't know?'

Aristide studied me, shook his head and said, 'If only one could tell whether a person is telling the truth or not.'

'It would make police work simple, and cause a lot of confusion in domestic life.'

Aristide nodded and then said, 'Search him, Albert.'

Albert came over, turned me round, perhaps out of respect for the dead, to face the door, and then went through my clothes. He did it very thoroughly and handed his find to Aristide. Aristide shuffled through the stuff, passport, credit cards, wallet and so on, and then handed the lot back to me.

I said, 'Look, Aristide, you know I didn't kill Max. That doesn't mean to say I'm not glad he's dead – but I didn't do it. What you

are doing is just falling for a gag – from another interested party –
to keep me from finding that car.'

'It could be true, *mon ami*, but it is equally true that I don't want
you to find that car, so . . . it is very convenient to have something
to keep you busy elsewhere for a time.'

At this moment there was a bark outside the door and the poodle
came bounding in. It ran a circle round the three of us and then
got up on its hind legs and danced, begging, in front of Aristide.

He beamed.

'*Mignon, non?*' His calloused, police heart was touched.

'Don't fool yourself, Aristide. He just sees you as one big chocolate
biscuit.' But as I spoke I was glad of the diversion. Both the men
were watching the exhibition from the fool dog with happy grins
on their faces. I stepped back to give the poodle more room for its
act and, putting my hand behind me, got hold of the neck of the
nearest bottle in the wine-rack. I jerked it out and slung it at the
naked electric light-bulb. There was a crash and the light went out,
followed by another, louder crash and a roar from Albert, but by
this time I was at the door and out, slamming it shut and turning
the key in the lock.

I sprinted for the kitchen and was beaten by the poodle. Trust a
dog to get the hell out of danger before anyone else.

I dashed through into the main room, picked up the shotgun, the
map from under the cushion, and my suitcase and headed for the
door, the poodle following. The cellar door was stout but I couldn't
give it more than five minutes of pounding from Albert's big
shoulders.

Outside I pumped both barrels of the shotgun into one of the
rear tyres of Aristide's car. The noise sent the poodle, yelping
hysterically, streaking for the woods, and then I ran for the Mercedes, wondering whether it was burgundy or claret which I had
slung at the light. Either way Aristide was going to be angry. Wine,
I was sure, was something which he always treated with respect.

The place where Otto and Tony had carried out the payroll robbery
was St Jean-de-Maurienne, a small town of about seven thousand
inhabitants on the N6, which is the road that runs eastwards from
Chambéry across Savoie to the Italian border at the Col du Mont
Cenis and then on to Turin. It had been well chosen because it left
them only about seventy-odd kilometres to reach the border. Fourteen kilometres east of St Jean there was a town called St Michel

and some way out from this on the road to the border they had
turned left-handed up into the mountains to their lake. From St
Bonnet it was quite a drive, and no direct route to it. I reckoned I
would make the lake sometime in the early afternoon. The payroll
robbery, I learned later, had been from a small light engineering
firm which had set up business on the eastern outskirts of St Jean-
de-Maurienne. And later still, I learned that Otto had had this
fixed pattern of hold-ups – knocking off a payroll in eastern France
and then making quickly for the Italian border.

Dawn came up with a slight drizzle as I left St Bonnet and
headed north. The rain slicked the road and cut down my speed.
I stopped for coffee around nine o'clock in a small town and also
bought myself a face-mask and snorkel, swimming trunks and a
rubber-jacketed hand torch. For all I knew the lake water might be
as clear as gin, but I wanted to be prepared. One thing I knew was
that it would be as cold as hell.

I reached the lake soon after midday. It was two miles up a side
track that climbed all the way through pine woods. It was still
drizzling and, as I got higher, wisps of cloud began to sweep through
the trees. The track ended, clear of trees, on a wide grassy plateau
that overlooked a lake almost as big as the one O'Dowda had back
in Sussex. On this side the ground was fairly level, broken with
large grey boulders pushing through the bracken and scrub. On the
other side – visible now and then through the mist – the ground
rose steeply to a small crest. The surface of the lake was still, and
the colour of gun metal.

I got out and walked to the edge of the palateau. Faintly in the
thin grass I could make out the marks of Otto's car, and at the
edge a big piece of ground had been broken fairly recently. There
was a sheer drop of about fifteen feet into deep water. Looking
down into it I could see nothing. It looked cold and uninviting and
I felt a thin rise of goose pimples move across my shoulders and
arms. I went back to the car, turned it round, and then stripped
and put on the bathing trunks and the mask and went back to the
bank. The cloud mist was thickening fast.

Somewhere down there was the car and Otto. I could rely on
that because I knew Tony would never risk a lie with me. I didn't
have to dive down and say 'hello' to Otto. I didn't have to grope
about and recover what rested behind the air-intake grille. I could
just go to the nearest phone and give O'Dowda the location and
then send in my bill. All I'd been hired to do was to find the car.

Whatever was hidden in it was no business of mine. O'Dowda and Aristide wanted it, and Najib wanted it for his employers. They could get on with it. It was no day for swimming and diving. All I had to do was to mind my own business. Simple. Except that few of us can resist minding other people's business – because just now and again it gives the chance of taking a commission on it. If Wilkins had been there she would have put her foot down firmly on ethical grounds and ordered me back to the car before I caught double pneumonia.

I scrambled down the bank until I was two feet above the water and then I jumped in feet first. I went in and nearly didn't come up. The cold hit me like a great hand squeezing the life from me. I surfaced, gasping for breath, blowing and swearing and in no mood to waste time. I didn't want my fingers to drop off before I could get down to that car.

I swam out a few yards, adjusted the mask and snorkel, took a deep breath, and went down, rubber torch in hand.

Underwater it wasn't as dark as I had imagined it might be, and I saw the car almost immediately. It was about ten feet away from me on the angle of my dive. It was lying tipped over to one side on the slope of the lake-bed. The driving-wheel side was the farthest away from me. I made it to the right-hand door, grabbed it to anchor myself and flicked on the torch. The window of the door was wound down. I beamed the torch around the inside and saw Otto at once. He wasn't a nice sight. He was wedged up like a grotesque carnival balloon against the roof of the car, his arms and legs dangling, marionette fashion, from the movement of my grasping the door. I took the torch off him quickly, swung it to the air intake to locate its position and then I let go and surfaced.

I trod water for a moment or two, wondering whether I was going to be sick, then took a deep breath and went down again. This time I worked without the torch, not wanting to see Otto buoyed up against the roof. I held the door with my right hand, shoved the torch into my trunks and reached in with my left hand. I got hold of the circular grille face and turned it. For a moment or two it wouldn't budge, then as the last of my breath was going, I gave it a jerk and felt it move.

I went up for a fresh supply of air and hung on the surface for a while like a played-out fish. The clouds had come lower and there was a dense, moving succession of mist wraiths wafting across the

water. Somewhere up the slopes on the far side of the lake I thought
I heard the soft tinkle of a cow-bell.

I went down again, and this time the grille turned easily and
came away in my hand. I dropped it and reached into the aperture.
I felt something flat and thick and pulled it out. It was about the
size of a good fat book. I groped around to make sure there was
nothing else in the compartment and then went up quickly without
taking time for a goodbye to Otto.

I surfaced, pushed the mask back, sucked in great gulps of cold,
misty air and looked at the object in my right hand. It was wrapped
in thick brown oiled paper and banded all over with scotch tape.
Shivering, hardly able to feel my hands or feet, I turned to make
for the bank.

It was then that I saw – standing up above me on the plateau
edge, a little fogged with the mist patches that swept by them –
Miss Panda Bubakar, and Najib Alakwe. They stood there and
watched me as I stopped swimming and trod water.

Panda had a short leather coat flung open, her hands on the hips
of a green mini-dress, her long, tight-encased legs seeming longer
from the angle at which I viewed them. She was so tall that at
times her head was lost in the moving patches of mist. But when
her dusky face was clear I could see that she was giving me a
cheerful, predatory smile and a chance to admire the sparkle of her
white teeth. Najib, though I had little time to be surprised about
it, was wearing a neat, sober grey suit and a dark tie on a white
shirt. He stood back a little so I couldn't check whether he still had
his ginger shoes. But I could see clearly that he was holding a gun
in his right hand.

'Hello, hello, Rexy-dexy boy,' called Panda. 'Just keep swimming.
You're on the right track. Big welcome awaits.'

'And be careful not to drop the parcel,' said Najib. Just to empha-
sise the need for care, he fired a shot into the water two feet from
me which made me leap like a running salmon, and he called, 'No
need for any alarm over personal safety. Just hand over the parcel
and all is forgiven.'

'And Mamma will come up with a big brandy and nice rub down
with rough towel. Whoof-whoof!' She gave that big dark brown
laughing bark of hers and did a couple of high kicks that would
have left a Bluebell girl grounded.

I shook my head. 'Sorry,' I said, 'but I promised myself I would
do a couple of lengths before I came out.'

'You come on straight out, lover-boy,' said Panda, 'otherwise you gonna freeze and lose all your accessories. Come on, come to Mamma. Mamma soon make baby warm.'

'Come on in,' I said. 'It's lovely. Don't know what you're missing.'

I turned, stuck the parcel between my teeth and flattened out into the nearest thing to a fast crawl that I could manage, heading away into the mist. I knew that Najib wouldn't fire at me. He didn't want me to drop the precious parcel. On the other hand that wasn't much consolation. I might make the other bank before they got round to it but I didn't fancy being stuck up in the mountains wearing only a pair of trunks. Even if I made a road I was going to have trouble thumbing a lift. The French aren't all that broad-minded.

After about twenty yards or so, I stopped, took the parcel out of my mouth and got some air. The mist hid the grass plateau now. That was good. But it also hid everything else. I hadn't the faintest idea which way to go. You can blindfold some people, dump them down in the dark and they can always tell where north is. Well, I could have been a homing pigeon but it still wouldn't have helped because I didn't have any home.

Just then, I heard Panda's delighted bark-laugh come through the mist and there was the crisp sound of a body diving into water. That scared me. She was after me, over six brown feet of human torpedo, impervious to cold water, and with a built-in radar device that could pick up a man and home on him from any distance. Once she got her long arms and lovely legs around me in the water I would have less chance than a minnow with a pike.

Parcel in my mouth, I went full ahead for a hundred yards, hoping to hit the bank. But I couldn't find any bank. I stopped, panting, no sensation in my body at all, and wondered how long it would be before Otto had company. From behind and to my right, some way away, I heard the water threshing as Panda screwed herself along. Then the sound stopped. All sound stopped. There was just the mist and the cold ripple of water around me. Then there was a sound. Up ahead of me I caught the brief tinkle of a cow-bell. I got moving. I swam thirty yards and then stopped. Somewhere behind me I heard Panda swimming. She didn't sound as though she were going fast; just heading steadily in my direction, keeping the blip on her screen dead centre. Over the noise of her swimming I heard the cow-bell tinkle again, but this time it was

away at an angle to my right and the unpleasant thought occurred
to me that there could be more than one cow browsing along the
far shore. I did the only thing. I took a mean between the two bells
and swam down it. Very sensible. In the circumstances. But not
good navigation. A mean course can land you in trouble. That's
the catch with averages, they always give you a cock-eyed answer
like the average English family has one and a half cars. I ran
straight into Panda, simply because I hadn't allowed for the acoustic
factor that sounds in a mist don't come from where they seem to
come.

She came out of the mist four feet ahead of me, went astern to
brake her way and gave me a big white tooth-flashing smile. Held
in her teeth was a nasty-looking knife. She took the knife out of her
mouth and said, 'Hiyah, honey. Come here often?'

I took the parcel out of my mouth, and through chattering teeth,
said, 'You come a foot nearer and I chuck this over-board.' I held
up the parcel.

She said, 'How we going to get warm if we don't get close?'

I said, 'Just switch your radar on the nearest cow-bell and lead
the way.'

She shook her head and said, 'We do it side by side, lover-boy.
And don't play no tricks on a poor girl what's achin' for love. You
drop that parcel and I'm gonna slit you from gizzard to crutch and
to hell with the waste of a good man.' She winked at me, and added,
'Anyone ever tell you you got nice shoulders? Kinda square and
sexy – and I like 'em that blue colour. Goes well with the red face.
Start tracking.'

We swam, four feet apart, and Panda just leading the way. I
wasn't concerned with what was going to happen. I just wanted to
get out of the freezing lake. My body was frozen, my mind was in
need of de-icing, and my arms and legs moved as though I were
swimming through mud. Only my eyes worked normally to help
me keep station alongside Panda.

She grinned at me and said, 'Kinda nice, havin' the whole place
to ourselves. Awful crowded in summer they say.'

I didn't answer. I had a mouth full of parcel. But I kept my eyes
on her as we swam on.

She was stripped to her bra and long tights, pink, with a little
balloon of trapped air swelling up over her backside, and every now
and then she twisted her head to give me a beaming smile, which
had a lot of mixed emotions bubbling in it. The least I could expect

when we got to the bank was to be raped, then knifed. I thought of praying but decided against it. It never did a male mantis any good in the same circumstances.

Panda's radar worked. We hit the bank dead on the cow. It was a big brown-and-white beast, standing between two pines, blowing great gusts of vapour through its nostrils and it watched us with large, liquid, uncurious eyes.

Panda slid out of the water, and said, 'Hi, cow! Nice lake you've got here.' And then, water rolling over her brown arms and shoulders and rippling down her tights, she held the knife at me as I stood in six inches of water and mud at the verge. 'Just come out nice and easy, man, and then toss the parcel to Mamma. Business before pleasure, uh?' She threw her head back and bellowed, 'Najib! Najib!'

From somewhere through the mist distantly came an answering call.

Panda stood waiting for me. She was no fool. I might not know what was in her mind, but she knew what still dimly survived in the icy depths of mine. I didn't want to give her the parcel.

'No tricks, honey. I like you a lot and anytime you say the word we'll shack up some place with a big bed and make the springs work double time. But first Najib must have his parcel. Okay?'

'Okay.'

I moved out of the water, but she stopped me after the first two feet.

'No more. Just toss it over.'

Somewhere up to our left Najib shouted. Panda shouted back. I looked down at the parcel in my hand, and remembered a lot of routines I'd been through in Miggs's gymnasium. Somewhere or other I guessed that Panda had been through even more routines, and she could give me inches in height, seconds in speed, and probably just as much in muscle, and she had a knife.

'Come on, honey. Flip it over. After that it's no hard feelings and loving kindness all round. Najib likes you and, what's more important, I like you and that spells a rosy future somewhere.'

Giving myself time to think, I said, 'Great help you've been – keeping Max on ice for me.'

'That? Honey, that was just for laughs. Come on, goose-pimples – give!'

I gave. I tossed the parcel to her and I deliberately threw it a little wide and a little short. It landed on the ground a foot in front of her and to her left. She flexed her gorgeous legs and bent, reaching for it with her free hand, her ample breasts sagging against the wet stuff of her white bra, and her eyes never left me except for the split second when eyes and hand had to co-ordinate to locate and pick up the parcel. It was the moment I wanted. I already had my hand on my trunks covering the bulge of the rubber torch inside. I had it out and jumped for her as her eyes came back to me. She made a good try. In fact she gave me a three-inch slash on my left arm but it was too hurried to be serious, just messy. I hit her as hard as I could just at the side of the right temple, really hard, and to hell with chivalry, and she went over on her back and stayed there.

I grabbed the parcel and ran, away round the lake in the opposite direction from which Najib's calling voice was coming. I didn't run for long, not in bare feet. But I kept going, hobbling fast, and luck was with me. I struck a small path, coated with dry pine needles and finally came back round to the grassy plateau.

Najib's Thunderbird was parked alongside my Mercedes. He'd left the ignition keys in so I took them and chucked them into the water. Then, without waiting to get dressed, I drove away, turning the heater up full blast. I couldn't wait to get to the nearest hot coffee and lace it with cognac.

As I drove down the track in the woods, and when I was almost in sight of the main road, a beaten-up yellow Citroen pulled suddenly out of the trees on to the track ahead of me and stopped. I braked to a halt about ten yards from it. Through the back window of the Citroen I could see a woman at the wheel. I waited for her to move on and while I did so, reached back for my shirt and trousers. I had them in my hand when the beaming, bespectacled face of Tony Collard appeared in the window across from me. He opened the door and got in, and, with a smoothness that astonished me, picked up the parcel from the seat and stuffed it inside his Windbreaker, reached back and got the shotgun, broke it and checked that there were no shells in it, and then, drawing a gun from his belt, said amiably, 'Just follow Mimi.'

He reached over and pressed the horn. The car ahead started to move. He prodded me in the ribs with the gun and I followed.

I said, 'If we've got far to go I'm not dressed for it.'

'We'll keep the heater going.' He looked admiringly at me and said, 'I had a bet with Mimi you'd make it. Five hundred francs.

Great little gambler that girl. This is the thing there's all the fuss
about?'

He held up the parcel.

I nodded.

'That's what your boss really wanted – not the car?'

'I wouldn't lie to you.'

'Course not, you're a *buono raggazzo*. But don't worry, Tony will
take care of you and everything. You're my friend, in a sense.'

'What sense?'

'That I got respect for you. My old man always said if you want
to succeed with people you got to work with their natures, not
against them. How was Otto?'

'No complaints.'

'Good. Mind you, Otto had his points. The master mind – that's
what he used to think he was, and he was to some extent. Do a job
in France and scoot back to Italy. Do a job in Italy and scoot back
to France. That's where we're going. A little hiding place we had
this side of the border. Old mill, not working now, of course.
Orchard with medlars and pears . . . lovely place for a kid to play.
And a stream. Course, now Otto's gone that makes me the master
mind. I can tell you, I had trouble with Mimi about it at first, but
she's come round to my way. Did you have to rub out either of
those two up there?''

We were out on the main road now and heading east.

'I was a bit rough with the girl.'

'Fix their car?'

'Yes.'

'Good. Then we can all relax.' He leaned back and lit a cigarette
and began to hum to himself. After a while, he said, 'I don't mind
being pushed around strictly in the way of business. Got to expect
it now and then. Don't mind if anyone pushes Mimi around a bit,
come to that. But—' he gave me a big smile and chuckled to himself
– 'I'm dead against any bastards that could push a little baby
around. That long-legged, dark number just chucked the feed bottle
out of the window. It takes a woman, you know, to be really cruel
to a little baby. You can see that's why I had to talk.'

'Absolutely.'

I knew it was no good trying to hurry him or force him to
put events in order, and anyway, I was dog-tired and longing for
something hot and fiery to be burning my gullet. I knew that I was
going to have to deal with him but it wasn't the moment and I

wasn't in the mood. His master brain had dreamed up some scheme but until I was dressed and in my right mind it would have to wait.

'My old man used to say,' he said, 'that a black child develops mentally faster than a white up to the age of twelve, and then it stops. They can't get beyond twelve. Something in it, I think, or that dark number must have thought I was an idiot. If he'd come down the road first I was going to take him. But I'm genuinely glad it was you.' He began to laugh. 'God, I'd like to see their faces now.'

Ahead of me, Mimi turned off the main road on to a B number.

Tony said, 'Make a lot of money in your job?'

'Enough.'

'Somebody asks you to do something, like, and you do it – no questions asked?'

'Sort of.'

'Must be interesting.'

'There's always something happening. Like now.'

That tickled him but he overlaughed it as usual.

Recovered, he said, 'I'd have liked working with someone like you instead of Otto. He was a randy, rotten runt. If you don't have nothing else in this life, my old man used to say, you've got to have respect for women. That's what he used to say, but he never acted like it. Some ways he was worse than Otto. Mimi's going to turn left up ahead. You'll have to get into low gear. Like the side of a house.'

I followed Mimi for a couple of miles up a steep, winding hill, and we came out on to a wide plateau, fringed on three sides by woods. As Tony had said, there was an orchard, full of moss-covered fruit trees, a small paddock and a tall mill-house standing at the side of a stream. Attached to the mill-house was a low cottage with a paved yard in front of it.

I drew the Mercedes up behind Mimi's car in the yard. Ahead of us she got out, reached into the car and brought out a carry-cot, and then went into the house.

Tony said, 'If you don't try any tricks we'll get on well. Nothing's going to happen to you and your boss won't be able to blame you.' He grinned, winked at me, and added, 'Let's face it, we've all got to have our failures.'

He got out and, gun in hand, marshalled me into the cottage. The main room was large, stone-flagged, and with a kitchen range against one wall. Mimi sat on a chair, gave me a nod, and then opened her blouse and started to feed the baby.

'There's not much here, Tony,' she said. 'With all the upset. Get the fire going and warm some up. But you'll have to do something with him first. The baby-food's in the case in the car.'

Tony went over to her, kissed the top of her head and kept his eyes on me all the time. Then he went to a door at the far side of the room, drew back bolts and opened it, motioning me to him.

'I think they wintered the goat or cows in here once. Kind of central heating for the house.' He chuckled.

He waved me in.

The room was stone built with one window about six inches square high up at one end. There was a broken-down wheelbarrow in it, a pile of old straw in a corner, an iron bed without a mattress against the wall, and a row of cobweb-draped rabbit hutches along the other wall. He shut me in, but was back again after a few minutes carrying my clothes and a bottle. Behind him Mimi came to the door, baby crooked in her arm, its wet mouth searching for her nipple, Tony's gun in her hand to cover me.

Tony said, 'Make yourself comfortable. Ring if you want anything.' He laughed, dropped my clothes on the floor and put the bottle in the wheelbarrow.

I said, 'Is it a boy or a girl?'

'Boy,' said Tony proudly. 'Two months. Fair-sized little pecker on him already. Gabriel we're calling him. Like it?'

'Heavenly,' I said and reached with one hand for my trousers and with the other for the bottle.

They left me alone and I dressed and drank. Then I pulled some of the straw out of the corner and spread it across the wire-spring frame of the bed and flopped down on it. A cloud of dust, smelling of cowdung, rose around me, but I didn't care much.

I just lay there, bottle handy at the side of the bed and stared at the ceiling. I've stared at a great many ceilings in my time, and mostly in the same kind of mood, feeling debilitated and incapable of sustained thought. I knew enough about the mood to realize that there was nothing to be done but to wait for it to pass.

From the other room I heard the sounds of Mimi and Tony and the baby . . . the clanking of pans, the wail of the child, and Tony's big laugh and Mimi's occasional chuckle. After a time the baby stopped crying, and suddenly, I heard Mimi give a loud exclamation and Tony began to roar with laughter.

I took another drink and went to sleep, but just before I went off I thought I heard the sound of a car starting up.

I woke late in the afternoon to find Tony in the room and with him a good smell of coffee and fried bacon. He'd put a plank across the wheelbarrow and there was a tray on it. He kicked an old box towards the barrow for me to sit on and then went and stood by the door, one hand inside his Windbreaker. I didn't have to be told what he was holding. He was friendly, but he wasn't going to take any chances with me.

He said, 'Keep your voice down. Don't want to wake the baby.'

I said, 'I'm not doing any speaking. That's up to you.'

I began to attack the coffee and fried bacon.

He gave it to me then, in his own laughter-punctuated, highly involuted way.

When he had come to visit me at the chalet, he had brought Mimi and the baby with him, leaving them parked in his car well down the road. He had brought Mimi, he explained, largely because they were inseparable and also because if there had been trouble it was easier to pass the frontier with a woman and a child in the car. Anyway, Panda and Najib had jumped him as he came back to the car. Najib had got into Tony's car, and Tony had to drive off with Panda bringing Mimi and the baby along in their car. Somewhere the other side of St Bonnet they had pulled up and the conference had begun. Najib had wanted to know what he had been doing at the chalet and who had been there.

'Honest, I tried to stall. Like I said, I got respect for you. He wanted to know everything – and he seemed already to know a lot – and then there was the baby. Mimi nearly went out of her head. Fact, I'm surprised she's got any milk left at all. That black tart was the worst, telling us what would happen. You can see, I didn't have any choice, and then on top of that he said he'd make it worth my while. Not that that by itself—'

'So in the end you told them about the Mercedes being in the lake?'

'Had to – and we had to take them there. Me with him, and Mimi coming behind with her. But I was thinking of you all the time. I wanted to give you a chance like, give you time to get there ahead. So I led him a dance, took the wrong roads and the long way round. You know once,' he chuckled, 'I took him round in a

big circle and he never noticed it. You can see I tried to protect
you, can't you?'

'I'm touched, Tony.'

'Well, I like you. You got a nice way. Still, I couldn't stall for
ever, 'cause I knew Mimi would be fussing about the kid's feed, so
I finally took him to the bottom of the lake road, and then he pays
me off and tells me to get the hell out of it.' He chuckled. 'Which
I pretended to do of course, but I didn't, and let me tell you if I
could have got my hands on the gun Mimi had in the kid's carry-
cot I would have blown their black heads off. Coloureds I always
thought were crazy about kids. Anyway, I'd been doing a lot of
thinking. Mimi and me wanted all the money we could for
emigrating. Nice touch we had from that bank, and a bit more from
the sale of the garage, but why not more? So I thought, what's in
that car they're all crazy about? Not just the car – so I decided to
hang around. First lot down the road will have it, whatever it is,
and whatever it is it's worth money and I'm going to have it. So
there it is. It was you – and I was real happy it was you. With
them I'd have had to be real rough in order to please Mimi.'

I finished the coffee and said, 'Don't go on, you're breaking my
heart. Just tell me what cock-eyed plan you've got now.'

'Nothing that will hurt you. Your boss will see that you tried and
you failed – on his behalf. He can't grumble.' He pulled the gun
from his Windbreaker. 'After all, what could you do? I'll explain it
to him when he comes.'

'When he comes?'

'To collect the parcel. Mimi's gone off for him now. Be back
tomorrow. Why you looking surprised?'

'Wouldn't you – if you saw a man jump into a bear-pit for a
friendly game of tag? My boss will tear you apart. Tony, my friend,
he's not the kind of man you can shake down. As your dear old
father would have said, you're good but you're not in his class.'

Tony grinned. 'You're trying to frighten me. I can handle him.
He's got to come alone. Mimi knows the terms.'

'Listen,' I said. "He's eight feet tall, four feet wide, and he's got
a fat touch of the Irish. He'll eat you.'

'Will he? Then he'll have to polish this off as a starter first.' He
joggled the gun. Then he gave me a kindly shake of his head. 'Don't
worry. You did your best. More can't be asked of any man. You'll
get your pay from him. You could sue him if not. And Mimi and
I will get our price for the parcel. You know what's in it?'

'No.'

'And a good thing for you, too.' He started to laugh. 'You ain't old enough yet. You should have seen Mimi's face. She's a first-class mother and wife, but that's not to say she hasn't been around – but she was shocked. She didn't even want to take the little bit of film I clipped off to show him, but I said she must. He's got to know we're genuine sellers. Anyway, it's all wrapped up again out there, just as it was, and you don't have to bother your head about it. And he's getting it cheap, five thousand dollars, used notes, and no fear of the police about it or he wouldn't have hired you.'

I gave him a look and went back to the bed. I picked up the bottle and took a deep pull, swallowed, breathed hard, and said, 'Wake me when he comes. I wouldn't miss the show for anything.'

'I will. You'll be right out there so he can see it weren't any of your fault. As my old man used to say, you take advantage of someone, particularly someone you like, then the least you can do is make sure they don't get more than their proper share of the blame. You just got outsmarted. I want him to know that. Then he can't hold anything against you.'

I didn't tell him that I was deeply moved – not for me, but for him. He and Mimi were a couple of Babes in the Wood, and O'Dowda would enjoy every minute he spent in this house.

I said, 'Did Otto ever tell you why he quit working for O'Dowda?'

'Sure. He'd accumulated some capital and wanted to get back to his own line of business.'

'How did he get the capital?'

Tony laughed and winked. 'Never asked him. Like my father used to say – never ask questions you know won't be answered.'

He went out, chuckling to himself.

I lay on the bed, later, and stared at the little patch of window. Through it a few stars were showing and now and again a brown owl screamed in the orchard just to keep the voles on their toes. It wasn't all that long a way from here to Evian. Mimi should be back sometime in the morning, and with her would be O'Dowda, alone. Mimi would insist on that, and O'Dowda would play ball. He would bluster and bully to begin with, threaten her with the police and so on, but in the end he would come, alone, and with the money because he wanted the parcel and he wanted it without any police interference. He probably knew already that the police, or Interpol, wanted to get their hands on it. Najib wanted it, Interpol wanted it, and O'Dowda wanted it. What did I want? Well, I had to be frank. I wanted it, too. But, in the first place, out of sheer curiosity to see what was in it. After I knew that, I could decide what to do with it. Ethically, of course, I should – if I ever got it – hand it to O'Dowda. He was my employer. But he'd only employed me to find the car, not to recover a parcel. And ethically, before allowing me to take his commission, there was a lot he should have put me wise to for the sake of my own personal safety, and personal safety was something by which I set a very high store. For the moment, ethics apart, I was prepared to be taken along by circumstances – in fact I had no choice – until I got a chance to dictate the running again.

I went to sleep, deep, complete, dreamless sleep, and woke to daylight and the fact that Tony was sitting hard and square on my shoulders, had my hands drawn back behind me, and was cording my wrists. If I had been one of those people who come fast out of sleep, brain clear, ready for action, I might have been able to take advantage of him. The truth was he had me trussed almost before I was awake. He got off me, rolled me over, and I yawned in his face. Outside the birds were singing and a shaft of sunlight came through the window.

Tony, beaming said, 'It's a great morning. Come on out and I'll feed you some coffee.'

He did, too, while I sat in a kitchen chair, and he did it expertly holding the cup to my lips. He should have been a male nurse.

'Thought you'd like to be present when your boss arrives. Tied like that he can see there was nothing you could do.'

I said, 'You're happy about meeting him?'

'Why not? He's coming alone, and I've got what he wants.' He tapped the parcel on the table with his gun. 'What's five thousand dollars to him?'

'You'd be surprised. He's got a gallery of people like you. Some there for less than five thousand, I imagine.'

'A gallery?'

'Never mind. He just doesn't like handing over money under duress.'

'Who does? But it happens. Just you sit there and don't move. I got things to do.'

He had. He warmed up some baby food, fed Gabriel, and then changed its nappy.

I said, 'You've skipped its bath.'

'Mimi said not to on account of its rash. All over its little arse. Powder's the job. Like I did before I put the fresh nappy on."

He settled Gabriel down in the carry-cot and I watched him with interest. Seeing me following his movements, he said, 'Haven't got Mimi's touch. He goes down right away with her, but with me he always yells for five minutes before going off. Don't let it worry you.'

I didn't. Gabriel yelled and I sat on my chair and stared at the parcel I had fished out of the Mercedes. So far I'd done all the hard work and it didn't look as though I was going to get much out of it. I should have skipped this job and taken a holiday. I'd have missed Julia, true. But at this moment that didn't seem much to lose. I yawned. What I needed was a tonic, something to pep me up and set me going again so that there was a bounce in my stride and a bright cash glint in my eye.

O'Dowda arrived three hours later. First there was the sound of Mimi's car. Tony went to the door and opened it. From where I sat I could see the yard. Mimi drew up alongside my car and came across to us, her red hair glinting in the morning sun, a spring in her step, and clearly everything all right with the world. As she reached the door where Tony stood, gun in hand to welcome her, O'Dowda's Rolls drew into the yard driven by him.

'He's alone?' asked Tony.

'Yes. I checked everything like you said.'

'Good girl.' He ran down her back and pinched her bottom.

She came in, gave me a friendly nod, and went to the carry-cot and began to fuss over the baby.

I said, 'What was he like?'

'Very polite and gentlemanly. No trouble.'

In my book that meant that he was saving the trouble for later.

O'Dowda came to the doorway, carrying a small case in one hand. He had a little billycock hat perched on top of his big head and was wearing a thick tweed suit which made him look even bigger. He gave Tony a fat smile and then seeing me inside, said, 'So you made a mess of it, boyo? Seems I read somewhere in your prospectus that nobody could outsmart you. Well, you're costing me five thousand dollars. You think I should deduct that from his fees?'

This was to Tony.

Tony, in a business mood, said, 'That's between you and him –

but he did his best. Just turn round, Mr O'Dowda, and lift your hands.'

O'Dowda did as he was told and Tony ran a hand over him from behind. Then, satisfied, he backed into the room and O'Dowda came after him.

O'Dowda looked around and said, 'Nice little property this. Could pick it up cheap and do something with it.'

Tony moved around the table, picked up the parcel and handed it to Mimi, his eyes never leaving O'Dowda. Well, at least that was something but he would need more than that to deal with O'Dowda. Nothing could convince me that O'Dowda was going to hand over five thousand dollars willingly and with that happy smile on his face.

Tony said, 'Your man did his best, Mr O'Dowda. Remember that.'

'Good of you to stress it. I'm sure he did. But it was a damned poor best – going to cost me five thousand dollars.'

He put the case on the table and then waved a fat hand at it. 'Just count it,' he said, 'and then your wife can hand over the parcel, and I'll be going.'

Tony said, 'No. You open it up. I don't want that lid snapping up and something going pop in my face.' He chuckled. 'My old man was an expert on booby traps, Mr O'Dowda.'

'You're right to be cautious, boyo. Let's be frank – if I could do you I would. But I know when to resign myself. I want that parcel too much to quibble over a few thousand dollars.'

He was too reasonable. I could sense that he wasn't worried, that underneath the mildness there was the real tough, don't-try-to-shake-me-down O'Dowda.

He opened the case, letting the cover flap back so that Tony could see the bundles of notes. I had a bet with myself that he would have a gun hidden under the notes. I was wrong. He picked up the case and turned it upside down, spilling the packets of notes on the table. From the far side Tony reached out a hand and picked up one of the piles. He handed it backwards to Mimi. She put the parcel in the carry-cot and began to count the notes. Then she came up to the table, and from a safe distance, counted through the piles.

'It's all there, Tony.'

'Give him the parcel. Don't go near him. Pass it to him.'

I had to hand it to Tony. He was taking no chances. He might not be a master mind, but he was doing his best. But there was one thing about O'Dowda he could never know, never believe, although I had in a way tried to tell him, and that was the man's courage. To be a millionaire you have to have it, you have to know that nothing can beat you, that anything you want is always in reach even if it means a moment or two of danger . . . for against danger there is always luck and, let's face it, luck is a snob and doesn't waste time on the poor and meek.

Mimi got the parcel and slid it across the table to O'Dowda. He picked it up and stuffed it into one of his big side pockets – and from that moment he didn't waste a second. The moment of pocketing the parcel was his deadline. As his right hand came out of the pocket he swept it forward, took the edge of the table and tipped it back at Tony, shoving it at him with all his strength.

As the table hit him Tony fired, but O'Dowda had already moved, and like a lot of big men, he moved fast. The bullet went high over him and hit the ceiling, showering plaster down. O'Dowda was round the table and, as Tony, on the floor, rolled over to shoot again, had one big arm around Mimi pulling her in front of him as a shield. Tony held his fire.

Panting a little O'Dowda said, 'Now you bastard, push that gun over here or I'll break your wife's neck.' He raised his free hand and grabbed the nape of Mimi's neck, screwing it round so that she gave a cry of pain.

Tony, lying on the floor, was lost. The game had gone against him and he had no idea of his next play.

'Tell him, Carver, that I'll do it,' said O'Dowda.

I said, 'He'll do it, Tony – and make it legal afterwards. Just kiss your five thousand goodbye. Do it, and don't be a fool.'

Tony looked from me to Mimi. Gabriel began to yell in the carry-cot. Tony slid the gun along the ground to O'Dowda. O'Dowda tipped Mimi over like a truss of hay and recovered the gun with his free hand. Straightening up, he gave a big smile.

'Well, now we can really do business.' He forced Mimi across the room to the open door of the cattle lodge. He shoved her in and then closed the door and shot the bolt across. Tony made a move to rise but O'Dowda waved him down with the gun and came back slowly to him.

He said, 'I'm a bit stiff from that drive, but I'm beginning to loosen up. All right, after business, pleasure; that's the order. Up you get.'

He put the gun in his pocket and stood back from Tony. Tony

must have thought he was mad to give him the chance. I could
have told him better. He came up fast at O'Dowda but before he
was off his knees O'Dowda drove his foot into his chest and sent
him sprawling and the shock whipped Tony's glasses from his face.
O'Dowda followed him up, grabbed him by the shirt front as he
rose, jerked him to his feet and smashed a fat fist into his face,
slamming him back against the wall.

It wasn't pretty to watch. Without glasses Tony was half blind
anyway. O'Dowda just used him as a punch bag. He held him in
the corner of the room and beat him until he couldn't stand on his
legs, and then he held him up and beat him some more, and all
the time Mimi was screaming like a banshee from the other room,
the baby was crying as though he had a fit, and I felt a murderous
rage running through me. Tony was not only getting what he had
asked for, he was getting far more.

I shouted, 'Lay off, O'Dowda. You'll kill him.'

O'Dowda, holding Tony, turned and looked at me.

'Not me, Mr Bloody Carver. I know the exact limit.'

He turned and slammed another blow at Tony and then let him
drop to the ground. Tony lay there, groaning faintly.

O'Dowda brushed off his hands, examined his knuckles and then,
the baby still crying, he went to the carry-cot and gently patted its
cheeks. 'Hush now, me darlin', your daddy will be with you soon,
though I doubt you'll recognize him.'

He came over to me and pulled a penknife from his trouser
pockets.

'Stand up and turn round.'

I sat where I was. Just at that moment I was enjoying myself. I
wanted him. I wanted to take him more than anything else in the
world, and the thought was doing things to my glands. Everything
had gone into full production again inside me. The bastard had
come in here, barehanded, and with just his mother-wit and the
knowledge that he could get away with anything, and it had worked
for him, as it had worked before. I just wanted to prove to him that
for once it wouldn't always work.

'Stubborn, eh?' He smacked me across the face and the chair
almost went over. 'And you think I believe his story about
outsmarting you? It would take a better man than him to do that.
No, it was a bright idea, boyo, right out of the old joke book. You
two got together. He shakes me down – then you split, and you're
still a hard-working but unsuccessful agent of mine entitled to full

fees. You think I fall for that? Stand up, or I'll knock your bloody head off.'

He hit me again and I stood up because I still needed my head. I needed it badly. I knew what he was going to do. He was going to free me and then he was going to play the same game with me that he had played with Tony. And I had an idea that, while it might take him a little longer, he could do it. He was all warmed up and ready to go, looking forward to the fun.

I said, 'You've had enough exercise for one morning, O'Dowda.'

'Don't believe it. All he brought out in me was a light sweat. You got to do better. Think you can?'

'You want to bet?'

'Why not?'

'Five thousand – dollars?'

He laughed. 'You're on, you cocky bastard. Now turn round.'

Slowly I turned round so that he could get my wrists, and I knew that from the moment he cut the cords I would have about four seconds in which to save myself. Four seconds. It doesn't sound much. In fact it's quite a long time, particularly against a man so full of self-confidence as O'Dowda was at that moment. In four seconds I had to finish him or he would finish me. I might be endangering my pay from him, plus five thousand dollars, but I was prepared to worry about that later.

He stood up against me at my back and sawed impatiently away at the cords and I kept the strain on them so that I would know the moment I was free. He was eager and impatient to be at me. I liked that. He was looking forward sadistically to his fun and an easy five-thousand purse, his mind full of it. That meant it didn't have room for too much caution. My only hope was to surprise and finish him in four seconds.

The cords went and I brought my arms round fast in front of me and, before he knew what I was doing, I had the back of the chair in front of me in my hands. I swung around, slamming the chair at him hard as I went. I got him full on the side of the head. He went over sideways and crashed against the floor. For once lady luck wasn't with him. Having seen him well and happily on his way, maybe she'd gone out for a drink. His head hit the stone-flagged floor with a crash and he just lay there, knocked out. I threw the broken chair from me and bent down by him. He was breathing. I took the parcel and the gun from him, and I didn't

waste any time. He had a head like an ivory ball and he wouldn't
be out long.

I let Mimi out, and said, 'Get out of here quickly, before he
comes round. Come on.'

She didn't need urging. I helped her haul Tony to the car. Then
I went back and collected the baby and my dollars. I put twenty
per cent of the purse in the carry-cot with the baby, and dumped it
in the car. Mimi drove off fast, sobbing to herself. I took O'Dowda's
ignition key and then turned my car and sat, window down,
watching the door of the house. A few minutes later he came
staggering out, holding his head.

I called to him, 'Great fight. I've taken my winnings. When your
head's better maybe we'll have a chat about things.'

I drove off and dropped his keys overboard a mile down the road.

I went north as fast as I could and by five o'clock I was at Talloires,
which is a small place on the east side of Lake Annecy. I got a
room at the Abbaye which overlooks the lake, and where I had
stayed before. I put a call through to Wilkins and caught her just
before she left the office. It was a long-winded conversation. She
was fussing like an old hen because she hadn't been able to get me
at Ansermoz's number.

She had no information, other than was public knowledge, about
General Seyfu Gonwalla or Mrs Falia Makse; that is that he was
head of his government and she was the wife of the Minister for
Agriculture. She could find no information at all about any Miss
Panda Bubakar. But our city contact had come across with the fact
that O'Dowda's United Africa company set-up had been on the
verge of obtaining monopolistic mineral rights and mining
concessions from the previous government to Gonwalla's. However,
a military *coup d'état* had brought Gonwalla in and negotiations for
the concession had been broken off. I could see how annoying that
must have been for a man like O'Dowda. That he would take such
a set-back lying down didn't strike me as likely. I had an idea that
the oiled-paper parcel on my dressing table would prove it.

She had seen Guffy, but had not been able to get anything more
out of him about anonymous letters concerning O'Dowda. He had
said, however, that he wanted to get in touch with me and would
she pass him any location or telephone number she had. I
considered this, decided there could be no harm in it, and gave the
Abbaye's number, Talloires 88.02. I then told her I had found the

Mercedes and would be back very soon to face the bills which had no doubt accumulated.

She said, 'Are you all right, personally?'

'Intact,' I said, 'except for a three-inch scratch on my left arm which I've bandaged with a very dirty handkerchief. I was chased by Miss Panda Bubakar. She was wearing just a brassière and pink tights. She's coloured, by the way.'

At the other end Wilkins cleared her throat but said nothing.

I said, 'Anything else to report?'

She said, 'A Miss Julia Yunge-Brown has telephoned three or four times wanting to know where you were. I decided it wouldn't be wise to say. Oh, yes, there is one other thing. There was an announcement in *The Times* yesterday of the forthcoming marriage of Cavan O'Dowda to a Mrs Mirabelle Heisenbacher.'

I said, 'Remind me to send flowers,' and then rang off.

After that I rang Durnford at the Château de la Forclaz. I gave him the location of the car to pass to O'Dowda when he got back. My job was now finished. I would be forwarding my bill in a few days.

He said, 'Did you go down to the car?'

I said, 'You any idea how cold those lake waters are, even in September?'

He said, 'If you did recover the package I'd like to talk to you about it, privately, and soon. After all, I did tell you where it was. And it could be, would be, to your advantage.'

I said, 'I'll think about it.'

He said, 'Where are you?'

I said, 'I'll tell you if you promise not to hand it on to O'Dowda.' I knew I was dead safe on that one.

'I promise.'

I gave him the hotel address.

After that I had the hotel send up a bottle of whiskey and a couple of bottles of Perrier water. I took the first drink into the bath with me and soaked for half an hour. Dressed, I fixed a second and undid the oiled-paper parcel. There was an inner wrapper of thick plastic sheeting, and inside this were two rolls of 16 mm. film and a tape recorder spool.

I took one of the films to the window and stripped off a couple of feet, holding the negatives up to the light. I wasn't really surprised. In this business you get to have a sixth sense, an instinct for anticipation that can sometimes take a great deal of pleasure

out of life. The short strip of film I held up featured Panda Bubakar
prominently, grinning all over her fun-loving face and stripped for
action. The man in the background, a coloured gentleman, looked
broad-shouldered enough to take the brunt of anything but, even
so, there seemed to be a slight nervousness about his attitude which
I could well understand. I didn't unroll any more film. Personally
I've found that if you must have pornography – and a little occasionally never did any harm except to make life a shade greyer than it
need be – then it was better after dinner with a couple of brandies.
I had promised myself that I would eat at the Auberge du Père
Bise along the quay and I didn't want to spoil my *gratin de queues
d'écrevisses*.

I wrapped the whole lot up, and wondered what I would do about
security arrangements. The next day I meant to hire a projector and
run the film and also a tape recorder to play off the tape. But that
was the next day. It would come all right. But I didn't want it to
come without my being able to take a dispassionate eye-view of
Panda and her friends and also to hear the tape which, I had a
feeling, would be more interesting because it would leave a great
deal more to the imagination than the film would. So I took the
whole lot, including my dollars in a separate packet, to the Auberge
du Père Bise with me and asked if they would keep them in their
safe for me overnight, which they said they would, without any
demur, which is always the sign of a first-class, well-run establish-
ment. My hotel would have done the same but I knew that that
was one of the obvious first checks that any official busybody would
make since I was staying there. The *écrevisses* were delicious. So was
the *omble chevalier poché beurre blanc* which followed them – and
although *ombles* are part of the great *Salmonidae* family, I didn't think
of O'Dowda once.

The next morning I was glad that I had taken my simple security
precautions. Around eight o'clock there was a knock on the door
and the chambermaid came in with my breakfast coffee, hot rolls
and croissants and two of those small pots of conserve, one apricot,
the other raspberry, and a big dish of butter curls. Behind her came
Aristide Marchissy la Dole. He looked as though he had gone
without sleep for a week and hadn't had his brown suit pressed for
a month. He had a little blue cornflower in his buttonhole and a
shaving nick on his chin with a little fuzz of cotton wool stuck to it
like penicillin mould. He gave me a slow, dubious smile and lit a
cigarette while he waited for the maid to go out.

I sat up in bed and said, 'There's one important thing I want to make clear. I'm hungry. So lay off my croissants.'

The door closed on the maid. Aristide came over, took a hot roll and buttered it, flicked the silver foil off the raspberry conserve, put a spoonful inside the roll, removed the cigarette from his mouth and wolfed the lot.

'I said lay off.'

He said, 'You specified croissants, which by the way, were first made in Budapest in 1686. That was the year the Turks besieged the city. They dug underground passages under the walls at night, but the bakers – naturally working at that hour – heard them, gave the alarm and Johnny Turk was thrown out. In return the bakers were given the privilege of making a special pastry in the form of the crescent moon which, I believe, still decorates the Ottoman flag. Fascinating, no?'

'Someday,' I said, 'I must buy myself a copy of *Larousse Gastronomique*.'

But I was fascinated. Not by what he had said, but by what he was doing as he spoke. I've turned plenty of rooms over in my time, and seen experts turn rooms over, but I'd never seen an expert like Aristide turn a room over. He did it without any fuss, restricting himself to the probable size of the article he was looking for. He was neat and he was fast and afterwards there wasn't going to be a sign that anything had been disturbed. He found the gun I had taken from O'Dowda and pocketed it without comment.

He disappeared into the bathroom and then came back and said, 'All right. Now the bed.'

Reluctantly, I got out. He searched pillows, sheets, mattress and the frame then replaced the stuff tidily and waved me to take up residence again, which I did. He buttered and jammed himself another roll.

I said, 'Of course, you've checked the hotel safe and my car?'

'Naturally. And of course, I know you've got it – somewhere. Let us just regard you for now as the custodian. If you lose it, of course, you could be in trouble.'

The roll finished, he came back to the tray, tipped the wrapped sugar lumps from the bowl, and said, 'Do you mind if I share your coffee? I've been driving since four o'clock this morning.'

'Ever since Guffy passed you my telephone number?'

'Yes. Your Miss Wilkins, of course. She had no option.'

'She didn't have to. She had my permission. That's why I've

been expecting you – though not so soon. Perhaps now you will tell
me on what score you are gunning for O'Dowda?'

He smiled. 'I understand you've finished your work for him.'

'I found the car, yes – and passed O'Dowda the location.'

'O'Dowda, I gather, isn't very pleased with you."

'News travels fast in these parts. You must have a line to
Durnford.'

'Yes. He's had communication with us before – first anonymously
– subsequently openly. He's not always been strictly honest about
his objective. Isn't now, quite. But he's been helpful.'

He raised the sugar bowl and made a horrible sucking noise at
the coffee.

I said, 'Was Durnford the only one who sent you anonymous
letters?'

'So far as I know. One came to me at Interpol. Guffy had two
others at Scotland Yard.'

'And naturally, even though there might not be any truth in
them, the police couldn't altogether ignore them?'

He nodded, squatted on the edge of a chair, and said, 'Guffy
passed his to us. The subject concerned was, in a sense, an international figure. More particularly for us, a European figure.'

'With a prototype in fiction?' Remembering Julia and the way
she had behaved about Otto, I didn't think it was a shot in the
dark.

'If it was fiction. There was the Chevalier Raoul de Perrault's
Contes du Temps.'

'Or Giles de Retz, the Marquis of Laval. Holinshed, I believe.
My sister used to scare me with the story at bedtime. For such a
nice, gentle, green-fingered person she has a macabre taste in
bedtime fairy stories.'

'All fairy stories, the best, are macabre.'

'Is this a fairy story, or fact?'

'It remains to be seen.' He stood up and looked out of the window,
at the terrace below with its cropped trees and the lake beyond.
'You have an expensive taste in hotels. *De la terrasse obragée belle vue
sur le lac.*'

'Poetry?'

'No, Michelin. It goes for any hotel near water. *Repas sous
l'ombrage, face au lac.*'

'You want to change the subject?'

'Not particularly.'

I said, getting out of bed and beginning to hunt for my cigarettes, 'I can understand Guffy, with murder in mind, telling me to keep an eye open if I were working for O'Dowda, but what I don't understand – from an Interpol point of view – is the interest in what may or may not have been in a submerged Mercedes?"

'No?'

'No.' I lit a cigarette, climbed back into bed and poured myself what was left of the coffee.

Aristide came back from the window. 'You have finished with the croissants?'

'Yes.'

He helped himself to one of the remaining pastries. He masticated slowly, smiling at me. Then he said, 'There are many differences between Interpol and the semi-honest little business you run.'

'Naturally. I don't get a pension at the end. That's why it's semi-honest. I have to work a handsome rake-off now and then.'

'Resist the temptation this time. Interpol is a police organization. The International Criminal Police Organization. Inevitably, it deals with more than crimes. Any international organization must occasionally accept some political influence from its members. The little parcel which – I concede you this – you have so cleverly found and so cleverly hidden, is a political matter.'

'And who are the interested parties exerting this influence?'

He cocked a sleepy eye at me and then rolled a grey lid down in a tired wink.

'That would be telling.'

'You can do better than that.'

'Not much – except that the interested governments prefer that neither Gonwalla nor O'Dowda should recover it. The interested governments could make good use of it – if they were ever forced to.'

'I'm sure. Though they would never call it blackmail.'

'In respectable hands, for respectable purposes, blackmail is a respectable weapon.'

'Put it to music and you've got a hit.'

I got out of bed.

He said, 'Where do you go from here?'

I said, 'To have a bath and a shave.' I stripped off my pyjama jacket.

He looked at my arm and said, 'You have been wounded.'

'You know what women are when they get excited.'

He said, 'You could finish up with more than a scratch. There could be a murder charge against you.'

I said, 'Even you can't say that with conviction. By the way, assuming I had the parcel, what sort of price would Interpol offer?'

'They wouldn't. Not cash.'

'They would. Tell them to forget the free pardon for murder and name a price.'

He sighed. 'I'll pass on your request. Meanwhile, I have to inform you that the parcel must be handed to us within four days.'

'Or else what?'

He grinned. 'A special disciplinary sub-committee is considering that right now. You don't mind if I finish the rest of the croissants?'

'Help yourself.'

I went into the bathroom and turned on the taps. When I came back to dress he was gone.

But that didn't mean I was going to be left unattended. The parcel had political significance. Interpol was a crime organization but – much as Aristide might hate any political pressure, which I was sure he did because he was a professional crime man – if a directive had been given then no employee could do anything else but obey it. That's where the real difference lay between Interpol and my semi-honest little business. I didn't have to obey anyone. I was my own boss. I just did what I thought was best – mostly for me.

I picked up the phone and put a call through to the Château de la Forclaz. If Durnford answered I was going to put a sugar lump in my mouth and do a little spluttering to disguise my voice. From now on, so far as I was concerned, Durnford had too many irons in the fire to be trusted. The call was answered by a girl on the château switchboard, and I asked for Miss Julia Yunge-Brown.

When she came on I said, 'This is Carver here. If you want to help me, pack a bag, get in your car and ring Talloires 88.02 from an outside phone as soon as possible. If you don't call me within the hour I shall enter a monastery. Probably La Grande Chartreuse – it's not far away. Incidentally, I had a brief meeting with Otto Libsch.'

I put the receiver down before she could say anything. Forty minutes later she rang back.

CHAPTER 7

'Rack well your hero's nerves and heart,
And let your heroine take her part.'
(Mary Alcock)

I packed my bag and left it in my room. Then I went down to
reception, paid my bill, said I wouldn't be in for lunch but would
be back around five o'clock just to pick up my bag.

Then I took a stroll along the lakeside and up into the village. I
picked up one of Aristide's men quite quickly. Not because I was
all that clever, but because he had meant me to spot him. That
meant there was another one around somewhere. I would be lucky
if I spotted him. The only thing to do was to isolate him, and I'd
already made arrangements for this.

The front man was a plumpish little number, wearing a beret, a
sloppy linen suit, and had a camera slung round his neck. He
worked overtime with the camera whenever I hung him up. There
was probably no film in it anyway.

I took him for a stroll around, hoping I might spot the other, but
I never did, and after an hour I gave up trying because it had
suddenly occurred to me that it wasn't a camera at all but a walkie-
talkie and he was just giving a running commentary to his chum
somewhere out of sight.

About one o'clock I went back to the hotel and got the car. As
I drove across the quay-side I saw the camera man sitting in a
parked car by the *pissoir*. He was lucky to have got a parking space
because the quay was crowded with visitors' cars. He took a nice
little shot of me as I went by – f.11 at 250, with a heavy cloud
overhead, what did he care? – to tell his hidden chum I was moving.

I drove along the road to Annecy for a mile and then turned left-
handed up to the Annecy golf course. I parked with three or four
other cars outside the little club house and went in and had lunch.

Halfway through, my camera man took a table well away from me and ordered beer and a sandwich. There were only a few other people eating and they had all been there before I arrived. That meant that number two was outside somewhere by now. I took my time. Julia had a longish drive ahead of her, even in the Facel Vega, and various things to do before we met.

Finally I went downstairs, paid a green fee and hired a small bag of clubs from the professional. I was wearing a pullover and thick brown shoes so I had no changing to do, but I went into the dressing room to see a man about a poodle. There was the usual notice over the place asking you not to throw cigarette ends into it. Some wag had added underneath: *Cela les rend si vachement difficile a fumer après.*

I was more interested in a camera that was hanging from one of the coat-hooks in the changing room. I didn't examine it, but I made a note of the brown suit jacket which was also on the hook.

When I went outside there was a man tapping balls about on the putting green. He was wearing brown trousers that matched the jacket inside. His shoes were suède moccasins. Never mind, like good policemen, they were doing their best. They couldn't have anticipated golf. He was a big man, with the height, bulk and look of a de Gaulle but with a nervous, hesitant smile on his face when I nodded to him that would never have done for a man of destiny. He didn't look as though he could say '*Non*' to anyone. But appearances are deceptive – or Aristide wouldn't have chosen him. He was going to stick to me. Just for a moment I was tempted to ask him to join me, set the stakes high and hope that I'd got a pigeon. Then I thought of Julia and gave up the pleasure.

I was lucky that I was operating on familiar ground. I'd once spent a memorable month in these parts and played the course a few times. I climbed the flagpole-decorated mound to the first tee and saw that my tail was wandering across to play round after me.

I didn't hurry. I couldn't have done because it was one of those days when I was right off my game. If I'd been playing the whole course – which I wasn't going to do – something in my bones told me that I would never break a hundred. I lost a ball on the first hole, in the long grass of the right-hand slope down to the green. I sliced one out of bounds on the second, over a stone wall and trees into a bungalow garden. On the third, which was a short hole of about two hundred yards, and the farthest outward point on this section of the course, I hit a lucky screamer to within three yards of the green. I wasn't too happy about that because this was the point I had picked for operations. I didn't want par golf, I wanted manly work in the rough, so I took a seven iron and chipped the ball boldly across the green into the bushes ten yards behind it. Then I started to look for it, and couldn't find it naturally. Behind me my tail hit a bad shot halfway down the fairway, and then a few more bad ones, working to the green and giving me time to find my ball and play out.

I stepped back from the bushes and politely waved him through. He had to come. It was a nice spot, low down and far out and not so easy to see from the clubhouse.

My tail holed out on the green, and then, with the camaraderie of an afternoon potterer, strolled across to me to help look for my ball. He came up with that nervous smile that meant nothing except that he wasn't going to lose sight of me, and I hit him, hard, with the side of my hand across his windpipe and again across the side of the neck as he choked and fell back. He went down with a rattle of irons from his bag and stayed down.

I ducked through the bushes and ran. Three hundred yards away, over a field and some small farm plots, was the road to Annecy.

The timing was beautiful. As I hit the road, a horn honked behind me and the Facel Vega came screaming down from the direction of Talloires.

A couple of miles further on, through Menthon on the road to Annecy, Julia swung hard right up the hill.

I said, 'Where are we going?'

She was driving fast, concentrating, and said without turning, 'I've got a ski-lodge near Megève. There won't be anyone there.'

'You collected all the things I wanted?'

She nodded.

I'd asked her to hire a projector and a tape recorder as she came through Annecy on her way down. She'd then gone to Talloires and picked up my bag from the hotel and the parcel from the safe at the Auberge du Père Bise.

When we hit Megève, some hours later, she stopped in the main street, near the Casino.

She said, 'There's no food in the place. You get coffee and bread. I'll do the rest.'

She was being very brisk and efficient, playing the role of assistant conspirator and enjoying it.

The shopping done, we went out of the town, along the road to Mont Arbois, past the golf course and then a mile further on she swung into a small open drive. Isolated in the middle of a small alp was a neat two-storey chalet, great stones wired to the roof, the façade polished boards, and the pink-and-grey shutters at all the windows cut with little heart-shaped openings. She parked the car round the back on bare gravel and we carried all our stuff in. There was a large main room with a tiled stove in the centre, comfortable chairs and a couple of settees, and an open stairway running up to the top floor. In a way it was not unlike Ansermoz's place.

When all our stuff was dumped in the middle of the floor, I said, 'I want a room to myself for half an hour. Okay?'

'You can take the big spare bedroom.'

I looked at her. She was worth looking at. She wore tight tartan trousers – I wouldn't know what clan, but there was a lot of red and yellow in them – a black sweater and a loose leather coat. On her head was a peaked black cap, shaped like an engine driver's. I could imagine the original photograph of it in *Vogue*.

She looked good; just the sight of her did things for me – but there was no getting away from the fact that our wavelengths were different. However, I had an idea now of the station she was more or less permanently tuned in to. As though to confirm it, she said, 'What about Otto Libsch?'

I said, 'We'll come to him in good time.'

I lugged the projector, tape recorder and the parcel up to the spare room. I took a sheet off the big bed, hung it cross the shuttered window and set up the projector. Then I locked the door and ran the two reels.

They were more or less what I had expected; *dramatis personae* – Panda Bubakar and, a safe bet for the other two, General Seyfu Gonwalla and Mrs Falia Makse. It had all been shot from a hidden camera somewhere high up in the room. Either Durnford or Tich Kermode, I thought, could have been responsible for that. More probably Tich. As a display of acrobatics it had its limitations; as a fillip for a tired businessman it was just run-of-the-mill stuff, but for private showing to Gonwalla's cabinet it would have been a bomb, particularly under the seat of the Minister for Agriculture. The public image set up for Gonwalla in his country was that of the stern father-figure, determined to stamp out corruption, immorality, and all social and economic evils. Given selective showing in the General's home country, I could see that the film would lead to a speedy change of government. Which, of course, was what O'Dowda was after.

The tape recorded a conversation between the General and Mr Alexi Kukarin. They were very friendly, referring to each other as General and Alexi, and it was all in English. And it had all been taped, I was sure, without their knowledge, otherwise the General would not have offered some of the comments he had about his government colleagues, and Alexi would not have made one or two beefs about his which would have made him very unpopular at home. The meat of the conversation, however, was that Alexi's people would be happy to supply aircraft, arms, and equipment against a guaranteed percentage – a large one, and at a cheap rate – of certain minerals, ores and chemical products, simple innocuous things like cobalt, aluminium ore and uranium, which were to be produced eventually by a state-owned monopoly of mineral and mining resources now in process of being established. In addition, Alexi was insistent that no compensation should be paid to existing European concerns already operating in the country. Straight appropriation was the ticket. The General stuck at this one a bit, but Alexi insisted – pointing out that the country had suffered decades of colonial exploitation, and there was no need to be soft-hearted. The General in the end agreed.

I must say that, from the tapes, their characters came over well Alexi – for all his charm and occasional jokes – had been given a brief and when it came to facts he was diamond-edged. The General was a nice enough chap outside of a bedroom, but he was a bit fuzzy around the edges, wanting things explained more than once. He had to have a big streak of simplicity in him, otherwise he would never have fallen for the invitation to use the Château de la Forclaz. O'Dowda, I knew, had made it open house for visiting members of the government for years and it hadn't occurred to the General to question the propriety of going on using it, as he had no doubt often done in the past when he felt the need for peace and quiet and the stimulating company of old friends like Panda and Mrs Makse. We all of us live and learn. It's a question of the proportion between the two. The General was miles away from ever breaking even.

I dismantled everything, and then packed the film and tape away in the parcel.

Downstairs the stove was alight, the room warm, and bottles and glasses had appeared on a side table. I could hear Julia moving about in the kitchen. I rummaged a desk, found paper and string and rewrapped the parcel. One thing was certain, I didn't want to have it around this place longer than I could help. I addressed it and then poked my head in the kitchen. She was doing something at the side of the sink with meat.

I said, 'Can I borrow your car? I want to go down to Megève to the post office.'

She looked at her watch. 'It'll be shut.'

I said, 'There are ways round that.'

There was. I went back along the road to the golf course and then turned into the drive of the Hotel Mont d'Arbois. It was pretty deserted because it was almost the end of the season.

I handed the parcel, and a hundred-franc note, to the clerk at the desk and asked him to post it for me. He said it wouldn't go out until the next morning. I said that that was fine, asked if they'd had a good season, was told that it had been so-so, and went.

Going into the chalet it was a nice feeling to think the parcel was well out of my hands. It was nice, too, to see Julia.

She'd changed into the dress she had been wearing in my office the first time we had met; it could have been design or accident. Anyway, just watching her move in it was enough to soothe away the strain of the last few days. I said what would she have and she said a gin-and-Campari with a big slice of lemon and a lot of ice, and it was all there on the table. I poured a stiff whiskey for myself. She squatted on the settee, drew her legs up, and took the drink with a polite little nod of her head. Something from the kitchen smelled good.

I said, 'You cook as well?'

'*Cordon bleu.*'

I said, 'You know why croissants are called croissants?'

'No.'

'Good.'

I stretched out in an armchair and lit a cigarette, sipped my drink and felt the first caress of whiskey go lovingly down. All was well with the world, almost.

Almost, because she was giving me her dark-eyed, gipsy stare, and I wasn't sure where to begin. Semi-honest, Aristide had called my business. He was right. Well why not, I thought, just for once, just for the hell of it, try straightforward honesty? Why not? It could pay off. It would hurt, of course, but I already had a four-thousand dollar purse to ease the pain. I decided to give it serious thought, later.

I said, 'Can you listen as well as I hope you cook?'

'You're nervous about something,' she said.

'Naturally. I'm considering being entirely honest. That's strange ground for me.'

'Take it a step at a time. It won't spoil what I'm cooking.'

I did. She listened well. Summarized it went like this.

1. I had been employed by O'Dowda to trace his Mercedes. In the course of my investigations I had learnt that a parcel – of importance to O'Dowda – was hidden in the car. O'Dowda had told me that the parcel contained Japanese Bank Bonds. I did not believe this.

2. While tracing the car it had become clear that two other parties were interested in finding it and obtaining the parcel it contained. They were, in order of activity: Najib and Jimbo Alakwe, working under the orders of General Seyfu Gonwalla, head of an African state; and Interpol.

3. I had found the car and taken the parcel, which contained certain film and a tape recording. (I didn't mention Otto or the Tony interlude.)

4. The film was a record, taken without their knowledge, of the sexual activities of General Gonwalla, Miss Panda Bubakar and a Mrs Falia Makse at the Château de la Forclaz.

5. The tape was a record, made without their knowledge, of a conversation between General Gonwalla and an Alexi Kukarin in which an exchange of arms, aircraft and equipment was agreed against a major proportion of the state's production of minerals, etc., in Gonwalla's country.

6. Clearly, the film and tape records had been secretly organized by O'Dowda for use in the General's country to stimulate the overthrow of his government and thus ensure the grant of a monopoly of mineral and mining rights promised O'Dowda by the previous government.

7. The Alakwe brothers wanted the tape and film in order to destroy it. O'Dowda wanted it to ensure his monopoly being granted. Interpol wanted it so that they could pass it to the custody of an interested government or governments. What the government(s) would do with it was pure guesswork, but clearly they weren't going to destroy it and so keep General Gonwalla

in power, otherwise there would have been a link-up already between Interpol and the Alakwe brothers. Equally clearly they weren't going to hand it over to O'Dowda, otherwise Interpol would have linked up with me. Probably then their intention was to let Gonwalla know that they had it, and could at any time they wished release it to his governmental opponents, but wouldn't do so as long as Gonwalla made concessions either political or economic to the interested government(s), and none to Kukarin's government.

At this stage, I said, 'You get that?'

She said, 'Yes. But I'm surprised that Interpol would do a thing like that.'

I said, 'Governments are outside morality. What is devaluation but defaulting on your creditors? Governments can short-change but not individuals. To go on to the most important point—'

8. Following the question of morality – I had the vital parcel. I ran a small semi-honest business, patronized mostly by clients who were non-starters in the Halo Stakes. Some of them were bad payers. It had become my habit, in selected cases, to supplement clients' fees by imposing substantial rake-offs for myself where possible. The money escaped tax, and I flattered myself that I spent it wisely and not all on myself and, let's face it, a fair amount of it did eventually go to the government in the form of Betting Tax. The real problem of the moment was – what should I do with the parcel? I could sell it at a good price to either O'Dowda or General Gonwalla. Or, I might sell it to Interpol, though they would never match the price of the others. Or I could destroy it.

'And what,' Julia asked, 'do you intend to do with it?'

'It's a testing question, isn't it?'

'Is it?'

'For me, yes. What would you do?'

'Put it on the stove right away.'

'Crisp, positive. If I had it here I might consider it. But it's in safe keeping.'

'That doesn't surprise me. It stops you doing anything impulsive like burning it here and now.'

'Bright girl.'

'Did you enjoy the film?'

I didn't like the way she said it.

I said, 'I've seen better. However, let's come to another point, which is more of a domestic matter. Interpol have another interest in all this – apart from the parcel. Somebody has been writing them anonymous letters about your stepfather.'

'It certainly wasn't me.'

'No, I didn't have you lined up for that. But would you have any idea what the letters might be about?'

She didn't answer, but I was sure that she did have an idea. Before the silence could become embarrassing, I went on, 'All right. Let's approach it another way. You've been wanting to talk about it for a long time. If I'd been on the ball I might have got it from you the first time you came to see me. In a way I'm glad I didn't because it could have complicated things then. Why didn't you tell me right away that Otto Libsch had once been second chauffeur at the château?'

'I didn't see that it was going to help.' She was ready enough with that one, but it was unconvincing.

'Look,' I said, 'I'm on your side. Just give a little. Okay, knowing about Otto at that time wouldn't have helped me much in the job I had to do. Oh, I can guess how he was linked up with Max. Zelia was the lonely type. Otto drove her around. They talked. She liked him. It was part of his form to have people like him. Maybe he took her to a discothèque or something in Geneva, gave her a pleasant time, and then eventually she met Max, and she kept the whole thing secret because it was her first big romance and that was the way she saw it. Something like that?'

'Yes, I suppose so.'

'Well, if so – there would have been no harm in telling me about it in Turin. But you didn't. And I know why.'

'Why?'

'Because you had a different interest in Otto. Right?'

She gave me a long look and then gently nodded her head.

'Good. You had another interest in him, but you weren't sure how to handle it. Not even sure you could tell me about it because you still weren't trusting me. You thought, maybe still think, that any private or confidential information I get I immediately look over to see where there might be a profit in it for me.'

'That's not true!'

'No?'

'No!' Her indignation sounded real and that pleased me.

'In that case, let's have it now. What had Otto got to do with the way your mother died?'

She put her cigarette down slowly and then stood up and came and picked up my empty glass and went to fill it, her back to me. It was a nice back, nice legs, and I liked the way that her dark hair fell about the nape of her neck.

'Slowly, in your own words,' I said, to help her.

Back to me, she began to talk.

'It was over two years ago. We were all at the château. My mother told me she was leaving O'Dowda. She was in love with someone else.'

'Who?'

She turned. 'She didn't say. Wouldn't say. I think, maybe, even then, she was scared to. She said we would know very soon. She was leaving first thing in the morning, and Otto was going to drive her to Geneva. This was late at night. I went to bed, and I never saw her again.'

'Why not?'

She came back and put the glass in front of me.

'I was told by my stepfather at noon the next day that she had been drowned in Lake Léman. He said that she had got up early, called for Otto to drive her down to the lake – we kept a couple of speedboats there – and she had gone out with Kermode and the boat had capsized.'

'Was it a likely story?'

'She loved boats and she loved speed. And she liked going out early. Any other morning it was something that could easily have been true. But not that morning. That morning she was due to go off for good with this other man.'

'And her body was never recovered?'

'No. But that happens sometimes in the lake. It's very deep.'

'I see. And Otto swore at the enquiry that he drove her down and saw her go aboard with Kermode?'

'Yes.'

'And Kermode told his story. Speed too high, tight curve, capsize, gallant effort to save her and so on?'

'Yes.'

'And you – and Zelia – have had your suspicions of O'Dowda ever since?'

'I think he had her killed.'

'And what about the man she was going away with? Did he ever show?'

'No.'

'And you've no idea who it was?'

'No.' She went and sat down, curling her legs up under her.

'I imagine that Otto left your stepfather's service soon after?'

'Yes.'

I said, 'You like me to tell you who the man was – the man your mother was going away with?'

'How can you possibly know?'

'Some of it's crystal-ball stuff, I'll admit. But not much. It was Durnford—'

'That's impossible!'

'No, it isn't. We're talking about love, and love comes up with some odd combinations at times. It was Durnford. He's the one who has been writing anonymous letters. His hatred of O'Dowda isn't the ordinary comfortable hatred of a secretary for a millionaire employer. He's so full of hate for your stepfather that he's buzzing around like a wasp trapped against a window pane. He's doing everything he can to bitch up O'Dowda – particularly over this car business. He must have been the one who tipped the Gonwalla crowd off about the film and tape in the first place. He'd do anything to spite O'Dowda. He was going off with your mother and, somehow, O'Dowda found out, and it would suit his sense of humour to get rid of your mother and keep Durnford on, half-knowing that Durnford would guess the truth and wouldn't be able to do anything about it. That's just the situation O'Dowda likes. That's why he has that waxworks. And Durnford has been trying to get at him any way he could. He's worked the ends against the middle so much now that he's got himself tied in a real Turk's Head – and if he's not careful Kermode will take him for a ride when O'Dowda's tired of the whole thing.'

'Durnford . . . I can't believe it.'

'I can. And I can believe something else. If your stepfather murdered your mother there isn't anything you or anyone else can do about it. Otto's dead, and can't give evidence of perjury. Kermode's alive and won't give evidence. She went to the lake, like they said. It can't be disproved. And that's not just my opinion. I've an idea that Interpol feel that way. So my advice to you is to forget it. You got money of your own?'

'Yes.'

'Then follow Zelia's example. Just get out on your own. Feeling as you do, you can't go on living under his roof.'

'That's just what I've done.'

'Done?'

'Yes. I'd have done it before, but this Zelia thing came up. But when you telephoned me yesterday I was packing to leave. This chalet belongs to me. I was coming up here anyway for a few days to settle things in my mind.'

'Did you tell O'Dowda you were leaving him?'

'Yes, in a letter which I left with Durnford . . . Durnford. I can't believe it.'

'I'll bet on it. Did you mention anything of your reason in the letter?'

'No. But he won't have difficulty reading between the lines. And I don't care a damn if he does.'

She stood up, smoothing the dress wrinkles over her thighs.

'Life's complicated,' I said. 'For the most part I like it that way. All this parcel business and then your mother . . . Phew, what a tangle. Sometimes a return to simple things is therapeutic. I'll pick the parcel up first thing in the morning and destroy it.'

She smiled for the first time, holding out her hands to the heat of the stove.

'You will?'

'I'll go and get it now if you like.'

'No, the morning will do. I'm not having the meal spoiled.'

She moved towards the kitchen door, then half-turned, her face serious again.

'You really think it's hopeless to do anything about . . . well, about my mother?'

'O'Dowda's a millionaire. He knows how to be careful. He can buy and sell, not only people, but truth. My advice is to forget it all. If he did it, it's written in the book against him and one day the charge will come home to roost. But there's nothing you can do.'

She nodded and went into the kitchen.

It was a good meal. We had *tranches de mouton* done in brandy and served with a *purée* of spinach, and then spent a pleasant evening together.

When we went up to bed, she stopped at her door and she said, 'You really are going to get that parcel and destroy it, aren't you?'

'First thing in the morning.'

She moved close to me and put her arms around my neck. I had to do something with my arms so I put them around her. She kissed me, and a little carillon of bells began to tinkle at the back of my skull. She drew back and looked into my eyes.

I said, 'What's that for?'

She smiled. 'To say I'm sorry for having been mixed up about you. You're not a bit like you want people to think you are.'

She kissed me again and then I held her away from me.

I said, 'You've no idea what I'm like, given the right stimulus. And it's working now.' I reached round her, opened her door, kissed her, fought against the one thing I had in mind, won, and gently armed her into the room. I pulled the door shut and, from the outside, said, 'Lock it. Sometimes I walk in my sleep.'

I waited until I heard the key turn. Then I went into my own room, telling myself that just for once I would do things in their right order. I wanted that parcel out of the way, destroyed, first, I knew me too well. I could have gone into the room with her, and had second thoughts about the parcel in the morning. After all, it was worth a hell of a lot of money, and money is real, so many other things fade and wither.

Before I undressed, I got out my four thousand dollars and hid the notes spread flat under the linoleum. If I were going to do the proper thing and all was to be right between us I knew that I would be back here soon. And if things didn't go right, well, it would still be here. After all, every winning fighter is entitled to his fairly won purse money.

I was down at the Hotel Mont Arbois by eight oclock the next morning to get my parcel before it was collected by the mail. I was too late. The post had gone. Well, I should just have to collect it at Evian – where I had posted it to myself *poste restante*. I drove slowly in the Facel Vega, wondering why I was throwing away the chance to collect a few more easy thousands for myself. So far as I could see it wasn't going to do me any good. I couldn't even detect the slightest beginning of any spiritual change in myself. Why was I doing it? Clearly, just to get a good standing in Julia's eyes. Some day, I thought, I might find myself in circumstances where I could do something out of pure principle, and no strings attached. It would be interesting to see how I felt then.

I parked the car round the back and hurried into the kitchen, looking forward to coffee and eggs and bacon. There was a good smell of coffee from the pot on the stove, but no sign of breakfast or Julia. I went up to her bedroom. The bed was made, but all her clothes and her suitcase had gone. In my room the bed had been made up.

I went down to the big main room, puzzled. On the table where the drinks were an envelope was propped against one of the bottles. I tore it open.

It was from Panda Bubakar.

Honey-boy,

We've borrowed your Miss Julia for an indefinite period. Don't fuss, we'll take good care of her. Tell her pappa that he can have her back just as soon as you return you-know-what. Ritzy pyjamas you wear.
A hatful of kisses. Yum-yum!
Panda.

I went into the kitchen and poured myself some coffee and sat on the table, thinking.

I had an idea that all this had stemmed from Durnford trying to free himself from the Turk's Head he'd got tangled in. He was prepared now to do anything to muck O'Dowda up and wasn't giving a thought to any consequences. If he couldn't get the parcel from me he was prepared to help Najib to get it. Anything so long as O'Dowda didn't get it.

I called the Château de la Forclaz and got him.

I told him where I was and went on, 'Did you know Miss Julia was going to be here?''

'Yes. Before she left she asked me to forward any mail to her there.'

'And you told Najib where he could find her?''

'What I do is my own business.'

'Well, all I can say is don't go out in any speedboat with Tich Kermode. You've made a real old muck of things. Where's O'Dowda?'

'He's back here and he wants to see you.'

'I'll bet he does. Tell him I'll be along pretty soon. Has he read Julia's letter?'

'What letter?'

'The one in which she says she's finished with him.''

After a pause, he said, 'Yes.'

'Pity.'

I rang off.

O'Dowda, knowing now that Julia had cut adrift from him, wasn't likely to consider that Najib and company had any great bargaining pawn in her. O'Dowda wanted that parcel badly. He wouldn't care a damn what happened to Julia – and plenty could happen to her because Najib was playing for high stakes on the Generals behalf.

I fried myself an egg and did some more thinking. It didn't get me anywhere. Then I went up and packed my things, including the ritzy pyjamas. I had a fair idea why Panda and Najib had not waited for me to come back from the hotel. They weren't interested in talking to me. They would go straight to O'Dowda himself.

Only one thing was clear to me. I had the parcel, and I didn't intend that any harm should come to Julia. That meant that I would have to hand it over to Najib. O'Dowda wasn't going to like that, and neither was Aristide. Both of them would do all they could to stop me. For the time being I decided that it would be best to leave the parcel sitting waiting for me at the Evian post office until I had got things straightened out.

I locked up the chalet and drove off in the Facel Vega. It was a good thing that I hadn't got the parcel with me. Just this side of Cluses, I was flagged down by a couple of police types on motor cycles. They were very polite, checked my papers, and then went over the car inch by inch. Disappointed, they asked me where I was going. I wasn't quite sure, but to keep them happy I said the Château de la Forclaz. They waved me on with a couple of gallant Gallic flourishes and sat on my tail for the next ten miles. But they must have been busy on the radio because, as I came down to Thonon on the side of the lake, a couple of fresh motor-cycle types appeared, slowed me down, took up station one at bow and one at stern, and escorted me into the town and on to the Quai de Rives where they pulled up. Aristide was waiting in a shabby old blue saloon.

He got out, dismissed the police, and came back to me and invited me across the road for a drink. He ordered a Pernod for himself and a beer for me and gave me a warm smile. The cornflower in his buttonhole was faded and he had cut himself in a different place on his chin shaving.

'Nice job you did at the golf course,' he said.

'I thought it was neat.'

'You have girls all over France you can call on for help?'

'Quite a few – but I'm not giving away any addresses. I'm not in a giving-away mood.'

'Pity. You spent last night with this Miss Julia Yunge-Brown?'

'Yes. She's a *cordon bleu* cook, and we had *tranches de mouton* with brandy. I don't know how she cooked it, but it took about two hours.'

He nodded. 'Could have been *à la Poitevine*. Should have had garlic with it. If only a touch.'

'It did.'

'Where is she now?'

'I don't know. I went for a stroll before breakfast and when I got back she had gone. A friend of ours left this note.'

I handed him Panda's note. He studied it without emotion and then put it in his pocket. 'What is so special about the pyjamas?'

'The design is made up of the flags of all nations.'

'Julia picked up the parcel for you, of course? I should have thought about the Auberge du Père Bise. And now you have safely disposed of it?'

'Yes.'

'Good. I would not want to think that anyone else could get their hands on it. That would be unfortunate for you.'

'Naturally, until I can hand it over in exchange for Julia.'

He shook his head.

'You are taking far too chivalrous a view.'

'If I didn't she could end up floating in a lake. General Gonwalla, fond though he may be of girls, isn't all that soft-hearted. He wants to keep his power seat warm, so he won't mind who he shoves out into the cold.'

'Power, politics – they are the bane of my life. It is nice to concentrate on simple things like murder, theft, forgery. Unfortunately one cannot always choose. I have the strictest instructions to obtain the parcel. Following your request, my organization have agreed to make a payment for it.' He sighed. 'Until now, I thought that it would be a simple little matter of bargaining between the two of us. You would not have got the price Gonwalla or O'Dowda might have paid, but since your heart is in the right place I know you would have foregone the extra profit in order to do me a favour. Now it is very much complicated by this kidnapping – and becomes very difficult for you.'

'You think so?'

'I know so, and so do you. I must have the parcel for my

employers. They insist, ruthlessly. Gonwalla may be ruthless and O'Dowda, too, but theirs is a personal form of ruthlessness. It does not approach the ruthlessness of an amorphous organization like a government or group of governments using a perfectly legitimate international organization. No individual would be personally responsible for the girl's death – not that we shan't try to find her and release her, of course – because it would be a bureaucratic necessity. It is very sad, is it not?' He drained his Pernod and called for another.

'You expect me to hand the parcel over and let what may happen happen to Julia?'

'That's what I've been saying.'

'You know that I won't bloody well do that!'

'I know that you will try to find a way around it.'

'What way?'

'That is up to you. I have no objection to anything you do, so long as I get the parcel. If I don't get it, you know, of course, what will happen to you?'

'Go ahead. Frighten me.'

'It will be out of my hands, of course. Happily another department will deal with it, so I shall have no guilt feelings. But you will be eliminated – out of pure bureaucratic pique, of course. I don't suggest that they will do it in any sadistic way, or make it particularly lingering. They will do it quickly and it will look like an accident. You are not naïve enough to think I'm being flippant about this?''

I wasn't. He was pressuring me, but behind the pressure was a fact, a simple, frightening fact. They would do just as he was promising. As a bureaucratic necessity. I would have to go. It was a straightforward situation. I had the parcel. If I gave it to Najib in return for Julia – then I would go. If I gave it to O'Dowda (which I couldn't see myself doing) – then it was ditto, with the addition of Julia. And if I gave it to Aristide, which I could do by motoring a few miles up the lakeside, then Julia would go because Gonwalla would have to make someone pay for the trouble that lay ahead of him. All I had to do was to find some way of getting my hands on Julia, freeing her, and then handing the parcel over to Aristide. That was all. Simple. I ordered myself a Pernod. Beer was too insipid in the circumstances.

Aristide watched me in silence. I downed the Pernod much too fast and stood up.

'I will have to think about this.'

'Naturally. You have my telephone number. Just call me.'

'And what,' I asked, 'are you doing about the other aspect of this O'Dowda affair?'

He shrugged his shoulders. 'That is a simple matter of murder. I have had instructions to leave it in abeyance until this far more important matter is settled. You are, I imagine, going to the château?'

'Yes.'

'Then please don't mention to O'Dowda our interest in this affair. That is between us.'

'Of course, I wouldn't do anything to embarrass you.'

He grinned. 'That is the correct attitude.'

It would have been nice to sock him on the nose before leaving. But it wouldn't have done any good. He had nothing to do with it. He was just a cipher. He took his pay and went through the prescribed motions and when he went home at night everything dropped from him, leaving him stainless. Just wipe the knife down with a wet rag and you couldn't tell that it had been used. As long as the correct official form had been made out, endorsed by the right department, and neatly filed in the correct cabinet, then there was nothing to worry about.

I drove along the lake as far as Evian, and then I phoned the château and got hold of Durnford. I asked if O'Dowda was around. He wasn't. He had gone to Geneva for the day. I told Durnford I was coming along to see him.

The last person I wanted to run into at the moment was O'Dowda.

I parked on the gravel outside the château, went in and across the big marbled floor to Durnford's office. He was sitting in a swivel chair, staring at a green filing cabinet, smoking, and, from the ash scattered down his waistcoat front, he'd been in that position for a long time. He just cocked his head at me as I came in and then went on staring.

I sat down and lit a cigarette. There was a photograph behind the desk of O'Dowda on the shores of some loch holding up a pike that must have gone all of thirty pounds.

I said, 'This is a purely private talk between us. We won't go into the muck-up you've made of things. We'll just stick to some straight answers – from you. Okay?'

He nodded and then reached down and produced a glass from an open desk drawer at his side. He took a generous swig, blinked his eyes at the filing cabinet and put the glass back.

'How long have you been on that?'

'Since lunchtime.'

'Then just knock it off until we've finished our business. First of all – have you had any communication from Najib Alakwe today?'

'No.'

'Did you know that he's grabbed Julia – and she isn't coming back until I hand over the parcel from the car?'

'No.' He didn't seem much interested. Well, whiskey can blunt the susceptibilities of the best of us.

'When you've wanted to get in touch with Najib in the past, how have you done it?'

He said, 'That's my business.'

I said, 'It's my business now. I want to know and I'm in the mood where I don't mind beating up a man some years older than myself. So give.'

He considered it for a while, then turned and fished in another drawer and passed a card across to me. I looked at it and wondered how many different kinds Najib had. It was the usual Mr Najib Alakwe, Esquire, of the import, export and specialities line, but this time there was an address in Geneva. I had to turn it over. You never knew what gem the Alakwe brothers were coming up with. I wasn't disappointed. The motto read: *A bon entendeur il ne faut que demi parole*. Well, I was hoping to have more than half a word with Najib – and soon.

Without looking at me, he said, 'All you had to do was to let me have the parcel, or destroy it.'

I said, 'I was going to destroy it – but you spoilt that. Things are a bit more complicated now.'

He shook his head. 'You would have kept it. Made money from it. I know you.'

'That's what I thought myself – but it didn't work out that way.' I stood up. 'You want some advice?'

'Not particularly.' He sounded completely apathetic, not the crisp number I had first known.

'Pack up and get out of here, get a long way away from O'Dowda. You were going to do it once with her and he bitched you. You should have done it on your own after that.'

He looked up suddenly, his eyes blinking.

'How did you know that?''

'It was a guess – until this moment.'

'He murdered her.'

'I'm inclined to agree. But there's nothing you can do about it. After what you've done, and when he learns the full story, you need to be thinking about your own skin.'

He said, 'I think I may kill him.'

I said, 'I wish I could think that was firm promise. But when the whiskey is finished your only concern will be how to get rid of a hangover.''

'Tich Kermode did it. He's an evil bastard – worse than O'Dowda. They get drunk sometimes, those two. Shut themselves up in that bloody great waxworks room with all the people O'Dowda hated. You can hear them laughing and pounding around. I kept it from the girls for years and years . . . but they knew in the end. . . . That's why they've left him.'

I made for the door. Then, a thought occurring to me, I said, 'Have you got a gun?'

'Gun?'

Why do drunks always have to give off echoes?

'Yes, a gun. It could be that I might need one – and for sure you won't.'

I think he fancied that I might be going to use it on O'Dowda because he co-operated by opening another drawer and tossing a gun to me. It's not an action I like. Guns are full of gremlins. I looked at it and said, 'What the hell's this?'

'It's all I've got,' he said, as he handed over to me a box of ammunition.

It was a .22 compressed-air pistol, powered by a Sparklet compressed air tube which gave about forty shots at somewhere around a muzzle velocity of four hundred feet per second. It could be nasty and looked like the real thing. I'd used one in Miggs's shooting range before. I hoped that it would be good enough to impress Najib and make him hand over Julia.

I went back to the car and sent up a fine shower of gravel going down the long drive. I wanted to be clear of the place before O'Dowda got back.

It was dark as I rode into Geneva. The address I had was in a cul-de-sac just off the Rue des Vollandes and not far from the Gare des Eaux-Vives. It was a top-floor flat and had a blue door painted with diagonal yellow stripes and when I thumbed the bell-push chimes inside played a simple melody that was vaguely familiar.

As I stood there trying to remember what it was, the door opened and Najib appeared. He'd gone back to his old style of dressing, ginger shoes, cream linen suit, red shirt and a yellow tie with garlands of multi-coloured roses trailing over it. It was a bit of a shock but I kept the air pistol firmly pointing at him.

'I'd like to come in,' I said.

The brown face beamed, the smudge nose crinkled, and the whiter shade of white teeth flashed.

'Certainly, Mr Carver. Damn glad to see you again. Welcome to not so humble abode.'

I said, 'You lead the way and cut out the music-hall patter.'

He went ahead of me down a softly carpeted hallway into a large sitting room. Not so humble it was. The furniture was all upholstered in black velvet, the carpet was pearly grey with great whorls of red in it. The curtains were green and the walls were covered with a paper that imitated great chunks of granite with thick white plaster marks in the joins. There was a sideboard nearly six feet long, covered with bottles and the things that go with them, a long table untidy with magazines, the covers of which were showing a lot of female flesh, and the place reeked of Turkish tobacco.

Najib turned, waved a hand around, and said, 'You like? No? Tastes differ. Some people say, just like a whore's parlour. Personally I have found many such parlours very comfortable and entertaining. What is your favourite tipple, sir?"

'My favourite tipple,' I said, 'is a large whiskey and soda which I'll fix myself in case you have any poison around. Personally I'm hoping that it's not a drink I shall have to linger over because I want my business cleared up smartly. Also, please cut out all the babu talk. You're probably a D.Litt. and, no doubt, could start at Chaucer while I pegged off at Shakespeare and beat me handsomely through to T.S. Eliot. So let's stick to a reasonable syntax, Najib, eh?'

He gave me that big, wide-open smile, and said, 'Actually, it's B.Sc.(Econ.) but I have not neglected the arts. Also, we should get the names right. I am disappointed that you have such a bad memory for faces. I am Mr Jimbo Alakwe, Esquire.'

I was so surprised that he went and fixed my drink for me while

I got over it. When I had recovered and the drink was in my hand, I said, 'What the hell are you doing here?'

'Temporary posting. Najib has a lot on his hands. Also, remember I now work for Mr O'Dowda so have to be on the spot.'

'You don't mean he actually took you on?'

'Why not? He doesn't trust me, but he likes to know where I am. Also, if he gets false information from me about affairs in my country, he probably guesses it is false and can make something from it. Wrong information can be as revealing as correct information. Mr O'Dowda is prepared to pay for both. Needless to say, my loyalty, my true loyalty, is to my country. I am inordinately proud of that. One of the things, I feel, which prevent you from becoming a success is that you have no loyalty to anyone but yourself. That can only lead to limited profits. What is your asking price for the parcel?' He held up a hand and went on quickly, 'Naturally the girl will be returned as well, but I realize that you will want something for yourself. But not as much, of course, as though we didn't have the girl.'

I said, 'No money passes. And no parcel passes. I want the girl.'

'I think,' said Jimbo, 'we had better discuss this situation a little more fully.'

'Let us do that,' I said, and sat down on a soft-sprung chair.

Jimbo reached for a cigarette box. As he opened the lid it began to play a tune. He grinned at me.

'*Au clair de la lune*. The toilet container in this place plays *Sur le pont d'Avignon*. This is really Panda's flat. You like her?'

'She's a great girl. Good swimmer, too. I'd like to know how she and Najib knew I was at Ansermoz's chalet, by the way.'

'It was very simple. They lost you so they made a phone call to the house. You answered the phone. Remember – you said to the woman caller that Max was in Cannes. So they knew you were there. After that they kept an eye on you from a safe distance.' He smiled. 'A man travelling fast, dreaming of profit, should look behind him occasionally.'

I said, 'You ought to print that on one of your cards.'

'Maybe.'

I stood up. 'All right, let's have a look round. You go ahead and don't make any sudden movements.'

He showed me round the flat. It was furnished throughout in Panda taste and it wasn't difficult to guess that she used the place for her professional entertaining. The whole place was probably wired for sound and film. One thing it didn't have, however, was any sign of Julia.

I took Jimbo back into the sitting room and he sat down and helped himself to another musical cigarette and waved his hand at the drinks for me to help myself.

Bottle in hand, I said, 'All right – she's not here. Where is she?'

He polished his ebony chin with the tips of his fingers and said, 'If I knew I wouldn't tell you, but the sad fact is that I don't know.'

'Why sad?'

'Because it shows that Najib, in a most unbrotherly way, doesn't altogether trust me. I have no means either of communicating with him. He phones me when he needs me. So please don't bother to exert yourself with any physical measures to make me talk. I have nothing to say. That is the most honest statement I have made for some weeks.'

I wondered. Then I decided to give him the benefit of the doubt. He realised it and gave me a sympathetic nod of his head.

'I should say, however, Mr Carver, that I am authorized to discuss details for a satisfactory exchange. What price were you thinking of?'

'I wasn't. I don't intend to do any deal.'

'Unchivalrous. She is a very beautiful girl, and – a little bird says – has some tenderness for you. Just think – for a parcel which is of no importance to you intrinsically you can earn yourself, say, a thousand guineas and her release. She will be delighted and, no doubt, eventually show her gratitude in the one way which constantly occupies men's minds. I am assuming, of course, that you still have the parcel and that it is in a safe place?'

I said, 'You can assume that. But you're not getting the parcel. Nobody's getting it.'

He shook his head. 'Not us, not Mr O'Dowda, or Interpol?' He gave me a big beaming smile of disbelief. 'You are, as they say, on the horns of a dilemma. A most unusual one, too, because this beast has three horns. I am sad for you. It is a predicament I should not like to be in myself. As I say, she is a very beautiful young woman. What you call, I think, the Celtic type. . . . No, no, perhaps Romany would be the word.'

He was right, of course. Not only about her physical type, but about my dilemma. At that moment I did not know which way to turn, what to do or where to go. Just for a moment I did reconsider using force on him in the hope that he might know more than he professed, but it was only for a moment. I could have taken him, but I didn't think he would speak before he passed out. Jimbo was a resolute type, inordinately proud of his loyalty.

I finished my drink and made for the door.

'Just sit there,' I said.

He nodded.

I went down the hallway and out. As I closed the door of the flat the solution to one question, at least, came to me. I realized that the tune the doorbell had played was 'Happy Birthday to You'.

A few minutes later, as I was about to get into the Facel Vega parked in the cul-de-sac outside the flat, Tich Kermode clubbed me over the back of the head and O'Dowda grabbed me like a sack of potatoes before I could hit the pavement. I passed out without protest.

CHAPTER 8

'No human being, however great, or powerful, was ever so free as a fish.'
(John Ruskin)

It was a Rolls-Royce. Kermode was driving and I sat in the back with O'Dowda. I felt in my pocket for the gun that I had borrowed from Durnford. It was gone. When O'Dowda saw that I had surfaced he handed me a flask without a word. I drank, then shivered, and blinked my eyes at the road unwinding before the headlights. We were climbing steeply through pine woods. Probably, I thought, the road back to the château.

Kermode had his chauffeur's cap pitched at a jaunty angle and was whistling gently to himself, happy at the thought of a good time ahead. O'Dowda was wearing a knickerbocker suit of hairy Harris tweed. There was a big bruise on his right temple.

Nobody spoke for a long time. Then, staring straight ahead of him, O'Dowda said, 'You're a bastard.'

It wasn't a good conversational opener, so I ignored it.

He said, 'You're a bastard. So is Durnford, but he's a drunken bastard. If it's of any interest to you, I've sacked him.'

'After twisting his arm to say where I was?'

'Both arms,' said Kermode over his shoulder.

The two of them had a merry chuckle over that.

I didn't relish the thought of the next few hours. O'Dowda wanted the parcel and he wasn't, I was sure, contemplating any kind of a deal – even if I'd been in a position to offer one.

He said, 'I hate time-wasting. Someone always has to pay for that, boyo.'

I yawned, closed my eyes, and leaned back against the genuine pigskin.

O'Dowda said, 'What makes you think you can sleep?'

I said, 'Try and stop me.' I slumped lower down and gave a drowsy grunt.

Kermode said, 'He should be fun, sir.'

O'Dowda said, 'Yes. Worth waiting for.'

From the corner of a half-opened eye I saw him pull out a cigar and light up. Despite the throb in my head, I went to sleep.

I woke as we turned into the driveway of the château.

O'Dowda said, 'Feel better?'

'Thanks.'

'Good. I want you in fighting trim. And this time I'm not taking bets.'

We went up the mile-long drive but we didn't go to the château. We turned off, down a side road, and climbed for about half a mile and then pulled up. Kermode dowsed the lights. Outside I got a glimpse of an expanse of water stretching away, steely blue under the moonlight. It looked like a lake, and that brought unpleasant memories.

Standing at the side of the lake was a small cottage with a boat-house attached to it. They took me across to it and into the large main room.

'My workroom,' said Kermode.

There was a long bench down one side of the room, an open fireplace at the far end and on a little plinth in the middle stood an unclothed life-size wax figure without a head.

'When it's finished,' said O'Dowda, 'it's going to be you. We'll use the suit you're wearing now, so just take it off.' He looked at Kermode. 'Turn up the heating, Kermode, so that he doesn't get cold.'

Kermode moved around the room, turning on three or four electric heaters. O'Dowda lit another cigar and went to a cabinet and poured himself a brandy.

'There's one for you,' he said, 'when you've got the suit off.'

I stripped my suit off. What else could I do? If I had refused they would have enjoyed doing it for me.

O'Dowda – going to get me a brandy – said to Kermode, 'Do we want his shoes?'

Kermode shook his head. 'Too scruffy.'

O'Dowda handed me my brandy.

He said, 'Don't be too long drinking it. We want to tie your hands behind your back.'

I said, 'Have you figured out a place for me in the rogues' gallery?'

'Not yet,' said O'Dowda.

'Do me a favour and keep me well away from the policeman. I'm allergic to them.'

'So you should be. I suppose Interpol have been telling you that you have to hand the parcel over to them, or else?'

'Something like that.'

'Powerful things, governments,' said O'Dowda. 'I should know, I practically own a couple. I also have two Interpol men on my payroll. By the way, as of this date, you are no longer on my payroll. What is more, I don't intend to pay you a penny of what I owe you for your work so far unless you hand over the parcel to me.'

'Why not? You employed me to trace the car for you. I did just that.'

'You did far more than just that. You walked off with my property.'

While we were talking Kermode was busying himself at a large cupboard. So far as I could make out he was sorting out a collection of fishing rods.

I said, 'Have you had any communication from Najib lately?'

He nodded, blinked his small blue eyes at me through his cigar smoke, and said, 'A phone call. To save unnecessary beating about the bush, boyo, let me say I am well aware of the whole position. Najib wants the parcel in return for Julia. Interpol want it from you – or else. And I mean to have it. Tricky. For you. You have my sympathy but nothing else. Oh, and there is the other thing, too. this nonsense about my late wife. That's pure poppycock. Just the kind of thing Julia would dream up and that a crazy fool like Durnford would jump at. Mind you, I knew he was having an affair with my wife just before her unfortunate accident, but it didn't worry me. I was going to divorce her anyway. I'd already instructed my solicitors to prepare a petition. One of life's little accidents saved me the cost of their fees. Tie his hands, Kermode.'

Kermode came over, politely waited for me to finish the last of the brandy, and then tied my hands behind me at the wrists tightly with thin cord.

Thinking it might interest me, he said, 'It's a piece of Corolene Dacron braided spinning line.'

'It cuts like hell,' I said.

'It's meant to.'

I looked at O'Dowda who was helping himself to another brandy.

'If I hand the parcel over to you – you know what will happen to Julia?'

'As the night follows the day. General Gonwalla can be a very mean-minded man.'

'And you don't care a damn?'

'She's not my true daughter, and anyway she has now formally severed all relationship with me. I have no responsibility for her. That's not to say that she isn't a nice-looking girl and it will be a sad thing. I wouldn't be surprised if you hadn't a soft spot for her. All this puts you in an awkward situation, but it is of no interest to me. Just hand the parcel to me, however, and I'll try and make Gonwalla see sense – though I can't guarantee anything.'

'If I do, then Interpol will rub me out.'

'Yes, I think they would do that. That's why I'm sure that I shall have to use some method to make you tell me where the parcel is. I couldn't expect you to do so willingly.'

Kermode looked towards O'Dowda. 'What do you think, sir. Let it get a bit lighter?'

O'Dowda nodded. 'I think so. Won't be as much fun then as a big sea-trout in the dark, but we mustn't expect too much. What rod do you think?'

'Salmon?'

'We'll try the A. H. E. Wood.' He turned to me. 'Of course you could save yourself all this by just telling me where the parcel is.'

'I destroyed it.'

He grinned. 'Not you, boyo. If you gave me an affidavit signed by St Peter I wouldn't believe that one.'

'What about St Patrick?'

'Less so. Think I don't know the Irish? No, you've got it some-where safe and I'm having it. Come to think of it, I'd rather force it from you. You need some of the spunk taken out of you. I wouldn't say that your manner towards a man of my standing is deferential enough. And even if I did, there's a well-developed sadistic streak in me that says go ahead and have fun. God, it's hot in here.'

He stripped off his Harris tweed jacket. Over by the cupboard Kermode was fixing up the salmon rod with a reel. I had a fair idea of what they might be going to do, but I couldn't believe it. I tried to remember what I could about the breaking strain of lines, and then I recalled reading somewhere that a good rod and line had stopped a really strong swimmer dead after he'd done about thirty yards. I stopped thinking about it. O'Dowda was right. It was hot in the room. The lake would make an unpleasant contrast in temperature.

Then I thought about the parcel. What the hell was I to do? The whole thing had me properly confused. Give it to O'Dowda and lose Julia? Give it to Najib and save Julia – but put myself in the soup? Give it to Interpol and save myself and lose Julia, and then have Najib and O'Dowda gunning for me out of sheer political and economic spite? If there'd been time of course I could have written to some lonely hearts column and got advice. 'In the circumstances I think this is a problem where you must squarely face your own conscience. . . .' Trouble was there was no sign of my conscience being around at this moment. It was that kind of conscience, never there when you really wanted it.

I sat and sweated. O'Dowda had a little snooze. Kermode – he was the type – kept busy, tinkering away at some metalwork job at a bench down the far end of the room. Now and again he went to the window and looked out to see how the light was coming along.

After a couple of hours he came over to me and strapped a leather dog-collar affair around my neck. There was a steel ring fitted into it just under my chin and attached to the ring was a three-yard length of line.

'It's a wire gimp,' he said. 'So you can't bite through. Some big pike have been known to – but you've got to have real teeth for a job like that.' Then he looked at O'Dowda and, believe it or not, there was a touch of gentleness on his craggy, monkey face. 'Pity to wake him. He needs his sleep, does the boss. Drives himself hard. Always on the go. Don't pay any attention to that sadistic talk. Heart of a lamb he's got really. If you just coughed up now, he'd call it a day. Probably hand you a bonus on your pay. What do you say?'

I said, 'He looks far too much overweight. The exercise will do him good – or give him a stroke. Want me to tell you which I'm cheering for?'

He went and woke O'Dowda, shaking him gently by the shoulder, and then holding his jacket for him.

And that was the beginning of the entertainment. They led me through a side door, Kermode carrying their equipment, into the boathouse.

We got into a rowing boat and Kermode took the oars and we

pulled out on to the lake. It was a beautiful morning; no sun yet, but the hint of it, and the sky pearly grey with a rosy flush in the East. Not a cloud in the sky and a few late stars still flickering in protest against the coming day. Some duck got up from the weed beds near the boat-house.

'Pochards and a few garganey,' said O'Dowda. 'We tried to keep goldeneye here, but they wouldn't stay.' As he spoke he leaned forward making the end of the reel line fast to the loose end of the wire gimp.

'Make sure the knot's good,' I said.

'Don't worry, boyo,' he said warmly, 'I've had my tackle broken but I've never lost a fish yet through a sloppy knot. All you have to do when you've had enough is just to shout. Don't leave it too long so that you're too weak to shout.'

I drove upwards with my right knee, trying to get him in the face before he could fix the knot, but he was too quick for me. One of his big hands grabbed my leg and held it. From behind me Kermode leaned forward and hauled me back, and O'Dowda straddled my legs and finished tying the knot.

From that position they didn't take any more chances with me. They took off my shoes and I was lifted and flung overboard.

I went under, and I thought I would go out with the sudden shock of the cold; and while I was still under I felt the strain come firmly on the collar round my neck. When I came up the boat was twenty yards away. O'Dowda was standing up, two-handing the salmon rod, and taking the strain nicely on me. Kermode was at the oars, not rowing, just holding the boat evenly.

I trod water and felt my shirt and shorts ballooning around me. The cold began to cut into me. O'Dowda increased the pressure through the line and my head came forward until my face was underwater. I was forced to kick out with my legs and swim towards the boat to get my face up into the air. I heard the reel take up the slack, and the pressure came on again as I stopped swimming. Again my face was dragged under. This time, I turned in the water, and kicked away strongly from the direction of the boat, knowing that the pull of the line would at least keep my head back and my face clear of the water. It did, and damned nearly choked me. I swam against it for as long as I could, and then the line pressure stopped me, rolled me over and I went down about two feet. If I'd been a salmon I would have come up in a great silver, curving leap, hoping to catch O'Dowda unawares and break line or rod tip. I came up like a sack of wet horse-hair, gasping and choking for breath, to hear O'Dowda shout, 'Come on, boyo, put some life into it. I've known a two-pound tench do better.'

I tried again. Not to please him, but in the hope of reaching the bank about fifty yards away. I swam towards the boat but at an oblique angle, hoping to gain a little ground towards shallow water. If I could once get my feet down and stand, I might have enough strength in my shoulder and neck muscles to hold them until I could turn round a couple of times, winding the line around my body and getting a grasp of it with my free fingers.

Kermode called, 'Watch him, sir. He's making for the weeds. Ah, he's a cunning one.'

The boat altered position and my face went under as O'Dowda tightened the line. I fought against it, jack-knifing my legs forward to bring my head up and then leaning back against the pressure of the line, taking the full power on my neck. O'Dowda held me like it for a few moments. I saw the arc of the rod bend more and I couldn't fight the power of the line and split bamboo rod. My face went under again and I had to kick forward fast to take off the full power of the line strain to get my mouth above water. I gulped in air, but before I'd had my fill, the boat moved away from me and the strain came in again. For five minutes O'Dowda played me, letting me have just enough air and respite to keep me going, but all the while I was getting weaker and more desperate, knowing that I was slowly being drowned. O'Dowda could have made a fast job of it, but he was taking his time. Now and again as I got my head up I saw them in the boat, and heard them laughing. I made a last, kicking thrust for shallow water, but I was stopped dead. Then the strain went off and I was allowed to breathe.

O'Dowda shouted, 'Well, where is it?'

He had me. There wasn't any question about it. Another five minutes of this and I wouldn't care what happened to me. But at that moment I was just conscious enough to care about the future. Quite frankly I didn't want to die, and I wasn't in any mood to make sacrifices for anybody. I wanted to stay alive. It's a powerful instinct and there's no arguing with it.

I opened my mouth to shout, but Kermode gave a couple of strokes on the oars and O'Dowda put more strain on the line and my face was under again. For a moment or two I blanked out from intelligent thought, just sinking into blackness, and stupidly telling myself that it was enough to put a man off fishing for life. . . .

They must have seen I was all in and ready to talk, because the strain went off the line. I surfaced slowly and lay in the water on my back, facing the gold and silver morning sky, seeing a flight of starlings skeined right across it. I lay there gulping in the lovely air.

The strain was right off the line now and I heard the boat coming towards me, the reel singing as O'Dowda took up slack line.

O'Dowda's voice called, 'Ready to talk?'

I rolled over and faced them. The boat was about four yards away. I trod water feebly and nodded my head.

O'Dowda said, 'Good. Where is it?'

'I'll have to go and get it. I posted it to myself,' I said.

'How long will that take?'

'Not long. It's *poste restante* at—'

Several things happened then to make me break off. There was the sound of a shot, O'Dowda ducked, raising the tip of the rod, and the strain came sharply back on to the line, choking the rest of my words silent.

Feebly I kicked to take the strain off. There was another shot from somewhere to my left. I slewed my head round to see three figures standing on the far bank. One of them plunged into the water and headed for me. At the same time one of the others raised a hand and I heard another shot. O'Dowda and Kermode went down flat in the boat and the strain was off me completely.

I made a few weak, token kicks towards whoever was coming out to me.

A few seconds later a familiar voice said, 'Hold on, honey-chile, while I get the hook out of your mouth. Yum-yum, fish for supper.'

It was, bless her black little heart, Panda Bubakar, heading for me at speed, a grin all over her face, her white teeth flashing, and, held between them, a knife.

She came threshing up to me, grabbed the wire gimp, worked her hand up to the line and slashed it with the knife. Then she turned me over on my back, grabbed the slack of my shirt and began to tow me ashore, while the two on the bank cracked off an occasional shot to keep O'Dowda and Kermode low in the boat.

When we reached the bank Panda pulled me out and helped me to my feet and went round behind to cut my hands free.

'Brother,' she said, 'have you got a thing for water! Your old lady must have been a mermaid.'

Standing higher up the bank were Najib and Jimbo Alakwe, both with guns in their hands. Najib, neat and tidy in a dark grey suit, beaming at me; and Jimbo in red jeans and a loose yellow sweat shirt with a man's head printed on it in black, a shaggy-headed, craggy-faced man with the word *Beethoven* under it. He beamed at me, too, but only briefly, turning away to give the row boat another shot.

My hands free, Panda gave me a wet smack on the bottom and said, 'Start running, handsome. Mamma show the way.'

She moved off up the bank. I followed, stumbling along, clumsy from loss of circulation, but now with enough interest in life to give more than a dull data-recording glance at her long brown, heavy-breasted figure clad only in briefs and brassière. At the top of the bank she stooped and jerked up a track suit and kept running.

'Be with you soonest,' said Jimbo as we went by.

'Sooner,' said Najib, and, nodding at me, added, 'Good morning, Mr Carver.'

Panda took me through the trees, along a small path and finally out on to the open space behind the cottage. Parked short of the Rolls-Royce was their Thunderbird.

At the car she jerked the rear door open and reached inside for a couple of rugs.

'Come on, honey,' she said. 'Get that wet stuff off and wrap up in these. And, boy,' she warned, 'no tricks. No jerking any torch out of your pants and slugging me. Jeese, was that something disappointing to a girl for a man to produce.'

She half-turned from me and began to slip out of her pants and bra' and then slid into her track suit. I stripped, too, and wrapped myself in the blankets and she bundled me into the car just as Najib and Jimbo appeared, running.

As they went by the Rolls, Jimbo put a shot in each of the back tyres.

Five seconds later we were streaking down the château drive towards the main road and my teeth were chattering in my head like an electric typewriter going at speed.

Najib, next to Jimbo, who was driving, handed a flask back to Panda.

With a wink, she said, 'Ladies first – which almost means me.' She took a good swig and then handed the flask over.

I took a deep pull, and she said, 'Keep sucking, baby. We'll soon have you in a nice hot bath and Mamma will give you a friction rub afterwards. Whoof! Whoof!' She put her long arm around my shoulder and gave me a great she-bear hug.

Driving, Jimbo said, 'That millionaire man sure has a thing about fishing. Only time I ever did it was with hand grenades in the river at home. Remember that, Najib?"

If Najib did, he didn't consider it worth recording. He turned back to me and said, 'Did you tell them anything?"

I said, 'Another two seconds and I would have done. I wouldn't have believed water could be so cold.'

Healthy, though,' said Panda. 'Early morning swim, wham, gets the old corpuscles stirring and ready for mischief.'

She leaned forward and tucked the blankets round my legs. She found her cigarettes and lit one for me, sticking it into my mouth and giving me a fat, almost motherly kiss on the cheek.

'Nice. Yum-yum,' she said, and to Najib added, 'Can I have him after you've finished?'

Najib said, 'Panda, for God's sake, throttle down.'

'She always like this?' I asked.

'Even in her sleep,' said Jimbo and chuckled to himself.

'I sure am,' said Panda unabashed. 'I've got over five hundred witnesses that'll testify.'

And from there, right to Geneva and Jimbo's flat she kept it up, ignored by the two in front. Her talk didn't trouble me too much. I had a lot to think about. But I had to fight off her long arms and hands occasionally as she checked now and then to see that I was comfortable inside the blankets and nicely warming up.

Nobody paid any attention to me as I went through the lobby to the lifts wrapped in blankets. Geneva is a cosmopolitan city. If a Zulu in war paint walked down the street everyone would know that he was just over to a conference hoping to get economic aid.

Panda ran me a bath, suggested we should share it, yelped like a disappointed puppy when I managed to lock her out, but was happier when I had to shout for a towel and there was no way of escaping the friction rub.

They found me a suit of Najib's, navy blue, and a white shirt and other odds and ends, but the only spare shoes were a pair of ginger suèdes.

Back in the sitting room, I said, 'Why always these suède jobs?'

'We get them wholesale from Panda,' said Jimbo. 'She has a small factory in Leichtenstein.'

Panda, coming in with coffee, said, 'Well, a girl has to do something with her profits. It's for my old age. When I retire from the entertainment business, round about eighty, I guess.'

She put the coffee tray down in front of me and the top half of her nearly fell out of the low-cut yellow dress into which she had changed.

Najib said, 'You two get off. You know where. I want to talk to Mr Carver.'

Panda winked at me. 'You want I give her your love, honey-chile? She's a peach. I'll hand you that – but she'll never have the touch I have with a towel.'

'Out,' said Najib.

Jimbo said, 'That O'Dowda might come along here.'

'Let him,' said Najib. 'And he can bring his fishing rod, too – but it won't do him any good.'

They went and I leaned back and sipped my coffee. I was feeling all right now, physically. Mentally, I was as scrambled up as ever over the problem of the parcel, except now I was beginning to feel bloody-minded, in fact, more bloody-minded than ever, towards O'Dowda. The man didn't care a damn for anyone but himself. Julia could go, I could go, everyone could go, just so long as he got his hands on what he wanted. With me, that just strengthened the desire I had to make sure that he never did get it. Just for once somebody was going to spit in his eye.

'How did you know I was out there?' I asked Najib.

'Jimbo saw them jump you from the flat window. The Facel Vega is still down there. But that's the past. You know what you're going to do, don't you?'

He was a different man, serious, calm, no babu talk, and it was easy to see him in his real role, an army officer seconded to an Intelligence position in Gonwalla's service.

I said, 'I never did believe in that old business of which would you save when the boat sinks, your wife or your mother?'

Najib nodded. 'I thought putting Julia in danger would work with O'Dowda. He's made it clear that it doesn't. That's the kind of man he is. But you're not that kind. Julia is in danger. I'm serious about that. I don't care for the situation particularly, but I have my orders. You'll never see her again – nobody will – unless I get that parcel. Life, a life, in our country isn't very important. Never has been, so don't think that I shan't carry out the order if you refuse to hand over.'

'I've got Interpol on my back, remember.'

'I know. But you've got to take a chance on that. In fact, your
Western philosophy or code demands it. You know that. Up to this
moment you've been trying to find a way round it – sometimes
there are ways – but not this time. So – there is nothing you can
do. I'm sure that you agree with me.'

I poured myself another cup of coffee and considered it. He was
right, of course. In cold blood he was nothing but right. Up there
at the lake, with the good air being choked out of me, I'd been
ready to give up, to forget all codes, but down here, under no
physical pressure, was thinking straight, and feeling straight. He
was dead right. I just had to get Julia out of trouble and then take
my own chances with Interpol. I could go to ground for three or
four months and they might decide to forgive me or forget me; they
might. But I didn't think it likely. The only thing that would make
them change their minds would be pressure, political or public.

Although my mind was made up, I said, 'When you've got this
parcel, what are the chances of Gonwalla putting pressure on
whoever is using Interpol? Would he? Could he?'

Najib considered this. 'When we have the parcel and it is
destroyed, then our government is safe. We have friends as well
as enemies amongst the world's governments. Many of them are
members of Interpol. I should say that there is a fifty-fifty chance.
But to be fair – and you must have thought of this – the individual
government which hopes to get this parcel through Interpol might
take its own private, vindictive revenge for a failure.'

They might. But that was all part of the chance I had to take.

I said, 'All right. How do we do it? It'll take me about an hour
to get the parcel.'

'You go and get it. When it's in your hands, phone here. By the
time you get back I'll have Julia waiting somewhere handy and
we'll do the change-over in the open, in the street outside. Satisfy
you?'

I nodded, and then got up to make a note of the telephone
number.

I said, 'You'll be here waiting for me to call?'

'Yes.'

'Good.'

As I went to the door, he said, 'We'll do what we can for you
afterwards. I'm in no position to lecture, of course – but it's difficult
to resist. You've only got yourself to blame for whatever the after-

math may be. You thought you could make something for yourself out of the parcel. Human greed. It's a constant problem.'

So it might be, I thought, as I went out, but without it the world would be a very dull place. Personally, at that moment I was all in favour of dullness. At that moment I would have liked to have been away on the holiday I had promised myself, sitting dully somewhere wondering what to do and knowing that if I thought of something I would never have the energy to do it. That's what holidays were for, to smooth you down to a nice, flat dull surface which you could take back for the rest of the year's events to mark up again.

It was a beautiful morning. The road out around the lake to Evian was choked with cars – parts of it were under repair so there was single-line traffic and hold-ups at lights which did nothing to ease down my impatience. All I wanted now was to get the parcel and have Julia back.

Away to the left, when I could see it, the lake was a great sheet of blue with the Juras somewhere beyond in the haze. Right-handed, somewhere out of sight, was Mont Blanc, and not far from that was the chalet where I had spent a night with Julia . . . Najib was right. Human greed. I promised myself that if I came out of this little lot with a whole skin I would really try to do something about it. I knew I wouldn't be able to cut it out altogether, but I would try to cut it down. For me that was a big promise. Money was such a comforting thing to have. The way things were I wasn't likely to get any fees or expenses from O'Dowda for this job. Wilkins would have something to say about that.

Good old Wilkins. I wondered what she would have made of Panda. I spent the rest of the journey imagining them together. For all I knew they might hit it off.

I parked the Facel Vega and went into the post office with my English driving licence, my international driving licence, and a banker's credit card, per favour of O'Dowda (all of which had been in my case in the car) in order to identify myself. Sometimes at *poste restantes* they asked you and sometimes they didn't. They worked on some system, probably their mood of the moment.

The woman behind the guichet had a pink nose, pink lips, fluffy blue-grey hair, and big moist eyes, doe-like, and reminded me of an Angora rabbit which I had once forgotten to feed for a week so that it died and my sister had leathered me with a slipper. Sensitive green fingers she had, my sister, even at the age of fourteen, but she also had the wrists of a squash player.

I spread out my *cartes d'identités* like lettuce in front of the girl.

She wrinkled her pink nose with pleasure.

I said, 'Carver. Rex Carver. I think there's a parcel here for me.'

She picked at the corner of the banker's card and said, 'Carvaire . . . ?'

I knew she would.

'*Oui,* Carvaire.'

She turned away to the rows of pigeon holes behind her, had a brief chat with a chum on her left, and then, starting on the lower row which ran backwards from Z, gave herself the trouble of a long ride up to C. There was a wad of stuff in it which she brought over to me.

'Carvaire?' She started to sort through it.

'That's right.'

She shuffled through the lot, and then shook her head at me.

'There is nozzings, monsieur. Caballaire, there is.'

'Carvaire,' I said. But my heart was right down in my ginger suède shoes already. Nothing she held in her hand looked the size of the parcel I had sent.

'I'm sorry, monsieur. Perhaps he comes the next collection?'

I shook my head and began to gather up the lettuce leaves. I was about to turn away – wondering what the hell had happened, the thought flashing through my mind that maybe Aristide had been at work (he could have made a check of every *poste restante* in the East of France by now and picked it up) – when the girl said with a sudden note of recognition in her voice, 'Ah, you are Mr Carvaire?'

'Yes.'

'Then it is explained. You are guest of Monsieur O'Dowda, no?' From the way she said it, it was clear that she knew Mr O'Dowda. Who wouldn't in this district? He owned half a mountain not six miles away.

I nodded, not trusting myself to speak. I was way ahead of her. But there was no stopping her. A guest from the château was something to relish and hold on to for a while.

'But Mr O'Dowda himself telephones this morning to see for parcel of his guest, Mr Carvaire. I say, yes, is waiting, so he send his chauffeur with passport for parcel. It is not long ago. One hour, maybe. Maybe a little more. The chauffeur I know well. Is a little man, much joking and winking the eye. . . .'

I didn't wait for the full description of Kermode. I was on my way out.

I sat in the car and lit a cigarette, smoking it as though I hated it, sucking the life out of it. Not Aristide but O'Dowda had done it. O'Dowda had had more to go on. He had my suit with my passport in it. I had told him that the parcel was *poste restante*. I had told him that it wasn't far away. He could have phoned every main post office around the lake in half an hour and his name would have waived aside all question of formalities. Monsieur O'Dowda's guest? Certainly. Mr O'Dowda's guests were always important . . . politicians, film stars, the famous . . . naturally one would send the chauffeur down with a passport for identification.

So what did I do now?

O'Dowda had the parcel. I could imagine him and Kermode, sitting up there in their wax works, laughing their heads off, and probably celebrating with a few bottles of champagne. It would be good stuff, too, as the occasion demanded. Veuve Clicquot, Brut Gold label, 1959, probably.

I chucked the cigarette out of the car window and swore. Aloud. One word. A good, coarse, satisfying one, and it did something for me. The key log in the timber jam slipped and the run began. O'Dowda was not going to keep the parcel. If ever God had made one man who was due for a disappointment it was O'Dowda. I elected myself as the chosen instrument to bring it about. I didn't know how, but I was going to do it. There wasn't any point in thinking of the hows and whys and whats. At this moment the only sensible course was to home on the target. But before I did I had to make sure of Julia's safety.

I went into the post office to the telephones and called Najib.

When he answered, I said, 'Look, there's a little hitch over the parcel. Nothing serious, but it might be rather later in the day before I can get my hands on it. Is that all right?' I tried to keep my voice normal. It wasn't easy.

Najib said, 'Let's get one thing straight, Mr Carver. I'm trusting you over this. But I cannot go on trusting and waiting forever. If you do not telephone saying you have the parcel by six o'clock this evening, my deduction will be that you will never have it. In that case I shall have to take other steps. Just which at the moment defeats me. But one thing is certain. If someone else gets the parcel

– then you know what will happen to Miss Julia. And, Mr Carver
– I shall know very soon if anyone else has it because they will not
delay in letting us know. Anymore than I should delay in letting
them know that I had it. Understand?'

'Don't worry,' I said lightly. 'You'll get it.'

I rang off and went out.

It was difficult to keep my speed low going through the town.
Once through, I put my foot down hard. But if I thought that speed
would wipe out thought, I was disappointed. All the way I kept
asking myself – how? How was I going to get the parcel? Long
before I got there it became clear to me that the last thing I could
do was to barge in empty-handed on O'Dowda. The man dealt in
force, understood power. The only way to deal with him was from
a position of strength. that was the logic. How did one translate it
into practical terms?

CHAPTER 9

'I rage, I melt, I burn . . .'
(John Gay)

I turned off the main road into the driveway to the château, but I
didn't go straight to the place. I swung off up the track to the lake.

The Rolls-Royce was standing outside the cottage on flat rear
tyres. I went into the cottage, looking for something that would
weigh nicely in the hand and give me a feeling of confidence. I had
no luck inside. My suit was there with my passport gone, and there
was a mass of fishing tackle, but I couldn't find a single sporting
gun or any other weapon. The best I could do was a heavy wrench
from Kermode's bench.

But outside, an idea struck me. I went over to the Rolls-Royce.
In the glove compartment was the compressed-air pistol which had
been taken off me when they had jumped me in Geneva. I took it
and left the wrench.

I drove back almost to the main driveway and then left the car
in the cover of some trees. I made the rest of the way to the château
on foot, keeping well off the drive.

A big shooting brake was parked by the entrance steps. I watched
the château from the cover of the trees, saw no movement, and
started to work my way around the back. I wanted to be inside
without anyone seeing me enter. I found a side door and enough
cover from a thick thuya hedge to get me to it unseen.

I went into a wide, stone-flagged corridor. When I was halfway
down it a door opened suddenly a few yards ahead of me and a
man came out and dropped a suitcase on the stone floor. It was
Durnford and he saw me.

I went up to him, gun in hand, and he backed into the room. I
went after him. It was a bedroom and one glance showed me that
he was in the process of packing up.

'Leaving the happy home?'

'Yes.'

He hadn't been drinking. He was stone cold sober. He was more than that. He was pure ice. Gone was the nervous flicker of the eyes, gone the bad-tempered officiousness. Something had happened to change him. Normally I might have tried to find out what, but at the moment I had my own problems.

I said 'Where are they?'

He turned and began to stuff shirts and underwear into another case. Over his shoulder, he said, 'On the second floor.'

'In the waxworks?'

'Yes. Celebrating. They had a case of champagne sent up.'

'Celebrating what?'

'I don't know. And if I did, I wouldn't tell you.'

He was right back to not liking me. And not only me. At this moment he wasn't liking anybody.

I said, 'How long will they be there?'

'Until they come out.'

'If they had a case sent up it might be a long time.'

'Yes. When they decide to get drunk, they take their time. They're both Irishmen. You know how drunk an Irishman can get.'

'I know how drunk anyone can get if they really set their mind to it. You've been sacked?'

'I handed in my notice.'

'Same thing. Can I get into that room?'

'Not unless they let you in.'

'But you've got some way of communicating with them – or they with you, surely?'

'Yes.'

'Lead me to it.'

'I'm not doing anything for you. You're as bad as they are. Money, that's all you're interested in. You never stop to think about anything else but that. Just money – and to hell with what happens to anyone else. People don't mean anything to you.'

I said, 'I seem to remember a coloured number called Joseph Bavana that you helped once – to something very unpleasant.'

'That wasn't me. That was O'Dowda's personal secretary carrying out orders.'

'Same thing.'

He swung round from his pile of candy-striped pants and shouted, 'It is not! He's gone! Now – this is me! A different man!'

I said, 'Work it out any way you want. I'm not going to argue. But I want to talk to them and you're going to show me how. If you don't, I'll just tell the police what I know about Bavana, and the new Durnford won't get very far. It's not something I want to do, but push me and I will.'

He looked at me in silence for a while and then he said bitterly, 'Yes, you'd do it. You'd do anything to get what you want. Just for a while I thought that you might have something that a man could respect. But I know better now. You're like them. You'd put up any front, tell any lie that would help you to get what you want.'

'It's an interesting point, but I haven't time to discuss it. Just show me how to talk to them.'

For a moment or two I thought he was going to refuse. He just stared belligerently at me, hating me, hating himself more probably, and his mind all twisted up with memories of the woman he had loved who had been drowned in the lake; a mind that had been warped and commanded by O'Dowda to the point of revolt. Beyond that in fact. At this moment he wasn't sane. He was capable of anything. If he refused to show me, I knew that I could never make him.

With a slow, cunning look, he said, 'What are you going to say to him.'

'That's my business. I've got to have a talk with him. Come on, show me how.'

He gave me a nasty little smile and said, 'You're still trying to make something for yourself, aren't you? Still after a profit – no matter who else suffers?'

'I've got things to do. For my own personal satisfaction.'

'Quite.' He snapped the word at me. Then, abruptly, he turned and walked from the room. I followed him.

We went through a rabbit warren of corridors and finally fetched up at the foot of the main staircase. He went up ahead of me and down the wide upper hallway to the tall leather-covered steel doors of the waxwork room and halted in front of them.

I said, 'Can't they be opened from this side? I'd like to go in unannounced.'

He shook his head. 'Not if they've got the trip over on the inside. And they will have. Always do when they have a drinking bout.'

He went to the side of the doors and opened a small recess let into the wall. He pulled out a microphone speaker, flicked a switch in the recess somewhere, and said, 'O'Dowda!'

The way he said it must have given him great pleasure. He put into it everything he disliked about the man and worked off just a little of the years of servitude behind him.

There was no reply.

'O'Dowda!' Louder this time, and knocking off a few more years.

This time there was a reply.

From a concealed loudspeaker over the top of the doors O'Dowda's voice boomed, 'Who the hell is that?'

'Durnford.'

'Then get the hell off my property!' O'Dowda boomed, and roared on, 'Try to steal my wife, would ya, you rabbit-eyed bastard! Get to hell with ya!'

He'd been drinking all right, not yet drunk but expansive.

I saw Durnford's face tighten as he held on to his control. He put the microphone to his mouth and said, 'Carver is here. Wants to see you. And one of these days I'll prove you murdered her, you black-hearted bog-trotter.'

'Carver!' The voice boomed, and then a great gust of laughter came over the speaker. He said, 'Well now, is he? Clear off, the both of ya.'

I said to Durnford, 'All right, you've done your bit, I'll take it from here.'

He handed me the microphone, and said, 'If you're wise you'll get out of this place. He's not drunk yet but he's in a mad mood. Whatever you want from him, youll never get it.'

'You're damned right about that, boyo,' O'Dowda roared.

'Make yourself scarce,' I said to Durnford. 'When they do open up you might find Kermode at your throat. Go on.'

He hesitated for a moment and then said, 'Even if you can, I advise you not to go in there.'

'Don't worry.'

'I'm not. If you don't want my advice, don't take it.'

He turned and went away down the gallery. I watched him go and then walked down to the head of the stairs to check that he was really gone. I went back to the microphone.

As I picked it up, O'Dowda's voice yelled, 'Are you still there, Carver?'

I said, 'Why should I not be? I'm going to take at least five thousand pounds off you.'

There was silence. There had to be. I'd mentioned money, and money to O'Dowda was important, so important that any mention of it aroused his curiosity.

'And why would you be taking five thousand pounds off me?' His voice had lost some of its kick.

'In a straight sale. That's excluding my fees, of course.'

'And what would you have for sale, boyo?' He was coming back a bit, but I knew that I had him hooked.

I said, praying it would be so, 'Don't tell me that you just collected that parcel from Evian and stuck it straight in your safe without checking it?'

There was silence, a long one, and a heavy one for me. It was the kind of thing he could have done. It was what I wanted him to have done, because it was the one thing which would give me the little edge over him that I wanted, the one thing which gave me the remotest chance of getting Julia back. The silence went on. I let it. The longer it went on the better it was for me. I let it run until I knew that I was betting on a certainty.

I said, 'Don't tell me that a careful man like you put it away without checking it?'

He tried to bluff. It was clear in his voice.

'Of course I checked it.'

I laughed. 'You're a bad liar, O'Dowda. You think I'm such a fool that I wouldn't keep one ace up my sleeve? Dealing with types like you, Najib and Interpol? And anyway, I'm like you, O'Dowda, I don't trust the mails. That parcel at Evian was a phoney. Sent there to give me a breathing space if things went wrong – which I'll admit they damned nearly did at the lake. Are you with it? Are you listening good and hard? You haven't got what you think you've got, O'Dowda. If the safes in there, check it and see – and then we'll talk.'

I sat down on an Empire chair by the door and lit a cigarette, blew smoke, and prayed. Hard. That his safe was not in the banqueting room. If it were my bluff was called.

I sat there, pretending to myself to be cool, knowing the runners were coming up to the last fence and mine leading, knowing that anything can happen at the last fence – and usually the thing you're praying will not happen. I blew a smoke ring and watched it spin up towards the loudspeaker over the door and then fade away like a grey dream.

Suddenly the big double-doors whined and slid back on their

runners. Kermode stood just inside the threshold and he was holding a gun on me.

He said, 'Come in slowly and keep your hands out in front.'

I gave him a beaming smile. Why not? I'd won the first round. I was feeling good, but being careful not to be over-confident.

I went in and he halted me. Holding the gun at my navel, he ran his hands over my pockets. Aristide wouldn't have thought much of the job he made, or Najib, I guessed. I'd got the compressed-air pistol stuck barrel first into the inside of my left ginger suède shoe and the turn-ups of the suit trousers came well down, hiding it. The pistol was ten inches long, three or four inches of barrel in my shoe and the butt just above my ankle. The only thing I had to be careful about was fast movement because it weighed just under two pounds and could be shaken loose unless I watched it. I wasn't worried. I wasn't going to make one fast movement until I reached for the gun. Kermode's hand came down my leg, over my calf and stopped short a couple of inches above the pistol. He stood back.

'Take a seat over there,' he said. He pointed through the crowd to a divan that stood just in front of the Cairo merchant or whatever who had gypped O'Dowda in a diamond deal.

I went over and sat down carefully, crossing my legs so that the inside of my left shoe was hard up against the front of the divan and out of sight.

I looked around at the wax figures and said, 'Same old crowd you've got, I see. Time you made some new enemies.'

O'Dowda was sitting at the far end of the room, just in front of the candelabra-flanked, oversized effigy of himself. He was wearing a loose oriental dressing gown for comfort, black patent leather shoes with elastic sides, and a white turtle-necked shirt. The dressing gown was black with silver peacocks on it. He was lounging comfortably in an armchair with a table at his side on which stood glasses and a champagne bottle, and a hand microphone with a flex that trailed away into a far wall recess.

He stared at me with his small blue eyes out of a very red face, and said, 'Don't worry – you'll join 'em soon, you bastard.'

I said, 'If you want to do a deal with me, you overstuffed bullfrog, just keep things polite, will you?'

I was in, and I was enjoying myself, and I was full of comforting hatred for him, a warm, intoxicating desire to see all the kick and egotism knocked out of him. I'd taken a chance so far and it had

worked. It had to be my day. I had that feeling that all men know
. . . that feeling that the moment you strike the twenty-foot putt you
know it's going to drop, that the moment you flick the line out with
a Blue Upright on the end and it settles like a fairy on the water
under the alders that a three-pounder is going to bulge up to it,
that the moment you swing the gun up as they come fast and
oblique down wind you're going to get one with each barrel. . . . I
was feeling good, optimistic, ready for anything.

O'Dowda reached for his champagne glass on the table, lowered
his head and sipped, watching me over the rim. Two yards from
him was another armchair and a table stacked with bottles and
glasses. That's how they liked it. To sit there, drinking, steadily
getting tighter and shouting comments and abuse at their guests.
Fun . . . once in a while.

O'Dowda said, 'You're a fool. You think I believe that stuff about
the parcel? You're bluffing. If you had the real thing you'd never
poke your nose in here.'

I gave him a friendly smile. 'If you really thought I was bluffing
you'd never have opened the door. You couldn't have cared less
about me. I'd come in the Julia category. By the way, I've decided
that I don't want anything to do with that either. Oh, I've got a
weakness for pretty women, but it never goes over the five-hundred-
pound mark. My price, exclusive of my fee, is five thousand pounds.'

Kermode said, 'If the parcel isn't genuine, boss, all we have to
do is persuade him, like before.'

'Do that,' I said. 'But it won't get you anywhere. The parcel's
with a friend in Geneva. If I don't call her within the hour, she'll
just phone Interpol and tell them I'm out here. They won't waste
any time getting here.'

O'Dowda said, 'Her? What woman?'

I said, impatiently, 'For God's sake what woman do you imagine?
How do you think I got out here, away from Najib? Miss Panda,
of course. We sort of got together, financially and otherwise, to do
ourselves a bit of good.' I reached for a cigarette in my pocket, saw
Kermode tighten up, reassured him with a shake of my head, lit
up, and said, 'Come on – check the parcel and let's get this over.'

I was doing well. I had them. I just told myself to go easy and
not get too confident. The difficult part was still to come. I wanted
the parcel brought back into this room for checking.

The champagne helped me. O'Dowda was comfortable in his
chair, he was used to having servants do things for him.

He said to Kermode, 'Go and get it. But give me that gun first.'
Kermode handed him the gun. Then he went out of the room.

O'Dowda held the gun on me with one hand and drew a new
bottle of champagne across the table towards him with the other.
He began to fiddle with the wire around the cork, one-handed, to
open it, found it awkward and gave up. Kermode could do it
when he returned. Behind him the lit candles surrounding his effigy
flickered and smoked a little in the draught from the open doors.

He said, 'You could have got a price from Najib.'

I said, 'Yes.'

'Or from Interpol.'

'Yes.'

'Why come to me then?'

I shrugged my shoulders. 'You're slow, boyo. Bejabbers, you're
slow, slower than an old bog donkey with a load of peat.'

He didn't like it, and I was happy. I went on, 'I want to take
you. I want to show you that there's somebody around who can
make you look like a shagged-out carnival giant. That's what you
like doing to people, isn't it? Rubbing their noses in it. Well, that
goes for me, too.'

Slowly, he said, 'I'm promising myself the pleasure of killing you
inch by inch one day.'

'And there's another thing,' I said, ignoring him. 'I want you to
have it. The moment you have, I'm getting on to my stockbroker
to buy me a fat slice of shares in United Africa Enterprises. I should
make a healthy profit from that when you begin to operate the
monopoly you will get when Gonwalla goes.'

For a moment he screwed up his face, as though he had a bad
taste in his mouth. He said, 'You're just like all the rest. You hate
my guts because I'm a millionaire, but all the same you'd like to
be one. But remember this, Carver, whatever happens – I'll get
you. You'll wish that you'd never been born.'

'We'll see,' I said. 'If I make enough money I might even have
my own waxworks. I can think of a lot of people I'd like to have
in it.'

I looked slowly around at the assembled company. Yes, I could
think of a lot of people for my own collection. I finished up with
my eyes on the steel doors. Kermode had left them open. When he
came back he would be sure to shut them, so that if I were bluffing
I couldn't make a quick departure. I wanted to see how the doors
were operated. I wondered just how fast and how accurate I could

be with the compressed-air pistol. As far as I could remember from sessions with Miggs, this type of pistol usually grouped at under three-quarters of an inch at twenty-five feet. It ought to do the job I had in mind.

From outside, far down the gallery, I heard the sound of footsteps on the marble. Kermode was returning.

I glanced at O'Dowda, and said, 'Remember, no bargaining. Five thousand plus my fees and expenses, and I'll need it in cash at the handover.'

He said nothing. His big head was lowered, bull-like, and he was watching me and the door behind me. I screwed round a little to keep the door in view. Just behind me a dowager-type with a little coronet perched on straw-coloured hair stared blankly towards the big wax figure of King O'Dowda on the raised dais.

Kermode came into view in the gallery, hugging my parcel to his chest. He came through the door, went to the right of it, raised his hand and pushed one of the two white knobs that were let into the wall – one for opening and one for shutting the door. He had pressed the one nearest the door. I would have to press the one farthest from the door to open it.

The doors slid across, and Kermode came up the room, past me and heading for O'Dowda. I knew the exact moment I wanted. It would be when Kermode handed the parcel over to O'Dowda for him to open and O'Dowda handed him the gun to keep me covered. I would have to shoot fast and move fast. I dropped my right hand low, just touching the inside of my left leg, feeling gently for the wide trouser turn-up so that I could get at the pistol.

Kermode stopped at the table by O'Dowda. O'Dowda ignored him and looked at me, gun in his hand still.

He said, 'Feeling nervous, boyo? You think I don't know you? You're playing a bluff right up to the last moment, hoping to get some advantage. I could even like you for it. You've got guts, all right. You sit there, smiling, but you're sweating inside.'

I said, 'You're the one who's nervous. You know you've been out-smarted, but you don't want to face the moment. Go on, open it. I want to see your face as you do.'

O'Dowda tapped the table for Kermode to put the parcel down. As he did so, O'Dowda handed him the gun.

'Keep that Anglo-Saxon bastard covered,' he said.

He was too late. As the gun rested between their two hands, butt towards Kermode, I jerked out the pistol and began to fire as it

came up from near ground level. I went for Kermode's legs, hoping
to make him fall. As I pumped away I was on my feet and moving
for them. My aim was something that would have made Miggs spit
with contempt. I saw wood-chips fly off the far leg of the table as
the slugs smacked into it, saw Kermode moving fast, swinging the
gun round, and saw O'Dowda throw up a fat hand to protect his
face against the flying chips, and then the god of battles – who often
makes up his mind far too late to be of any help in a just cause –
came up trumps for once. Still firing, I swung the pistol left to get
Kermode's legs and the movement made me fire high. The lead
slugs smashed into the bottles of champagne that stood on the table
and they went off like bombs. Froth spouted high, spraying over
O'Dowda and Kermode. Shards of glass whined through the air
viciously. I saw a red streak suddenly appear down the side of
Kermode's face. Despite himself, he raised his gun-hand to it and
by then I was in amongst them. I grabbed at the gun, got it, and
wrenched it round until he had to let go to save his arm from being
broken. It came free in my hand and I kicked out at his feet and
he went down, thudding into the table, sending glasses, broken
bottles and parcel flying.

By the time they had sorted themselves out, I was standing ten
yards back from them, pistol in my pocket, parcel in one hand, and
their gun in the other.

O'Dowda, who had been knocked backwards, picked himself up
and stood shaking his head and rubbing at his eyes. Kermode sat
on the floor, face wincing with pain, grabbing at one of his legs –
in the last second a couple of stray slugs must have got him. An
ugly line of blood ran down his face from a glass cut.

Suddenly O'Dowda came out of his shock. He looked at me, his
face purpling and he roared, 'You bastard! By Jasus . . .' He started
to come for me, crashing through the wreckage of the table. I fired
at his feet, obliquely. The bullet hit the stone floor and ricocheted
away, thudding into the stomach of the policeman effigy. It tottered
and then fell to the floor.

O'Dowda pulled up fast.

'You come a step further, O'Dowda,' I said, 'and I'll let you
have one where the bobby just got his.'

He teetered there, mad with frustration, and it was touch and go
whether he came on. Then he saw wisdom and moved back a little
and looked down at Kermode.

'You useless sod. I told you to keep him covered.'

Kermode didn't say anything. Buddies they might be but he still knew when not to argue with his master.

I said, 'Don't fuss, Kermode. You can pick the pellets out with some tweezers later. Just get on your feet and sit somewhere where I can see you. And that goes for you, O'Dowda. Sit down somewhere and keep your hands in the open.'

They did it slowly, under protest, but they did it.

I stood there, watching them dispose of themselves, and I was feeling good. I had O'Dowda exactly where I wanted him. And I was human. I had to tell him so. It was a pity, but there it was. I just had to tell him. It would have been better if I had been magnanimous in victory and just cleared off. I should have stuck to action and left the preaching to others.

I held up the parcel. 'You were right, O'Dowda. I was bluffing. This is the genuine article. The blue films and a nice roll of tape that's political dynamite. How do you feel, master mind? King O'Dowda outwitted by one of the palace servants. O'Dowda, with men and money at his command; O'Dowda, who, if he wants a thing a certain way, fixes it that way and no expenses spared. . . . How does it feel to sit there now, feeling the wind going out of you?'

I should have known better. It was schoolboy stuff. Gloating stuff. When you've got what you want, get out quick is the motto. I ought to have known that, but then, again, it wasn't often that I had a chance to cast myself for the role of boy David, or Jack the Giant-Killer, with a touch of Sir Galahad thrown in.

I began to back to the door, covering them.

'Know what I'm going to do with the parcel? I'm handing it over to Najib in exchange for Julia. No money, just a straight exchange. That means you'll never get a thumb in Gonwalla's pie, ever. Means, too, that I'll lose my fee from you, but it will be worth it. Oh, yes, it'll be worth it. Every time your name comes up somewhere, I'll have a little chuckle to myself. I'll think of the oversized O'Dowda that I put in the hot seat to melt down to size.'

He sat there and looked at me. He said nothing, but I knew that he was feeling a lot. Close to him Kermode, still shaken, dabbed at his face with a handkerchief. Behind them, on their tall holders the candles flickered around the giant, throned effigy of King O'Dowda, lording it over his once-rebellious subjects, over the people who had thwarted him, or tried to out-cheat him from cheating them.

Then he said, 'One of these days, I'll get you, Carver.'

I backed to the wall by the door. 'Oh no you won't. The moment

I'm gone, you'll want to forget me. You'll make a good job of it, too. You'll bribe your memory to make it a blank. But every so often it will come back.'

'Get the hell out of here!' He bellowed it at me.

'Gladly, O'Dowda.'

I tucked the parcel under my gun-arm and reached behind me for the wall knobs, found them, and pressed the one to open the door.

Nothing happened.

I pressed again. Still nothing happened. I pressed the other knob in case I had got them mixed up. Nothing happened.

Stupidly, I said, 'The damned door won't open.'

O'Dowda with a flicker of new interest said, 'That's your problem, boyo.'

To Kermode, I said, 'These are the pushes, aren't they?'

O'Dowda said, 'They are.'

I tried them again. Still nothing happened.

Just then there was a crackle from the loudspeaker over the door, and Durnford's voice came booming into the room. He sounded in good spirits as he announced a servant's farewell to a well-hated master.

'Be happy in there, you bastards! I'm glad to think that I shan't see any of you again. Goodbye – and the devil take you!'

'Durnford,' I shouted.

The loudspeaker gave a click and went dead.

'How the hell could he do it?' I asked.

Kermode said, 'He's pulled the main fuses from outside.'

'The doors are inch steel. You couldn't force them, Carver. You're stuck.' O'Dowda had begun to sound happy.

'The man's mad.'

'I'm inclined to agree. What the hell does he think this will achieve? Not that I care.' O'Dowda smiled. 'I'm just content to know that you're not away yet, Carver.'

After victory never preach. I could have been out of the place if I had kept my mouth shut.

I moved away from the door, covering them.

'I'm going to be very nervous if either of you two makes a move.'

I went slowly round the room. All the windows were closed barred on the outside. The glass could have been smashed but no one could ever have squeezed between the bars. Keeping the two men in view, I went up as far as the curtained throne and looked behind. There was no other door leading out of the room. I went back to the main door and sat down.

'You were doing a lot of gabbing about master minds, Carver. Let's see you tackle this one.' O'Dowda got up and began to move towards the upturned table.

'You sit tight,' I said.

'You go to hell,' he said. 'You stay up there. This is our half of the room. And I'm thirsty.'

He salvaged a bottle and a glass and poured himself some champagne and then sat on the foot of the throne under his own outsized figure.

I said, 'Kermode. Get over to one of the windows, break it and the moment you see anyone outside give them a shout.'

Kermode looked at O'Dowda.

O'Dowda said, 'Do as the master mind says.'

Kermode went over to one of the windows, jabbed a lower pane with the leg of a chair, placed the chair by the window and sat down.

O'Dowda wrapped his loose robe tighter round himself and said, pointing, 'See that smooth city type.'

He indicated an elderly, distinguished-looking man in pin-striped trousers and black coat; a man with a square, honest face and nicely greying hair.

'Floated a company with him once. He was clever. Brilliant. And he got me to the point when he thought he had me on toast to the tune of thousands. He damned near did. As near as you are at this moment to doing me. Know where he is now? Doing time – eight years – for fraud. It must be bitter for him because the fraud was mine not his. I heard that his wife committed suicide. No kids, thankfully. I don't like hurting children until they're over eighteen.' O'Dowda rose and came halfway up the room carrying a bottle and a spare glass. He put them on a chair. 'This may be a long wait. No reason why you shouldn't have a drink.'

I said, 'If you come past that chair, I'll shoot.'

O'Dowda said calmly, 'I know you will.'

He went back to his throne and sat down. He filled his glass, raised it to me, and said, 'It'll take some time, but eventually I'll be missed and one of the servants will be up here. We'll get out – and then I'm shouting for the police, for Interpol, the whole boiling. I'm laying charges. Assault, armed robbery, the whole book. I'll make such a fuss that Interpol will have to back out because they'll

be scared of the publicity. They will forget the parcel. Even they
have their limits. Yes, boyo, one way and another it's you sitting
in the hot seat. Ever been in a French prison? No coddling like in
ours. French are a practical people. Punishment is punishment.'

I said, 'Before that happens I'll set fire to this lot.' I tapped the
parcel.

'Yes. I see you'd do that. I'll accept that. But I'd still lay the
charges. Eventually, boyo, I'll have you keeping my city friend
company. Pilch his name was. Eye for the women, he had, too. Not
that his wife ever knew, or she might not have committed suicide.'

I said, 'What happens up here if you want someone, want to
have something sent up?'

'Good question,' said O'Dowda. 'And I'll be honest with you.
Nothing. This is my place. When I come up here, I make sure
there's everything I want here. Only two men have permission to
disturb me up here, Kermode and Durnford. They use the loudspeaker. But if we sit here long enough, Kermode will spot someone
from the window.'

I stood up and walked towards the champagne.

He grinned. 'Thought you might get round to it. If I'd known
I'd have had some non-vintage stuff up here for you. Veuve Clicquot
is only for friends. But this time I'll overlook it. You get a wine
issue in French prisons, you know. Probably only plonk. So enjoy
that while it lasts.'

I went back and sat down, put the parcel on the floor between
my feet, and opened the champagne one-handed, steadying the
bottle between my knees.

I was in a jam. I drank some champagne and tried to think. Lots
of thoughts came, but none of them seemed to have much comfort
to offer in the present situation. I was really in it, up to my neck.
We might be stuck here for hours. All day, all night. They could
take it in turns to cat-doze. They were two to one. Eventually they
would get me. There was no question about that.

I looked at my watch. We'd already been locked in for half an
hour. I was feeling hot and tempted to take another glass of champagne, but I put the temptation from me. At any time O'Dowda
or Kermode might try something. I couldn't afford to be fuddled.

Maybe some such thought had occurred to O'Dowda for he raised
his glass to me and beamed over the top of it.

Across the room at the windows, Kermode kept watch on the
outside world. If he did see anyone he probably would not say so,

not yet, because he, too, must know that the waiting game up here was the one which would pay off for O'Dowda.

I picked up the parcel and, with the gun in my other hand, went over to the windows and pushed a chair into place. To Kermode, I said, 'You get back with him.'

He quit his place without a word and went over to O'Dowda. He sat down, rolled up his trouser leg and began to examine his pellet wounds. I sat at an angle, so that I could cast an eye outside from time to time and also keep the two of them in view. Outside it was a beautiful late September day, and miles away I could just glimpse a corner of the lake and a huddle of white houses shimmering in the heat haze on the far side. It was hot in the room. I ran the back of my hand across my forehead.

O'Dowda said, 'Finding it warm, eh?'

I said, 'You don't need the heating on on a day like this.'

He shrugged his big shoulders. 'On all the time. But there's an automatic control. Constant temperature of sixty-eight. You're only feeling hot because you're worried, Carver. You don't know what to do. Things are going to be much hotter for you before we finish. Pity – because if you'd played ball with me, I could have learnt to like you and put a lot of work your way. I might even have taken you into one of my organizations and made a fortune for you. But not now . . . oh no! I'm going to see you fry. I'm going to have you regretting that you ever knew me.'

I didn't answer. I sat there, enjoying the coolish air through the broken window. But for all the draught, I was still hot.

After a while I got up and moved so that I stood above one of the grids that covered the underfloor heating. Warm air was flooding up through it. For my money, it was a damned sight more than sixty-eight in the room. Something must have gone wrong with the thermostat. I went back to the window.

It grew hotter. There wasn't any doubt about it.

O'Dowda had noticed it too. He loosened the front of his oriental gown and said, 'What's that thermometer say?' He nodded to a wall space between two windows close to me.

I got up and checked the thermometer.

'Something's wrong with your system. It's seventy-two. Where's the thermometer?'

'In the gallery outside.'

'Well, if it gets any hotter you'll have all your guests here melting on you.'

He grinned and drank another glass of champagne.

I lit a cigarette, and glanced out of the window, and was rewarded with a sunny world in which nothing stirred except a pair of black-birds kicking up soil in a worm search on one of the garden beds.

Kermode and O'Dowda refreshed themselves with champagne, and I sat smoking, one sticky hand holding the gun across my knees, and thought about the closed steel doors. Durnford was crazy. What the hell was the point of shutting us all in here? In fact, if he'd known that it was going to help O'Dowda, then he would never have done it – because O'Dowda was the man he hated. Then, why the hell be content to go off just leaving us all locked in? It was like throwing a snowball at a tank as far as O'Dowda was concerned. He really was crazy – yet crazy or not he was basically an intelligent man and intelligence did not just disappear in a mad moment of hatred. Usually it reinforced the crazy action. He didn't have a very high opinion of me – largley because he thought that I'd failed him in mucking up O'Dowda's plans. But he didn't hate me as he hated O'Dowda. He'd advised me not to come in this room and see O'Dowda.

I stood up and loosened my tie, opening the neck of my shirt. Then I walked over and had another look at the wall thermometer. It was now reading eighty. I really was worried then because some-thing had begun to nag at me.

I looked at the copper grid in the floor by the window. There was a line of them all round the room, set about two feet back from the walls. This one was fastened to the floor by a couple of screws at each end. Hot air streamed up through the ornamented grid work, very hot air.

I looked at the thermometer again. It now read eighty-two. Ever since Durnford had closed the doors on us the temperature had started to rise. When I had first come in here the place had been at a comfortable room heat. Now it was hot enough to grow orchids.

I looked across at O'Dowda and Kermode. O'Dowda, his gown flowing open untidily, was leaning back in his chair, glass in hand, watching me, the light from the candles behind him on the raised throne burnishing the stiff stubble of his red hair.

Kermode was sitting on the edge of the throne, a small, bent-up grasshopper of a man, the side of his face caked with dry blood, his dark eyes on me, full of interest, promising himself, no doubt, some dark pleasure of revenge when the moment came.

O'Dowda, imagining I was about to say something, said, 'Not so cocky now, eh? But don't waste your breath trying to make any deal. You're here and we're here and we're going to get you. So no deals.'

He was right. I was going to speak, but not about deals.

I said, 'What's the temperature limit on this heating system?'

They both looked surprised at the question, then Kermode said, 'Somewhere around ninety-five.'

I said, 'It's gone up from seventy to over eighty in the last ten minutes.'

'So what? It's that bloody fool Durnford. He's locked us in and turned up the regulator,' said O'Dowda. 'The mans gutless. He doesn't like us and that's all he can think of doing. I'd have had some respect for him if he'd pulled a gun on me – even though he was talking through his hat about all that murder stuff. Sit down, boyo, and take your jacket off and finish your champagne. Might feel like a nice sleep afterwards.' He chuckled to himself.

I had it then, of course. For the last few minutes it had been at the back of my mind, but now I had it clear. Durnford was crazy, but he was no fool. And there wasn't any question of his being willing to wound and afraid to strike.

I said quickly, 'Remember the first time I was in this room, O'Dowda? I handed over a thermal bomb to you. A big overweight beast of a thing that could blow this room to bits. What did you do with it?'

He wasn't any fool either. He was with me at once.

'I gave it to Durnford to get rid of.'

'Well, my guess is that he has. Somewhere in this room. Probably, on the pipes under one of the floor grids, that bomb is sticking like a limpet waiting for the temperature to hit the right mark. Durnford has pulled a gun on you all right, and the rest of us.'

They were both on their feet.

I said, 'Kermode, go quickly round this room and see if you can spot any grid screws that have been scratched or tampered with.'

'The windows,' said O'Dowda, and now there was alarm in his voice. 'Smash 'em open, that'll bring the temperature down.'

'Only the air temperature. It won't affect the bomb. It's clamped against a pipe somewhere.'

'We can take up all the grids and turn the heat off at the individual radiators,' said O'Dowda.

He was panicking now.

I said, 'There are about two dozen in this room and we need a screwdriver. The only thing to do is to spot the grid he used. We can rip that up, maybe.'

As I spoke Kermode was already on his way round the room, examining the grids.

I checked the grids along the window wall. None of them showed signs of having been moved. The thermometer on the wall now read eighty-five. What would he have set the temperature control at on the bomb? Ninety? Eighty-seven?

Kermode came out from behind the throne and said, 'I can't see any grid that's marked.'

'Pull 'em all up,' shouted O'Dowda. 'Come on.'

He went to the nearest grid, bent, got his huge fingers in the ornamented copper-work and pulled. The soft copper face bulged upwards, stretching under his power, but the screws at either end held. And they would hold, I knew that. He was a millionaire. Millionaires don't tolerate shoddy work. In any suburban house the screws would have come out as though they had been set in soap. Anyone who worked for him was forced to give full value for money. That was his epitaph. I couldn't bother with mine. I checked the thermometer again; it was eight-seven. I put what might be my last bet on Durnford having plumped for ninety and headed for the door. The grids ran all around the room except across the door end. If any spot was going to be safer than another, it might be this end. Also it was well away from the windows. I didn't want momentarily to survive the blast and have a sheet of glass take my head off.

Kermode stood, lost, at the foot of the throne and shouted, 'What the hell do we do?'

I said, 'Come down here and fix yourself some cover.'

As I spoke, I toppled over a duchess and laid her lengthways as a barricade. I piled a gent in diplomatic corps dress on top of her. At least I was observing social levels.

Kermode began to move, but O'Dowda, panicking, not believing that there wasn't something that could be done, working on the old millionaire's principle of maintaining immunity from everything unpleasant, shouted, 'Give me a hand with this!'

He was tugging at another grid, the sweat lacquering his red face. Kermode hesitated, glancing towards me as I broke the social code and put a Coptic bazaar merchant on top of the diplomatic corps man.

O'Dowda roared at Kermode again and Kermode went to him.

He had to, he had to bank on survival, and that meant he had to be in O'Dowda's good books. Master and man, it's a bond that lasts right up to death, when the master is a millionaire. I was glad I was my own master and man. There was no quarrel between us. I added three more bodies and then propped a tall, thin, ascetic-faced university don with a fur-tipped robe against the pile. I wondered what he'd done to annoy O'Dowda. Voted against him in convocation, maybe, when the others wanted to give him an honorary law degree in return for some new university building.

Between them, they ripped up the grid at last, buckling it back. The screws were still holding but they gained enough room to feel inside. O'Dowda bent and groped and almost immediately was up and reaching for another grid. He was a trier. With luck – and it would have to be the luck of the Irish – he might strike the right grid this time, might even get it opened up and have his hand poised, but he was running a race with ninety degrees Fahrenheit and my bet was that it was pushing the eighty-nine mark already.

Gun and parcel in either hand, I settled behind my barrier and shouted, 'For God's sake be sensible. Get some cover away from the grids!'

Kermode, straining at the grid with his master, turned and looked at me. All he could see was my head behind the barricade. His eyes were full of longing, but he dared not leave his master.

Then suddenly he straightened up, taking his hands off the grid.

'KERMODE!' roared O'Dowda angrily.

'Wait a minute.'

Kermode turned and ran towards the throne. There was a strip of fine Persian carpet across the floor four yards away from the monstrous effigy of O'Dowda. He ripped it aside. There was a grid underneath it.

'I'd forgotten this one. . . .' He bent over, examining the screws. 'This one! This one!'

O'Dowda moved towards him, gown flying, knocking over a table as he went, shoving a Rajah-like figure, turbanned, white-suited, out of his way.

'The screws . . . look!' Kermode pointed.

And then they were at it, fingers gripped in the copper work, both of them putting their backs into it. The bomb had to be under there. That's where Durnford would have put it. Under the monstrous effigy, and close to where O'Dowda normally sat. If Kermode had remembered that grid at the start. . . .

I yelled, 'Give it up! Get down here!'

They took no notice of me. Big man and little man, sweating at
the grid, master and man, linked by so many things in the past:
loyalties, villainies, drinking bouts, fishing trips, rough houses in
the old days, sophisticated manipulations as the master grew richer,
and always the one thinking he was untouchable, his own law, and
the other knowing himself safe in the shadow of the other's power.
And they didn't listen to me. They had forgotten that I was there.
You don't sit down and let unpleasant things happen to you, not
an O'Dowda, you fight and you overcome. That was how it had
always been and that was how it would be, had to be, or life was
not worth living.

I dropped behind my barrier, snuggled in against the cold, bare
wax back of the duchess and then pulled the don down on top of
me.

As I did so it happened. The end of the world. There was a bang
as though a jet had broken the sound barrier in the room, and
everything moved. I was slammed backwards, tangled up in
duchess, diplomat and don, towards the steel doors. I should have
been killed. I thought I was killed, ears ringing, all breath gone
from my body. The steel doors waited for me, waited for the shock-
wave to slam me against them and flatten me. But the wave must
have hit the doors a second ahead of my body and flung them back
like untidy crumpled wings. I slid twenty yards down the gallery
and lay flat, eyes closed, waiting. . . . And in the waiting I heard
glass crashing, heard plaster and stone and wood falling and
breaking.

I came slowly to my feet and, dazed, rubbed dust and grit from
my eyes and face. On the floor at my feet was my gun and the
parcel, and the severed head of the duchess with a six-inch glass
splinter sticking out of her right cheek. I stepped over a red-tabbed
general, half of his white moustache torn away and one glass eye
shattered, and made for the door.

The room was full of smoke and dust and I could only just see
the full length of it. There was no sign of O'Dowda or Kermode.
But there were heads and arms and legs scattered all over the place.
Most of them were wax. As I went over the threshold, staggering,
not really knowing what I was doing, a gentle rain began to fall on
me from the remnants of the fire sprinkler system in the roof. I
went through it to the throne. The curtains and woodwork on both
sides were burning away, and the robes of O'Dowda's effigy were

blazing. The flames licked up around its face as it lay on the floor, one arm and one leg severed. I stood looking at it from a distance, and wondered if I were still really alive, or trapped for ever in some nightmare of death. O'Dowda was burning and melting away.

The wax of the face began to run. With the heat beating at my face, still full of stupidity from the shock-wave, I watched the great figure slowly melting before me, melting down to size, melting down to less than size. The sprinkler rain fell on my bare head, streaking down my dirty cheeks like tear-runnels, and the blaze burned fiercely at my skin so that I slowly began to step back, my eyes on O'Dowda's wax face. As the features ran away into shapelessness, I watched in horror at the thing that came swelling up through the wax into the flickering flame-light. Slowly, like a film developing, another face surfaced, grimacing up at me through the running, bubbling wax, another face, fleshless, eye-sockets first dark, then filled by the fire and alive with hissing little flames. A mouth grinned, tight, and then slowly fell open as the jaw broke away and slid to the floor with burning wax spurting little red and yellow tongues from it.

Behind me, miles away it seemed, I heard voices shouting, heard a great stir of life, bells, sirens, and the clatter of feet.

I staggered to a far wall, bent over and vomited, knowing that the horror was going to be with me on many a night ... the sight of a small, fragile skull slowly coming back into the light as O'Dowda's face melted away.

As I straightened up, I saw the real O'Dowda. When the bomb had exploded Kermode must have been shielding him. He had been slammed away across the room to hit the window wall like a two-hundredweight sack of corn. He lay huddled against the wall and floor angle, naked from the waist up, his head cocked horribly to one side and his one remaining leg twisted back up under his body. In the fingers of his right hand, outflung, was still held a large, jagged piece of the copper grid-work.

I went back, out of the room, leaving the fire flaring away around the throne. I picked up the parcel, nearly falling from giddiness as I did so, and then staggered away down the corridor, tucking the parcel into the waistband of my trousers and buttoning my jacket-front over it.

Sitting in a red velvet chair at the head of the stairs was Durnford, smoking, quiet, composed. He looked at me, nodded, as though congratulating himself on a neat piece of arrangement. O'Dowda and Kermode killed – main targets. Carver, shaken, contrite – minor target; and he, himself, not caring what happened now, because no one could ever take away from him the savour of the last hour, content to wait, no man able to touch him.

He said mildly, 'I phoned the fire brigade. They're arriving now.'

I said, throat dry, words coming like the dry rustle of old reeds, 'I don't feel in the mood for company.'

He pointed to a side door beyond his chair. 'Go through there. Down the stairs at the end and you'll find the garage.' Then, as I braced myself for the move, he said, 'How was he at the end?'

I said, 'I thought it was panic, but it wasn't. He just knew, as always, that nothing could ever beat him. He missed out by about five seconds.' Then I went to the door and, my hand on it, added, 'When the police get here they won't let you into that room. If you want to make your farewell, do it now.'

'To him?'

'No, to her. She's on the throne, waiting for you.'

He looked at me, not understanding for a moment, and then he got up slowly and began to move away, up the gallery towards the smoke-veiled and water-sprayed room. I found my way down to the garage and out across the grounds, knowing that I had been lucky. The exception. I had got away with something that belonged to O'Dowda. That was a record. Even the things he owned but no longer wanted, he kept. Just as he had kept her, locked up in himself. . . .

CHAPTER 10

'Kissing don't last: cookery do!'
(George Meredith)

The Facel Vega was still where I had left it. I crawled into it like
a hermit crab going back to its shell and drove off. A fire tender
nearly put me into the bushes before I reached the main gates.
Nobody can accuse a French *pompier* of not driving with panache.
A police car nearly did the same for me as I turned into the main
road. Somebody shouted at me through an open window. I didn't
stop. It could have been Aristide Marchissy la Dole.

I went down to the lake and along to Geneva, and I kept seeing
that melting wax face, bubbling and seething, and the horror
coming up through it. I was going to have bad dreams for a long
time unless I got away and grabbed my long-promised holiday.

I stopped at a call box and rang through to Najib.

I said, 'I've got the parcel for you. How long will it take you to
get Julia?'

'No damned time at all.'

'I'll meet you outside the west end of the Cathedrale de Saint
Pierre in half an hour. Okay?'

'We'll be there, and as a bonus you'll also get two thousand
pounds.'

'You're slipping,' I said. 'The Alakwe brothers always pay in
guineas.'

'Guineas,' he said.

I drove to the cathedral and waited.

They made it in twenty minutes, so they must have been holding
Julia in Geneva somewhere.

They came trooping across to me in a merry family party, the
Alakwe brothers, Miss Panda Bubakar and Julia.

I stood by the car and waited for them.

Jimbo patted Julia on the shoulder and pushed her gently towards
me. He was wearing a green corduroy jacket, black trousers, a
yellow shirt and a red tie with a great leaping salmon on it. He
couldn't have known that the salmon touch was the reason for my
frown.

He said anxiously, 'You tell him, missee, we treat you with every
respect and courtesy.'

Julia came into the crook of my arm. She didn't have to tell me
anything. It was all in her face.

I handed the parcel to Najib. He fingered it, and I knew he was
itching to open and check it.

'Go on,' I said, 'It won't offend me.'

'I trust you,' he said.

Panda semaphored her teeth and eyes at me and said, 'You never
gave me a chance. Everything I had I was ready to trust you with.
Don't forget, lover-boy, when she throws you back in the pond you
come swimming to Mamma. Whoof! Whoof!' She did a high kick,
pirouetted, and tossed me a fat envelope.

'American dollars,' said Najib. 'All you do now is avoid the arm
of the law.'

I shook my head. I said, 'You can twist it a bit for a while, but
never avoid it.'

We drove off, heading for Bonneville and then the road to
Megeve.

She said nothing for a long while.

I said eventually, 'Where do you want to stop and do the
shopping?'

'Anywhere. You sold the parcel to them?'

'No – it was a straight exchange for you. I didn't ask for any
money. But when it was offered I thought I had earned a bonus.'

I went on and told her all that had happened since I had last
seen her. Before I had finished her hand was out just touching me
on the arm, and when I had finished she said, 'But what happens
about you and Interpol now?'

I said, 'I don't know and I don't care. I'm just not going to think
about it. What are you planning to cook for dinner?'

We had *poulet sauté aux olives de Provence*. While she was making it
I had a bath and changed and laid out my ritzy pyjamas, and then
I came down and sat and drank and got up each time she called
from the kitchen for her glass to be refilled and it was on the second
refill that her arms went round my neck and her lips found mine.

'I'm a shy girl, really,' she said. 'I always need time.'

'Don't rush anything.'

The *poulet* was delicious.

As she disappeared to make the second course, the telephone rang.

It was Aristide.

He said, 'I thought I should find you there. You have company?'

I said, 'She's just served me with *poulet sauté aux olives de Provence.*'

He said, 'Did she serve the chicken on top of the hot sauce, or pour it over the bird?'

'On top.'

'Treasure her.'

'For the time that is left to me, I shall.'

'Ah yes, it is of that which I wish to speak. You had much trouble with O'Dowda, of course?'

'Of course.'

'The whole room was gutted, including many valuable paintings. However, enough was left to establish the secondary matter of murder. My people are pleased about that.'

'I am so happy that they are.'

'They were disappointed about the parcel, though.'

'Naturally.'

'Until I explained that you were, in fact, making an heroic effort to recover it for us, and that it was not your fault that the flames consumed it. On your behalf – and you will understand that I can think of no one else for whom I should do such a thing, and not a very strong reason why I should do it for you, except that, of course, I have a sentiment for you which, illogical though it be, I am forced to acknowledge, since I feel – and you will bear with me in this—'

'I can bear with you, Aristide, but somewhere I have lost myself in your sentence.'

'*Enfin,* I have persuaded them to abandon any drastic action. You were trying to get the parcel for us, you failed. Disobedience is punishable, but not failure. So you should be happy now, yes?'

'Very.'

'Good. But also you must not go unscathed.'

'It's a good word.'

'Najib drew a large sum of American dollars today, we are informed by his bank. I presume they are in your possession?'

'You speak officially or privately?'

'Both. Interpol have a charitable fund with which they do much good. Often it receives anonymous contributions. May we expect another soon?'

'I will send the money to you.'

'I am delighted. Money is always to be treated seriously, and talking of money, I would advise you, if you can bring yourself to it, to marry this Miss Julia. She will undoubtedly inherit much wealth from O'Dowda. She will have you, and you will have her and her money, and I shall never be bothered with you again. We shall all be happy.'

'Except Miss Julia,' I said. 'If you keep me on the line after she brings in the *omlette soufflée aux liqueurs*, which she is now making.'

He gave a deep sigh, and said. 'In the village of Inxent in northern France there is an inn where they make it perfectly. If she does not bring it to the table frothing and on the point of spilling over the dish, do not marry her.'

It came to the table, as he had said it should, filling the room with the aroma of fresh eggs, sizzling butter and the warm, heartening smell of liqueurs.

There were many times in the next two weeks when I knew that I would marry her, and then there were days when I wasn't sure, and in the end I agreed with Meredith, *Kissing don't last: cookery do!* But who wants to spend his life just eating?

So, in the end I retrieved my four thousand dollars from under the linoleum and went back into the big swim, wondering how long it would take to get my fees and expenses from O'Dowda's executors, and hoping that Panda was nowhere around. But Wilkins was, and no smile or warm word did I get from her until she came into the office one morning to find an electric typewriter waiting for her.

She beamed, and then almost immediately frowned.

'Why did you buy a German machine? British makes are just as good. Not that I've got anything personally against the Germans but one really should support . . .'

I shut my office door on her. You can't win.

JOHN O'HARA OMNIBUS

PAY JOEY is a wondrous creation, characteristically American, funny and frightening – Mr. O'Hara at his sharpest and most merciless.

'Mr. O'Hara's great talent creates a very bright light that clearly illuminates Joey and all that he is.' *New York Times*

'Completely uninhibited – Pal Joey tells all!' *New York Herald Tribune*

HOPE OF HEAVEN is another vividly realistic example of this outstanding author's work. Reviewing the original edition, *Time and Tide* said: 'There is bite and to spare about Hope of Heaven . . . In three or four pages the author manages to turn somebody inside out, show up self-deception, solid selfishness and permanent heartache behind the glittering facade.'

The New Statesman summoned it up succinctly: 'Mr. O'Hara is slick, vital, vivid, realistic, brutal, humorous, honest, tireless, readable, fearless, and generally swell.'

SERMONS AND SODA WATER is about life and love – always true life, occasionally true love. The principal intoxicant is marriage on the rocks.

'No one writing can bring back the lost generation and its heirs as vividly as Mr. O'Hara, and he is in magnificent form here. *The New York Times*

HENRY CECIL OMNIBUS

BROTHERS IN LAW is about Roger Thursby, called to the bar and promptly plunged into practice. He finds himself pitch-forked into a court without the most shadowy notion of his brief; knowing that he must get to his feet and address the Judge, but not having the slightest idea what he is to say. This funny, wise, sympathetic book must obviously be read and studied intently by all law students. But to the reader whose knowledge of law is the average man's *Brothers in Law* should prove exhilarating.

'Full of charm and humour, I think it is the best Henry Cecil yet.'
P. G. Wodehouse

FRIENDS AT COURT, like *Brothers in Law*, is extremely funny.

'No one has ever caught more precisely or wittily the atmosphere of litigation.' *Cyril Hare* (*Judge Gordon Clark*) in the *Daily Telegraph*.

SETTLED OUT OF COURT, which had a successful run as a West End play, is recommended reading for all law-makers, law-breakers and law abiders. Mr. Cecil has a persuasive way of presenting the most outrageously improbable situations, and getting away with them by dazzling entertaining dialogue.

CHRISTOPHER LANDON
OMNIBUS

ICE COLD IN ALEX – The thought of ice-cold lager, as served in Alexandria, haunted Captain Anson living on whisky – and his nerves – in doomed Tobruk. It became an obsession when he, his sergeant-major and two nurses set out in the ambulance Katy to break through Rommel's encircling panzers. Their desperate journey ran full tilt into action, excitement, personal drama – and Captain Zimmerman, who claimed to be a South African . . .

'The tension of this nighmare drive will grip you.'
Manchester Evening News

'Finely imagined, finely told.' *Birmingham Post*

'Wholly realistic and believable.' *Guardian*

DEAD MEN RISE UP NEVER is a novel of suspense with a dramatic courtroom twist and a tense finale aboard a sardine trawler off the coast of Spain.

THE SHADOW OF TIME – Anger, love and, above all, fear – these are the emotions that drive the characters in *The Shadow of Time* to their various fates. Christopher Landon is a master of suspence, and he keeps the reader on tenterhooks until the very end.

ANDREW GARVE OMNIBUS

MURDER IN MOSCOW – Verney had been sent to Moscow to report on changes in the Russian scene. When the leader of a British peace delegation is murdered, Verney discovers only too quickly the sort of changes that have occurred; the authorities produce a pseudo-criminal – and Verney soon sees why the truth doesn't make a scrap of difference.

'Convincing and fascinating.' *Illustrated London News*

'An authentic peek behind the curtain.' *New Statesman*

THE ASHES OF LODA – This is the story, told at a gripping pace, of how a man struggled single-handed and in alien surroundings to uncover events, intrigues and passions long buried in the 'ashes of Loda' – and of what he found.

THE CUCKOO LINE AFFAIR – When a highly respected citizen is accused by a pretty girl of assaulting her in a train, and two unimpeachable witnesses say they saw him do it, his position is serious. The incident was only the beginning of troubles for Edward Latimer, sixtyish, lovable and slightly quaint, on a journey to the Essex village of Steepleford by the ancient single-track railway known locally as the Cuckoo Line.

Andrew Garve is undoubtedly one of the most successful writers of detective-thrillers to emerge since the war. This is largely due to the vivid atmosphere he evokes from the varied and authentic backgrounds against which he sets his stories.